For everyone who enjoyed the first book: here's your sequel. Keep reading.

Copyright © 2014 Meghan Namaste

All rights reserved

This book or any portion thereof may not be reproduced or used in any manner whatsoever without the express written permission of the publisher, except for the use of brief quotations in a review.

This book is a work of fiction. Names, characters, businesses, organizations, places, events and incidents are either a product of the author's imagination or are used fictitiously.

Cover photo © Faisal Haroon

Cover design by Erica Naomi Braymen (artificechild.com)

Team Dark Horse

Prologue

Marian

Faint, young sunshine had begun to appear through the cracks in the blinds. I closed my eyes, but I was conscious now, and my mind hummed and whirred with the usual concerns. There was always a jolt, a mild panic that shot through me every time I woke up in this bed. But I remained beneath the covers, never leaping up and hurrying away, because it was better here.

From behind, Fiske draped his arm over me, rolling closer to rest his head on my shoulder, his lips on my spine. I knew we were both in the same place. Awake, but refusing to acknowledge it. Refusing to surrender this peace we had together.

In time he moved, rising up on his elbows to brush his lips against my ear. "Morning, Mari."

I let my head fall back so I could see him. I smiled. "Do you have to leave?"

"Soon. But not now." Fiske lowered his head, kissing me fully, and in seconds my whole body moved into him, each part of me somehow seeking, needing, sliding over him in the perfect way without even thinking. It took only minutes before I gasped and the hot swell of rushing, pounding sensation took over me and rendered me thoughtless, writhing, until I came to rest. Calmed.

For a while we lay there, lingering, until I rose, reaching out and trailing my hand over his chest. Fingering the russet hair. "I have to go," I said, regretfully and matter-of-factly.

Fiske nodded. "I need to head to work anyway," he said in a similar tone. Fiske sat up, and neither of us moved for a moment. His eyes held me to him. "I love you," he said.

I smiled. "I love you too."

It was routine by now. But it still sent a thrill through me, saying that.

I kissed him softly. "I'll see you tonight."

I drove through LA along my chosen route. It meandered quite a bit and took up a lot of time, but it took me away from major freeways. It still made me nervous to drive in heavy traffic. The houses seemed to expand and tower as I covered the miles, their scale and stature multiplying by millions.

I made the final turn, and my foot lightened on the gas pedal. The Porsche sucked back, the engine whined. I put on the gas again and it revved happily. Flanked by photographers on all sides, I drove up to the wrought iron gate, heavy bars and eighteen foot spikes in the air. I rolled down the window, reaching out to type in the security code. The paparazzi flung themselves at me, jostling, straining, snapping ferociously. I smiled reflexively. The gate swung open.

I was met by Geraldo, who took the car for me. I walked up to the door, where I tapped out another, even more fiercely guarded code. I waited for the answering click, and when it sounded I opened the door and stepped inside.

My clogs patted the floor, the tread squeaking softly on the glowing hardwood flooring. I'd all but stopped wearing heels. The sleek, vinyl-bright appliances in the kitchen caught my eye as I moved my head looking for something normal to do. *Maybe I'll bake something.* I walked with purpose now, opening cupboards and lining up ingredients on the counter. I reached to turn the oven dial to pre-heat when something stopped me.

Footsteps, echoing, resonating in the still, icy, conditioned air. They came down quickly, harsh against the floor. I straightened up and looked into the face of my husband.

He was approaching hurriedly, his face tight. I gave him a placid smile. "Hello, David," I said.

He stopped at the counter's edge, grasping it and leaning toward me just a bit. "Where were you last night?" he demanded.

I widened my eyes at him. "I was out."

A tic of annoyance swept across his face. "I *know* that. You were supposed to accompany me to the premiere." David abruptly turned, stalking across the room. "I had to tell everyone you were tending to your sick mother. So that's the story, if anyone asks. Please stick to it."

I gave him a nod, turning my attention back to the eggs and sugar before me.

I heard a flurry of movement at my back. "It's just that it doesn't look good when you don't show up," David went on, butting in. His speech was getting faster. The words carried more desperation.

I nodded again in silence, tapping an egg against the edge of the mixing bowl. *Crack.* I watched the yolk slide down over the glass, giving it my full focus.

David was moving about. He couldn't let it go. "All I ask is that you show up at my events. You left me stranded. Please don't let it happen again."

My head flopped back. I sighed. I turned around. I began to sift through my head, locating the things I always said. The things that would calm him, talk him down from this maelstrom of anxiety. I was having trouble finding them. There was so much I wanted to say instead.

David's deep brown eyes focused on me, traveling down my oversized button-down and slacks. The clothes that I'd borrowed from Fiske. "When you came in," he said tremulously, "were there photographers?"

I rolled my eyes. "There always are."

His eyes widened. "You can't...how can you dress like that in *public*? God, are you even wearing makeup?" He broke away from me and started walking, doubling back and retracing his steps. "You are my wife, Marian. You have *got* to make an effort to be presentable."

This was the part where I would apologize, running meekly to my room where I'd put on a lovely, trendy frock, and spend hours pressed up against the mirror perfecting my painted-on face. This was the part where I would go back to being perfect. And I waited for that to happen, for the guilt to come and mold me into something that fit his ideal. His image.

I kept waiting, and then I did something different instead.

"Why don't you like the clothes I'm wearing?" I asked, looking right up into his face.

David rocked backward, his eyebrows nearly meeting in the center of his forehead. He struggled for a moment. "How...they're hideous! The fit is all wrong. They're frumpy. They make you look like a common housewife...I don't even want to think about what the fashion bloggers will have to say."

I stepped forward, right up against him. "You're a fucking *idiot*."

Silence expanded in the air with enough pressure to splinter the walls. David fell back, staring, mouthing words that did not make it out of his head. I stood strong, enjoying this. Both the feel of the obscenity on my tongue, and the power.

"H-how do you mean?" David finally stammered.

I was all too happy to clarify things. "Here you are fretting over my *frumpy* outfit and what snarky things they'll say about me on TMZ. And here I am standing in front of you in *another man's clothes*. Did you even notice, David? Did you even think about what this means, or are you too afraid to even consider the possibility?"

David looked at me, I saw it connect, and the blood slowly left his face.

It wasn't as if he'd been blindsided. In the beginning, I had been careful. I was careful almost to the point of obsession. Only leaving the house when David was away, never missing a premiere or awards ceremony. Stealing brief moments with Fiske, never spending the night, never waking up with him. Never leaving a hair out of place. But over time, I became less careful. And in these last weeks, I'd been downright reckless, almost defiant. I'd spent the night with Fiske, many nights in a row, coming home in the same clothes the morning after. I'd been gone more than I was home. And I never once offered an explanation for all this, and David never asked. I came home each day with my heart bursting, waiting for a confrontation, almost seeking it out. And David never said a word.

I had never been a brave person. I was weak, spineless, timid. I was intrinsically a coward. I knew fear fully, intimately. It drove me, herded and cornered me like a sheepdog. Fear had brought me to this life, this marriage. It would probably always have a place in my head. But for the very first time, I began to understand that I would never know fear like David did.

He was looking at me now, rising up to his full height. His broad chest and thick arms were clenched. His face was hard as a rock. The smooth, flat hair on the top of his head even quivered. "You...*whore*," he spat belatedly. "How can you *live* with yourself? You go around with your hair a mess, reeking of him, in his *clothes* even. Have you no shame?"

I couldn't back down. I was an addict now, and adrenaline was filling me. "Makes you wonder, doesn't it? Why I was never like this with *you*."

David lunged forward, grabbing the mixer from the countertop. I kept myself from flinching as it smashed and watched the pieces scatter over the floor.

"Make yourself scarce," David muttered, leaning over the counter. "I can't look at you right now."

I took a deep breath. "Then get the fuck out of my kitchen."

In an instant, he put his fist through the microwave, crunching it in on itself. He was breathing hard. I knew what that fist could do to my skull, if he finally crossed that line. I still didn't move.

"Did you think you could just keep this going forever?" I shouted. I was moving now, bearing down on him. "This marriage is a sham. It's a fucking *front*. I only went along with it for so long because I had *nothing*. I was scared and weak, and you provided for me. That worked for a while. We made a pretty little family for a while there, didn't we?" I spat those last words against his ear, and he ducked his head, cowering. Hiding.

"*Stop hiding!*" I screamed, and my fists were drilling into his head, over and over, pummeling him until he lurched away and ran out into the foyer. I tore after him.

"You robbed me of my son!" I screamed at his back. I was sobbing now. I'd demolished the final barrier.

He stopped running abruptly. As my words went through him he stiffened like I'd shot him right in the spine. I ran up to him and wrenched his arm, grabbing it with both hands, turning him to face me.

I could hear sirens. Someone had called the police. Maybe Gabriella, the housekeeper. I didn't let it distract me.

David's face was crumbling in my gaze. He was losing it. I still held his limp arm in my hands. I threw it back at him.

"You robbed me of my son," I repeated. I was convulsing with rage and adrenaline and relief. "I was wrong too. I let it happen. *But you robbed me of my son!*"

The cops were at the door, banging away and shouting. I turned and stumbled to the walk-in closet nearby, where my fingers grasped the bag I had packed 24 hours before. I yanked the door open and pushed past the police officers, striding right into the ravenous lenses of forty cameras. Geraldo had my car ready and waiting. I choked out a goodbye and drove straight to the nearest freeway, where I flung myself into the snarl of speeding cars. I had no time to waste.

Part One

Erica

A pan of bacon popped and sizzled on the stove, filling the air with that slightly scorched pancakey smell. The beep of the microwave shrilled and I hit the button, popping the door open. I took out a warmed-up muffin, peeling off the paper. *Mmmm.* I bit the entire top off and chewed it up, reveling in the silence. I never failed to appreciate a judgment-free breakfast.

Lawrence wandered out of the bedroom, deftly flipping the strips of bacon. They landed with a hiss, and he dodged the flying grease. "Hey," he said, eyes lighting on the partially consumed muffin I held. "That looks good."

I shook my head, keeping him at bay with a flick of my hand. "Last one. Not up for grabs."

Lawrence grinned, sidestepping my outstretched arm and coming up behind me. His hands slid down, gently holding onto my hips, and he breathed a path from my earlobe to my collarbone. As my pulse quickened and my every muscle went slack, he licked his way back up that same path. My mind went all swirly and hot.

"Here," I managed, handing him what remained of my breakfast.

"That's *not* what I was after," Lawrence said against my neck. "But thank you."

He whipped around, pulling the pan off the stove before the bacon could turn into charcoal. As it cooled on a plate, Lawrence backed me up against the counter. I sought out his mouth, and we kissed with increasing intensity.

"You're missing out on breakfast," I pointed out as I took a quick breath somewhere in there.

"Screw breakfast," Lawrence said in a tone that made my core temperature rise by at least a few degrees.

There was a sharp thud out front, and a few of the horses called out for some reason. I didn't think anything of it. Then the doorbell trilled through the house.

I leaned back, breaking away from Lawrence. "Who could that be?" I said breathily.

"Hell if I know." Lawrence glanced halfheartedly toward the door, then back at me. "Let's pretend we're not home."

I shook my head. "I should go see who it is." I pried Lawrence off me with difficulty and walked to the front of the house. Fortunately I was still decent, in sweats and one of Lawrence's ratty long-sleeved dress shirts. I stepped to the door and pulled it open. And a little gasp slipped down into my throat.

Because the eyes I looked into were the same eyes I looked into every morning. I had seen those eyes, stared into them, close as they were, as Lawrence and I made love just hours before.

The woman standing in front of me was absolutely, achingly beautiful. She had a pale complexion and silky, thick black hair that lay around her face, touching her shoulders. She wore a simple, dark navy trench coat tied at the waist. Her hands were hidden in her pockets. And her eyes, her deeply set, intense, nearly black eyes were open wide as she peered at me. She appeared almost to be trembling.

She started speaking. "Is Harry..." She sort of shook her head at herself. "Is Lawrence here?"

I turned, stumbling back into the house. Lawrence came toward me, halted almost immediately by the look on my face. I could feel the unnatural hugeness of my eyes, my lack of color. "What is it?" He demanded.

I tried to focus on him. "Your mother is here."

Lawrence looked at me in total disbelief, like I'd told him we won the freaking lottery or something. He gave a quick shake of his head. "What makes you think it's my mother?"

I stared at him incredulously. I marched up to him. "Go look for yourself," I said, and I shoved him at the door.

Lawrence

I stepped out onto the porch, and there she was. I'd forgotten how much I looked like her.

She looked up at me, and her hand went to her mouth, which had fallen open in a smile. She rushed forward, but only for two steps. Then she stopped herself. She backed off and waited for me to choose how this went.

All the noise in my head evaporated. I felt like I was outside of myself, shrinking, staring at this sudden reunion from a great distance. There was an absurd expectation in the back of my mind for how this was supposed to go. But I had no idea what it was.

My mother's eyes were on me. Searching. In my clouded and quickly retreating mind, I saw the widening fear on her face. Already her eyes were overfilling.

Somehow, I fought through the haze of denial. *Okay. Just start.*

"Mom." The word cracked in my throat. "What are you doing here? How..."

I looked at the little Porsche in my driveway. I looked around for a chauffeur. "Since when do you *drive*?"

"I started," she said simply.

"Does...does *he* know you're here?" I couldn't say his name. I definitely couldn't give him a title.

My mother seemed to rise up. "I left your father." There was a quiet, hard-earned smile on her face.

Those four words went off in my head like dynamite. I gaped at her, almost unable to believe it. I never thought she would leave him.

"How did you...what happened? Why?" My thoughts were all screwed up and fighting to get out of my mouth.

My mother looked at me with level eyes. "I've been sleeping with another man for over a year. I quit wearing heels. I left the house without makeup. I missed his fucking *premiere*. Leaving was the only thing left to do."

I stared. *My mother* - my mother - *is having an* affair?

My mother drives a car?

Never mind all that. My mother says "fuck"?

I could not comprehend this. Any of it. The woman I knew was a total doormat. She was quiet, nearly mute much of the time, and light of foot, tiptoeing around her own house. She was the kind of person who listened to easy-listening music at low volume. She was easily manipulated, weak-willed and passive. She had no fight in her. The woman I knew would never have taken a stand, not one this big. I didn't know this woman at all.

But I kind of liked her.

I needed more answers. I hesitated, pulling back, distrusting this need. But I gave in.

"How did you find me?"

"I hired a private investigator," she said softly. "Six months after you left. I went behind your father's back. I couldn't stand it, not knowing if you were okay." My mother took a small step toward me, still holding her arms around herself. "Fiske…the man I hired found you at the polo club. He would travel there periodically, observe and report back to me. He told me he thought you were doing well. He said you had a gift with horses." She smiled, but I saw the pain behind her eyes. "It was such a relief to know you were happy, and that you had someone looking out for you. Wilson did a better job of raising you than I ever could have."

At the sound of Wilson's name, my head jerked upright. I was filled with a strange iciness. She had been there all along. Only I never knew. I tried to figure out if that made everything better or worse.

"How much do you know?" I demanded.

She glanced away. "Only pieces. I followed your career of course. I saw all your matches. I was so proud." She blinked several times. "I tried never to be too intrusive. I always wanted to respect your wishes. So I left you alone."

I looked down. *My wishes. Right.*

My mother's eyes were seeking mine. I blinked away from them. "I am so sorry," she said fiercely. "I know how much I failed you. And look at you. You're twenty years old now. You've made a life for yourself. I don't expect you to allow me into your life. I know it's too late for us." She was starting to

11

cry now. "I just wanted to see you. I just wanted to apologize for not being brave enough. For not being your mother when you needed one. You deserved so much better, Harry." And she dissolved.

I watched it happen, and I said nothing. I was hard, unmovable. I was frozen.

A sob tore through her. Clutching herself, she stumbled away from me, head down, intent on her car.

Something broke in me, freeing me. I was off the porch without even realizing it. I caught up with her in a couple strides. She stopped gratefully and turned around. Tears ran down her face, unchecked.

"Do you want to meet my girlfriend?" I said.

Erica

They were outside for quite a while, or maybe it just seemed longer than it was. I spent however long it was flitting around the front of the house, hovering close to the windows. My heart jumped around, and I moved about clumsily in tight-limbed shock. I stared through the window, watching what was happening out in the yard. Occasionally I did wrench my eyes away, because staring would be wrong.

There was a lot of distance between them at first, and now there seemed to be a lot of crying going on. Sobbing even. *Is that normal? How long has it been since they've seen each other? Why all these heightened emotions?* I realized, with a slight uneasiness, that I had no answers.

Okay. This is not productive. Do something! Freaking find something to do, Erica! In a desperate haze I wandered to the nearest pile of stuff. *Okay! This is good. I'll just move these things over here. Closer to the window.* I picked up the first thing which was a folder of some sort. *Mine or his, I wonder? Hell if I know.* Casually I let the unknown thing fall to the floor, and I let myself look out the window again.

Roving back and forth, I shifted countless random things around in a dull, manic state, until I heard them come onto the porch. I stopped what I was doing with a jolt, and the door opened.

Lawrence entered the house first. He stepped toward me. He was unreadable. His mother followed a couple paces behind, stepping daintily around the new pile of stuff I'd made. She was clearly nervous, in that twitchy scared-little-bunny way. But she walked right up to me.

All I could do was stare from one to the other.

Lawrence forged valiantly ahead, unstopped by my mute delirium. "Erica, this is Marian. My mother."

One of my eyebrows sank low. *No duh,* I wanted to snap at him.

His mother held out one of her previously hidden hands. "It's so good to meet you," she said warmly.

Slowly I got my arm to move, and I shook her hand limply. "Thanks," I said dumbly. "It's good to meet you too," I quickly added, finding my lost social skills at the last second.

His mother was looking at me intently. "Lawrence was just telling me all about your horses. It's so wonderful that you share the same passion."

I smiled and nodded. She was so sweet. I could've kept talking to her, but it felt like I wasn't needed. "I'm gonna check on the horses," I said breezily. "You guys keep catching up. It was great meeting you."

I slipped past the two of them, and they didn't stop me, so I stuffed my feet into my boots and headed out the door.

I made my way to the paddocks, weathered, slightly bowed wooden fencing containing so much. My past, present and future. This small gathering of horses, this strange assortment of personalities and potential was everything to me. These horses were both my daily grind and my wildest dreams, and it all depended on what I could make of them. They stood in the morning mist, calm-eyed, watching me. They made no sound except for the occasional snap of a swishing tail or the rhythmic crunching of their molars as they grazed, and it didn't matter. I didn't need them to acknowledge me. I didn't seek praise or reassurance. In their presence I was whole.

I kept walking until I got to D.M. The huge gelding I'd trained and grown with since my teens thrust his head over the topmost fence rail, blowing softly into my outstretched hands. "Hey, buddy," I said softly.

I reached up, giving his blaze a good scratching. Little white hairs rained down on me. The gelding never seemed to stop shedding on his face, no matter how obsessively I groomed him.

"You won't believe what happened today," I said, shaking my head and smiling slightly at the look on his inquisitive face. I stayed with D.M. for a while, letting my horse restore some normalcy to the morning.

When I looked up, I saw Lawrence's mother get into her car and drive off.

"I guess I should go talk to him," I murmured. I gave D.M. a final distracted pat and turned away.

D.M. stayed by the fence, stretching his neck out as far as he could, as if he could hold onto me by simply lessening the distance between us.

I leapt up the rickety steps and entered the house. My eyes searched for Lawrence, finding him without difficulty. He was right in the main room, pulling on his boots.

"Hey." I reached forward, touching him gently on the shoulder. "What happened with your mom?"

"We talked some more," Lawrence said, completely matter-of-fact. "And she left."

His seemingly chill demeanor didn't fit at all with the passionate (and teary) exchange I'd just witnessed between them. "Is she…gone forever?" I asked.

Lawrence shook his head. "No, she'll be back. At some point." He shrugged, straightening up.

I stared at him, totally thrown for a loop.

He seemed to notice. "Hey. It's not a big deal." He gave me a peck on the cheek. "I'm gonna go ride before it heats up out there. Harry can't afford to sweat off any more weight. He's lean as a greyhound as it is."

He darted out the door, leaving me alone with a slamming screen door and my own swirling thoughts.

"Okay then," I said to the empty house.

I watched from the window as Lawrence retrieved Harry from the paddock he shared with Lawrence's other polo pony, Vegas. The black gelding's coat glittered in the sun like patent leather. His walk was as fluid and focused as a jungle cat about to pounce.

With a sigh, I gathered my riding clothes and changed into them. Zipping up my riding boots, I put a lock on any intrusive thoughts about what had just happened. I had work to do.

Down at the barn, I set out all my gear while Lawrence quickly saddled Harry. Pausing to pick up a mallet, he rode off to the field. The gelding leapt around, impatient, displaying his usual brilliant, focused hyperactivity.

I chose Soiree for my first ride of the day. The lovely young ex-racehorse greeted me with her cute customary nicker. It made me smile, and I segued into my normal routine.

While I was in the barn with Soiree, I heard Amber arrive. The guttural uproar of her truck was unmistakable. A minute later she appeared in the barn doorway, with her mare Maude dragging at the end of the lead rope. "Hey," Amber said brightly. She had slowed her pace to account for Maude's recalcitrance, and her baggy cargo pants scraped across the concrete aisle. Her T-shirt had motor oil down the front. Despite all this, she still looked airbrushed.

"Hey, Amber." I clucked to Soiree and led her forward, vacating the cross ties.

Amber grinned. "Thanks." She pulled Maude over and clipped the ties to her halter. The ancient mare's ears drooped in bored resignation. "So what's new?"

I raised my eyebrows. And I told her the morning's events.

"You're *kidding*," Amber screeched, throwing a saddle over Maude's bony back. "His *mom* showed up?"

"Uh-huh." I fastened the noseband on Soiree's bridle. The cavesson was askew for some reason, and I shifted it. "Right in the middle of breakfast."

"And by breakfast, I take it you mean morning sex," Amber said astutely.

"Not full-blown, no. But we were working up to it." I gave up on Soiree's cavesson and reached down to tighten her girth. The young mare sweetly nudged me in the ribs.

"Damn." Amber shook her head. "That was unexpected. The mother showing up, I mean."

"Yeah." I stood at Soiree's head, pulling on my riding gloves. "I just...I never even knew he had one, you know?" I grimaced a little. "I know that sounds really stupid. Of course he has a mother. Everybody has a mother. But we just never talked about his parents. Not one word. And now I realize how strange that is."

Amber ducked under Maude's neck, fastening the girth on both sides and pulling it snug. The old mare threw in a few cow kicks, and Amber slapped her in a way that was barely harsher than a caress. "I've known him for years, and he never really told me anything either. I know he was estranged from them. He was sixteen when I met him, and he'd already been in Lexington a couple years. I think his dad was an asshole in some way."

Amber unsnapped Maude from the cross ties, and the metal snaps struck the walls. I flinched at the loud, sharp sound. "Was he...abusive?"

Amber shrugged. "I dunno. Maybe. Maybe just controlling. Whatever it was, it was bad enough that he wound up shoveling shit at the LPC and sleeping in a five-by-ten storage room. And he never called them and begged them to come get him."

Amber clicked her tongue, rousing Maude from her sleep. The mare followed her out. I just stood there until Soiree gave me a little push with her soft nose. Then, slowly, I led her outside.

That night, after the horses were brought in and fed, Lawrence and I were finally alone together. He made dinner, and took dessert out of the freezer to soften, while I watched him, softly, all the time. And I saw nothing in him that tightened me up inside. I drew no suspicions from the look on his face. He was happy and bright, and I brightened as well, falling easily into the joyful ease of our simple interactions.

It wasn't until we were climbing into bed that I remembered the things Amber had said. It was only then that I freshly remembered all the things we had never talked about. All of the jagged white spaces that framed our union like drapery. The spaces I just left hanging there, because I could not break the spell.

I sat up in bed. "Lawrence?"

His eyes followed me. "Yes?" He asked, soft and low.

"Why did she call you 'Harry'?"

He didn't retreat or duck away or even flinch. "It was a nickname," he said. No hesitation. No elaboration.

He touched me, pulling me close, and I instantly gave in to the familiar, exciting sensation of his hard, corrugated torso settling against me. I let the swarm of heat and blankness take over my head. When it was over, only when it was over and he was curled up against me, as still and trusting as a sleeping child, did I realize that this time it had felt like premeditated avoidance.

Lawrence

My wallet was on the seat of my truck where I'd left it. I riffled through it, seeing if I had enough cash to make a feed store run. *Barely.* I set it back down and started the engine. Barely was enough.

I had just shifted into reverse when the burgundy Porsche slid across my rearview mirror. I threw it in neutral and shut it down. The truck jerked a little. I opened the door and stepped out of the cab.

My mother was standing just outside her car. Her eyes darted, landing on me. "I hope I didn't catch you at a bad time," she said worriedly.

I shook my head. "You didn't. It can wait."

"Oh, good." She smiled up at me. "I just came to say goodbye."

I fell back a little on that one. "You're leaving?"

She grimaced a bit. But she nodded.

I moved closer to her. I was finding I didn't want her to leave. Strangely, I wanted to drop to her feet and become a lead weight around her ankles. "Are you coming back?"

"*Of course* I will." My mother reached out to me, smoothing a rogue strand of hair. "I have some pressing matters in California that need to be resolved. I'd rather not have all that hanging over my head." Her eyes went harsh. "So I'm going to take care of that, and then I'll be able to move forward with my life." She looked at me tenderly. "And I want you to be a part of it. I *will* come back."

She embraced me, holding me strongly, then releasing me and stepping back. Saltwater clung to her eyelashes like dew. My own vision was starting to get waterlogged.

"Thank you for letting me back into your life," my mother said. She was walking backward, unwilling to look away even as she took steps toward her waiting vehicle. "You're a wonderful man, Lawrence." She stopped with her hand on the door. "I know I have no right to be, but I'm damn proud of you."

She climbed into the Porsche like her limbs were bound. The engine started, and she shut herself inside the car. I could see she was crying, but it looked like the best possible kind. The Porsche crept down the driveway in reverse.

I picked up a useless arm and waved stupidly at her, because it felt better than just standing there. She waved back enthusiastically, laying on the horn as she shrank in my retinas. And then she was gone.

I should have been able to just get on with my life. But I was stuck, tethered to the spot. Eventually, my head got too heavy, and my legs got too tired, so I bent a knee, easing down onto the rough surface of the driveway.

I was still sitting there when I heard gravelly footsteps. I turned my head slightly. It was Chuck. He must've walked over from Mandy's. I didn't see his Jeep.

Chuck was looking at me with some concern, which is something, since I used to fuck his fiancée. "Are you okay?" he said.

I looked up at his reedy frame, his wispy grey moustache. "My mom, who I haven't seen in seven years, just left."

"Oh," Chuck said. He moved his cowboy boots around a little. "I reckon I'll leave you to it."

"Thanks," I said.

After a while I picked my ass up off the ground. Then I wiped my face on my sleeve and drove to the feed store.

Erica

The bed was warm as we both shifted, our internal clocks firing, pulling us out of sleep. *Six AM*. In the barn, the horses would be at the ready, alert and watchful for anyone capable of opening the feed room door.

I lay still for a moment longer, letting my to-do list pile in my head. Slowly, my body wound tighter, and all restfulness evaporated. I was running out of time. I was officially awake now.

I sat up rather violently, untangling myself from the sheets and Lawrence. Once free, I moved off across the room, hunting for clothes. Warily I picked up a pair of jeans and held them to my hips. In a sleep-deprived moment I had once attempted to put on Lawrence's jeans. They hadn't make it past my knees. I had no desire to redo that mistake. Ever.

I heard a creak from the mattress, and I turned. Lawrence had rolled over in bed and was now propped up on one arm, with a sheet draped carelessly over his taut body. I stepped toward him, my hold loosening on the pants.

I reached him, leaning over to kiss him. "Hey."

"Hey." Lawrence's arm crept around my back, and I fell gently into him. I softened, and for a long moment I gave no thought to anything except breathing and being here in this loving, rapturous silence.

"What's the hurry?" He asked me, smiling loosely.

I looked into the warm blackness of his eyes. "Show season starts in one week."

Lawrence whistled softly. "That close?"

"Yeah." I lowered my head, moving my lips over his neck, feather light. "It's almost here. And I still have so much to do. My trailer isn't organized. I don't know if my clothes still fit." I grimaced a little on that one. "Plus this is the last chance I have to put the final polish on Soiree. I want to make sure to do her justice."

"You will," Lawrence assured me. He lifted my chin with a single finger, looking in my eyes. "You'll kill it."

I smiled.

Team Dark Horse

I felt Lawrence's abs rise and fall beneath me. "I guess we better go feed," he said.

"Yeah." I stood up, quickly throwing my pants on. Lawrence appeared at my side, zipping up his fly. Soon we were more or less dressed, and together we went outside.

The sun was strong on my skin already. As we walked to the barn, Harry stood in his paddock, waiting. He made no sound, but he pricked his ears and trotted up to the fence, pressing his chest against the boards. Lawrence slipped his hand around mine.

As soon as my boot passed over the barn threshold, the building reverberated with noise. Horses on both sides of the aisle thrust their heads over their stall doors, nickering throaty greetings or outright demands. Soiree, serene and loving at all times, merely stretched out her neck to say hello. The polo ponies were a bit more keyed up, bobbing their heads with increasing intensity.

Further down the aisle, Assault loomed over his stall door, 16.3 hands of well-muscled contempt. He greeted me, as usual, with a foul expression and threatening ears. Lawrence shot the gelding a look, and Assault backed down, putting on a pretty face that vanished as soon as Lawrence looked the other way.

I followed Lawrence into the feed room. We worked together in a well-worn system, carrying pre-measured meals to the waiting horses. While they ate I filled cans for the evening feed, and Lawrence fed Harry. We then reconvened in the aisle and began turning out the horses. I led Soiree outside first, giving her a chance to stretch her legs before our morning ride. Lawrence turned Vegas out with Harry, and the two geldings engaged in their usual (and somewhat violent) reunion. I watched them for a moment with a smile, then reversed my steps.

Assault was straining against his door, testing the latch. It held, so he escalated the abuse, striking the door with his front hoof. The thunderous crack seemed to please him. He got in a few more blows before I reached the stall and threw my hands in his face. "*Back off,*" I growled.

Assault twitched his lip, showing his teeth, but he did take a step backward. I clipped a lead to his halter and unlatched the door. Assault rose up as if on tiptoe. "*Wait,*" I ordered him.

Lawrence materialized at my side as if summoned. Wordlessly he stepped in and took Assault's lead from me. The gelding's eyes focused, and he deflated, all his contempt and bravado leaving him. There had been an instant palpable shift in the chain of command.

"That's better," Lawrence said caustically to the gelding.

I sighed. "Thanks. I don't know what's gotten into him today."

"He's a jerk," Lawrence said. "This is just his natural form." He led Assault down the aisle.

I turned to the next occupied stall, finding a much more cooperative face. "Hey, D.M."

My draft cross sniffed me, his big head hanging over the stall door. I scratched the white hairs of his blaze, then wrapped my arms around his head.

I glanced downward, my eyes traveling below the little brass nameplate to where a single green rosette had been tacked to the stall door. That was the sum total of our wins last season. One brilliant round. One sixth place ribbon.

D.M. was ten years old now. He was nearing the end of his prime, and he had not set foot in the Grand Prix ring. I hadn't either. I tried not to dwell on our failures, but with show season approaching it was hard not to think back and analyze.

When I looked at D.M.'s career from an emotionally sterilized, purely professional standpoint, I could see that he had probably reached his apex. He'd given me all he had to give, and then he'd pushed and clawed his way even higher because that was his nature. That was why I loved him.

I knew in my pragmatic mind that D.M. was never going to be a Grand Prix horse. He was not going to carry me into the ring for my Grand Prix debut. We would not be there together as I won my first $50,000 prize. Love and dedication had taken us far. But we were not going to achieve the impossible. The impossible just was.

I had already begun to move on in little ways. Mostly inside my own head. I was changing my focus. I had Soiree, my lovely prodigious hunter. And I had Assault, who possessed every bit of ability D.M. lacked, though none of the kindness. I had a shot at Grand Prix. Assault could take me there; I was reasonably confident.

But for all my rationalizing and planning and moving on, there was something I couldn't shake. I couldn't stop the hope, and then the dismay, and after a while they began to feel just the same.

I slipped a lead around D.M.'s neck and he followed me outside, breathing warm air on my shoulder.

Lawrence

Vegas stood in the yard looking around, craning his plain neck with the thin strip of just-clipped black mane. I turned the hose on, aiming the stream of water at the dried sweat on his neck and shoulders and the dark patch where the saddle had been. When he was clean and dripping I whisked away the excess water with a sweat scraper, then turned him out with Harry to dry in the sun. He trotted off, breaking into a gallop when Harry came at him feet first.

I turned and headed for the house, feeling the familiar strain in my right arm. Already the muscles were developing unevenly, with my right bicep filling out my shirt sleeve more than the left. I liked it that way. Anyone in polo with even arms was probably riding their horse's mouth too much.

I jogged up the front steps, wrenched open the screen door and stepped inside, where I looked around for Erica. I didn't have to look far. She was sitting on the floor, surrounded by a pile of show clothes, rulebooks and about eight million different leg wraps.

"Getting organized?" I asked, smiling slightly.

Erica's head came up. She looked at me a bit wild-eyed. "I'm so sorry. I know I'm in the way here." She picked up a random jumping boot, looked at it, and set it right back down. "When I stopped showing last year, I kind of just threw everything in a big pile. And then with the move…I don't have a freaking clue where anything is. And I have to find what I need for Saturday…it's just a nightmare."

I held up a hand to stop her. "It's okay," I said reassuringly, easing down to the floor beside her. "Do you want some help?"

"I don't know if you *can* help," she answered dubiously. "But go right ahead."

"Okay." I took a sweeping look at the pile. "You have a lot of show coats here. You have to pick *one* to wear, right?"

"Yes."

"Okay, well, what about this one?" I picked one up, sliding it out of the dry-cleaning bag. "This one looks nice."

Erica glanced at it for about a microsecond. "That one doesn't fit."

I looked at her blankly. "It doesn't fit? Are you sure?"

"*Yup.*"

"Well, then if it doesn't fit, why don't you just get rid of it?" I asked reasonably.

Erica shot me a look. "You don't understand." She dove back into the pile.

I sat there a second. Then slowly I leaned over, breathing softly against her neck. "You're working too hard."

Erica shook her head, still distracted. "I'm just disorganized."

I picked up a knee, moving in front of her, straddling her lap. "Let me take care of you." My hands slid down her sides.

Erica's eyes snapped up to mine. I kissed her deeply, moving closer to her body until she could have no uncertainty about my intentions.

When I finally pulled back, her hand was at my inner thigh. "You're killing my productivity," she groaned.

"You'll work better if you're relaxed," I justified, hastily unzipping my jeans.

"So relax me." Erica lay back invitingly, spreading the pile of show clothes to cushion the floor with one hand and unbuttoning her shirt with the other.

In the blink of an eye I was on top of her, settling into her, rocking gently back and forth as the sensations steadily built, and we clung to each other, riding out the spasms as they grew overpowering.

Finally, I groaned and slid off her, landing face first on the oak flooring, which hardly dimmed my euphoria. Rolling over, I saw Erica sitting up unsteadily.

She glanced around, her eyes still somewhat hooded. "Whoa."

I smiled loosely. Years of experience told me I should wait at least a full minute before attempting words.

Erica's eyes landed on me. "I can't believe we *did it* on my show coats," she said, almost contemplative. "I'm gonna be ironing all day now."

I sat up slowly, collecting my clothes. Clumsily I put them on.

Erica took immediate notice. "Where are you going?"

"Well, I thought I'd leave you to your ironing," I said jokingly. I leaned over and kissed her, then stood up.

She didn't laugh. She watched me walk over and grab my keys. "Seriously, you're leaving?"

I stopped. I didn't like talking about this with her, even indirectly. She didn't know anything, and it was better that way. But this put me in the position of having to come up with a decent explanation for why I had to take off. And right now I had zero mental ability.

"I just remembered I have to stop in at the polo club," I said. "I'll be back in an hour probably."

"Oh. Okay. I didn't know."

"I'll be back as soon as I can," I said. "I love you."

"I love you too."

When I left the house, Erica was still sitting on the floor, watching me go.

Elaine

My lungs heaved, and I was abruptly awake. My mind went into overdrive, reacting faster than my body could. I blinked hard, and the grey walls around me went fuzzy like mold. I sat up anyway, finding the uneven firmness of the mattress with my hand.

I heard it again just then. A soft click, the faintest rattle of the wooden door frame settling into the wall. *Someone is in here.* My hand flew up to my hair, ritualistically smoothing the short, patchy strands. I frantically shifted the oversized T-shirt on my body. Defining my waist.

It was ridiculous and truly sad that even now, in my panicked state, my first instinct took me straight to vanity. My overwhelming fear at the thought of seeing another person had nothing to do with my safety.

I was sitting upright but somehow still clouded with sleep. And someone was standing over me with his back to the door. Disoriented, I moved my slow, heavy head and focused on him. My body had moved into a crouch.

"It's just me," Lawrence said.

"Oh." I sat down heavily.

"I'm sorry I didn't knock," he said. "The barn is full of people. It would've looked really weird if I'd gone up to an empty storage room and started knocking."

"It would've," I said. I shifted a leg up, laying my hands on top of my knee. "I just…I thought it was someone else. One of them."

Lawrence nodded. He left the door and started looking around. He always did that when he was here. He never sat down. "Are you low on anything?"

"Not really. I've still got enough sugar cereal to choke a horse." I stretched upward without moving my arms. "I could use some shampoo though." My hair had finally grown out enough to warrant lathering and not just rinsing.

Lawrence looked up from the fully-stocked milk crate in the corner. He gave his head a slight twitch, freeing his eyes of hair. "Any special kind?"

"I don't know. Whatever the salon brand knockoff is right now. Don't you dare get me some cheap shit like Suave," I warned.

"Okay," Lawrence said. His lips curved amusedly. I looked at his mouth and forgot everything. It all went away and I was empty, a clean slate with nothing but white noise in my head and my heart rising in my chest.

"Elaine?"

My pulse faltered. I looked up hurriedly into his coal-black eyes. The virgin silence in my head was gone. There wasn't anything unspoiled in me.

"Yes?" I breathed, excitement blocking out the blind terror.

Lawrence hesitated. There was a beat of uncertain recognition between us. Slowly, he came around and sat down beside me.

"You're going to have to leave this room eventually," he said.

My head dropped. My eyes went with it, and I stared straight into the concrete floor. I couldn't move.

"I know," I whispered.

Lawrence

I stood under the drugstore lights, looking over the paltry assortment of shampoo. I could feel the minutes leaving me, and I just kept standing there like an idiot. I had no knowledge of shampoo brands. I always just bought whatever was cheapest. It was a good system. It made shopping fast.

I should just go ask a salesgirl. I knew any woman could glance at this store shelf for two seconds and tell me exactly what to buy. Even Amber could do that. Right after she finished calling me a sexist bastard.

I knew exactly what I should do, but my feet remained on the floor. As a man, I was doomed to fail at things like this, yet I was hard-wired to try. I could not admit defeat on anything, even a stupid errand, and just suck it up and ask for help. I was forced to stand there as the minutes piled up and my day became more and more shot, until I finally cracked, hastily snatching a random product and inevitably making the wrong decision.

A salesgirl wandered over, saving me from myself. "Need some help?"

"Uh, yeah." She was a cute blonde with chunky highlights. "I'm picking up some shampoo for a friend. What's the best kind to get?"

The girl glanced at the selection. Not even for two seconds. "Suave is good. Salon quality on a budget. I use it myself." She flashed a smile, running her fingers through her hair.

"Excellent," I said. I picked up a bottle. "Thank you for your assistance."

"No problem. You need anything else?" She asked a bit too hopefully.

"No," I said. "Thanks, though." I went to the counter and paid up.

I drove back to the Lexington Polo Club. The lot was full, so I took the handicapped space. I tucked the shampoo bottle under my coat and walked nonchalantly into the stable. The flurry of activity hadn't died down. There were ponies all over the aisle, most of them with grooms crouched by their legs, wrapping them in white polos, feeling them for heat or applying poultices. I deftly stepped through the maze of ponies, intent on getting to my old room. Without glancing around I moved straight across the aisle. My hand was on the doorknob.

"What are you doing, Cavanaugh?"

I turned back. Paul Miller was standing right in front of me. The look on his face was less cruel and more confused, but with Miller, cruelty was never far below the surface.

"I'm visiting my old room," I said to Miller, completely straight-faced. "I do that sometimes. I think it's important to remember where you came from."

Miller stared at me for a moment. I watched it fly right over his head. Then he turned away, muttering loudly to himself. I opened the door and quickly shut it behind me.

Elaine was sitting on the bed. She'd put on a pair of jeans and an Ohio State Fair tee. "Was that Miller out there?"

"Yeah," I said. "He's an asshole for sure."

There was a clatter out in the aisle, and both of us tilted our heads, listening. I opened the door a crack and peered out. A flash of bright chestnut whirled by my eyeballs.

"They're bringing Firewall in," I said. "He's keen to go."

Elaine smiled a little. "Maybe he'll run down his owner."

She stood up suddenly, then bent down, picking up a box of cereal. Carrying it with her, Elaine sat down on the bed and unfurled the bag. She began taking handfuls of cereal and putting them in her mouth. Slowly she chewed. Her face was completely blank.

Elaine was as thin as a Parisian runway model, but even that was a vast improvement over how I'd found her. The clothes I'd bought for her fit closer to her arms and legs. There was more color in her face now. She was getting better all the time. But sometimes, her eyes were still the eyes of a person who was starving.

I listened at the door. It was quiet out there. I took the shampoo bottle out from under my jacket. Elaine's eyes glued themselves to the brand name.

"Here's your Suave," I said. "It's the current salon brand knockoff."

"You're *kidding*."

Erica

The ground sped by, far below me. My only reality was the maze of fences, red and white striped and shining like plastic. Made up of nothing but standards and precariously balanced poles, they were capable of looking chintzy. Toy-like. But each one stood as tall as a petite woman. These fences were set at four feet.

Assault churned beneath me, pulling at the reins. I could feel his hind legs quickening, building up some considerable firepower. Assault barreled down to the first fence, taking off early and clearing it anyway. I leaned back, engaging my core, and he settled into a less flat-out pace. The next takeoff was much better. I turned Assault almost before he hit the ground and rode on to the next fence, which we jumped at an angle, setting us up perfectly for the in-and-out that was next on the hit list.

As Assault flew over the *in* portion of the in-and-out, I noticed my mother standing outside the arena. She was staring intently at me behind her laughably huge Calvin Klein shades. I groaned.

Assault left the in-and-out behind, driving on eagerly to the next fence. I checked him with the reins, stopping his momentum. He fought me, slewing around as he tried to keep going. I leaned back, throwing all my weight against his mouth, managing to stop him.

Assault was motionless for a fleeting second. Then his ears snapped back, and he lashed out with his hind legs three times in a row before I could blink. I booted him hard in the ribs, and he scurried forward, stomping and carrying on like a spoiled child. Which is basically what Assault was. When he didn't get his way, his brain shut down, and he became angry and irrational. Unfortunately, Assault weighed 1,300 pounds, and that kind of shit could not be tolerated.

I lunged for a rein, grasping it only inches from his mouth, and hauled his head around. "You *quit!*" I roared directly into his ear.

Assault's eye got a little bigger. He set his feet down and stood still.

I released his head. "Good boy," I said, my voice a few octaves lower than normal. I turned Assault around, heading for the rail.

I halted the sullen, fuming gelding and looked around for my mother. It didn't take me long to find her. She was hurrying into my field of vision, her ankles wobbling above the trendy, torturous footwear she insisted on strapping on every damn day.

"I still don't like the idea of you riding that horse," she said primly. "He doesn't look safe."

I rolled my eyes. "Of course he's not safe. But he's talented."

My mother didn't say anything. She looked around the yard; her eyes darted to the house, and I saw all her features tighten and narrow. She didn't have to say anything. My mother made it clear how she felt.

Assault raised his head, neck muscles bulging. He lifted one front hoof, just an inch, and began to drag it across the sand, back and forth. It was a loaded gesture, coming from Assault.

I glanced at my mother. "Do you have something to say?" I threw the words at her like a clod of dirt. I imagined it bursting across her face, covering her with grime.

My mother slowly turned to me. "No," she said, almost sadly. "I just came to see you. I never see you anymore."

I was speechless for a second. "Well, great. Thanks." I pushed Assault back into a canter. His hooves ripped through the sand, tossing up a cloud of dust.

Lawrence

Harry's eyes stared into the blackening sky. They wobbled in his head. I watched the flickering emotions on his face, the eloquent tension in his neck, flung upward and held rigid in a backward curve. His shoulders rippled mechanically, supple skin and black hair sliding over muscle and bone. Already, sweat shone through in places.

I reached the edge of the yard and stepped in between the shuddering maples. Harry followed, so close he buffeted me gently as we walked. Beyond the thin line of trees, the field lay bare, reaching farther than I could see. I knew where the field ended. I knew every inch of this ground. Harry did not.

I knew what I was asking him to do. It was like asking a person to walk back down the alley where their best friend had been shot dead. But if Harry had been human, I could have talked him through it. I could have explained to him why this was necessary. I could've helped him understand.

I swung onto his back and nudged him forward. The sky heaved. Thunder cracked with the force of a bullwhip. Harry ducked his head, cowering, but his eyes strained ahead. He searched for the lightning. And when it cut the sky in two, Harry came to a trembling halt. Terror flooded his veins, and mine, circling back and meeting at the heart of us. I gave Harry the reins and waited, hunched near his withers. He would either stand strong and learn to break free from the fear that had controlled him all this time, or he would turn around and run. He might kill us both.

Harry thought of one thing constantly. Most horses did. But the thing most horses thought about was food, and Harry thought about *this*.

The moment I released him, when I lightened my fingertip hold on the reins and breathed my leg inward against his lean sides. It was no longer an aid; there was no effort in it. The effort was in holding back. All through the long minutes of waiting, when I wrapped his legs and he stood perfectly, unwaveringly still. The warm-up period. All the times we circled the field at a sedate walk, then a trot, then a canter. Harry never pulled on the reins anymore. He remained straight and true at all times. He waited. But I could feel it in his mind always. The insane focus. The longing.

It was down to a mere thought that flickered through me, somehow reaching Harry. When he felt it, the very instant he felt it, Harry came alive, giddy, charging and fearless. Everything he had held back came bursting forth, a whip-lashing surge of relentless drive. His hooves slashed against the grass, flinging him everywhere at once. His head ticked back and forth, his eyeball straining in its socket. When he'd been at it a while and his nostril began to flare red from exertion, he looked mad. But to be this good in polo, a horse has to be a little crazy.

Team Dark Horse

I closed my fist against the reins, connecting with Harry's mouth. He shook his head, fighting to go on, but when he felt the unrelenting pressure, he stopped in mid-leap. I let the reins out all the way to the buckle, and Harry stretched his neck downward, walking with clear resentment. He wasn't even breathing that hard. "You are something, Harry," I said to him.

He walked on underneath me, crossing the field, treading lightly on the scuffed-up grass he'd torn over just moments before. You could trace the line of play from the torn and flattened grass we'd left behind. The field told everything.

I leaned forward out of the saddle as Harry climbed a small hill. "Whoa," I said, and he stopped at the apex. Here we could see all around. Harry stood motionless as my eyes followed the path we had made.

There were intersecting lines over nearly every square foot of the field. I had expected to see a mess, and the scene was chaotic. But the most evident thing was the accuracy. The lines Harry had left were improbably straight, as if machine-made. But they didn't go on indefinitely like plowed rows on a farmer's field. They went on for five feet, or twenty, maybe. And then there were the corners, abrupt changes in direction that lay starkly before me, often too tight, it seemed, to allow the bulk of a horse through. My eyes swept through the steep, limitless patterns. My adrenaline, which had calmed, rose.

Harry shifted restlessly under me. I gave the field one last glance and let him turn for home.

Erica

The sun was a vast orange orb in the sky. It left dark purple scribbling across my vision, but my eye was still drawn in. When I was a kid, I considered this kind of sunrise a positive omen. Now, as an adult, it did little to reassure me.

Nothing had gone wrong as I loaded up and pulled out. Everything was fine. D.M. and Assault were aggressively prepared for the level of competition they faced. Soiree, I had left home. She would make her debut in one week, when I could focus. I owed it to the mare to pilot her well. Soiree was a phenom. Assault and D.M. were whatever they were. Anyway, I had to start somewhere. I had to leap back in.

I drove along, keeping one eye on the rearview mirror, alert for any unusual shifting or rocking of the trailer. Focused on the subtle sway and lean, I nearly missed the first turn. My hands frantically spun the wheel, and I heard more than one thud from inside the trailer as the horses struggled to stay on their feet. Cringing, I felt the urge to leap out and check for damage, but no distressed whinnies reached my ears. Taking a fluttering breath, I stared grimly at the tarmac ahead, newly riddled with show nerves.

I had to focus on my driving, and not just because I couldn't keep slamming my poor horses around. The route to the show grounds was emblazoned in my memory, or at least it should have been. I used to drive the whole way by feel. But this time, nothing was familiar. I found myself leaning forward, peering through the windshield as I searched for road signs and landmarks. More than once, my foot eased off the gas pedal, and my truck lost power.

When I reached an intersection I knew comfortably at last, I breathed out in happiness. A right turn would take me straight to the show grounds. On the way back, a left turn would take me home.

I realized something, and it settled on me with a strange heaviness. I'd had trouble finding my way because I had always come from home. My *parents'* home.

I checked both ways and quietly drove the rest of the way. When I saw the open gate and the field stuffed with trailers, anxiety seared through my stomach.

After getting my number from the show secretary, I drove a few laps around the field until I found a spot. As soon as I maneuvered in I threw down the ramp and scrambled up it. D.M. blinked languidly at me as I hastily searched his legs for cuts or swelling. A veteran of many shows, D.M. could withstand just about anything. My nerves failed to penetrate him. They rolled off his close-shaved coat like water on a newly waxed car. In the front of the trailer, Assault's neck was craned, his rope taut and vibrating from the steady, calculated pull. The gelding loomed before me, even bigger than his natural height, moving his feet rather menacingly. *Clearly, he survived the trip.* I sighed, unhooking D.M. and leaving Assault behind. At the moment, I didn't have the energy to battle with him.

As I tied D.M. to the side of the trailer, I cocked my head, listening to an announcement read over the loudspeaker. There was still a ways to go before my first class. I fetched a hay bag and put it within D.M.'s reach. Assault began to paw, grinding his hoof against the trailer floor. In response I picked up the ramp and shut the door, blocking out his hostile face.

I decided to take a walk around, giving myself a chance to scope out the competition. I started off down the first row of trailers, noting those in attendance. It was the usual crowd, with some seasoned horses I recognized, but mostly new prospects. I glanced appreciatively at finely shaped heads and keen eyes. Various grooms and trainers were bobbing around the horses, saddling them or giving them more polish, and I gave them a nod and a smile as I passed. I was met with a blank stare each time, followed by a quick twist of the head as they removed me from their field of vision and focused on the task at hand.

The first couple of times, I brushed it off. Show folk were chronically eccentric and self-centered as a rule. It just came with the territory, and I had long ago learned to avoid taking it personally, or reading much into it. But when it happened repeatedly, without exception, paranoia began to creep in. I began shrinking, avoiding eye contact, my very presence apologetic. Fueled by my growing unease, I wound up scurrying between the trailers like an unpopular kid, desperately searching for a familiar face among the large and unfriendly crowd.

When I turned a corner, the familiar colors of the Newberry barn presented themselves. I lunged for the eggplant-and-green trailer, feeling my pulse settle down.

Jennifer was about to mount up on a tall, narrow bay. She placed her feet on a tack trunk, one at a time, and a groom swiftly wiped the dust from her close-fitting boots. Her elegant silhouette was complete with tan breeches and a grey pinstripe coat. Her long blonde hair was contained in a net beneath a black velvet hunt cap.

I hurried over, smiling. "Jennifer, hey."

Jennifer's head snapped over to me. She smiled without moving her face, said a short "hi", and mounted her horse. She rode straight past me.

Jennifer's father came out of the dressing room. Upon seeing me, his acknowledgement was polite, and nothing more.

I turned around and hurried quietly back to my trailer with Jennifer's cold reception echoing around in my head. I didn't allow it to land anywhere. I couldn't deal with a conclusion right now. My eyes held steadily to the path in front of me. I registered the noises and movement on all sides, but it seemed a great distance away. There was so much distance, it was almost all I could feel.

I had often felt invisible before. But not here. Never here.

I reached my trailer and brought Assault out into the light. Tying him up short, I saddled him numbly as he twitched around, looking for a fight. Once he was saddled and booted up, I changed into my show clothes, which, for the first time ever, actually brought relief. I seized the chance to stop dwelling on the profoundly uncomfortable events of the day, and focused on the more trivially uncomfortable sensation of having to stuff myself into breeches that hadn't fit last season, and sure as hell didn't fit now that I was living in a house that inevitably had several varieties of cake in the fridge. After fighting my way into the unforgiving fabric, I zipped up my boots, squeezed into my show coat and staggered out the door.

I put on my helmet and gloves, then bridled Assault and led him to the warm-up ring, a simple task that was complicated by Assault's continual aggression toward other horses. By the time we reached the warm-up ring, my class had already begun. I hurried onto Assault and gave him a short warm-up. The gelding's ears were flat to his skull as we circled the ring. The other riders gave him a wide berth.

When my number was called "on deck", I left the warm-up ring and brought Assault over to the in-gate. I watched as the last few jumps were ridden, but I wasn't overly concerned. Assault was overqualified for this height. My main issue was going to be keeping him under control.

When the rider before me exited the ring, we rode in. I rode my opening circle with a firm hand, half-halting strongly. Assault blew over the start line like an eventer going cross-country. He made a clumsy leap over the first fence, not even bothering to pick his legs up. The rails didn't wobble. I pulled back and tapped him with my crop, and he gathered himself a bit more before the second fence. His form was all over the place and he pulled against me the entire time. But he didn't touch a rail.

I left the ring, feeling many eager eyes on Assault. I rode the gelding away. Assault was infuriating to deal with, but he was precious to me. I needed him if I was ever going to get anywhere.

I waited a short while for the jump-off, and when my number was called I rode back in. This time, I let Assault loose, and he screamed over the fences, barely even looking at them. A couple of times, his takeoff was so bad I was sure he would knock a rail. But Assault's insane, brash ability carried him through.

I waited, and watched the carnage as others tried to beat our time. Only a few tried. The others just rode clean and slow, ceding the win to us. As the last rider approached the in-gate I took Assault back to the trailer. I quickly stripped off his tack and retied him, placing a hay net within reach of his mouth. Somewhat calmer now that he'd had a chance to expend some energy, Assault stood still.

Careful not to let my guard down, I stood at his head for a moment, softly laying my hand on the long slope of his shoulder. Assault's head dropped a few inches, and his ears fell forward.

A second or two went by, and Assault quickly shrugged me off, reaching for his hay. I stepped away from him and went on foot to collect our ribbon.

I made my way back to the show ring, contented. The buzz of activity around the trailers had subsided. As I looked ahead, I saw the reason. The trainers, my colleagues, were gathered mainly in the vicinity of the ring. And as I approached, my steps slowed, twisted, and stopped.

They were huddled in groups, discussing their horses, offering condolences, congratulations, and envy. The groups split and combined as they moved freely amongst themselves. I couldn't have walked up and joined in if I'd had a battering ram.

There was an unspoken order to this little world, this social class. And for the first time, as I stood off to the side, completely alone, I felt a barrier between me and them, as solid and unyielding and *real* as the fence I now leaned against, too drained of energy to stand tall and too despondent to even try.

I wasn't a part of this world anymore. I was an outsider.

Lawrence

I lay across the couch, concentrating fully on the Oreo cake in front of me. All my horses were ridden. It was late afternoon, and nobody needed to be fed yet. Nothing was required of me, and I took full advantage. I was relaxed and tired, the best kind of tired. Well, okay, not the *best* kind. But one of the top five kinds.

I must've fallen asleep, because I was suddenly aware that the light was different. I glanced down at the plate on my chest. There were still a few crumbs left, and I tipped the plate up to my mouth. Then I set it aside without getting up.

The door opened, and I craned my neck to see. Erica closed it softly, leaning on the door for a moment. Erica looked over at me. She looked tired too.

"Hey." I smiled. "I didn't hear you drive in. Do you need help unloading?"

"No. It's done." She walked over to the kitchen, moving slowly.

"So how'd it go?" I said.

She stopped walking. Her head fell back a little. "It was….okay. Assault won his class."

I nodded. "What about D.M.?"

"He didn't quite make it into the ribbons." Erica leaned on the counter, blindly reaching for a box of cereal.

"Well, it's only the first show of the year." I lay my head back down. "Sounds like a decent start."

"Yeah, I guess so." Erica's footsteps padded softly over to me. She sat down on the arm of the couch. I lay there in comfortable silence for a while.

"Oh, hey." I stirred suddenly, remembering something. "A really good friend of mine is coming to the area next week. She's planning to stop by. She wants to meet you."

Erica turned her head sharply. "Who is she?"

"She's just an old friend," I answered.

"What's her name?"

"Marla."

Marla

The freeway stretched unchanging before me like a treadmill, rolling on and on. Beyond the black leather interior, patchy trees and mundane cornfields blurred, vanished and reappeared. The subwoofers throbbed with Lady Gaga's "Bad Romance", carrying me along, the relentless beat filling me with false energy. I had driven all night, and I wasn't about to stop now.

A tightly-spaced pack of cars languished up ahead at a sedate 80. I was gaining on them as if they were idling. They grew larger in my windshield, bunched up together, occupying both lanes. There was no way around them. But as I eyed the wall of vehicles, I decided there might be a way *through* them.

I was nearly on top of the first car, tailgating aggressively. It was the moment when I would have to slam on the brakes, or drive straight into the back of the Prius in front of me. So I cranked the wheel left, stepping on the accelerator. The car leapt into the passing lane. With a close-lipped smile I called on every ounce of performance the Mercedes had to give, shoehorning myself through the crush of cars, fishtailing between the lanes as the other drivers panicked, swerving out of my way. I smiled as the freeway opened up, my foot pressing against the accelerator. The engine rumbled, and I was once again gaining ground, impeded by nothing.

The Mercedes chewed up a few miles before the cop car appeared in my rearview mirror, tiny swirling lights and a black blur. I rested my foot on the floor, no longer feeding the engine. Slowly, I coasted over to the shoulder and stopped. I held down a button, and my window receded into the door. I sat and waited for the cop to get there, occasionally checking his progress in the rearview. I shook my hair out a little, even though that was unnecessary.

Eventually the cop sidled up to my window. He was young and soft. He seemed short of breath, as if he'd been pursuing me on foot.

I turned my eyes on him. "Ever had a high-speed chase before?" I asked with a low smile.

He stared for a second, the blood rushing to his face and elsewhere. "No," he admitted.

"Well, I'm glad to be your first." I blinked coolly up at him.

He struggled, red in the face. Then he seemed to snap out of it. "You've been traveling at a high rate of speed," he said like he'd memorized it. "I've received calls that you've been driving erratically. Dangerously."

I shrugged, drawing my shoulders back just so as I widened my legs on the seat. My skirt crept up, increasing the skin visible between it and the thigh-high boots I had on.

I leveled my eyes on him, unrelenting. My gaze was unapologetically full of heat.

"I'm in a bit of a hurry to get where I'm headed," I said to the cop. "But I can assure you that I'm an *excellent* driver."

His eyes, which had been crawling all over me, snapped up to meet mine. I held his gaze and curled my hand around the gearshift, rotating once, twice, three times as I turned the key and moved it into drive.

I stepped on it, leaving rubber behind. He stood there and let me go.

Erica

I halted Soiree by the mounting block. She stood calmly with loops in her reins as I got on. I patted her and gave her a touch of leg, and she walked on.

I had a few jumps set up in the arena, but I wouldn't be taking Soiree over them. I jumped the young mare only one day a week, and the rest of the time I worked her on the flat, slowly building her up. Soiree's delicate build required finesse. She had already recovered from a stress fracture sustained during her time as a racehorse. Soiree's talent wasn't an issue.

The mare could jump beautifully, consistently, and she never lost her sweet, enthusiastic expression. The challenge in moving Soiree up in the competition ring would always remain the same: preserving her soundness while asking her to jump higher and more difficult courses. That balancing act was an integral part of training, but each look at Soiree's eager face and slim, refined legs was a sharp reminder.

After traversing the ring at a walk for ten minutes, I picked up my outside heel, lifting Soiree into a canter. She floated around the ring, pulling softly at the bit, seeking the comforting sensation of connection. Soiree's canter transitions were now solid, and I was beginning to test her endurance with longer durations of the faster gait. She needed to be able to sustain a canter through an entire course without fatigue. I followed her motion with my seat, listening to her breathing, feeling for changes in her rhythm. When her breathing quickened and she began to slow, I squeezed her sides, keeping her going just a bit longer. Stretching her. Then I patted her, letting her walk. I let the reins lengthen, and Soiree dropped her head and snorted repeatedly. She walked at a steady pace, catching her breath quickly.

I heard the far-off rumble of Amber's truck. I almost felt the vibration of it through my saddle. A couple minutes later I actually saw it. Barely decelerating, she cranked the wheel expertly and sailed into our driveway.

I halted Soiree and dismounted, hurrying to the arena gate. Amber slammed her door and headed our way. Soiree picked up her head and nickered adorably.

"Soiree, look at you," Amber said lovingly, meeting the mare with outstretched arms.

I stood off to the side, impatiently holding Soiree's reins. When Amber finally looked up from the mare's face, I seized my opportunity.

"I need to talk to you about something," I said.

Amber looked slightly thrown, but she recovered quickly. "Sure. What's going on?"

I hesitated. I was at the point of no return, where I'd finally know for sure. I had thought I wanted to know. But I was finding that I really, really didn't.

I sighed. "Lawrence said some woman named Marla is coming to visit." Amber's eyebrows arched toward her hairline. She sort of opened up, taking a step forward. "*Marla's* coming? He said Marla, right?"

"Yeah. I thought you might know her. He said she was a really good friend."

Amber just stared at me for several long moments.

"Oh, boy," Amber finally said. She didn't say anything else.

Erica again

I was trapped in front of the mirror, staring disparagingly into the reflective surface. It was quickly becoming rather unfocused at the edges. My head was starting to hurt.

I reached down, flipping open my cell phone. Time was running out. I returned to my reflection with shaky resolve. My entire limited closet was piled around me.

I'd been flipping between two different shirts for some time now. I didn't have that much in the way of nice clothes. I had always shot down my mother when she tried to buy me stuff. Undeterred, she'd bought things for me anyway, but I had left it all in my old room when I moved out. I'd almost thought about calling her for advice, but I just couldn't open that door again.

Back to the stupid shirts. The one on the floor at my feet was your basic short sleeved button-down in navy. All my stupid shirts were navy. The one I had on was a little fancier, a department store brand. The material was satiny. It was basically a fancy T-shirt, with a plain, slightly embellished neckline, but it zipped up the back. Unfortunately, it only zipped up the back under great duress.

I guess I've put on a little weight since last summer. I didn't own a scale; I assessed my physical condition based on the fit of my clothes. No less humiliating, just a different take on self-punishment. I shuffle-twirled around to get a better look at the fit. I couldn't breathe in the thing, and it highlighted several areas I wasn't too pleased with, now that it was tighter than shrink wrap. But it felt like surrender to just wear the button-down...

Team Dark Horse

I checked my phone. Five minutes until we should leave. I felt my respiration increase. *I guess I'm committed to this shirt,* I conceded. *Especially since I think I'm going to have to cut myself out of it.* I backed away slowly from the mirror, glad to be rid of my stuffed-sausage-like image. *Okay.* I was as ready as I knew how to be. I'd been at this for hours. I'd showered earlier and washed my hair. It was dry. I'd even peered at my fingernails to ensure they weren't overlong and full of grit. I stood there, fidgety. I felt like I should apply makeup, but I didn't own any cosmetics, and I sure as hell didn't know how to apply them.

I heard a creak to my left, and it turned my head. Lawrence banged through the screen door, right on schedule.

"Hey." He peeled off his sweaty T-shirt, picking a clean (or at least dry) one off the back of the couch. Without stopping he pulled it over his head and walked over to me. "You look hot."

"Really?" I swiveled my head to gawk at him. "You don't think it's too tight?"

He grinned. "Not possible."

"Okay then." I snatched up my phone and Lawrence's keys. "You're driving. I can't move my arms in this thing."

Fifteen minutes later we were parked outside of Angelina's, a ramshackle club in the "bad" part of town. It had been popular when I was in high school, but it had gotten kind of rundown. I hadn't been there before. The whole building was painted in flaking midnight blue paint, and the black lettering of the sprawling sign blended in. I sat in the cab of the truck, letting Lawrence walk around to open my door. I wasn't in a hurry.

I stepped out and walked in the door, taking a look around. The place was deserted. It was wide open, with limited seating and a massive stage with a pole in the center of it. The high ceilings made our footsteps echo. I was severely out of my element but I walked around checking things out anyway, emboldened by Lawrence's hand on my ass.

Soon we had seen all there was to see of Angelina's, and we stood down near the stage. I pulled out my phone. "What time did you say we were meeting her?"

Lawrence shrugged. "Noon. I'm pretty sure."

"Well, she's late," I stated snippily.

"If she doesn't show up soon, do you wanna make good use of that stage?"

I glared at him. "I will *not* pole dance. I refuse."

"So sex is an option?"

I twisted my head to face him. I was so not in the mood. "Shut up. Someone could hear us."

"There's no one here."

A door swished open somewhere in the building. Both of our heads snapped up.

She was on the upper level, far above me. She paused for just a moment, surveying the scene. Then she made her way down, each step deliberate, long and fluid. Her eyes were on Lawrence like she'd sighted in on him and was coming for him.

I stood, comatose, fragile as paper. Steadily she grew bigger in my frozen eyes.

She was slim and voluptuous at the same time, with curves in all the right places and no excess fat elsewhere. Her reddish brown hair billowed around her, reaching halfway down her back, flowing, gyrating and sparkling. She wore leather shorts and a sheer white dress shirt with a black bra underneath. She didn't wear heels. She didn't need heels. Her legs went up to her collarbone without any enhancement.

She came across the room, striding out like it was a runway. She smiled at Lawrence. Looking at her eyes as she looked at him felt like watching porn.

"Marla." Lawrence stepped right up to greet her.

She put her arms around him and kissed him full on the mouth, right in front of me.

When she pulled away, Lawrence turned to me without skipping a beat. "Marla, this is my girlfriend, Erica. Erica, this is my good friend Marla."

I just stood there like a deaf mute. Horrifying realizations were going off like a gong behind my eyes.

Marla's lip twitched in clear amusement and probably satisfaction. She extended a hand. "I'm so glad to have finally met you in person," she said, her tone subtly mocking. "The girl who tamed Lawrence Cavanaugh. This I *had* to see."

I took her hand clumsily and gave a little tremor of a handshake. I was slow and heavy. I was fat, and I was stuffed into my shirt. I was inept and clueless.

Marla's eyes skimmed over me, quickly growing disinterested. I was wildly aware of my rolls, my cellulite, my acne scars. I felt the sweat marks on my shirt, the chopped hairs on my head. I felt it all like a caustic substance that raised smarting welts wherever it landed.

"Very interesting," Marla said out loud. She turned away.

Marla

I'd spent so long imagining, crafting this girl in my head. *The girl who lured Lawrence Cavanaugh into monogamy.* My mind had gone wild speculating on what features she must possess. Such a girl would have to be extraordinary, I had surmised. Almost inhumanly so.

I'll bet she's had work done, I had long decided. *Fake tits, probably ass implants too.* Lipo on the thighs and mid-section, all to present the right hourglass ratio. She'd probably spent years on the carving board to look that way, too. *Guys never pick up on that stuff.*

Or maybe she's one of those super thin, super healthy vegan types who's all wholesome and shit. One of those perky, maddeningly earth-conscious girls who are so beautiful you just want to slug them and force a fast food burger down their righteous little throat.

There were many other possibilities I entertained. But I couldn't imagine such a girl. I couldn't come close.

I entered Angelina's through the back, feeling no effort in my muscles as I ascended the stairs. Pushing through a door, I saw them on the ground floor. I saw *him*, and I was flooded with enough adrenaline to dive over the railing. My feet pummeled the flight of stairs. I was almost there.

I was about to find out who Lawrence had chosen. I was about to *see* this girl, in the flesh, and find out who she was. What she had that I didn't.

It had been infuriating, all this time, not knowing the slightest thing about her. But now I would know. I would know everything.

But first, I had to see Lawrence. He was standing right there, right before me, in a tight T-shirt and jeans. I could smell the unshowered sweat on him, drawing me in like pollen.

Lawrence smiled. "Marla," he said with that voice. That silken gravel tone.

I stepped right up and kissed him brazenly. His girlfriend, whoever she was, did not rip me away by my hair or even speak up, which told me something about the girl.

I pulled away a few seconds after the kiss had become inappropriately long. Lawrence introduced us. And I finally got my answer.

The girl was perfectly, astoundingly ordinary. She had the haircut and physique of a homely lesbian. I would never have picked her out of a crowd, unless I was coaching rugby. I stood there in delighted shock, trying not to laugh in her scared, mousey face.

Well, this is going to be easier than I thought.

Erica

I sat in silence the whole ride home. As soon as we got there, before Lawrence had even shut the engine off, I pulled out my phone and shakily rattled off a frantic text to Ashley as he sat there in blissful ignorance.

Ash! Call me! Immediately!

I thrashed out of my seat belt and stalked around the yard. I knew I couldn't expect a quick reply. Ashley had a life, and I hadn't been a part of it for a while. I hadn't even talked to her in months. But she was all I had.

Lawrence slammed his door and glanced at me. "Erica, you coming?"

"No!" I almost screamed. Quickly, I attempted to rein in my voice and my crazy eyes. "I'm, uh, gonna be outside for a bit. I have…I have an urgent text I have to respond to!" *There! That explains everything!*

"Okay," he shrugged, going on his stupid merry way. The screen door opened and shut, and he was hidden from my sight.

Good. I threw my full attention at my phone, holding it in both hands, head bent low. *Come on, Ash. Come on, Ash.*

Suddenly, the phone buzzed in my hands. The incoming call popped up on the screen. *Ashley.*

Thank God. I hit the answer key like it was a game-show buzzer, and I was winning a million dollars. "Ash."

"Erica. What's going on?"

I was immediately, fully hysterical, my control gone. "Ash. Oh my God. I'm *freaking out.* I just met Lawrence's ex, and she is freaking *perfect.* I just…I can't believe he just sprung this on me with no warning! Like it's no big deal! Ash, it was *humiliating.* To have to stand next to her and look at them together…" I ran out of words to express my panic and just stood there hyperventilating.

"Erica, calm down," Ashley said soothingly yet forcefully. "Just hold on. So you met his ex?"

"Yes," I dry-sobbed. "And she's…she looks like a freaking supermodel. Except hotter."

"Oh, come on," Ashley cut in. "She can't be *that* pretty."

"No, Ash, you don't understand," I said firmly. "She *is.* She is."

"Okay," Ashley acquiesced. "But so what if she is? He's with you now."

I had walked all the way over to the line of maple trees without even noticing. I let myself slump against one, hitting the solid trunk so hard that it nearly knocked the wind out of me.

"Yeah," I said. "We'll see how long that lasts."

Lawrence

The LPC was shut down for the night, with just a few faint bulbs lighting the drive and illuminating the sign out front. Wilson abhorred stable lights because he felt they interfered with the horses' sleep cycles. It was after eight and the imposing metal gate blocked the way in. It was just like the first time I'd stumbled onto this driveway when I was a 14-year-old runaway.

Team Dark Horse

Except now I had a key.

I unlocked the gate, and it creaked dully as it eased forward to let me in. I drove up to the barn, where Wilson's decrepit Chevy still stood. That wasn't unusual. Wilson didn't have much of a life outside the barn. He lived nearby in the caretaker's cottage, but I doubted he even made the drive over there most nights.

It felt even less legit to be coming here to visit Elaine after dark, but I hadn't been able to get away all day. A few of the ponies whickered when I padded down the aisle, but I remained intent on her room. I didn't want to be gone for too long, since I was only supposed to be on a gas run.

I passed Wilson's office, where the distinctly orange glow of candlelight flickered at the edges of a slightly ajar door. Soft jazz was playing.

Something was wrong here. Wilson did not approve of playing music in a stable.

In an instant I doubled back, facing the door. Something was not right here. *Wilson's either losing his mind or…* I searched for another possible explanation. *Nope. Wilson's lost his mind.* I tried to recall the last time I'd spoken to the man. I couldn't remember. *Shit. I totally dropped the ball here.*

Screw it. I'm going in. Boldly, I pushed the door open and stepped inside, bracing myself for whatever I might find.

I was not prepared. Wilson's office *was* indeed lit up by candlelight. There was actual soft jazz playing from an actual record player. But Wilson was not delirious or alone. Well, delirious might've been the word, actually. But he sure as hell wasn't alone.

Several things happened just then. Shocked out of my mind, I exclaimed, "Barbara!" causing Wilson and Barbara to jump back from one another. Wilson's eyes snapped onto me, and he proceeded to stare at me with cold hatred, which he was absolutely within his rights to do in that moment.

"*Cavanaugh,*" he growled.

Barbara blushed hard but still managed a polite smile.

At my back, Elaine said, "I was about to warn you not to go in there. But I guess you found out for yourself." And she disappeared back into the night.

I cleared my throat. "Okay, well, sorry about the interruption. You kids have fun!"

My attempted bolt lasted about two strides before Wilson stepped out of his office, closing the door behind him. "*A word*, Cavanaugh," he intoned.

I stopped and turned around. "Yes?"

"*Not here*," Wilson snapped. "It'll disturb the horses. *Come with me*."

I was about to point out that what he and Barbara had been working up to would likely be equally disturbing for listening equines, but I thought better of it.

Wilson stopped in front of Elaine's room and thumped on the door. She opened it. "Yes?"

"Cavanaugh and I need a *private moment*," Wilson said through his teeth.

"Of course you do." Elaine stepped aside, leaving the door wide open.

"*In*," Wilson snapped, and I obeyed.

Wilson shut the door behind us. "*Sit down*."

I stared at him. "Seriously?"

He started looking murderous, so I sat down on my former bed.

"*What the hell*," said Wilson, "were you *thinking*?"

I looked up at him. "Honestly? I thought you were having a psychotic break."

"*What*?"

"The jazz, the candlelight - an open flame in a stable! I was concerned for your mental stability."

Wilson appeared to be struggling. "Did it *ever* occur to you that I might be entertaining a *special visitor*?"

I considered that for a second. "No. It did not."

"Even after all the times you brought some girl back here, and I was expected to deal with it...I can't even *tell* you how many awkward run-ins I had to endure, in *my own stable*...girls in various stages of undress, running through the aisle..."

"Yes, and that's my point exactly! Seeing some girl in a bed sheet was the most action you ever got! You can't expect me to just instantly go there, because *this is unprecedented!*"

Wilson was silent. He still looked perturbed, so I waited until the crackle went out of the air between us. Slowly a smile split my face.

"So," I said. "*Getting it on with Barbara Wellings.*"

Wilson turned red. "Don't be weird, Cavanaugh."

"I'm not being weird," I argued. "You're the weird one here. It's *weird*, for instance, that you are not *jumping up and down*, screaming from rooftops, and standing a foot taller, because you are now fucking Barbara Wellings, and *that*, my friend, is fucking *awesome*."

I stood up, clapped him on the back, and left the room.

Elaine was hanging out with Free Bird, one of the elderly polo ponies. "So," I said on my way past, "I take it you don't need anything."

"No, seeing as you provided the nightly entertainment."

I raised one arm over my head, and I was out of there.

I hauled ass on the way home, but Erica was still worriedly pacing the window when I pulled in the drive. She met me at the front steps. "What kept you?"

I raised my hands up to her face and kissed her apologetically. "I know. I'm sorry. I got waylaid at the LPC."

"I thought you were making a gas run."

"I was. But Wilson needed my input on something."

"Oh."

I steered her back into the house. "Hey, do you wanna know something crazy?"

"What?"

"Wilson and Barbara got together finally."

Her eyes brightened. "When?"

"I don't even know. He never told me. But I found him *entertaining* her in his office."

"His *office*?"

"Yeah. Candlelight, soft music, and file cabinets." I snorted.

"Oh my God." Erica was laughing now. "That's kind of sweetly pathetic."

"Whatever works," I shrugged.

Erica

Lawrence was off stick and balling on Harry, and I was sitting on the front porch with Amber, doing what I'd done for the past two days. Obsessing.

"I just can't believe he didn't even give me fair warning," I said, grinding on a particularly galling point. "I mean, had I known, I could've gone in prepared. I could've, you know, *done* something!" *Like gone out and bought a better outfit, for instance.* I shuddered. "It was horrible."

Amber nodded along monotonously. I got the feeling she was quickly tiring of my obsessing and grinding. At that moment, though, I didn't care.

"I just can't help but think about them...*together.*" I drew back, revolted. "And I can't stop thinking that if *she* was in his past, and he dumped her, how can he possibly be happy with *me*?" A sudden, horrifying thought struck me. "Do you think she's better in bed than I am?"

Amber shrugged. "Probably."

I gasped out loud and twisted to face Amber, gaping at her with wounded eyes.

"One of the most important friendship qualities is the ability to use a well-placed lie!" I yelped at her. "Which you clearly *do not have!*"

Amber twitched her shoulders. "Sorry. I'm not really the problem here, though, am I?" She glanced pointedly at Lawrence, who was returning from the field with Harry.

I chose to ignore the very reasonable point she was making. "Yeah, but...you're not helping! So go away."

Amber hopped off the porch with an enthusiasm that stung a little. "Maudie!" She sang out, jogging over to her mare's paddock.

I sat there, alone and unhappy. I was becoming a person nobody liked. I didn't want to be like that. *Maybe I should just calm down. Maybe it'll be alright.*

Having calmed myself, I got up and went to meet Lawrence and Harry as they walked down the driveway. Over the crunch of Harry's hooves on the gravel I heard a smooth but powerful engine.

Team Dark Horse

Lawrence turned his head to see the chrome-colored sports car as it whipped into the driveway. Amber rushed forward, not wanting to miss out on the show. I stopped moving and lost all initiative. Even without looking in the driver's seat, I knew who it was.

Marla stepped out into the expectant sunlight. This time she wore thigh-high boots and a miniskirt that barely covered her ass. Above that, she had a white tank on and a long gold necklace.

"I was in the neighborhood," she said coyly, not even trying to make it not sound like a line.

Lawrence grinned. I could almost hear Amber salivating. They both left me behind and closed in on her, drawn. I stayed back. Watching.

I noticed something in the unforgiving glare. Marla was not, actually, without her flaws. When I looked at her makeup free skin, I saw the fine lines, the gathering creases at her eyes and mouth. She was older than I'd thought, perhaps in her early 40s. But none of this comforted me for even a moment. In fact, it seemed almost like a taunt. She stood there, showing her age, flaunting it, hiding nothing. Those lines on her face didn't diminish her appeal. If anything, they made her even more attractive. She was a sex fantasy, and she was *real*.

No one called me over, so I ignored them, fully invisible. Instead, I walked surreptitiously over to get a better look at the car. I admired the streamlined, muscled-up exterior. The interior was gleaming black leather, and I could see one hell of a stereo in the back.

I was about to turn around and go back to the house when I saw the emblem. My head fell forward in disbelief and outrage, and I walked away quickly, firing off a text to Ashley, because Amber was too busy slavering over Marla.

She has a Mercedes. I'm going to kill myself.

Lawrence

I pulled up alongside Amber's apartment. It was the worst house in a seedy neighborhood. The siding appeared to be turning into sawdust. The

50

roof looked like bedraggled cardboard.

Amber was pacing in the narrow yard, stewing and occasionally throwing seething glances at the Harley. She didn't seem to notice me, so I shut the truck off and stepped out.

I crossed the sidewalk and right when my feet hit the grass, Amber stopped in mid-pace. She raced up to me. "Thank God you're here. Fuck my fucking truck." She glared sharply at the still form with its open hood.

I was still staring up at the house. "So this is your shitty apartment."

Amber turned her patented Death Stare on me. "No, I live in a fucking mansion. I just come here for the *ambiance*." She shook her head once, whipping her straight hair against her face. "Now let's *go*."

"Aren't you going to show me inside? I came all this way..."

Amber's knuckles quivered. "*Fine*." She lurched over to the door and yanked it open, shoving me inside.

I quickly scanned the room. The walls were so discolored I couldn't tell what was a stain and what was the actual paint. The floorboards were warped and sticking up in places. Near the back of the house, the sunlight fought to get through a single grimy window.

I stared at Amber. "It looks like a crime scene. And it smells like something died in here."

"Yes. I know. Okay, can we get *going*, please." Amber was using her lower register.

I gladly left the house, inhaling the fresh air. Amber ran full out to my truck, sending me nasty glances when I failed to speed up my walk.

Soon we were on the road. Amber didn't relax. She was jumpy, moving in her seat like she'd been carjacked and was trying to escape. Her eyes leapt wildly between the clock display on her phone and my speedometer.

"Can you *please* step on it a little?" She whined after maybe 30 seconds.

"I could, but then my engine would fall out. Also the brakes are iffy, so I don't like to go over 45."

Another glance at her phone. "I just don't want to miss Soiree's class."

"We won't miss her class. I just talked to Erica right before I got to your place. We have plenty of time." I reached over and patted her shoulder

51

reassuringly.

Amber swatted my hand away. "I really hate when you drive," she muttered.

"Because I don't break the sound barrier."

"You drive like a fucking granny. You get *passed* by fucking grannies. And they give you the finger."

"You won't miss Soiree's class," I said soothingly. "We have plenty of time."

"Fuck you."

Amber

Lawrence pulled into a space at the outskirts of a large field. I was out of the cab and on my feet before he shut the motor off. I moved quickly, my cargo pants scraping the ground under my heels. I didn't see a single horse or rider. I didn't hear a sound. My heart beat frantically in my chest, and I pushed onward, even though I had no idea where I was going.

A distorted human voice came on the loudspeaker. Through my rattled breathing, I listened hard. I didn't hear a class number or anything, but I caught the words "working hunter". And I accelerated into a run.

Going flat out, I covered the distance in several very long moments. I could see the rings now, one with many horses milling about and the other with a course of jumps and a single horse that was not Soiree. That didn't comfort me, though. *What if she already went?* I surged on, the anxiety at full force. *I'll strangle Lawrence, that's what if.*

Then I heard a nicker.

I whirled around, and there was Soiree, walking toward me with Erica on her back. I gasped out loud. "Soiree," I said softly, my voice stifled with emotion. "You're beautiful."

The mare had always been gorgeous, but Soiree was so obviously in her element here that her beauty was underscored. Her coat glowed like an incandescent light bulb, and the simple, elegant tack she wore was similarly shiny. The D-ring in her mouth was blindingly bright, and her pale golden mane was done up in tiny, perfect braids that showed off her long, shapely neck.

I just stared at the mare for a few moments, and then I reached out to hug her neck, being very careful of her braids. I looked up at Erica, suddenly finding my words. "*Wow*. She looks awesome! You haven't gone yet, have you?"

Erica grinned, shaking her head. "Nope. I'm on deck. You didn't miss anything!"

"That's good," I said, able to smile again. "Otherwise I might've killed your boyfriend."

She laughed.

Lawrence ambled up just then. "See? Right on time," he smirked at me.

I exchanged a glance with Erica. "I might still," I said darkly.

The loudspeaker started up, and Erica sat up in the saddle. "That's us," she said as Soiree's number was called. "See you in a few!" And she steered Soiree toward the in-gate.

I moved closer to the ring with Lawrence at my side. Finding a good vantage point, I stopped and watched Erica circle Soiree at the start of the course. My whole body was alert, and my throat prickled with emotion as Soiree leapt over the first fence, carefree and content. But most of all, she was *alive*.

Lawrence put an arm around my shoulders, and for once I didn't shake him off. "We did a good thing saving that one, didn't we?"

I nodded. I was overcome and starting to sniffle. "Yeah, we did."

Erica

Soiree was with me. Every muscle was supple and tuned in, right up to her brain. I felt the thoughts in her head, beautifully clear and free of outside influences. I felt only compliance, with an edge of pure joy.

I touched her with my leg and she stepped into a canter, reaching into the bit, the power from her hind legs rocking through her, unburdened like a wave. I circled her, unhurried, savoring. And we began.

The hunter course we faced was simple. No heroics were required. In fact, quick turns and harried jumping efforts were practically outlawed here. In the jumper ring, style counted for nothing. Here, it was everything.

Soiree cantered down to the first fence, ears pricked as she contemplated the dimensions. I felt her plan and prepare, and without changing anything, she stepped into her take-off spot, rounding up over the fence with slow, relaxed precision. Ears up, she moved on to the next obstacle, carrying me along as she completed the course.

There was no deviation, no falter in her technique. Each jumping effort was indistinguishable, a continuation of that first leap. The rhythm of her stride was mechanically precise. She was almost too accurate, too perfect. Yet there was no drudgery to her performance. She was not overly rehearsed or sour. Soiree glowed.

As we crossed the finish line, after what had been the most flawless hunter round I had ever seen, much less ridden, I was somewhere far above myself. Somehow I reined in Soiree, falling on her neck, caressing her and thumping wildly, and we left the ring. I was aware of a sudden crush of people surrounding us. Surrounding Soiree. They flocked to her, unable to keep back. The mare stopped and stood, foursquare, head gently bent as she welcomed the love. She basked in it.

I let her stand there until the trainers and onlookers returned to their own horses and the path cleared. I gave the moment to her, because it was her moment. I had done nothing to help her along in the ring. I had simply been there with her, and Soiree had done what she was born to do.

Gradually, the crowd parted, drifting back to their own horses. A path formed, and I rode Soiree through it. My eyes focused ahead on the only two people who really mattered. Soiree raised her head and whinnied.

Amber rushed over to Soiree, burning a trail of dust in her wake, her face open in a grin. "*Soiree!* You were *awesome* out there!" She exclaimed, wrapping her delicate arms around the mare's head.

Lawrence was close behind. He glanced sideways at the tableau of Amber and Soiree, smiling quietly. Stopping alongside the mare, he reached out for my hand. "I guess she likes her new job."

"I guess." I realized I was grinning from the sudden cramping in my cheeks. I couldn't stop.

"I knew you would do something great with her," Lawrence said, turning his ever-present bedroom eyes on me.

I shrugged. "It's all her," I said. "It's all her."

Amber's head suddenly popped up. Strands of hair stuck to her damp cheeks. "Thank you, Erica," she said earnestly. "I always knew Soiree was special, but you made her into something amazing. She looked like she belonged out there."

"Yeah, and her bascule was terrific," Lawrence threw in slickly.

Amber rolled her eyes. "Do you even know what that stupid term means?"

"It's her arc over the fence," Lawrence recited promptly with a glimmer in his eye.

Amber stared at him for a moment. "Well, shut me up, then."

I dismounted, landing lightly beside Soiree. She reached around to snuffle me with her nose. "You were *so* good," I said. "I better get you untacked, huh?"

Amber stepped eagerly forward. "Can I take care of her for you? Please?"

"Of course," I said, and I gave Amber the reins. Throwing an arm over the mare's neck, she led Soiree off.

Alone with Lawrence now, I turned to him. "Wow. That was something."

"You were amazing out there."

"*I* didn't do anything," I reminded him. "It's a hunter class. The horse is the star."

"Well, it's a good thing I don't judge hunters. Because I didn't even see the horse."

I moved closer, my grin spreading. "So all that talk about her bascule?"

"Educated guess."

"You can judge equitation anytime, then," I murmured. "Eq is all about the rider."

"I like watching you ride." He kissed me, holding onto me, which was good because my sense of gravity was slipping away. The universe went silent for a time.

When we broke apart, I was almost startled by the typical, raucous horse-show sounds around me. I looked around, dazed and somehow on edge.

"So are we done now?" Lawrence asked me.

I paused. *Are we? Wait, no.* I hadn't picked up my ribbon. "I'll be just a minute," I said. "Why don't you go ahead and I'll meet you back at my trailer."

"Sure." Lawrence walked off, negotiating this foreign territory like an old pro. I smiled, jogging to the ring.

Ribbon in hand, I walked briskly through the spotty crowd. I got a few lingering looks here and there. *Not so invisible anymore, am I?* I smiled to myself, vindicated.

Mark DeWayne stepped in front of me purposefully. I halted, immediately on guard. Mark had never been in good stead with me since he'd gone behind my back to try and snatch up Assault.

Mark's eyes were pinched, and he was looking off in the distance. "That guy…" he said sharply. "Is that *Cavanaugh*?"

I stepped back clumsily, thrown. "Uh…yes?"

Mark's shoulders rose. He shook his head. "He's got some nerve showing his face here," he finally sputtered and abruptly stalked off.

I stood there holding my ribbon to my chest, staring after Mark. I couldn't read that much into it. Horse people were crazy. I didn't even like Mark DeWayne. He had never once done or said anything of value. I couldn't read that much into it.

I walked slowly back to my trailer. From a distance, I could see Amber at the end of Soiree's lead. The mare was eating grass. Lawrence was on one knee, devotedly wrapping her legs, keeping the perfect tension on the white cotton even as she moved about.

I walked headlong into the familiar, loving scene, letting Mark's cryptic remark fade into the background.

Lou

I carefully opened the etched-glass door and was immediately engulfed by my mom. She hugged me fiercely for several seconds, then leaned back to get a look at me. "Oh, it is so *good* to see you again," she enthused, burying her face right back into my shoulder.

I looked up and saw my dad approach on my right. He stepped right up and gave me a warm, one-armed hug. "It's good to have you back, son. If only for a week."

I smiled at them both, feeling my mind relax. Riding Grand Prix dressage in Germany was a dream, an honor, a necessary prerequisite on the path to the US Olympic team. But the pressure was intense and constant. The European judges demanded brilliance, undeviating brilliance at all times. Anything less was an excuse to put me, a startup kid on an Irish Thoroughbred, in my place.

I didn't care particularly for that world. It wasn't me. But I was a resident of that world, like it or not, and it changed people. It changed me. It got in my head, winding me up, pushing me, driving me away from humanity. If not for my nightly calls from Marisol, I probably would have lost myself entirely. But she kept me holding on.

These brief visits home were wonderful. Even though much of my time was spent on business - teaching clinics and the occasional private lesson - I always made family a priority. They had seen me through so much, and I never wanted to lose sight of all they had given me.

After we'd all stood misty-eyed in the foyer for a while, we went to the dining room, where Helga was proudly setting out my favorite meal. I thanked her warmly, and she beamed.

I made my way to the table and sat down. My dad was already seated at the head, with my mother across from me. I dove into my salad. She smiled behind her forkful of greens.

"So, how's business?" I said, directing the question at my dad.

"Still quite good." He chewed a bite of roast chicken. "I've had to cut back a bit on my training horses. But quality is selling."

"That's excellent. I'm glad to know the family name is still prospering." I poked some more spinach leaves with my fork. "And how is Erica doing?"

Two forks clinked to a halt. The silence was pointed.

I looked around suddenly, scanning the table. My head jerked up, and I looked at my parents. "Where *is* Erica?"

My dad slumped down in his chair, making himself scarce. My mother spoke up instead. Her voice was all nasally. Pinched.

"Erica doesn't live here anymore," she said, and she stabbed her salad with a deafening clink.

Erica

It was Sunday morning, and we were all still high from Soiree's magnificent debut. Amber had been out already, pitching in with chores and taking both Soiree and Maude out to graze on the lush, overgrown lawn. When she had to leave for work, Lawrence and I had gone inside. And we hadn't left the house since.

We hadn't even bothered cooking a "real" breakfast, since, as Lawrence so helpfully pointed out, if this wasn't a time for celebratory cake, nothing was. So in between rounds in the bedroom, we'd devoured the triple-fudge brownie cake in the fridge like piranhas on a dead cow.

Eventually, I was looking at a mere slice of cake, the equivalent of a normal-person serving. A very small twinge of guilt hit my veins, carried along on a flood of sugar. "This was a whole cake when we started."

Lawrence shrugged. "We'll burn it off," he said from somewhere behind me, hot breath landing on my neck.

"*You'll* burn it off," I reminded him. "*I* won't fit in my show breeches next week."

He was undeterred. "I think I read somewhere that an orgasm burns 200 calories."

I turned my head around. "Where did you read *that*?"

"In one of those chick magazines. Cosmo or something."

"You read Cosmo?"

"I skim through it occasionally. To make sure there's nothing I don't already know."

I snorted. "Well, I think it's going to take more like 2,000 calories to make a dent on *this*." I gestured to the almost-empty cake tray.

Lawrence flipped me around expertly, and suddenly I was on top of him. "Well, we better get a move on it, then."

Team Dark Horse

I laughed out loud, and his mouth was on mine, and we were well on our way to getting a move on it when there was an unmistakable knock on the door. I jerked my head up and let out a groan, while Lawrence turned his face into the pillow and swore fluently.

"If that's Amber, I'm putting Maude on the grill, and we'll have a block party," Lawrence said dryly after a moment's pause.

I shook my head. "Amber went to work, remember? It's probably another of your long-lost relatives."

"Not likely."

I got off him and went to answer the door, pulling on the button-down I wore so it covered what it needed to cover. I was beginning to think it was probably Marla at the door, and in the back of my mind, I was rather pleased to show her that Lawrence's and my relationship didn't lack for passion. Or cake.

I threw open the door without another thought, and I instantly regretted that action, because the person I revealed myself to was not Lawrence's Barbie-doll-sex-freak ex, or one of Lawrence's relatives.

It was one of mine.

My brother was standing there, and he looked at me with slight shock in his eyes, but not nearly what I would've expected. There was more resignation in his face, the confirmation of something already known. Then it smacked me right in the face. He'd been to our parents' house. Lou had already heard the tale from our mother, or her version of it anyway. The anger revved in my abdomen.

"Lou," I said inadequately.

He didn't answer right away. His eyes swept over me. They weren't harsh, but they weren't exactly generous either. Finally, he looked up into my face.

"I did not expect to find you here," he said. He seemed to say it very carefully.

My eyebrows lowered. "Didn't mom tell you?"

"No," Lou said. "When I asked her, she just said 'Erica doesn't live here anymore'. She wouldn't tell me anything. She seemed really pissed off, though. So when I got out of there, I called your cell phone. You didn't

59

answer, so while I was waiting for you to call back, I drove over here. Then I saw your truck in the driveway..." my brother trailed off for a while. "I was just coming to say hi to Lawrence. I had no idea...you would be here."

I paused for a few seconds. I really had no idea what to say. "Well...it's nice to see you again?"

"Yeah," Lou said uncomfortably. We both looked away just then. I couldn't believe this. I couldn't talk to my own brother.

A very tight moment passed by. Then Lou spoke up again. "I just hope you've thought this through, Erica," he said quietly.

My eyes snapped onto him in a heartbeat. "What the hell does that mean?"

He peered up at me, worried. "It's just...this isn't like you. This is very sudden."

"What was I supposed to do?" I snapped. "Stay with mom forever? She was bad for me, Lou. You know that."

"I know that, Erica," Lou began.

I cut him off. "I never interrogated you like this when you hooked up with Marisol," I said harshly. "I don't see why you shouldn't extend me the same courtesy."

He tried to speak up, but I was already turning around. "I'll tell Lawrence you're here," I said, and I left him standing there.

I walked back to the bedroom. Slowly. My head was pounding with rage only slightly diluted by confusion and sadness. I couldn't understand why Lou was being like this. I got that I had changed a lot. I got that this was unexpected, given my track record. But why did everyone expect me to just stay a hardworking ambitious virgin for the rest of my life? And why did everyone seem to think that just because I was in a relationship now and having regular sex, my priorities and ambitions had fallen out the window? I got that I was different, but I was still the same person. Why couldn't anyone see that?

Lou had always been so supportive. Why had he stopped now, when I needed him the most?

Lawrence was still waiting for me in bed, but he no longer looked hopeful about the prospect of round four or whatever number it was.

"Lou is here," I said. "I expect he wants to talk with you."

Lawrence

I made my way to the front door with considerable dread and the tentative, lingering footsteps of someone in avoidance mode. One look at Erica's face when she came back from answering the door had put me ass-deep in it. I wasn't looking forward to this conversation.

I was at the door too quickly. *Damn this little house.* I let myself have one more second of hesitation, then I stepped bravely out into reality.

Lou was at the bottom of the steps. The blonde hair down to his chin and his denim jacket were the same as always. But the look in his ice-blue eyes was not promising.

I badly wanted to cling to the high ground on the porch. But I made myself walk down to his level. As it was, I still had the height advantage.

Lou looked up at me guardedly. "So, you and Erica," he said. "That's...weird."

I coughed a little. I could feel myself becoming defensive. "It's not that weird."

Lou was studying me carefully. "When did this happen?"

"Last fall." I could hear him adding up the months in his head, and it pissed me off.

Lou straightened up and looked at me full on. "Lawrence, I know we go way back and all, and I should be cool with this, but I'm not. I don't like this."

My hackles raised. "Oh, really? You don't approve, do you?"

"She's my sister," Lou said, staying firm. "And I'm not gonna say she's naïve, but she doesn't have a lot of experience with guys."

"So you don't think she's capable of making her own decisions? Or you think I just took her inexperience and ran with it? You think I took *advantage* of her?" My blood was heating up.

"No," Lou said, setting me back a little. "I don't think that. But I know how you are, Lawrence. I know how many girls you hook up with all the time, and how sometimes you have one you kind of care about - like

Team Dark Horse

Amber, back when. But it never goes anywhere. I know it, you know it, and I just want to make sure my sister knows it. Because you might be okay with having her be your latest fling or whatever, but Erica doesn't operate that way. She might tell you she's okay with it, and she might try, because she really wants to be with you, but she's going to get hurt. And she doesn't deserve that."

Lou looked at me forcefully. I looked at him in relief. "No, she doesn't," I said. "And I'd rather die than hurt her, Lou."

His features started to soften. "So she's not just your latest fling?"

I shook my head. "Absolutely not."

Lou cracked a smile for the first time. "That's wonderful." He glanced downward. "I probably owe both of you an apology. I was just concerned."

"You didn't know any better," I said, feeling more generous now that things were cleared up.

Lou looked back at his rental car. "Well, I'd better get going. I don't think I should subject Erica to any more of my presence after I was such an ass." He turned to go. "Just tell her I was wrong and I'm sorry, okay?"

I nodded. He started the car and drove off with a wave.

I went back into the house, fully intent on telling Erica what Lou had said. But when she met me at the door, she didn't look like she was in the mood for talking. Her eyes were lowered, her face clouded over. She led me straight to the bedroom, where everything fell out of my head when she threw me against the wall and had her way with me almost defiantly. Then we went on with our lives and never talked about it.

Yvette

I awoke in a lavish king-size bed, surrounded by silken curtains half drawn. I lay beneath sheets of an undeniably high thread count, and I tore them off as if they contained shards of glass.

I dressed quickly, walking directly to the refrigerator, where I opened and drank a protein shake. Another two steps took me to the treadmill, which I turned to the highest setting. I ran until I was bathed in sweat, and then I showered, dressed once more, and grimly stepped outside.

The house I had just left was merely one of many structures on this sprawling piece of land. There was a gazebo in the lavish garden, and a tennis court nearby, complete with a retractable roof and seating. Of course there were the stables, perfect in every way, fully stocked with ponies and equipment. There were grooms on-site 24/7. A regulation polo field sat in the center of it all, with perfect, lovingly maintained footing. Even as I looked, it was being watered with the precision of someone performing surgery.

My eyes drifted unwillingly up the hill, to the main house, larger than all else combined. For I was staying in the guest house. None of it was mine.

When my sponsor, Jean-Philippe, dropped me, I lost more than my place on a team ranked number one in the Women's Polo Federation. I lost my independence. Without cash prizes and endorsement deals, I could no longer earn a living. I clung to my apartment in Wellington for as long as I could, then was evicted. So, even though it appealed to me much less than the prospect of sleeping in my car, a subcompact environmentally friendly missile made of aluminum, I accepted Courtney's offer and came to live in the guest house on her father's estate in Vermont.

My days were without deviation. I stuck to my stringent exercise schedule. I kept to my diet. I rode Courtney's ponies, one after the other, for hours on end. With the time that was left over, I prowled websites, attempting desperately to remain within earshot of the world I had left. The world that had been taken from me. It was futile, but I could not stop. I could not accept defeat and move on, because there was nothing else out there for me. Not a thing.

I bent over a computer screen, fully focused on the item in front of me. It was a regular column, a brief, gossipy recap of matches, year-end standings, and the like.

Rahor Has Excellent Season, the headline read.

Brandon Rahor led The Pony Express to an improved national ranking of #4 this past season. Rahor, who took over the #3 position on Team Pony Express after Lawrence Cavanaugh's abrupt departure last spring, has proved quite industrious, if not the stylist that Cavanaugh was in his brief reign. Coming from out of nowhere, Cavanaugh left with the hearts of many fans and a perfect record, as well as a staggering five Most Valuable Player awards in a row.

Cavanaugh has yet to be heard from since he left for Lexington, KY with his injured pony, Eloise.

My eyes read no further. I was motionless, staring into the screen. My hands trembled, my pulse exploded, and I felt a rush of adrenaline within me, expanding, carried along on a blast of absolute clarity.

I did not pause. I did not question it. I slammed the computer shut with a bang, and I hurried to find Courtney. *Enough fucking around,* I thought manically. The polo field was empty, as was the tennis court, so I sprinted up to the main house. I entered without knocking and pelted up the stairs to her room.

"Courtney!" I roared as I fell against the door.

I heard something, and she opened the door. "Yvette? What's going on?" She peeped out from eight inches above me.

I lurched into her room, my eyes lighting on her. "We are leaving."

Courtney's eyes widened, even more than usual. "What - why? Where are we going?"

"Kentucky," I announced, and my lips drew back in a smile.

Courtney blanched. "Why?" She said again. She was starting to look like Bambi.

I shook my head once. "It does not matter. I have a plan."

"Oh," Courtney said, and she nodded. That was all she needed to hear. "My dad went out to breakfast. We'll have to wait 'til he gets back so I can let him know."

"You may call him from the road. We have no time to spare."

"Oh," Courtney said again. She was beginning to look slightly panicked. "I guess I should go get the Hummer ready."

"We are *not* taking the fucking Hummer, Courtney. *Think* of the gas mileage."

"But I don't fit in your Voyage."

I stared at her, incensed. "It does not matter. We will make it work." I strode around to the highboy, yanking upon all the drawers until they lay open. "Pack all of your shit and let's go."

Courtney stumbled over to the dresser and began to sift through her clothing. She looked at me plaintively with big wounded eyes as she lifted a handful of hot pink thongs. I turned my back on her.

"You have ten minutes," I said on my way out. "And then I will leave without you." I turned back once more. "And pack lightly," I said viciously. "Because we are *taking* the Voyage."

I returned to the guest house, where I swiftly packed up everything I owned. I stuffed it in the Voyage's trunk and chugged another protein shake as I waited for Courtney.

She came staggering down the hill at exactly ten minutes from the time I'd left her, carrying nothing more than a small backpack. She looked near tears. I moved the passenger seat back as far as it would go, allowing her a few more scant inches of leg room.

Courtney got in, struggling to buckle the seat belt with her knees hiked up to her chest. I put it in drive and roared out of there, cutting off some guy in an SUV. He passed me and flipped me off, so I passed him, and we battled for a few miles.

Eventually, I looked over at Courtney. Her eyes were downcast and she appeared to be sniffing a little. I kept my eyes on her until she looked up.

"Cheer up," I said. "I have a plan."

Erica

I stepped out of my truck, lowered the ramp and looked in on my little string of horses. From the front of the trailer, Soiree turned her head and nickered, the sound echoing pleasantly off the metal walls. Assault cranked his head around, tied tight as he was, and stared pointedly at me while dangling a front hoof in the air. D.M. provided a buffer between the two horses. It had been a nerve-wracking trip, listening for sounds of scrambling, in-fighting and general hell breaking loose, but it appeared that the three horses had come to no harm.

Assault began tapping the trailer wall with his hoof while looking me right in the eye. He was testing boundaries. I sighed, squaring my shoulders as I went to his head. "Put it *down*," I growled in his ear, and he stood with four on the floor as I untied him. He had learned *something*.

I re-tied Assault to the side of the trailer and shoved a hay bag in front of his face. Then I unloaded D.M. and Soiree, tying them on the *other* side of the trailer. They could be within reach of each other. *They* were civil. That left Assault totally isolated, and he pulled a bit at his lead, but the gelding wasn't seeking companionship. He just wanted something to sink a hoof into when the mood struck him. As usual, I ignored him as much as possible in the period leading up to his class.

When the time came, I tacked him up impersonally and we began the long walk to the ring. I had parked at the far reaches of the field this time. I wasn't seeking approval, and I didn't want to talk to anyone.

From the outset, though, I couldn't help but notice that I was getting a very different reception than I had two weeks ago, when I couldn't get a single person to look me in the eye. This time, people I had long known and people I barely knew looked up as I went past. Their eyes seemed to bore into me even as I stared straight ahead, remaining determinedly on my path to the ring. And I knew somehow, by educated guess or by feel, that their lingering stares were not complimentary.

It was unsettling. I almost preferred my prior invisibility. I wanted it back.

Assault pulled at the reins, and I hurried to keep up. I had a job to do. I needed to get this horse into the ring on time. I refused to stop. I refused to be dragged under by the multitude of people trying to catch my eye.

Then I ran right into a wall. That wall was called Mark DeWayne. *Of course.*

"I see you didn't bring that scumbag with you again this week," he said acidly.

"That scumbag is my boyfriend," I reminded Mark, drawing myself up tall and trying out Amber's Death Stare.

Mark threw me a condescending look. "He wouldn't be for long if you knew what he did to my cousin."

I wasn't sure I wanted to know. Scratch that, I definitely *didn't*. "Okay, well, I've got to go *warm up this horse*," I said, enunciating clearly. "You

Team Dark Horse

know how Assault gets, don't you, Mark?"

With perfect timing, Assault flattened his ears and showed his teeth, causing Mark to stumble away, muttering something under his breath. I was pretty sure he called Assault something, and I was certain it was a lot less flattering than "scumbag". I wasn't about to correct him.

I smiled, patted the gelding on the shoulder, and turned for the warm-up ring. I was almost there when Ben Miller neatly blocked my entry, mounted on a chubby roan mare. He was smiling down at me like a gargoyle.

I looked up at him, contempt rippling through my body. "If this is about my love life, Ben, you can save your breath."

Ben tipped his head back in faux surprise. "You know I never have a bad word to say about anyone, Erica," he said, his voice saccharine. "I'll admit I was…taken aback by your choice in romantic partners. But then again, your choices have *always* been questionable."

He rode off smirking. If I hadn't been surrounded by people, I would've given him the finger.

I thought the worst was over, since my two main enemies had already done their best to get under my skin. But from there it was just a collision course with people I'd known since birth, all of whom seemed to somehow know intimate (and sometimes extremely unflattering) details about Lawrence and his past transgressions. I managed to escape without hearing too many specifics, mostly because I was fighting to maintain control over Assault the entire time. But the sheer volume alone was horrifying.

Finally, my number was called, and I leapt onto Assault. I had never been so glad in my life to ride into the big, open, solitary show ring. Without even a warm-up, Assault pounded over the course, clearing everything in sight even as he pulled, lurched and screwed around the entire time. By the end of the course, he was nearly pulling me out of the tack. I sat up and gave him a firm jerk on the outside rein, and he settled into a walk as we left the ring.

I kept Assault moving as we waited our turn in the jump-off. I kept him far away from the prying eyes of my so-called friends. I had already heard more than enough today, and I charged away from anyone who even

Team Dark Horse

looked my way.

I let Assault loose in the jump-off. I sat up, held on, and aside from pulling him this way or that when he threatened to veer off course, I let him go, and I watched almost in slight amusement as the rails remained firmly in their shallow cups while Assault tore around in his usual madcap fashion.

We took the blue back to my trailer, where I took off Assault's tack and tied him up again. Before I began to get Soiree ready, I scratched D.M.'s class. I didn't have enough energy, and I just wanted this day to be over.

Soiree lowered her head agreeably so I could peel off the stretchy neck cover that protected her braids. Gradually, her pleasant demeanor managed to influence my mood, and I went about the final, frantic hoof-polishing and dust-removing preparations with a new resolve. By the time I mounted up, we both looked the part of class-A champions. I was more than ready to get out there and show.

I rode a cursory warm-up, rejoicing in what I held in my hands. Soiree moved under me, poised and confident. I settled into her metronomic rhythm and listened for our number.

When it was called I left the warm-up ring, smoothly bringing Soiree to the in-gate. I was glad to see people sit up and take notice. Apparently, Soiree had made an impression in her sparkling debut.

We completed our courtesy circle. Soiree sighted in on the first outside line like she'd spotted an old friend. She moved with a skip in her step, a delightful, youthful exuberance that made me break out in a smile. Her body rounded up over the first fence, knees up to her chin, ears pricked forward. She felt thoroughly alive, almost rambunctious by hunter standards. The discipline was fraught with tales of horses being malnourished, or longed into submission, made good and tired before a round to produce that automaton rhythm, the flat-kneed, relaxed way of moving. In contrast to some of the "made" hunters I'd ridden, Soiree felt as if she was about to light up like a firecracker.

If I hadn't known the mare like I did, my impulse would have been to check her. But here in the ring, I trusted Soiree implicitly. She was reliable. She knew her job, and she loved it. I would not raise my hand, or put so much as an ounce of pressure on the reins, unless she gave me a clear reason to. This spark that she had, this passion, was something pure and special. I cherished it. I would guard it with my life if I had to.

With the first line down, I bent Soiree through the corner, making a neat turn onto the diagonal. Soiree switched her lead seamlessly, looking ahead to the next fence. She continued the course with elegant jumping efforts, and swept over the finish line, her body electric and calm at the same time.

Positive tension, I thought. It was the same feeling I got from riding Harry. He could have run, he wanted to run, but he held back, giving only what was asked of him. I could get on Harry, even now, and put him through his paces. Walk, trot, canter. He was obedient, never taking one step faster than the pace I dictated. But he felt as though lighting was conducting inside of him.

Positive tension was difficult to create in a horse if they didn't have the impetus. It wasn't something you could force. You had to just try, through good, patient training, to help it along. But I was learning that the truly great horses, the superior performers, had it inside them already.

I waited to hear the results, sitting on my horse, conspicuously off the one side. The other trainers grouped together loosely, moving among each other with ease. I was stiff as a board, right there, but not really present in the true sense of the word.

I didn't let Soiree down. She earned another blue. Bending her neck graciously, she allowed the ribbon to be pinned on her bridle. I gave the mare a pat, allowing her a moment before giving her a touch of leg. She pivoted on her haunches, leaving the ring behind as we made the long walk to my trailer.

As I loaded up in my far corner, I watched the typical bustling activity going on up ahead. I saw the camaraderie between the rival barns, and while much of it was pretext and totally fake, I still missed being part of it. I thought about all the different sensations of being alone, and how I had never felt this particular one back when I was single.

I felt like crying as I loaded up and drove out of there. Usually, after a hard day I just wanted to get home. But the concept of home had gotten convoluted, and I didn't know what I wanted.

When I pulled in the drive, Lawrence wasn't there. It was almost a relief, and I clung to the simplicity of that feeling and didn't delve any deeper. I unloaded my horses and turned them out, pausing to scratch D.M.'s blaze. I apologized to him for dragging him along for nothing.

I stood there looking out at my horses in their little paddocks. I didn't feel like riding, and I didn't feel like sitting and waiting either. Almost without thinking I dug in my pocket for my phone. It had uttered not a beep all day.

I dialed and waited.

"Hello?"

"Hey, Maggie, it's Erica."

"I *know* who it is. I have caller ID."

I smiled. "Do you want a lesson? I have some free time."

"Okay, sure!"

"Get Twinkle ready. I'm heading over now."

Lawrence

Erica was gone, at a horse show. I was unmotivated and off to a slow start. My two polo ponies stood idle. I'd spent most of the morning shoveling shit and the past few hours working with Trucker. The gelding still had major fear issues since a dressage trainer had spurred him bloody, trying to force brilliance out of him. But Trucker was different than the usual abuse cases I'd dealt with over the years. He didn't thrash in a panic at the slightest touch; he didn't rear when I tightened the reins. He didn't come at you with teeth and hooves, ready to mow you down. Trucker did absolutely nothing to defend himself, and his giving nature had only escalated the abuse he'd suffered.

He was able to hang out and be a horse now at least. I could pet him, brush him even. I could lead him around. But when I got on his back, he reverted to that frozen mess of terror he'd been when he first stepped off my trailer. He locked up and couldn't move. And he needed to get past that somehow.

Trucker couldn't just stand in this paddock forever. He was a sound, healthy, good-natured horse who could have a job. He could have a future.

If I could get him over this crippling phobia.

So I'd taken to sitting on him, as much as possible, sometimes for hours at a time. I'd lead him out to the lush grass behind my house, halt him and climb onto his back. And I sat there, asking nothing of him, until finally he relaxed and lowered his head to eat.

I had just finished with Trucker and turned him out. Harry was pacing his fence line, staring at me and wearing a trench in the soil. I was starting to think about bringing him in and tacking him up when the horses all turned, seeing something. My head followed.

Up the dirt road, a tiny, beetle-like silver car was driving straight down the middle at an improbably fast clip. A plume of dust stretched out behind it, hugely tall and wider than the car itself. I watched in slow fascination as it careened into my driveway, fishtailing a bit on the gravel.

I got a mere glimpse of the driver before she stepped out of the miniature cab. Her hair was back in a severe ponytail, and she wore large sunglasses, but her face did not change when she took the sunglasses off.

Yvette looked at me for a few moments, and the contempt on her face was just as strong as I remembered. Her small shoulders were held rigidly back, and her short, tight strides carried her along efficiently. She offered no greeting.

Yvette came to a tidy stop. "He dropped me."

"What?"

"That son of a bitch." She rolled her eyes, waving a hand. "Jean-Philippe. He dropped me."

"Oh," I said. "That sucks."

"You are not kidding."

Yvette heaved a sigh, her eyes scanning the yard. I saw her eyes light on Vegas and Harry, and just as quickly, they ticked back to me. "So. What have you been doing all of this time?"

I shrugged. "Training. Stick and balling. Keeping my edge," I added somewhat proudly.

Yvette scoffed. "*Keeping your edge*. What good is it? I train and train each day, as hard as I ever did, all to *keep my edge*. What good is a fucking edge? What use is there for a blade, if not to *sink it into the throats* of your competitors?"

Her eyes were a bit mad. I remembered she was intense, and I could tell the months-long dry spell wasn't helping. She was like a rabid dog staked out in the middle of a flock of chickens. Lunging and being yanked back. Lunging and being yanked back.

An idea slipped into my mind. It was only natural. I didn't question it. I looked at my two polo ponies, all legged up and ready to go. I looked at Harry, who with all his brilliance and eagerness, was still ignorant. He needed to learn the game, really learn it. He needed to get out on the field with another horse just as focused on the ball as he was, and he needed to take it away from them.

I looked at Yvette as she stood in front of me, her mind positively twitching with the exact same idea. I was looking at one of the finest polo players in the world.

"Fancy a rematch?" I said to her casually.

She gave no response. She didn't have to.

I smiled and went to hook up my trailer.

"I will *not* be sleeping with you," Yvette said primly as I walked away.

"That's what you said last time."

Yvette

The bay gelding stood underneath me, but even his stance held the promise of considerable power. The wind coursed through the deserted polo club. Not a soul was here, and that suited me. For I was not seeking an audience. I needed only the game.

For a high goal polo player, sustaining one's self and maintaining one's *edge* on solitary stick and balling was tantamount to a prison inmate living on gruel. You could survive this way, but things became very grim indeed. Galloping about and whacking upon a ball that only went where I placed it quickly became monotonous. Lacking the opposing crush of players, the rattle of mingled hoof beats, the bitter scramble and the havoc, it was empty. A dreary, suffocating shell.

Team Dark Horse

Polo was about destruction. With no one to destroy, it may as well have been croquet, for all the thrills it offered.

Cavanaugh had mounted up on his pony; they moved slowly across the field. With a sigh, I turned the bay and allowed him to walk on. I never cared for this warming up phase. My mind idled while my body remained poised, my hand firmly clenched upon my mallet.

At last, Cavanaugh gave me the signal. He looked at me, black eyes boring through me with clear intent, and he dropped the ball onto the center of the field. Quick as could be, we moved away from it, shunning it, eyes averted. The ponies' step elevated. Cavanaugh's gelding rolled his eye in the socket, fixing it on the stationary ball.

As we reached the goal, we turned the ponies around. They made the turn on their hind legs alone, rising above the flat earth with anticipation and need.

We began as we had the last time, nearly a year before. With each halting step our ponies took, we watched each other, neither tipping their hand. Making not a twitch. Nearly in unison, we stalked each other, and our ponies' heads rose higher and higher, both straining for the barest signal, the lightest touch of leg upon their taut sides. All around us, the universe slowed, and the sound went away, so complete was our focus, so overpowering was our concentration on one another.

I feinted to the left, and Cavanaugh's pony leapt forward. He checked him, and in the split second that their momentum stalled I slapped my heels into the bay, and we were out ahead.

There it was, the glorious noise of hoof beats, coming down heavily as a pile driver. I moved the bay to the side, attempting to block Cavanaugh's path, but he was too fast for me, so we wove across the field, close enough to spit in each other's faces. My leg buffeted Cavanaugh's leg, his pony's flank, his churning shoulder. The ball was nearing; we were almost there, and I directed the bay to slam into Cavanaugh's pony, to knock him out of the way, but the young horse dug in and pushed back even harder. We galloped over the ball locked in a tussle, and neither of us could swing. The ponies doubled back as one. The young gelding's eyes were pinched. His tail lashed like that of a caged tiger. I saw Cavanaugh prepare to strike.

He had the greater reach. I would not beat him to the ball. With a growl and a push from my leg, the bay made a mighty leap, and I hooked Cavanaugh's mallet with mine, stopping him dead.

Feeling the resistance, the young gelding ducked his shoulder and spun, freeing his rider. But he moved one step too far, and he lost the advantage. He allowed me in.

One should never allow me in.

My mallet hissed through the air, striking the ball with the ease and deadliness of a cobra. The bay gelding shot forward, and as the ball touched the ground, he brought me there to give it one more shove in the direction of the goal. It went in without hesitation.

I pulled up and just looked at it lying there, not unlike the last time when Cavanaugh had been victorious. When I heard him come up behind me, I slipped the reins and the bay began walking. Cavanaugh's pony fell into step with him.

"He handled himself very well," I said in regards to the young gelding. I could afford to be civil. I had won.

Cavanaugh nodded, obviously pleased with his startup. "You won't get by him again," he said surely.

"We will see about that," I said.

Erica

The dainty, white-socked Welsh pony wasn't going in the water. Each time he crept up to the edge of the large, shallow puddle, his eyes opened wide, and he quickly jumped back to the perceived safety of the marshy ground he now stood on.

"You're going to have to wait him out," I told his rider from the other side of the puddle.

Maggie wrinkled her nose. "Wait him *out*?"

"Yes. Twinkle doesn't know anything about water. He's used to walking on firm ground or the sand in the arena. You can't force him to go through it when he's frightened. But if you turn around now and give up, he'll learn

74

that he can get out of doing things." I stepped off the trail and leaned against a maple sapling. "So what you need to do is just sit there. Sit there on his back and keep him facing the water. Don't pester him, don't try to make him go forward. If he tries to turn around, stop him and make him face the water again."

Maggie had kept her attention on me throughout my whole speech. The second I stopped talking, her sparkly pink helmet bobbed up and down. She set the reins down on Twinkle's withers. He stared suspiciously down at the stagnant water. "How long do we wait for?"

"However long it takes for him to get bored. Anywhere from a minute to a few hours."

"If we're gone *that* long, my mom will call the FBI." Maggie looked rather pleased with the idea. "I should've brought my phone. It's got season one of *Game Of Thrones* on it."

Must be Maggie's latest TV obsession. I hadn't heard of it. "Did you finally find something more age-appropriate to watch than *True Blood*?" I asked.

Maggie looked at me shrewdly. "Sure," she said vaguely, with a smile that was not at all reassuring.

I sighed. "Have you ever tried watching a show aimed at your actual age group, Maggie?"

Maggie's little face darkened. "You mean like *Fetch With Ruff Ruffman*? *Dora The Explorer*?" She threw the titles at me with such scornful force that I was reminded of Amber.

"At least Dora is bilingual," I pointed out.

Maggie gave me a look that was unsettlingly condescending. "I already know how to say 'do me now' in six languages. I read *Cosmo*."

"Okay!" I said loudly, limping away from the conversation. "Let's just focus on Twinkle, shall we?"

"You're the one who brought it up," Maggie said, nimbly reverting to innocence.

I glanced at Twinkle. He was stretching his nose out, trying to get a better look at the dark water. "Try it again," I told Maggie. "Just give him a little nudge."

Maggie picked up the reins and pressed her legs into Twinkle. The gelding stepped right up to the puddle's edge, hesitating, staring into the dark water. Then with an extravagant heave, he flung himself up and over, snatching his legs right up against his belly as he cleared the wide, flat puddle. He would've easily cleared a 2-foot oxer.

As Twinkle's little hooves settled into the dry land directly in front of me, Maggie straightened up in the saddle, looking triumphant and whiplashed. "Hey, I finally got to jump!"

We spent the next few minutes getting splashed with mud and water as Maggie rode Twinkle through the puddle, back and forth. At first, he trotted through with great animation, snapping up his legs like a Saddlebred in an attempt to stay clean and dry. But after some repetition, he seemed to realize he was getting wet anyway, and with a slightly worried expression, Twinkle resigned himself to walking through the rippling, chocolaty water.

From there, we went on to a trail in the woods, which looped around, bringing us back to the puddle. Once again, Twinkle regarded it with considerable distrust, but now that he faced homeward his refusal was short-lived. Twinkle's walk was brisk, and I was sweating as we headed back to the Allsteens' estate.

After our time in the woods, the transition to emerald green grass, ostentatious landscaping and topiary girl and pony sculptures was all the more nauseating for me. Even Maggie slumped in her saddle a bit, looking studiously away from the icons of her.

Juan stepped out from behind a particularly ghastly bush. It dwarfed him in size. "Hello, miss Maggie. Did you have a pleasant ride?"

"It was great!" Maggie exclaimed. "Erica helped me get Twinkle through a *puddle*. The first time he *jumped* it! Then he just splashed right through." She beamed.

"I can see that," Juan said. He eyed the muddy pony like a housewife assessing a messy kitchen, Lysol in hand. "Would you like me to take him now?"

Maggie shook her head. "No! I mean, no thank you, Juan." She glanced at me, ensuring I noted her politeness. "I'm gonna give him a bath. You can clean the tack if you *really* want to." She poked Twinkle with her heels. I grinned at Juan and went with her. We got about two strides further and were halted by a sudden shriek.

"Oh, shit," Maggie muttered, and she didn't even bother to correct her language. Neither did I.

Mrs. Allsteen had come bustling around the corner, and she regarded us in open-mouthed horror, unconcealed by her enormous sunglasses. We stared back quite similarly.

"What in *heaven's name* is going on?! Maggie, you are *soaked*! And just look at the state of your pony! *Dripping* wet with *mud*!" Mrs. Allsteen recoiled. "*What* have you two been *doing*?" She seemed to guess the answer. "Maggie, I have told you a thousand times. I will *not* have you running around in the woods like a...a common *fiend* when you have a perfectly nice arena to ride in! With the same footing they use at the Olympics, I might add. The same kind!"

Maggie jumped off of Twinkle. Her teeth were already bared. "It's *boring* in the arena!" She screamed. "And CROSS-TRAINING IS BENEFICIAL FOR THE HORSE AND RIDER!"

Juan wisely stepped in and took Twinkle, and I ran for my truck. Maggie would pay me next time.

Lawrence

It was nearly dark by the time I heard her truck drive in. The horses had been fed and cared for, and I lay on the bed, savoring the ache in my right arm and thinking about Harry. His first real test had come, and he'd excelled. Sure we had lost, but we lost to Yvette on Vegas, a top class made pony. Harry had fought every second of the way. He'd handled being slammed into at top speed and getting tangled with Vegas as they'd wrestled for the ball. He'd kept his head beautifully, showing quick thinking and reflexes. And he had learned a valuable lesson, one that would serve him well as he began to learn strategy. Never let anyone in. Always put yourself between them and the ball. I knew Harry, and I knew he wouldn't make that mistake again.

I saw the headlights darken out front, heard the dull squeak of the door, and Erica came through the house. She dropped something heavy just outside the bedroom door, looked at it for a second, and then stepped into the room.

I sat up a little. "Hi."

"Hi."

"How was your show?"

She seemed to put some thought into the answer. "It was fine. The horses won their classes."

"Wow. Even D.M.?"

"Nah. I didn't ride him." She wandered over to the dresser, pulling her sweatshirt over her head. I watched raptly as she systematically removed her clothes and put on my threadbare robe.

She looked over at me, and I smiled. "Come here."

Erica shook her head. "I need a shower. I ate dust all day at the show grounds, and then I went to Maggie's and got splashed with mud. It was Twinkle's first water crossing."

I nodded. "You probably want to shower alone." I looked at her hopefully.

"No, you can come too." She turned and walked away. I caught up with her quickly.

Later, we lay together in bed, slightly chilled, damp, and close. Her arm was hooked over my back, her head weighing down my shoulder. The nerve endings prickled, and I ignored them.

Erica sighed, her gentle breath skimming across my chest. "Sometimes, I wonder if I'm doing anything right."

"You're too hard on yourself. You're amazing at everything you do."

Erica turned her head, gazing up at the ceiling. "I just wonder about all these decisions I've made. I just think, was it right? What if I had done something else?" She went quiet.

I kept silent for a minute. I didn't want to just charge in with those typical, breezy phrases people use to get someone to feel better. She deserved better than that.

"I know you're carrying the majority of the burden keeping us going," I said. "You have no idea how much I appreciate that. I know it's not easy, and I'm so grateful you believe in me enough to give me this chance. Because it won't be like this forever."

"Things are going to change," I said.

Courtney

The Days Inn we were staying in was mildewy. It was dark and altogether too damp in our shared room. I slept on the floor because Yvette wouldn't spring for a room with two beds. She had gotten really weird about finances. I wouldn't have minded, but she took the bed and wouldn't negotiate. So every night I was right on the fungi-infested carpet, breathing in the mold spores.

I didn't know what exactly we were doing in Georgetown, Kentucky, and Yvette wouldn't tell me. She disappeared for hours, and I stayed in the room watching TV or listening to Britney. We'd been here three days, accomplishing nothing, as far as I could tell. Well, she'd accomplished nothing. I hadn't tried.

There was a sliding click, and Yvette barged in. I looked up from my position on the bed. "What are you doing back already?"

"I am merely back from the gym," Yvette snipped. "Now, I am going out for real."

She marched over, grabbing her wallet from the nightstand. I sat up, wrapping my arms around my legs. "Yvette?"

She jerked to a stop. "*What.*"

"Why are we here?" I breathed in slowly. "Why did you make us leave my dad's estate for a Days Inn that doesn't even meet the health code? What are we doing in Kentucky?"

Yvette stared sharply at me. "I am networking," she said guardedly.

"*Here?*" I asked incredulously. "But all the power players are in Florida."

I saw Yvette's fingernails dig into her leather wallet. "I am not a fucking *moron*, Courtney." Her eyes went harsh. "And I do not recall asking you to go along with me. You *chose* to join me, because without me you are lost."

She shook her head. "*You* do not get to question me, Courtney."

I nodded meekly. "You're right. I'm sorry. I just really hate it here. My sinuses are all stuffy, and I've been coughing. I'm sure there's black mold in the walls, and probably asbestos too."

Yvette rolled her eyes. "Courtney. No one gives a shit about the fucking black mold."

"Black mold is carcinogenic," I protested. "It can kill you."

"Well, if I have to hear the words 'black mold' one more time, *I* will kill you. And you will not have to worry about cancer anymore." Yvette turned to go. "Have a good time with Britney," she said, a little softer.

I lay on the bed, flipping between MTV and VH1 for a while. Eventually, I got up and went into the bathroom, where I undressed quickly and stepped into the rickety shower. I had to duck on my way in and crouch at an angle to fit. After rinsing off, I dried myself with an overly detergent-smelling motel towel. I hastily put my clothes back on.

When I walked back out into the main part of the room, I inhaled and it came out in a sneeze. I swallowed, and I could feel a sliminess in my throat.

I snatched up my room key and bolted. I didn't look back.

I ran down the dingy hallways until I found a door, and I burst out into the fresh air. Well, it was fresh air laced with fumes from an idling Suburban, but it still went down easily. *Ahhhhh.* I looked around, considering my options. This part of town was pure, crass development, filled up with chain motels, gas stations and fast food restaurants. I stood there, feeling kind of stupid just standing there in the Days Inn parking lot. I had no plan. I didn't even have my phone. *Nice going, Courtney.*

I glanced back at the motel I'd just left. Even the outside looked discolored and fuzzy somehow. *Screw it. I'm not going back in there.* I started off in some random direction. *I'll just go for a run. That's a perfectly reasonable thing to do in a strange town when you don't know where you're going and have no way to call for help.*

I shook off that rather dire train of thought and just ran. I sprinted at first and then coasted, falling into my distance-running pace. Running was easy. It was automatic. I could run all day, almost unconsciously, trusting my body. It was easy to trust my body, once I got out of my head.

Team Dark Horse

I left the crush of stark, garish storefronts behind, coming out on the interstate. I ran along the ditches, my shoes pushing against the soft, weedy terrain, listening to the cars and semis blasting by. I just kept running until the next exit, and then I got off the highway and pushed onward, past a Citgo station and the obligatory McDonald's.

Once I reached the outskirts of whatever town this was, I slowed my pace, downshifting until I was walking flat-footed. I looked around, seeing no real landmarks. In fact, it wasn't too different from the place I'd run from. I was just further away from where Yvette could find me. And further away from my phone.

Wow, it was really *smart of me to come here. Really freaking brilliant.* I quickly cut across a gas station parking lot, head down, eyes racing around. Every innocent bystander who happened to be filling his tank right then took on the form of a serial rapist. In my widened, panicked eyes, they all seemed to be leering at me. *Walk away quickly, Courtney. No, don't. That incites his predator instinct. Wait, I think that's for dogs. Okay, keep going. Get to a well-lit public place, like that gas station right there. You'll be safe there. Just keep walking with purpose. Don't walk like a victim, and you won't become one. And no matter what, never let him take you to the second location.*

All the self-defense sound bites that had stuck in my head over the years were going off like a car alarm. Dropping my fake self-assured posture, I lurched up onto the sidewalk and lunged for the door. I flew inside, my breathing nearing hyperventilation. *I made it. I'm safe now.* I stood under actual, protective walls, in amongst the shelves of brightly packaged chips and candy. I smiled. I looked up into the eyes of the gas station clerk, all the way across the small building. He smiled back. In a creepy way.

In about a fifth of a second, I was back on the other side of the door. My heart was pattering away like a little rabbit's. I looked out at the array of potential sexual predators and saw a new vehicle pull in. It was a maroon pickup, and it wasn't new at all.

Moments later, Lawrence Cavanaugh stepped out of the cab. He spotted me and came right up to me, leaving the door hanging open.

Team Dark Horse

"Courtney. Hi there," he said, acting for all the world like the last time he'd seen me, we hadn't had three days of near-constant, screaming sex.

He gave me a quick, one-armed hug, and stepped back. "How are you?"

I just stared mutely at him. My thoughts were at a higher decibel. *Does he not remember the sex? All the sex? Is it possible he forgot? Why would he remember my name and not remember we had sex? That seems unlikely.*

My heart was going so fast that the beat had almost accelerated to a vibration. "I'm...good," I said absurdly.

Lawrence tilted his head sideways. A shock of black hair fell across his forehead. "What brings you here?"

My tongue was slow and leaden in my mouth. "Yvette is networking."

"Really?" Lawrence looked at me. He looked amused. "She never mentioned it. Well, say hi to her for me," he said, turning to select a fuel grade. "And tell her how much I enjoyed our rematch."

Dougie

You are now chatting with a stranger. Say hi!
krypton1000: hi
cutesexy317: hi :D
cutesexy317: what u doing tonite
krypton1000: bored and lonely, trolling the internet for sum1 to talk to. obvi.
cutesexy317: lol
cutesexy317: how old r u
krypton1000: 21
cutesexy317: nice u out of school?
krypton1000: yup. got my own place, working part time in tech support n various internet schemes. taking a different online course every other week for some light reading. lol
cutesexy317: u sound really smart wanna video chat?

Four minutes later
cutesexy317: u still there?
krypton1000: yeah. my webcams broken. sorry ☹
cutesexy317: oh ok
cutesexy317 has signed off.

Courtney

I ran back, not at my distance-running pace, but in an all-out sprint. When I reached that disgusting motel room and banged on the door, my heart was slamming around alarmingly in my chest, and not just from the exertion.

The door was wrenched open by Yvette, who struggled to hold its iron weight and keep it from slamming shut. "*Courtney*. Where the fuck have *you* been?"

I stalked through the open door and heard it close loudly behind me. When I looked at her again, Yvette had her hands on her narrow, pointy hips and was staring at me. "You do nothing, you go nowhere, and all of a sudden you take off! What am I supposed to think when I come in here and you are *gone*? And without even your fucking cell phone!"

"I know. I left it here."

Yvette's eyes flashed. "I *figured that out* when I called your number and *Britney* began to assault my ears."

I walked off. Yvette followed. "You did not answer me. Where the *fuck* did you run off to? And why?"

I doubled back. "Why? *Why*? I told you, I can't stand being in this...this freaking room anymore! I'm getting sick, and I hate it here, and there's nothing to do! Why *should* I stay? Stay and just wait for you? *Screw that!*"

Yvette rolled her eyes. "Courtney, there is no reason to have a fucking temper tantrum. We all know you are trapped in adolescence, but you must refrain from regressing any further."

I whirled on her, my hands moving into fists. "*You've been lying to me!*" I screamed.

Yvette stared at me. "Now what is *this* about?"

"You've been lying to me," I repeated, as calmly as I could. "You dragged me here and *you said you had a plan*." My voice was getting screechy. "You said you were networking, and all you've been doing is playing polo with Lawrence Cavanaugh!"

Yvette's pinched mouth dropped open. "How - how could you *possibly* know that?"

"I freaking - no, screw that, I *fucking* ran into him today at the gas station! And he said 'Tell Yvette how much I enjoyed our rematch'! He said you never even mentioned any networking, so he must've been the whole reason you came here!" I paced the squishy carpet furiously. "And damn it, Yvette, I have a right to know these things! This is both our lives you're playing with here!"

Yvette had waited through my tirade, and only now did she speak again. "Are you done, Courtney?"

I looked at her critically. "Are you going to admit that you're trying to start a team with Cavanaugh?"

She looked as though she'd heard a high-pitched sound. The pain on her face was strong. "No."

"Then yes," I said. "I'm so fucking done."

I left for the second time that day. I took my phone this time.

Erica

I cruised by the Allsteens' front gate, and Maggie was there waiting for me. The little girl stood still as a rock, her blonde hair pulled back in a bun, pink sparkles reflecting in the muted sunlight. I pulled over, hopping the curb, and hit unlock. She jerked the passenger door open, propelling herself into the cab with a mighty leap.

After she buckled her seatbelt, Maggie reached in her pocket and pulled a 50. "For last time," she stated.

"Thanks," I said. "Did your mom ever calm down?"

Maggie made a sound in her throat like she was congested. Or disgusted. "She made some noise about 'finding me a *real* instructor'. But I shut that down with some screaming and smashing things."

I looked over, slightly alarmed. "What did you smash?"

Maggie shrugged. "You know. Vases, art and stuff."

"Why not just dishes?"

Maggie glanced at me. "You know I can't reach the cabinets."

"Oh, right," I said. "I forget that you're small."

Maggie smiled, leaning back against the seat. "That's why I like you."

I drove the meandering route to Lawrence's, listening to the radio and not offering much in the way of conversation. As I covered the miles, I mentally planned Maggie's lesson for that day. Some instructors' lesson plans were meticulously thought out and charted months in advance, with everything neatly documented. I wasn't one of those instructors.

As we pulled in the drive, Maggie sprang into action, releasing her seat belt and kicking open the door while the vehicle was still moving. She hit the ground running and took off for the barn just as Lawrence peered out from behind the door frame. He waved lazily at her, and she accelerated. I finished parking the truck and went to join them.

I decided she would ride D.M. for the lesson. He hadn't gotten out in a while, and he would certainly ride differently than Twinkle, or even Vegas. Plus, I knew I could trust him with her, which could not be said for some of the horses on the farm (namely Harry and Maude).

I went to D.M.'s paddock, picking up the halter that hung on the gate. He looked at me for a moment, almost like he wasn't sure if I were serious. Then he ambled right over.

I hugged his enormous face for a moment, breathing in his slightly dusty horse smell before haltering him and leading him up to the barn.

Lawrence had Maggie crouched underneath Vegas, feeling his tendons for heat. The seven-year-old stared intently at the gelding's plain black legs, her eyebrows lowered in concentration as she felt along the vertical ridges.

I dropped D.M.'s lead shank on the floor; he stood quietly. Then I walked over to Maggie and shook her awake. "*Hey,*" she protested, getting to her feet.

"You're riding D.M. for this lesson," I said. "He's trained for jumping, so he'll be a little different from what you've ridden before. As you can see, he's a very large horse, so you'll have to be very correct with your aids and use your body properly. You won't be able to guide this horse using brute strength."

Maggie strode right up to D.M., looking up at his massive form. The gelding stared down at her, and he began to stretch his nose downward, little by little, until finally she could reach him.

Maggie rubbed his inquisitive nose. "He's *very* nice," she said approvingly. "Is this *your* horse?"

I nodded. "Yes, he's my boy."

Maggie's head whipped around, an evil grin on her face. "Can I *jump* him?"

Lawrence snickered, and I shook my head violently. "Maggie. *No.* You *are* about ready to start learning to jump, but D.M. is not the horse for you to learn on. First of all, his jump is way too big. It would unseat you."

"Twinkle jumped big over that puddle!"

I snorted. "*Please.* D.M. could use Twinkle as a cavalletti pole."

"Oh, all right. I just wanted to see what you'd say." Maggie picked up a brush and went to work on D.M.'s knees, which was about all she could reach. "Can we go trail riding then?"

"If you want to." I thought about trying to keep up with D.M.'s stride on foot and swiftly vetoed the idea. "I'll ride along on Soiree. She could use a hack."

"Okay. I'll saddle my horse." Maggie went to the tack room door. "Which stuff is his?"

"Just look for the really big saddle and the bridle that's dragging on the floor," Lawrence offered dryly.

"And how on earth do you think you're going to saddle D.M.?" I asked.

Maggie cocked her head to the side, as if she was just now considering this conundrum. "I'll need a stepladder," she said slyly. "Or a very tall and handsome groom."

I choked on a reluctant (but robust) laugh, and Lawrence went to D.M.'s side, ready and waiting (and smirking). I shook my head at him.

"Maggie, I'm begging you," I said as she appeared from the tack room, staggering under the weight of D.M.'s extra-large tack, "don't do his ego any favors."

I brought Soiree in. Soon the horses were tacked up, and we were heading for the fields. Maggie looked improbably tiny on D.M.'s broad back, her feet barely reaching beyond the saddle flaps. But she sat up straight, looking quite at home on his back. D.M. marched out happily, bobbing his head with the swing of his walk.

Maggie laughed out loud. "His *walk* feels bigger than Twinkle's canter!"

I smiled. "That's the feeling of a horse with a lot of reach in its stride."

When we reached an appropriate meadow, I turned to Maggie. "You can trot here if you'd like. Just make sure to keep a strong core and control your posting so you don't end up pitching forward. He's going to have a lot more impulsion than you're used to."

Maggie nodded. "Right." She gathered up the reins and touched D.M. softly with her calves. He moved smoothly into a trot, and in the first few strides she was thrown off balance, but she quickly sat up and regained control of her body. She asked him to extend his stride, sending him forward while maintaining a steady contact with his mouth, and soon she had him nicely balanced between her leg and hand.

I halted Soiree and watched them move around me. After a few minutes, Maggie asked D.M. to walk. She turned him and rode over to me, grinning and breathing hard. "That was awesome! He's so fun to ride!"

I smiled. "You did a great job establishing a proper connection. That's a lot of horse for you to put together. You should be really proud."

Maggie nodded, still a bit out of breath. "Can we keep riding?"

"Definitely. Let's see where this next trail goes."

We rode on for quite a while, and I kept absolutely no track of the time. We trotted and cantered the fields and wide, open trails with good footing, walking the trickier paths. D.M. and Soiree, both being sweet, sensible horses, didn't spook at birds that exploded from the bushes, or even deer leaping across our path. D.M. plodded through stream crossings, stepped carefully over logs and didn't even panic when his legs got tangled in a pile of brush strewn across the trail. Maggie was in heaven.

"He's *such* a great trail horse!" She raved as we made our way home.

"Yeah, he really likes getting out." I thought back to his younger years. "I even considered taking him to a competitive trail ride one time."

Maggie swung around in the saddle. "You can *compete* in trail riding?" She wanted to know.

"Oh, yes. They have rides of all different lengths, but the beginner ones usually start out at like six miles. There are different obstacles you have to complete - hills, bridges, gates, stuff like that. Judges score you at each obstacle based on how your horse does. I don't know that much about it because I never went, but it sounded cool."

Maggie was pretty quiet the whole way back. I just knew she was planning something.

Yvette

Courtney did not come back. She refused to return to the Days Inn, even to talk, so I was forced to track her down.

I did not call Courtney, or her *daddy*, to demand her whereabouts. I did not have to call. I knew Courtney well enough to know exactly where she would be.

And so I got into my Voyage and drove to Lexington, weaving into and out of traffic, running many stoplights and cutting many people off. It was Kentucky, so most people allowed me through with a wave. This did not please me. Nothing pissed me off more than polite fucking drivers.

Eventually, I found it. The largest, gaudiest, most expensive premium hotel in Lexington. *The Davenport Hotel*, it read on the enormous exterior.

I parked in a location that would surely earn me yet another ticket. A genial man opened the door for me as I stepped inside the lobby. The façade, the walls and even the ceiling lights were in the style of elegant art deco.

I walked up to the front desk, stopping in front of a clerk who was probably just out of school. "I am here to see Courtney Silva," I said.

"May I please have your name?"

"Lawrence Cavanaugh," I told her, completely expressionless.

"I'll call her room right now. One moment..." the girl began to sift through a large computer database of room numbers.

"I will wait over here," I said vaguely, and I walked away.

Five minutes later, I heard the bing of an elevator, and Courtney descended upon the lobby. She wore her usual wide-eyed look of slight panic, in addition to Adidas pants and a polo shirt bearing the insignia of our former team.

Courtney looked around wildly, clutching her hands together. I walked up to her, abruptly ending the suspense.

Courtney stared at me, her eyebrows lowering. "You used Lawrence Cavanaugh's name at the desk, didn't you."

"I knew it would work. You are hopelessly predictable, Courtney, and you cannot let go of your stupid fan girl obsession." I took her arm and steered her toward the elevator. "Now let us talk."

Once we were both in her room, I shut the door behind her. "Now. What do you want?"

"I want to know what your plan is. It's not enough to just *say* you have a plan. I want to know what it is."

"The plan is irrelevant this early on."

"So you don't have a plan."

My teeth gnashed. "I *have* a fucking plan," I said viciously.

"So you *do* have a plan. But you won't admit to it. You can't even admit it to yourself in your head, because you hate the idea of it so much. So you're lying to yourself and me and everyone."

I stared blankly at her, momentarily at a loss.

Courtney blinked coolly at me. "You're thinking of starting a team with Cavanaugh. He's a free agent right now, he's an incredible player, and no one wants him. It's not a bad idea. It could be a great idea. Are you going to admit that's what you're thinking?"

I looked at Courtney, sitting on her bed. I hated her. I wanted to kill her. "No," I said loudly. I couldn't think or say anything else. "No."

Courtney did not pay any attention. "I'm going to come along the next time you have a practice. We need to see if we can all work together. If the chemistry is there."

"Cavanaugh does not have another pony for you," I snapped. My blood was burning my skin from the inside out.

"Then I will send for Hermione." Courtney turned her back to me, picking up the hotel phone next to the bed and dialing. "Hello? Daddy?"

Amber

I didn't want to be in my shitty apartment all afternoon on my day off, and I'd already been to see Maude. And because my life sucks, I had nowhere else to go but this shitty suburb. *Fuck my life.*

Block after block of identical beige houses were bathed in the Harley's diesel fumes. At each window, pasty, average-looking people ripped back their drapes and stared, as if they'd never heard a truck with no muffler and a dying engine before. I stared right back. *Yeah, whatever. Have fun with your boring nine-to-fivers and your fucking soundless Toyota Camrys.*

At the end of Sherman Street, I cranked my wheel, earning myself a stressed-out screech from the power steering, and made the difficult right turn into the narrow-ass driveway. The Harley's broad front end connected with the bumper of the parked car in front of me, a white minivan. Cursing, I threw it in reverse and let it roll back a few inches before cutting the engine. I let myself into the house without checking the van for damage.

The house opened to a narrow entryway and a kitchen. There was nothing in it, as usual. He was down to an open bag of Doritos that was mostly crumbs. The skeleton of a twelve-pack of Mountain Dew sat in the fridge, holding only one bottle.

I shut the fridge door and hung a left, walking into the living room. It was big and open, mainly because there was no fucking furniture in it. There was a desk chair, and a desk that stretched the length of one whole wall. On it, there were four different computer monitors, plus several tablets, an e-reader, and an iPhone. Another wall was filled up with a plasma flat screen that was about 10 feet long and hooked up to various gaming systems and DVRs. The third wall served as a sound system, with an

Team Dark Horse

elaborate display of speakers that stretched from floor to ceiling.

This was Dougie's world.

He was sitting in his desk chair. I had never walked in here unannounced and not found him in his desk chair. He was crouched over his desktop computer Photoshopping some funny shit onto yet another cute cat picture, while simultaneously Tweeting on his iPad and playing Night Of The Gummies on his phone. He was never not playing Night Of The Gummies.

I walked over. "You shouldn't leave your door unlocked," I said. "Someone could just walk right in and steal all your fancy electronic shit."

Dougie looked up, raising his pockmarked, white-blue face. "You are the only person who ever walks in here, Amber."

I shrugged. "Just saying." I peered at the screen. "What're you working on?"

Dougie's eyes ticked back to the computer. "Just getting my posts queued up on Tumblr for the next week. And adding fuel to the controversy on Twitter over *Celebrity Dog Swap*."

"Excuse me, *what*?"

Dougie leaned back in his chair, fingers still typing. And playing Night Of The Gummies. "*Celebrity Dog Swap*. It's like *Wife Swap*, but with celebrities and their dogs. It's the most popular reality show this minute. Anyway, these two rival pop stars had to swap their dogs - one has a Great Dane; the other has a teacup Yorkie. The Yorkie got stepped on and had to have surgery on its paw, and everyone thinks the girl did it on purpose."

My mouth went slack. "She was used to a fucking Great Dane! It doesn't matter if you step on them! And they gave her a *toy breed*?!"

"Like I said. It's great television. But not so great for Bubbles."

I stared.

Dougie glanced at my face. "Bubbles is the Yorkie."

"*I think I knew that.*"

I went back to the kitchen, opening the barren cupboards. "You have no food," I called out. "Again. It's no fucking wonder you're so skinny."

"Sometimes I forget to eat."

"I know. Just like you forget to go outside. And just like you forget to sleep."

Suddenly, Dougie rolled his desk chair away from all the vibrant, addictive computer screens he was forever shackled to. He stood up, wincing as his spine unbent, and came over to me. He still held himself in that odd, self-loathing, low-shouldered way, but he met my eyes, and it was like some deep-buried, prehistoric social cue had suddenly come to the surface and struck him on the head.

"Do you want to watch a movie?" He asked me.

I felt myself brighten. Movies were my weakness, and I hadn't seen one in forever. I would pick something good and classic, like *Thelma & Louise* or *Harold & Maude*. Or maybe just something with a lot of hot chicks and no plot, like *Sucker Punch*. So many possibilities.

"Sure," I said.

Erica

Assault careened around the first turn to a narrow vertical, throwing me off balance with his back-cracking leap. Feeling me rock forward, he rooted at the reins, slowing down his front end and preparing to buck. I walloped him with my legs and gave the gag snaffle in his mouth a good tug, and he brought his head back up just in time to meet the next fence, an in-and-out combination with tricky striding. With no preparation, he merely gave it a glance and bounced right through, earning a pat from me.

Next was a long gallop to the liverpool, and at the takeoff, I half halted, compressing Assault so his lofty jump wouldn't carry us any further than necessary. A tight rollback turn awaited on the other side of the still blue water. Assault cleared the liverpool, landing just as I had wanted, and I quickly spun him around to meet the last fence, a maxed-out oxer that several of my biggest rivals had reduced to kindling just minutes before.

I opened my hands, and Assault snatched up the entire length of the reins with one toss of his head. His power rose, unchecked, uninhibited, and my spine swayed jarringly like a tree in a hurricane. Assault's hooves smacked the ground, and he paused, every muscle aligning and tensing at the same time. Then he was airborne, like a hollow shell fired from a gun.

We spilled across the finish line, Assault's head in my face, his ears flat back and tail wringing as I pulled him down with difficulty. When Assault finally conceded and came back down to earth, I glanced at our time preserved on the clock as an afterthought. 68 seconds. We were winning, and we were getting faster.

I walked Assault along the perimeter of the ring while the winners were announced. The other trainers were grouped together, smiling and talking. When I rode by, when I looked at them, their faces frosted over.

It shouldn't have bothered me, and I meant not to let it. I had never cared that much about social standing. But I cared about my business, and my future as a rider and trainer. That was why I was here. I had the right horse, in both the hunter and the jumper ring. I was consistently coming out on top, and no one would acknowledge it. No one was stepping up and hiring me, or even handing me a horse to catch-ride. And that was something I couldn't ignore.

I thought it was all about winning. That winning was key. And now I was winning, and I was still getting nowhere.

I opened the door and walked into the house. Lawrence was intent on digging through one of the massive piles of stuff that littered the house, and he didn't notice me right away. I started banging through cabinets, because I needed something to eat and it was also somewhat satisfying to make a lot of noise.

Lawrence's head popped up from the avalanche of clutter. "Hey. How was your show?"

I turned around, feeling my hair rise. "Not so good!"

He looked perplexed. "What happened? The horses didn't do well?"

I shook my head, feeling the crazy seep into my eyes. "The horses did awesome. *I'm* awesome. I'm *good* at this!"

"Okay..." Now he was actually starting to look a bit worried. "So...what happened?"

I didn't answer immediately. I had located the Cookies 'n Cream Crunch, and I stuck my hand into the bag, grabbing as much as I could fit into my mouth. As I chewed, I wondered idly why anyone bothers doing drugs when there is such a thing as sugar.

Lawrence was still waiting. I took a breath. "I am just *sick* of the politics, the popularity contests, and the petty freaking *bullshit* I have to deal with every weekend. I *grew up* on this show circuit. Everyone has known me since I was a *baby*. I had a good thing going, you know? I knew everybody, I catch-rode for everybody, we bought and sold and traded each others' horses. It was a good life."

Pausing to inhale more Cookies 'n Cream Crunch, which didn't calm me down all that much, I continued. "And what I do *not* understand, what I do *not* get, is why you had to go and screw around in *my* inner circle, absolutely indiscriminately, with no regard for anything, and piss off all my fellow trainers! Everyone *hates* you, and now they hate me by association!"

My crazy rant over with, I strode off into a corner to stew some more. I heard not a sound for about a minute, and then Lawrence came up behind me. Without even flinching, he leaned in close, his breath trickling down to my collarbone while his hands closed on my waist. I was instantly gone.

"They're idiots," Lawrence said, his voice soft against my neck. "They're fucking idiots, and they're probably pissed off that you have all this talent, and these kickass horses, and you're actually going to get somewhere."

My body sagged into the floor. "You think so?"

Lawrence turned me around gently so I faced him. He held me with his eyes, that magnetic coal. "You're going to get out of this show circuit, Erica. You're gonna go way beyond it."

I smiled. "Okay."

"You'll get more clients," Lawrence said, stretching up to kiss my forehead. "People are noticing you. Trust me."

His cell started vibrating, and after a moment, he went to look at it. He flipped it open, glanced at the caller ID, and closed it again.

"Who was that?" I asked.

Lawrence shrugged. "Just Marla."

Marla.

The very mention of her name shoved me right back into my horrible mood. "What is she still doing in town?" I demanded.

"She's thinking of investing in some real estate," Lawrence said perfectly casually. Like it was *no big deal.* "You know that club, Angelina's? She's gonna buy it and restore it to its former glory. Or knowing Marla, she'll make it even better."

Fighting to maintain a hold on my raging bitchiness, I said, "And how is she affording all this? Does she even have a *job*?"

"Marla's independently wealthy. Something about the sale of a resort in Antigua and a bunch of stocks? I never understood it. So she works as a freelance journalist mostly, but nothing steady. She has houses all over the place. So she can pretty much settle wherever she wants."

Clearly oblivious to the fury rising to my face and manifesting itself in blotches, Lawrence returned to the pile he was excavating, and I went outside, because otherwise I was going to club him over the head with something.

After slamming the screen door, I leaned over the railing, fuming to myself and listening to my respirations get really, really shallow.

Yeah, she can pretty much settle wherever she wants.

And I know exactly where she'll be settling, I thought grimly.

I was still standing there when Lawrence banged through the screen door some time later. I glanced up half-heartedly, and as he clattered past me, I did a double-take.

He was dressed in a way I hadn't seen since the clinic, way back when. In tall boots that fit excruciatingly well, white breeches that were snug without being skintight, and a polo shirt with a number and an official team logo. He had a helmet in his left hand, but not his usual schooling helmet that he wore every day (well, since I had guilted him into doing so). This helmet was more egg-shaped, with a visor and a metal face guard.

He was obviously intent on his destination, striding out and covering ground quickly. "Hey!" I called out. I had to call out to get him to notice me.

Lawrence stopped short and looked back at me, his momentum stalled.

"Where're you going?" I yelled.

"The LPC. I'm hauling Harry and Vegas over for a few hours," Lawrence said.

"Dressed like *that*?"

He cocked his head. "What d'you mean?"

"What do I *mean*?" I stared at him incredulously. "You're all *fancy*. You never dress like that for anything!"

Lawrence looked at me a bit edgily. His eyes didn't quite settle on mine. "Well, I think it's time for me to get serious."

I was silent, and slightly thrown. "Okay," I finally said. I struggled to say it. "Well…have a good time."

Lawrence grinned, moving past the uncomfortable moment with remarkable ease. "Thanks. Love you."

I tried to follow his lead, but it felt like trying to move a ring-sour horse past the out-gate. "Love you," I said to the still air.

I watched him back up his trailer and load up Vegas and Harry. And for the first time, I noticed how good he looked. It wasn't just the clothes or the boots. It was his whole being. His passion.

That was what I loved about him. But I was used to feeling the full intensity of it, basking in it and lying in the glow of it when we were together. Now I saw it speeding away from me in some unknown direction.

Lawrence

I pulled into the LPC, and there they were. Just as I remembered them from two winters back, when The Women had descended on the International Polo Club. Lacking a pony, Yvette looked no less menacing, tapping the ground relentlessly with the toe of her boot and giving her mallet an occasional twirl. Courtney stood a few paces back, still towering over Yvette, her blonde hair in a high ponytail. It swished around as her head turned nervously, from me to Yvette.

Courtney held the reins of Hermione, her well-traveled pony. Hermione was muddy brown in color, rather dull-coated despite top-class care, and she looked a bit like the sketches you find in old-time horse books displaying every conformation flaw known to man. But in motion on the polo field, as I recalled, she was a thing of beauty.

I parked and slammed the door behind me, leaving the ponies on the trailer. Mallet in hand, I walked up to the two women. Not one of us was aligned with a team, but we were all wearing uniforms.

"Hello there," I said, extending my free hand. "Nice to see the two of you again. Together."

Yvette made a strangled sound in the back of her throat, but Courtney's hand crept forward, and I shook it. Her wrist flopped limply.

"Hi," Courtney whispered. Her eyes were large and flitting around.

"Hi yourself," I said to her.

Yvette thrust herself between us. "You have brought my pony, I am assuming." Courtney fell back and began busying herself with Hermione's breast collar.

I smiled down at Yvette, blowing through the open hostility on her face. "Yes, I brought my spare for you."

Courtney shot me a look of panic, but Yvette just stared at me, her face contorting minutely. After a moment, she stalked away, taking Courtney with her.

I walked around to the rear of my trailer and let the ramp fall. Harry's quivering eyeball greeted me as he swung his head around, staring intently. He knew this place now, and as I backed him down the ramp, I had to remind him to place his feet down slowly and carefully. Harry danced beside me as I led him to the barn. He knew exactly what we were here for.

With Harry securely locked in an empty stall, I went back for Vegas, throwing as much gear as I could carry over my left arm. Vegas followed me obediently. I stuck him on the cross ties and went back one more time for the rest of my shit.

Yvette was pacing the aisle when I returned. I let myself into Harry's stall and started wrapping his legs.

I could feel her eyes in the back of my head, and I straightened up for a moment. "Yes?"

"What about my pony?"

"What about him?"

"Aren't you going to saddle him as well?"

I shook my head, going back to Harry's left front. "I can't saddle two horses at once."

"But I do not - "

"I know," I interrupted. "You don't saddle your own horse. Well, I don't saddle two horses at once."

I caught a glimpse of Courtney through the stall bars. She looked positively ashen.

"You did last time," Yvette argued.

"That was an exception," I calmly stated. "But it's pointless for me to saddle two horses at once while you sit there and do nothing. So you might want to get a move on it."

Courtney sucked in a breath that I heard clear across the aisle. Yvette's boots scuffed to a halt just behind me. I turned.

Her face was savage. "You are *supposed* to saddle horses!" Yvette shrieked. "You are a fucking *groom*! It is your fucking *job* to saddle horses, individually or all at once! It does not matter!"

Courtney rushed forward, dragging a somewhat alarmed Hermione along with her. "Yvette, calm down. I'll saddle the pony."

"*You* are supposed to be watching Hermione!" Yvette thundered. "You will do no such thing!"

Abandoning Harry's front leg, I stepped out of the stall and closed the door. "Both of you! Shut up for a second."

Their heads swung, locking onto me.

"I have a solution. I think. I'll be right back."

I left them standing there and I walked down the aisle. Softly, I knocked on the door to Elaine's room. She opened it within two seconds.

"Can you saddle a horse?" I asked her.

She rolled her eyes. They weren't quite so large in her sunken face anymore, I noticed. Her face wasn't so sunken. "Of course I can."

I led the way down the aisle and gestured to Vegas standing naked in the cross ties. Elaine walked straight through and began saddling Vegas matter-of-factly while Courtney and Yvette stared wordlessly at her sudden appearance.

Soon, both Harry and Vegas were tacked up, and as I led Harry past Vegas, I checked Elaine's work. Even the polo wraps were applied correctly. I glanced at Elaine, my eyebrow raised. "Very nice."

Elaine shrugged. "It's not that difficult. Any idiot should be able to do it." She smiled sweetly at Yvette and disappeared down the aisle in her grey sweatpants and Kellogg's Corn Flakes T-shirt.

I took Vegas' reins and placed them in Yvette's frozen hand. "This is *my* pony that I'm letting *you* ride," I said clearly. "And if we're going to work together, you're going to have to stop using me as a groom."

I looked them both in the eye, and neither of them looked away. "Now. Let's do this."

Courtney

Hermione stood solidly as I mounted up and settled onto her narrow back. My feet found the stirrups, and I asked her to walk on, heading straight across the field. Nearby, Yvette was warming up Vegas, a look of distaste on her face. Yvette was scary good at polo for a reason. She hated everything *but* polo.

Ever since we had planned this meeting, my body had been chugging with nerves. Now that we were all on the field, I felt myself relaxing into Hermione's movement. *It's nice to be part of a team again.* I caught myself quickly. There was no team. We were just three singular people gathering to partake in a common interest. *Just like bingo, or karaoke night. Not that I've ever been to a karaoke night. I don't even like to go out at night, for any reason, so I'm not sure why I even thought of that. Okay, this is pointless. The point is, there is no team. Not yet.*

Not yet.

The thought powered me forward, and Hermione moved into a trot, reading my mind like she often did. Up ahead, Yvette moved the bay up to a trot as well with a click of her tongue. I stared down, lost in Hermione's rhythm as we circled the field. My mallet hung on my right, an extension of my arm, swinging softly in time with Hermione's gait.

Suddenly, I could hear the approaching rumble of hoof beats. I looked back and saw Lawrence cantering up on his black gelding. The horse's white-rimmed eyes and white blaze drew my eye to him.

Team Dark Horse

"I like your pony," I called to Lawrence over the soft pounding of the horses' hooves.

"Thanks," Lawrence grinned, coming up on my left. "He's something else."

"What's his name?" I asked, faltering slightly in the black warmth of Lawrence's stare.

"Harry," he told me, and Harry fell into step with Hermione. The ponies moved together, nearly in unison, and so close that Lawrence's leg brushed against mine repeatedly. I relaxed, leaning into him ever so slightly, until Yvette's sharp eye pulled me away and I straightened up again.

"*Are we going to do this shit?*" Yvette shouted as she thundered past on Vegas.

"Sure." Stealthily, Lawrence pulled a ball out of his pocket and tossed it out in front of Harry's nose. "Try and catch *this.*"

And just like that, every one of us exploded into movement. It was like he'd detonated a bomb, or tripped a fuse or a wire.

Harry surged at the ball like he was connected to it by an industrial-strength magnet, and I allowed myself to stare, just for one second, at the sickly accurate trajectory of Lawrence's arm. He didn't even bother to look at the ball, just swung smoothly, casually and hit it dead on. I gave Hermione a kick and she launched herself in the direction of the airborne ball, doing her best to get out in front. Harry wasn't having it though. He was right at our side, steadily, subtly pushing us off our line. Hermione pinned her ears and shoved back, and from my position atop this tangle of churning bodies, I felt both horses lock up and dig in.

We were gaining on the spot where the ball lay, but neither of us would be able to actually hit it, not with our ponies locked in a tussle. Lawrence knew this as well as I did. I looked over, and I saw his grip relax on his mallet. I saw the plan forming in his head. He was going to ride it out, then ditch me as we passed the ball. He was thinking he'd just roll back and recapture the ball when he was rid of me.

I knew precisely what he was thinking. And I knew exactly how to screw him over.

I gave Hermione a cluck and a shove with my leg, and she redoubled her efforts, pushing Harry even further from the ball. *Just far enough.* And then, shifting my crushed right leg with difficulty, I put my spur into her *other* side.

Hermione wheeled away from Harry, whose head shot up in a panic as he staggered, trying to regain his footing now that the solid, unrelenting pressure he'd been leaning against had suddenly vanished. With Harry floundering, Hermione moved on unimpeded, and I enjoyed a clear shot at the ball.

It didn't last. Lawrence's knee slammed into mine within three seconds, but by then I'd already scored the first goal.

I could hear an ominous rumble of hoof beats in addition to Harry's and Hermione's. *Oh, shit! I forgot about Yvette!* I hastily moved Hermione out of the way as she descended on Lawrence.

"Think you are fucking *cute*, motherfucker?" She snarled at Lawrence as they galloped by at full speed. "Think you will just sneak one by me, do you?"

"If you can't keep up, get off the fucking field," Lawrence shot back, cutting her off effortlessly so Vegas was forced to slam on the brakes.

I watched, transfixed, as he took control of the ball, holding it, keeping it in the air, doubling back and toying with it while keeping one step ahead of Yvette. Then finally, as if bored, he sent it flying into the goal.

He stopped his horse, coming face to face with Yvette. She was panting, both from the exertion and from sheer, unadulterated fury.

"I told you you wouldn't get by him again," Lawrence said, patting Harry on the neck. Then he stepped off and began walking Harry cool while Yvette and I both stared after him.

As soon as I could speak, I turned to Yvette. "We have to work with him," I said breathlessly. My breath was excited and my heart fluttered somewhere up near my collarbone.

Her head snapped back like I'd slapped her across the face. "You fucking bitch."

My eyes flew open, and I jumped down from Hermione. "Yvette."

She dismounted quickly, throwing Vegas' reins at me. She left me with two horses and walked off the field.

Erica

I walked Soiree around the deceptively simple little course I'd made, letting her take a look at it. The lines were easy enough, all outside/diagonal, typical hunter fare. But I'd bumped each one of the fences up by two inches, so that by the end of the course she would be facing four feet. If she was going to compete in the Hunter Derby Finals Soiree needed to be comfortable jumping much higher, and she couldn't afford to lose any of her perfect form.

I was hoping to ease her into it this way. She would have a gradual buildup to four feet, and if at any time I felt her floundering, I could pull up and adjust the fences down. I hoped that wouldn't happen.

After ten minutes of walk on a long rein, I began to trot and canter Soiree, suppling her and letting her stretch down. I wanted to ensure she was loose and relaxed before tackling that course. Finally satisfied, I turned her off the rail and pointed her at the first jump.

Okay. Now or never.

I kept my hands low and my seat quiet, and Soiree's ears pricked forward, locking onto the obstacle in front of her. She lifted up, and I felt the arc of her bascule, just as steady as ever. *So far, so good.*

She landed in perfect balance and remained that way over the next two fences. But now the jumps were markedly taller than anything she'd faced before. Listening and feeling for any sign of nervousness in her, I had to remind myself to keep riding her forward toward the jump. Sizing it up, Soiree calmly put a bit more power in her step and cleared it easily. I gave her a quick thump on the neck, and then all my focus went straight back to that final, 4-foot fence.

Soiree's head lifted as she gave the obstacle a good long look. I closed my hand on the reins, ready to check her, but she didn't flatten and run at it as so often happens. Her long, sweeping stride seemed to inflate a bit, moving her forehand even higher off the ground. In the critical strides before the jump, she began to spring, nearly floating, and I hardly felt the takeoff. She swept over the jump, light as air, landing catlike with her rhythm intact.

I dropped the reins, patting her neck wildly with both hands. Soiree snorted, enjoying the praise, and I pulled her up and jumped down, chills running over my back from the thrill of that *jump*.

"*Good* job, Soiree. *Good* girl. You are amazing." I went on and on as I stepped back to look at her. She peered at me from beneath her blonde forelock, and her puzzled gaze made me laugh. *What's the big deal? I could see her thinking. This is what I do. This is easy.*

Still smiling, I threw an arm over her neck and led her to the barn.

When we got there, my phone was buzzing, right where I'd left it by the cross ties. I lunged for it, snapping it up just before it rang out. "Hello?"

"Hi, Erica. It's Maggie."

"Maggie. Hey." Holding the phone to my ear, I wrestled with the sliders and keepers on Soiree's bridle.

"Are you busy this weekend?"

"Um. No." I'd decided to take a week off from showing, and this session had definitely justified that decision. If Soiree kept going like this, I could probably move her up a division by the next show. Same with Assault, come to think of it. "Why do you ask?"

"I need a ride for Twinkle and me. I found one of those trail riding competitions you told me about, and I entered us."

Having gotten the bridle undone, I let the bit drop from Soiree's mouth. "That's great. But why don't you just have Juan take you?"

"Because my mom can never know about it."

I let out a short laugh. "Ah. I see."

"So can you give us a ride or what?" Maggie wanted to know.

"Sure. But I can't stay and coach you," I warned her. "I don't know enough about competitive trail riding, and I'm way too busy with my own horses this week. So if you really want to do this, make sure you study and *practice* beforehand, and don't expect it to go perfectly."

"That's *no* problem," Maggie said surely. "I rode Twinkle on the highway before I even knew what I was doing on the trail. Remember?"

I shuddered. "I try not to."

"Okay, well, we'll be *fine*," Maggie said. "See you on Saturday!"

Dougie

New SMS Message

Sent From: Amber

My lease is up. Landlord raising rent again for this shit hole. Fuck my life.

Reply

That definitely sucks. Ever thought about moving?

Send

New SMS Message

Only all the fucking time. Can't afford rent anywhere else though, so I'm stuck handing over my paycheck to this dickbag.

Reply

You could come and live here with me.

Send

Incoming Call: Amber

One Missed Call

New SMS Message

If you are going to drop a bomb on me like that, then you are going to talk to me ON THE PHONE like a normal person and explain yourself.

New SMS Message

NOW, Dougie. Not fucking around here.

Wearily, I picked up the phone and tapped the call icon. Amber picked up after a fraction of a ring. "Okay. What the hell is going on in your brain? Tell me."

"You're awfully jumpy about this," I said. "Considering I'm just trying to help you."

"I'm jumpy? Well, maybe that's because you just *randomly* sprung this on me, and I can't get a clear read on your intentions or *anything* when you refuse to use your actual voice and actually talk to me on the phone!"

"I'm not refusing to talk on the phone. I'm talking on the phone right now."

I heard Amber release a very loud breath. "*Okay,*" she relented. "But will you *please* tell me what your deal is with this?"

"My deal is not that complicated. I have a spare room we could fix up for you. It's just sitting there, doing nothing, and it makes no sense for you to keep paying that asshole to rent that shit hole, surrounded by sexual offenders -"

"Hold the fuck on. *What?*"

"Oh. Yeah. So I was bored and ran your address. Your neighborhood is full of red dots."

"*Seriously?*"

"It's pretty much just a red blob. Anyway. It's stupid for you to throw all your money into that train wreck, when you could pay me a nominal fee to rent my spare room, and live in peace and comfort. That's what I'm thinking. *That's all.*"

"That does sound nice..." Amber sounded downright wistful. "But how is that going to work? With our history."

I sighed. "Amber. That doesn't matter. You're gay, and I'm..." I couldn't finish that sentence.

"You're a wonderful person who deserves to be happy," Amber said lovingly.

"Yeah. Okay." I closed the conversation with two short words.

Erica

The state park entrance was still filled with horse trailers, but many were departing. I looked fondly at the reliable Quarter Horses and draft crosses as they were loaded up by their riders. *D.M. would fit right in here*, I found myself thinking. *It's too bad I'm so busy with Soiree and Assault. It would have been nice to ride along with Maggie, and to get D.M. out for a change...*

I shook off that rather pointless thought and maneuvered into a space. I was here for Maggie anyway. This was entirely Maggie's deal. I shut off the engine and went to look for her. I hadn't seen any sign of her or Twinkle, and she'd been pretty cryptic on the phone. I hoped nothing bad had happened.

Just when I was starting to get that throb of anxiety in my stomach, I saw a group of riders up ahead, and in the center, looking incredibly out of place among the cow ponies, with his impeccable braids and glistening English tack, was Twinkle. He wore his usual post-trail-ride look of mild terror. Beside him was Maggie, chatting with the other competitors as she held the pony's reins.

I walked up to the edge of the loosely grouped circle. "Hey."

Maggie's head turned and her face perked up. "Hey, Erica!" To the others, she said, "That's my ride. I gotta go."

"Okay, Maggie, hope to see you again! Good job today!" Several of them called out.

As soon as we were out of earshot, I stopped her. "So. Out with it. How *did* you do today?"

Maggie smiled coyly. "*First place* in the novice division."

"*No* way! Seriously?"

"Uh-huh. Twinkle was *awesome*. He handled everything, and I think he liked having the other horses there. He wasn't as nervous. The hardest part was when we had to open a gate. The latch was *way* over my head." Maggie held her arm up and stared at the sky, exaggerating.

I laughed. "I'm sure they gave you points on that one."

"It was so cool. It was a really pretty trail too. They even allowed us on a special one you normally can't ride on, just for this ride."

"It sounds great. I wish I could've come along."

We reached the trailer, and I quickly unsaddled Twinkle and exchanged his bridle for a halter. However heroic his performance on the trail had been, the pony still leapt onto the trailer with an eagerness that seemed to indicate a clear preference for his manicured, climate-controlled home turf.

Back at the Allsteen's estate, we quietly (and swiftly) unloaded Twinkle and unhitched his pony-size trailer, putting everything back where it belonged (with Juan's timely assistance) in about five minutes flat. Maggie's mother would never know.

Maggie was grazing Twinkle on the lawn and giving Juan an animated recap of the day's adventures. I watched them, leaning on my tailgate, when my phone rang.

I pulled it out slowly and peered at it, somewhat befuddled because Maggie was pretty much the only person who ever called me. I didn't recognize the number, and I figured it was probably going to be a "wrong number" kind of call, but I finally decided to just answer it.

"Erica Rimwork speaking," I said, adding a shot of professionalism just for kicks.

"Erica, hello there. My name is Martha Gross, and I'm calling about a horse of mine that I'd like you to train."

Every bit of professionalism, every trace of *together-ness* I'd managed to obtain in the span of my stagnant career went freefalling straight into my stomach with a *clunk*. This was the sort of call that I had dreamed about, wished for, and bitterly lamented the absence of. This was the kind of call that normal, successful trainers get all the time and think nothing of. This was *what I'd been waiting for.*

Struggling to speak, I of course said, "Yes, well, I do training."

Bless her heart, the nice lady went on even as I furiously kicked myself in my own shin. "Delusion is a four-year-old Thoroughbred who was to be my daughter's horse, but he wasn't fast enough for her liking. She enjoys barrel racing, and I guess if you're going to do that, you have to have a crazy horse. I don't understand it at all. But Delusion is a very nice horse with a good heart, so I decided I would start riding again. I gave up my riding when I married and started a family."

I nodded, finding my voice again. "Tell me about your aspirations for this horse. What would you like to do with him?"

"I've just been riding him on the flat, and he walks, trots and canters nicely. He has very smooth gaits, and everyone keeps telling me he would make an excellent hunter. So, I've been going to the shows to see the local trainers ride. I saw you ride your mare, and I love what you've done with her. I can tell you have a special bond. I can see you would do a wonderful job with Delusion, and I hope you will train him for me."

I waited a second until the knot of emotion cleared in my throat. "Absolutely. I would love to take him on."

We spent a few more minutes on board and training fees, which I had to come up with on the fly, and I gave her directions and a good time to haul him over. Then I waved goodbye to Maggie, jumped in my truck and flew out of there. I had only one person I wanted to share this with.

When I pulled in the drive, I saw immediately. He wasn't there.

Lawrence

We stood on the flat green field, Courtney on my left with Hermione's reins folded in her arms. Harry and Vegas were shoulder to shoulder, both motionless, heads hanging low as they waited at my side. The world was full of agonizing stillness.

I shifted, resting one overworked heel. Courtney worked her reins into a hopeless tangle as her eyes darted from the empty driveway to the unmarked turf in front of her.

I gave in. "Did Yvette say anything to you? She won't return my calls."

Courtney shook her head balefully. Her blonde ponytail sagged. "I had to rent a car." She gestured to the white Malibu sitting in the parking lot. "I haven't seen her. She won't talk to me."

"Do you even know where she is? Could she have left town already?" I wondered out loud. "She lives with you at your father's place though, that's right. She couldn't have left without you."

Courtney shook her head. "Yvette can do whatever she wants."

I was silent. Courtney's arms wrapped around her torso, and Hermione moved closer to her, adopting a stance that was almost protective. I looked back at Harry and Vegas standing there. *I'm gonna need to untack one of you,* I thought.

There was a light crunch of gravel in my ears, but I didn't bother to turn my head. It was Courtney's sudden intake of breath that caught my attention.

I looked over to see a tiny silver car slide into a parking space. A solitary figure made its way onto the field.

Courtney and I watched Yvette carefully. Not one of us made a sound.

She stopped just before us, hands in the pockets of her hooded sweatshirt.

I nodded to Yvette, acknowledging her return. "Are we good?"

"Yes."

I smiled fully. "Then let's do this shit, motherfucker."

Part Two

Elaine

Once it began, everything quickly changed. Seemingly overnight, a new string of horses moved into the LPC, wearing matching stable sheets in Hummer yellow. I got to know them at night, roaming the aisle. The ugly mare had the sweetest temperament and an old soul.

They began practicing every day, sometimes twice a day. They would come at off-peak hours, so during the spans of time when I usually lapsed into a boredom-fueled slumber, the barn was now full of life and energy. I was lured out of my room by it, and I found myself breaking my rule, venturing out in the light of day to watch them. It was impossible to stay away, and as I sat in the empty stands with the strong sunlight on my tired skin, I felt happy and almost exuberant again.

Yvette and Courtney had been unsure about my presence at first, but they accepted me now as the horses did. With nothing to do all day, I helped in any way I could, walking ponies cool, tacking up or untacking them, even cleaning tack. With a purpose, my body suddenly rebounded. My color returned; the sagging flesh on my arms firmed up. The contours of my skull became less apparent.

Courtney, Yvette and Lawrence had left for the day, and I remained, poulticing the legs of one of the hard-ridden ponies. She stood in the cross ties with her lead on the ground as I smeared the clay over her cannon bones.

I heard the scuff of a boot on the concrete directly behind me. I startled badly, and looked back to face Wilson.

"Elaine," he said in his usual greeting. His eyes were on the pony, not me.

"Hi, Wilson." I turned back to the task at hand, my heart rate settling.

Wilson walked around to the side, inspecting the pony's legs. His eyes swept around the aisle, taking in the half-dozen saddles, cleaned and oiled, sitting on racks. "You've been working hard."

I shrugged minutely. "I like having something to do."

Wilson nodded. "Have you ever thought about doing this for a living?"

I laughed silently. "I don't know that anyone would hire me."

Wilson looked at me squarely. "I would."

My head jerked around, and I stared up at him. "Do you really mean that?" I asked disbelievingly.

"I don't say anything I don't mean," Wilson said. He started off down the aisle.

Erica

I sat at the kitchen table (or what we called the kitchen table; it was really just a random table, since it wasn't even in the kitchen or anything) waiting for the arrival of my new training horse. His owner and I had talked on the phone extensively, and I was pretty sure I knew what I was getting into, but I hadn't seen the horse in person yet. *What if he's completely different in person?* I wondered. *What if he's not the well started, up-and-coming hunter dreamboat that she described? Then what, Erica?*

The truth was, I didn't really know. I came from the world of buying and selling, where you had the option of walking away if the horse you went to try out wasn't as advertised. What could you do if, in this instance, a misguided owner brought you a horse that was clearly unsuited for their chosen sport? Were you obligated to try and make something of the animal, or could you back out?

What could I say to the eager owner? Was I allowed to say, *I'm sorry, Mrs. Gross, but your horse is not at all suited to the hunter ring. If you'll go out and get a different horse, I'll consider becoming your trainer. Any horse will do. You can't possibly find a worse horse than the one you currently have, even if you try. In fact, go ahead and bring back a zebra; it will still be easier to train.*

My runaway thoughts were surpassed by the unmistakable sound of a horse trailer pulling into the drive at a slow rate of speed. I bolted up from my chair, shoving my feet into my boots, and hurrying out the door to meet Martha and Delusion. Despite all my worries, my veins were filled with pure excitement as I jogged down the front steps.

Martha had parked her truck and lowered the ramp already. She was a petite, athletic 50-something with short grey hair, wearing jeans, a long-sleeved tee and paddock boots. She disappeared into the rig while I waited anxiously. The horse inside wasn't kicking or carrying on, which I noted as a definite plus. Then Martha emerged from the Sundowner trailer, leading Delusion.

Easing his way down the ramp, he stopped once his feet were on flat ground, looking around the yard with calm interest. He was wearing a head bumper, lightweight sheet and shipping boots, but I could judge his build through all the gear. His eyes looked my way, wide and bright on his well-carved head. His stance was classic: a leg at each corner, correct angles, fitting neatly into an imaginary box. He was pure OTTB-show-prospect material.

His owner extended a neatly manicured hand. "It's so nice to finally meet you in person, Erica," she said warmly. "Now what do you think of Delusion?"

If he jumps like he ought to, he'll be hard to beat. "Based on first impressions, I'd say his future looks promising," I said less cockily, not wanting to over-promise when I hadn't even seen him in motion yet. He could still be a secret paddler or have some other fatal flaw. But I was growing more confident by the second.

"If you'd like to turn him out while we unload your other stuff, I have a paddock ready for him." Small, peaceful, within sight of the other horses but lacking any shared fence lines, it was ideal for a newcomer. It was also the place where Trucker had lived, until Lawrence had moved him just this morning.

"How lovely! He'll enjoy that for sure." Martha smiled gratefully, and I walked her and Delusion over. Once there, we stripped off his gear, and she turned him out. He trotted once around the perimeter announcing his presence to the other horses, who mostly ignored him. Then he settled down to eat.

I smiled. *No paddling,* I rejoiced.

Martha's trailer was both spotlessly clean and impeccably organized. Its living quarters were stuffed to the gills with everything a fledgling show horse could want - a close-contact saddle flocked to fit his back, a generous supply of schooling and show pads, leg wraps both timeless and trendy, and a grooming kit of perhaps 30 or more brushes, mitts, and currycombs. None of the brushes were grimy. In fact, they did not appear to have ever been used on a horse. The inside of the kit was similarly sterilized. None of the pockets were dusty or dirty. No horsey skin cells clung to the hunter green industrial fabric.

I helped Martha carry her things into the tack room, highly conscious of the saddles on the racks that had gone several rides in a row without so much as a wipe-down, and the sweat-stained pads that hung before them, air-drying in lieu of an actual cleaning. Spying my grody grooming kit sitting in plain sight, I surreptitiously kicked it into a dark corner. *I promise I will give you a proper bath later, and reacquaint you with that thing called bleach. But right now, just don't draw attention to yourself.*

After reorganizing the tack room to accommodate Delusion's equipment, we moved on to the feed room, where Martha set out his feed. He had his own special diet, 12% forage pellets infused with vitamins and SmartPaks brimming with coat supplements, hoof supplements and low-dose preventative joint supplements.

Martha made one last clean sweep of her trailer. "I think that's everything," she said, closing the door and making sure it was secure. "When will you start?"

"Tomorrow at the earliest. I'll give him a little time to settle in first. Although he seems pretty settled already."

"Sounds perfect." Martha reached into her purse, handing me a check for the first month's board and training. "I hope to come and visit him regularly, but I'll try to stay out of your hair and let you do your job. I sure don't want to interfere."

I held my arms against myself, looking at her earnest face, thinking of the people I knew, the stories I'd heard. The absentee owners who would write a monthly check and never look in on their horses, the aspiring competitors who blindly accepted a trainer's rough methods and gimmicky shortcuts as gospel. That last one hit especially close to home.

"Don't ever worry about interfering," I said to Martha. "And if you ever have any concern, no matter how small, about how your horse is being cared for or trained - by me or by anyone - don't dismiss it. Ask questions. Be persistent. And if you don't get an answer, if something doesn't change…take your horse and get out of there."

"You sound like you're talking from experience," Martha said, her face compassionate.

"The last person I gave that advice to didn't take it," I told Martha. "I hope you will."

"I doubt I'll have to, as long as you're my trainer," Martha said kindly.

"That's what Angie Wellman thought about her choice of trainer," I said. "And she ended up with this."

I was walking, with Martha in tow. I led her past happy, inquisitive horses, to the paddock on the outskirts of the property, where Trucker Hat lived.

He was outwardly normal. Smallish, bay. Unremarkable. He was eating grass. Until he saw us, and his body changed. He went rigid, bracing for impact. Everything froze over, except for his eye. Wide-open, worried, and tracking our slow, calm movements. That eye spoke volumes.

Martha stared at him in concern. "What's wrong with him?" She asked quietly. "Why is he hiding?"

"Because it was the only thing that worked." I turned away from the gelding, focusing on Martha instead. "This horse doesn't have a mean bone in his body. He doesn't have it in him to fight back. So he went inside himself after a while, and he hid. And now that's all he knows."

She looked at me, comprehending. "How awful. How unthinkable."

"And how preventable." I turned away, starting the long walk back to my house. After a moment, Martha caught up with me.

"Be an advocate for your horse," I said. "Always."

Lawrence

I shut the engine down and leaned my head back against the seat, sitting still in the near darkness. I was good and tired. After a particularly bruising practice with Yvette and Courtney, plus all the care and maintenance that went into a string of polo ponies, I looked forward to nothing more than falling into bed with Erica. Not that I ever *didn't* look forward to that.

I rested my eyes for one second before the rapid-fire sound of Harry trying to kick my trailer to bits snapped them open. "I'm *coming*, you little fuck," I muttered under my breath as I opened the door and stepped out of the cab.

Grasping a halter in each hand, I led Harry and Vegas to their stalls, where I fed them their dinner, ignoring the curious gazes of the other horses, except for Eloise. I went to her and rubbed her face, causing a few grey hairs to fall. She turned away from me, aloof as ever.

I left the barn and bounded up to the house, eager for a better reception. I walked straight to the bedroom, taking off my shirt and boots on the way.

Erica was lying in bed, and the light wasn't on. I thought she was asleep, but she sat up immediately as I came into the room.

"Where were you so late?" She asked as I unzipped my jeans.

"The LPC. It was an epic practice today. Multiple chukkers, working out strategy and shit. And then of course, aftercare for the ponies." I slipped in between the covers, rolling over to face her.

She turned onto her stomach, the sheet wrapped tightly around her. "So, what's happening with this, anyway? Are you, like, back on the team now?"

"No. I'm not officially with a team right now. We're starting a new team."

Erica looked at me, her blue eyes harsh and empty in the dimming light. "Who's '*we*'?"

"Me and...two other players."

"Only two? But don't you need four on a team?"

Team Dark Horse

"We'll add a fourth member somewhere down the line. I'm not too concerned about it. The main thing is, we're all free agents right now, and we work well together."

"How did you meet them? Did you know them from before?"

"Yes. From Florida."

"So you've played with them before?"

I hesitated. "No. We were never on a team together. They were...affiliated with a different governing body of the sport."

"Huh." Her eyes were unblinking.

"They're women," I said finally.

Her eyebrows shot upward. "Wow. Okay. Is that why you've been so secretive?"

"Erica. No." My hand brushed her wrist, soothingly, I hoped. "I was going to take you to meet them. I just wanted to make sure this thing was real before I brought you into it. I didn't know if it would go anywhere."

"But it's going somewhere."

"Yes. It looks that way."

"So when can I meet them?"

I leaned over and kissed her softly. "Tomorrow, if that's what you want. There's no reason to wait."

I met no resistance, so I kept kissing her, but before I could move my mouth lower, she pulled away.

"Lawrence?" She asked, guarded.

"Yes?"

"How well do you know these women?"

"Not the way I know you," I murmured, moving on top of her, feeling myself getting hard against the soft heat of her thigh.

She was unwavering. "But did you have sex with them?"

I sighed, pushing myself up with my arms. "Yvette, once. Courtney..."

Courtney

Our excursion to the International Polo Club had been simple enough,

Team Dark Horse

initially. We arrived, we made our statement (well, Yvette made a statement, and the rest of us averted our eyes and silently freaked out). We represented. For my part, I thought I'd done pretty well. I showed up for our appearances. I looked people in the eyes when I introduced myself. I played brilliantly during our exhibition. Basically, I totally avoided embarrassing myself for a few glorious days.

Until I ran into Lawrence Cavanaugh on a trail ride, and had sex with him on the ground, like an animal, with two actual animals watching. His polo pony, Eloise, and my mare, Hermione.

After I galloped away from him in a panic on Hermione, I avoided Lawrence like crazy. I went back to my usual routine of staying in my room all the time like a hermit, and when I was forced to make an appearance with my team, I spent the entire time looking around nervously in every possible direction, so he couldn't sneak up on me. When I did see him, I panicked, moving away from him and jerking my head away from his gaze like I had epilepsy. I knew he was trying to make contact. I could feel his eyes on me; I could see it in the way his body turned toward me as I ran away.

The worst part was that I felt bad for running away. I knew he wanted to talk to me, and I knew that by refusing to talk to or acknowledge or even remain in the same room with him, I was probably giving him a complex.

And that made me sad, because I didn't want to give him a complex. I didn't want him to think I didn't like him or that I thought he was repulsive. I especially didn't want him to think that he was bad at sex, because he wasn't at all. He was amazing at sex, and that was why I couldn't deal with seeing his face anymore.

It wasn't a good idea for me to have sex. It wouldn't end well. It never ended well. Well, it hadn't ended well the one time I'd had it, until now.

So I hid from him everywhere. In the banquet hall, in the Mallet Grille, in my room. Hiding in my room worked the best. Until it didn't work anymore.

Until he knocked on my door.

And even then, really, I could've avoided him. I could have called security and had him thrown out. But that really would've added insult to injury, and I couldn't do that to him. So I told myself I would be an adult, and

Team Dark Horse

I threw that door wide open.

"I'm sorry," he said immediately when our eyes met. "I know you don't want to talk to me."

"I don't not want to talk to you," I said feverishly. "I know that's what it looks like, and I know this is what people normally do when they don't want to talk to someone. But that's not what it means. I'm sorry." By now the words were falling as quickly as my panties had a few days before. Oh, wait, that metaphor doesn't work, because he never even took my panties off. He just pulled them aside because I wear thongs. Because they're comfortable.

"I never wanted you to feel uncomfortable," Lawrence was saying, looking into my face. "That was never my intention."

"Oh, I know," I mumbled. "That's, ah, not your fault. I get uncomfortable easily. I have a high level of discomfort."

Lawrence stepped closer, laying a hand on my arm. My arm hair stood up in response. "I just think you're really sexy, and amazing, and I loved riding with you and talking and everything, and it made me want to be with you, you know, in that way." He smiled tenderly. "But we don't have to do that ever again. I like you, Courtney. And if you're okay with it, I'd like to hang out with you sometimes, and talk horses and polo and feminism." He grinned loosely. "If you'd be comfortable with that, that is..."

We were practically the same height; he was just a little shorter. It was too easy for me to do what I did next. Which was kiss him. And the thing about kissing is it usually leads to other things.

Usually very quickly in my limited experience.

Within seconds, our hands were all over each other, and I practically jumped him. He withstood the addition of my weight quite admirably and staggered to the bed with me half on top of him. We struggled out of our clothes (including panties, this time, on my end), and just as I began to consider the fact that we didn't have protection, he pulled a condom out of the pocket of his jeans and rolled it on.

"Wait," I demanded as he began to pull me onto him. "If you came here to reassure me that we didn't have to have sex, why did you bring a condom?"

Lawrence grinned, leaning over me. "Well, you can't be too careful."

I gazed into the coal-black depths of his eyes, feeling the head of him lodged against me. "Okay," I said with a small nod. "Don't wait."

He entered me, remaining completely still for a moment, until I wanted to scream from the anticipation. Then suddenly, he pulled out, moving me to the very edge of the bed, spreading my legs wide, standing with his feet on the floor.

"I want you like this," he murmured, pushing inside me again, his eyes on me, watching every part of my body at once as I lay sprawled across the bed, completely open. I watched him too, and I felt my timid, juvenile inner self retreating as I saw him moving in and out of me, slick and hard. At the same time, he was stroking me with his thumb. I even saw my body begin to rise and spasm before my head fell back and my eyes closed and I simply rode it out until he pulled away from me, helping me down onto the floor with him, guiding me on top of him. And then it happened some more.

Then we moved to the window, and my rapid, open-mouthed breathing fogged up the glass until it was impossible to see through, which was probably a good thing, and then it happened some more.

The quick, sharp click of a room key sliding into place jolted me back to reality. Seconds later, Yvette burst into the room, slamming the door with excessive force.

"Do you have to be so *loud*?" I whined, letting my head fall back against the motel pillow marked *Soft*.

"I am not being loud. The door is loud. *All* motel room doors are fucking loud," Yvette stated as she stomped around the room, dropping her keys and her purse onto hard surfaces, and kicking off her boots.

"Well, you could've at least told me you were coming home," I muttered sourly. "I wasn't expecting you this early."

Yvette barked out a harsh laugh. "Why on earth would I inform you of my plans, Courtney? You do nothing all day long, so it does not matter what time I come home. I cannot possibly interfere!"

"I was trying to take a nap," I lied ineptly.

Yvette's hawk-like gaze quickly swept over me. "Then why are your cheeks flushed?"

I rolled over onto my stomach, away from her eyes, burning with shame. "It's hot in here," I mumbled.

"I am sure it is hot in there," Yvette said sagely, looking me up and down. "It has been a long time for you."

Not as long as you think, I thought.

"Anyway," Yvette redirected, "you will need to make yourself presentable within the hour. Run a brush through that hair of yours. Perhaps even a shower would be advisable."

I rose up onto my knees, turning around on the bed. "Why?"

Yvette pulled out a compact and began to apply eyeliner with surgical precision. "Because we are going out."

"Why?" I repeated myself.

"Because Cavanaugh would like for us to meet his girlfriend."

I was glad I was still on the bed, as I sank weakly into the mattress, my knees giving way. "Why? Why does he want that?" I demanded at the volume of a stage whisper.

Yvette shrugged, still contouring her eyes. "He did not say. But I am sure it was her idea, not his. She will want to get to know us, to get a feel for the situation. To ensure that nothing inappropriate is happening."

"Wow," I said dully. I felt like I had just been taken down by a 300-pound lineman. I had no air in my lungs.

Yvette reached for a tube of mascara. "It is not a big deal," she said perfectly casually. "It is not as if we have anything to hide. Neither of us have been intimate with him."

I jumped off the bed, my head swaying with horror and dizziness. "I need to shower," I said loudly.

"Don't take too long in there," Yvette warned as I wobbled past her. "I do not want to be held up and have us show up late because your fucking hair takes forever to blow-dry."

"Don't worry," I mumbled. "I'll be quick."

I stumbled into the bathroom, where I locked the door and turned on the shower so it would make that noise. Instead of getting in, I sat on the floor with my arms wrapped around my knees, and I had a panic attack.

Erica

Delusion stood amicably as I fastened the halter - leather, with a brass nameplate proudly bearing his name - behind his ears. He'd had time to adjust to his new surroundings, and I was excited to see what he had to offer under saddle.

In the barn, I moved a brush quickly over his shiny coat, my fingers feeling for any abrasions or galls that would be irritated by the saddle. Finding none, I bent to inspect his hooves. He picked up his feet obediently and held them for as long as it took me to pick out his hooves and check the clinches on his shoes to ensure none of them were coming loose.

I set the saddle pad (so white it cast a shade of blue, like people's teeth when they drastically over-whiten) on his back, following it up with the saddle. I slid it back into the right place, making sure it cleared his scapula. Then I reached for the girth. The sheepskin still looked brand-new, presumably because Martha had actually bought that special sheepskin-fluffing brush and used it religiously after every ride.

As I led Delusion down to the ring, I found myself feeling grateful for the lack of eyewitnesses to this first training session. Despite my insistence that Martha should be a presence, and an advocate for her horse, I had to admit that this initial assessment would go much more smoothly without the additional pressure of the owner's eager face at the rail.

I tightened the girth one final time and mounted up, holding the reins on the buckle. Delusion waited patiently, maintaining his halt instead of walking off the second I settled into the saddle, or even sooner. I gave his sides a small squeeze, and he obediently picked up the walk.

Nice, I thought.

Delusion kept to the rail without having to be micromanaged, staying straight and bending his body through the corners. His walk had a sweeping, well-oiled quality to it. I left him alone entirely for ten minutes, then slowly picked up the reins, establishing contact with his mouth.

Because he was still fairly young, I avoided asking for too much connection at the walk, focusing on maintaining his pure, four-beat rhythm and allowing him to carry himself in a light, natural frame. As I asked him for the trot, I gathered the reins, picking him up a bit more, asking him to flex at the poll. He met my contact agreeably, his head steady. His soft back muscles lifted to gently rock my seat, and I could have sat the trot easily had I wanted to.

I rode him through a large figure-eight, testing both trot diagonals. He showed no traces of residual right-bend difficulty, the cross that so many ex-racehorses must bear.

Turning him back onto the rail, I slid my outside leg back and asked for the canter. Delusion's ears flicked backward and he stepped into it lightly, maintaining the roundness over his spine. He had a good natural canter with a little jump in his stride. He was the kind of mover who would find it easy to go over fences.

I transitioned him to a walk, giving him a break while I thought about my next move.

Delusion was a gem on the flat. I could find no holes in his training up to this point, and there was nothing I needed to add or take away. This meant my job was simple: start him over fences, and work him up to the point where he could comfortably carry his amateur owner over a full hunter course.

I had a line of trot poles in the arena, set for an average stride. But I felt that Delusion could handle more of a challenge. I halted the gelding, asking him to stand. After glancing back to make sure he was stationary, I moved several of the poles, leaving more space between them. Then I dragged the other three over to the far side of the arena, setting them closer together.

"Okay, Delusion," I said as I got back into the saddle. "Let's see if you can lengthen and shorten." I turned him onto the rail, establishing a rhythmic trot before pointing him at the first line of poles. His ears pricked forward, sizing up the poles, figuring out the spacing. His brain was in gear, and that was exactly what you wanted to feel from a horse as you rode down to an obstacle, whether it was a few trot poles or a 6-foot fence.

Delusion bounded over the sand, his trot stride expanding as he stepped over the carefully spaced poles lying on the ground. I circled him back around, taking him over the line of poles on the other side of the arena. He shortened his stride seamlessly and without stutter-steps.

Delusion was everything his owner had promised. He was a dreamboat, free from physical or mental pathologies, the kind of horse that would make my job easy. He had everything going for him, including a rock-solid foundation of training. And I had the honor of polishing him up and readying him for the show ring.

I dismounted, leaving Delusion in the center of the ring, and reset several of the poles to fit a canter stride. After a few minutes of canter circles, I turned the gelding and rode him over the canter poles. I felt him hesitate slightly on the approach, but as he stepped over the first pole, he seemed to relax and trust that his feet would carry him over.

Satisfied with our session, I halted Delusion and stepped off. After untacking him, I decided to let him graze a little. He had been my last ride of the day, and I was in no hurry to return to an empty house.

I leaned one arm over his back, my hand resting lightly on the lead rope. Delusion was an erratic grazer, moving here and there, sampling a bit of everything.

I was still standing with the gelding when Lawrence's truck drove in. He cut the engine and slammed the door, walking right over to me.

"How was he?" Lawrence asked, nodding at Delusion.

I smiled. "He's a wunderkind. He's going to make me look very, very good."

"Excellent." Lawrence grinned at me. "Are you done with the horses?"

"Yeah, he was my last one."

"Okay. If you want to turn him out, I thought we'd go to dinner."

"Really?" I perked up at that one. "That sounds nice." *It's been a while...*

"Yeah." Lawrence started up to the house. "I figured it was time you met Courtney and Yvette. I'm gonna go change, and you can think about where you want to eat. It's your call."

I stared after him, utterly deflated. *Right. A nice dinner, just you and me. And your exes. I'm so looking forward to this.*

"Come on, Delusion," I said grumpily. He picked his head up from the grass. "I wish I could just stay here with you," I muttered.

Amber

I hadn't been entirely sold on the idea of moving in with Dougie, even after he persuasively argued for it, bringing up all the ways in which we would both benefit. I'd resisted hard, even after he attempted to scare me with sex-offender statistics and building code violations. Even after he insisted he was over me and that it wouldn't be weird. Even after he promised me he wouldn't look, touch, or think about touching.

He could have promised me that a billion times, and I still wouldn't have believed him.

But eventually, after weeks of staring at my moldering walls, overpaying rent to my sexist bastard of a landlord, and sleeping with a knife under my pillow, I caved. I folded. I threw all my shit in the back of the Harley, and I went to live with Dougie in suburban hell.

And so far, it was looking like the best decision I had ever made.

Dougie was a quiet, unassuming roommate, polite to a fault. He mostly lived with his computer, so I had the whole rest of the house essentially to myself. He let me rearrange his stuff to suit my needs (and unlike Cavanaugh, he didn't have useless shit like horse coolers and bridles piled everywhere, so there was actually room for my stuff). He let me watch whatever I wanted on his flat screen, and he started keeping the fridge stocked with quinoa and kale. "It's for both of us," he said, but he and I both knew he had no intention of eating anything but Doritos for the foreseeable future.

After coming home from my job at the track, I lay on the couch (another purchase he'd made on the DL after I'd bemoaned the lack of one) snacking and watching the LPGA on Golf Channel. Dougie was on his computer (and his iPad, and his phone) raking in the Likes.

"I just hit 50,000 on my last post," he reported. It was the first time he'd spoken in well over an hour.

I craned my neck to glance at him. "Do you announce these things even when you're alone in your house?" I asked facetiously. "Or did you suddenly remember I was here?"

"I've known you were here all along, Amber." Dougie swiveled his chair around, wincing as his posture shifted slightly. "I just thought you'd be interested."

"Okay, I'll bite." I got up from my couch-burrow with some difficulty. "Show me this incredible work of genius."

Dougie pulled up an image on the screen, and I leaned over his shoulder to look closer. It was a photograph of a misprinted street sign, with the words spelled backward. Underneath it, the bold, Photoshopped-in words read *Go home, sign. You are drunk.*

Dougie was looking at me expectantly. I retraced my steps and flopped back down on the couch.

"You're wasting your life with this shit," I called out as I propped my feet up and went back to watching the lady golfers.

From his chair, Dougie was looking at me. I caught his eye, expecting to see hurt on his face, but instead, there was mirth.

"And so are you," Dougie said.

Erica

The only good part of having to meet Lawrence's exes he was now working with was that I got to pick the restaurant. The Home Stretch had been my favorite place to eat out when I was growing up, and the setting for many celebratory family dinners. It was also $30-entrée pricey, and I intended on ordering the filet mignon.

I'd gone clothes shopping since the whole Marla debacle, and I was kind of okay with the outfit I was wearing (dark wash jeans and an empire waisted top in satiny turquoise). It was visually slimming, or at least not fattening. At any rate, it was a marked improvement.

Lawrence's eyes were on me as he held the door for me. "You look great," he said, grinning.

"Thanks," I whispered as I slipped past him. He followed me closely as we entered the restaurant, his hand descending into the vicinity of my ass. I felt the smile on my face. *Maybe tonight won't be so bad.*

The hostess was a girl I'd known for years, but she barely acknowledged my presence. "Good evening, sir," she trilled in that too-eager soprano that had become all too familiar to my ears. "Just the two of you this evening?"

"Four, actually. The reservation's under Cavanaugh."

"Oh, of course. The rest of your party is waiting. Right this way…"

Yvette

"Well," I said, settling into my seat at the cheap-looking burgundy-clothed table, "*we* are not late. They are late."

Courtney did not say anything. She appeared anxious, holding a water glass and occasionally sipping from it, setting it down with a clunk, and then snatching it back up.

Ignoring her antics, I began to peruse the menu. "She must be under the impression that Cavanaugh makes more money than he really does," I remarked upon reading the prices.

Courtney took another panicked sip. "He doesn't make any money," she said suddenly.

I nodded. "Precisely." I set the menu down on the table. "I hope you remembered to bring your *daddy's* credit card."

"I always carry daddy's credit card," Courtney said, but without irony.

I smiled behind my glass. "Good girl."

Some distance away, the door of the restaurant opened, revealing a tall, husky girl wearing an exceedingly bright shirt. Beside her was Cavanaugh, with his hand molded to her ass. "It looks like they are here," I remarked.

Courtney's torso stiffened abruptly, causing some of her water to slosh over the rim of her glass. "How do I look?" she asked, her eyes widening like the zoom lens on a camera.

Amused, I gave her the once-over. "Well, you are wearing a pink Nike tracksuit in a sit-down restaurant, so if I am being completely honest, you look ridiculous."

Courtney's eyes dropped to her thighs, which happened to bear the word *Nike* in exceedingly large letters. "I was trying not to overdress! I didn't want her to be threatened."

"I see no reason why she would be threatened by you," I smirked. "But if the girl is insecure, she will find a reason to be threatened by any girl, even one covered in logos."

Courtney's face fell, and she clutched her water glass with both hands.

"Cheer up," I said, as Cavanaugh and his hulking girlfriend made their way to our table. "At least your hair looks nice."

Courtney

I could see Lawrence and his girlfriend from across the restaurant. Soon I could see them clearly. They were getting closer. They were coming to our table to sit down.

The girl was tall, and she had short dark hair and piercing blue eyes. Her eyes were looking at me, and they were narrow.

When they reached the table, I stood up, pushing my chair back and almost upturning it. "Hi," I said unintentionally loudly, thrusting my hand out at her. "I'm Courtney."

She stared at me, saying absolutely nothing. Then, she kind of reached out and brushed my hand away without really shaking it. I had to look away, so I looked down at Yvette, who hadn't stood up when I did. She was sitting there, absolutely motionless, with a growing smirk on her face.

And I realized I had just made things five hundred million times more awkward than they already had been. And the initial degree of awkwardness had been sky high, what with the secret sex and all. I flopped down on my chair, folding my arms over my chest, covering up one of the many logos on my body.

Lawrence just smiled, putting his arm around his girlfriend like nothing out of the ordinary had happened. He was pretty much immune to awkwardness, because when you have casual sex, awkwardness is basically guaranteed to happen at some point.

Team Dark Horse

I mean, I had only ever had it that one time, with one guy, and look where it had gotten me. Here at this dinner, making a fool of myself in front of the guy's new girlfriend.

Which is something they should really make note of in those "just say no" campaigns.

Lawrence addressed the table. "Courtney, Yvette...meet Erica."

I bit down on my tongue to stop myself from spewing out some other dumb greeting. *I will let Yvette take the lead from now on. I will not speak unless I am directly addressed, and even then, I will proceed carefully.*

Silence ensued. First to the point where I became uncomfortable, and then it progressed to the point where even a normal, non-anxiety-prone person would notice the social breakdown. I looked at Yvette, and her lips were pressed tightly together. Her eyes were gleaming.

Yvette was doing the thing where she deliberately said nothing, forcing me to sit there, in so much discomfort that I wanted to claw my eyes out, until I finally broke down and filled the silence.

I resisted for about another ten seconds, and then I crumbled like a California mansion under the weight of a mudslide.

"It's *so* nice to meet you!" I exclaimed, prompting stares from half a dozen of the nearby tables. "So what do you do?"

Erica

We walked across the room, skirting tables, and I looked for the one our hostess would zero in on. Most of them were already full. Large, rectangular tables with carefully arranged families, the father invariably at the head, mixed with smaller, more intimate tables tucked away in corners. Couples sat across from each other, perusing the menu or each others' faces, displaying every possible degree of awkwardness that might eventually lead to intimacy.

I found our table even before the hostess pulled out the chairs and slapped menus down where we would be seated. It was a square table obviously set for four, with two women sitting on the same side.

They were so different physically that it was almost comical. The girl on the left was a slim, petite brunette with her hair pulled back in a tight bun. She sat bolt upright, with impeccable posture, and the look on her pointed face showed both keen assessment and preemptive disdain.

The girl on the right towered over her companion. She had to be at least my height. She was what the average person would call "athletic", a sort of veiled insult often directed at taller, more heavily built girls. But even though she was seated, I could tell she had escaped the curse of the athletic girl - the heavy bone, the graceless distribution of muscle. Her breasts were pert and full. She was ample and toned, in all the places where you want those qualities.

I knew she was Courtney. I knew it before we even sat down.

We got to the table, and she bolted up from her chair, leaning across the table. Her wide blue eyes and long blonde hair glittered at me, a cruel representation of the feminine ideal. "Hi," she said almost breathlessly, reaching for me. "I'm Courtney."

I shook her hand briefly, sitting down. Courtney looked flustered, and she sat down as well.

Lawrence remained standing, taking charge. "Courtney, Yvette…meet Erica."

I stayed seated. I didn't look up, smile, or offer anything in the way of conversation. It took a lot for me to lose all my social cues. I had been in many uncomfortable situations over the course of my life. I'd participated in a lot of awkward, potentially volatile conversations, and usually, I always tried to go along with it. I wasn't always the smoothest or the quickest on my feet, but the point was, I tried.

Right now, I just didn't feel like trying.

I didn't even care that the silence was expanding and pressing down over the table, enveloping us all. Apparently, Yvette didn't care either. She sat across from Lawrence, watching the awkwardness unfold, her eyes lazy, a small smile on her mouth.

Maybe Yvette and I could get along, I started to think. Then I remembered that she'd been with him too.

Abruptly, Courtney shattered the quiet. "It's *so* nice to meet you!" She exclaimed phonily. "So what do you do?"

It was on me now to carry the conversation. I picked up a menu even though I knew what I was getting, buying myself a little time. "I'm a trainer," I said dully. "I work with hunter/jumpers."

"Erica's got some exciting prospects moving up the levels right now," Lawrence elaborated on my behalf. The eagerness and pride in his voice thawed my icy core, just a little.

Yvette glanced at me for the first time. "What is your end goal?" She asked, and I was surprised by the crystalline softness of her voice, and her strong accent.

"I don't know," I said, fully aware that it made me look stupid. "I'd like to make it onto an international team."

Yvette nodded. "Many say that," she said succinctly.

"I have the drive, and the experience. It just takes getting a leg over the right horse."

"What about the horse you have now? Your exciting prospect?" She was testing me, a boorish horse rooting at the reins. Picking, picking, picking at your resolve, until your balance shifted, and they could run away with you.

"He lacks experience in the upper echelon of competition," I told her. "He was started in another discipline. But he's made for the jumper ring. He'll get there."

I said the words confidently, but the truth was, I didn't know if he would. The question gnawed at me every day when I schooled him and felt his simmering resentment underneath the saddle. Every time he blew through a line, or chipped in to a fence, or locked his jaw against my half halt, it was there, blatantly obvious. *What am I doing with this horse?*

"I think it's great," Courtney chimed in. "I used to ride hunters in middle school. It was a blast."

"Why only middle school?" I asked, because I really didn't want to hear about her undoubtedly sparkling success in the ring. "Why did you stop?"

Courtney looked down at her napkin. "Well, I was involved in a lot of other athletics, and when I was a freshman in high school I decided to try out for the football team. I made the team, and after that, it took up a lot of my time."

"You made the boys' team?" I asked, my curiosity piqued in spite of myself.

She glanced upward. "There wasn't a girls' team."

"What position did you play? Kicker?" I realized as I said it that it would come out kind of condescending. That hadn't been my intention. It was just, in every news article I'd ever read about a girl player on a boys' team, she'd played that position.

Courtney shook her head. "Defensive tackle."

Our waitress cut in, and I ordered my drink somewhat distractedly. The others did the same, and when the waitress left I leaned forward, unwillingly fascinated by Courtney's story.

"Did you play football all through high school, then?" I asked.

Courtney took a sudden gulp from her glass of water. "No. I only played the one season."

I stared at her in surprise. "So, all that work to make the team, and you just quit after a single season?"

The table was quiet. Courtney shrank back a little from the abruptness of my question. Yvette's eyes flashed at me, and though she didn't open her mouth, I could tell she wasn't happy with the way I was interrogating her teammate.

Courtney looked up at me, not quite meeting my eyes. "It just wasn't for me," she said. Her voice was small.

I nodded. "I can understand that," I said. "I had other sports I pursued for a while, but they didn't compare to being with horses."

Courtney nodded. "The summer after I quit the team, I started learning polo," she said.

Our waitress was back, setting down drinks both alcoholic and fizzy. "Are we all set to order?" She asked.

"I'll have the filet mignon. Medium rare." I handed in my menu.

"I will take the same, as rare as you will serve it." Yvette sat back watching me with some sort of challenge conveyed in her eyes.

Lawrence ordered a burger, and Courtney ordered some sort of salad, which made me distrust her all the more. As we waited for our food, I found myself watching Courtney, and considering the strange trajectory of her athletics career.

She'd been involved with horses before, but had chosen to pursue football above all else. Then, after one short season, she'd walked away, finding her way back to horses, starting fresh with a whole new sport. Something that would have taken considerable concentration and dedication to master.

I looked at Courtney, sitting there in her pink tracksuit, her giant eyes flitting around the room, never landing anywhere for too long. She'd obviously found success in her new sport, but her mannerisms and her way of being didn't mesh with the image of a confident, successful world-class athlete. She seemed to me like a teenager. Restless. Fitful. Trying too hard.

What happened during that one season? I wondered.

We fell in and out of small talk. Eventually our food came, and I cut my meat into thin strips, watching Courtney dig into her Caprese salad with actual enthusiasm. Beside Courtney, Yvette ate her steak in large bites, occasionally shooting me a loaded glance over the spreading pool of blood on her plate.

The waitress appeared, right on cue. "How is everything?" She inquired.

"Couldn't be better," I mumbled, and no one called my bluff.

Lawrence's headlights illuminated the road as he pulled out of the parking lot. I sat silently in the passenger seat, watching the dimly lit scenery as it passed by me, buildings and empty lots fading into the darkness.

Lawrence was the first to speak. "Well, I think that went well," he said, leaning back in the driver's seat with one hand on the wheel, secure in his declaration.

I wondered about that. *Did it go well? By whose standard? His? Mine? It didn't go badly. It could have been worse. But isn't the essence of good based on more than the absence of disaster?*

I shrugged noncommittally. "I guess."

He reached over, squeezing my hand. "So do you feel more comfortable with my working with them now that you've met them?"

I wanted to tell him that, yes, I did feel more comfortable now. I wanted to tell him that I didn't feel threatened, that I was entirely okay with it. It seemed like that was how a caring, secure girlfriend should feel.

I nodded slowly. "Well, I know them now."

I didn't say whether that made it harder or easier for me, and he didn't ask.

When we got home, I felt a strong instinct to shut him out. To turn my body away from his, to roll over and pretend to sleep while he lay there all worked up and restless, shifting beneath the covers.

But as we got ready for bed and I saw him strip in the moonlight, I found myself drawn to him as much as ever. When I felt his hands at my hips, his hard-on pressing against me from behind, I went limp, feeling myself getting wet even before he touched me there.

He reached around, and I heard the familiar sound of a condom wrapper opening. Then his arms were around me, guiding me exactly where he wanted me, gently throwing me down. Our bodies coiled together, each of us in total agreement, our voices rising steadily as the pressure inside me built up, and the need for release drove every conflicting thought out of my head.

When we were alone, everything was right. It was easy, fluid, undeniable. I couldn't give it up, couldn't resist. He was relentless, and I was powerless to say no.

I'd never turned him down, never failed to respond to him. It hadn't happened once.

Afterward, as he lay sleeping, I held him close, draping myself over his still form. I wondered why I hadn't gone through with it, why I hadn't pushed him away when every cell in my body had called for me to do so.

It wasn't just because of how much he turned me on or how good it felt when he was inside me. I craved comfort and reassurance, now more than ever. And with the absence of a support system, I turned to him. Even though he was the source of my pain, he could still provide me with what I needed.

I went to sleep and woke up a few hours later. I remembered clearly the dream I'd had, which was strange because it wasn't especially action-oriented or detailed.

I was driving along on an empty highway, running on empty, my vehicle slowing to a crawl. I'd pull over to a gas pump and fill the tank just enough for the level to rise above the *E* line. Then I'd get back on the road, running on fumes, until I could locate the next meager supply of fuel.

Elaine

It was strange having a job now, a purpose, after spending so much time shut away. In a storage room. On the corner of Hewitt and Aachen. In a mansion, in a marriage. In a shithole town in Indiana. In my own soul.

For the first time in my life, I was doing work that I enjoyed. It felt good to me, the steady routine of horse care and cleanup. It was intensely physical, grueling, especially with my wasted body. But at the end of the day, I could step back and see all I had achieved. It was purposeful, and I had been floating for some time.

This job was my tether, and I clung to it with frail, scarred hands.

I knew Wilson had entrusted me with a lot, and not just because of the high dollar value attached to the ponies. I knew he would face derision from those around him, those who knew me from before. I was a joke in that crowd, a salacious scandal. They wouldn't expect me to reappear here, of all places. Here, where this whole thing started, when I saw Lawrence hand-walking that pony.

Now I held the lead rope, and I could feel what it must have been like for Lawrence, just starting out knowing nothing, working with these creatures and falling in love with them. The absolute focus on their welfare, the strange intimacy of walking side by side, maintaining the proper distance between the pony myself. I spent so much time with the ponies that I felt as though I could live among them, mastering their subtle body language, learning their code. I went days without speaking to another human being, and the click of my tongue or a quiet, hushed "whoa" were the only sounds I made.

As a consequence of my work, though, I could no longer hide. I could no longer avoid the people I did not want to see. Wilson was depending on me, as were the ponies. When I saw a face from my past walk through the stable doors, I had to be brave.

The thud of a car door, or the sound of human voices laughing and talking loudly, caused my heart rate to spike. I glared at visitors or looked away, resting my eyes on the comforting ripple of my pony's shoulder muscle. I had become a hermit like Wilson, edgy and unhappy in the presence of human beings, at ease in a dark, quiet stable.

Eventually the inevitable happened. I was standing at the wash rack, hosing down a pony, when my ex husband walked in with a young blonde on each arm.

I had thought I would run or hide when this happened. That was how I imagined it, the first time I saw him since he kicked me out and I nearly died. But that's not how it went.

I stopped what I was doing, and I watched him. I scrutinized him, my eyes sliding over every inch of his body. I ignored the girls. They didn't matter to me. As he continued to walk up the barn aisle, I stared, almost in fascination. I could feel myself becoming bored, even as I looked at him. He was so unremarkable.

Arnold didn't notice me, didn't look my way, so I was spared an awkward exchange. I wasn't especially relieved, nor was I disappointed. I was completely, utterly neutral, and the sensation was so alien that it shocked me.

As I stood there contemplating what had just happened, engine noise reached my ears. It wasn't smooth and quiet like the sponsors' cars. It was Lawrence's truck.

And just like that, my heart went into overdrive.

Arnold didn't turn me inside out. But I knew who still did.

Lawrence

I breezed through the door of the LPC, fully intending to make it quick. Hermione had been running a slight fever, and I promised Courtney I would look in on her. Even though I trusted Wilson, he had a lot on his plate, and no one knows horses like a former groom.

I saw Elaine on my way in, and my pace slowed. She was standing by the wash rack, holding a pony in one hand, a running hose in the other. It wasn't unusual to see her doing that, but the pony she held wasn't one of our string.

My footsteps stopped. "Hi," I said.

"Lawrence. Hi."

"I thought you should know something," I said. "You've got the wrong pony there."

She looked at me, unblinking. "No. I don't."

I looked back cluelessly. She must have seen this, because she quickly opened her mouth again. "I work for Wilson now."

"Wow. For how long?"

"A week, so far."

I nodded, comprehending a few things. "So that's why I haven't seen you at practice."

"Yes. I'm sorry to miss it, but..." Elaine trailed off, looking at her hands.

"No, it's great," I said, smiling. "I was just surprised. But it's great. It'll be great for you."

"It already has been." She smiled slightly, then turned back to her pony.

Hermione's temp was normal. She looked normal in every way. I called Courtney and told her that, and then I made a beeline for Wilson's office.

He was in there, of course, half-buried by paperwork as usual. I knocked on the wall as an afterthought when I was already inside the room. Wilson rolled his eyes.

"I'm ass deep in work, Cavanaugh," Wilson declared. "Keep it brief."

"You're always ass deep in this stuff," I said, glancing around the messy, dim office. It looked like the human version of a rodent's den. "You need a secretary."

Wilson sighed, running a hand through his hair, russet with ever-increasing patches of grey. "What do you want, Cavanaugh?"

I decided to get to it. "I didn't know you hired Elaine."

Wilson nodded. "Well, I did."

"That's really great of you, Wilson," I said honestly. "I was worried about her. I really was. But this will get her out of that room, out in the daylight. Back on her feet, maybe."

"She's good at her job," Wilson said, brushing off my little speech. "She's meticulous, focused. She'll give it a hundred percent. And Wayde just quit on me. Eloped with his girlfriend to Antigua."

I chuckled silently. "Well, it sounds like it all worked out."

Wilson peered at the papers on his desk, his brow furrowed. "Like I said, Cavanaugh, I'm real busy here..."

"Yeah, I know. I need to get back to Erica anyway." I headed out the door, raising my hand as I did so. Wilson jerked his head slightly in my direction.

Walking back through the deserted parking lot, I felt around for my keys. They had crept into that no-man's-land between the pocket and the fly, so I stopped walking and gave the extraction my full concentration. When I succeeded, I looked up and immediately noticed something I hadn't before. There was another car in the lot, and I suspected it had been there all along.

It was a red Mustang. Just like Barbara's car.

I had a sudden vision of Wilson at his desk, overloaded by work, and how dismissive and snappy he could get when he was stuck underneath all that office drudgery.

I moved toward the car slowly, dreading what I might find.

As I got closer, I could see that the person behind the wheel was definitely Barbara. She was crying, and from the looks of it, she'd been crying a while.

My shoulders sagged. "Wilson, you dumb idiot," I muttered as I hurried to the car.

Barbara didn't look up as I approached, so after I spent a few minutes leering outside of her vehicle like some creep, I finally just tapped on the glass. Predictably, she jumped, and then she hastily opened her car door.

"*Lawrence*, hello," she exclaimed in an attempt at a cheerful voice that was pretty damn strained. "I'm so sorry, I'm such a mess right now..." she trailed off in embarrassment.

"I noticed that," I said. "I mean, I noticed that you seem upset. Is anything wrong?"

A couple new tears ran down her cheeks, adding to the salt water already dripping down her neck and staining the collar of her shirt. "Oh, it's nothing, I suppose. I really shouldn't be so upset, but Jeff and I, we had planned a nice evening tonight, just the two of us, and I was really looking forward to it..." and she dissolved into more tears.

"Go on," I said, patting her gently on the shoulder. "What happened?"

She sucked in a very noisy breath. "Well, I came here to pick him up, and he said he had work to do and he couldn't make it! Just out of the blue! He's never done that before...." Barbara looked at me desperately. "And I've been through this before, I know exactly what it means...he's cooling off, he's checked out of our relationship!"

I stood there a second, and then I gave her a hug, both because she was really upset and because I wanted to buy myself a bit more time before I had to explain Wilson's unbelievably stupid behavior to her. Her body heaved a few times, but then she seemed to calm down a little, so I released her and looked into her watery eyes.

"You're not stupid," I said, "so I'm not going to bullshit you. I'll admit, that tactic is a particularly dick move that guys are known to do when they don't want to be in a relationship anymore. But Wilson's not like that."

Barbara looked at me searchingly. "He's not?"

"No, he's not. Wilson's a straight shooter. He can be gruff sometimes, but he's never going to lead you on. If he wanted to end things, he most certainly would. But this is not him ending things."

Barbara looked almost hopeful. It was working. "I mean...I just didn't know how else to interpret it."

I nodded. "Trust me. Wilson's not a game player. If Wilson tells you he has work to do, then he has work to do. No interpretation required."

"Whew!" Barbara flapped her hands in front of her face, as if that alone would dry it and reapply her makeup. "Thank you, Lawrence." She laughed in clear relief. "I feel a little foolish, now."

"Don't be. I'm just glad I was able to clear it up." I smiled at Barbara. "It's the least I can do for Wilson. He's a good man."

"Now if you'll excuse me," I said, "I need to go back in there for a minute. I think I left my keys."

I turned around and walked straight back into the LPC. My boots hit the floor heavily, in an ever-increasing rhythm. When I reached Wilson's office, I threw the door open and strode right up to his desk, so I was standing over him.

"Are you aware," I said through clenched teeth, "that your girlfriend is sitting in the parking lot, crying in her car?"

Wilson peered up at me, his entire face slackening with shock, and, I was glad to note, horror. "She is?"

"Well, not anymore. I stopped her from crying and sent her on her way. She's all right now."

Wilson nodded slowly. He looked dazed but relieved. "Well. Thanks, Cavanaugh."

My teeth connected, harder this time. "*That's not the point*. The *point* is that I just had to do damage control with your girlfriend and explain away your behavior. Which, by the way, is appalling. Your behavior, that is."

Wilson gave me a blank look. "What on earth are you talking about, Cavanaugh? What did I do?"

"What did you *do*? Okay, let's explore that. Let me see, you cancelled on a 'nice evening' with Barbara - which, by the way, is code for getting all kinds of laid - at the last minute, and you gave her some lame-ass excuse about having *work* to do…basically, you acted like a big dick, and not the kind that wins you fans and notoriety."

"It wasn't an excuse," Wilson said, looking browbeaten. "I do have work to do."

"*I* know it wasn't an excuse! But Barbara doesn't know that. You have a girlfriend now, Wilson! You have to tread carefully, and be sensitive to her needs, and maybe fucking make her a priority once in a while! You can't just act like a dick and expect her to go along with it."

I fell silent, and even though I was exhausted, a small part of me was kind of digging on the fact that I had just given Wilson a lecture, when usually it was the other way around. Mostly, though, I was just exhausted.

Wilson's elbows were propped up on the desk. His chin fell to his waiting hands. "Okay, Cavanaugh. I get it. I'm sorry."

"Just try to be more careful, Wilson," I said as I left. "I don't want to have to talk your girlfriend off the ledge all the time."

I started off down the aisle yet again. Elaine was cleaning tack, and she glanced up at me questioningly. "What's going on? Why are you back?"

"Wilson's a clueless idiot," I said as I passed her. "I just saved his relationship."

Elaine smiled, biting down on her lip. "Well, some people are better at some things than others. Wilson has other gifts."

It's true, I thought as I walked out into the lot, now empty except for my truck. I thought of Elaine, myself, and Eloise. *Like saving lives.*

Erica

Barn Traffic, the sign read. My trailer rattled as I drove gently down the pockmarked road that led to the network of outdoor arenas. It was the only spot on this desolate fairgrounds that was humming with activity, even when no rides, games or funnel cakes were in sight.

I found a wide-open spot and parked. It was wide-open because it was nearly at the far edge of the field, and no one wanted to be inconvenienced by having to walk that far. So, everyone always crammed their trailers as tightly together as possible, in a somewhat underhanded fight to get closer to the action. I had never enjoyed the endless circling and close quarters, and today I just didn't feel like participating. If I was going to be an outcast, I might as well have my space.

I hopped down from the cab, straining to hear the announcer's grating voice. *Good. Plenty of time. No rush.* I eased the ramp down and looked in on Soiree. The mare turned her golden head and nickered, the pleasant sound echoing off the metal walls.

A huge gooseneck rattled past me, the driver intent on finding a space. I knew what would be going on in the clustered mass of trailers. Edgy horses would scream and paw. Grooms would be wrapping legs, tightening girths and ensuring everything remained shiny. Trainers would stalk around, eyeballing each others' strings and exchanging pleasantries, meaning not a word of it.

I turned my back on it all and climbed into the trailer. I left everything and I went to my horse.

"We're moving up today, Soiree," I said.

Yvette

Every Saturday, we could count on getting in an early morning practice. Cavanaugh's girlfriend would always be at a horse show, so he would have no distraction preventing him from meeting us at the Lexington Polo Club at the appointed hour.

I sat on a chair overlooking the polo field. Countless divots lay upon the grass, chunks of turf uprooted by steel-shod hooves, a visual reminder of what had transpired there.

Cavanaugh caught my eye as he passed, leading his pony, the gelding Harry, and mine. The sweat-soaked animals fell into line behind him, walking in tandem so their legs moved in the same sequence, like pistons firing seamlessly.

I had made many compromises in this new venture. I was living in a Podunk town with absolutely no culture. The roof over my head was that of a Days Inn, which Courtney constantly reminded me was not up to code. And I now saddled my own pony, because I had conceded that we could begin our practices in a more efficient manner if Cavanaugh was not burdened with the task of saddling two horses at once.

But I did not, and I would not, walk my pony cool. After we finished, after the chukker was over, and my pony was spent, sweating and panting with its mouth open, I was done with it. I walked away, leaving it in the care of whichever groom happened to be available. I did not care for it, worry over it, and worship it, because I was a player. The pony was a vehicle, a piece of equipment. A rather crucial piece, but nevertheless, it was one, and as such it bore no more significance than my hand-stitched boots or my mallet.

Team Dark Horse

There were, of course, players who thought differently. There were players who came to the game because of horses, not the other way around.

I was looking at one of them right now.

Some people carried the opinion that this insane love of horses, this unmatched devotion, made Cavanaugh a better player. To my mind, it had only held him back. It was this insane love that had prompted him to leave the International Polo Club, to abandon his coveted spot on a winning team and hand it all over to someone else. Had he been sensible and stayed on at the IPC, I could have used his status and inarguable record to gain sponsors and allies as we embarked on this team-building exercise. I could have been 50 steps ahead, instead of scrambling from the bottom.

Love is never advisable. When you love, you give up your power to someone else. You allow them a certain clearance into your wellbeing. And once you do that, you have no leverage anymore. You give it all away and hope they don't fuck with you.

Cavanaugh had halted the ponies in front of me, uncomfortably close. I lifted my feet up onto the chair, mindful of their shod hooves.

"Your pony's cool," Lawrence said. "If you rub him down, I can tend to Harry."

I shook my head once, succinctly. "I will not 'rub him down'. I do not *rub* things."

I saw Cavanaugh's face veer between pure amusement and actual annoyance. The former won out, of course. "That's a shame."

I looked at him coolly. "I do not think it is."

"That's why you're single."

A smile twisted my mouth. "If your implication is that my lack of enthusiasm for rubbing objects makes me an unskilled and ungenerous lover, you would be dead wrong."

Cavanaugh's face perked up. "Oh, really?" He said casually, trying to appear disinterested even as his whole body leaned in my direction.

I smirked up at him. "I do not *rub* things. But I do other things, specifically one thing, and I do it exceptionally well."

Cavanaugh was silent for a moment. "I never got that thing from you,"

142

he said.

I smiled. "That was not accidental."

His eyes flicked skyward. "Well, since you're not going to be rubbing down this pony, you can hold onto Harry." He dropped the horse's lead rope in my lap and walked off.

My mouth fell open in protest, but he was already gone. "Fuck it all," I muttered, taking hold of the lead.

I looked up into Harry's bony face, my eyes tracing the bold white blaze that adorned his head from the point of his eyes to right above his nostrils. He had a strong profile, a slightly roughhewn look to his head. He was aggressively fit but not weedy, almost plump-looking by polo pony standards. His eye tracked me as I assessed his features, never letting me go.

I knew that with a single twitch of his head he could pull me out of this lawn chair and fling me into the dirt. It made me want to stand up and plant my feet on the ground. Even more than that, it made me not want to be holding onto him.

"You are a fine specimen, Harry," I said to the air. "But you are still a vehicle."

He swished his tail, fighting back against the diminutive assault of a biting fly. His ears flopped to the side, and he turned away from me as far as the lead would allow. I slouched in my chair, and he slouched on his hooves, both of us in agreement that the company we had been forced to keep was anything but stimulating.

My eyes nearly closed, and then they shot open. Courtney was walking quickly toward me, dragging Hermione along with her. She looked near tears, blonde hair flying around her face.

"What the fuck is going on with you?" I nearly shouted.

She stopped in front of me, clutching her forehead with one hand. "I have to tell you something. I can't keep it a secret any longer!"

"Courtney. What on earth…"

"I had sex with Lawrence!"

Erica

I kept my total focus on Soiree the entire time as we prepped for our class, our big move to the 4' Working Hunter division. And when I slowed down, when I wasn't racing from horse to horse, ring to ring, and feeding into all the craziness happening around me, I noticed things. Like how blissfully happy Soiree was to have her hooves painted, because I was paying attention to her. Like how she watched all the other horses, and her eyes got big and expressive, like a cartoon character's, when she saw one putting up a fight or acting out. I noticed the little strut she put on when we got near the grandstands, probably a lingering habit from her racing days. She had been a poor runner, but I was sure she had always tried to put on a good show.

And, focused on Soiree as I was, I began to adopt some of her inborn traits. Instead of haphazardly dressing myself, squeezing myself into my show clothes hurriedly and praying I didn't rip a seam, I took my time, carefully buttoning my coat, dusting lint off my breeches, and applying a final coat of polish to my boots. I took pride in my appearance, because I was with Soiree. I was an extension of her, and I would make sure we both glowed brightly.

I took the long way around, eschewing the dangerous, tightly packed maze of trailers and avoiding questioning glances from people who used to be a part of my life. It was unorthodox, but it felt right, and I didn't waver. I even did the thing I never did, steering clear of the crowded ring and warming up on the hill instead.

Soiree felt good underneath me. I felt calm as a lazy ocean tide on her back. The wind moved along, causing the immature evergreens to sway. I could just hear the loudspeaker from the hill, and when it called my name, I smiled.

"Number 398, Erica Rimwork on Soiree For Two. This is your last call."

I cantered down the hill, lifting my torso slightly, maintaining my balance. Soiree's hindquarters were engaged underneath me. I tested her with a half halt, and she responded, coiling even more. She was ready.

Team Dark Horse

We cantered into the small group of waiting riders, gathering stares and surprised looks. I looked through the in-gate, and without circling, I began the course.

These hunter courses were always the same, and Soiree knew them well by now. My job was reduced to staying out of the way and giving her a clean ride. It was as effortless as driving a sports car on an empty, gently winding freeway, and as exhilarating.

Soiree soared. She had always been good, but as the fences got higher, she was getting better. I hadn't felt her struggle once. She was a gifted and talented student who was thrilled to skip a grade and move ahead. But I felt like Soiree could advance straight to college.

Straight to the Hunter Derby Finals.

When we left the out-gate, I rode far away from the arena, back to my trailer. I no longer cared about collecting my ribbon. It was one of many. I had become a true competitor. Our turn in the ring was over, and now I looked ahead to the next competition.

I was content just to be with Soiree, pampering her, taking her braids out, and spending half an hour fastening her shipping boots just right. But I kept being interrupted by people who wanted to talk to me. Most of them wanted Soiree, of course. I was offered five-figure amounts that I swiftly turned down.

But then there were people who had horses they wanted me to consult on. A lady was interested in having me travel to her barn to give monthly clinics. One man wanted me to take a road trip with him and help select which yearling hunter prospects he would buy.

They all found me, even though I was far away from the inner sanctum. They sought me out, even though I was alone and on the fringe.

And just as I lifted the ramp and slammed my trailer door shut, I turned around to see Jennifer's face.

"That was a beautiful round," she said to me, her face generous. "I don't even think Silken and I could have beat it, back in the day."

The moment I stopped caring, the moment I turned my back on them all and focused solely on my horse, was the moment they wanted me back.

Courtney

Yvette didn't let me say another word until we were off the LPC property. She stuffed me into her Voyage without even moving the seat back and flew out of the parking lot. She hit the road and just kept accelerating.

"When? When did this happen?" She snapped over the low hum of her eco-friendly engine.

"Two winters ago," I sniffled, "when the Federation sent us to the IPC to give our presentation and stuff."

I heard her exhale loudly. "So, when I thought you were simply hiding in your room, you were fucking him."

"Not at first. We were there for…a couple days, before….it….happened."

Yvette was silent for a moment, staring straight through the windshield. "I am curious to understand how this happened," she said quietly. "Since you never leave your room, he must have been quite determined to get inside you."

I shook my head. "No, I did leave my room. That was my mistake. I should never have done that. But I decided I should get out and *do* something! *Not* stay in my room the whole week! So I went on a trail ride, and he was on a trail ride, and…things happened."

Yvette nodded curtly. "I see. So this was an isolated incident? I should hope so."

I let my head fall forward. "No. It wasn't isolated."

Yvette's head twisted to the side. "You fucked him after that?" She demanded. "How many times?"

I struggled for a minute. Part of it was I didn't want to have to tell her. And part of it was, I didn't even know how many times it had been. I couldn't even ballpark it.

"A lot, okay!" I finally wailed. "It happened a lot!"

She didn't say anything, so I did that thing where I panic and just keep talking more and more. "And I felt really guilty about it, Yvette! Especially since I know how you hate male polo players, and Lawrence even more for some reason, and I knew you wouldn't approve at all! And I felt so ashamed, Yvette, like why did I even leave my room; why couldn't I just stay there and watch bad TV and listen to Britney and stuff, but I didn't. I left my room, and then I let things happen…and I wanted to stop, I tried to stop, but it just kept happening, and I just…couldn't stop."

"You couldn't stop," Yvette said slowly and pointedly, "because you didn't *want* to."

I raised my eyes. Anxiety was searing my stomach. "Yvette," I pleaded.

She looked over at me and held my gaze, even though she was going 75 mph on a backcountry winding road. "So, when we boarded the plane, and you sat there the entire flight, not saying one word, with that glazed-over look on your face that I attributed to you blasting that one Britney song over and over into your earbuds…"

"Yvette," I gasped, trying to cut her off.

"….you were behaving in that way because you had come straight from your hotel room, where Cavanaugh had just finished fucking your brains out."

My hand had formed a fist of its own accord, and I felt my nose pressing against my knuckles, harder and harder, to the point of pain.

Yvette glanced at the road for one second, then back to me. "Is that accurate?"

What could I say? "Yes," I whimpered.

"Then I can accurately call you a cunt."

Dougie

Congratulations! You've reached a personal best in Night Of The Gummies. *Would you like to play again?*

Yes.

Loading….

I heard the Harley roll up, and my head turned. Even though I heard it all the time now, I still reacted to it like it was a rare occurrence. My heartbeat rose, and anxiety bloomed, resulting in pinpricks of sweat all over my skin.

Amber's door slammed, and her feet pounded up the stairs of my porch. My phone dinged, and I didn't look at it. Amber's hand twisted the doorknob. I looked at my computer screen, so I wouldn't be looking at her when she walked in.

lifeonplanetg is now following you.

It was weird. Whenever there was a person in my house, I always felt this strong need to get up and do something. There were things you did when another person came through the door. Things people did without a single thought, like say hello. Offer a snack. Ask how their day was.

Ada Johnson wants to be friends on Facebook.
Confirm request.

I spent a lot of time being afraid, much more than most people. Like right now for instance. I was afraid that staying in this chair, not looking up or acknowledging Amber or asking how her day was, made me a dick. I was always worried about that, and I always expected her to call me out on it.

I could have remedied this. I could have taken this day, this moment, and changed the pattern. I could have gotten up, asked things, and maybe felt better about myself when it was all said and done.

But there was a greater fear, a more consuming fear at play. The fear that by not getting out of my chair and socializing I was being perceived as a dick, was superseded by the fear of trying something and screwing up.

It was a kind of induced paralysis, a cunning little trap I rigged for myself all the time. I was uncomfortable being in this chair constantly. My body and my mind ached to get up and move. I thought about getting up and trying things. Cooking, asking about someone's day. In some rational part of my mind, I knew I could do those things.

But when I thought about doing things, I thought too long. I thought too much. I thought of every possible thing I could do, and every possible way it could go wrong. Then, there was the potential of doing the right thing but not at the right time, and after a while, nothing seemed attainable.

The fear of trying and failing overpowered the fear of doing nothing. So I stayed in the chair.

Erica

Maggie was still talking about Twinkle's triumph in the competitive trail ride. It was all she could think about.

"And then we got to go on this *bridge*, and it was all wooden so you couldn't see through it, but you could see over the sides, and the horses could hear the rushing water." Her words became muffled as she bent over, currying vigorously between Twinkle's front legs. "Some of the horses were *freaked out*. I just let Twinkle stand on one side for a minute, and then I gave him a squeeze and he walked right onto it." She gave the pony an affectionate hug. "He was all wobbly, and I thought he was gonna stop and not want to go, but he didn't. He kept going."

"He's a very brave pony," I agreed, casting a glance at his fine, dished face and teacup muzzle. "Have you thought about what you want to do in our lesson today?"

Maggie glanced at me, fishing a strand of blonde hair out of her eye and wiping some horse dirt on her face in the process. "What are my options?"

"We can either do some more work on the trail, or we can work in the ring, which Twinkle might appreciate after his recent adventure. You could even start learning to jump, if you want to," I offered.

Maggie shrugged. "I'd rather go on the trail. I don't really care so much about jumping anymore, to be honest. It's more fun to be out in the woods."

I nodded. "Well if you want to hit the trails, you'd better tack up your pony in a jiffy. Your mother will be back in a couple hours, and we don't want to risk another screaming match."

Maggie stared at me. "Who even says 'jiffy'?" She asked impertinently. But she did hop to it.

Ten minutes later Maggie swung onto Twinkle's short back, and I walked alongside, towering over both girl and pony. If nothing else, these lessons-on-the-trail were decent cardio. Not that they were rendering my pants any looser or anything.

From my particular vantage point, I had the advantage of observing Twinkle, something that was hard to do from a horse's back. As we left the outskirts of the manicured grounds and stepped onto the forest path, Twinkle's little eyes bugged out from beneath his bushy forelock. I could almost feel his hesitance as he picked up his feet, never quite sure if they'd come back down on solid, quiet ground, noisy leaf litter, or squelchy, sticky mud.

For her part, Maggie was content and relaxed. She moved in the saddle with an ease beyond her years, having achieved that elusive centaur effect. She gazed up at the leaves and branches, her face serene, her petulance and occasional flat-out brattiness left behind somewhere alongside the topiary sculptures. Maggie was in her element here.

I had hoped that Twinkle would follow suit and develop a zest for trail riding somewhere along the way. It could take a while for ring-bound horses to expand their comfort zones, but sooner or later, most of them learned to love the open land. Only a select few never became comfortable with it, and would always prefer the safe, even ground of an arena.

When Twinkle stepped in a puddle and got mud on his socks, his pink-tinged nose scrunched up in misery. Each time they reached a corner, his nostrils flared with worry. He kept going through it all, propelled by his good training, Maggie's good riding, and probably most of all, his love for her. But his discomfort was easy to read, from the nervous, repetitive chewing of his bit, to the spots of sweat popping out on his chest and his flanks, to the tight, uneasy clamp of his fluffy tail to his hindquarters.

A sparrow burst from the undergrowth in that jarring way that birds have of making their appearance. Twinkle shied violently, leaping backwards and nearly sitting down. Maggie spoke to him softly, sitting lightly, leaning forward over his withers, and he slowly rose to his feet but continued to tremble.

"Easy, Twinkle," Maggie intoned, stroking his neck. "It's just a silly bird. It's okay."

Twinkle sighed, stretching his neck and snorting loudly. Maggie gave him a bolstering thump on the neck, gathered her reins, and asked him to walk on. She sat upright in the saddle, her shoulders and back relaxed. Putting the spook instantly out of her mind, she looked ahead to the next bend in the trail.

Maggie had certainly found her niche. But I wasn't sure Twinkle had.

Lawrence

Eloise galloped down the edge of her paddock, cornering effortlessly and doubling back. Her front end was elevated, her neck arcing out of her shoulders and rising to her poll. The sunlight stuck to her, held in each shaft of steel-colored hair. She reflected the light like a hood ornament.

Now she was circling something, dogging it, sitting back on her haunches like a cutting horse. Abruptly, she took off again, peeling around the corners before spinning once again to face the unknown thing.

I moved closer to the window, straining to see what she was after. At first, I didn't see anything, but then she wheeled to the side and I saw it. There was a rock on the ground, nearly white in color and shaped like a tiny boulder.

She was trying to play the game. Elle was using the rock as a ball. But there was no one on her back to send it away, so she just kept circling back, determined and almost maniacal in her intensity.

Erica had come up to the window and was watching beside me. She shook her head. "Lawrence, that mare needs a job."

It was true. Eloise could not just sit around. She didn't have the capacity to just stand and do nothing. She'd been forced into early retirement, but her brain was unwilling to make the adjustment. Her body wasn't really cooperating, either. She hadn't been ridden hard in over a year, and she still looked like she'd just stepped off the polo field. She was lean and fit as a racing greyhound. She hadn't gone soft or lost a bit of condition. The only thing holding her back was that damn left hind. The awkwardly mended bone.

Sometimes, I thought of just getting on her, throwing out a ball and letting her go. There were times when I looked at her, keen and restless, going crazy in her skin, and I wanted to forget it ever happened. To go back in time and just ride.

I knew I couldn't do it. One bad step, one quick turn while balancing both our weights, and her life would be over. The fear was too strong. It was all-consuming. I'd tried, before, to let her have a little taste of polo. And I wound up pulling her back, slumped at her withers in the fetal position, shaking in terror and grief as she fought me.

Eloise needed a new career. Something more than our infrequent trail rides. Something that would use her mind and body, but without the bruising impact of polo. Something new that she could focus on and lean into. Elle needed a job, and she needed it to be full-time.

But what, exactly, does she need? I was at a loss. I'd gone in circles thinking about it, just like Elle with her rock. And I had no answers.

I left the window and went to go take that rock away from Eloise. Erica's eyes followed me out.

Erica

Delusion stood patiently in the cross ties as I moved the brush over his coat in long strokes. He'd graduated to small cross rails recently, and while he hadn't demonstrated the phenomenal ability of Soiree, he had hopped over the tiny fences agreeably. I was confident his form would improve with time and higher fences. For now, he was on the right track.

Amber bustled through the barn door, her arm stretched out to accommodate Maude's grumpy pace. Several seconds later, the old mare appeared at the very end of the lead, scuffing her toes on the cement. When they reached her stall, Amber dropped the lead rope, and Maude stopped moving as abruptly as a wind-up toy with the battery pulled out.

Amber glanced over at Delusion. "Is that your new training horse?"

"Yup, this is him," I answered, my voice slightly muffled as I leaned down to brush underneath his belly.

"He's nice looking." Amber walked over to inspect him. "Thoroughbred?"

"Yeah. He came from the track, but I don't think he ever raced. I don't think he's done much of anything."

"Not from the looks of those legs." Amber nodded at the clean, tight lines of Delusion's tendons, his slim ankles. "Nice to get a project that hasn't been beat to shit."

"It makes it way easier. I'm not picking up the pieces; I'm just starting from the bottom." I unclipped the cross ties from Delusion's halter. "Nothing wrong with a good problem horse, though," I added.

"Yeah, but you've paid your dues. You trained Harry." Amber snorted quietly. "Enjoy yourself. Enjoy working with a horse whose mind isn't a shit storm."

I smiled. "It is nice. But not as interesting."

I clucked to Delusion, and he followed me outside. As I turned the gelding out and locked the gate behind him, Lawrence's rig pulled in. I stayed where I was, watching him unload Harry and Vegas. Holding a lead in each hand, he began walking toward their paddock, and the two horses fell into step with him. He slipped off their halters and closed the paddock gate. Hard-ridden and happy, the geldings leaned on each other, shoving and squealing halfheartedly before settling down to nibble at the sparse grass.

Lawrence watched them for a minute, then turned away, slinging the halters over one shoulder. He spotted me for the first time and came jogging over.

"Hey." He kissed me, glancing over my shoulder at Delusion. "How was he today?"

"Very good. How was practice?"

"Kinda weird. Courtney and Yvette aren't speaking for some reason." He shrugged.

"How come?"

"Oh, they're probably in a fight about black mold or Britney or something. Same shit as always. They'll work it out." He slipped his unhaltered arm around my waist, and we walked to the house. "Actually, I was gonna ask if you wanted to come with me this Saturday."

I peered at him. "Where?"

"To the LPC to watch us play. Well practice. I thought you should see what we've got going on. We can do an evening practice, after you get back from your show."

"I'm not showing this weekend." I slipped out of his grasp so I could make eye contact. "I'm flying out to Fort Worth with this guy to look at yearlings. He's shopping for hunter prospects, and he wants me to evaluate them. I won't get back 'til Monday."

Lawrence looked at me in slight surprise. "Oh. Well, that's good. He's compensating you for all that, then?"

"He's paying me $800 for the weekend, not including meals or my flight, which he's covering."

"Awesome." Lawrence leaned in, giving me a quick squeeze. "I knew people would start taking notice."

I smiled a little. "It should be fun. I've never specifically gone out and evaluated a bunch of young horses, but I do it all the time with training horses. Watching them move, figuring out what they're best suited for. So this will be a great experience, and it'll be one more thing for my resume."

"You'll kill it," Lawrence said surely.

"Are you sure you'll be okay taking care of things here? I probably should have talked to you before I said yes to the guy..."

"Don't worry about it," Lawrence cut me off gallantly. "I'll take care of everything around here."

I let out a breath I realized I was holding. "Good. Thanks a lot."

He grinned mischievously. "I'll make sure all the horses are dead or lame by the time you get back."

"Great." I shoved him a little, and he darted into the house. I remained on the porch looking out at our little array of paddocks.

I was thinking ahead to the weekend and mentally tallying what needed to be done before I could leave, but in an increasingly large portion of my brain, I was thinking about what Amber had said about problem horses.

I had worked with a huge variety of horses over my 22 years. Most had problems when I picked them up. It was the nature of the training game. You bought damaged goods, patched it up, and flipped it for a profit.

Most of these problems were pretty minor, the result of inexperience or the wrong kind of experience. When you knew what you were doing, you could fix those typical, pesky problems in a little over a month. Quick and easy. Lucrative.

I'd only ever come across a few true "problem horses" in my career. Horses whose minds, as Amber put it, were a shit storm. Quite simply, it was hard to screw up a horse's mind that much. Horses put up with a lot. They withstand things that would cripple a person physically and mentally. With most horses, if you peeked in their braincases, it would be clear skies and smooth sailing.

The few times I'd had a stormy-minded horse in my hands, I had been captivated by them. I'd worked harder and longer and pushed myself further than ever before. My thoughts had been consumed with them, an endless loop that played day in and day out. I thought so much that my head ached and my eyesight blurred, and even then, I could not stop.

My thoughts were always the same. *How can I reach you? What are you running from?*

With Harry, the eventual answer had come, literally, in a storm. Later, his breeder provided all the answers. Harry had put his trust in humans and followed their orders, against his better judgment, a decision which led to the tragic death of his best friend.

Such an event would unhinge a person completely. Horses can withstand trauma much better than humans, but even they have their breaking point.

I never did save Harry. In the end, Lawrence stepped up and brought him through to the other side. I would never have done what he did, riding Harry out into that field, showing him he could face the storm. I never would have thought of that, not in a million years.

I couldn't save Trucker, either. I couldn't even touch him, after all this time.

I used to judge horses, and people, by the damage they had sustained. Subconsciously, I was attracted to a damaged soul and to the strength I perceived it took to still be standing after a rough past, a traumatic event. I was drawn to a stormy mind and a strong exterior. I sought it out, and when I found it, I was unable to walk away.

My theory, at least when it came to stormy-minded horses, was that it gave them a little extra in the way of performance power. That was certainly true of Harry. Every ounce of will he used to exert fighting, he now used on the polo field, and it was breathtaking.

But now I questioned things. Was it truly a boon to have withstood hell? Did it really make you better, stronger, more capable? Were those mental scars, those mended cracks, really the mark of power and potential? Or was it better to be unbroken and whole?

Soiree had endured hardship. She had been run into the ground by a callous trainer, and she'd cracked, literally, under pressure. Soiree had been inside a double-decker cattle trailer, the very definition of hell, hemmed in with countless other throwaway horses. Yet, she never wavered in her sunny demeanor. The trailer had been intercepted, and Soiree got off, never to reach what would've been her final destination. Soiree had been lucky in more ways than one.

No one could say Soiree had an easy go of it early on in life. Yet she never lost that spark in her eye, that love and generosity in her heart. She hadn't been affected by the pain. It had rolled off her spine like water.

Maybe that was the real key to success. Some horses (and people) latched onto the pain, worrying at it and holding it inside. Others seemed to deflect it.

Lately, I'd felt a slow shift within myself. No longer romanticizing the challenge of holding onto and loving a troubled soul, I moved through life with a growing sense of reality. I wasn't a young adult living with my parents and having all my expenses paid in exchange for a modicum of work. I was a real person now, and real life was tough. It was challenging and always uncertain.

Maybe that was why I found myself seeking out horses like Soiree and Delusion. I leaned into my work with those two, now more than ever, basking in the sweet silence of an untroubled mind.

I was about to silence my whirling thoughts and go inside when D.M.'s large form caught my eye. His eyes were half closed as he let one hind leg rest, snoozing in the sun. His hard-won muscles were slackening. His belly drooped from lack of use.

He was perhaps the only horse on the farm who truly fit the bill for an easy, unspoiled soul, and I'd sent him into early retirement.

Amber

Dougie was in that fucking chair when I walked in the door. He was always in that fucking chair. And today I decided I was going to get him out of it.

"Get up," I hollered from the kitchen.

"What?" Dougie called out, even though there was no way he didn't hear what I said. I was loud.

"Get. Up." I freed a couple bottles from the six-pack I'd just picked up. "You've been in that chair all day. You are going to get up, walk yourself across the room, sit down on the couch and have a beer with me."

I watched his back stiffen and his chair swivel around very, very slowly. His face, white skin and vicious acne, peered at me as I stood there with a beer in each hand and a determined look on my face.

Dougie was slow to open his mouth. "I'm working," he finally said.

"You're blogging. Not the same thing."

"Thousands of people depend on my posts to brighten their day."

I snorted. "First of all, never say 'brighten their day'. Secondly, get up."

Dougie looked at me in clear surrender. He got up, slowly unfurling his 6'3" frame. His spine cracked audibly in several places.

"That is not good," I said as he grimaced in pain. "You should really get that looked at."

Dougie took a beer from my hand and wandered into the kitchen to find a bottle opener. "It's just from too much sitting," he said. "When I used to go outside and move around, it never happened."

I caught Dougie's eye. "Then why don't you go outside?"

I could feel him trying not to hold my gaze. "Because when I went outside, other things happened."

Deftly, he located a bottle opener and popped the cap on his beer. He passed it to me, and we walked to the couch in tandem.

I grabbed the remote and flipped through the sports channels, hoping to find women's beach volleyball. I had to settle for the LPGA.

I sighed, propping my feet up. Dougie tried to follow my lead, but he wasn't flexible enough.

"Life is passing me by," I announced in the general direction of the screen.

Dougie's head whipped around in surprise. "Why do you say that?"

"'Cause it's true." I took a long sip and turned to face him. "Look at my life. I mean, yeah, I have a job. I'm good at it. I like it. I have an old, cranky horse that I love more than anything. I have a falling-down truck, I wear clothes that aren't mine, and I live in Suburbia with you. I'm 23. Shouldn't there be something *more*?"

Dougie was quiet for a second. "Like what?"

"Well, okay." I paused, drinking my bottle down to the halfway point in a matter of moments. "I feel like I never do a goddamn thing. I'm stuck. I mean, I go to work, I go ride my horse, I go to the grocery store, and I come here. That's it. That's all I ever do. My life is just this endless circuit."

"That doesn't sound so bad," Dougie offered. "At least you go out."

"That's not the point though," I argued. "You're stuck, but I'm just as stuck as you. My box is just bigger. It extends beyond this room. But it's still a fucking container. It contains me."

I tipped the bottle back and didn't raise it up until I'd gulped every last drop. Dougie's eyes widened as he watched me.

"Maybe you should pace yourself," he suggested feebly.

I slammed the empty bottle down on the coffee table, harder than I'd intended. "And you know what the really shitty part is?"

Dougie shook his head wordlessly. He hadn't touched his beer, so I took it from him.

I took a dainty sip to show him I knew my limit. "It has been three years since I determined I was gay. You know that? Three fucking years. And in all that time, I haven't even kissed a girl."

"I haven't either," Dougie said hurriedly, in an adorably eager and dreadfully misguided show of solidarity.

"You fucked a girl though," I pointed out.

"Yeah, but not for very long," he joked feebly. "Kissing a girl, though, that's a big one. I think about it all the time."

"Kissing's overrated," I said, drinking another gulp. "Fucking is overrated. Foreplay is overrated. Everything is overrated."

"That's because you did it with guys," Dougie pointed out.

"That's true. Guys suck." I raised my bottle again. "Guys are such dicks," I added somewhat redundantly. "Not you. You were nice."

Dougie's head tipped downward. "You need a nice girl."

"You're fucking right I need a nice girl." I waved my bottle around for emphasis. Fortunately, it wasn't full enough anymore for anything to slosh out. "How do I do that, Dougie? How do I make that happen?"

He considered that seriously. "I'm no expert, but I think maybe if you went places other than your job, the place where your horse lives, and the grocery store, you might have a better chance."

I held my hands out to stop him. "Containers, Dougie. Containers."

"Right." He leaned back, resting his head on the back of the couch. "How did we get here?"

"I don't know." I followed his lead, allowing gravity to do most of the work as I drained my second beer. "But it's nice that we're here together."

His head snapped up, and I felt his eyes on me hard.

"I mean, I'd rather we were somewhere else, separately, with a nice girl," I clarified.

His head fell back. "Right. Yeah. Of course."

"But this is nice," I said.

"It's alright," Dougie agreed.

Courtney

I was sitting alongside the field, my hands in my lap and my head tilted downward. Hermione was on the hotwalker. I was too exhausted to walk her myself like I usually did.

I heard quick, light footsteps behind me, and Yvette was suddenly standing over me. She held an armful of bridles out in front of her like she was carrying firewood.

"You may clean these," she said curtly, and she dropped them on me.

A stainless steel bit whacked me in the head and left a trail of green slime and horse spit through my hair. I wanted to cry, but I waited until Yvette smirked and walked away. Then, I bent my head and let my tears soak into the leather. Which isn't very good for leather, incidentally.

Yvette had been like this ever since I'd told her what happened with me and Lawrence. She had always been mean, but this had made her downright cruel. And she was only getting worse.

In practice we were totally out of sync. She usually focused on one-upping Lawrence, but now she focused on me. Yvette was ruthless. She worked me over. Yvette knew my strengths and weaknesses intimately, and now she exploited them. She made me look dumb out there, like I didn't know what I was doing. She chipped away at me until I felt like a shell. She never got tired of it. It was like she didn't even care that she was systematically dismantling all the hard work we'd put into building this team. She just wanted to wreck me.

I wrapped my arms around the bridles and myself, rocking back and forth. *I just want to go home,* I thought despondently. *I'm sick of the Days Inn; I'm sick of Yvette being so mean. I'm sick of feeling this way. Why should I stay here? I shouldn't. I should call Daddy and have him send a car for me. I could call him right now.*

I lifted my head to search for my phone. Too late I saw Lawrence. He was looking right at me. He was stopping what he was doing. He was coming this way.

In a dull panic, I estimated that I had about two seconds to try and pull it together, which wasn't nearly enough time. *He's coming over here, and he's going to see me sitting on the ground, covered in tack, crying, with horse slobber in my hair. Crap.*

Lawrence walked swiftly, reaching me in a few sweeping strides. "Courtney. What the hell is going on?"

I looked up at him and tried to take a deep breath, but it came out as a sniffle. "Yvette gave me these bridles. I'm supposed to clean these bridles."

Team Dark Horse

He rolled his eyes. "I don't give a shit about the bridles. What the fuck is going on with you and Yvette? She's out for your head on that field, and I don't understand. I thought you guys were allies, and now all of a sudden she's..." He looked at me with a flicker of comprehension in his eyes. "She's treating you like me."

I burst into tears. Not a trickle this time, just full-on tears streaming down my face. "It's my fault, okay! It's all my fault. I told her. I told her everything."

"About what?" Lawrence knelt down so he was on my level. "What did you tell her?"

"Yvette knows. About us." I raised my soggy face and looked at him, even though the act of looking at him made my insides burn with shame and other things. "She knows we were...together. And now she hates me. Because I'm a slut."

Lawrence's face went hard. "If Yvette thinks you're a slut because of what we did, she should take a look in the mirror."

I froze, confusion drying up the tears.

Lawrence looked at me directly, unwaveringly. "I fucked her, Courtney."

My mouth fell open. It was completely dry. "Who?" I gasped, not believing what he seemed to be telling me.

"*Yvette.*" Lawrence shook his head at me. "Wake up, Courtney. She's not some superhero. She's a person, and she's not even that great at being one. And yeah, I fucked her. The same week I met you. We met up for a practice together, I got one past her, and a few hours later, she knocked on my hotel room door. She came to *me.*"

I was mute. I could do nothing but stare at him.

Lawrence stood up. "You're not a slut, Courtney," he said to me as he left. "But you seriously need to grow a pair."

I sat there as he disappeared from view. My body felt so heavy, like it could sink into the ground if I stayed here long enough, the weight of exhaustion and what I knew and what I felt pressing down on me.

Then something ignited in me. I stood up, knocking the bridles onto the ground. I left them in a heap, and I began to run.

Courtney again

I whipped into the Days Inn parking lot, parking my rental car haphazardly and leaving it straddling the lines.

I stormed into our hotel room, where I found Yvette chewing on a PowerBar and talking on her phone. She gave me her usual look of superiority, and I saw her preparing to cut me down in some way.

She didn't get the chance.

"YOU *BITCH!*" I screamed from across the room.

Yvette looked startled, though she didn't stop chewing. She stared at me for a moment, then spoke into her phone. "I will call you back," she said, pressing the End button.

Yvette turned to me with a look of annoyance on her face. "Now what is this about?"

"I know you had sex with Lawrence." I shook my head at her in a way that conveyed quite a lot of judgment.

Yvette's face seized up. "Why do you say that?"

"*Because he told me.*"

Yvette's lip curled until she resembled a small, food-aggressive dog. "He is lying."

"No, he's not." I crossed my arms over my chest, widening my stance. "He's a lot of things, but he's not a liar. He wouldn't just make stuff up. He's telling the truth."

"Cavanaugh is only telling you this to turn you against me. He wants to break us up."

My blood boiled. Without even meaning to, I ripped the tacky Wal-Mart lamp out of the wall and threw it at her.

"Shut *up!*" I yelled. "You are so full of shit. Why on earth would Cavanaugh want to split us up? He's trying to make a *team* here, Yvette. We're all trying to make a team, and the only one who's set on destroying it is *you!*"

Emotion flickered on Yvette's pointy face, but she soon shut it down. "What do you want from me, Courtney?"

I leaned against the door. "I just want the truth."

Yvette looked at me for a long moment. She looked very small all of a sudden. "Yes, I fucked him, Courtney."

My body deflated. I slid down the door until I was squatting, looking at the mildewy carpeting. My face was hot. I expected the tears that spilled over my cheeks to evaporate with a hiss, like water thrown on a hot stove.

"You have been so horrible to me," I choked out.

I heard Yvette expulse a breath. "Courtney. Can we not do this right now?"

"You've always been mean to me since I've known you," I said slowly. "But this is *beyond*."

"Of course you will do this right now." Yvette walked to the window, pacing steadily back and forth. "You are always so dramatic."

The steady current flowing from my tear ducts stopped instantly. I stood up and walked over to her.

"I may be dramatic," I said carefully. "I'll own up to that. But that doesn't mean what you did is excusable."

Uncharacteristically, she stood still and waited for me to finish.

"You abused me," I said to her. "You maligned me; you degraded me. You made me feel less than human. And you acted all superior, when in reality, you had the same secret I did. You just didn't have the guts to tell me to my face."

Yvette heaved a sigh. "I am sorry you feel that way," she said tersely.

What a bullshit apology.

"*You made me feel like a huge slut!*" I screamed in her face. "And there's no way that we can work together now. This team we worked so hard on, this *dream* that was supposedly the most important thing to you? Well, it's over. It's not going to happen."

Yvette stared at me, and just for a second I saw a little fear creep into her eyes.

"It's not because of me, and it's not because of Lawrence. You did this, Yvette. You fucked this up with your obsession with making other people look bad. You *always* have the be the best. You can never let anyone else have any glory. And you know what? That doesn't work in a team sport.

You have to give yourself to the team, because you can't win unless the team does."

"It doesn't matter that I fucked Cavanaugh," I said on my way out. "And it doesn't even matter that *you* fucked Cavanaugh. What matters, in the end, is that by focusing on who fucked whom, you fucked yourself, Yvette. You fucked all of us. And worst of all, you fucked the team."

Erica

The rain fell in sheets, blowing sideways at times, but mostly it just poured straight and fast. Every article of clothing I wore was wet, down to my skin. It wasn't cold, but after standing in it for hours, I was steadily getting a chill.

It was ironic, given the deluge, that the whole reason we were here in the first place was persistent drought. The guy who owned the ranch was selling his entire herd - young stock, broodmares, studs - because his pastures had dried up from lack of rain. The guy next to me, one of his hired hands, kept mentioning that this was the first real downpour they'd had in two years.

The rain needled into the drought-hardened ground, working hard to soften the surface. It was mostly running right off the top. Puddles had formed anywhere there was a depression. The guy looked at the dusty water pooling at his feet and sighed.

"Not the kind of rain we needed," he lamented, looking up at the dreary sky. "A real steady, light rain would soften that ground. This'll just pool up and burn off when the sun comes out again."

I nodded in solidarity, but my eyes were on the pen of yearlings in front of me. Wet, bedraggled and miserable-looking, each one muddy bay in color, these were my top choices out of the dozens of young horses I'd sifted through over the previous day and a half.

They were exceptionally well built - leggy, attractive and upstanding, with straight legs, balanced bodies and gorgeous, arched necks set high. Expressive faces blinked and shook away the rain, and they huddled together, choosing warmth and comfort over establishing dominance.

Jim, a hired hand barely out of his teens, appeared at my side with a halter and rope. "Do you want me to bring 'em out for you then?"

I shook my head. "No. I'll go in myself."

"All right then." He handed me the halter and lead.

I smiled. "Thank you."

I walked to the gate, my fingers slipping on the cold metal latch. After letting myself in, I carefully closed the gate behind me. The yearlings watched me. Friendly at first, they had been moved around so much and had stood for so long in bad weather that they were now a bit wary. Their good humor had been spent.

I approached the first of my choices, a colt. He took a look at the halter in my hand and darted behind the others, sandwiching himself between their bodies and the fence rails. There were others easily within reach, but instead of going for a quick grab, I stepped into the small herd, lifting my arms to scatter the yearlings.

They moved away, exposing my chosen colt. He looked at me balefully, pivoting on his hindquarters and facing in my direction.

I stretched out a hand, and when he didn't move, I carefully stepped forward, rubbing his face, his neck. His trust restored by the gentle touch, he allowed me to slip the halter over his head.

I patted him softly. "C'mon, babe, let's get you out of the rain."

Jim opened the gate, and I led him through, up and over a small hill to a covered arena nearby. The colt looked back a few times, craning his neck to check on the whereabouts of his buddies. He didn't balk once, though. He was insecure, but he trusted.

Once we were inside the arena, I halted the colt, reaching for a coiled-up longeline hanging from a hook. The colt flinched a little at the sound of the rain on the roof, and when I pulled the longeline down, he startled. But as he came to the end of the lead, he gave to the light tension and stopped in place, ears forward. I tugged lightly on the rope, and he moved closer. I patted him and rubbed him lightly with the longeline, and he relaxed.

"Good mind," I mouthed to Stewart, the guy I was shopping for. He stood in the corner, well out of the way, but his eyes followed my every movement. He was tall, silver-haired and a stylish dresser, and he took notes on a notepad instead of an iPhone.

I clipped the longeline to the colt's halter and sent him out on a circle. Some of these babies had been worked with more than others. With young horses like this, you never knew when they would decide to take off on the longe or just straight up leap into the air. You had to really pay attention and anchor yourself against any sudden movements.

The colt took a tentative step and then stopped, confused by the increased distance between us. He shook his head slightly, feeling the weight of the longeline, and looked back at me. I clucked to him encouragingly and stepped strongly toward his hindquarters, driving him forward. He began walking in a nice rhythm, maintaining a slightly wobbly circle. His eyes and ears flicked back to me repeatedly. *Is this okay? Is this what you want?*

I clicked my tongue again and began jogging, encouraging him to pick up the trot.

He lifted his shoulders and made a smooth transition to the faster gait. He moved naturally in a good balance, with his hindquarters underneath him and his front end elevated. His suspension propelled him off the ground; he seemed to linger in the air.

I tugged gently on the longeline, and he stopped quickly. I sent him in the other direction, hoping things would be different. But I already knew it would be more of the same.

I stopped the colt and rubbed his face. He snuggled up to me, and I felt my insides hollow out.

"Nope," I called to Stewart. "Not this one."

The colt's powerful suspension and elevated movement would serve him well as a dressage horse, or perhaps even a show jumper, if he had the ability over fences. But as much as it killed me, I couldn't steer my client wrong. This colt was all wrong for the hunter ring. He walked trustfully by my side as I led him back to the pen, where I handed him off to Jim. The colt was led off to the pastures, where he disappeared, just one of many.

I picked out my second choice, a dainty filly. She looked a little like Soiree, but with a coarse black mane instead of a sleek blonde one. I took her up to the arena and went through the motions as I had with the colt, but with a little less enthusiasm.

This filly already knew how to longe, and at the end of the line, she displayed movement that was far different from the colt's. Her hooves remained close to the ground in a "daisy clipper" style of movement. Her stride was long, flat, and smooth.

I kissed to her, and she picked up a canter. No elevation here. Her canter was long and reachy, and when I sent her over a small fence, she picked up her feet and jumped round.

"That's what you want." I nodded to Stewart. "Her and a few others like her."

Lawrence

Harry shifted edgily as I tightened the girth, stopping just short of pawing at the concrete floor. Down the aisle, Hermione was in a similar mood. Normally perfectly complacent, she swung her hindquarters left and right in a show of impatience that Courtney was too kindhearted to punish.

The ponies had gone three days without a real practice, and the downtime hadn't done them any good. Courtney and I had finally agreed to meet up at the LPC and ride a bunch of our string, because what choice did we have? Yvette hadn't left us a whole lot of options.

Elaine came down the barn aisle. She had bits of hay and pine shavings stuck to her clothes, and she was eating a sandwich like it was a timed event. Clearly she was on break.

She stopped at our stalls and looked around. "Where's your other player?"

Courtney spoke up before I could. "I'm not working with her anymore," she stated tightly.

Elaine raised her eyebrows. "Wow. You finally got tired of her bullshit?"

Courtney shook her head. "I didn't just get tired of it, I got finished with it."

Elaine nodded slowly. "Well, good for you."

"Yeah, except now we're even further away from having an actual team," I cut in.

"That's true." Elaine looked at our fired-up horses and weary faces and sighed. "She was a great player. Too bad she's such a terrible human being."

She walked away, leaving me alone with Courtney. I threw Harry's bridle on and led him outside. He wouldn't stand still, so I vaulted onto his back and began to warm him up, carefully keeping him in check. Courtney soon joined me on the field with Hermione, and we lapped each other repeatedly without saying a word, hands holding tightly to clamped and uneasy mouths. Harry's rigid neck bobbed in front of me, locked against me in a steady pull. He just wanted to fly.

We'd barely finished our walk set when Courtney reined in Hermione abruptly. She let out a gasp. "What is *she* doing here?" Then her eyes went black. "What is she doing with my *pony*?"

I followed Courtney's eyes and saw Yvette on the edge of the field, riding Courtney's gelding, Hedge Fund. Elaine was hot on her heels, even though it was clear Yvette was trying to shake her off.

Yvette rode into our midst and halted. She wore her usual look of ambivalent defiance.

Courtney was staring at Yvette, her face bunching up. "You've got some kind of nerve showing up here."

Elaine reached the field, only slightly winded from her chase. "I told her she had no right to use your pony, Courtney," she said, casting a livid glance at Yvette. "I tried to stop her. But she *has a bit of a listening problem*!" She shouted that last bit at Yvette.

I nodded grimly. "Thank you, Elaine. We'll take it from here."

"Good fucking luck." She walked off the field, looking daggers at Yvette.

Courtney turned Hermione, riding up beside Yvette. "Get off," she ordered, her voice shrill. "Get off my pony right now!"

Yvette's eyes flashed. "Do not be a child, Courtney."

"Don't fucking talk to her that way." I closed my legs on Harry's sides, and he moved toward Yvette. Hermione moved closer, too, the two ponies closing her in.

"What are you even doing here?" Courtney demanded. "Why did you come back?"

Yvette considered the question. She looked pretty comfortable for someone who was hemmed in by two fit, angry polo ponies and sitting on a third. "I came to see what you two are doing in my absence."

"We're cleaning up your mess," I said harshly. "Or trying to."

"You appear to be getting on just fine without me." Yvette glanced at both of us in turn. "I am sure you prefer this arrangement greatly, Courtney. Especially since Cavanaugh's girlfriend is conveniently out of town."

My grip tightened on my mallet. Courtney's lips were set in a thin line.

I don't know who cued their pony first, or if any of us did. But a second later Harry, Hermione and Hedge Fund burst forward. Close enough to touch, they stayed together, ears flat and running full out. All I could feel was the vibration of the ground and the deep churning energy of the three ponies, combined like some massive locomotive, barreling downhill with no sign of stopping.

Someone, probably Yvette, threw out a ball, and just as quickly as they'd joined together, the ponies split, leaping at it and shoving each other aside. Courtney and Yvette were locked in a grudge match, slamming into each other, hooking mallets, playing dirty. In a pairing this evenly matched, this advanced, someone had to blink before the other person could get past them and score. No one was blinking.

I watched them, and a realization crept into my mind. Before I could question it, I reined in Harry.

"Stop!" I called out.

Shockingly, they both stopped and broke apart. They faced me, slumped over their horses' withers, out of breath.

"Stop fighting," I said clearly. "We know defense. We know offense. We can go into attack mode whenever. But we don't know how to be a *team*."

Courtney sat up in the saddle. Yvette did too.

I walked Harry around them in a large circle. "Let's do some long-distance drills. Enough with this close-up, aggressive play. Let's practice passing."

They were still paying attention, so I kept going with it. "Courtney, you ride down to the goal on that side like you just intercepted the ball. Backside forehander it to me. Be precise. Remember, I'm surrounded by opposing players."

Yvette spoke up for the first time. "And what do I do?"

"What you do best. You score a goal. They'll be guarding it, so get in close. Give yourself every chance to make it."

Yvette nodded. She was taking it seriously.

I rode up to the untouched ball, sending it down the field. It settled just ten feet away from the open mouth of the goal.

"That's how precise you've got to be," I said. "Go, Courtney."

It only took a few seconds. Courtney put her heels into Hermione, and the mare leapt forward. She rode a meandering line, just like she would if her path were full of opposing players. As soon as she reached the ball, her mallet snaked out, quick as lighting, sending it flying backwards in my direction. Harry surged into a gallop, and we met the ball in mid-air. I scooped it up, balancing it on the end of my mallet for a delicious second before making my shot. Yvette had tucked herself in tight, and she reached back deftly, giving the ball a final tap and finishing the trajectory almost matter-of-factly.

Courtney rode up beside me, and we joined Yvette at the goal. The three ponies stood close together, ears up, relaxed. They were sated.

I looked at the two women beside me. "Now how did that feel?"

"Amazing," Courtney said, breathless.

"It was not bad," Yvette said primly.

"Good. Because we're going to be doing a lot more of that." I set my reins on Harry's neck. "We're great individually. Now we have to be great together."

"We already are." Yvette dismounted, landing on her feet beside Hedge Fund. "That is what I am doing here." She gave Courtney a loaded glance.

"You two, sort it out." I shook my head at them. "And Yvette...no more bullshit. Ever. Or we *will* make this thing happen without you."

"I am sure it will be very easy to replace me," Yvette said with a smirk. She reached up, passing Hedge Fund's reins to Courtney. "You may take your pony now," she said, and she walked away from us.

I turned to Courtney. "Are you okay with this?"

She looked at me, her eyes strangely unfocussed. "We have something here."

I nodded, looking out over the torn-up field. "Yeah, we actually do."

Erica

I left the airport with my carry-on bag slung over my shoulder, craning my neck as I scanned the sea of cars for my emerald green F-150. I could never remember which section I'd parked it in, which led to a lot of unnecessary walking around. This was why I liked to avoid going to places with large parking lots. Like malls, or supermarkets. Basically stores.

As I wandered, my mind did too. *I hope I find my truck soon. What happens if I never find it? I wonder if that has ever happened. How long do you keep looking before you just give up?*

I spotted a green Ford truck and was about to give a celebratory cheer, when I pressed the Unlock button and the headlights failed to flash. Slowly, I walked around to the back of the vehicle. *B3Z 78A*, it read.

"Yup, not my plate," I said aloud. I looked at it in defeat for a second, then trudged onward.

I hate when that happens. It's the worst. I'd almost rather not find my truck at all than have that keep happening.

I reached into my pocket and turned my cell phone on as an afterthought. A few seconds later, it vibrated, uncharacteristically.

"Hello?" I answered distractedly.

"You're back." Lawrence sounded pleased, and I melted into the phone just slightly.

"Yeah, I just got off the plane. Now I'm circumnavigating the lot looking for my truck."

"How did your weekend go?"

"It was fine." I shifted the strap on my shoulder. "It rained torrentially the entire time, but the yearling crop was really nice. I think I picked out some great prospects. Oh, I think I just found my truck." I pressed Unlock again, grinning in relief when the lights came on. "Yup, I'm good now."

"Listen, do you want to meet me at the LPC?" Lawrence inquired. "I'm just wrapping things up here. You could stop in if you want, and then we can grab dinner in town somewhere."

"Yeah, that would be nice." I stepped up into the cab, settling into the driver's seat.

"Great. I'll be here."

I drove to the LPC with my radio up along with my spirits. I was looking forward to spending some uninterrupted time with Lawrence. It seemed like we hadn't seen each other at all lately, other than at night when we fell into bed together. We operated so separately, each with our own horses and our own projects, that we rarely spent much time together over the course of the day. It was a stark change from the days when we were training Harry, when we spent all our spare time focused on a singular mission.

I pulled into the LPC lot and looked around for Lawrence. His truck was there, but I saw no sign of him, so I parked and went to look for him.

On my way to the barn, I saw Courtney in skintight breeches and a polo shirt that was straining against the onslaught of her boobs. I tried to change course, but she saw me and waved, gathering herself to make a beeline for me. I groaned.

"Erica! Hi!" She chirped, while my mood plummeted straight to the floor.

"Hi," I said stingily.

"Lawrence is in Wilson's office," Courtney said. "I guess he's having woman problems, or something. Wilson. Not Lawrence." She tittered girlishly. "He said he'd be done soon. Lawrence did."

God, she was overly helpful.

"Thanks," I said, feeling a little bitchiness creep into my voice. "I guess I'll just wait for him, then…"

"Did you have a good weekend?" Courtney asked. "You were in Texas, right? Looking at hunters?"

She was also depressingly eager. For a second, I warmed to her slightly. "Yes. Well, future hunters. This guy hired me to go through some yearlings and tell him which prospects he should buy."

Team Dark Horse

"That's really neat." Courtney seemed to be balancing on her toes, hovering over the ground. "That must be fun. Recruiting future talent."

"Well, it pays the bills," I said matter-of-factly. I smiled insincerely in her general direction as my whole body walled off. I didn't want to hear anything more.

I could feel her hovering. I could feel the weight of her eyes on me. How could someone's eyes be that heavy? How could I feel them that much? They bored into me, pushing against my body like fists. I just wanted to leave.

Lawrence came out of the barn just then, saving me. "There you are," he said, pulling me into him and giving me a kiss. "Sorry I kept you waiting. Wilson's an idiot." He rolled his eyes.

"I'm starving," I said, kissing him back. "Let's get out of here."

His arm settled around my lower back, and we walked in sync. We walked straight past Courtney, leaving her standing there with her boobs and her long blonde hair and her big stupid eyes.

You may have him during the day, I thought as we left. *But I'm the one he comes home to.*

As I got in my truck, my cell phone buzzed with an incoming text message. I clicked *Open,* peering at the small group of assembled words. I'd never liked the design of my phone's inbox, how it showed the contents of the message before revealing the name of the sender. It made it confusing and potentially dangerous to respond to vague queries (like the popular "Hey, how's it going?"). But there was no mistaking the sender of this message.

Code red. Mother on warpath. She found out about the trail ride.

Lawrence

I was sprawled on the sideline of the polo field, working saddle soap into the crevices of a sweat-crusted bridle. Courtney sat near me, her legs tucked up underneath her. Yvette had parked her lawn chair on Courtney's left, and she sat, as usual, with her legs crossed and her airborne foot tapping incessantly.

Courtney's face was relaxed, her eyes bright as she tipped her head back and stared into the sun. "I love it out here," she said.

"Out there, perhaps," Yvette snipped, looking out across the field like a lion would glance hungrily at an zebra. "Out there is where the action is. Out *here*, it is boring as shit." She re-crossed her legs and began her foot calisthenics all over again.

"It's not boring," Courtney said, her voice uncharacteristically mellow. "It's comfortable." She leaned back, stretching out over the grass and shaking out her hair. The breeze kept it moving even after her head stilled.

"This has been nice," I agreed, setting the bridle down. "Now we just need to get someone to join in."

Yvette sat up straight, fully participating in the conversation for the first time. "It is impossible," she said gracelessly. "No one wants in. I have already put out feelers to everyone…Delgrange, Pieres, Rahor…"

"Why should they?" I cut in. "They're all part of established, winning teams. They have success, fame, sponsors, and women draped all over them. Hell, that one guy's got a perfume ad that's running on national networks all day long. Why should they give that up for the unknown?"

Yvette looked put out. "Because our team is *better*," she snapped, turning her pointy chin up.

"Our team isn't a team," Courtney stated obviously. "It's three quarters of a team."

"And it could be half a team *very* soon," Yvette said murderously.

I lay back, pointedly ignoring the tiff like I'd gotten so used to doing. "What we need to do is add a girl."

The bickering stopped. "*Another* girl?" Courtney asked, unblinking. "That would make three girls and one guy."

"That's the way I like it." I turned my head, letting a shock of hair fall over my eyes, grinning at her loosely.

Neither of them laughed. "That's never been done," Courtney said. "I mean, occasionally you'll see the odd girl in men's polo. Eleo Sears…it happens. But there's *never* been three on a team…"

"It would be unprecedented," Yvette agreed.

I stared at them, my eyebrows descending. "You know, the two of you are the *last* people I would ever expect to give me pushback about this idea. All this talk…'We are equal! Give us a chance, and see what will happen!' But the second I throw out the idea of adding a girl, you freak out!"

"It is not simply a question of male versus female," Yvette said primly. "There are logistics involved."

"You said it yourself. The men don't want to play with us."

"The women do not want to join us either." Yvette sprang out of her chair and began pacing the sideline. "You saw when I gave my speech. I put it all out there. And Courtney was the only one who would stand by me. The others scattered. They do not want to make history. They are content where they are."

"Those aren't the women I'm thinking of." I held Yvette's eye as she slowed to a standstill. "I'm not talking about trying to get someone established to jump ship. That's never going to happen. I'm talking about recruiting someone new. An up-and-comer. Someone whose mind hasn't been corrupted by politics and petty bullshit. Someone unsponsored, who's in it for the love of the game. Someone who's hungry."

I saw a flicker of recognition in Yvette's beady eyes. She understood hunger.

"We find them, we take them under our wing, and we make them fill the void," I said. "We can make them into whatever we need."

Elaine

I didn't see too much of Lawrence anymore. Now that I was earning my keep, he no longer had to provide me with the basic necessities of life, which is why it was strange when he made a beeline for me on a random Wednesday afternoon.

"Come with me," he said, walking past me at a brisk pace and doubling back when he finally realized I had not followed.

"I'm on break," I said, "but only for five more minutes. Whatever this is, it better be quick."

"I told Wilson he could spare you for a couple hours," Lawrence said. "So he's sparing you for a couple of hours." He started walking again.

I hurried after him. "*Why?*" I nearly shouted at his back. "What are we doing?"

"Getting you a vehicle." Lawrence reached the parking lot, pulling out his keys.

I followed him to his truck, which had rust creeping halfway up the doors. "I don't have the money for a vehicle."

"I know. I'll get you on the road, and then you can take it from there. It won't cost much, especially if you don't drive it a lot. But you need a vehicle."

He wrenched the door open for me. I climbed into the cab and sat down, staring at my hands in my lap. "It's too much. I can't let you do that."

Lawrence started up his engine. It made a noticeable knocking sound. "I didn't say it would be a nice vehicle."

30 minutes later, we were in a used car lot that was also a junkyard. The junkyard part of it seemed to be the more dominant side. Cars lay in pieces all over the lot, and even those that were whole had a look of imminent death about them.

Lawrence seemed to be in his element, looking under hoods and stepping on fenders. I followed him mutely, occasionally breaking my silence to voice another well-reasoned argument.

"I don't even need a vehicle," I protested, watching flakes of rust rain down from yet another car. "Where do I ever go?"

Lawrence glanced up at me, hair falling over his forehead in that way that always sent my heart pattering. "Exactly."

He stood up, walking to the next sad sight on the lot, a huge, white Chevy pickup with no doors. "You live at the barn, you work at the barn, your whole life centers on the barn. That's not living. It's a start, and I'm glad you're out of that fucking room, but you need more. You need your independence, and you need the freedom to go somewhere. To leave, to come back. Or to not come back." He paused and then shook off whatever train of thought he'd been on. "Anyway. I want this for you. I want to make this happen for you. I'm bankrolling you, just like you did for me a while back."

My body stiffened up, and my pulse throbbed dully at the sudden acknowledgment of our strange, sordid past.

I took a breath. "Lawrence, if this is all because of you thinking that I ended up on the street because of you...that it was your fault..."

He looked me square in the eye. My insides quivered. "You're telling me that it wasn't?"

I had no way to answer that without giving up everything. Or lying.

I stayed silent, and the moment passed. Lawrence popped the hood on the Chevy, and after a careful inspection, he slammed it shut. "I think we should try this one."

I blanched. "It doesn't have *doors*."

He shrugged. "A cosmetic issue."

"Not in the winter!"

He looked at me, confident, refusing to be thrown. "So we'll get you a fur coat."

He disappeared into the garage, returning with a key. I climbed up into the driver's seat. "I'll drive."

Lawrence looked at me, doubt crossing his face. "Are you sure?"

"If it's going to be my truck, I should fucking test drive it," I snapped crossly.

He threw the keys at me and jumped up into the cab. "I like this no door thing," Lawrence said, fastening his lap belt. "Easy access."

"I bet you do." I turned the key, and a fairly healthy-sounding engine roared to life.

I drove down a country road, bringing it up to speed, testing brakes and steering on the sudden curves. I could hear the road noise of the gravel under the tires, and I listened for clanks and thumps.

It wasn't a pretty truck, and it definitely had a story. It had done some hard living, seen some better days, but there was life left in the frame, and under the hood.

I reached the end of the farm road and took a left onto the highway. "I'm

Team Dark Horse

just taking a little detour," I said to Lawrence's questioning eyes.

As we approached a Hardee's, I signaled and made the turn into the cramped parking lot. Lawrence watched, wide-eyed, as I negotiated the tight, curving drive-through without hitting a single curb.

"You really know what you're doing," he said, once I was done placing my order.

"Well, these fast-food menus are pretty user-friendly," I joked.

He rolled his eyes. "No, I mean with the truck."

"I drove a truck like this in Friedmont," I told him. "When I was a teenager."

I put the truck in Park and settled in to wait for my order. "Then when I married Arnold, he gave me a Jaguar."

"And now you're back to a truck."

"Full circle." I smiled ironically. "It all fits in a tight little box. I always liked continuity."

Lawrence shook his head. "I don't think your trajectory is done. Not by a long shot."

I know it is, I thought. *It has to be.*

The girl who brought out my order was a cute, button-nosed brunette with a bob. I thanked her, and I ate my burger while staring grimly through the windshield.

Erica

Pulling the key from the ignition, I sat in the cab of my truck for a minute, bolstering myself for the ordeal ahead of me. If I could've stayed there, I would have, the doors, windows and frame providing an ample shell, keeping me safe from the tyranny of Mrs. Gloria Allsteen.

Unfortunately, that wasn't a viable option. I exited the vehicle, squaring my shoulders, projecting a look of confidence and fierce determination. I had to be strong for Maggie's sake. As Maggie's instructor, I was obligated to look out for her welfare and stand by her preferences, even if that meant disagreeing with her parents. Somehow, I had to convince Mrs. Allsteen that this trail riding thing wasn't equivalent to Satan worshipping.

And in the process, I had to try not to get fired.

I didn't have to look far to see Maggie. She was sitting on Twinkle's back in the outdoor arena. Her mouth set in a sour line, she looked out at the freshly-dragged arena footing with clear disinterest. Juan stood on Twinkle's off side, wiping the dust off Maggie's boot with a well-worn rag.

For a second, I wondered why Juan was putting on such a show of dedicated service. Slowly, unwillingly, my eyes drifted upward to the gazebo on the hill overlooking the ring. They rested on Gloria Allsteen, feet up, clad in a sundress, sipping red wine far too early in the day. Sunglasses and a cigarette completed her look of rich white trashiness.

She'd parked herself up there to observe her daughter's lesson. I was going to have to be exceedingly careful.

I opened the gate, letting myself into the ring. Juan returned to the stables, leaving me alone with Maggie.

I glanced at her. "When did your mom take up smoking?" I asked.

Maggie shrugged. "She only smokes when she drinks," she deadpanned.

"Okay, start your warm-up, I guess." I watched Maggie slip the reins out to the buckle. Twinkle began walking, gravitating toward the rail on his own and following it faithfully. His neck stretched downward, free of tension.

After a few times around, Maggie picked up the reins and rode Twinkle at a medium walk, circling in both directions. She moved him up to a trot, turning across the diagonal, sitting two beats in the center of the ring as she changed direction.

I watched Twinkle curiously. I'd forgotten what a good mover he could be, sedate, steady and flashy. How well-trained and confident he was. As he trotted past me, I glimpsed his eyes, bright and happy underneath the white fuzz of his billowing forelock.

Twinkle was in his element here, and Maggie looked as if she'd been chewing on glass.

"Take him up to a canter," I offered. Maggie sat the trot for a stride, moving her hips to mimic how Twinkle's back would swing in the canter. The pony smoothly picked up the new gait.

"Try a figure-eight with a simple change," I said. "Before changing direction, transition to trot for a stride or two, then have him pick up the canter on the new lead."

"Sure." Maggie ably turned Twinkle off the rail, bending his body to follow the curve of the circle. After completing the first figure, she half halted, bringing her shoulders back and raising her torso. Twinkle dropped back to a trot. Maintaining perfect straightness in Twinkle's body, Maggie lifted her seat, cuing him for the canter. Twinkle jumped into it, his hocks underneath him. Maggie's eyes looked ahead, planning her turn. She rode an accurate figure in the new direction and returned to the rail.

"Very well done," I said, slightly stunned. "Your circles were even, and they were round. That was very well executed."

Maggie glanced at me. "You don't have to sound so *surprised*," she snorted. "You were the one who kept yelling at me about it. '*Look ahead! Plan your turns!*'" She mimicked.

"Your flatwork is just really solid," I clarified. "And we haven't been working in the ring at all. That's why I'm a bit taken aback."

Maggie shrugged. "This ring stuff is easy," she said.

Except it isn't. Not by a long shot. I watched Maggie canter along confidently, and I allowed myself a brief moment of celebration. The kid who couldn't get her pony to trot when we started now looked like a million bucks out there. The bratty, mouthy little girl who was so certain she knew absolutely everything had taken my instruction even when it bordered on verbal abuse, and come away a rider.

So what if she wanted to trail ride? If that was what she wanted to do, in my mind, that was what she ought to do. It wasn't as if she was going to medal in Equestrian at the Olympics right this minute. She didn't lack talent, certainly, but the top athletes in our sport didn't get there by talent alone. Success required drive. To succeed, you not only had to tolerate spending long hours in a ring, you had to love every second of it. If Maggie didn't feel that way about dressage, or jumping for that matter, I saw no reason for her to be forced into it.

I flagged Maggie down. "Give Twinkle a walk break," I told her. "I'm going to talk to your mother."

Maggie's face was apprehensive. "Don't get fired," she ordered me.

"I won't. But I'll make sure she listens."

Maggie regarded me dubiously. I dismissed her doubts, hopping over the fence and making the hike up to the gazebo, heart pumping, carried by bravado and the silly, steadfast belief that my principles would remain intact and would not be sullied when this conversation was over.

Mrs. Allsteen watched me from beneath her shades, stabbing her cigarette into the ashtray. She nodded coolly at me, but she failed to move from her chaise lounge.

"Mrs. Allsteen. Hi." I sat down across from her in a wicker chair. "I'm so glad you could be here today to see Maggie ride."

"It is nice, isn't it, to be able to watch your daughter ride?" Mrs. Allsteen took a sip from her glass. "Heaven knows I wasn't comfortable watching her disappear down that *trail path* every day."

"Yes, that's actually what I wanted to talk to you about," I said, jumping in headfirst. "I know Maggie's really developed a preference for trail riding, and I know it isn't exactly what you envisioned for her, but trail riding is a growing sport, and it's one of the most popular pastimes in the US. If you knew more about it, I think you'd feel more comfortable with Maggie pursuing it. If you have any questions, I'd be happy to answer them."

Mrs. Allsteen stared at me, and I wasn't sure if she hadn't understood what I'd said or if she was just waiting to make sure I was done talking. "So, did you have any questions?" I asked stupidly.

Mrs. Allsteen put her fingers to her forehead, and I had absolutely no idea what that was supposed to mean. Luckily, a hired girl quickly rushed forward with a hand towel that she used to blot the perspiration off Mrs. Allsteen's forehead, and that cleared things up for me.

"Children can be so headstrong at times," Mrs. Allsteen dramatized, gulping another sip of wine. "That's why you must always do right by your children and make good decisions for them, no matter what they might want."

"That's...one way to put it," I said cautiously. "But isn't it better to support them and enable them to make decisions, good and bad, for themselves?"

Mrs. Allsteen peeled off her sunglasses, so I could see that she was for sure giving me the snake eye. "Do you have children, Erica?"

Damn it. I knew she was going to bring that up. "I don't," I admitted. "But I do know horses. I know equestrian sports inside and out, and if Maggie wants to focus on trail riding, I see nothing wrong with that."

Mrs. Allsteen shook her head, keeping a tight grip on her wine glass. "My daughter is too talented to waste her time on this trail path thing. Why, anyone who can sit upright on a horse and not slip off the other side can ride down a path! From the day she was born, Maggie has displayed superior athletic ability. She should be competing, earning ribbons and recognition, not yahooing around in the woods like some inbred trailer park child!"

I stared at Mrs. Allsteen, caught in a mire of dread and loathing. *You probably were that inbred trailer park kid. You just managed to marry well.*

"I still don't think you've considered all that trail riding has to offer," I said reasonably. "It's become a competitive sport. The sanctioned events are well-attended and judged by respected individuals. The trails and obstacles require good horsemanship and quick thinking. It teaches self-sufficiency and creativity, and it's a great bonding experience for horse and rider."

"There are also prizes and money to be won," I added. "Maggie won her division in her first competitive ride."

"Which you took her to, unbeknownst to me, and against my wishes," Mrs. Allsteen stated flatly.

I fidgeted uncomfortably. She had me there.

"And with all due respect, Erica, Gary and I didn't spend $30,000 on a fully-trained English show pony so Maggie could use him like a dirt bike," Mrs. Allsteen snipped.

I gasped. "Gloria...Mrs. Allsteen...that is *hardly* a fair assessment of your daughter's horsemanship. These trail outings are planned in advance and well thought out. Trail riding, done correctly, is actually *less* taxing on a horse's body than ring work."

Mrs. Allsteen flapped a hand in the air. "Never mind all that. The fact of the matter is, I have been far too lenient up until this point. I have been blinded by love, and I have allowed this nonsense to go on far too long. But now it ends," she declared, fixing me with a steely eye. "Maggie must enter a proper show, and she must do it soon. Her equestrian career needs to get back on track, and I will see to it that it does not fall off track again."

Mrs. Allsteen set her glass down on the table in front of her. "And if you, as her instructor, are not willing or able to keep Maggie focused on her goals, I can certainly find someone who is."

"I see." I leaned back in the wicker chair, wishing it would topple over, landing me in the grass, where I'd slide back down the hill. I wanted to go back in time, to rewind these last few minutes of my life. I wanted to have never had this conversation.

Before my eyes, Mrs. Allsteen transitioned easily into her former, benign self. The sunglasses went back on, joined by an accompanying smile. She reclined, languid, acting as if nothing remotely unpleasant had happened.

Maybe that was how it was if you had enough money. When you didn't have that fear in your heart, clawing at your back, pushing you onward, everything just leveled out. If you were rich enough, maybe it all really was just a game, and everything became trivial, even the things that really affected other people. If your life was that worry-free, perhaps it was too hard to relate to the struggles of those around you. Maybe empathy was like a muscle you didn't use enough. After a while, it just went soft. And then it hurt to use it, so you tried not to.

I looked at Mrs. Allsteen, the soft lines around her mouth, half-hidden by makeup. The relentlessly teased pouf of blonde hair that swirled around her head.

She hadn't come from money, I was sure. At some point, she'd known how the other half lived. Now, she was so disconnected, it was like she'd never set foot outside the gates of her husband's estate.

How could you just forget your upbringing? Was it really that easy?

Maybe it is if you don't want to remember.

Mrs. Allsteen's eyes followed Maggie as she grudgingly traversed the ring on Twinkle. "She rides like a dream, doesn't she?" The woman asked, her voice tinged with motherly pride.

"Yes," I agreed, biting down on the inside of my lip. "She does."

I left the gazebo and began the long walk back to the arena. My head was heavy.

Noticing my return, Maggie halted Twinkle by the rail. She studied my face. "You didn't get anywhere, did you?"

I swallowed. "I got nowhere. I'm sorry, Maggie."

"That's okay. I know you tried." Maggie leaned forward, her hands on Twinkle's withers. "You're not fired, are you?"

I exhaled. "No. Not just yet. But she's insisting that you enter a horse show. A 'proper' show."

Maggie considered this. "What are my options?"

I stared at her in surprise. "For horse shows?"

"*Yes*, duh. I'm not about to get you fired." Maggie shook her head at me. "So what are my options?"

"Well, this weekend there's a AHJSA-sponsored show. Like I took you to last year. You haven't learned to jump, so you'd have to ride in the flat class again. And I think I saw an advertisement for a dressage show. You ride by yourself, executing specific gaits, transitions and movements, and they score you on each portion of the test. You can either ride one of the tests of your level - you'd be competitive at Training Level, for sure - or I think there's an option to ride a freestyle."

"What's that?"

"It's where you ride a test from your level to music. The required movements are all the same, but you can do them in whatever order. You have to choreograph it to music, and they score you according to how well you ride the test, as well as accuracy and artistic appeal."

"I'll do the dressage thing," Maggie said casually. "You can enter me in the Training Level freestyle."

"Okay." I studied her face, pleased but slightly unnerved by her calm, poised demeanor. "What are you going to ride to?"

A smile glimmered on her mouth. "You'll see," Maggie said.

Lawrence

I walked into the LPC, fully ignoring everyone in my path - grooms, ponies, sponsors, hangers-on. I had one mission, which was to follow up on a lead. Wilson had heard of a polo club in Illinois that had gone bankrupt, and some of the ponies there were decent - maybe better than decent in the right hands. Yvette needed a string of her own that wasn't Courtney's, and I was always in the market. So, understandably, I wanted to jump on it.

I was aware of footsteps behind me, oddly close, but I didn't pay them any mind. Suddenly I was aware of my arm being snatched and my body spinning around.

And then I was aware of Barbara in my face, holding onto my arm and looking really, really pissed.

"Can we have a word?" She asked.

I couldn't exactly say no, so I followed her outside. *Wilson, you fuck, what did you do now?*

"What did he do now?" I asked Barbara when we were alone.

"Oh, he hasn't done anything," she said exasperatedly. "It's what he *won't* do."

Now I was confused.

"We've been together for more than six months now," she said, holding her arms to her chest and pacing in a short line. "That's a long time, isn't it? That's pretty long."

"I mean...yeah." I watched her, still confused as all get-out. "It's solid..."

Abruptly she stopped pacing, stopped fidgeting and looked at me. The universal signal of a woman cutting to the chase. "You'd think we would've made love by now, wouldn't you?"

My mouth was dry. This had just gotten beyond weird. "I mean...I mean....yeah. I would."

"Well we haven't." Barbara resumed her repetitive pacing, staring down at the manicured grass she was slowly trampling into powder. "And it's not for lack of trying. I've done everything I can think of. Nice dinners, champagne, lighting...I've worn nice lingerie, I've just plain thrown myself at him! And nothing! He won't do it. It's *humiliating*." A tear trailed down her face. "I mean, I know I'm not 20 anymore, but I'm desirable, right? I'm not *unattractive*...but apparently I'm just not good enough for him."

"Wow." I shook my head, completely at a loss. "That's crazy. That makes no sense."

"Well, I just wanted you to know that I tried. And now I'm giving up." Barbara reached into her purse for a Kleenex and delicately blew her nose.

"D'you think it's maybe, I don't know, medical?" I was grasping here. "I mean, he's kind of old, maybe he has that thing where you can't get it up? Or low testosterone or something? There are so many commercials about it, it must be kind of common..."

Barbara looked at me sagely. "That's *not* the problem," she said. "Trust me. I *know*."

"Okay then." I slunk away from the topic as quickly as I could. I really didn't want to think about Wilson getting a boner, although I was glad he still could.

Barbara stuffed the used Kleenex back in her purse and gathered herself. "Well, I'd better be going," she said stiffly. "I'm sorry for bringing you into this, Lawrence. It just helps to release the frustration."

"Oh, uh, no problem," I said eagerly, even though it kind of *was* a problem, and it was actually sort of interfering with my daily life right now. "You should probably tell Wilson, though, if you're actually leaving him."

Barbara smiled bitterly. "I already did," she said, and she walked swiftly to her car.

Before she was even in it, I sprinted to Wilson's office.

He looked up as I burst in, and I quickly assessed his condition. He looked upset. He was obviously upset enough to not even comment on the fact that I barged into his office without knocking. He wasn't crying or anything, which was kind of a relief. Mostly he looked resigned. Like he'd been waiting for this to happen.

And I realized something. Wilson *wasn't* the clueless idiot I'd made him out to be. He'd known exactly what he was doing, and he'd known that eventually Barbara would get fed up and leave.

That really pissed me off.

"I just saw Barbara," I said.

"We broke up," Wilson grunted. He shifted some file folders around to make it look like he was actually doing work.

"Why did you break up?" I asked him.

"She just said she was done." Wilson peered under his desk for no reason whatsoever. "That's all."

"Are you sad about that?"

Wilson rolled his eyes at me. "Of course I am, Cavanaugh. But I understand why she did it."

"Did you try to reason with her? Did you tell her you would make changes, work things out, whatever? Did you even try?"

"Wouldn't do any good." Wilson opened his desk drawer, shut it, and opened it again.

I was losing patience. "What the fuck, Wilson?"

He stared balefully at me. If there's one thing I hate, it's people who stare balefully.

"Why won't you fuck Barbara, Wilson? Why the fuck not?"

Wilson sank into his seat. "That's personal, Cavanaugh."

"I know it's fucking personal, Wilson, it involves fucking. There's not a lot that's more personal than fucking."

Wilson wheeled his chair away from me until he hit the back wall. "This does not concern you."

"It does too concern me. Because this is affecting my quality of life, too. When your *girlfriend* is crying in her car in a parking lot, and then crying all over *me* in a parking lot, it affects my quality of life. And when your *girlfriend* is so frustrated and so upset that she corners me and tells me intimate details involving whether or not you can get it up, *it affects my quality of life.*"

Wilson stared at me in horror. I took advantage of his silence.

"So really, now that I'm this fucking involved, the least you could do is tell me why you don't want to fuck your girlfriend. I'm *all ears.*"

Wilson's head, his torso, his everything seemed to compress and sink even further into his desk chair. If he could've tunneled under the floor, I think he would have.

"It's not that I don't want to," he said. "I'm just very...hesitant. I'm nervous."

"Why?" I blurted.

Wilson looked at me for a long moment. He seemed to be rearranging his words. "Because I've never...been with a woman. In that capacity."

The realization rolled around in my head for a minute, and then it clicked jarringly, just like when Erica told me. But Erica had been a 21-year-old girl, and Wilson was a 40something guy.

"This would be my first time," Wilson clarified.

I held out my hand to stop him, so he didn't just keep saying it in different ways. "You have to tell her, Wilson."

He shook his head. "I can't tell her that, Cavanaugh. Why should she want to be with me if no one ever has? She'll think I'm a relic."

"Right now she thinks you don't find her desirable. Anything's got to be better than that."

Wilson picked himself out of his desk chair and looked me in the eye. "With all due respect, Cavanaugh, you don't know shit."

Erica

The USDF-recognized show was well attended, and as I searched for Maggie, I found myself flanked by massive Warmbloods. They power-walked along, their overstep clearly visible in the hoof prints they left behind. Their hooves raised up a little puff of dust with every step, as did my boots, slowly eroding the loose, sandy soil underfoot.

It had been a while since I'd stepped onto the dressage scene, and I never could get over how big these horses were. The jumper ring had its share of giants, but they were typically piloted by strapping men. In dressage, it seemed, the basic model for success was a petite five-foot-something woman mounted on a 17-hand horse whose heavily shod and padded hooves were roughly the same size as her skull. A really effective rider could overcome the disparity in size and get her point across using finesse, not brute force. That was what good riding was all about. But I couldn't help thinking some of these women were over-mounted, plain and simple.

I rounded a corner, coming upon Maggie's rig by sheer luck. Twinkle looked sleek and elegant, the giant pouf of his mane and forelock contained in tight, meticulous braids. He wore Maggie's sparkling, oft-unused dressage saddle and his cannon bones were wrapped in white polos that would be whipped off just before he entered the show ring. He looked the part of a true dressage pony, and he looked at peace in the bustling show environment.

"Morning, Twinkle." I reached out to give him a scratch. "Where're your peeps?"

A door flew open, and Maggie jumped down from the trailer's living quarters, not bothering to use the steps Juan had so carefully set up for her. She landed sharply, but because she was a little kid, she didn't grimace in pain and hobble away with jammed ankles. *I long for those days.*

"Hey, Maggie," I said. "Where's Juan?"

"He went off to get my number. My ride time's in half an hour."

"Oh, okay." I looked at Twinkle, who still needed his bridle put on, and at Maggie, who needed her stock tie re-tied. "We should probably think about getting you to the warm-up ring."

"Please. Twinkle needs like a five-minute warm-up." Maggie sat down on the steps, totally relaxed. "You're as bad as Juan, fussing around with my tie every minute."

"Well your tie is crooked, so Juan's efforts are probably justified," I noted.

"As long as my entry and halt at X aren't crooked, I think I'll score just fine," Maggie rationalized.

"You learned the test," I said, pleased.

Maggie rolled her eyes, like she often did when I opened my mouth. "I may not *like* this show stuff, but I'm not about to go out there and look like a complete idiot. I owe it to *him* to ride well." She nodded at Twinkle, standing patiently with his ears pricked.

We both looked up as Juan came walking down the narrow lane between trailers. He wore ironed pants with a belt at all times, and he was clean-cut, without a hint of facial hair. He was skinny, a little wisp of a person, and he held his five-foot-five frame perfectly straight, with an air of quiet authority balanced with deep humility.

"Stand up straight, Ms. Maggie, so I may pin this on your back," Juan instructed, his quiet, slightly accented voice calm and soothing, not rushed. "Then we must see about getting that stock tie tied correctly, and by then it will be time to bridle your pony and take him to the warm-up ring."

He nodded sideways at me. "Good morning, Ms. Erica. You're here just in time."

I watched him work, concentrating deeply on the task of affixing Maggie's number to her show coat with safety pins, and I thought, not for the first time, *Juan really is a class act.*

Since I wasn't doing anything, I moved over to Twinkle, fetching his bridle and slipping it on. Juan finished with Maggie's tie, looking pleased.

"We should be all set from here," I said, grateful for his efforts. "Why don't you go relax for a little while?" I offered, knowing full well there was nothing relaxing about a horse show. There wasn't even good food available or anything.

Juan smiled. "I will wait by ringside in case I am needed," he said. "But I appreciate the offer."

Maggie mounted up, Juan gave her boots a final swipe with a cloth, and the four of us headed to the ring.

Canned classical music played as a small girl on a 16-hand Warmblood rode out of time with the beat. I directed Maggie to the appropriate warm-up ring (she was forever trying to warm up with the upper echelon riders in some show of toughness, or simple disregard for the rules), then stood back and watched her. She worked Twinkle through a textbook warm-up, giving him time to stretch, then moving him out and bending him in both directions. The pony moved forward, tracking up nicely, supple and responsive. Maggie wore her slight frown of concentration. They were both on.

Soon Maggie's number was called. Juan stepped in, swiftly removing the polo wraps, and she rode Twinkle to the show ring, walking him around the perimeter of the marked dressage arena. The bell dinged and she calmly brought him around, entering at A.

Expectant silence filled the air. I stood next to Juan, watching Maggie closely. "What is she riding to?" I asked him.

Juan shook his head. "She would not tell," he said. "She wanted it to be a surprise."

I glanced at him. "Didn't she practice it at home?"

A smile crossed Juan's mouth. "She made me take a drive so I would not overhear."

I laughed softly. "What a kid."

Juan hesitated, dragging a boot toe through the dust. "I wanted to tell you, Ms. Erica, how grateful I am for your work with Maggie. When I first started this job, the parents were difficult, and Maggie was worse than both of them put together. But after you began teaching her, she changed." He straightened up and looked at me. "She is a better individual for knowing you."

I didn't know what to say. "Wow, thanks, Juan," I said, slightly choked up.

The opening chords of Maggie's freestyle blared out of the speakers. It was a throbbing, highly synthesized beat I didn't recognize at first. But then I did.

"Is that..." I looked at Juan for clarification.

He nodded. "Miley," he said, grinning. "Of course."

Maggie circled around, sitting erect in the saddle, her seat quiet. Twinkle, unlike the previous horse, was completely on beat. His little legs touched down precisely with the music, and he and his rider were as poised and solemn as soldiers, while the lyrics to "Can't Be Tamed" spewed out.

I go through guys like money flying out their hands...they try to change me but they realize they can't.

Maggie brought him up to a canter as the verses built, laying down perfectly round circles. Her geometry was completely accurate. As if to stab the point home, she threw in crisp, seamless transitions between gaits, leaving no points up for grabs. Twinkle was moving beautifully, his tiny ears swiveled back in concentration. His face on the vertical, his back round and his strides full, Twinkle epitomized the Training Level horse.

And if you try to hold me back I might explode...baby by now you should know, I can't be tamed.

Maggie's eyes seared into the small crowd, seeking someone out. I almost felt the contempt coming off her, chugging into the atmosphere like steam from a locomotive. Following her eyes, I saw the unmistakable form of Gloria Allsteen sitting in the stands, watching her daughter with blind love and senseless greed in her eyes.

I can't be tamed.

Maggie circled around for her big finish, half halting and squeezing a little extra out of Twinkle. The pony dug in and went to work for her. They headed for their final centerline, straight and true.

I was overcome by it all. The events leading up to this point, the range of characters involved, and the sweet dichotomy of Maggie laying down a beautiful freestyle on her perfect pony with a look of screaming contempt on her face, Mrs. Allsteen in the stands, pleased as punch and already envisioning her daughter's Olympic debut, and Maggie's song selection. The perfect protest.

I can't be tamed.

Maggie halted Twinkle straight from a trot without any walk steps. His feet were as square as table legs. With a final vengeful glance at her mother, Maggie patted her pony on the neck and walked him out.

Lawrence

Erica was sitting at the kitchen table when I got in. "Hey. How'd it go with Maggie at the show?" I asked, suddenly remembering.

She grinned. "Maggie went down fighting. Sometimes I really love that kid…"

"That's good." I moved around the house, distractedly looking for food without much of a real game plan.

"Yeah. Picture this: we show up, Maggie warms up, she's in the ring on time. Twinkle's perfectly turned out by Juan, per usual. Maggie's dressed to the nines, a mini dressage queen. And what song comes on the speakers as she starts her freestyle? 'Can't Be Tamed', by Miley Cyrus." Erica snorted. "She rode perfectly, but the whole time, that song's blaring in the background and she's staring daggers at Mrs. Allsteen. Who was beaming in the stands, by the way. You're preoccupied," she added as I darted around the room. "What's going on?"

"Oh, nothing important. Well, kind of." I turned around to face her, giving up on my search. "Barbara broke up with Wilson."

"Oh no! Why?" Erica looked genuinely concerned. "Was he being an idiot again?"

I shook my head. "See, I thought Wilson was an idiot, but it turns out he's just scared."

"Of what?"

"Of..." I got bogged down and had to start over. "Okay. This is awkward. And weird. Wilson...Wilson's a virgin."

Erica's hand went to her throat. "Oh. My. God." She stared at me, her eyes as big as Courtney's. "That actually really makes a lot of sense."

"How does that make sense?"

"Lots of ways. Wilson's not very social. He's shy. He's awkward. And he's a workaholic. He spends all his time in that stable; he practically lives there...it's probably hard for him to meet women."

"Yeah, but..." I struggled for a minute. "He's *old*."

Erica shot me a look. "Adult virgins *aren't* unheard of. And it doesn't mean they're damaged, or undesirable, or anything. Sometimes, the opportunity doesn't present itself, or the right person hasn't come along...so you wait."

Erica stood up from the table. "So Barbara broke up with Wilson because he's a virgin?"

"No. Barbara broke up with Wilson because he wouldn't sleep with her."

"*Ohhhh*. Of course." Erica shook her head. "He's got to tell her."

"I know. That's what I told him."

"And what did he say to that?"

I looked at her coolly. "He said I didn't know shit."

She didn't laugh or act offended on my behalf. She nodded. "Well, you don't."

"What?"

"You don't know shit. About this. You have no idea what Wilson's going through."

"I don't know how that makes any difference. I'm still right."

Erica looked at me straight on. "How old were you when you first had sex?"

"I was 11."

Her face twisted. "Oh my God. That's sick."

"Well, you asked."

"Was she older? Was it consensual?"

I rolled my eyes. "Yes, she was older, and of course it was consensual. I was horny as shit. There was nothing weird about it, okay? It was normal."

"Except that you were 11." Erica sighed. "See, this is why you can't talk to Wilson about this. You have no concept of what it's like to be an adult virgin. You have no idea of the emotions involved."

Her face lit up suddenly. "I know what I should do. *I* should go talk to Wilson."

"*Why*? Why would you do that?"

"Because I understand what he's going through."

I tried not to roll my eyes, and I kind of succeeded. "Erica. You were 21 when we hooked up. *21*, okay? Wilson is in his *forties*. That's a *lot* different."

"No, it's not." Erica wasn't even paying attention to me anymore. She was doing things. Like grabbing a coat and finding keys.

"What are you doing?" I yelled, even though I already knew.

"I'm going to talk to Wilson!" She yelled back.

"If he knows I told you, he'll kill me," I pointed out.

She darted over, giving me a quick kiss on the cheek. "No, he won't."

"How come?"

"Because I'm going to help him."

"I think this particular situation may be beyond help."

"Nothing is beyond help." And she burst out the door.

Erica

The Lexington Polo Club wasn't really my territory, but I walked down the aisle like I belonged there. I kept my eyes out for Wilson, and his unusual posture gave him away - walking briskly, straight ahead, torso at a steep angle as he peered critically into each of the stalls he passed.

I intercepted him swiftly. "Wilson. Hi."

He looked startled. And suspicious. "Erica," he said in greeting, as he attempted to dodge me.

I wasn't that easily thrown. "I wanted to talk to you about something."

"It better not be what I think it is," Wilson muttered.

"Something that you might be struggling with, that I might have also struggled with in the past. Something that I know something about."

Wilson stared at me with haunted eyes. "I don't think so," he stammered, and he turned and kept walking, attempting to disappear into the organized chaos of the busy stable.

I shook my head. "I wouldn't do that, Wilson," I said, loud enough for him to still hear me. My voice rose as the distance between us increased. "Because if you keep doing that, I'm going to have to start *shouting things at your back*."

He jolted to a stop like he'd been shot in the spine. Slowly, he turned around and came trudging back to me.

"That's better." I patted him on the shoulder encouragingly. "Is there somewhere private where we can talk?"

Wilson nodded once. We walked a few paces and we were inside his office. He shut the door behind me and sat down in his desk chair.

"So I take it Cavanaugh told you," Wilson grunted.

"He did." I nodded deeply. "And I'm glad he told me, because I can help you."

Wilson looked at me sideways, like he didn't quite understand what I was getting at.

"Lawrence doesn't know what you're going through," I said. "He has no idea. But I do. Because I was a virgin before…before him."

Wilson eyed me critically. "And how old are you?"

"I'm 22," I admitted. "I was 21 at the time. But age is really irrelevant in this situation. The basic emotions and fears involved are the same. The waiting, the wondering, the resentment that you've somehow been left off this train that everyone else is unquestionably on...the pervasive fear that there's something inherently wrong with you..."

I stopped talking and looked at him levelly. "You have to tell her, Wilson. It sucks. It's embarrassing. It's humiliating. But you have to tell her the truth."

I could see Wilson's mind shutting down. As I would with a horse, I backed off and tried a new tactic.

"What about Barbara, Wilson? Doesn't she deserve to know?"

Wilson's eyebrows jumped in surprise. "I don't think this is anyone's business but mine," he grumbled, but he didn't sound all that certain.

I shrugged. "Yeah, but this affects her, too. Are you so afraid of having a slightly uncomfortable conversation that you're willing to let her live the rest of her life thinking that you don't love her? That you don't want her? This relationship was hard for you to start, but you went there anyway, because she was worth it. Are you telling me she's not worth putting yourself out there one more time?"

Wilson struggled for a minute. Then he actually looked at me. I could see his resolve wavering like a dandelion in the wind. "But what if it doesn't do any good? What if she decides I'm too old to just be learning the ropes? What if she gives up on me anyway?"

"That's a risk," I said. "It's a risk every time you put yourself on the line for someone. But if that happens, that's on her, not you. You walk away hurting, but at least you walk away knowing you gave everything. You tried *everything*."

"That's how you really find out if someone cares," I told Wilson, delving into my own past. "If you try everything, and they give you nothing, then you realize they're not in this with you. And there's nothing you can do to recruit them. But with the right person...you won't have to try so much. You can reach out, and they'll meet you halfway. You can mess up, and they'll take you back. Things aren't so fragile when two people really care about each other. But to get to that point, sometimes you just have to fall back and hope they'll catch you."

There was a tear in my eye, and I wiped it away on my sleeve. Wilson was looking right at me. He was with me.

"Don't protect yourself," I told him. "I tried that once. It doesn't work. I got to the point where I didn't trust, and I was tired of hurting, and I just wanted to protect myself. And if I hadn't gone back, just that one last time..." I shuddered. "I would've missed out on the best thing in my life."

I stood up to leave. "Go tell Barbara, Wilson. Don't keep *yourself* off the train just because those other people did."

Lawrence

The road in front of me was really, really straight and long. The thing about Kentucky was that it was a beautiful state surrounded only by really shitty states, like Ohio, or Indiana. Right now I was driving through Indiana.

It was the kind of place that just had nothing going for it. The gas stations and stores I'd been in all had a thin layer of filth over everything. You couldn't even find a decent station to listen to. It was all old-timey country and conservative talk radio.

I'd been making good time until I hit a detour near Friedmont, the town where Elaine had grown up. They were tearing up the freeway, scattering chunks of asphalt everywhere and having a lot of fun with their heavy equipment. And because it was Indiana, they had rerouted me miles out of my way, and now I was on some middle-of-nowhere stretch of road, staring at cornfields and searching for street signs that never materialized.

I will never see Illinois. At this rate, I was definitely going to be late to meet the guy and check out those ponies. I reached for my phone, but of course I didn't have service. *Fuckin' Indiana.*

About a million more cornfields went by, and they all looked pretty much like normal cornfields. And then I saw the strangest thing. It made me take my foot off the accelerator.

It was a girl on a horse. More specifically, it was a girl on a horse, galloping full-out, and holding a hockey stick.

I slammed on the brakes, causing the guy behind me to almost run into me. Drivers peeled around me, pressing down on their horns and showing their middle fingers as I sat in the middle of the road.

I ignored them, focusing fully on the girl. She sat lightly in a Western saddle, poised over the withers of a grizzled, somewhat reedy-looking Quarter Horse who reminded me of Maude - ears flat back and running hell-bent. The girl was bareheaded, with long chestnut hair down to her lower back in a ponytail. She held the split reins in one hand, lightly neck-reining the horse as her eyes peered ahead at something hidden in the mown-down cornstalks.

Quickly, I stepped on the gas and pulled over to the narrow shoulder. I drove along the edge of the road, keeping up with the girl. I wanted to see if she was just riding with a hockey stick at hand because that's just what people did in these parts, or if my hunch was right.

Sure enough, she gathered herself and let her arm whip through the air. The hockey stick made a smooth trajectory and connected with something small and white, scooping it up and sending it onward.

Holy shit. Is she stick and balling? She is. She fucking is. Fuck. The girl was picking up speed now, and I drove at a reckless pace on the pockmarked side of the road just to keep up with her. *What is she playing with? Is that a golf ball? It can't be.* My mind was whirling. *It's gotta be, like, a softball or something. Yeah. That would make way more sense. And be easier to hit.*

All of a sudden, I felt the distinct sensation of my front bumper slamming into something. I looked through my windshield, and saw that the first fucking road sign I'd seen in 20 miles was now bent over and unreadable.

The impact knocked some sense into me, and I threw it in reverse and backed up by 10 or so feet, so as not to immediately incriminate myself should a cop drive by. Then I shut down my truck, threw the keys on the seat, and went out into the field on foot.

The girl was circling back on her rangey horse. Intent on making the shot, she didn't notice me, so I was able to concentrate fully on her movements. She wasn't fooling around out there. She was accurate, precise. Her technique was solid. She waited until she was in the right place, half-halted her horse for a beat, and hit the ball.

And now that I was out of my vehicle, right up close, I could hear the distinctive sound her hockey stick made when it connected with the ball. I could see the dimpled surface. *It really is a golf ball. Holy shit.*

She had the wrong equipment, the wrong horse, the wrong saddle. But she had everything. She was everything we needed.

She was our girl.

The girl stopped her horse, noticing me for the first time. I hesitated, not sure of my first move. I wound up going for the big stupid grin and cheesy wave, because it was the first thing that came into my head.

The girl urged her horse into a jog, riding right up to me with a big smile on her face. She was pretty. Very pretty. She had a rider's build, long legs and a slim torso.

And even though she was sitting down, I got the sense that she could really fill out a pair of jeans, if you know what I mean.

"Hi, stranger!" The girl exclaimed, leaning over and reaching out a hand like a rodeo queen. "My name's Delaware."

"Delaware. What an unusual name. I like it." I shook her hand warmly.

"Oh, there's a story behind it. See, I was born in Delaware, but then we moved shortly after. I've spent my whole life in Indiana, all except for the first six months." She brushed the tale aside with a swipe of her hand. "What's *your* name?"

"I'm Cavanaugh. Lawrence Cavanaugh," I said, trying to make it sound as cool as possible.

"*Ooh*," said Delaware, her eyes widening. "It sounds foreign. Are you foreign? You *look* foreign."

"I think it's Irish. I think. But no, I'm not," I admitted. "I grew up in California."

Her eyes lit up at that. "Did you live near any famous people?"

"Oh, yeah. Very near." *I lived in his house, actually. The prick.*

"Wow." Delaware set the reins on her horse's withers and looked at me. "So what brings you to my daddy's cornfield?"

I looked her straight in the eye. "You did."

"*Me?*" Delaware raised a hand to her chest. She also filled out a T-shirt really nicely.

"Are you aware that you're playing polo? Or practicing polo?"

Delaware glanced around, and ended up looking at the hockey stick in her right hand. "What, with this?"

"Yes."

She giggled. "Heck no. I'm just foolin' around, really..."

"Are you aware that polo is a sport? Do you know what it involves?"

Delaware shook her head. "I know it's a brand. Like shirts and stuff. And perfume! That one guy in that ad is super hot..."

I seized my opportunity. "Well, he's a professional polo player. And so am I."

"*Really?*" Delaware's eyes sparkled. "That's impressive."

"But anyway. Back to you for a second." I studied her face. "You're really not proficient in polo? You haven't had any lessons or anything?"

"Where would I find polo lessons around here?" She laughed out loud.

"Well, that's really remarkable, because your form and technique are spot-on. It's hard for me to wrap my head around how good you are."

Delaware shook her head. "That's very nice of you, but I honestly don't have a clue what I'm doin'. I just do it 'cause it's fun." She shrugged.

I was unrelenting. "How did you even get started? Do you just like to make up crazy, difficult things to do on horseback when you're bored?"

"*No,*" Delaware protested, laughing. "It all started 'cause I was messin' around with this stick, hittin' golf balls with it and seeing if I could get a hole in one, 'cause we didn't have a golf club no more 'cause my brother threw it so hard it broke in half." She rolled her eyes. "So then he saw me hit a hole in one with this thing, and he said he bet I couldn't hit a hole in one on Toby here." She patted her horse. "So I jumped right on and did it right then, just to show him. And it was real fun, so I just...continued."

I stared at her, transfixed. "You need to come to Lexington with me."

Delaware burst out laughing. "*Why?*"

"Because two of the top players from the Women's Polo Federation and I are starting a polo team. And we need you."

Delaware was incredulous. She also looked flattered. "*Me?*"

200

"You're the missing piece. You have raw talent, you're gutsy, you're fearless, and you're also a really cool chick." I was totally ad-libbing at this point. My pulse hadn't been this elevated since back in the day when I was doing drugs. "You're perfect."

Delaware eyed me, seated on her horse. "This isn't *Dateline*, is it?"

"What d'you mean?"

"I mean, you're not tellin' me all this stuff to get me in your *van* or nothin'?" She was giggling, but at the same time, the way she surveyed me was all business.

"I can assure you this is not *To Catch A Predator*." I smiled. "I realize this is strange and unexpected, and I'm sure I sound totally crazy right now. I wish I had rehearsed this better, but I never expected this. Not here, not today. But it's happening. And I'm so excited."

"I'm excited for you," Delaware said. "I just don't understand how I'm gonna help you guys out. I'm telling you, I don't know what I'm doing!"

I brushed her remark aside. "Are you in school?"

"Nope."

"Do you have a job? Family obligations?"

"No and no."

"Do you have a boyfriend around these parts?"

"No!" She started laughing.

"Then you have absolutely nothing holding you back from taking a trip to Lexington with me and meeting the rest of the team. I'll put you up, I'll cover all your expenses…meals, shopping, whatever. You can spend a couple weeks training with us. I'll teach you the ins and outs of the game, put you on a real polo pony, teach you the shots…and if it doesn't work out for whatever reason, if the team doesn't gel or if you just decide it's not for you, I'll bring you back home to your family and you'll owe me nothing."

Delaware swung off her horse. She approached me, and I saw the keen interest on her face.

"And what if it does work out?" She asked me.

"Then your life changes forever. In the best way."

Delaware didn't hesitate. She threw her arms around me. "I'll do it!" She shouted.

I grinned, holding onto her tightly. "You won't regret this."

"All I know is if life hands you an opportunity, you'd be a fool not to try it." Delaware stepped back. "Just let me take care of Toby. I'll be back in fifteen."

"You can take longer if you want," I said, slightly dazed. "If you need to pack a suitcase or anything."

"No need." Delaware was already heading for the barn. "Baggage weighs you down."

I watched her go, only starting to grasp the craziness of the situation. *I fucking love Indiana,* I decided as I stood out in the middle of a cornfield, giddy enough to jump up and down.

I pulled out my cell phone, and by some miracle I had reception. While I waited for Delaware, I called up Yvette.

"How are you in Illinois already?" She demanded without saying hello. "How are the ponies?"

"Fuck the ponies," I responded. "I found something *even better.*"

"What in the hell are you talking about?" Yvette spat into the phone.

I stretched my free arm up toward the sky. I may have allowed myself a little twirl. "I found our girl."

Erica

It was the time of day I dreaded the most. No matter what I did, no matter what I tried, it was always an ordeal.

Riding Assault.

If I brought him out first, when I was fresh, he'd put me in such a bad mood that it affected my dealings with my other horses. If I rode him last, I'd be in a good mood, but I'd be tired, just weary enough for him to zero in on my weaknesses and take full advantage. You couldn't win with this horse.

Assault was so sour, so easily bored, that the best strategy with him was as little schooling as possible. When he was showing in the low jumper classes, I hardly even rode him over fences. Just a light flat schooling here and there, and I'd pull him out for the shows and win every time. But now he was moving up in the ranks. The fences were getting higher, the courses more technical. His job was more physically demanding. I could not let him sit, and then ask for peak performance. I had to keep him in peak physical condition. I simply had to ride him.

Assault trotted along the rail, ears swiveling around. His back was up underneath me, gently cupping my seat and providing a smooth ride even as his limbs powered along. His neck telescoped out from his withers, every muscle in play as he held the bit in a quiet, receptive mouth.

It was the very image of harmony, grace and good training, and I felt like I was holding it together with a thread. Assault was like a bomb that I constantly had to try to diffuse, and when it inevitably blew, I had to pick up the pieces.

Assault glanced into the center of the ring where I'd set up some grids, medium to low height. Grids and gymnastic exercises were how you built and kept fitness in your jumpers. You didn't go pelting around courses all the time. Assault hated grids. He liked to plow through them, or duck out and refuse. That was his way of making it more interesting.

I moved him up to a canter, staying in a full seat, making him engage fully. Then I rose into a half seat and pointed him at the first grid. Assault jumped through it, but grudgingly. I patted him generously, and he rooted at the reins, jerking my arm. I put my spurs into him and growled, and he shook his head at me. His muzzle was clamped tight. Sullen.

A flash of chrome distracted me, and Assault quickly threw in a couple bunny hops. I reined him in hard and stared even harder at the car that had just pulled in the drive. Marla's Mercedes.

"What the fuck is she doing here?" I demanded in the general direction of Assault's ears.

I thought she might see that Lawrence's truck was gone and just go back the way she came. But no. She got out of her car and came right for me.

She was clearly dressed for the beach. In fact, she was wearing nothing but a string bikini and a black mesh cover-up. Why they even call it a cover-up is beyond me, though, since it really doesn't cover anything up at all. Especially not in this case.

"Lawrence is out of town," I said bluntly. *Not that you should be visiting my boyfriend anyway. But we both know that's the only reason you're here.*

"I know." Marla gave me a disconcerting smile. "I just thought I'd drop by." She spread out her arms, leaning against the rail.

"Well, I need to school this horse," I said tightly. Assault's neck rose higher with every minute that went by, and his nostrils flared like a dragon. "You can watch if you want, but don't expect much in the way of conversation."

"Words are overrated," Marla said, stretching up toward the sky. "I'm much more interested in action."

I looked at her critically. "Aren't you a writer?"

"Yes," she said, straight-faced. "But it doesn't define me."

"Then you must not be very passionate about it," I muttered under my breath.

"I'm passionate about a lot of things," Marla said, smiling disturbingly. "But they don't involve anything as cold and clinical as letters on paper."

"Okay then. Good to know." I gave Assault some leg, and he wheeled away from where she stood. Glad to be rid of her, I stood in the stirrups and let Assault cruise for a minute. When I sat back and asked him to collect, I had an entirely different horse underneath me.

The feather light connection was gone. Assault had become a pile driver, barreling full speed ahead with no sign of stopping. He ignored my aids, so I pulled back hard on the outside rein, twisting his head around. A clear demand.

Assault's pinched eyeball glared at me. He grabbed the bit and continued. He just flat-out said "No."

We lapped the ring several times, steadily pulling against each other, both our mouths set in a thin line. Marla leaned on the rail, watching critically. "He's loading his forehand," she called out as we thundered by. "Get him off the right rein. Make him carry himself."

I thought there could be nothing more irritating than Lawrence's older, more experienced, more worldly, zero body issues, natural redhead ex, I mused darkly. *But hey, she's also knowledgeable about horses. Isn't that great?*

"I'm aware," I snapped at her the next time we passed by. "Why don't you get up here and try, if you think you can do better?"

"I'm not really dressed for it," Marla smirked. "And I'm sure you have it all under control."

Yeah. *It really seems that way.* My horse wouldn't stop, and my arms were wearing out. So I did the only thing I could think of. I pointed him at the smallest, dinkiest grid I'd set up. *There. That should take the wind out of your sails.*

Sure enough, upon seeing the tiny fences, Assault dropped back to a crawl. "No, I don't think so," I said to him, and I wrapped my legs around him, spurs and all. "You are *going* to jump through this grid."

Assault humped his back and lashed out with his hind legs. Once, twice, three times. I stayed with him, but he knocked me off balance. My hands slipped forward, a tiny door opened, and Assault being Assault, he barged right through.

I was prepared for him to stop or wheel to the side, but that's not what he did. Before I knew what had happened, Assault charged forward in a full-on, flat-out gallop. He left the ground from an impossibly long spot, catapulting himself into the air and attempting to jump all the fences in one bound.

It was an impressive effort, that was one way to look at it. Assault was completely sure of himself. He really thought he was going to clear that grid.

Of course, what actually happened was Assault landed square in the middle of the grid. He completely demolished it. Poles and standards keeled over underneath him, and the gelding scrambled to keep his footing. Twice he almost went down, but he righted himself and kept going. I heard the crack of splintering wood under his feet, and I began to see a new set of jumping standards in my future.

When Assault's feet touched bare, non-wood-strewn ground, I looked back to see the damage. Assault had annihilated the grid. Not one piece of the intricate jump exercise I'd so carefully set up that morning remained standing.

Assault stood still, content for the moment now that he'd made a big mess. He was a lot like a toddler in that way. He liked to dismantle things, and then watch you pick them back up.

We were face to face with Marla. I was breathing hard. She looked at Assault in amusement and slight awe.

"Is this a problem horse you're retraining?" She asked me.

I shook my head. "Nope. This is my up-and-coming Grand Prix horse."

"Huh." Marla considered this. "Things certainly have changed since I rode jumpers."

I made no comment. I didn't particularly want to hear about her undoubtedly illustrious past life competing in the jumper ring. There would always be comparisons, I was realizing. I would constantly be trying to measure up, and failing. Nothing was mine alone.

"Is my horse bleeding anywhere?" I asked Marla coolly.

She peered at his limbs, his body. "No. I don't see any blood."

"Then we have some work to do." I pivoted Assault on his haunches, shutting her out.

Much as I wasn't paying attention to Marla, I did notice that she had left the rail. I did hear her car start up, and I did see it drive off.

With a loaded sigh, I steered Assault toward the remaining grid. I didn't over-aid him, trusting that he had learned his lesson from the earlier debacle.

Assault cantered down to the grid, straight and true. He jumped through it cleanly and answered my half-halt at the end, coming back to me.

"You couldn't have done that *before*," I growled at him as I patted him softly on the neck.

Lawrence

Delaware sat laughing beside me in the passenger seat. Having her in the cab with me made the miles go by a lot faster. Even the schlocky country music sounded better. She sang along, but only on certain parts. Usually the most hilarious ones.

Delaware leaned back, propping a foot up on my dashboard. She was wearing Daisy Dukes, a tied-up Western shirt that bared her midriff, and hot pink cowboy boots with a pointed toe and 4-inch, dagger-thin stiletto heels.

"I want to make a good impression," she'd explained as she got in the cab. "And if I'm gonna leave home with just the clothes on my back, they better be these ones."

Now, as we crossed over into the state of Kentucky, Delaware scooted to the edge of her seat, taking in the scenery. "Holy mother of pearl," she exclaimed. "It's downright gorgeous here."

I shrugged, playing it cool. "It's alright."

Delaware stared out the window, her head swiveling around to catch all the sights. I guessed that someone who'd spent her entire life in a tiny, corn-growing town in Indiana would find this state to be a revelation - the greenery, the sleek cities, the sprawling, classic-looking horse farms. I wasn't as easily moved by the place I called home. I'd found my way here by accident, settled here out of necessity, and I'd stayed because it worked for me. Pure and simple. When it didn't work for me anymore, I would leave without a thought.

The important things in my life, the people closest to me, and my horses, could all be moved. We could achieve just as much in another city. Or depending on the location, we could even achieve more.

I smiled. "You should see Florida."

"I hope to." Delaware turned her gaze away from the window. Her eyes were a very deep shade of blue, about five shades darker on the color wheel than Erica's or Courtney's. "But I guess that all depends on how I do in Lexington."

"This is where it starts," I agreed, flicking on my blinker and exiting the highway.

I took the scenic route, winding my way through downtown Lexington, past the life-size bronze racehorses of Thoroughbred Park. Then we were deep into the countryside, and soon the wrought-iron gate of the LPC beckoned. I parked, and we walked up to the stable, Delaware's heels clicking against the smooth asphalt.

One thing was certain: Wilson ran a tight ship. The LPC grounds and stables weren't terribly lavish by polo club standards. Back when we traveled for away games, I'd played at many venues that clearly had more money behind them. Most clubs in the region were bigger and better than what we had going on here. But Wilson more than made up the difference with good, if obsessive, management. He was constantly on his employees about cleanliness, all day, every day, and some people up and left because of it. But the ones who stayed caught on quickly, and they learned to take pride in their work and not half-ass it. Because Wilson would *always* notice.

With Wilson's sharp eyes roving over everything, dust rarely settled on any surface. The barn walls glowed. The concrete aisle looked freshly poured. Everything, from the beams holding up the roof to the stall floors, was sparkling clean.

Delaware walked through the stable with her mouth agape. "Holy shit," she whispered. "Horses live here, right? *Horses.*"

I spotted Wilson at the end of the aisle, taking a walk-through like he always did. Checking to make sure no one screwed anything up. "Wilson," I called out.

He abandoned his mission and walked over, noticing Delaware for the first time. Wilson looked her up and down, then looked at me, an extremely odd look on his face.

"Wilson, this is Delaware. Delaware, this is Wilson. He manages this place."

Delaware quickly stuck out her hand. "It's a pleasure," she trilled.

Wilson grunted a vague "hello". His eyes were lingering on Delaware's high heels and exposed legs and belly, but not in a leering, creepy-old-man way. If anything, he looked somewhat critical of her appearance.

"Cavanaugh. What is this?" he muttered as he broke their handshake.

"This is Delaware," I repeated myself. "She's trying out for the team."

"Uh-huh." Wilson glanced back at Delaware one more time and then shook his head, locking his eyes on mine. "Be careful there, Cavanaugh," he said cryptically, and he moved on.

I shook myself. *Well. That was weird.* Shrugging it off, I took Delaware out to see the ponies. Hermione came up to the fence to be petted, but most of Courtney's string just turned their butts toward us and walked away. I could imagine what they were thinking. *Oh good,* another *rider. Even less downtime for us.*

Delaware was looking around. "So where's the rest of the team?" She asked.

I looked at her, surprised. "I thought you'd want to settle in first."

"I can settle in later. I want to meet them."

"That can be arranged." I felt in my pocket for my phone.

Courtney

Yvette came bursting through the door of our motel room. She was never quiet about anything. "We have to go to the polo club," she said, her words barely audible over the gunshot-loud sound of the door slamming shut behind her.

"Why?"

"Because Cavanaugh is there with this new woman who is supposedly our missing piece." Her brow crinkled distrustfully. "She wants to meet us. And I for one would like to see what kind of player he could have possibly unearthed in a place like Indiana."

"I guess Indiana has just as much likelihood of producing a polo prodigy as any other state in the union," I theorized diplomatically.

Yvette rolled her eyes. "Let's just go meet this train wreck, Courtney. Perhaps you will get along. Perhaps she will like *Britney*."

"Lots of people like Britney," I protested, grabbing my room key.

Lawrence

From our vantage point on the bench out in front of the stable, I saw Yvette's Voyage as it sped into the parking lot. Yvette leapt out of the driver's seat and began walking speedily in my direction, while Courtney struggled to remove herself from the tight quarters.

Delaware jumped off the bench, her face eager. Yvette caught sight of her and slowed way down. Courtney caught up with her, and they both stopped moving entirely and just looked at Delaware, their faces unreadable.

Annoyed by their cold reception, I grabbed Delaware's hand and led her up to them. "Guys, this is Delaware," I announced in an attempt to control the situation. "Delaware, meet Yvette Sauvage and Courtney Silva."

Delaware grinned and went in for a hug, but Yvette brushed past her. Courtney being Courtney, she followed Yvette.

"We should talk," Yvette hissed urgently at me, with a cutting glance in Delaware's direction.

"Yeah," I said. "We should." I grasped her arm and dragged her out of Delaware's line of hearing.

In a few seconds, we stood in the mouth of the stable, framed by the open door. Yvette ripped her arm out of my grip and glared at me sullenly. Courtney just looked worried.

I ignored her, focusing fully on Yvette. "What the fuck?"

She looked at me coolly. "So that is it. Your big solution."

"Yeah, she is. And she's awesome. So why are you treating her like shit? You don't even know her, Yvette. This is low, even coming from you."

"You expect me to jump up and down in celebration? Because you picked up a low-rent floozy from the shit hole capitol of the world?" Yvette spat at me. "If I respected your girlfriend more, I would have half a mind to call her up and inform her of your cheating ways."

Her words hit me with the force of a tire iron. "*That's* what you think this is?" I asked harshly. "That's what you think is going on here?"

Yvette stared up at me defiantly. Courtney shifted uneasily at her side. "It...doesn't look good, Lawrence," Courtney whispered tentatively.

My eyes narrowed. "Oh, is that you, Courtney? Did you finally decide to participate in this conversation?"

"Get off her," Yvette snarled with surprising force. "She doesn't deserve your abuse."

"But she deserves yours?"

Yvette didn't even blink. She gathered up Courtney, and in a split second they were facing away from me. I had to chase them down.

"What are you *doing*?" I demanded, catching up with them.

Yvette turned back. "I am not sticking around to witness this," she said bluntly. "We are done here."

All the air went out of me. I stood there, completely thrown. "You really think that's what's going on here? You honestly believe that I would bring this girl here because I want to fuck her?"

Yvette folded her arms in front of her. "Look at your history. And look at her."

I followed the line of Yvette's stare. It led to Delaware, who was sunning herself on the bench, head tipped back, looking like a mudflap girl.

I looked back at Yvette. She gave me a twisted smile. "You see?"

I shook my head hard. "You're wrong."

Surprisingly, she seemed to consider this. But soon her gaze turned to lead. "So what if I am. This girl is ridiculous. She is a backwoods hick from the butthole of the Midwest. What can she possibly have to offer?"

I stood there at a loss for words. Anger was building up in my head and turning everything dark, like a storm cloud.

"Give me one week," I said hotly. "At the end of that week, you'll be eating those words."

Yvette took a step back. She regarded me with amusement, like someone listening to the fancies of a small child. "All right. I can't wait to witness this miraculous transformation."

She left, shadowed by Courtney. I stared at her in contempt. *What a bitch.*

I shook off that unhelpful thought and went to Delaware. "Today is the start of your basic training," I said. "I'll be working with you alone this week, and at the end of the week we'll start to incorporate you into team practices."

Delaware looked up at me, her eyes shadowed. "They don't like me, do they?"

I sighed deeply, sitting down beside her. I could have lied to protect her, but lying doesn't prepare you for anything.

"When you're first starting out in this sport," I told her, "you'll get the skeptics. The people who think you can't do it because you didn't come from money, or you came from the wrong side of the tracks. The people who think you can't do it because you're too young or too green. And you can let that get to you. You can let it seep into how you view yourself and let it affect how hard you try. You can let it box you in."

I met her eyes. "Or you can work harder, and try harder, and you can exceed everyone's expectations. You can make them look really, really stupid."

Delaware brushed her eyes with the back of her hand. She looked at me with unmistakable hunger in her eyes. "Hard work never killed anybody. And I want to cover as much of this ground as I can before I'm put in it."

I clapped her on the back. "Let's go find you some clothes and get this show on the road."

Amber

My shift over, I leaned against the shed row, stretching out my back. After a morning of working strong, fit racehorses that pulled against me with every stride, my shoulders were so tight they were painful to the touch. Not that anyone was touching them.

I'd been working here a while, and it was pretty much like a job. It was a good job. The work was intensely physical, which was good for me. And it didn't involve much in the way of human interaction, which was also good for me. I'd had a string of retail jobs when I was growing up, but they never lasted more than a few weeks. I got hired easily enough, as long as my interviewer was a guy. But between the mind-numbing, sedentary nature of the jobs, and the moronic nature of the customers, my brain would become so stupefied that I'd eventually just start mouthing off at will. And that didn't fly.

Track jobs were my bag. You didn't have to be nice. You didn't have to keep it clean. All they cared about was your ability to preserve the soundness of the racehorses. If you were effective, you stayed.

Some days, I peeled out of here right when my shift ended, and some days I lingered. Recently, one of my horses had been laid up, so I'd taken to visiting her. She was a dark liver chestnut with a coppery mane and tail, and a thin stripe down her face. She had the unfortunate name of Kahuna

Matata, so I called her Kay, but even that nickname brought up images of tacky jewelry commercials. It didn't do her justice.

Kay raised her head when she spotted me, a few strands of hay dangling from her mouth. The slow feeder attached to her stall door was half empty. "Ooh, you're so *hungry*," I said in that egregious baby-talk voice that some women use on their boyfriends.

Nobody was around, so I ducked into the stall. Slipping an arm over Kay's back, I stood with the filly as she gobbled up pieces of hay, a few at a time. There was something so relaxing about the sound of horses chewing.

That sound was cut off by the sound of boots on the concrete floor. I stiffened in alarm, hoping I wouldn't get shit for being in the stall with this horse, which was technically not where I was supposed to be right now. There wasn't much I could do, so I just kind of stayed where I was and tried to look like I belonged. And I listened. The footsteps stopped right outside Kay's stall.

"Hey, gorgeous, you are just going to town on that hay bag. Looks like you need a refill."

I relaxed. *Oh. Just Kelly.* She was a groom, not some uptight trainer or official. She probably wouldn't give me shit about being where I wasn't supposed to be.

"Hold on, let me get in here," Kelly said, pushing the filly's head aside as she unbuckled straps on the hay net. She looked up suddenly. "Oh, hey, Amber. I didn't see you there."

"Yeah, I'm just visiting my favorite girl," I explained.

Kelly gave me a sincere nod. "I feel ya. I've definitely spent some off-the-clock time in this stall. Especially lately."

A normal person would've responded to that by saying something like *Oh, is something bothering you?* Or not said anything at all. But because I was me, I just came right out with it. "Why lately?" I asked bluntly.

Kelly didn't seem offended. She stuffed a flake of hay in Kay's slow feeder and closed it back up, resting her arms on the top of the stall door. They were tan, muscular and covered in red scratches, undoubtedly from putting up hay in a tank top. "Oh, I just broke up with my girlfriend of two years. You know."

Girlfriend.

Hang on, back up a second. What?

She broke up with her girlfriend?

I stared at Kelly. My heart was thudding, and I was getting that crazy, overstuffed, too-many-thoughts feeling in my head. Kelly and I had never been close. We worked at the same track, for the same trainer, but our relationship amounted to knowing each other's names and passing each other, me on a horse and her leading one. Racehorses walked fast.

I'd never studied her face, never really committed it to memory. I looked at her closely now. She was petite, stocky. Her limbs were muscled and hard from the kind of work she did. Her body looked like you could just fall into it. She looked soft and ample in the places where you want those qualities.

Her nose was pert, her lips full, and her light brown hair fell in tightly spiraled ringlets. My body felt unnaturally warm all of a sudden.

I had a choice, and once again, I chose directness over tact. "You're gay?" I demanded.

Kelly shrugged. She didn't seem oversensitive about it. "Yup. Always have been."

"I am too." I sucked in a quick breath and blinked at her, trying to calm myself. I'd never really told anyone before. Except Lawrence. But that had been a mercy thing, to show him that I was a dead end.

"Really?" Kelly stepped back, considering this. "My gaydar must be way off."

"I don't *have* fucking gaydar." I rolled my eyes. "I'm pretty sure it's a myth."

"Maybe. I can usually get a read on people, though." Kelly looked me up and down. "Huh. I never would've thought."

I let myself out of the stall, wanting to remove the barrier between us. She didn't retreat, and I moved in close, into that inner sanctum of personal space normally reserved for close friends or lovers. Not casual work acquaintances. My hands hung at my sides, and I kept them there through force. There were so many things I wanted to touch on her.

"So you're gay, and I'm gay..." I trailed off, leaving it to her to finish the sentence.

"Well then." She looked up at me, reaching up to smooth my hair back with one hand. My breath caught.

"Well then," I repeated her words.

Lawrence

Delaware was mounted on Vegas, and I was on foot. We had retreated to the field next to my property, where there were no witnesses, no questioning glances. No cutting remarks. Just her, me, and a made pony to show her the way. This was all we needed, and this would be the center of our lives for the next seven days.

Delaware let Vegas move out at a walk, getting used to the pony's sweeping stride and the flat, close-contact seat of a polo saddle. "My legs feel all over the place," she remarked, swinging them back and forth and adjusting her foothold in the stirrups.

I nodded. "That's the idea. You need the freedom to be able to move - standing up, leaning backward, forward or sideways - in order to make the shots."

"I see." Her eyes narrowed in concentration, Delaware positioned herself over Vegas' withers, reaching down to his chest with her free hand, then standing upright. She twisted her torso, laying a hand on Vegas' rump. "It's just a different feeling than I'm used to."

"You'll get it." I watched as she settled back into the saddle. She moved Vegas up to a trot, her seat lightly rising and falling in time with the swing of his back.

"You know how to post," I said, overjoyed. "Most Western riders sit the trot."

She laughed. "Toby has a rough jog. Like a pile driver my dad used to say. It's get out of the saddle or die on him."

Delaware trotted around me in a large circle. Tall boots and breeches had replaced her cowboy boots and Wranglers, and she wore a polo shirt. My helmet sat on her head, a concession to Erica's preferences, and because falls are common when you're learning your way around a polo field.

"Try a canter," I called out to her. "Or a lope, or whatever you people call it."

Laughing, Delaware kicked Vegas, who made a bold leap into the three-beat gait. Delaware sat in the saddle, her mouth open. "He's so *smooth!*" She gasped. "Are they all like this?"

"Not as good as Vegas, no. But you won't find too many rough-gaited ponies. Makes the job more difficult than necessary." *And it's already plenty difficult.*

"Ride him out to that tree line," I pointed off to the west. "Take him out, open him up, and bring him back."

"Alright then." Delaware pointed Vegas in the right direction, and I watched his body lengthen and flatten out. Delaware leaned over his withers, her hands smoothly following the rapid movement of Vegas' head and neck. They disappeared from view, descending into a valley. It was a minute before they returned.

Vegas was still traveling at a pretty good clip, and Delaware began to rein him in. But she over-aided him, and Vegas obediently slammed to a halt, skipping all the gears in between. Delaware fell forward, nearly nose-diving onto Vegas' neck. But she recovered quickly and sat up, breathless. And I looked into the face of someone who was hooked on the unique sensation of pelting around on a fast horse in a huge field.

"That concludes your English training," I said. "Now you start to learn polo."

She nodded, fully absorbed.

"You won't be going that fast again for a while," I said as I walked around to Vegas' off side. "We begin from the ground up."

"Now, let's start with equipment. You need a lot of horses to play polo competitively, but you don't need much else. You need the clothes on your back, a ball to hit, and a mallet to hit it with. Mallet selection is intensely personal. You need the length to suit the reach of your arm and the height of your pony, as well as the type to suit your style of play. Some people like a whippier, more flexible mallet - they've got more striking power, but they're harder to control. Since you're used to something with virtually no give, I thought I'd start you out on a mallet that's more rigid."

I handed her the mallet I'd been holding onto, and she took it in her hand, twirling it and giving it a few experimental swings. "It's so *light.*"

"I think you'll see it has a lot of heft to it when you start stick and balling." I walked around to Vegas' other side.

"You'll hold the mallet in your right hand, and you only swing with your right hand. That keeps you from hooking mallets with other players - unless you want to, that is. But that comes later."

Delaware nodded. "Right."

"The first thing you'll learn are the shots. There are seven of them, and you'll learn them at a standstill, then a walk. You'll master them on your own until you can reliably execute them at a full gallop. Then, and only then, will you be in a position where you can ride with a team."

"We'll start with the off side forehand. It's the most commonly used shot, and it's the easiest. You already know how to do it."

Delaware perked up. "I do?"

"Yup. Hit the ball forward or to the side. Make sure the mallet's on the right-hand side of the pony."

"That I can do." Delaware touched Vegas with her leg, and he walked forward. She sighted the ball, took aim and made contact.

"Good." I walked alongside Vegas picking up the ball and repositioning it. "Ever tried a backwards shot?"

Delaware shook her head. "No…"

"Well, you're about to. Offside backhand. What you just did, but backwards."

"Okay." Delaware turned Vegas, setting him up to meet up with the ball. Once he was lined up, she glanced back and hit the ball. Her reflexes were good. She got it done.

"Good job," I said. "Once you get better at those, you'll be able to hit them blind."

She nodded, pivoting Vegas on his hindquarters. "What next?"

"The near side shots. Forehand and backhand." I smiled. "This is where it gets a little tricky, because you're reaching across your pony's withers with your mallet hand. It's awkward at first, and you're going to feel like you're fumbling. But it's essential to master them, particularly the near side backhand. It rounds out your skills as a player and makes you way more deadly."

Delaware didn't respond. Her face set in deep concentration, she repositioned her arms and rode up to where the ball lay. Her rein hand was tight and restrictive on Vegas' mouth, the result of nerves or just having too much to think about. The gelding tried to help her out, staying on a diligently straight track even with his head cranked in to his chest, but as she readied to swing, her right arm came down on her rein hand, jerking Vegas in the mouth. He lurched to a stop, and her mallet ran into the ground and shuddered.

"*Oof.*" Delaware untangled her limbs and released Vegas' mouth, patting him in sympathy. She turned to me. "You weren't kidding when you said it'd be awkward."

"You'll get there. Everyone starts out this way." I walked over to Vegas' head, looking Delaware in the eyes. "Don't rush it and get aggressive. Think smooth and slow. Be soft. That ball weighs a few ounces. You don't need brute force to get it off the ground. You need to be accurate, and you have to give yourself the time it takes to be accurate."

"Okay. I get what you're saying there." Delaware squared her shoulders, crossing her mallet diagonally over Vegas' withers. "I won't jerk on you this time, I promise," she told him. The gelding walked forward decisively, taking a cue from his rider.

Delaware stayed relaxed. She kept an eye on her target, giving herself time to prepare adequately. She planned ahead, and this time when her mallet hissed through the air, the only thing it ran into was the ball.

Delaware turned to me, grinning. I gave her the thumbs-up. "One hundred percent better."

"So the off side and near side shots, that's four. What about the other ones?" She asked me.

"Okay. This is where it gets crazy." I approached Vegas. "It's probably easiest if I hop on him and demonstrate."

"No problem. I'd love to watch." Delaware halted Vegas and

dismounted. I tweaked the stirrup length to account for my longer inseam and climbed aboard.

I took Vegas up to a canter immediately, and he eagerly obliged. "So you have your near and off side shots," I said, firing them off in succession and speaking over the soft pounding of Vegas' hoof beats. "But you also have your neck, tail and belly shots. They'll give you the full range of motion you need to get yourself out of tight spots and fully master the ball. You'll need them all in your repertoire before you even think about team competition."

Whipping Vegas around so he faced Delaware, I rode down to where the ball lay, reaching over Vegas' withers and dipping the mallet underneath Vegas' churning neck. Flicking my wrist, I scooped up the ball, much like you'd hit a chip shot in golf, and repositioned it so it settled further down the field. Moving my mallet back to the off side, I leaned forward, hitting the ball in front of Vegas.

"Those are the neck shots," I called out, probably unnecessarily, "and this is the tail shot." Vegas surged forward, and I leaned back as he cleared the ball, reaching behind his rump with my mallet. With a quick snap of my wrist, the ball flew clear.

I didn't provide any more commentary, simply concentrating on what lay ahead. With a touch of my outside leg, Vegas positioned his body over the ball, and time slowed down for me.

Making this final shot was a little like grasping in the dark. When you first started out, you were going to come up empty. A lot. It could be elusive, sometimes maddeningly so, if you didn't have the degree of feel it took to know exactly where all of your horse's legs are at any given second.

It was a little like sex in a way. You couldn't see what was happening, you had to go by feel. The smallest shift in angle, timing or technique could make all the difference.

Once you got it down, you knew it forever. It was in your muscle memory. And it felt really, really good, always.

I waited, poised, until the moment before the moment when Vegas' legs would be off the ground. That beat of suspension was my point of entry. I swung, Vegas' hooves rose, and my mallet slipped into the space they'd left behind.

The ball spun off into a new direction, coming to rest at Delaware's feet. She looked up at me, slightly awed. "Wow. How do I get that good?"

"Practice on a live horse every second you can. When you're not on a live horse, be practicing on a wooden horse. Sit on the horse, have a bucket of balls, and practice all the shots. Over and over. Practice until your arm feels like it's about to fall off, then do it some more."

"It's got to be automatic, Delaware. That's the biggest thing, because it only gets more complicated from here. There are rules, intricate rules that have to be followed. There's strategy, and there's melding with your teammates and picking apart your opponents. There are 8 players on a field, sitting on 8 ridiculously fit, fast ponies. There are over a hundred things that could happen at every second. And it's all at a balls-out gallop."

I stepped off Vegas. "So this week you learn the shots. Get them in your muscles, in your brain, so you don't have to think about it. And then we throw everything else at you."

I gave her a questioning glance. "Think you can handle it?"

She mounted up, going through all the shots in the order she'd learned them. And when she ran into trouble, when her mallet caught air or tangled with Vegas' legs, she backed up, took a different approach, and tried again. She deconstructed the movements, the steps, the setup and follow-through. With minimal support from me, she figured it out.

She answered, loud and clear.

Amber

When I got home, I ran into my room without saying "hi" to Dougie. My keys slipped from my hand, crashing to the floor and making that sound. I cringed, but I didn't bother to pick them up. I went to the dresser where I kept my clothes, and I threw every single drawer open.

Cargo pants and oversized drawstring sweatpants revealed themselves to me. I rifled through the drawer, knowing exactly what I would find, but somehow still hopeful that maybe, just maybe, I had some long-buried, presentable thing hidden in here. I almost screamed in relief when I found a pair of jeans, only to discover that they had a massive hole in the vicinity of the back pocket. Like, a hole roughly the size and shape of my right ass cheek.

Okay. So that concludes the pants selection. I shoved the drawer back into the dresser without finesse and moved on in my search.

The T-shirt drawer was an archeological exploration into my dating history. I hadn't purchased a single one of these shirts. I'd lifted them all off ex-boyfriends, whether they knowingly gave their permission or not. As a consequence, they were all ridiculously big on me. That was what I did. I wore baggy, grungy, not-made-for-my-gender clothes. And that was fine. But it wasn't fine right now, because I had a date tonight.

Struck by a sudden burst of inspiration, I tore out of the room and honed in on Dougie. He was in the same place as always. He was a sitting duck.

"Hey, do you have any clothes I could borrow?" I asked him loudly.

Dougie turned his chair around to look at me, his skeletal frame engulfed by an XL T-shirt with Pac-Man graphics on it and stiff blue jeans that looked like they'd walked themselves out of the 1950s.

"Never mind," I groaned.

Dougie watched me circumnavigate the house a few times. "What's going on?" He called out.

I came to a stop in the kitchen/entryway. "I have a date!" I yelled, a little louder than I'd intended.

Dougie's eyes widened. "A date? Like a lady date?"

"*Yes*! What other kind of date would it be?"

"I don't know." Dougie looked embarrassed. "But, I mean, wow. That's great."

"Yeah, except all my clothes are abominations." I stalked away from his eager eyes. "How am I going to do this? I don't know how to *date*!"

"Didn't you, you know, date before?" Dougie sounded confused. "You've dated, haven't you?"

I snorted. "I dated *men*, Dougie. Guys are easy. I never had to put forth any effort whatsoever. In fact, I had to try *not* to get dates. And if I said the wrong thing, or did the wrong thing, or if the guy just straight up decided he didn't like me anymore, it was no big deal. Because it didn't really matter to me anyway."

I raked a hand through my greasy hair. "This matters."

Dougie nodded. "It's good that you care."

I stared at him. "You think so?" I asked tremulously.

"Yeah. I mean, if you don't care, you can't get anywhere." He stopped suddenly. "That was dumb. It rhymed." He rolled his eyes. "Anyway. I'm just saying, you've been waiting a long time for this. Of course you're excited, and nervous, and when you roll up to wherever you're meeting her, you'll probably be a total hot mess. But the point is you're feeling things. And you deserve to feel things."

My vision got all watery. "I want to feel things. All these years I've just felt dead inside…like there was no feeling in me. My heart never picked up; my body never felt on fire. There was no electricity ever, just this horrible nothingness. And now that I'm faced with the possibility of something else, something *more*…it scares the living shit out of me, Dougie."

Dougie nodded, staring into the subtle glow of his computer monitor. "I'm no expert, but I'm pretty sure that's how you know it's truly real."

Erica

I was standing in the barn, holding Delusion for the farrier, when my cell phone buzzed to life. It was Lawrence, so I answered it.

"I've found the answer to all our prayers," he said, before I'd even said hello.

"Really?" I asked, excited. "The ponies were that good?"

"I didn't make it that far," Lawrence said. "But I found something way better."

Now I was curious. "What?"

"I found our fourth member. The person who'll round out the team."

"Wow. That is great news." I held onto my phone in one hand and Delusion in the other, thankful that he was so well behaved. I could not have managed this with Assault.

"I can't wait for you to meet her. Her name's Delaware, and she's terrific."

The farrier had begun nailing the shoe to Delusion's right front, and in the sharp silence that followed, I clung to the hope that the loud, metallic sound of hammer on nail had distorted Lawrence's words.

"She's a girl?"

Delaware was indeed a girl, and not only that, she was a girl who was now all over my house.

She slept on our couch, because it was cheaper than putting her up in a motel, and it gave them more time to train. My freezer was now filled with her favorite foods, because for some reason, she seemed to prefer things that you cook from frozen, like corn dogs, fries and Anytizers. Her long hair was collecting in my shower drain. And it went on.

On the second day, I called Ashley for moral support. She listened to me vent, and after a long pause, she asked, "So you're actually letting this random girl stay in your house for a week?"

Somewhat embarrassed, I said, "Yes..."

"Wow, Erica." Ashley sounded dumbfounded. "You sure are...tolerant."

"Well, it benefits the team," I explained. "Which is really important."

"So are other things," Ashley said quietly.

I pretended like I didn't hear her, and the conversation petered out.

All things considered, Delaware really wasn't a bad houseguest. She didn't have a ton of luggage stacked everywhere. She was gone for long periods of time, stick and balling on the horse outside, so Lawrence and I had our alone time. And even though she was practicing like a fiend all day long, she still found the energy to pitch in around the house. So in spite of myself, I couldn't dislike Delaware. She was a nice girl and a hard worker. And Lawrence seemed really happy to have found her. He sure talked about it enough.

This is the best thing for the team. She rounds out the team perfectly. This is what the team needs.

The team. Everything was about the team. In the early days, he'd been so secretive about it that I'd had no idea what was even going on. I'd been completely shut out. Now, I couldn't go a day without hearing about it, without witnessing its progress. The team was all over my house too. I thought this would be better than the total lack of knowing. I never liked being in the dark before. But I didn't like this either. I liked it even less, which was surprising.

I was gone a lot, so I never really witnessed Delaware's training sessions. All I knew was that she and Lawrence would disappear into the field for hours on end. She'd be on Vegas, and he'd be on Harry or just on foot. The tree line eclipsed my view, and I never followed them. Our lives were separate. He had the team, and I had my horses that earned prize money, and my clients that paid. I had to earn money. One of us had to keep the place afloat.

By my calculations, it was nearing the end of the week. I was cantering Delusion around his first little hunter course when I saw them leave for the field. I finished my session with Delusion, brushed him, and put him back outside. Then I stared at that tree line for a solid minute.

I shook myself. *No. You have work to do. You don't need to see what they're doing.*

You're right. I went to Assault's paddock, trying to put the thought out of my mind. Assault met me on his hind legs. He sensed my indecision, and he was having a field day with it.

I stood there, staring into his hateful, smug face, and I cracked. I dropped the halter and lead on the ground and ran across the yard. Slipping between the trees, I stepped onto the grass.

I didn't have to wait long before Delaware came into view. Vegas was cantering strongly, and she moved in the saddle with ease and grace, hitting the ball from every possible angle. She didn't look down, yet she connected with the ball every time, as if her mallet was magnetically drawn to it.

She was good. She had it. And clearly, they'd been working really hard. I slunk away before I could be seen. *What did you expect?* I thought angrily. *What did you think was going on between them?*

Of course nothing was going on between them. I'd known it all along, and now I'd seen it for myself. But that didn't make me feel any better about what I *had* seen.

Yvette

We drove to the Lexington Polo Club at the appointed time. Courtney fidgeted in the seat beside me, sliding a gold ring up to her knuckle and back down again.

"What a fucking waste of our time," I muttered under my breath.

"It might not be," Courtney said.

"Oh, are you on his side now?" I snapped.

"No, I'm not on his side," Courtney hastened to say. "I'm just saying, maybe he actually saw something in her, other than the fact that she looks good in her jeans."

"Cavanaugh? Not likely." I parked the Voyage and opened the door in quick succession. Heaving a sigh, I waited for Courtney to extricate herself. "Hurry up," I said tersely. "Or you will make us late."

"What does it matter if we're late?" Courtney grunted as she struggled out of her seat. "It's just a freaking waste of our time, you just said..."

"The sooner we have made our appearance and witnessed this atrocity, the sooner we can leave." I began walking, and Courtney caught up with me quickly.

"You mean go back to the Days Inn?" Courtney asked, her voice tentative, floating above my head.

"No, I do not mean we will go back to the Days Inn." I stared straight ahead. "As soon as we are finished here, we are going to check out of the motel. We are going to leave Lexington and return to your father's estate. And Cavanaugh can have his little slut prodigy all to himself."

"Oh my," Courtney quavered. She did not say anything else because we had reached the bleachers and Cavanaugh was standing there waiting for us. He nodded respectfully at Courtney, and then he and I exchanged what could only be described as a look of contempt.

I folded my arms. His jaw tightened, and he stepped to the side, extending an arm. "I present to you, Delaware Freeman."

That name! I clutched my sides and a laugh escaped me. In better company, I would have suppressed the sounds of incredulity and maintained composure. But in that moment, I saw no compelling reason not to allow myself a small chuckle, given the circumstances.

Courtney's hand pushed forcefully into my back. "*Stop*," she hissed.

My head jerked upward, and I saw the girl ride out onto the field. She rode Cavanaugh's bay gelding at a full gallop.

As I watched, she hit the ball, sending it between the goal posts. She did this many times, using every shot known to man. She did not miss once. Each time, she struck the ball and sent it straight into the unguarded goal.

My brain was on fire. My entire head sizzled with activity, from the grey matter within my skull to the hair follicles that stood on end.

Cavanaugh and Courtney were looking in my direction, each of them wanting something from me. In response, I turned away, taking off toward the stable at a dead run.

I pulled one of Courtney's ponies from its stall, snapping the cross ties onto his halter, running my hand down his legs in a cursory check of soundness. Hands flying, I saddled the pony in the span of a few minutes and led it outside. Picking up a stray mallet, I mounted up wearing slacks and street shoes and rode to the field.

Delaware had halted Vegas. She watched me with curiosity and slight apprehension in her eyes. I rode right past her, curling my mallet around the ball and taking it with me.

"See if you can get this from me," I said to her over my shoulder.

Delaware trotted up behind me, her hand loose on the reins. She obviously thought I would be playing on her level.

Fine, then. We will see just how incompetent you are. I put my spur into the pony's side, and he pivoted on his forehand. Delaware hastily pulled up, just before her pony ran face first into my pony's haunches.

Gamely, she tried a new tactic, leg yielding to the side, trying to cut in from that direction. When that didn't work, she rolled back, feinting left and right and picking up speed. She circled around me, accelerating to a gallop and coming straight for me.

I held her off without breaking from a walk.

As she bumbled around me, I stole a glance at the bleachers. Lawrence and Courtney stood side by side, their expressions pained.

"Enough of this," I said gaily. I pulled up, and Delaware did as well.

"I will give this to you." I tapped the ball and it rolled up the field, coming to rest at her pony's hooves. "And you must try to get it into the goal."

"Past me," I added.

Delaware nodded. She took control of the ball, moving away from me. Giving herself space.

I moved into position and she turned, looking right at me. Watching me. She sighted in on the goal, and she hit a perfectly lovely shot. Which I then sent right back into her face, as swiftly as if it were a tennis match.

Delaware dug in. I could see the look of determination on her face, with a bitter edge of pure frustration, like so many opponents I had faced. She rode right up beside me, controlling the ball with a light touch on her mallet, keeping it in her corner. She kept an eye on me, looking for a break. Willing me to lose focus.

If only it were that easy. I would show her that it was not.

I took my eyes away from her and stared off into the distance. I could hear her excited intake of breath. Feel her gather herself, and make the shot.

My mallet flew through the air. I stopped the ball cold without even looking at it.

I turned my head to see her face. She appeared crestfallen. But there was admiration there, too.

"Wow," Delaware said. She sounded out of breath. "How do you do that?"

I regarded her calmly. "I can do it," I said simply, "because I live it."

I rode to the edge of the field and dismounted. I dropped the reins on the animal's neck and looked meaningfully at Courtney.

I saw her sigh. Slowly she walked down from the bleachers and collected her pony. Lifting the reins over his head, she led him to the stable.

Leaving Delaware on the field, I walked over to where Lawrence stood. I came within a foot of him and stopped, facing him head-on.

"She has a long way to go," I said to him.

Lawrence eyed me, his forehead drawn. "I never said she didn't."

"You said that you would find us someone un-sponsored. You never said it would be someone who is completely green."

"She knows all the shots," Lawrence said defiantly.

"Yes. She knows all the shots. And she can execute them, by herself, in a field." I raised my arms. "So what? That does not make her a player!"

Lawrence shook his head, clearly growing impatient. "So she needs work. She's never played with a team before! She needs more practice. Give her a break."

I pressed myself up close against him. "We *never* agreed to this!" I cried.

I stalked away from him, sitting down heavily upon one of the benches. I stood up quickly, doubling back.

"We do not have the *time* or resources to train someone from scratch," I said quietly. "She may have potential. She may have some raw talent. But the gap between what she now knows and what she must learn is insurmountable. We cannot make her into what we need. There is not enough time. Another winter season will pass us by, and she will still be working out how to score a heavily defended goal."

Lawrence looked down at me, his eyes clear and critical. "You don't get it, do you?"

"I do not get what exactly?" I spat.

Lawrence shook his head at me. "There is no one else, Yvette."

"What do you mean, there is no one else?"

"Your points are valid. I get what you're saying here. But I'm telling you, that girl learned in one week what it took me months to pick up. And I'm supposedly this great prodigy."

Lawrence stepped down from the bleachers onto bare ground. "And if you're serious about getting a team together for the winter season, then you need to be investing a large portion of your waking hours into making Delaware the best she can be."

I could only stare at him.

"Because she's *it*, Yvette. She's our chance to make this team happen. No one else is going to step up and play for us. Like it or not, this whole thing hinges on Delaware."

My insides writhed. "But you saw her out there. I just wiped the floor with her. She was absolutely helpless."

"Yeah, I saw that. And you know what, Yvette? It's really comforting to know that you have the capability to wipe the floor with someone who's been playing polo for a whole *week*. Really proves you haven't lost your *edge*, doesn't it?"

"Fuck you," I said, my voice low.

"And you know what else, Yvette? The whole time you were toying with her, basically taking her for a fool and laughing in her face, she didn't give up. She didn't cry; she didn't lose her cool...she kept on trying. You can't train that into someone, Yvette. It's not something you learn; it's something you innately have. It's that hunger I keep talking about. You have it, I have it, and she has it too. She may not have the knowledge and the training, but we can give that to her. And once she has it, she's going to be every bit as good as either one of us on the field."

Lawrence turned away abruptly and went to Delaware. I was left staring at them, together on the field, united. I sat in the bleachers, my head spinning like one of those infernal carnival rides until I let it drop between my knees.

Courtney found me like that some time later. She peered at me in confusion and concern.

"So are we leaving?" Courtney asked me timidly. "Are we going back to Daddy's house?"

I looked at her for a long moment. "Not just yet," I said resignedly.

Erica

It was high noon and the sun loitered in the sky, a dull orb barely showing through the haze of humidity. I was ready for a break, and I needed to fuel up before dealing with Assault. The gelding's cunning disobedience and an empty stomach were never a good combination.

I opened the door, finding Delaware slumbering on the couch. She was almost always in the same place, either lounging on the couch or standing in front of the microwave. She always watched as the high-frequency electromagnetic radiation super-heated her Tyson boneless chicken chunks, taking them from flash-frozen to steaming hot in around a minute or so. I imagined she found the process compelling and somewhat mystifying, much like a Labrador would view a tennis ball being lobbed back and forth.

I clomped past her sleeping form, rummaging through cabinets and pouring cereal into a bowl. The big bowl, because the other bowls were dirty. And also because I wanted the big bowl.

Splashing some milk over the cereal, I set the bottle back in the fridge and walked to the couch, tucking Delaware's legs up underneath her so I had room to sit at one end. Delaware was a heavy sleeper in a class of her own. You could reposition any part of her body to accommodate your need for space, and she wouldn't even twitch.

I almost drifted off myself, falling into a nice cereal haze. I was so focused on the rhythm of spoon to mouth insertion, I didn't even hear a car drive up. But I did hear a knock on the door, and I did yell "Come in!"

A second later my mother stepped across the threshold. Her eyes took in the scene before her, the tableau of Delaware and me on the couch. True to form, she seemed to focus primarily on the large bowl in my hand and the chocolaty contents of my spoon. Her priorities were always in order.

Eventually, her eyes rerouted, and she glanced at me, then back to Delaware. "Who is this?" She asked.

"This is Delaware," I said.

She appeared to be working something over in her mind. "Is this a friend of yours?"

I shook my head. "Nope." I did feel slightly bad for phrasing it that way, even if it was the truth. It wasn't that I *disliked* Delaware.

"Huh." A thin smile had formed on her face. She was wearing one of those goth-looking burgundy lip stains. "I never pegged you for an open relationship. But I'm guessing it probably wasn't *your* idea." Her mouth twisted.

I rolled my eyes. "You've been watching too many soap operas. Delaware is Lawrence's new recruit. He's training her for his polo team."

My mother looked surprised. "I never would have thought." She laughed slightly. "You can understand the conclusion I drew though. She's very pretty."

I raised an un-plucked brow. "So an attractive woman can't have any merit other than relative fuckability?"

My mother blanched. "The words you put in my mouth, Erica! I never said such a thing."

I nodded. "That's true. You merely subscribed to society's unspoken prejudices." *Because you have no thoughts of your own.*

She recovered quickly, batting away my comment like a cat chasing a dust bunny. "How long has she been living with you?"

"A little over a week."

"What happens if she makes the team? Where will she go? Is there a long-term plan?"

I shrugged, lowering my face to the level of the cereal bowl. "I assume there is."

My mother took a step backward, untying and re-cinching her Burberry trench coat at the waist. "My, you're tolerant."

Dougie

Text messages. Inbox (9)

Waiting at the restaurant. SO fucking nervous. Why did I get here early, again? Just so I could fit in the time to have a panic attack in the parking lot?!

Sent from: Amber

I'm not sure about this outfit I picked out. I'm not sure what my personal style is. Aren't I supposed to have personal style as a lesbian? My personal style is basically "long-haul trucker", from what I can tell.

Sent from: Amber

I'm still early. She's still not late. I hope she's on time, because I don't know if I can sit here for too much longer. I'm alarmed by the sheer number of words I'm typing right now, and I'm sure you're really thrilled to be reading them. I'm sorry. I can't stop.

Team Dark Horse

Sent from: Amber
Wow, that was a lot of words. Can't. Stop. Typing. Words.
Sent from: Amber
OMG. She's here! She just drove up. I can't get out of my truck. I don't think I can walk. OMG eeeeeeee!
Sent from: Amber
I'm doing this thing. Wish me luck!
Sent from: Amber
Okay. Bathroom break. I'm NOT doing that thing where you type under the table while you're on a date, so don't yell at me. I'm also not doing that thing where I text you while I'm on the toilet, so don't yell at me about that either. Things are going well. We've talked a lot about our horses, and she wants to meet Maude. And it was hilarious because of course I ordered vegetarian, and according to Kelly, I'm the first lesbian she's ever known who's actually a vegetarian. Apparently that's a well-known lesbian myth. The things I don't know, right?
Sent from: Amber
We're getting ready to head out. I'm nervous. This is usually the time when people kiss, if they're going to. I really want that to happen, but I also don't know if I'm prepared for it. What if girls do it differently? What if I fuck it up? I also kind of want to open the door for her, but I don't know what the protocol is. Is chivalry gay? Is chivalry dead?
Sent from: Amber
OMG. OMG I DID IT I KISSED A GIRL! AND IT WAS AWESOME!!!!!
Sent from: Amber
Options
Select All
Delete

Courtney

Hermione pulled lightly on the reins, expressing impatience and resignation as she stood in the middle of the field. We weren't alone; in fact,

Team Dark Horse

we were surrounded by players and ponies assembled in a neat line. Lawrence on Harry, Delaware on Vegas, and Yvette on Hedge Fund. There were four of us, and I took comfort in the evenness and continuity of the number.

"Set aside your differences," Lawrence was saying, his eyes sharp as he peered out from underneath the brim of his helmet. "From now on, we put all our usual team drills and priorities aside, and we focus on bringing Delaware up to our level. Cut down on your stick and balling, halve your workouts, and use that time to coach Delaware. Everyone should be working with her, not just me." He looked pointedly at Yvette.

I saw her hand tighten around the reins, and Hedge Fund began mincing backward from the pressure. She let up on his mouth and glared at Lawrence with eyes that could cut a rough diamond.

Delaware gathered her reins. She was grinning excitedly, seemingly unaffected by the bristling undercurrent of hostility coursing through the air. "Thanks so much for taking me under your wing, you guys!"

"Let's just do this shit," Yvette deadpanned in her lilting accent that made everything that came out of her mouth sound delicate, even obscenities. Which came out of her mouth quite frequently.

"Alright." Lawrence moved Harry up to a trot, and the rest of the ponies swiftly fell into step with him, relieved to be moving out.

"The objective in polo is to move the ball downfield, into the opposing goal," Lawrence explained, posting smoothly, his seat rising and falling in time with Harry's stride. "Everything is determined by the line of the ball - the trajectory of the ball as it travels downfield. The player who controls the ball has the right of way, and you can't cut directly in front. You stay on either side of the line of the ball, and you look for a way to gain entry without fouling the other player. When fouls happen, the other team gets a free shot at the goal."

"And you don't want that," Delaware said surely.

"No, you don't." Lawrence grinned at her. Throwing a ball onto the field, he picked it up smoothly with his mallet.

"Come on my right, and practice following the line of the ball. When you feel you've got it down, you can attempt to cut in and steal it."

Yvette pulled up abruptly. "I believe I can sit this one out," she said acidly.

"No, you can't," Lawrence snapped. "She needs to get the feel for riding in a group, in close quarters. You're staying right next to her."

Yvette shot him a murderous look and fell back into formation. For a good half hour she rode in perfect silence as we traveled up and down the field at a sedate trot, with Delaware edging out in front, taking control of the ball, and passing it back to Lawrence.

The sky was sunny and hazy, and I was relaxed, sinking into the familiar rhythm of Hermione. Delaware cued Vegas to canter, and as he loped along, she backhanded the ball to me. I spun off in a new direction, and she was hot on my heels, ably giving chase. Lawrence sat in the corner on Harry, beaming like he was watching his daughter play in her first Little League game.

Yvette bowled between us, shattering the moment. She slapped her mallet down, claiming the ball like someone would grab the last dinner roll in the basket, and slamming Hedge Fund to a halt.

Stunned silence followed. "Okay," Delaware piped in, "what she just did was *definitely* a foul."

Yvette ignored her. "I cannot *participate* in this bullshit anymore," she said coldly, turning to Delaware. "You and me. To the goal. *Now.*"

"Yvette, what the *hell* are you *doing*?" Lawrence shouted from across the field.

Yvette lifted her mallet into the air, leaving the ball on the turf, undisturbed. Unguarded. She looked Delaware straight in the eye, a clear challenge.

"I am going to teach her how this game is played!" Yvette thundered. With another searing glance at Delaware, she cantered down to the goal.

"Yvette, no! She isn't *ready!*" Lawrence came barreling in on Harry, exasperation clouding his eyes. "Delaware, stay where you are!"

Delaware hesitated for a split second. Then she snatched up the ball with her mallet and roared downfield.

Lawrence and I huddled together, watching and waiting.

Yvette accelerated, keeping Hedge Fund light and balanced with a sure hand on the reins. This time there were no theatrics. She didn't shut her eyes or stare into the sky. Her eyes were locked on Delaware and her body was poised to block the shot.

My eyes shifted to Delaware, and I saw her do something surprising. In the heat of the moment, she checked Vegas. She half-halted, giving herself a moment to think.

Then she raised her arm over her shoulder and followed through.

I could tell the sheer velocity of the hit from the sound it made. It was a resounding crack, the kind of sound that would stop the heart of your opponents when they heard it. The kind of sound that soaked my body with chills, from my scalp to my tailbone, whenever I made it happen.

"Holy shit," Lawrence muttered. We stared at the ball as it traveled forward, undeviatingly heading for the goal.

Yvette did everything right. She didn't fumble; she didn't bobble. She tried to stop that thing. She tried her guts out. And it slipped right past her.

She knew what had just happened, and she couldn't believe it. I saw her pull up on the spot, and she just stared into the sullied goal.

I glanced at Lawrence, and he looked at me. Slowly, we both started grinning, and after a while, we just couldn't stop.

Delaware cantered around to us, a hopeful look on her youthful, radiant face. "Was that good? That was good, right?"

Lawrence struggled to speak. "I think I'll let Yvette answer that one for you," he said smugly.

We turned. Yvette had dismounted and was leading Hedge Fund up the field. He stepped out smartly at her shoulder, and she trudged along at the pace of a funeral march.

We parted as she walked into our midst, and Delaware watched her, clearly apprehensive.

Yvette came to a stop. Her teeth were clenched, and her lips were tight against her skull. Her entire body radiated intense loathing. She looked positively radioactive with it.

"*Well played*," Yvette hissed, her voice strained.

"Thank you, Yvette," Lawrence said condescendingly. "I know how hard that was for you."

She gave him the finger and led Hedge Fund away.

Lawrence turned to Delaware, his cheeks colored from excitement. "Do you know how many people are able to do what you just did?"

Delaware shrugged. "Not a lot?"

"You can't just get one past Yvette," I affirmed. "That doesn't happen. Like ever."

"She looks pretty mad now," Delaware commented reasonably.

"She'll get over it," Lawrence said dismissively.

"No, she won't," I corrected. "She'll always hold a grudge. But that doesn't mean she won't be an effective team player."

"Does that mean you want me for the team?" Delaware asked.

"*Hell* yes," Lawrence said, reaching out to give her a friendly squeeze.

I looked around, trying to see where Yvette had disappeared to. Hopefully she was taking care of Hedge Fund, and I wouldn't find him fully tacked up in a stall, ready to put a leg through the reins or scrape his saddle on the manger. I thought about rushing off to console her, but instead I leaned over Hermione's withers, slipping my arms around her narrow chest and breathing in her salty, warm, leathery horse smell.

The team was real now, and I was a part of it.

Part Three

Wilson

Dusk was approaching and the lights out in front of the stable had come on. They burned a dull, occasionally flickering orange swath of light, and I never did understand how that was supposed to deter intruders. It sure hadn't stopped Cavanaugh, way back.

The ponies were in for the night, and the aisle was dark and quiet. The only thing audible was the steady crunch of equine molars mowing down hay. The only pony who wasn't eating with her usual enthusiasm was Platinum Choice. Head in the corner, she stood stoic, with her belly clenching and unclenching periodically. Occasionally she would lick and chew, submitting to the pain, or perhaps just keeping her mouth moist like a person would.

I leaned over the stall door, finding Elaine sitting in the corner on Platinum's untouched hay.

"How is she?" I asked.

Elaine looked up at me, unsurprised by my appearance. We had seen each other from this vantage point many times over the course of the day, and since the other workers had gone home, she hadn't moved from the stall.

"Gut sounds are present and remaining consistent. Skin maintaining its elasticity, no dehydration. Mucous membranes are pink and moist. Manure output is intermittent, but considering her decreased appetite, it seems reasonable. She's definitely not impacted."

I nodded, watching the mare carefully. "A bad heat," I said.

"Looks that way." Elaine smiled tenderly. "I can sympathize. Cramps are a bitch."

I rested my elbows on the stall door. "Do you mind keeping an eye on her for me?"

Elaine looked at me in surprise. "Do you have somewhere to be?"

I blushed, my eyes slipping away from hers. "I'm supposed to be meeting Barbara tonight. Of course, I can cancel," I hastily added. "She would understand."

"No! No, that's okay." Elaine drew her knees up to her chest. "I don't mind watching Platinum. I just didn't think you would want me to. That's all."

"You know what you're doing," I said. "And you care. That's good enough for me."

"Well, thank you," Elaine said quietly. "That means a lot."

I stood up, stretching out my back, forever tight from too much office work. "Call me if anything changes. If she starts to get fractious, or depressed, or if you even suspect something is changing. Don't hesitate to call."

Elaine nodded. "I will." She smiled at me from the stall floor. "Have a good evening with Barbara."

"Thank you," I said.

I started to leave and turned back just as quickly. "Elaine?"

Her eyes flicked upward. "Wilson?"

I hesitated, and then I went through with it. "We're…the club is having a fundraiser a week from Saturday. At the Davenport Hotel."

"Hmmm." She looked like she wasn't quite sure why I was telling her this.

I wasn't sure either. *This was a stupid idea.* "What I mean is, you're invited. If you want to come."

She stared at me.

"There will be food there. It's catered." *This was a really bad idea.* "And there's an open bar."

She laughed briefly. "An open bar. All the more reason for me to stay away."

I glanced down at her, sitting in hay, her hair grown out to her chin, her skin luminous. So different from when Cavanaugh brought her in.

"Well, as a valued employee of this club, I would be happy to have you there," I said. "But I understand if you would rather not go."

Elaine was silent for a minute. "Thank you, Wilson," she said slowly. "I'll think about it."

She wrapped her arms around her stomach and stared into the line of tightening muscle on Platinum's belly.

Erica

I was facing the last lesson on a Tuesday. My final obligation before I could go home and work with my own horses. The promise of freedom spurred me onward, while the growing realization that it was already 6 PM drove me down and made it harder for me to get excited about it.

The student, Anna, a college girl who seemed to ride with a great deal of ambition but no focus at all, was longing her horse in the middle of an outdoor ring that desperately needed a pass with a harrow and about fifty gallons of water sprinkled over the surface. Her horse, a flea-bitten grey with elaborate pinto markings that only showed when he was soaking wet, orbited her haphazardly, swinging in and out on the circle with his body bent in the wrong direction.

She turned around when I approached. Her horse slammed on the brakes and walked right up to her, nearly entangling himself in the longeline. I didn't see a saddle anywhere in sight, and I began mentally tallying the minutes it would take her to get ready.

"I don't know what's gotten into him today," she explained, her tone stopping just short of a whine. "I need to longe him some more. He's too forward."

It's a nice night. The air's crisp. He's in a good mood. Why shouldn't he be forward? "I thought we talked about our plan for today," I said diplomatically. "We were going to work on channeling the forward. So it might help if we *kept* some of the forward."

Anna shrugged. "Okay. I'll get him saddled." She walked away, coiling up the longeline the wrong way, so if her gelding took off it would tighten around her hand and she'd be dragged into next week. Her horse slouched along behind her, putting the bare minimum of effort into his steps.

Her horse wasn't even that forward. It was the classic example of someone who nagged and pushed and prodded their horse ineffectively, making the animal as responsive and peppy as a car parked on blocks with the head gasket removed. So they complained about how their horse wouldn't move forward, but as soon as it moved forward at all, they freaked out and couldn't deal with it.

If I had liked Anna enough, I would've facilitated a real teaching moment and put her on one of my horses who *did* move forward. She would never experience a truly forward ride on her gelding, not if she kept training him the way she did. And she really needed to experience the sensation, to have her eyes opened.

There were clients, like Maggie, who had something going for them. That spark, that drive. The dedication.

There were clients you went out of your way for, and there were clients who just paid the bills.

Anna emerged from the barn with a fully tacked horse. Joining me in the ring, she mounted up and gave her gelding's sides an obvious squeeze. He shuffled into a walk.

She started to gather up the reins, and his head tipped in toward his chest. "Let him walk on a long rein for a minute," I called out. "I want to talk about what we're looking to achieve here."

Anna let the reins out, and her gelding dropped his head. His stride lengthened.

"Everyone knows they want their horse forward and on the bit," I said. "But most everyone goes about it the wrong way. They'll take up on their horse's mouth, focusing on the frame above all else. And then, when they have the outline they want, and the horse looks to be in the correct shape, they'll try to add the forward. It doesn't work, because the aids are conflicting. The hand is holding back, saying 'stop', while the legs say 'go'."

Anna glanced at me. "But isn't that how collection works?"

"Yes. Collection does involve conflicting aids. It's a balancing act between seat, leg and hand. But true collection starts with forward movement. Before anything else, you must make sure your horse is freely moving forward. And then you channel that energy. You take it in your hands, compressing it and containing it. Little by little, you shift your horse's balance back to his hindquarters."

"So let's start." I walked alongside Anna and her gelding. "Take him up to a trot. Collection begins with impulsion, and the walk has no impulsion. That's why collected walk is a more advanced movement, one we'll save for later."

Anna booted her gelding in the sides, and he pulled himself into a lazy trot. Instinctively, her hands crept up the reins.

"Leave his mouth alone," I said loudly. "Throw away the contact, and focus on getting him forward. You want him to feel quick, even a little out of control. Just get him *forward*."

She gave me a quizzical look, but she dropped her hands and pushed him on. I watched as they circled the ring, keeping my eyes on his feet, looking for that lengthened stride, for the bending of joints.

"Okay," I called out, beckoning her closer. "This is where the fun starts. Keep him moving forward. Sit tall. Think of the balance you want him to have, and create that in your body. Take a light feel of his mouth, and elevate your hands slightly. Think of catching the energy and holding it, rerouting it back into your body. You're not stopping it. You're containing it and *lifting* it, just a smidge."

Even as I said all that, I knew what she would do. Sure enough, she snatched up the reins and set her hand, catching him in the mouth and causing him to lose all the energy he'd built up, as quickly as the air would gush from an untied balloon.

"Try it again," I said. "Softer this time. You're not stopping him, you're *containing* him. Be subtle."

She pushed him forward before I could even remind her to ease up on the reins. He raised his head, gaping his mouth, and her fists tightened. The gelding balked, raising a hind leg in frustration.

She turned to me. "I don't think he's getting it."

"Get off," I said.

She peered at me, her eyes critical underneath the brim of her helmet. "*Excuse* me?"

Breathing out slowly, I said, "I think I should get on him and show you what I mean."

"If you can." Anna dismounted, rolling her eyes at the gelding.

I strode up to him, adjusting the stirrups to accommodate my longer inseam. "May I borrow your helmet?" I asked pleasantly.

"Sure," Anna shrugged, handing it to me. Her head was slightly more egg-shaped and narrower than mine, but I let out the dial, and it settled onto my head well enough.

I mounted up, picking up the reins at the buckle and asking him to walk with a soft brush of my calves. When he failed to respond, I put my heels into him, a quick, sharp jab. He startled into a walk and I dropped the pressure, ruffling the hair that lay over his meaty withers.

My legs were not the legs of a beginner - clumsy, inept, and often nagging. My legs were educated, able to lie perfectly still against a horse's sides, and in the next instant, deliver a pointed message. Riding was a delicate balancing act of tact and gentleness, assertiveness and control.

My eyes shifted to Anna as she stood in the center of the ring, watching me with her arms folded. As an instructor, I tried never to do this. Oftentimes, it was a cheap shortcut for a trainer to take, getting on the horse and making it look good in the short-term, instead of really buckling down and walking the student through the problem, giving them the tools to make changes on their own. But Anna just wasn't getting it.

I was reminded of what she'd said about her horse. *He's just not getting it.*

I asked him to trot the same way I'd asked for the walk, a feather-light request. He was quicker to answer me this time. The arc of my seat rising and falling mirrored his stride as it steadily quickened. My calves hugged his sides, pulsing on and off, asking him for more.

I left him alone up front and moved him up to a good working trot, just as I'd instructed Anna to do. Then I picked up the reins smoothly, connecting with his mouth. At the same time, my legs touched him. My eyes looked ahead, not down at his neck.

He moved forward with nary a bobble.

Approaching a corner, I sat up, engaging my core, bringing my weight back toward his hind end. My inside leg squeezed his side, bending him strongly through the curve. My outside hand lifted, holding gently but firmly to his mouth. My inside hand softened. Its only purpose now was to occasionally vibrate, maintaining the proper flexion at his poll.

For two beats I closed my hand. Lowered my posting. Through the saddle, and down through his body, I felt his hind leg pause and gather beneath him.

I closed my leg again, maintaining my own balance, keeping the contact but easing my hands forward by about an inch. He whooshed forward, raising his back underneath me, his neck a wonderful, soft crescent, his compliant mouth as soft as butter.

He flew down the long side, and at the next corner I half-halted again, rebalancing him, shortening his stride through the short side. I transitioned to a walk in the corner, then brought him smartly back up to a trot, working him through bent lines and straight lines, halts and rein-backs.

I was unaware of the passage of time. I was unaware of the fact that I was supposed to be teaching a riding lesson, not schooling this horse. I was caught up in the feel of it, the heady rush of being completely in tune with an animal. I was intoxicated by the brilliance of two separate beings working as one, striving for the perfect balance, overcoming all our combined imperfections. Together.

Only the shadow of dusk approaching could bring me back.

I let out the reins, letting the gelding stretch as he walked on the rail. "That's a good boy," I said softly. "Those muscles are going to be a little sore tomorrow I bet. This is probably the first time you've ever used them, huh?"

He paused and shook himself, blowing though his nostrils contentedly.

I let him walk for a full five minutes before bringing him over to where Anna stood. I dismounted, hopping once as I landed to lessen the shock of slamming into the hard-packed dirt.

"So, that's kind of what you're looking for," I said to her. "He's obviously capable, as you see." I tried not to look gleeful at her expense. "Now that you have a visual of what you're going for, it should be easier for you to achieve it. We'll have you guys looking that good at your next lesson," I finished confidently.

Anna took her horse's reins from me. "Oh, I don't know about that…"

"Of course you'll be able to," I argued on her behalf, even though I wasn't entirely convinced myself. "It just takes a little practice. It's a lot going on at once. But we'll practice all the aids in sequence, and then you'll put them together. You'll do fine."

"Oh, I didn't mean it like *that*," Anna said, stopping me short. "I saw what you did. It didn't look that hard. I'm sure I can do it on my own now."

White noise engulfed my head. I stared at her numbly. *Really? That's what you took from that?*

Anna started leading her horse out of the arena, further signaling that she was done with me. "You can leave the helmet on that gate post," she said over her shoulder.

I stood there for a minute, watching them leave. Then I did the only thing I could do. I unfastened the helmet and left it on the gate post, just as I'd been told.

When I started my truck, the headlights came on automatically, burning a bright path through the growing darkness.

I got on the road to home, a meandering stretch of two-lane highway. Thickly lined by trees on either side, it was prime deer habitat. It was never wise to push the speed limit here.

As I drove, darkness descended. The trees became mere silhouettes, black trunks and craggy branches looming menacingly all around. Through the spaces between tree limbs, the sky lit up in a pale, bruised red.

I pressed my foot down on the accelerator, and suddenly I was barreling down the narrow two-track, leaning on the wheel, staring out helplessly at the nightfall.

And I knew I was never going to win.

Delaware

Yvette hadn't gotten any nicer since I'd started living down the hall from her. I saw her all the time now, usually when I was on my way to the microwave. Instead of having one in every room like some of the better chains, this Days Inn had only one microwave down by the lobby. I didn't mind that at all, because going down to the lobby meant there was always someone to talk to. Like other people using the microwave, for instance, or the motel clerk, so I got a nice conversation along with my meal.

Being in the lobby also meant running into Yvette a lot. She always seemed to be getting back from someplace, and when I saw her, it was always the same. She'd stare at the food in my hand like it was something rotten, and she'd walk past me without a word. It was like we didn't even know each other.

The only time she acknowledged me was when we went to practice. She'd started driving me and Courtney over to the polo club separately, because her car only fit two people, and she wouldn't let Courtney drive her Hummer because of the environmental toll or something. So, every day she made two trips from the motel to the polo club and two trips back again.

Right now she was banging on my door, so I hopped off my bed and opened it.

"We are leaving in five, Podunk," she greeted me in her usual way.

"I'm ready now," I said brightly.

"We leave in five," Yvette snapped, and she shut the door in my face.

I sat around for a couple minutes, and then I went down to the lobby to wait for her. Soon, she was at my back, and her short, tight stride overtook mine. She started up her car, buckling her seat belt and pulling out of the parking space before I'd gotten my door closed.

Yvette played her music loud the whole way, canceling any chance of a conversation. She liked weird music by a girl with a wailing voice who sang about knives and coffins and girls with one eye. She did have one track I enjoyed, though. It was a song with a joyous rhythm, a strong drumbeat and a line that went, "The dog days are over, the dog days are done, the horses are coming, so you better run".

As usual, Yvette dropped me off at the stable and shot back down the driveway in reverse, peeling out onto the roadway without pausing or looking. She drove like I'd only seen people drive in movies. I walked into the stable humming the "dog days" song.

Vegas was waiting for me in the cross ties. He'd been brushed already and his legs were wrapped, so I went to work putting his saddle on.

I was just about to bridle him when Elaine walked past me. "Delaware, your girth's on backward," she said without stopping.

"Oh, crap." I pulled on the straps again, unhooking the girth and putting it back the right way. "I can't get a handle on this English tack."

Yvette arrived just then with Courtney trailing her. "Why are you not ready?" She demanded. "I bring you here first so you may have extra practice time, not so you can fuck up the saddling process."

"Give her a break," Courtney muttered. "She's never ridden English before."

"Precisely."

Courtney sighed, letting herself into Hermione's stall, pulling off the mare's yellow stable sheet. In the stall next door, Yvette saddled Harris, another pony of Courtney's, with the blank-faced enthusiasm of someone slicing cold cuts at a deli.

Soon, we joined Lawrence on the field. Harry was antsy, anticipating the session ahead, so Lawrence rode him out to the edge of the field and cantered him in different figures to take his mind off things. Harry chewed the bit, dropping wads of white foam onto his chest and the grass, ears back as his body lifted up. His hooves seemed to hover over the ground, and when he passed me, the sound they made was as soft as a roll of toilet paper landing on the floor.

When our ponies were warmed up, Lawrence rode Harry over to us. I fingered the mallet in my hand, a slightly nervous habit I'd developed. The real work of the day was about to begin.

Lawrence looked over at me. "You ready, Delaware?"

I forced a smile. "As I'll ever be," I replied.

Harry's hooves, which had patted the grass so softly moments ago, ricocheted off the turf and sent chunks of it flying. He leapt into the air, and then his body dropped low, crouching down and moving impossibly fast.

All the ponies around me, and the one under me, did the same thing. They were moving full-out, like mustangs on the prairie, feeding off each other, racing together like a solid wall of wildfire. They were under control, but just barely.

The ponies rumbled down the field, packed tightly together. The sound of their hooves slamming into the ground was deafening. Vegas was smooth, very much a Cadillac to old Toby's pile driver, but at this speed the force of his steel-shod hooves hitting the turf radiated up into my spine, jostling my whole body. And out ahead of us on this field, there was a ball.

I peered ahead, trying to focus. I needed to get out in front, but Yvette was steadily pushing me off my line. I tried to push back, and it seemed to be working. *I just need to gain a little more ground...*

Yvette put her spurs into her pony and was off like a shot. I tried to give chase and Courtney blocked me. My pony slammed up against hers and Yvette captured the ball.

Just like that, the action ground to a halt.

"Sorry," Courtney mouthed at me.

"It's alright," I said. "I botched that one up pretty good..."

"Don't worry about it," Courtney said, moving away from me on Hermione. "Everybody makes mistakes when they start out."

That was the thing. I was starting out, and there was still so much I didn't know. There were rules, complicated rules to this game, but Lawrence hadn't talked me through them all yet. He said he wanted me to take it one thing at a time. He didn't want to overload me with facts when what I needed was feel. But sometimes not knowing things meant that I wound up looking like an idiot on the field.

Polo was more intense than anything I'd ever done. It was a physical workout that knocked the stuffing out of you, and a mental workout more challenging than the ACTs, all rolled into one like a Hot Pocket. I had to have eyes on everyone at once, and if I looked at one player too long, someone else would sneak in. It was like driving on the interstate, except there were no lanes and no exits and people could run into you at will.

"Let's try another scenario," Lawrence's voice broke into my thoughts. "Give Delaware some space. Yvette, leave the ball upfield."

Yvette was playing her own private game with the ball, turning it back and forth, and she paid him no mind.

"*Yvette!*" Lawrence shouted.

Team Dark Horse

"I can *hear*," she bellowed liltingly at him, leaving the ball and cantering downfield.

"Okay." Lawrence turned to me. "You've broken away from the pack. Now set yourself up and make your shot. Remember, the opposing goal is downfield, near us."

"Right. Okay." I cued Vegas and he shot forward.

I didn't really think about it, I just rode up to the ball, and when I got near it, I raised my arm and prepared to backhand it.

"Turn it!" Courtney shouted at me from downfield.

I didn't know what that meant, so I wavered and hit a terrible shot. The ball skittered sideways, and even as I whipped Vegas around, I knew Yvette would be right there to claim it.

She was.

She fired it off into the goal and then turned to face me, looking smug.

"When the field is wide open," Yvette started in on me, "you must *turn* the ball so it faces the goal, and hit a forehand shot. Give yourself every chance to succeed. Because you will need it," she threw in cuttingly.

"Thanks," I said, because at least now I knew what *turn it* meant. "I guess I'm just not at the top of my game today."

"That must change," Yvette said clearly. "Up your game, Podunk. Or the game will go on without you, as will this team."

She rode away from me. I sat on Vegas with my arm at my side. Every muscle in it was stretched and aching. My hand stung.

I wanted an adventure. That was why I came here. But I hadn't come here to lose myself, and right now I was a long way from the carefree girl in that cornfield.

Amber

Kelly and I lay in bed together side by side. We were close enough to touch, but we hadn't yet. Kelly had propped her head up with one arm and her other hand lay tucked beneath her body as if she were keeping it there by force. The overhead light was off, and the room was dimly lit by a bedside lamp with a single bulb.

Expectations fluttered around the room, mine and hers. All the while, I struggled not to have them.

Kelly leaned in a bit closer. "We can take things slow if you want," she said gently.

I let her words settle on my brain. *Does that make it better? Is that what I want?*

"No," I said urgently, deciding something. "That's not what I want." And I rolled on top of her.

I kissed her, settling into the familiar, swirling rhythm of her tongue in my mouth. Breaking away for a moment, I quickly maneuvered out of my clothes. Kelly made an attempt to do the same, but her hands were slow and fumbling, and as she stared at me, they stopped moving altogether.

"Here," I murmured, reaching over and yanking her shirt over her head. Setting it aside, I tucked myself into her waiting arms, feeling the heady, comforting sensation of flesh on flesh.

Kelly sighed deeply beneath me, an exhalation that stopped just short of a moan. "That's more like it."

I took a deep breath and continued.

I had been afraid, all this time, that I wouldn't know what to do next. That being with a girl would throw me off. That I would appear helpless, or inept, or just plain incompetent. I had resented the implied learning curve, the return to square one.

But as I slipped my hand down her belly, I realized something. In all of my previous relationships, I'd been awkward, unsure. A lot of the time I'd chalked it up to a lack of interest in sex, but more often, it was just me straight up not knowing what to do next and waiting for the guy to take the lead. Which they did, usually very poorly.

I *had* been clueless. But now, I knew exactly what to do.

My fingers moved against her, mirroring the touch I used on myself, and I felt her body go limp. She opened herself up to me, and I explored thoroughly, gently at first and then harder, my hand slick with wetness. I moved my fingers steadily, feeling her muscles loosen and change shape, allowing me further inside.

Excitedly, I pulled back, dropping low and pressing my mouth against her. Licking steadily, I tasted her tangy, cushiony flesh, delving inside her with my tongue and then returning to encircle the tiny ridge of her clitoris with its firm point.

Pulsing my tongue against her, I increased the pressure as she arched into me, moving her hips in time with my mouth, her hands pulling my hair. I moaned softly as I felt her muscles start to quiver, reaching a hand between my own legs and rubbing vigorously, breaking through the wetness, finding some friction.

Everything inside me tightened, the pressure building as I stroked my engorged clitoris. I held back until Kelly's body relaxed and sank into the mattress, and then my vision went hazy as I came roughly, abruptly.

When it was over, I flipped my hair back behind my shoulders and crawled back up to lay beside Kelly.

She looked at me, her eyes hooded. "Was that really your first time doing that?"

I shrugged happily. "Yup."

"Goddamn." Kelly shook her head in wonder. "You're a natural."

I settled in behind Kelly, turning her over and pulling her close. Resting my chin on her shoulder, I placed a hand over one of her breasts.

We lay there for a while. Eventually, I felt her stir.

"I'm sorry I didn't reciprocate," she said. "I was going to, you just took me by surprise, and then…"

"It's okay," I cut her off. "We'll have time for that later."

"Okay," Kelly said, reassured.

She snuggled into me, and we fell into silence. I felt our breathing sync up.

"Right now I just want to do this," I said.

Lawrence

Delaware sat on a bench outside the LPC, her chestnut hair fluttering over one shoulder. She looked up when I approached. "Where are Yvette and Courtney?"

"Yvette's not coming back, and Courtney's not coming, period." I sat down beside her. "I'm giving them the day off, because I wanted you to have a special one-on-one session."

Delaware dropped her chin into her hand. "I know! I'm a mess out there lately. I don't know what I'm doing, and it shows."

"No, that's *not* why I'm doing this." I reached behind her and thumped her on the back a couple times. "Get dressed. I'll saddle Vegas."

"Aren't you riding?" Delaware asked.

I shook my head. "Nope. I have to give Harry a day off every once in a while. Not that he appreciates it."

She cocked her head. "So how is it a one-on-one if you're not riding with me?"

I smiled slyly. "You're riding with someone *else*."

Her eyes got big. "*Who?*"

"Go get dressed," I said, laughing. "You'll see in a minute."

I wrapped Vegas' legs in a clean pair of white polos, stretching the cotton material over his cannon bones. After each leg was wrapped, I tightened the girth by one hole. By the time Delaware came jogging down the aisle, Vegas was ready.

"Start your warm-up," I told her as we walked the short distance to the field. "Your victim should be arriving shortly."

Delaware twisted in the saddle. "What d'you mean, victim?"

I bit back a grin. "You'll see."

I stood on the sidelines resting one leg while Delaware put Vegas through his paces. The sunlight caught in his coat, burnished bronze moving over the bright, Astroturf-green of the field. Lean, with a hint of ribs showing and the muscle lying flat over his skeleton, Vegas was in peak condition.

Delaware stood in the stirrups and Vegas' stride opened up underneath her. She was already developing a rapport with him that was visible to the naked eye, a language of aids that communicated more by saying less. Despite my history with the gelding, I had already begun to think of him as

Team Dark Horse

Delaware's horse.

When I was able to catch her eye, I flagged Delaware down. She trotted over to me.

"I know it's been tough on you," I said. "I brought you here, away from everything you know, and I'm asking you to do the impossible. I'm asking you to rise up and play polo at the level that our team needs. And it's hard. I get that. But I'm asking you to do it because *I know you can*."

I went on. "Your learning curve is steep. It's not really even fair to call it a *curve* at this point. You're playing with 9- and 10-goal players. You're playing with two women who are inarguably the finest players the Women's Polo Federation has ever had on their roster. And that might discourage you. That might make you think you aren't any good or that you don't belong here."

I looked in her eyes. "But you *do* belong here. And I'm going to show you how good you really are."

She was about to respond, but we both fell silent as a keyed-up pony with a bright chestnut coat and pinned ears took to the field.

Firewall.

Paul Miller sat astride him wearing his usual attire. Pressed white breeches, embossed knee guards, Austrian-made boots and a cocky smirk. Sandy hair fell around his ears in waves. He never wore a helmet for stick and balling, and if you asked me, he'd been hit on the head a few too many times.

And I had a pretty good grasp on that figure since I'd hit him a fair number of times in my day, on and off the field.

"That's Paul Miller, the star player of Lexington Polo Club's senior team," I said. "Say hello."

Without hesitating, Delaware rode Vegas up to him, while I slipped into the stands, unseen.

"Hi, I'm Delaware," I heard her say. She stuck her hand out, a big smile on her face.

Miller looked her up and down, seemingly baffled but pleased by her sudden appearance. "I'm Paul Miller. Nice to make your acquaintance," he said slimily.

Team Dark Horse

Delaware shook his hand, then sat upright in the saddle. "Do you want to play one-on-one?" She asked brightly.

Miller actually guffawed a little. "Sure. Why not?" He said, in the general direction of her tits.

"Great!" Delaware threw in the ball, following the line of it like a hound on a scent trail. Miller loped along beside her, seeming to take it for granted that she wouldn't be able to make the shot. He watched, seemingly dumbfounded, as she hit a perfect shot and followed it up, sending the ball to rest between the goal posts.

Delaware turned the ball, bringing it back into play. With a toss of his head, Firewall yanked Miller's hand forward and leapt up to attack the ball. Miller raised his mallet, preparing to strike.

He didn't get the chance. Vegas moved deceptively fast, meeting Firewall head-on. Delaware hit a neck shot while Paul Miller's mallet caught air. Firewall's teeth gnashed, his incisors snapping shut mere inches from Vegas' ear.

"Your pony sure is spunky!" Delaware sang out as she wheeled Vegas away from the pissed-off chestnut. Firewall tore off after them, lugging Paul Miller along as he sat in the saddle with a dazed look on his face, totally ineffective.

When Delaware captured the ball for the third time, Miller snapped into action, booting Firewall with his spurs. In response, the gelding ducked his head and let fly with both hind feet, nearly pitching Miller off headfirst. I could hardly blame the gelding. Actually, I felt like applauding him. Miller was behaving like a spoiled child, and Firewall had just taken the wind out of his sails.

Miller settled back into the saddle, and began the task of chasing down Delaware. He let Firewall open up, until he was tailing her, staying alongside the line of the ball like Delaware had been doing in our drills. But this time, instead of being the one who inched along and fumbled and fought for a way in, Delaware was the seasoned pro in command of the ball, and she held him off effortlessly.

Miller tried to force her off her line, implementing the ride-off and running Firewall into Vegas repeatedly, staying between the gelding's hip

Team Dark Horse

and shoulder. Instead of fighting back, Delaware used the empty field to her advantage and turned the ball. Vegas cornered efficiently on his hind legs, and Delaware backhanded it into the goal before Miller had even gotten his pony turned around.

"Come on!" Delaware laughed. Her smile was huge, her face radiant. She filled up the whole field - her beauty, her happy, carefree nature, and the complete ease with which she slayed Paul Miller. "You're *letting* me win! You can try harder than that!"

In the beginning, Paul Miller had maybe decided to play nice and let her win. But now he was trying his guts out. The amusement had gone out of his face, which was slack from exertion. His hair flopped at the back of his head, damp with sweat. His hands formed tight fists, and his movements became increasingly jerky as the minutes passed.

Vegas had come alive under Delaware, his quick-flying feet skipping over the ground as he skirted Firewall like a snake charmer faced with a cobra. Almost hypnotically he moved in, a stride-length away, then even closer. Firewall would lunge for him, and Vegas would feint to the side, dropping back to passage when he'd regained the distance between them.

Through all this, Delaware kept the ball. They worked together, two bodies on the same mission. Delaware put her faith in Vegas to take them where they needed to go, and she controlled the line of the ball, no matter how fast Vegas' feet moved. Her brain moved just as fast.

Finally, Paul Miller pulled up. Firewall fought his hold, gnashing his teeth against the bit. Even when Miller got him stopped, he still inched toward Vegas with a look of venom in his eye.

"If you'll excuse me," Miller wheezed, leaning over the pommel, red in the face, "I need to get back to practicing."

Delaware lifted her rein hand. Vegas halted neatly. "Why, sure!" She smiled. "It's all yours."

And she passed the ball to him.

Unable to contain myself any longer, I leapt down from the bleachers and strode onto the field. Miller saw me immediately. His eyes narrowed.

"I see you've met Delaware," I called out. "My new protégé." Coming up alongside Delaware, I rested an arm over Vegas' withers. "Tell me, Miller, did you enjoy your one-on-one time?"

He didn't answer, just turned Firewall around and flipped me the bird.

"Classy guy." I turned to Delaware. "Anyway, I thought you should know. That guy is the star player of Lexington Polo Club's senior team. And you just made him look like he hadn't played a day in his life."

I looked in her eyes, grinning. "That's how good you are."

Erica

Keeping one eye on the clock, I pulled on my boots and began the nerve-wracking task of zipping them up. These zippers had gone almost a full year without breaking, and they had certainly seen better days. Many of them.

"Don't break, don't break, don't break," I hissed as I gently forced the zipper upward, closing the boot over my calf. "Not right now, not right now, not right now...."

By luck or prayer the zippers held, and I was officially dressed. Heaving a sigh of relief, I took one last glance at myself in the mirror, confirming that nothing was out of place. Then I stepped out of my trailer's dressing room and back into the unfolding horse show.

I'd left Assault at home, and you could immediately discern his absence by the scene of complete serenity around my trailer. Soiree, the veteran of nearly half a season stood contentedly, watching the goings-on with the horsey equivalent of an eager grin on her face. Delusion was tied next to her, stuffing his mouth full of hay. Two model citizens.

11 a.m. Right on schedule, Martha appeared, dressed up in cream-colored slacks and a white blouse. "How's my boy today?" She asked, glancing fondly at Delusion.

I gestured to where he stood, quiet as a whisper. "What can I say? He's perfect."

She grinned at me and handed me a plastic cup with a straw sticking out of the lid. "I got you a Coke at the concession stand. Figured you might need a pick-me-up."

"Thanks," I said, reaching for the beverage even though it was pure sugar and highly unlikely to calm my nerves. "I appreciate it."

"Well, you're working hard," Martha said kindly. "You deserve a little support."

I'm glad someone thinks that, I thought as I smiled gratefully at her.

The loudspeaker crackled to life, and I listened for the current class number. If there was one thing I'd gotten out of all my years working with horses, it was a finely-tuned, superhero-worthy sense of hearing. Between deciphering garbled (and extremely far away) loudspeaker announcements, listening for unevenness in my horse's stride as I rode, and straining to hear whether a rail that had taken a hard rub would stay in the jump cups while I was on course, my hearing was definitely above average. Despite my mom's insistence that listening to my music too loud would make me deaf.

The classes were moving quickly. I turned to Martha. "I should get Delusion tacked up." I reached for his saddle pad, freshly laundered and Oxy-Clean-bright white. Once it lay smooth over his back, I placed the saddle on top of it. After I fastened the girth and tightened it once, Martha went to his head, slipping off his halter and easing the bit into his mouth.

"It's that time again," I said to the gelding. Mounting up, I settled into the saddle, stepping into my right stirrup so it sat straight over his topline.

"Will Soiree be okay here by herself?" Martha asked.

"Yeah, she'll be fine." I glanced back at the mare as she pricked her ears in my direction. "If you want, you can untie her and bring her along. If you don't mind holding onto her. She likes to watch stuff happen."

"That sounds like a lovely idea." Martha pulled the quick-release knot on Soiree's lead rope, inviting the mare to walk on with her. Soiree eagerly obliged.

Delusion walked calmly as we picked a path through the trailers with Soiree and Martha in tow. I kept him on contact, riding defensively through the crowd. Keeping an eye on every errant horse, I piloted Delusion safely to the warm-up ring. I paused for a second, then rode into the fray.

The ring was already teeming with horses from Delusion's division. Young, inexperienced horses crossing paths with each other in a space as tight and pressure-filled as a kettle. Delusion had brains and good sense on his side. Quite a few of these horses didn't.

Delusion blanched, losing the momentum in his stride. Staring at the swirling mass of horses, he bobbled, unsure of himself. I wrapped my legs around him, looking ahead, finding our path. My hands were steady. My heart was steady. My whole body was steady, fueling Delusion with its steadiness, giving him the courage to proceed.

Delusion trotted on. He was wobbly, still a bit taken aback. But he joined the horde, and as we made it around the ring without incident, he moved taller, with more panache. I directed his feet, and he showed himself. He shrugged off his worries like a pesky stable fly.

I saw Martha at the rail with Soiree. She waved at me, a big smile on her face.

This was what Martha was paying me for. My experience, my countless hours on the show circuit gave me the skills that she would probably never have. It gave me the ability to take her young horse into the show ring for the first time and give him a good, trouble-free ride. I wasn't chasing a ribbon or prize money. I was laying the foundation for many happy years of showing for Delusion and his owner. To an adult amateur like Martha, my service was priceless.

I chose a short, to-the-point warm-up, not wanting to drill the gelding unnecessarily. I wanted the spring to remain in his step for his first course. I took him out of the crowded ring and onto the surrounding hills, where I worked him through easy transitions, focusing his mind and getting his balance in order.

When they called my number, my mind was strangely calm. I knew it was a big moment - Delusion's debut in the hunter ring, my first course with a client's horse, with Martha watching eagerly from the rail - but I didn't allow those thoughts to take hold. I was focused on the task at hand, and I knew we were ready.

Other things, like judging or recognition, were out of my control. Being competent, and confident, didn't guarantee success. That was the thing about real life.

But I had finally put my anxieties aside, and I knew I belonged here.

I guided Delusion into the ring and made my courtesy circle, concentrating on establishing that perfect 12-foot stride.

Then we were on course, approaching the first outside line of fences. I felt Delusion perk up a little, his adrenaline chugging. My instinct told me not to check him, and I stilled my seat instead, breathing deeply. Delusion simmered down, losing none of his momentum, and we met the first fence perfectly. If nothing changed, we would have a stellar round.

Delusion picked up his feet over the second fence, lifting his topline and showing a good bascule for his level of training. As we came to the corner, I held him between my aids, focusing on getting the proper bend to set us up for the turn onto the diagonal line. As the far standard of the last fence on the line came into view, framed by the standards of the first fence, I smoothly turned Delusion onto the diagonal. He bounded over the jumps in a clock-like rhythm.

We jumped the second outside line cleanly, and I poured Delusion through the corner, wanting to hit the second diagonal as accurately as possible to leave a lasting impression in the judge's mind. We left the corner without a hitch, meeting the diagonal line dead-center.

This last line faced the out-gate, which could make some horses anticipate and speed up through the line. Delusion pricked his ears, giving me pause, but his stride didn't change. Trusting him to complete the course, I turned my focus on myself, wanting to give him a good ride over those crucial last two fences. If he was even the slightest bit flat or uneven, it could cost him the top prize.

As we passed over the finish line, I slumped over Delusion's withers. I realized the pressure *had* been enormous, and I *had* felt it. I'd just done what I had to do, and ignored it.

We were met by Martha and Soiree. "Well done, Erica! He looked amazing out there," she gushed. "I can't believe that's my horse!"

I shrugged. "He was always a good boy," I said. "He was great out there. He jumped well, and he kept his rhythm all the way through. He should have a really good shot at winning."

"Oh, I don't care about that," Martha said fondly. "What matters is that he did a good job. And he enjoyed himself out there!"

"That attitude will serve you well," I remarked. "Horse shows are hard to enjoy if it's all dependent on winning. Although," I added, "I don't think you guys will be doing very much losing."

The rest of the class wrapped up as we watched, and then came the painfully slow process of announcing the ribbon winners.

Delusion's number wasn't read as they announced the lower placings. I knew it wouldn't be. It wasn't until they announced the second place horse that I was sure we had it.

"In first place, number 443, Erica Rimwork on Delusion, owned by Martha Gross."

I swung around in the saddle to look at Martha. "*I told you,*" I mouthed. She stared at me in shock. "Well...I never! How wonderful."

I rode in to collect the ribbon. Delusion handled having it fastened to his bridle like a seasoned pro, while Mark DeWayne's horse, in second, nearly flipped over on him from the shock of red satin coming near his face.

We returned to Martha, who had her iPhone at the ready. "Smile!"

I grinned cheesily, and she took our picture. "What a wonderful surprise," she kept saying.

"See, winning is alright," I teased her. "If you stay for Soiree's round, you'll see me do it again."

"You know what?" Martha said, smiling. "I think I'll do just that."

Elaine

I cinched my truck into a curbside parking spot and jammed a quarter in the meter. The cab of my truck revealed itself through a gaping hole on either side where the doors had been. Instead of leaving things up to chance, I traveled light, with all my essentials scaled down to fit in a satchel by some knockoff Target brand. I couldn't seal off the wound, but I had made sure that if someone did infiltrate, they would leave empty-handed.

I walked about half a block, the dull scuff of my work boots on the cement replacing the aggressive, pointed click of the stilettos I'd strapped to my feet in my previous life as a millionaire's trophy wife. And before that I was wearing sensible orthopedic clogs, when my cleaning job kept me on my feet for long hours.

How many times can someone rebuild themselves? It was easy on the outside. New hair, new clothes. New mode of transportation. New address. New shoes.

It was funny walking down the street in this neighborhood, not far from where Lawrence had picked me up all those months ago. In a many ways, I was what society would see as a successful, functioning human being. I had a job and a roof over my head. I had a vehicle. I looked plain, even slightly unkempt, but I was out in the world and moving forward, walking tall over the concrete.

I still felt as if I'd just stepped off it, a rack of bones with filthy, matted hair.

I pushed on the door and entered the salon. The façade wasn't all that nice, and it wasn't very busy on a weekday evening, which gave me pause. But I'd never stooped so low as to give myself a hack-job haircut while staring into the bathroom mirror. I wasn't going to start now.

A receptionist with brassy red hair glanced up from her smartphone. "Hello! What can I do for you?"

"I'm just looking to get a cut." Idly, I fingered my graceless, all-one-length strands.

"Okay, we can take care of that for you." The girl leaned over the counter without getting out of her chair. "Theresa!" She called. "Do you want to help her out?"

The stylist who emerged from the back was middle-aged with side-swept bangs. She didn't have chunky highlights, so I felt okay with having her touch my hair.

The lady fell back a little when she saw me. "Oh, my," she said. "Did you have to get chemo?"

It's worse than I thought. I shrugged. "I've been living off the land," I said, my voice tinged with evasiveness.

She clucked disapprovingly. "Oh, well. I'll soon fix you up."

She took me over to the sink, where the water came out in thin streams from a contraption much like a detachable shower head. I flinched when it touched my head, and she pulled back quizzically. "What's the matter?"

"The water's a little hot," I said.

She looked at me funny. "It's actually lukewarm."

"Well, can you make it a little *more* lukewarm?"

She shrugged. "Whatever you say."

I'd grown accustomed to showering in the wash rack at the barn, which *wasn't* heated all that well, despite anything Lawrence had to say about it. But I didn't tell Theresa that. I just kept my head low while she washed my hair, feeling like it was on fire.

She sat me down in the heavily padded fake leather chair, pumping it up with her foot until it put me at the optimum height. Another stylist, who had wandered out of the woodwork, smoothed the cape over my shoulders and fastened it around my neck.

Theresa slid a comb through my hair, parting it deeply on one side. Taking careful aim, she clipped the first layers.

The other girl had taken my hand in hers and was turning it over, staring at the state of my fingernails. I had forgotten how people would touch you when you went into a salon. It had become a strange, foreign land of soft music, heavy scents and human touch.

I used to go every single week.

"What have you been doing to these hands?" She asked me, her heavily-lined eyes wide open.

I glanced downward, seeing what she saw. The torn cuticles, the scratches and blemishes that came from handling horses and hay. The nails clipped as short as I could make them but still dirty. And the heavy, rosy scars on my knuckles, a reminder of that final night in the Davenport Hotel when Lawrence ended our arrangement.

"I work with horses," I said. Horses were big, strong animals, intimidating to most non-equestrians. Horses explained away a lot.

"Oh, my," she said. "That's a lot of hard work, isn't it?"

"It's a job," I said.

"I'd love to give you a manicure," she piped up. "Those hands could use some TLC."

"It's not really in my budget," I told her.

She nodded sincerely. "How about if it were on the house?"

I glanced at her, only partially aware of the hair clippings falling onto my shoulders. "I can't let you do that."

"Please? At least let me put some lotion on and tidy up those cuticles for you."

"It would be a wasted effort," I said. "I'll just be going right back to work after this."

She grinned. "I didn't hear the word 'no' in there."

I almost cracked a smile. "I suppose not," I said.

She was back in a flash, and I leaned back in the chair, trying to enjoy the sensation of scented lotion being rubbed into my dry, chapped hands. She filed my nails and trimmed back my ragged cuticles, and afterward, they did look nicer.

I was about to say thank you when Theresa turned on the blow dryer and began running it through my hair, pausing occasionally to spritz some product on it.

It was difficult to avoid my reflection. The mirror was tall and wide, positioned directly in front of me. And as Theresa finished with my hair, I began to see a reflection that I didn't mind facing. She'd styled my hair in a jagged, spiky pixie cut, with bangs that swept to the side, partially covering one eye. My hair, previously lank and luster-less, had regained some body at the back, and fell sleekly, longer near the front, framing my face.

I didn't look ancient and rundown anymore. I looked maybe 25.

"I love it," I told her honestly.

Theresa reached for a tub of pomade, handing it to me. "If you do one thing for yourself, get this product. You'll be able to put it on with your hair wet from the shower, and once it dries, it'll look like you've spent 20 minutes styling it."

I nodded. "I'll take it."

The receptionist rang me up; I paid and stepped outside.

There was still time on the meter, and I didn't feel like leaving it for someone else to take advantage of. Plus, one thing was still nagging at me.

I walked past a few clothing boutiques, but they didn't appeal to me. I knew they'd be out of my budget, and the clothes seemed to be trying too hard. They were designed for women of a certain age who thought, misguidedly, that they could still be every bit as trendy and provocative as teenagers.

Nestled between a coffee shop and a burned-out storefront that had once been a seedy haven for lowlife musicians (and drug dealers) was a used clothing store. I'd never set foot in one (although every single article of clothing I now owned came from thrift stores, thanks to Lawrence). It was something I just didn't do, right up there with cutting my own hair.

But I needed something to wear, if I was actually going to this stupid fundraiser. So, I went inside, drawn in by some vague, otherworldly pull.

I saw it right away, displayed at the end of a rack full of dowdy, unremarkable dresses. If I hadn't seen it right away, I probably would have turned around and walked out.

It was a long-sleeved dress with a simple, modest neckline that I could tell would fit me impeccably. It was also completely sheer.

I fingered the gauzy fabric, considering the implications of such a garment. I could wear something else, something plain and chaste, and I could escape from the party entirely unseen. Or I could wear something like this, and make an entrance.

I thought of my truck, sitting on the side of the street with no doors. I thought of my reputation, trashed beyond repair. I thought of my soul, blasted open.

I snatched the mesh gown off the rack. It would be the centerpiece of my outfit, and I went looking for the pieces that would make it whole.

Lawrence

The tail end of a scarlet sunrise was still visible but fading fast in the morning light. For the first time since I'd brought her to Lexington, Delaware and I rode together with no one else in sight. Her seat rested lightly in the saddle, following the movement of Vegas' back as it dipped and swayed.

Beneath me, Harry covered the sloping terrain of the field with ease, as surely as he moved on the flat, groomed ground of a regulation polo field.

It was almost more satisfying to be out here on this vast stretch of rolling land. When you stepped onto it, you couldn't see the end. It made me feel limitless and power-hungry.

Harry dropped his head low, snorting loudly. I could feel his body ramping up. He could count. He knew we were close to the end of the warm-up, and he knew the fun would soon begin.

I turned to Delaware. "You're probably wondering why I wanted to bring you out here," I said.

She grinned. "Oh, I'm sure you bring all the girls around to this field."

I cracked a smile. "You've done well with everything I've thrown at you so far," I said.

Delaware shrugged. "I try."

"You have the shots in your muscle memory, like we talked about. And you're learning what it takes to be on a team. It's not always easy, but you're finding that you can hold your own in what is inarguably a formidable group of players."

"Well, that's the idea." Delaware picked up the reins, and Vegas smoothly transitioned to a canter. She rode around me in a large circle, remaining precisely the same distance away even as Harry moved forward.

I watched her for a moment. "I want to add one more skill to your arsenal," I announced.

"Oh, really? Do tell." She changed rein, Vegas swapped leads, and she began a new circle.

"Ball control." I halted Harry, who raised his head somewhat crossly. "You have it, but you can have more of it. Specifically, I want you to learn one of my specialties. Something that I've perfected."

Delaware brought Vegas to an elegant halt, her face keen with interest. "Show me."

Harry sprang into motion. I checked him, holding him to a collected canter.

"You can control the ball in two ways," I said. "You can reposition it on the field, or you can keep it from touching the ground."

I rode up to a line of balls atop a hill. Scooping one up, I let it fly over to where Delaware sat watching.

"The easiest way is to do what I just did," I called out. "But what makes it easier on you also makes it easier on your opponents. So a skilled player will often employ a different method, particularly in close quarters, or during a hotly contested match."

Harry brought me right to the ball, a true heat-seeking missile. Right in front of Delaware, I swung my mallet again. But this time, instead of going for a strong blow, a long-distance hit, my touch was softer. More delicate. The ball stayed with me, hovering in the air. I kept my mallet under it, giving it a tap whenever it started to fall. Still riding at speed, I kept it in mid-air, and when I felt the time was right, I sent it flying.

I raised my hand, giving Harry a clear signal to stop and turn back. He still fought me, compelled by his almost magnetic need to follow the line of the ball.

Delaware was staring at me, her mouth open. "*Wow.* That was sick."

I grinned slightly. "It's not too shabby."

She still shook her head. "It's like you can just keep that thing up *indefinitely.*"

I managed to not make a really inappropriate (and way too easy) joke. "Most players will only keep it up for a beat or two. It's almost impossible to maintain it for longer than that. But the advantage you'll gain is huge."

Delaware nodded. "It's harder for the other players to steal the ball," she said, contemplative. "If they have to snatch it out of the air."

"Exactly."

"I want to try it." Delaware rode forward, her eyes on the line of balls.

I watched her first try. She picked the ball up expertly, but when she tried to keep it up, she hit it with far too much force, and it sailed away from her.

"Light touch," I called. "You can't imagine how soft it needs to be."

Undeterred, she tried again. I watched her botch it up in every way possible, which is what happens when you first start trying to do this.

Taking a breather, she rode over to me. "I don't think I have the feel for it."

I shook my head. "You have all the feel you need. You're just overdoing it."

She looked at me, puzzled.

"It's the hardest thing in the world," I said. "When you're out on the field in possession of the ball, your adrenaline is up sky-high, and you've got players on all sides of you who are gunning for that ball. It's the hardest thing, and it goes against all your instincts. But you have to slow down. Dial it back. You have to be so relaxed, and so soft...."

I reached for Delaware's hand and moved it gently, quickly. She watched the head of the mallet snap upward, and in her mind I knew she saw it connecting.

"That's the feel you need," I said. "It's completely different. It's alien. But try it and you'll see what happens."

Concentration taking over her face, Delaware aimed Vegas at the ball. Her body was slower, her arm looser. When she hit the ball, she let it pop upward, swinging without the usual force and follow-through. With a tiny flick of her wrist, she sought out the ball, finding it again and flicking it up.

She didn't give it quite enough height, and it sank to the ground before she could touch it again. But she'd done it. And I could tell by the look on her face that she'd do it again, until it was so deep in her muscle memory that she could do it without looking, without hearing, on a field where the only thing audible was the rattle of hoof beats.

I made a move to congratulate her, but some movement at the edge of the field caught my eye just as Harry spooked, darting forward. I turned him around, my eyes finding Wilson as he walked toward me.

I dismounted, filled with fear. I didn't know why he would track me down like this. "What's going on?" I demanded.

Wilson looked a bit startled. "Nothing's gone wrong, Cavanaugh, if that's what you're ripping my head off about."

The air went out of me. "Well, why else would you come all the way here?" I muttered edgily.

"Occasionally, I like to get out of the office, Cavanaugh." Wilson shook his head. "And I had some news that I thought you might like to know."

"Oh, really? What's that?" I asked.

Team Dark Horse

"You know the club is having a fundraiser on Saturday, of course," Wilson said.

"Ah, of course," I said. "I remember those...open bar, bored housewives, coatrooms...the good old days."

Wilson rolled his eyes. "I try not to remember your debauchery, Cavanaugh. It's been wonderful not to hear about your constant escapades now that you've settled down." He paused, getting back on track. "Anyway. The thing I'm here about is this. I've invited Elaine to the event, and she's decided to go."

That stopped me in my tracks. "Really?" I said, incredulous. "It's at the Davenport Hotel, right?"

"Yes."

"And...*people* will be there, won't they? Like Arnold, for instance? And everyone else from her past?"

"Yes." Wilson's gaze shifted, resting on me. "That's why I need you to be there."

I stared at him. "You want *me* to be there? How is that going to help anything?"

Wilson eyed me steadily. "I don't know, Cavanaugh. The whole thing might be a disaster. This isn't my line of expertise." He dragged the toe of his boot through the grass. "All I know is she's going. She's putting herself out there, in front of all those people. And she needs someone there who's on her side." Wilson reached out, gripping my upper arm firmly. "Someone from her present."

I was silent, looking at him. "I'll do it," I said surely. "I'll be there."

"You better be." Wilson dropped my arm, turning away. "Because you brought her here, Cavanaugh. You got her to where she is. You fed her, sheltered her, and gave her a start, and she's better. But she's nowhere near well."

Elaine

The house was a huge, elaborate cage with fine art on the walls. I'd put myself in here, lobbied for it and worked on him shamelessly. My eighteen-year-old self had sought higher ground and inadvertently committed suicide. When I left my hometown, I slipped away from one slow death and walked right into another.

I stood, locked in my bedroom, motionless in front of the gilt-edged mirror, motionless except for the hand that was putting on my face. The layers of makeup cemented my expression, made me into who I needed to be. Lovely and radiant, kind and loyal. A good wife, a stylish dresser. Intelligent enough to be a good conversationalist. And no more.

I set down the brush, and even though I meant not to, I looked at myself. I was a girl in a painting, someone else's ideal. I had no life in me anymore, no spirit, barely a pulse. I was flat against a canvas, hemmed in by the unyielding rectangle of the frame.

I stood in the grimy bathroom of a 7-Eleven, applying Cover Girl drugstore cosmetics to my face with the unsure hand of a preteen girl. The fluorescent light bulbs above the mirror cast a sickly highlighter-green hue that made it impossible to know if I was achieving the right balance of toner and blush, lipstick and eyeliner. Eyeing myself critically, I hoped the end result wouldn't make me resemble a transvestite. But surely it had to come out better than anything I could have achieved at the stable. I had no mirror in my room. I had no need for one, and I probably never would.

Peering at my face, I decided it was time to leave well enough alone. I stuffed the cheap cosmetics back into my cheap Target brand clutch and unlocked the door.

I didn't want to be unfashionably on time, so I loitered in the aisles for a while, inventorying the array of travel-friendly junk fare. The mini boxes of cereal that cost as much or more than the real thing, bags of chips that were mostly air, generic trail mix and bags of nuts with racially offensive spices. Oriental Mix. Mexican Mix.

I drew a few stares from the customers who flowed in and out, and it took me a while to realize their meaning. I'd gone so long assuming that any person who looked at me did so out of pity, disgust, or morbid curiosity. But I realized now that my appearance actually did not resemble the mess I was on the inside. My haircut and makeup created the image of a person who took care of herself. My trench coat was simple, lacking a designer label, but it fit well, tied at the waist, pulling my look together.

I'd forgotten what it felt like to be the best-dressed person in the room. As always, it was that sensation of false power, the flimsy lie that you were somehow better than everyone else. It was a dangerous belief, even when you had the social standing to back it up. It would have been laughable had I subscribed to it now.

I picked up a mini box of Cookies 'n Cream Crunch and walked to the counter.

The cashier had floppy, sandy brown hair and a nametag that said *Ron*. He eyed me up and down, and I was almost startled to see a flare of heat in his gaze. "You're dressed to kill."

I gave him a muted smile. "I'm attending a function at the Davenport Hotel."

"No way." He scanned my cereal box with deliberate slowness. "Are you one of them high-society ladies, then? You look too young to be a lady."

I skirted his eyes. "I used to be one of them," I said. "I kind of fell out of favor a while ago."

Ron nodded. He looked at me, and his face turned serious. "Why go back?"

I studied him. He wore a graphic tee and jeans. Nice ones. He had a pleasant sort of everyman vibe to him. If I hadn't been shut down for life, he might've been a nice guy to go on a few dates with.

"I don't know," I said. "I guess just to show them that I'm not dead. That I'm still in this thing."

"Well, I hope you march in there and do yourself proud. Whatever your past, you look mighty capable tonight." Ron took my money and handed me the change. "That's a great choice," he added, nodding at the Cookies 'n Cream Crunch.

I walked into the softness of night, broken up by the harshness of floodlights. I sat in my open-air truck, eating my cereal piece by piece.

I still didn't have the hunger. After all this time, my body couldn't come back, couldn't return to normalcy. I kept thinking I'd feel it one day. But I hadn't even felt a twinge.

It was like something had gone wrong during the procedure, and they'd scraped out more than the embryo. It seemed like everything went back to that day. Because that was the day I stopped caring whether I lived or died.

I'd aborted the child for many reasons, some of them inherently selfish. But mostly, I'd done it because I couldn't stand to bring a life into the world under those circumstances. That baby was the product of a messy affair, a sick arrangement I'd designed so I could get what I wanted. What kind of a life would that child have had?

I used to have hunger. I used to be ravenous, so blindly hungry that I'd crash into things and demolish whatever I needed to in order to satiate myself. A mere thought of Lawrence, and the pleasurable burn of his touch, and I'd lose control, like a wolf with blood on his lips who continued to rip the throats out of a flock of sheep, even when he couldn't possibly eat so many.

I didn't allow myself to have those thoughts anymore. I just kept them under the surface, floating in the murky bottom of my subconscious. And if they attempted to come up, I beat them back down.

But sometimes, I would dream about Lawrence or our baby. I'd wake up with my face and neck soaking wet with tears, and I'd flip over, shudder, and try not to scream.

And that was when I knew without a doubt that the hunger was still there. It tore a hole inside me, as large as the life I might have lived.

Lawrence

I hadn't had an occasion to break out the tux in quite a while. It had been so long, I didn't quite remember how to tie a tie, but I muddled through and left the men's bathroom looking the part of someone who gave a damn.

Team Dark Horse

    I hadn't missed these fancy gatherings. There had been a time in my life when my attendance had been mandatory. Often, I even had to get onstage and give speeches, because Wilson hated the public eye, and he always played the "I took you in off the street and put a roof over your head" card.

    Steering clear of drunken housewives, I mingled without really mingling. I was hoping mainly to avoid having to interact with Arnold. Fortunately, he was easy to spot. All I had to do was look out for the matching blonde girls who were perpetually on either side of him. Taller than Arnold even without the stilettos, they were easy to pick out in a crowd.

    Wilson appeared on my right, holding a glass of elaborately garnished water pretending to be vodka. "Any sign of her yet?" He asked.

    I shook my head. "I'm keeping an eye out."

    "As you should." Wilson moved off across the room. I saw him find Barbara and loop an arm around her waist. She laid a hand on his chest and gazed up at him, and I could see that Wilson had gotten the deed done.

    I considered going to the bar and taking a shot of Jameson, but it was a long walk in a crowded room. When I glanced back to the lobby, I saw Elaine.

    But I didn't know it at first.

    She stood, grounded, surveying the scene of the party before her. Her hair was cut in jagged, glossy pieces that surrounded her face and ended in a sharp point. Her lips and eyes were bright, her cheeks blooming in color.

    My eye was drawn to her in that moment not because I knew her. It was simply drawn.

    A butler came forward to help her out of her coat, and there was something about the way she reacted to him - a look of surprise, even slight fear, that transitioned quickly to boredom - that let me know it was really her.

    Elaine pulled on the end of her trench coat tie, and the butler slipped the coat from her shoulders. She stepped forward, bursting forth as the dark cloth of her coat was whipped away.

    She wore a slim-fitting black pencil skirt that fell to mid-calf level. Above it, her entire upper body was encased in black mesh, revealing the narrow band of a strapless bra.

She stepped out under the lights, bringing herself into full view of everyone at the party. She was luminous, absorbing the light and reflecting it, moving like a candle flame. I watched the articulation of her joints, her lean muscles bursting through the sheer material. Her body was healthy. Powerful.

I wanted to go to her, but I held myself back. Somehow, I knew Elaine had a plan. I knew it didn't involve me.

She picked up her head and threw herself into the partygoers, walking across the room through the vast center. The crowd parted with an almost choreographed flow. She took up the whole room, and not a single person could look away from her.

I saw a glimpse of the old Elaine, vibrant and cunning, relentless in her pursuit of money and toxic love. I saw the essence of the person who had tormented me, pushing me to my limit. The person I had sought to destroy.

And I felt like standing and applauding her return.

Erica

Under the blazing midday sun, it was a hundred degrees, with a hundred percent humidity. It was too hot to ride the horses. It was too hot to even longe them. So, I sat in the barn aisle, trying to feel the nonexistent breeze, and I did something I hadn't yet done but needed to.

I began outlining the show schedule for my horses the old fashioned way. Pen to paper.

Soiree needed to earn a minimum of $500 in Hunter Derby classes if she was to compete in the Finals. With a solid competitor like Soiree, I didn't need to fret about donating my entry fee, but the fact of the matter was that fees were higher in the qualifying classes.

Earning money showing horses was a fallacy. Anyone who generated an income in horses did so by training, teaching, or breeding. While it was rewarding to be handed a check along with a blue ribbon, when you factored in entry fees, membership costs, and transport to and from the show venues, you were lucky not to lose your shirt.

I scribbled away on my battered notepad, scrutinizing the show schedule and making careful, cryptic notations. Each had to do with some underlying factor - distance, footing, judging, even basic things, like proximity to a convenience store.

I paused, wiping a trickle of sweat away from my eyeballs. There was no relief from this heat. Not even the concrete was cool today.

Staring at my sheet of notes, I pieced together a show schedule on a new blank page. I'd planned a somewhat aggressive campaign for Soiree, with a few optional events I could drop if I thought she needed a break. Burnout was a very real threat in a show horse, and something I desperately wanted to avoid with Soiree. But there was also the fact that I was sitting on a treasure, and time was of the essence. If I qualified Soiree, her value would soar.

If I timed it right, Soiree could fund my venture with Assault. My shot at the Grand Prix.

I sat on the sweating concrete, the possibilities reeling in my mind. I'd talked about it for so long. I'd thought about it for longer. *Grand Prix. The big shows, the Worlds. The Olympics. Gold.*

Now it almost seemed like it could happen. For a second, I allowed myself to go there.

A loud snort from one of the stalled horses brought me back. They'd been so quiet, stupefied by the heat, I'd forgotten they were there.

I glanced down at my scribbled show schedule, covering two pages. Two pages of events that we could win or lose. Two pages of potential for all kinds of mishaps. A trailer accident. A twisted ankle.

The word "almost" covered a lot of sins when you were talking about horses.

I picked myself up off the concrete and walked down the aisle, looking in on the horses. Their eyes flickered at me, sloth-like and subdued. I peered at water buckets, topping off those that needed it, and threw each horse another flake of hay. Each of them dug in, except for Soiree. She continued to bob around her stall door, ears up, her face curious and lively even in the oppressive heat.

Team Dark Horse

I smiled. "Do you need some loving?" I asked her, stepping closer.

Agreeably, Soiree thrust her head into my outstretched arms. I wrapped them around her face, pulling her in tighter, and she sighed, satiated. I stood there, feeling the bony warmth of her skull pressed against my body. I thought of something my dad had told me, a long time ago, the first time I ever had to sell a horse I really cared about.

When you make your passion into a business, it hurts sometimes.

And I remembered that the hardest part of the plan I'd outlined wasn't the qualifying, or the budgeting, or being lucky enough to avoid a mishap. It was what would come at the end.

I rested my head on Soiree's face, right above her eye socket. The tears came, not in a torrent, but in a steady, knowing trickle. After a while I realized Soiree was holding me up now, instead of the other way around.

Lawrence

I headed down Main Street at a brisk pace, nodding casually at the shoppers when I passed them. I came to this part of town pretty regularly to hit up the bakery, *Indulgence*, but that was my singular mission. These other kitschy shops didn't interest me.

The male-to-female ratio was especially skewed on this block due to the array of store fronts grouped together within this small radius. Back in the day, I had worked the ratio hard, and it had worked out very well for me at times. It made perfect sense: besides *Indulgence*, where you could get a delicious dessert to squelch even the most random sugar craving, you had your beauty parlor, your dry cleaning service, and probably half a dozen places where you could spend anywhere from $10 to $200 on a pair of shoes.

That's why I was more than a little surprised to see a guy on the sidewalk ahead of me. Even more surprising, it was a guy I halfway knew. And if I recalled right, this particular guy didn't like to leave his house.

Shoulders slumped forward, he was avoiding eye contact. I intercepted him anyway. "Long time no see. Dougie, right?"

After a long pause, he shook my hand awkwardly. "Yeah. Hi, Lawrence."

"So what brings you out into the light of day?" I asked, trying to be friendly and realizing, too late, that I was probably verging on douchey.

Dougie's head flopped forward. "Yeah. I'm not much for outside," he admitted. "But I needed to get away. Have some peace and quiet..."

A siren wailed to life two blocks down. I looked at Dougie critically. "Don't you have your own place?"

Dougie glanced at me. "Amber lives there now," he said after a moment's pause. "Didn't you know that?"

"No. Amber doesn't pick up the phone." I considered this new development. "Yeah, I lived with Amber once. It wasn't too good for my blood pressure."

"Amber was fine," said Dougie almost protectively. "I liked having her there."

"So what changed?" I asked, well aware that I was being pushy. But I wanted to know what was up with Amber, and Dougie sure as shit looked like he needed someone to talk to.

He appeared to struggle with the vague morality issues that came along with this kind of exchange. Then a sigh whistled through his skinny, caved-in torso. "I suppose there's no harm in telling you. Amber got a girlfriend."

My eyebrows leapt up. "Not a platonic girlfriend?"

"Very non-platonic."

"Wow." I stood there grinning while a couple of irritated joggers were forced to cut around us. "That's great for her. This is a long time coming."

"It is. And she's taking full advantage."

I looked at him levelly. "So, like, all the time then?"

"My house sounds like I dubbed in the audio from an endless loop of girl-on-girl porn," Dougie said, completely straight-faced. "Which you'd think would be great, but it just so happens it's not. I can't concentrate on my work; I can't relax in my own house. I'm hard *all* the time." Dougie dropped his eyes away from mine like he hadn't meant to throw that detail in there. The skin on his face that wasn't covered with cystic acne reddened considerably.

"I'm not surprised," I said, amused. I knew a thing or two about how to carry an awkward conversation. "When Amber does something, she does it big." I remembered how she'd rendered my house unlivable with her soulless blaring pop music. "At least you're not listening to an endless loop of Lady Gaga," I pointed out.

"I actually like Lady Gaga," Dougie said uncomfortably.

"You would." I started off again in the direction of the bakery, and Dougie followed. "You should probably have a talk with Amber about boundaries."

"Boundaries?" He looked at me in bewilderment, like I'd tossed out some obscure scientific term that he would probably actually understand.

"Yeah, boundaries. She's living under your roof. You make the terms. She'll be all dramatic about it, and yelling may happen, but if you put your foot down and don't cave, she'll come around."

Dougie appeared doubtful. "I don't know if I can do yelling."

"Just think of it as collateral damage," I shrugged. "You have to have a temporary dustup sometimes. For the greater good."

"I guess I could try talking to her," Dougie said in a tone of voice that implied he was in no way going to talk to her at any point in this century. "How are things with you? Still doing those horse clinics?"

I shook my head. "No, that's a thing of the past. I've moved on to bigger and better things. I'm building a polo team."

"Who's on it?"

"Me, the two top-ranked players from the Women's Polo Federation - before they left, that is - and our real wild card, an undiscovered up-and-comer named Delaware. Found her in a cornfield in rural Indiana. She's going to come on the scene and shock everyone."

"Interesting," Dougie said. "Do you have a sponsor?"

"Not yet. We're working on it."

"Does your team have a presence on social media?" Dougie asked. "Do you have a Facebook page? Are you posting videos of your players and your practice sessions to generate interest?"

I shook my head. "We don't have time for that crap, Dougie. We're building a *team* here. It takes work, and focus. Dedication."

"So does all the stuff I just mentioned," Dougie said, his voice surprisingly strong. "And if you're starting from the ground up and lacking a sponsor, you can't afford to have that attitude about the value of social media."

I glanced at him. He'd drawn himself up unknowingly to his full height. His back was straight. This sudden change was oddly compelling.

"Go on," I said.

"It's very simple," Dougie said. "The internet has really taken off in recent years. It's sucked everyone in. You can be forgiven your ignorance because I feel like you've spent way too much time in horse barns, and you probably don't keep up with current events. But hear this. The internet - Facebook, YouTube, Twitter, Instagram, all of it - is huge. It's not going away. The age of smartphones is upon us - people have access to the internet 24/7! The average person checks their phone every 15 minutes. Smartphone dependence, information overload...this is the new addiction of the 21st century."

"Anyone who's got something to sell - a book, a clothing line, an idea - has to have an online platform. It's mandatory. No one's going door-to-door at record companies and singing their lungs out anymore. Everyone's getting discovered on YouTube! People are documenting every waking moment of their lives and attaining millions of followers, book deals, their own show...and these are just normal, ordinary people with a slightly quirky way of looking at things! They're not even that interesting! But they're entertaining, and people lap that shit up."

I stared at him. "This...all sounds very intriguing."

"As people become more and more disconnected from their own lives, they become increasingly dependent on the internet to fill the void. They identify with strangers. They live vicariously through celebrities and cute cat videos." Dougie looked at me somewhat gravely. "People kill themselves because of a mean comment they read on Facebook. That's how powerful the pull is. And that's how much ability you have to exploit it for your own personal gain."

I looked at Dougie's earnest, slightly breathless face, trying to let it all sink in. "I still don't understand what this has to do with the team."

"Let me give you one more example." Dougie smoothed the sleeves of his shirt. "I'm a permanently single, middle-class tech geek with bad skin, not a hint of abs, and considerable 'issues'. In real life. On the internet, however, I have over 2 million followers on Tumblr, Twitter, and Facebook who lap up whatever I post on any given day. My site traffic is constant and heavy. I have dedicated Anons - those are anonymous posters who send messages and ask questions - who worship me. I get marriage proposals on the regular."

"That's all just me. That's what I've made of myself. And if your team is as awesome as you say it is, with those girls on it and their compelling stories - top players starting over, a corn-fed sweetheart on a fast-track to the big leagues - imagine what that could be."

Dougie shook himself abruptly. "I should get going," he said. I watched him fold himself over, and he was just an awkward kid again.

My words were all jumbled. I fought to sort them out. "You've certainly given me a lot to think about," I said.

Dougie nodded. "It's worth thinking about," he said. "Because in this day and age, if you don't exist on the internet...you don't exist."

My mind was working now. "If you ever need to get out of the house, you should come see us play," I offered.

Dougie looked unconvinced. "Will there be a lot of people there?"

I shook my head. "The stands will be empty."

"I'll think about it," Dougie said as he slipped away from me.

"It's worth thinking about," I repeated his words.

He just barely smiled; then he turned away, painfully thin and stooped over the pavement.

Erica

The first thing I noticed as we made our way to the warm-up ring was the sheer quality of the horses. Not a single capped hock or blemish could be found on them. No horse toed in or out; none were over or back at the knee. I saw nothing but straight or concave profiles and large, bright eyes. They circled around the warm-up ring, passing each other agreeably at a sedate canter, occasionally making a smooth leap over a practice fence. Toned yet slightly plump and undeviatingly turned out, they presented a picture of polished, easy skill, tight button braids lying flat against the line of their crests.

"We're in the big leagues now, Soiree," I whispered, noting with pride that my off-the-track rescue snatched off the kill buyer's truck looked right at home here. But I hadn't paid my exorbitant entry fee just to blend in. We'd come to shine.

I mounted up in the corner and entered the current of hunters in motion. Soiree drew a few covert glances as she joined the mix, which I'd come to expect. Our recent domination of the Working Hunter classes couldn't have gone entirely unnoticed.

I looked for an opening and let Soiree take a bead on a practice fence. She gracefully cleared it and returned to the rail, falling seamlessly into step with the other horses.

I took her over the fence a couple more times, if only to ensure that she was limber. Then we exited the warm-up ring and joined the group of assembled horses waiting for the Hunter Derby class.

The first horse I watched on course went foot-perfect. The second suffered a minor loss of rhythm, but it was clear that the competition was several notches above anything we'd faced previously. The riding here was mixed. Some people rode like stylists, their equitation solid, their posture perfect, while many tended toward the more extreme showmanship that had become a fad in recent years, leaning over their horses' necks, hands flung forward, reins loose and draping. Perhaps it was meant to convey their horses' self-sufficiency, the ease with which they completed the course with little to no help from the rider. But it seemed to me that anyone with an ounce of respect for their mount would sit up and ride with poise, not drop heavily forward onto the horse's withers just as their bascule was reaching its apex.

The atmosphere near the in-gate was reserved, lacking the quips and small talk I'd become accustomed to. Whether that was the norm for this level of competition or simply a way of freezing out the new kid, I couldn't say.

It didn't really matter. I wasn't here to make friends. I was here to earn money.

Soiree's name sounded from the loudspeaker, clear as a bell. I picked up the reins and she bounded into the arena. I let her have her head and she settled, but I felt the anticipation and excitement within her, skittering around just below the surface of her flesh.

It was the age-old question, to check or not to check a fresh horse? I knew what the riders who were watching me would do. Many of them were probably digging their nails into the palm of their hand to keep from yelling it out. *Check her.*

It was a gamble, absolutely. But I'd come this far believing in Soiree every step. I couldn't stop now.

"Easy, mare," I murmured, letting my fingers skim the soft skin lying over her withers.

I turned her onto the first line, feeling for that rhythm, that optimum 12-foot stride. *There it is.* I smiled.

With soft, floating reins, Soiree skipped around the course, all grey and white fences and lavish decorative brush. Her hooves leaving tiny imprints in the vast sandy ring, she demonstrated what she was capable of. She didn't falter.

Soiree had made a firm case for a winning score. It remained to be seen whether the judges would award it.

We returned to stand with the other competitors. A previously icy trainer turned in the saddle to nod at me. "Well done."

"Not too shabby for a yahoo jumper rider," I said, tongue-in-cheek.

Another trainer spoke up. "My heart was in my throat when you started. She looked like a fireball out there. But you just sat it out, and she came right back to you." He smiled at Soiree. "That's good training."

"What's your plan with her?"

"I'm qualifying her for the Finals, and then I'll put her up for sale," I said regretfully.

"That's smart. Bring her value up, make the most out of your investment." He nodded approvingly.

"*If* I can get her qualified," I pointed out.

The conversation halted as we listened to the loudspeaker talk. It named Soiree as the first place horse.

The trainer grinned at me. "Well, you're off to a solid start," he said, turning his mount on its haunches. "Not bad for a yahoo."

Elaine

I prowled the aisle, stealthily creeping past stall doors and peering in at the occupants. Everyone was either happily engaged in eating their last wisps of hay or settling down to sleep, so I signed off on night check and slipped into my room, wishing for a life as uncomplicated and vital as the ponies I cared for.

Despite Lawrence's generous gift of a truck, my life was more or less dictated by my job. I worked early mornings that lasted well into the night. And then there was the fact that my body was on lockdown. So I'd taken the necessary steps to avoid contact.

When it came down to it I was an industrial machine, outwardly benign but full of dangerous gears and untold hazards. The way I moved, the way I acted, the firm, careful way I held myself indicated strongly that I should be avoided. I was wary of appearing too accessible. If I could have strung myself with red caution tape, I would have.

The dress I'd worn at the fundraiser hung on the wall, its sheer material gathering the light from the overhead bulb. Shaming me. I hadn't worn it since that night, when I strutted through the ballroom, not speaking to a soul, but flinging my very presence in their faces. *I'm alive. I'm living.*

My eyes lingered on the clock, its hands showing 11. I normally fell into bed right about now, to catch a scant six hours sleep before my shift began anew.

I decided to try something different.

I rifled through the drawers of clothing in the little dresser Lawrence had gotten me, pulling out a small black tank top and some tight black jeggings that looked like leather if you weren't accustomed to nice things. I stripped off my barn clothes, setting them down where I'd find them in the morning, and put the jeggings on, realizing that I finally filled them out. The tank top clung to my body, its thin straps emphasizing the cut of my shoulders.

I applied my makeup quickly and with a loose hand. Where I was going, the lighting would be dim.

As I left the barn, a few ponies raised their heads, noticing the click of my heels against the concrete, the curious outline of my hurrying shadow.

"Go back to sleep," I told them. "I have nothing for you."

Hermione watched me closely, the bulge between her eyes even more bulbous and protruding in the dark of night. Her large eyes seemed to convey an almost maternal concern for my wellbeing. The little wrinkles by her mouth and eye sockets were pronounced, even more than usual.

"I'll be safe," I said to her, blowing a kiss that was meant for her muzzle. "You'll see me again at feeding time."

Hermione laid back her ears like a discontented donkey, still pouting as I disappeared from her view. *You better be*, her expression seemed to say.

As my truck ate up the miles, and the night air whistled through the interior cavity, I wondered if it should be alarming or comforting to me that I didn't feel the slightest chill.

I parked outside of Angelina's, its towering exterior blocking out the moon and promising a seedy, dim, pulsating nightclub. *Grand Re-Opening*, a neon sign announced. I wasn't aware that Angelina's had ever shut down.

I wasn't asked for my ID at the door. My stance and the set of my face indicated I was a woman, both hard-ridden and hard-lived. I stepped into the mass of people, bodies rubbing together in every way, from the focused, sexual grinding of couples on the dance floor to the inadvertent brush of limbs as strangers wove their way through the tight, crowded spaces.

I made my way to the bar, stepping up to the long slab of painted metal, glossy black. Beyond the bar, rows of shapely, attractive bottles stood attentive, glowing, backlit by iridescent blue strips of light.

Without bothering to order anything, I stood up on an empty bar stool, my heels leaving indentations in the seat. Climbing up on the bar, I stood above everyone else. I let the music throb through me, finding its way into all my sensory regions. And I let it move me.

Hands above my head, I whirled, keeping pace with the snappy club beat. A sheen of sweat appeared on my belly, visible as my tank top crept upward toward my ribs. My hips came loose, operating separately from my body, finding the supple rhythm of two beings coming together. Shakily, my hands crept down my body, fingers skimming over my collarbone, my breasts, down my belly to the slim, oblong firmness of my thighs.

My eyes swept over the crowd. Mouths slightly parted, the men watched me, taken in by the show. In a flash, I realized what power I held. I was unattainable, just out of reach. I could be seen but not touched. Up here, I could let myself go.

My body soaring, I gave in to the music. It seared through my body, reaching everywhere. My movements became more distinct and focused. The easy sway of my hips became the heavy thrust of a piston, rhythmic to a fault, jutting out from my body in a heavy arc.

When the song ended, I looked around, my vision clearing. Standing at ease among the men, a woman sought me out with her eyes. She was wearing a tight silver bandage dress. Red hair spiraled around her face and upper body, catching more light than the glittery fabric of her dress.

"I'd like to make you an offer," the woman said.

I leapt down from the bar like I'd exit a hayloft, landing lightly with my knees bent. "Who are you?"

"Marla St. James," she purred. "I own this place, and it's been missing something. I think you can fill the void."

"I'd be surprised if I could fill any void," I said honestly. "But what are you referring to?"

A slim smile on her face, she pointed to the main stage, looming beyond the bar in the center of the cavernous ground floor. A vast, empty space graced with a single pole.

I looked at Marla, equal parts shocked and excited. "But I don't pole dance."

Marla shrugged. "So learn."

"I don't know how..."

Marla cut me off. "Come back here on a weekday afternoon. No one's around then. And practice. See if you like it." She smiled, turning and hurrying back to the dance floor, where she was engulfed by writhing bodies.

My eyes lingered on the solitary pole. No one touched it or went near it. It was just there, conspicuously waiting.

Dougie

As had become commonplace on a weekday afternoon at 4:30, Amber and Kelly descended on my house. They paused briefly in the kitchen, kicking off their work boots and grabbing a bite from the fridge, and then they tore up the stairs to Amber's room.

I stuffed in my earbuds and turned the volume up on Adele, raising the decibels until they were strong enough to shatter the tiny hair-like follicles of cilia within my ear, permanently altering my hearing. It blocked out everything that was happening up in that room, but somehow I still couldn't concentrate.

I thought about my run-in with Lawrence, and his polo team. I'd been having those thoughts a lot ever since our conversation. They crept into my mind in quiet moments, sneaky and determined.

I'd done some preliminary research on the sport and culture of polo. It had once been an Olympic sport, but it no longer was, and that seemed to have halted any mainstream appeal it might have otherwise garnered. It maintained a reputation as an elitist sport, an elegant pastime enjoyed by the idle rich, the old and stodgy. Despite being action-packed and full of handsome young men on horses, it just wasn't on the radar of young people. But when Prince Harry played in a match, it made the national news.

Polo needed a champion. It needed a leader, a recognizable, charismatic face to blaze a trail of promotion and notoriety. Someone compelling enough to get the nation behind them.

The sport needed to be thrust into the public eye. It needed to be visible, and even though I lived a tightly contained life, I knew a thing or two about achieving high visibility.

I looked at the time, sterile numbers on the lower right-hand corner of my desktop. I'd been sitting here for six hours without a break. My bones were molding to the shape of this chair, slowly conceding to the slumped posture I insisted they maintain. My body was breaking down. Over time, if I kept this up, I would become less and less mobile. Eventually, I would be chair-bound not by choice, but by necessity. I would be physically disabled, and I would always know in my heart that it didn't have to be that way.

I wasn't sure what was drawing me to that polo club. It didn't make much sense. I didn't like horses, and I didn't like sports. Horses had big teeth, big feet, and they really didn't watch where they were going. They were basically a good way to get killed or broken. And sports were...sports.

Whether or not it made sense it got me out of my chair, gritting my teeth in pain the whole way, and into my van. I typed "Lexington Polo Club" into the GPS and followed the clear, calm instructions of the automated voice.

At the polo club, I walked the grounds looking for signs of life. Horses - technically ponies - moved about in small fenced yards, mowing down grass with their sharp incisors. I gave them a wide berth.

Gradually, I came upon the stands and the field, a huge flat square with a sheen of green grass bright as Astroturf. Tiny sideboards marked the boundaries.

"Look alive, Podunk!" I heard someone shout.

I scurried up into the stands, taking a seat in the corner. Confident I was somewhat hidden, I looked out, letting my eyes settle over the action.

Four ponies were stretched out over the field, traveling close together, a vast locomotive of charging, breathing flesh. Mallets stuck out high above their necks like quills, raised with warning and the intent to sink into something.

All four players seemed to be converging on one small patch of turf, moving so tightly together, it seemed improbable that any of them could hit anything. It seemed unlikely that they could breathe.

At the last second, one of the players dodged away from the pack.

Sending the ball careening off to one side, she raced after it, her long reddish ponytail flowing behind her. Others immediately positioned themselves to block her, landing in her path like large boulders. The girl looked up, clear-headed, not missing a beat. Her horse angled himself sharply, nearly leaning on his side as he whipped his hindquarters around.

She lifted her mallet high and brought it down. The ball streaked across the field, cutting a precise path in between the two players on defense. Upfield, Lawrence eased up alongside it, making an easy shot into the goal.

"Good job, Delaware," he called out, turning his mount around. "Do you concur, Yvette?"

His question was directed at a slender brunette. Now that they were standing still, I could see that she was the smallest person on the team by far.

"It was a fine shot, *Podunk*," she allowed, turning her pony and moving pointedly downfield.

There's friction on the team. They were obviously capable of working well together, but there was enough bad blood between Yvette and this Delaware chick to drench the whole field.

"Let's try another drill," Lawrence cut in. He was clearly the ringleader. "Why don't you practice your goal-tending, Courtney."

I was aware of the fourth player for the first time as she rode forward. She was a tall blonde on a funny-looking horse, muddy brown with crooked legs.

As she passed by, she looked up into the stands. I shrank back against the steel. I don't think she saw me, but her eyes lingered. They were wide and blue, impossibly expressive. Her blonde hair fell down her back, gathered in a high ponytail.

I felt something jarring within me. A twinge, some sort of pull. As she galloped down the field I stood up, no longer caring if I was spotted.

She waited by the goal, cool and collected. Soon she was under siege as Delaware, Lawrence and Yvette all took turns firing shots at her. Eyes half-lidded in concentration, she blocked all but one.

"Nice, Courtney," Lawrence said approvingly.

Courtney. That was her name. I tried to let it settle in my brain, but it just sort of leapt around in there, flashing on and off like a neon sign.

Yvette suddenly twisted in the saddle. Her eyes went right to me, narrow as slits.

"There is someone watching," she declared.

Courtney

"There is someone watching," Yvette snapped, her jaw set firmly.

"Where?" Delaware asked, turning around and looking.

Yvette's eyes rolled. "*In the stands*, Podunk."

I glanced up nervously, my muscles on alert. "Who would be watching us?" I asked shakily.

"Someone in particular, I'm hoping," Lawrence said, riding to the edge of the field. "DOUGIE!" He hollered.

Yvette and I exchanged a glance. *What now,* I could see her thinking.

Whoever-it-was didn't appear right away. Slowly, I caught the outline of a tall, thin man. He made his way out of the stands, pausing around ten feet from the field.

Yvette stared at him, incredulous. "What in the hell is *this*?" She spat.

"At ease, Yvette." Lawrence stepped off Harry, chucking his reins at me and approaching the stranger. "Dougie. Glad you could make it."

"I've been watching," Dougie said, shuffling his shoes. "What you have here is impressive." His eyes landed on me for the faintest second, then they tipped downward again.

Lawrence's back was to me, but I could still sense his keen interest. "So what do you think about coming on board?"

This was too much for Yvette. "Coming on *board*? In what capacity?" She challenged. "What does this *kid* have to offer?"

"A service you desperately need," Dougie said, his voice surprisingly firm. "P.R."

Yvette hacked out a disapproving sound. "How does *that* help us?"

"Finding sponsors. Recruiting fans. Money. Notoriety. Power." Dougie shifted on his feet. "It all starts with visibility. From what Lawrence tells me, none of you have done a damn thing to build buzz on social media. You don't have a platform. You don't have shit." He looked Yvette in the eye. "Since you disassociated from the Women's Polo Federation, you've been living under a rock. Internet searches of your name turn up old news from a *year* ago. In the eyes of polo's royalty, you might as well be dead."

His words hit Yvette right in the chest. He silenced her, knocked the wind right out of her. And that was a hard thing to do.

"You guys have something compelling here," Dougie said. "You've got a story that people will identify with. You've got looks, determination, and talent. But someone needs to put you in the public eye. Someone needs to get your story out there. While you're practicing, I could be doing that."

Delaware zeroed in on him, her eyes clear and assessing. "What's your angle?" She asked, not unkindly, but not flippantly either. "What are you getting out of this?"

Dougie considered this. "I've been looking for something to invest in," he said. "Something beyond myself. I want to do what I do on a much more vast scale." For a second, his face fell into shadow. "And maybe I want to live. Maybe I want an adventure."

Delaware nodded, satisfied. "I can understand that," she said.

"What about financially?" Yvette had finally come out of her stupor. "Surely you will expect compensation."

Dougie shook his head. "If you make it big, like say you get a reality show, I'll take a cut. But I don't expect anything up front. I'm financially stable. I can support myself. I'm not here for any of those reasons."

"So you are bartering your time and talents for us to whisk you away from your caged-in life?" Yvette smoothly articulated.

Dougie looked embarrassed. "Essentially."

A silence fell, everyone in their own head, contemplating the chain of events, forming opinions. I watched Dougie standing there, painfully out in the open, half-hidden by the enormous baggy clothes he wore.

Some people were unlucky enough to have it all on the outside. Like Dougie. Who knew what a fine mind and pure soul could be in there, obscured by acne-ravaged skin and knobby knees.

It went both ways. You could have someone like me, athletic, attractive, with a body that worked in every way it was supposed to, a well-maintained vessel. And you could look in my mind and see that every single moment I appeared to have it together, it was all a house of cards.

"Well I think we should at least give him a trial run," I said.

Everyone looked at me, slightly startled. Rarely was I the first person to speak.

"Yeah, what could it hurt?" Delaware said.

"I'm all for it," Lawrence said. "So it doesn't really matter what Yvette thinks."

"*What I was going to say* was that we ought to give him a chance. Some of his ideas are valid." Yvette clucked to her pony, cantering primly away.

Gradually, the group dispersed, and it was only me and Dougie standing there. Well, he was standing and Hermione was standing. I was sitting.

Dougie ran a hand down the back of his head, clutching a chunk of short hair just above his neck. "Thanks for saying that," he said.

"No problem. I meant it." I fiddled with my reins like I meant to go somewhere. Hermione, knowing me all too well, didn't move a hair.

Dougie's eyes stayed on me. He rocked back and forth slightly on his feet. "You looked good out there," he said. "I mean, you played well," he quickly clarified.

"Uh, thanks." I shortened my reins and even moved my legs a little. Once again, Hermione didn't flinch. "I was pretty rusty for a while there. It's good to have a team going again."

"Does it have a name?"

I glanced down at my little mare. "Hermione."

He blushed slightly. "No. I meant the team. That's a pretty name, though."

I smiled. "She's not much to look at. But she's a great girl." I thought for a second. "No, the team doesn't have a name. I don't even think we've passed around any ideas."

"Well, we'll need to come up with one. Something recognizable." Dougie let his hands fall to his sides. "Maybe you should think on it."

I let my reins slacken. "Why me?" I asked.

Dougie shrugged, looking at me full-on. "Why not you?"

Erica

Maggie sat in the passenger seat, her small face firmly set in a scowl. Her thumbs pressed down feverishly on her phone screen, undoubtedly composing a blistering Facebook status that her friends could all Like within minutes. Soon she finished and stuffed her phone back in her pocket. She crossed her arms over her chest and huffed out a sigh.

I didn't press her to talk, I just drove along in contemplative silence. Eventually, when we turned onto Lawrence's road, and she began to see the familiar landmarks - the brick farmhouse, the old stone wall, the chickens - Maggie's face perked up again.

"Thanks for bringing me out here." Maggie glanced at me as we pulled in the drive. "I just really needed to get away from my mom."

I nodded deeply. "I understand."

The truth was I had been eager to whisk Maggie away. I had missed spending time with her lately. Our lessons had dwindled due to my other responsibilities, and when I went too long without seeing the kid it made me question everything all over again. Maggie grounded me. She reaffirmed my convictions. And she would always be my first and most loyal client, the one who kept me going when I was starting out on my own.

Meanwhile, Mrs. Allsteen was her usual controlling, misguided, entirely ineffective self. When I showed up for our lesson, she and Maggie had been in the middle of a row. Despite hitting a brick wall every time, Mrs. Allsteen was still hung up on her crazy conviction that Maggie should be riding in shows so that she could end up in Madison Square Garden, or the Olympics, or the Grand National. No matter how many times Maggie told her that she didn't want to show, and she didn't want to jump, she just wanted to trail ride, Mrs. Allsteen refused to let go of her dream that Maggie would become the next Velvet Brown.

Then there was the sad, unavoidable fact that Maggie was fast outgrowing her pony, Twinkle. Not in height - Maggie was 8 years old, slender and petite. In experience. Twinkle was, and would forever be, a pretty, perfect, push-button hunter pony. He was great, and safe, but he was boring. Maggie wasn't a huntseat princess. Maggie was a gutsy, determined aspiring endurance rider. She wanted to ride for miles in desolate terrain, subsisting on handfuls of nuts and Powerbars and camping with her horse. I hadn't had the heart to tell her yet, but Twinkle was never going to be that horse.

So I'd brought her here to get her away from it all, and to get her up on another horse, something she could be challenged by and have fun with. But as I parked my truck and surveyed the array of horses clustered in paddocks, I experienced my typical conundrum. *What can I actually put her on?*

Delusion was out. I couldn't use a client's horse as a lesson horse, not without permission, and he was basically Twinkle in a bigger, younger package. Trucker was out, for obvious reasons. The rest of the horses were either too valuable or too volatile for me to put Maggie on. *Or both, in some cases,* I thought as Assault shot me a nasty look. I noticed he'd kicked down another fence board.

While I mentally debated, Maggie took charge. "I'm gonna go pet Soiree." She took off running. "Hi, Lawrence!" She shrieked as he came out of the house.

Lawrence raised a hand and flashed a smile in her direction. She staggered in mid-stride, caught herself, and kept running. *Horses, not boys.* Maggie had her priorities in order.

Like I used to.

Lawrence sidled up next to me. "What's the kid doing here?"

"I thought I'd put her on a different horse. Twinkle just isn't cutting it anymore." I gestured at the paltry selection. "But I don't have that many options here."

Lawrence snapped to attention with surprising speed. "Use Eloise."

I gaped at him. "*Really?*"

"Why not? She's been sitting for weeks now. She needs a job, and I haven't had the time to take her out, what with the team and everything. She's as safe as they come - she doesn't spook, doesn't put a foot wrong, unless you get up in her mouth. But Maggie's got good hands." He paused, nodding slightly. "And Elle loves trail riding."

I nodded, excitement settling onto my face. "Maggie would love it. The chance to ride Eloise...*Eloise*!" I looked at him searchingly. "I just never thought...I know how much Elle means to you."

"I just want her to be happy." Lawrence stared out at the small paddock where Eloise spent her days. "And she's not. She's miserable standing around. And if I can't use her, someone should." He slipped his arm around me. "Maggie's a good kid. I like her. And if there's anything she needs to learn, if there's anything you haven't already taught her, Elle will make sure she learns it."

I hugged him tightly. "*Thank you*. She'll be so thrilled."

"You bet." Lawrence gave me a squeeze. "I've gotta run. Let me know how it goes."

I watched him as he stepped away from me. "Anything I should tell Maggie?"

"Light hands, and enjoy the fuck out of my horse."

"Okay." I laughed, standing still as he disappeared into his truck and down the road.

I went to the barn and picked up Eloise's halter, butter-soft, faded leather. I walked to the paddock where she stood, a cagey look on her face and every muscle in her body on alert. She turned around and greeted me with the snap of her teeth and pinned ears that had become her default. Humans had become unwelcome in her eyes, justifiably villainous, never letting her run, always moving her from stall to paddock, from box to box.

I wanted her to know that things were different this time. I left the halter on the gate and went back to the barn. I came out with a bridle instead.

At first, Eloise's reaction was the same. A threatening click of her incisors, a grimace. But as I slipped the reins over her head and held the bit under her nose, she changed, dropping her head, sniffing the leather, the stainless steel. She opened her mouth and took the bit in, chewing it as I fastened the straps. Her eyes large and soft, she peered at me, not quite trusting, but unmistakably hopeful.

"Come on, Eloise," I said, opening the gate, leading her by the reins. "Let's get to work."

Elaine

Wilson didn't give me any grief when I came up to him out of the blue and asked for a weekday afternoon off. If anything, he seemed pleased. He even grunted "Have a good time," at me as he saw me on my way out the door.

I fingered my hair as I drove, brushing it back from my eyes as the warm air buffeted me. Angelina's was vastly different in the light of day. It was completely deserted, and I left my truck sitting in the middle of the sloping, potholed parking lot.

The only reason I'd come out here at all was to get this idea out of my head. The most absurd thing I could do would be to let this belief have a foothold. To entertain the possibility that I had a destiny, or some such bullshit. I'd found my niche. I had a job that consisted of menial labor and meticulous observation. It kept my body exhausted and my head clear. It kept me down in the trenches where I belonged.

I walked in, noting that the vast interior was comfortingly dim. There really wasn't much charm to this place. It had the atmosphere of a dive bar on the scale of a stadium. The sunlight pushed through a single window, determined, reaching all the way across the room in a thin strip that came to rest on the pole.

I dropped my bag on the floor, bounding up onto the stage. I reached out, grasping the pole and leaning back. I really didn't know how to do this.

I wondered what Marla had seen in me, what her expectations were. I knew I didn't intend on stripping. There was nothing inherently wrong with it, and I certainly couldn't judge those who made a living at it. But I couldn't see myself up here, nearly naked and shimmying around.

I wanted to be fully clothed, unattainable, and unashamed. Like I was the other night.

I backed up a step or two and leapt at the pole, hugging it and clinging to it without a shred of grace. I hauled myself up with my arms, climbing higher until I was perched near the top, looking down at a lot of open space. Making sure my feet were securely hooked, I let go, bending my body backward. My head swung through the air, staring up at the ceiling. With a single hand, I grazed the surface of the stage.

I pulled myself up again with difficulty, becoming more aware of my body and the ways I needed to use it. I slid partway down, stopping myself and climbing up high again. I leaned far to the side, reaching out, my fingers lit up by errant sunbeams. None of my movements were coordinated or beautiful. But as I pushed myself, I found my body responding.

An hour later, I sat on the floor, sweat pooling in the small of my back. My work-hardened hands hurt from gripping the metal. A back muscle spasmed periodically.

I heard a noise, and I jumped to my feet. Marla had appeared from nowhere. I hadn't even known she was there. She was barefoot in a men's dress shirt and not much else.

I wondered if she'd seen my fumbling. "I don't know what I'm doing," I said honestly. "You've probably got the wrong person."

Marla appeared unbothered. "How soon do you think you can put a routine together?" She asked me.

I thought for a moment. "Probably within a couple of weeks. If it's going to work, I'll have it down by then."

"Okay then. I'll start getting the word out. Two weeks from Friday you'll debut."

I stared at her. "But what if I'm terrible?"

Marla shrugged. "It's just entertainment. No one's life is at stake here."

"I guess you're right," I said. But my heart was beating so fast it felt like mine might be.

Erica

When Maggie found me in the barn I was leaning under Eloise's belly, whisking the dust and grit off the mare with a body brush. I could see Maggie attempting to read the situation. Her eyes narrowed and she leaned back on her heels, carefully watching me.

"I thought you said I was gonna ride," Maggie said.

"You are." I straightened up, walking over to a saddle rack. I picked up Eloise's saddle, smoothing the pad beneath it, and set it on her back.

Maggie's hand fluttered up to her collarbone. "But...that's Eloise."

"Lawrence is very busy now with the polo team, so he wanted you to ride her. She needs a job," I explained, tightening the girth and walking around to Eloise's other side.

"Oh my God." Maggie walked over to Eloise's head, staring up at the mare as if she were an icon. "I get to ride Eloise?! *Eloise*. That's insane. She's, like, famous."

"She'll be a step up from what you're used to," I commented, adjusting the stirrups for Maggie's short legs. "But you've ridden D.M., you've ridden Vegas. Those are both highly trained, sensitive horses."

"But they're not Eloise." Maggie was giving me that slightly pitying, almost condescending look that was particularly disconcerting on such a small, young face. "This horse is *beloved*. There are photos of her all over the internet. She has legions of fans, Pinterest boards, groups on Facebook...people were devastated when she was injured." She smiled wryly. "Lawrence is probably still living off the contributions from her fans."

"Huh."

I bent down to wrap Eloise's legs, not pausing until I was finished. Maggie's last remark hung in the air, and it bothered me, although I didn't know why it should.

When I stood up, Maggie was watching me intently. "Get your helmet, and we'll be ready to start," I said.

She jogged off to retrieve it from wherever she'd set it down and returned with the gaudy, sparkly pink protective gear strapped to her head.

"One more thing." I knew Maggie had good hands, but I wanted her to have a more visceral understanding of why that was so important. "When you ride this horse, you need to be especially mindful of how you use your hands. You can't get tight on her. Because of this...."

While Maggie watched, I hooked my thumb in the space between Eloise's teeth. She resisted at first, bracing against my hand, but I persisted, and she relented and opened her mouth.

Maggie stared, her eyes darting from Eloise's scarred tongue to me.

"What happened to her mouth?"

"Someone was very rough with her," I answered, releasing Eloise's head. She mouthed the bit in relief.

Maggie's eyes darkened. "A *bit* did that? That's sick."

"That's why you never use more force than you have to. With a horse like this, only fingertip pressure on the reins is necessary."

I led Eloise outside, lifting the reins over her head and setting them on her withers. "Here, I'll give you a leg up."

Eloise stood still as Maggie settled into the saddle, nestling her feet into the stirrups and finding her seat. She looked at me. "Are we going in the arena?"

I looked at them together, and I made a decision. "Elle hates the ring. Let's go on the trail."

Maggie grinned openly, and with a touch of her leg, Eloise moved out. Her ears pricked as we left the outskirts of Lawrence's property, and she did not glance backward, even when the other horses called out. Maggie sat loosely in the saddle, with one hand on the reins, and the wind fanned out their hair, blonde and silver. They looked like they'd been together for years. And I walked alongside them, even though they didn't need me there. Eloise had replaced me as Maggie's teacher, and she now stepped in with the same desire and flair of her younger years, when she'd shown Lawrence how to play the game.

Lawrence

For the second time in my life, I stood inside Dougie's house. It hadn't gotten any homier since the addition of Amber as a roommate. But I guessed Amber had probably been too busy screwing her girlfriend to worry much about Dougie, or the depressing state of his bare walls and nearly empty rooms.

Yvette stood next to me, arms tightly crossed, foot tapping soundlessly. She'd come along with me to check up on Dougie's progress (or, as she put it, "to see what that kid has done for our team"). Delaware had elected to stay at the Days Inn. "I trust y'all's judgment," she'd said sweetly when I offered to give her a ride.

I didn't know why Courtney had stayed behind. Usually where Yvette went, she'd follow. Maybe they were having another tiff or something.

Dougie leaned over a desk, opening up web pages and images on different monitors. All the while his thumb jerked around on his phone screen. "Here's some of what I've been working on," he said.

I stepped forward, stooping over to look at the first screen. Yvette shoved past me, wriggling into the space between me and the desk, determined as ever to be the first to know.

She looked at the screen for a long moment and just sort of froze. I saw her jaw slacken.

"How...did you do all of this?" She demanded, clicking through tab after tab.

I moved to the next computer, wanting an unblocked view. A video of one of our recent practices was playing. It had been edited flawlessly to show us at our best, and it played in high resolution.

I stared at the monitor. "We have a YouTube channel?"

"When were you even filming us?" Yvette asked with slight alarm.

Dougie shrugged. "I stay quiet," he said. "Out of sight. But I'm always there."

"That's a little creepy." I looked at the next screen, a gallery of high-quality photos. "But this is awesome."

"You have a Facebook page, a Flickr gallery, and obviously the YouTube thing to start with," Dougie said. "I've also made a Twitter handle for each of you, and I'm tweeting daily on your behalf." He looked at our shocked faces. "Don't worry, it's all very benign, nothing about your personal lives. It's all about getting people invested in the team. To do that, they have to feel like they know you. Twitter is another way of making that connection, and it's more effective if each of you are speaking to the populace. I could've made a generic handle for the collective team, but that reads as phony. In that case, people assume some undercover writer is composing the tweets, and they lose interest."

Yvette scanned through the photo gallery, her finger rhythmically tapping the mouse. "You have done beautiful work here," she said softly, completely disarmed.

"It's a start," Dougie said. "If I continue with you, I'll want to make it more interactive. I'll step up the tweeting, as well as having you do some interviews on camera. Maybe even start posting videos in reality-show format, just tailing you and filming in real time. Your stories and goals are admirable and compelling, but there's nothing wrong with dishing the dirt as well. Everyone loves a good fight."

I turned away from the computer screen. "Well you've sold me on it." I glanced at Yvette, who was still motionless. "What do you say?"

She ignored me, turning the full intensity of her gaze on Dougie. He flinched, slouching low and reducing his height by several inches.

"When did you decide to call it Team Dark Horse?" She asked him.

"The other day, after I left the polo club," Dougie said. "I knew it needed a name. Something recognizable that people could latch onto. They might not know all your names, but they'll remember Team Dark Horse and what it stands for. You're coming from nothing. You're overlooked, undervalued, untested. Each of you has something to prove. And you're working restlessly to come bursting onto the scene, out of nowhere, and achieve a long-shot win."

He looked nervously at us, from one face to the other. "But if you don't like it, I can change it. I should've asked first. I'm sorry."

"Do not be sorry," Yvette snapped, raising her voice for the first time. "It is perfect."

Courtney

Dougie was always around now. He was easy to overlook, slipping in behind the scaffolding on the bleachers, or crouching at the sidelines for the optimum shot. During breaks in the action when we switched to fresh horses, he would pull out his phone and start typing. He never let any of our pages go silent for too long.

Dougie was easy to overlook if you weren't looking for him. Whenever I passed by him, I was self-conscious of the lens of his camera staring me down. I noticed when it was on me, and I noticed when it pointed away. Somehow, those moments were the worst.

"Silva!" Lawrence bellowed. "Get over here!"

I clucked anxiously to Hermione, and she carried me over to where the rest of Team Dark Horse was assembled. "Sorry," I mumbled.

"*Someone* really likes the camera," Delaware commented with a friendly smile.

"Indeed." Yvette gave me a crushing smirk. "And the camera likes her as well."

I clutched my reins, breathing unevenly. *Is there some deeper meaning behind that? Or does she just mean I look good in my pictures? She did see the pictures. Maybe that's all it is.*

Yvette watched me for a moment. "Be careful there, Courtney," she said warningly.

My torso drooped. *Okay, no. She doesn't just mean that I take a good picture.*

"Don't worry," I mumbled, eyes downcast. "I'll just stay in my room and listen to Britney."

Delaware's head was cocked to the side. She looked confused and also kind of relieved that she wasn't in on the conversation.

"Today I want to talk about team roles," Lawrence's self-assured voice cut in. "Of course we need the ability to play all the positions and adapt to the flow of the game. But it's clear to me that we have an extremely well-rounded team here, and each of you are really shining in your roles."

"Position number 1, the glory position. That's you, Yvette." He smiled as she puffed up, looking fiercely happy. "You're a beast when it comes to offense. You're on the attack, and if there's a goal to be scored, you'll get in there and get it done. You can do anything, but this is where you really shine."

"That is true," Yvette said without a hint of modesty.

"Number 2, primarily offense, backing up the number 1 player while also working with the number 3 player on defense. You really have to be a chameleon of sorts to do this well. It takes a very versatile, very cool-headed player. Surprisingly, that's turned out to be you, Delaware."

"Which brings us to number 3, the most revered position." He paused for dramatic effect. "Responsible for stopping the opposing offense and passing the ball to the number 1 and 2 players. It requires a lot of accuracy, a lot of experience. The person in this position will have the highest handicap." He grinned from ear to ear. "And I do."

Eyes rolled simultaneously. Delaware even jokingly put a finger down her throat, earning an approving glance from Yvette.

"Anyway." He straightened up, looking serious again. "Rounding out the team is Courtney on number 4. Heavy defense, goaltending, and the ability to accurately hit a shot halfway up the field to reach Delaware or me. You've got it all, Silva. You get it done."

Yvette gathered her reins, picking up contact with Hedge Fund's mouth. "Now that we have all congratulated ourselves, can we get back to work?" She asked humorlessly.

"I'm way ahead of you on that one." Lawrence peeled away from her, arm outstretched as he chased the ball. She swore loudly, pursuing him. I watched them, sighing deeply.

I turned in the saddle, looking back at Dougie. He was looking right at me, and he quickly raised the camera to his eyeball. But I didn't see him take a picture.

Dougie

Team roles.

Lawrence

Team leader, the lone guy. Rags to riches backstory, bad-boy appeal. Womanizing past. Flawless, dedicated horsemanship. Only one on the team with experience playing internationally. Highest handicap.

Yvette

Foreigner with a chip on her shoulder. Smallest girl on the team and the most vicious. #1 ranked in the Women's Polo Federation, dropped when she dared to dream.

Delaware

Lovable all-American girl. Corn-fed, country-proud. Plucked from a cornfield and now poised to make her debut in international-caliber competition. Tons of raw talent and determination, but entirely untested. Wild card.

Courtney

Here was where I got hung up every time. I didn't know where Courtney fit in. Team-wise, sure, she had her place. But what was her *story*?

All I knew about her was that she came from privilege. She had her every expense paid for by her doting father, and she played second fiddle to Yvette in every aspect of her life. She was dynamic on the field, but in real life she was a pushover. That didn't make for a compelling story.

Everyone else had a clear role they filled. But Courtney didn't. And I was starting to realize just how much that bothered me.

I stared at the document for a while longer, and because I wasn't getting anywhere with it, I opened up the gallery of photos I was editing. Page after page of thumbnails stared me in the face.

They were overwhelmingly photos of her. I needed to get a handle on that.

The only thing that truly jumped out at me about Courtney if I put myself in the place of a casual bystander was her beauty. And even that she carried unconvincingly. It could have been effortless, but instead it seemed to weigh on her. When I looked in her eyes I saw the blank, frightened stare of someone who didn't know how to handle the world they lived in.

I looked again at the picture of Courtney on Hermione. I tried to think of what people would see in her when they were getting to know the team. What role they would automatically put her in. What value she would be assigned. I already knew the answer, but I wanted something better for her. I closed out the gallery, and the document laid itself bare on my screen.

Courtney

Sometimes there just isn't anything better.

Courtney

The T & A, I wrote below her name. Brutal honesty. People would see a pretty girl, and not much else. There wasn't too much else to see.

The T & A

I clicked "Save", and tried to pretend that was all she was to me too.

Maggie

Erica dropped me off at the barn and got back on the road to teach some of her other clients. Nobody was there but the horses, and I was allowed to tack up Eloise all by myself and go for a ride. It was just like having Twinkle, but better, because my mom couldn't butt in all the time.

And because it was Eloise.

"Eloise, Eloise!" I sang out her name when I skipped down to her paddock carrying a halter. She wasn't sure about my singing, but she came right to the gate and stuck her head in the halter. The cool thing about Eloise was she liked to go for rides.

Eloise was a fast walker, which I didn't mind. She wasn't mean about it either. Whenever she got to the end of the lead, she'd slow down so I could catch up. I tried to walk quicker so she wouldn't have to do that. She was taller than Twinkle too, so I had to stand on a mounting block to do stuff like brush the top of her back and put the saddle on.

Eloise wasn't like the other horses. She didn't care about the kind of things they did. When we went on rides, she'd march right past the other horses and she wouldn't look back. She was kind of a loner, I guessed. She didn't really have friends and she didn't seem to care about making any. She liked what she liked and that was it.

Twinkle did what I wanted him to do because he was trained for it. It was like a job for him. For Eloise it was a passion.

She would go along the road, with cars passing by her, no problem. She passed all the houses and the mailboxes like they weren't there. She wasn't even afraid of the chickens. But when we got to the woods, that was when she got really good.

Eloise went through water, through ditches, up and down hills. She could find the best footing in any situation. If there were trees in the way, she'd slip between them or just bowl them over. She actually liked crashing through the underbrush and would do it at any opportunity. No trail was too rugged for her. When the going got tough, she just powered through.

Sometimes I'd lose track of time, and we'd be out for hours. It was just so comfortable being with her. She was so safe, so in control. But she wasn't boring. Not at all.

By the time we got back, it was pretty late in the afternoon. Erica was back, and so was Lawrence. After I untacked Eloise, I decided to give her a bath. She had dirty sweat marks on her coat.

I dropped her lead rope, and she stood still the whole time, even though there was grass all around her. I poured the soap on her sweaty areas, rubbing it in until she was all foamy. Then I rinsed off her whole body, paying extra attention to her legs where the leg wraps had been. She stood in the sun, water dripping off her silvery coat, looking down at me in her special way. Like she didn't quite understand why I was there, but she accepted it.

I decided to take her to eat some grass over by Lawrence's house. I always did that, and I always stayed with Eloise until Erica showed up and told me it was time for me to go home. I always made her come and find me, which she didn't always appreciate.

This time Lawrence came to find me. I looked up and saw him. He smiled at me, but he didn't tell me it was time to go so I just waited for him to say something.

"Did you have a good ride?" He asked me.

"Oh yes." I nodded happily.

"That's good." He leaned against the side of the house, watching Eloise eat grass. "I'm glad she's working out for you."

"She's great." I patted her on the shoulder. "It's so cool that you're letting me ride her. I almost feel like she's my horse. But I know she's not," I added.

"Actually, that's kind of what I wanted to talk to you about." Lawrence cocked a hip, resting one leg, a lot like horses do when they're standing around. "Eloise will always be my horse, as far as ownership goes. I'll never sell her. But I can't use her, and it's hard for me to give her the time she deserves. That's why I wanted you to try riding her. I wanted to see how the two of you would get along. And you seem to be getting along very well."

"I really like her." I patted Eloise again. "I don't know if she likes me."

Lawrence shook his head. "She likes you. Trust me. Elle is not a warm and fuzzy kind of horse. She doesn't go for petting or physical contact. She tolerates it." He leaned back, gazing up at the sky. "That's how I knew I couldn't leave her. When she got hurt, and I went to see her in the large animal hospital…she was still recovering from the anesthesia, but when I let myself into her stall, she looked right at me, walked up to me and put her head right on my chest. Just stayed like that for a good ten minutes."

He shook himself a little. "Anyway. Erica told me about your competitive trail riding. Is that something you want to keep doing?"

"Yes." I nodded my head. "Then I'd like to start doing Limited Distance rides and eventually, 50-100 milers."

"Elle can do that. You'd have to condition her, obviously, and it's a lot of work to maintain a horse at that level of fitness. But it's nothing you couldn't do. And it's well within Elle's capabilities. She can't gallop, can't handle the sudden stops and tight turns of my sport. But a steady trot over terrain…she can do that. And she'd love it."

I stared at him. "But…what about Twinkle?"

"I know you've been doing a lot of work with Erica, getting Twinkle used to the trails. And I know you could probably keep him going for a while. But Twinkle's not a trail pony. He's a show pony. You get a lot out of him because he loves you, but it's clear to Erica and me that he's not comfortable in this sport. So as hard as it is, I think you should consider selling him to a kid who does want to show and ride in arenas. And you should consider Eloise yours on indefinite loan."

My hands were shaking. I almost dropped the lead rope. "*Eloise*? Mine?"

"I mean, if you're interested." Lawrence grinned at me.

"Of course I am!" I shouted.

"Well, there you go." Lawrence smiled. "Works out for everybody."

"Everybody except for my mom." I felt my grin fading. "What's she gonna say when I tell her I want to sell Twinkle? She'll *never* go for that."

"Endurance is an Olympic sport. Just tell her that, and say you've got the use of a horse who's a seasoned international competitor."

"That could work."

"You bet it could." Lawrence grinned at me. "Oh, and Erica says you need to go home."

"Ugh." I pulled gently on the lead, and Eloise picked up her head. I hugged her neck, and she sighed, gazing off at her paddock in the distance.

"We're gonna do things, Eloise," I whispered.

She pricked up her ears.

Erica

In the pinkish light of dusk, I rode Assault, flexing him and keeping his back round. The surge and ebb of his stride revealed his displeasure with the exercise, and a tightness crept into the spot between my shoulder blades, a small mutiny from my body as it carried the burden of reining him in.

I kept experimenting with Assault, trying to find the work schedule he would tolerate. I'd attempted gallop drills to take the edge off, and all they did was render me exhausted, as floppy as Gumby, while he was still piping hot and ready to run even more. I'd even given him several days off in a row. It had done nothing to improve his attitude.

I hadn't intended on giving him time off. I'd just run out of time and energy one day, and I found that once I stopped working him it was hard to start again. I'd spent the time I should have used on Assault traipsing around on D.M., letting the quiet steadiness of his stride restore me.

But it was now or never. Soiree's winnings were adding up. She was close to qualifying, and once she sold, my entire focus would be on campaigning Assault.

A thin cloud of dust rose up from the under-watered ring, contributing to the hazy atmosphere. Assault's neck rippled as he curled behind the bit, dropping his back out from underneath me and mincing along.

"Cut that out," I growled, lifting him up with my calves. "Step up."

Headlights arced onto the drive, courtesy of a new-model Ford truck. My dad stepped out of the driver's side, carefully shutting the door and pressing the Lock button even though he was way out in the country.

"Hey, Dad." My voice was dry and somewhat croaky. "What's up?"

"I haven't seen you in the ring lately," he said, leaning over and resting his torso on the top rail. "I thought I'd come see how you were doing."

"I've been qualifying my hunter mare," I explained. "That takes precedence over Assault right now."

My dad eyed the gelding. I'd halted him, and Assault had thrust his head straight up in the air, nostrils billowing like a dragon. I gave the outside rein a light tug, and Assault ignored it. Rather than get into a scene with the gelding in front of my dad, I gave up. My dad had never considered Assault safe.

"Well, don't let me keep you from your training," my dad said. "Keep doing what you were doing. I'll be your eyes on the ground."

That was exactly what I'd been trying to avoid.

I pushed Assault into a canter, and he made a nice transition. Disarmed for a moment, I reached forward to pat him. Assault gathered himself to hump his back, and I slammed my butt into the saddle. "*Quit,*" I ordered.

Assault moved along, disgruntled and in a broken rhythm. He overreacted to my aids, careening off the rail and flipping his head when I touched his mouth. His eyes were wild, like I'd flogged him within an inch of his life or something.

My dad shook his head. "He's still as rank as he ever was," he said, watching him.

"He's better in the ring." I sat up and aimed him at a fence. Assault ran at it, jumping crookedly. He didn't rub a rail, but I could tell it was an ugly effort.

My dad was watching intently. "He's laying on his side and hanging his left knee," he called out.

"He's just screwing around. He can do it right when he wants to." Assault sucked back, boarding up his body, his flanks unresponsive to my kicking.

"But that's the thing. He doesn't want to." My dad sighed, watching Assault's jarring transition from hypersensitive to dead-sided. "A horse can have all the physical ability in the world, but if they're not there with you mentally, it doesn't matter how great they look on paper. You have nothing to work with."

"He just hates training. He's great in the ring. We just have to get through this." I tried to speak with conviction as my dad continued to shine an ultra-watt beam on all the collective doubts I'd ever had about this horse.

My dad squared up, turning away to pace the fence line. "All I know is that when you reach the upper levels of this sport, it's going to be more intense than you can even imagine. The things you'll face, the physical feats you'll have to attempt and the split-second decisions you'll need to make are more daunting than you realize. In that world, you're in a wormhole of horse showing. Everything is heightened. When you're just starting out, it's all you can do not to dissolve into a puddle of nerves when you realize what you're up against. And in that moment, the only thing that's going to get you through is having a good horse under you."

My dad's eyes swept over me, pale blue and clouded with worry. "The partnership is *everything*. That's all you have. And I'm concerned you don't even have that."

I looked away. My eyelids battled to contain the heavy moisture behind them. "We'll work it out," I said firmly. "We have to."

My dad nodded grimly. He stared at Assault's aloof posture with something bordering on loathing. "I just wish you had something better."

My eyes looked out through the falling darkness, catching Lawrence's headlights as he pulled up to the house, two hours after he said he'd be back from the polo club.

"Yeah," I said roughly, dabbing my eyes with the back of my gloved hand, ruining the leather with my tears. "I do too."

Lawrence

Eight ponies were scattered around the stable in various stages of aftercare, standing in cross-ties with clay smeared on their hard-worked legs or making endless circles on the hotwalker. I looked fondly at the people gathered around, the pieces of Team Dark Horse that had fallen into place so perfectly. Somehow, the addition of Dougie, quietly typing away in a corner with fierce, somewhat insane dedication, made all the difference.

"Let's think about our next move," I said to the group. "We have a fully-formed team. We have a name. We've got PR covered. What next?"

"Perhaps," Yvette said icily, "we should aspire to attain some additional ponies before Courtney's entire string collapses from burnout."

"I was wondering about that," Dougie's voice floated up from the corner. "You guys are seriously under-horsed."

They were both right. With meticulous care, Courtney's string had been shouldering the burden admirably. But they couldn't keep going like this forever.

"This is where it gets tricky." I leaned back against a stall wall. "We've got to get some money behind us."

"Well, I do not think *you* should be in charge of obtaining it," Yvette said haughtily. "Based on your track record, you will send potential sponsors running for the hills. Or they will expect sexual favors."

"What now?" Delaware piped up, her eyes wide.

"Ancient history," I said dismissively.

"What's that you're calling me?" Elaine had appeared in a doorway, smiling slightly while trying to look disgruntled.

"I am trying to convince Cavanaugh he does not have the ability to recruit a sponsor," Yvette snipped.

Elaine raised her eyebrows. "*You* were dropped by your last sponsor. How does *that* look?"

"I don't think Yvette should be the one to talk to potential sponsors anyway," Delaware cut in. "I know from my fund-raising days that it pays to be friendly and nice, and Yvette just doesn't have it in her."

Yvette turned stone cold. "I'll have you know, you small-town bitch, that I secured a million-dollar contract with my former sponsor, Jean-Phillipe. And I did it without help. I know something about dealing with people."

Delaware shrugged. "Like Elaine said. He dropped you."

I raised my hands. "This is going nowhere."

"Actually, this is kind of awesome. I should have been filming it," Dougie's disembodied voice announced.

"So if Lawrence cannot reach out to sponsors, and if I am so *unqualified* to do so, then who will do it?" Yvette asked thunderously. "Certainly not Courtney. If we are talking about poor people skills..."

"Hey!" Courtney protested weakly. "That's a low blow."

Yvette sent her a withering glance. "I had to place your *order* at Taco Bell last night because you clammed up."

I sighed. "Well, if anyone has any leads, or even the slightest hint of one, we need to get on it right away. And maybe we should start attending these LPC-sponsored get-togethers. We need to be proactive, not just wait for money to fall into our laps."

In the silence that followed my statement, I became aware of a new sound. As it got louder, I recognized it as the rapid-fire clicking of two pairs of stiletto heels moving in tandem. Stilettos attached to a matching set of young, vapid blondes escorting Arnold Windzor down the aisle.

"Cavanaugh!" The small, homely man beamed at me, wrestling his arm away from one of the girls and holding out his hand for me to shake. He was developing a slightly stooped widow's hump posture.

"Hello, Arnold," I said with great unease. I just couldn't get used to his misguided gratitude no matter how hard I tried. "How's things?"

"Excellent, excellent." Arnold grinned like a Cheshire cat. What else would he say?

"I, uh, haven't seen Wilson around." I made a show of craning my neck to look in all the most unlikely places, including up in the rafters. "I think he's out at the moment."

"That's fine, fine." Arnold looked at me straight on. "I actually came to see you, Cavanaugh."

"Oh, really?" I swallowed hard. "To what do I owe the honor?"

Team Dark Horse

Arnold glanced at his matched set of girlfriends. He looked like a poor man's Hefner. "Darlings, if you could excuse yourselves for a moment. We're talking business here."

Obediently, the girls dispersed. Arnold turned back to me. "I hear you've got a team now."

"This is it." I swept my arm around to indicate all the girls, who were staring at Arnold with shock and thinly veiled disgust. "Team Dark Horse."

Arnold nodded, his beady eyes sizing up Delaware and especially Courtney with creepy approval. "But do you have a backer?"

A thin needle of pain seared through my brain. "Not yet."

Arnold grinned, clapping me weakly on the back with his miniature hand. "Then today's a lucky day for both of us."

Some time later, he collected the two girls and drove off. Dougie had disappeared, leaving me with Courtney, Yvette and Delaware. The four of us stared at each other, shoulders slumped, as downtrodden as the ponies after a rough practice.

Courtney spoke first. "If he's our sponsor, he's going to want to *hang out* with us," she said, voicing all of our most violent fears. "And we're going to have to let him."

"How can we be seen with him?" Yvette asked murderously. "We will be a laughingstock. Team Dark Horse will be a *joke*."

"We need the money, though," Delaware said glumly. "I don't see anyone else showing up and offering us millions. Sometimes you have to make compromises to achieve your goals."

I shook my head, standing up tall. "No, we don't. We will *not*."

The three women looked at me.

"We're *not* giving up that easily." I grasped a stall bar for emphasis, feeling like I could crush it in my hand. "We're going to the LPC meet-and-greet on Friday night. We're going to dress up, we're going to arrive as a team, we're gonna look like a million. We're going to mingle, schmooze, and kiss a lot of ass. Because I'm *damned* if I'm going to let us get saddled with Arnold fucking Windzor. We deserve better."

Yvette met my eyes, rising to the challenge. "What should we wear?" She asked.

I cut to the chase. "Slut it up as much as you can, but keep it somewhat classy. Not full-on street whore. Shoot for high-end whore, maybe. Like the kind that politicians get caught with."

"All right." Yvette turned to Delaware and Courtney. "I believe we have a plan."

Elaine

I dropped my music off with the lighting and sound guys and went backstage to get ready. I wiped the last of the dust from my face with a towelette and went to work on my makeup, painstakingly filling in the fine lines and blemishes so I wouldn't have to think about anything else.

I hadn't showered before leaving the barn, but it scarcely mattered because once I went to work on the pole I'd be sweating all over again. It felt more authentic anyway. My performance aesthetic had evolved since I'd put in more practice time. I wasn't this perfect, unattainable girl. I was raw, almost unkempt, pouring my heart and soul into this inanimate object because I had nothing else in the world to lean on.

I hoped it looked like art. I hadn't shown my routine to anyone, hadn't filmed myself. It was the best I could do, and I hoped that it had meaning, but there was this pervasive fear that it would only ever mean anything to me.

I shook myself. *Five minutes.* I finished the last contour and turned my back to the vanity mirror. *Inhale. Exhale. No one's life is at stake here.*

My legs were all wobbly, making me think of the time I walked through the parking lot into the abortion clinic, my body pulling me desperately in some other direction. *Any other direction.* I just overrode it. I forced it to comply.

No one's life is at stake here.

The generic club music cut, and I heard Marla take the mic. I started toward the stage. This time, I followed the pull. It took me right there.

"This stage has been empty for far too long," Marla's voice echoed. "I'm pleased to announce that we have a new performer ready to fill it. She's prepared a routine especially for tonight, so give her a warm welcome."

Loud, drunken applause picked up where her voice left off.

I stepped onto the stage. *Okay.*

My music began, and I leapt up to the pole, grasping it, pulling myself close. Swaying gently, my back to the audience, I spread my arms, keeping myself upright with my legs. Leaning back slowly, I surrendered to the gravitational pull as if someone was holding me and I implicitly trusted them to keep me safe.

Eventually, my head flopped back, coming within an inch of slamming into the floor. My eyes snapped open, and I stared at the audience upside-down, shock and hurt registering in my eyes. A gasp rippled through the crowd.

Gathering myself, I lifted my upper body, returning to the pole. My body nestled intimately with it; my head pressed against it. I climbed higher until I was near the top.

I loosened my grip, looking benevolently up at the ceiling. My body slipped down several inches and I caught myself. As sure as ever, I let go again.

My body dropped dramatically this time, sliding down several feet, creating a breeze that ruffled my hair. My spine arched, and I started to let go, throwing my body backward, repeating my past mistakes.

Again I fell. My hand skimmed the ground as I rolled across the floor, coming to rest at the edge of the stage. The faces in the audience were shocked and riveted, and I couldn't tell if it was because I was getting my point across or if I just looked like a hot mess up here.

I pulled myself up, crawling painstakingly back to the cold, unreceptive pole. I reached out to touch it softly, looking up, my gaze plaintive.

The audience sucked in a breath.

I stood up, shoulders squared even as they shook with the strain of physical effort and the emotions I was accessing in order to make this believable.

I leapt higher, landing halfway up the pole, clinging to it like a child, holding on desperately. I raised my hands, clasping it like I'd hold the back of another person's head, pressing my forehead into the hard, icy metal. I breathed in and out, gathering the last of my reserves.

This last part was the toughest. I'd botched it plenty of times in rehearsal. I was at my weakest by now, my muscles spent and quivering, and the move required both power and precision. It also required a certain fearlessness. I had to take all my limbs away and willfully fall, taking a bruising impact.

I gave the pole one last hopeful stare, and then I launched myself away with enough speed and force to make it look like I'd been thrown. Letting my body go limp, I soared through the air, crumpling into a heap on the hardwood floor. My arm stretched out toward the audience, my palm open. It closed tightly around nothingness, and then my fingers parted, surrendering to the inevitable.

I let the moment play out, remaining still. Then I rose smoothly to my feet.

There was another moment of silence, and then the clapping started. It went on, not drunken, but reverent.

Lawrence

I rolled up to the Days Inn in Dougie's van, because it was the only vehicle that would seat all of us since Yvette had outlawed Courtney's Hummer. I left it running and stood outside the door waiting for them.

Courtney was the first to come out. She wore a short black skirt and a black top cut from the same flowing material. Her hair was down, shimmering to its full effect, and she wore ample gold jewelry on her hands, wrists and neck.

"You look gorgeous," I told her, giving her a kiss on the cheek.

"Thanks." She clasped her hands in front of her. "Yvette will be right out."

Not a moment later, Yvette stepped outside. Her look was the opposite of Courtney's in every way. Her hair was pulled back tightly in a bun and shellacked to her head. It wasn't going anywhere. Her gown was floor-length, skimming her body, glittery silver with spaghetti straps.

"Who are we waiting on?" She spat, looking around. Her face assembled into a scowl. "Of course."

"She'll be here," I said evenly.

"She had better be," Yvette threatened.

The door thrust open, and our heads turned. Out clattered Delaware, precariously balanced on sky-high wedge heels. Her hair bounced around her face in big-barrel curls, and she was in a bronze-colored, heavily sequined getup. It was strapless, molded to her body, showing ample cleavage and even more leg.

"Sorry I'm late, y'all." She skipped over to us, skidding to a stop and nearly twisting her ankle. "I am so *excited!*"

Yvette looked at her, showing a range of disgust and pity. "He said to shoot for *high-class* whore, Podunk."

"I think she looks lovely," I fired back, offering Delaware my arm. "Let me get the door for you."

"Why, thank you!" Delaware twisted her head around to grin at me. "Such a gentleman."

"Don't fall for it, Podunk," Yvette said warningly, rolling her eyes. "He is just waiting to get a glimpse up your skirt when you climb into that van."

"I'll shut my eyes," I promised.

"And you will be picturing it the whole time," Yvette said, opening the door and hopping into the passenger seat.

With Courtney and Delaware seated in the back, I opened up the driver's side door and put the van into reverse.

"This had better work," Yvette muttered beside me.

"We'll give it our best shot," I said confidently.

"What happens if Arnold's there and sees us schmoozing with everyone else?" Courtney asked. "Won't that be weird?"

I shook my head. "Arnold's pretty oblivious. He overlooks a lot."

"Like when you were fucking his wife in exchange for a string of ponies financed by his money?" Yvette asked fake-sweetly.

I cracked a smile. "Precisely."

"Damn." Delaware's eyes were wide in my rear-view. "And I thought Friedmont had its share of drama."

"Consider this your not-so-warm welcome to the world of high-goal polo," Yvette deadpanned. "The higher you rise, the dirtier it becomes."

"Let's hope we make it that far," Courtney said, biting down on a nail.

Yvette

The mood in the stable was decidedly grim. We were each seated upon bales of hay or tack trunks. Knees spread, we stared at the floor. Not one person had expressed interest in backing Team Dark Horse, with the exception of Arnold Windzor. Time was running out for us to make a decision. But no one wanted to be the one to pull the trigger.

"We're going to have to hang out with him," Delaware said, pulling on a limp strand of hair. Her eyes were as glum as I'd ever seen them.

"He is going to expect to tag along wherever we go," I said. "Like a sick, glassy-eyed puppy. We will constantly be tripping over him."

"At least you're not his type," Courtney said thickly.

"He did marry a brunette," I pointed out.

Lawrence raised his head. "Yeah, but once you go blonde, you never go back."

"He does have two of them now," Delaware said. "That probably means he likes them extra."

"Shut up!" Courtney yelped. "This isn't a laughing matter. You guys don't have anything to worry about. *You're* not the one who's going to get sexually assaulted."

"I'm pretty sure you could just deck the guy if he ever tried to get physical," Delaware said sensibly. "For reals, though. He's definitely going to make a pass at you."

"Uggghh. I don't think I can deal." Courtney buried her face in her hands.

I scanned the room, taking in everyone's faces as they wallowed in despair and resignation.

"I am just as unhappy as the rest of you are," I announced, standing up.

"I find this man loathsome. The idea of having this fucker around, breathing my air, makes me want to fucking murder both him and his slut bookends."

"But we need his fucking money," I finished. "We have no choice. We do not have enough ponies, and we do not have the resources available to move to Wellington. We are stuck with this lowlife prick bastard, or we are just stuck."

Three baleful faces stared at me. "Nice pep talk, Yvette," Lawrence said. "Very peppy."

"You know I am right." I sat down again, facing him. "We have no choice."

He let out a sigh that moved his entire body. "You're right. Give me a few days, and I'll tell him we accept his offer."

"Why a few days?" I snapped.

"Well, you never know," Lawrence said without a hint of humor. "Money might fall from the sky."

Delaware

There were only two registers open at the Sav-On, and I stood in a line that was five deep. We'd just gotten back from a practice, and I'd hoofed it over here from the motel, still fully decked out in my polo duds.

I held the cold Tyson bag between two fingers. The white frost slowly melted off and dripped to the floor. Behind me, a guy joined the line. He didn't fidget or dart around or crowd into me like people were apt to do. He just calmly walked up and stood there, maintaining a respectful distance, his feet flat on the linoleum floor.

I turned around, angling my body so I could see him. I felt a sense of curiosity and a sort of welcoming pull, even though he hadn't said a word to me. The way he commanded and occupied his own space drew me in. He was just that type of person.

I gave him a friendly smile that he instantly returned. He had a remarkable build, both tall and powerful, with thick arms and large hands. His black hair was neatly, professionally cut, and his eyes looked warm, black as night with little flecks of golden brown that glinted like sunbeams.

He had a body that could crush steel and cause all sorts of problems, but there was an overwhelming gentleness about him that made me suspect he had never raised a hand to anyone.

He nodded at me, taking note of my attire. "I like your boots," he said approvingly.

"Why, thank you." I stretched out a leg, lowering my heel deeply. "They're Austrian leather. Gen-u-ine."

"I couldn't help but notice," the man said. "You're dressed for polo. Do you play?"

"I sure do." I offered him my hand, noting that his handshake was just about ideal - firm, assertive, but not bone-crunching. "Delaware Freeman. I play #2 position on Team Dark Horse."

"Team Dark Horse?" He leaned inward just slightly, his eyes searching and eager. "I haven't heard of it. Do you play around here?"

"We only just joined together this summer," I explained. "We're getting ready for the winter season. You like polo?"

"Always have," the man said. "I grew up playing it, and I had some aptitude, but once I hit my late teens that kind of went out the window. I don't really have the right build for the sport."

He had a point. I couldn't really see him fitting on a short, wiry polo pony. "I never really thought about that. It must be hard not being able to play anymore."

"It was at first. But I stay involved with the sport in other ways. You don't have to be on the field to make an impact."

"That's very true." I smiled up at him, and we both shuffled forward as the line finally got moving. I set my Anytizers on the conveyer and slapped down a plastic divider.

"If you like polo, you should come see us play sometime," I offered. "We're practicing every day at the Lexington Polo Club."

The man looked at me with clear interest. "I would be happy to. If you're sure it wouldn't be an imposition…"

"No, not at all!" I shook my head. "Just come on down and find yourself a seat in the stands. Afterward I'll introduce you to the rest of the team."

Team Dark Horse

The man nodded. Suddenly, his face turned downcast. "I apologize, I was so captivated by your story that I completely forgot to properly introduce myself. I'm -"

"No need for that." I waved a hand to cut him off as the impatient store clerk cleared her throat loudly at me. "You can tell me your name when you come to see us play."

"Okay." He stared at me, slightly taken aback, but slowly a smile appeared on his face. "I'll do that."

"Seriously, you should come see us play," I said as I reached in my pocket for my money. "We're awesome."

"Here, let me get that." Smoothly and decisively he handed the cashier a gold card. Looking somewhat confused, she swiped it and handed it back to him.

I picked up my bag, preparing to go. "Thanks for the Anytizers," I said politely.

He looked slightly embarrassed. "It was my pleasure."

I walked away, looking back just once, taking in his tall, regal bearing and sad, almost haunted eyes. I noted how out of place he looked in the cheap, fluorescent-lit Sav-On, but most of all I wondered if there even was a place where he would look as if he fit in.

Dougie

Lawrence and I were in the trenches, sorting through my growing archive of photos and choosing which to edit and which to move to Trash. I didn't really want him here, and I didn't need the help, but I couldn't exactly say no.

Lawrence eyed the galleries, the many pages of files. "There are a *lot* of pictures of Courtney here."

"She's the T & A," I said blankly, staring at the screen. "I have to take lots of pictures of her."

"Do you?" Lawrence asked point-blank, delving deeper into the most recent folder.

"She's the T & A," I repeated myself, watching helplessly as the images piled up, one after the other, closing in on her face, her hair, catching her in quiet moments between chukkers, hugging Hermione, or just sitting there, her eyes plaintive.

"Huh." Lawrence leaned back in the chair, his hand idle on the mouse. "I don't see much of the T *or* the A in any of these."

"Well, maybe that's because you're crass and you don't understand art." I went right in for the cheap shot, hoping to take the pressure off myself.

Lawrence wasn't swayed. "I think something else is going on here," he said, looking at me sagely.

"Wow." I sat back like a flopping fish. My bones had gone all rubbery. "You're really gonna make me do this, aren't you?"

He remained steady. He showed no remorse.

I took a breath. "Okay, fine. I like Courtney." The words sounded stupid, so painfully obvious, so of course I added more. "It won't affect what I'm doing for the team, so don't worry about that. She never has to know. No one ever has to know. I'm fully secure in the fact that nothing is ever going to happen between us. It is what it is. I'm fine."

Lawrence just looked at me, quietly waiting me out. I knew I wasn't fooling him at all.

"Just let me have this." I looked at the vast array of electronic devices on my desk, all full of Courtney. "I'm not Photoshopping her into porn scenes or anything like that. I'm not that type of guy." I turned my head away from his face, looking into the corner, where I desperately wanted to be. "Just let me have this, and I'll be fine."

Lawrence stood up. "Courtney might surprise you, you know," he said cryptically.

I shook my head at him. "Just go."

He finally did as I told him, and in the crushing silence he left behind, I spent the next two hours turning over that comment in my mind.

Courtney might surprise you.

Lawrence

The ponies spread out over the field in a V formation with Harry at the front, his skinny neck bobbing along as his pace increased. The gelding always walked as fast as he possibly could, but he never jigged, knowing I would soon shut that down with a firm half halt.

"Is Dougie here today?" I asked, twisting around in the saddle.

"I don't think so." Delaware looked around, scanning the stands and the surrounding area. "I don't see him anywhere."

"Just because you do not see him, it does not mean he is not here," Yvette said, cruising past Delaware.

"That's true," Delaware allowed. "But I really don't see him anywhere."

They went on slinging the same argument back and forth at each other. I moved away from the girls, letting Harry's stride create some distance. He knew the warm-up routine by now, and he stepped into a trot as soon as the ten minutes were up. I let him do it. I trusted Harry's internal clock more than any timepiece.

The wind rushed in my ears as Harry cruised around the edge of the field. My eyes sharply assessed our string, and I noted that Hermione, Hedge Fund and Vegas were a little on the thin side. Even with all the food Wilson and I had been pushing on them, the increased workload was starting to take its toll. Even Harry looked more angular. He had one of those air fern metabolisms and tended to be a little chubby by polo pony standards, but from my vantage point aboard his back I could see the sharp line of his shoulders and croup.

I'll track down Arnold today, I thought grimly. I couldn't stand the man. None of us could. But I was just prolonging the inevitable by waiting, and the welfare of the ponies had to come first. I would not compromise the health of our string by biding my time and waiting for something better to come along.

Harry launched into a canter beneath me. I saw the other ponies follow suit.

My head turned as we passed the stands, drawn by a subtle shift of movement. There was a lone figure sitting there, and it sure wasn't Dougie. This stranger sat in the middle, posture erect, eyes forward. He watched the ponies on the field with the eyes of someone who knew what he was looking at.

I urged Harry forward, closing in on the girls who were cantering in a tight cluster. "Who is that?" I called over the patter of hooves.

"Who is what? Where?" Courtney glanced back in alarm.

Delaware looked up toward the stands. Her face opened in a grin. "Oh, it's that guy! I met him in the Sav-On. He likes polo, so I invited him to watch us play. It's so nice that he came!"

Yvette pulled Hedge Fund up, forcing Vegas to make a panic stop to avoid running into his hindquarters. "You invited some *random* guy to watch us play?"

Delaware looked affronted. "He's not just some random guy," she said. "Well, he is kind of random. But he's nice. He liked my boots."

"I bet he did," Yvette said nastily.

"*And* he paid for my Anytizers," Delaware added, as if that closed the case right there.

"Well, he must be extremely well-off. If he can pay for *Anytizers*." Yvette rolled her eyes. "In the future, please refrain from doling out invitations to total strangers. We are not an exhibition. We are not *entertainment*. Unless someone expresses a genuine interest in becoming our sponsor, *we do not* associate with them. Is that clear?"

Delaware set her chin, standing her ground. "All I know is sometimes it pays to be nice."

I glanced up into the stands, watching the mystery guy. He was dressed well in nice slacks, a pressed button-down and a sport coat. He didn't look like a degenerate. I shrugged, turning to the group. "Well, he's here at any rate. Let's at least give him a good show."

"I never said I planned on doing otherwise," Yvette said haughtily.

Delaware

We started out sedately enough, with some drills, some passing, a little goaltending. After that, everyone went one-on-one, trading off and seeing who could get one past the other. It was always hotly contested, but there were never any hard feelings. Except when I played with Yvette.

She was seated on Hedge Fund, outwardly patient. I could see the look in her eye, though, and I wasn't fooled for a minute. I knew it would soon be war.

The presence of the mystery guy in the stands had made her crankier than ever for some reason. She stewed beneath the brim of her helmet, her mouth tilted in a grumpy scowl. I saw her body tensing up like a crouching tiger, preparing to strike.

"Delaware, you're on offense." Lawrence's voice boomed out. "Yvette, you're defense. Try to keep her from scoring."

"Yes, do try," I sang out, snatching up the ball with my stick.

A hiss of anger slipped from between Yvette's teeth. It was soon drowned out by the rapid-fire sound of hoof beats as Hedge Fund leapt forward, ripping up clods of turf. I hit the ball closer to the goal and gave Vegas a kick. We beat her to it, just barely. She was breathing down my neck, within spitting distance of me.

Trying to hit it into the goal from this far off was too risky. If it came up at all short there was a chance she could block me and redirect it. In a situation like this, ball control was the only answer. It wasn't the easy way out, for sure. The only easy way out would be to walk off the field.

I took a deep breath, slowing my body down. That part was the hardest. I had to pretend time was standing still and let my surroundings get fuzzy.

I picked up the ball, keeping it off the ground, reaching under it and tapping it to keep it afloat. Once you got in a rhythm with this, it got easier. Every stride, a tap. Every heartbeat, a tap. Eventually, everything just kind of pulsed together, and it stopped being a thing I had to think about. It just happened, as natural as breathing.

Yvette was dogging me, waiting for me to slip up. Measuring the distance between myself and the goal, I reached back with my mallet, swinging forward, connecting with the ball. It made a satisfying *whack* before flying into the goal.

"Good try," I said sweetly to Yvette.

"Nice stick handling, Podunk," she admitted, her eyes in slits.

"I think that's enough for these ponies," Lawrence said. "Start the cool-down process."

I jumped off Vegas, patting his skinny neck. He pricked his ears, a happy look on his face. Vegas had the best moves of any horse I'd been on. Even after a hard practice he'd get a little strut going if we'd done especially well.

I was about to start leading him around, but I saw the man from the Sav-On heading down from the stands. I stopped and watched him as he made his way to the field. The other players halted around me. Even Yvette picked her head up and eyed him with grudging admiration. He just had a presence.

"Thanks for coming down," I said, giving him a hearty wave.

"My pleasure." He nodded at me, including the rest of the team with a turn of his head. "You play exceedingly well, Ms. Freeman. I must admit I was surprised, and very impressed."

"Thank you." I let the moment ride, knowing how Yvette's ears were surely burning. "I learned from the best."

"You certainly have. I'm glad you know how fortunate you are." He smiled, looking around at Lawrence, Yvette and Courtney. "I never thought when I came here today that I would see the three of you together. But it makes perfect sense. I'm glad to see you playing again."

The air stilled as the three of them glanced around at each other. "Who exactly are you?" Yvette demanded.

The man shook his head at himself, looking remorseful. "I apologize, I've neglected to introduce myself. I'm John Spencer. I've been an avid fan of the sport since I was three years old, so of course I feel as though I know all of you. But you don't know me."

Lawrence stepped forward, easily blasting through the awkwardness of the situation. "Good to meet you, John."

"Same here," Courtney said, extending her hand after Lawrence and John were done shaking. Yvette remained suspicious.

John looked around at the riderless ponies. "You are done for the morning?" He said.

"Yeah." Lawrence loosened Harry's girth, and I did the same for Vegas. "We don't really have a lot of ponies. Or hired help."

"How big is your string?" John asked.

"Courtney owns eight. And I have two." Lawrence smiled ruefully. "That's it."

"You've been making do with 10 ponies between the four of you?" John looked mildly shocked.

Lawrence shrugged. "You do what you have to do," he said.

John's eyes swept over the four of us. A fire seemed to light behind his eyes. "I take it you don't have a financial backer then?"

My heart leapt up to full speed, filling my body like the beat of drums in a Fourth of July parade. My eyes flickered to Courtney and Lawrence, then to Yvette. They each had the same look of longing, fear and wonder, like a little kid straining on tiptoe to reach for the highest shelf. *Can this be possible?*

John smiled. He looked the happiest I'd ever seen him. "You do now."

He went on for a few minutes, discussing details with Lawrence about contractual things and other important-sounding business stuff. They planned a meeting for the following morning, shook on it, and he left as silently and unassumingly as he'd come.

We looked around at each other and our sweaty ponies, who were probably wondering why we were just standing around and not taking care of them.

"Did that really just happen?" Courtney asked, her face contemplative.

"We have a sponsor." Lawrence stared up at the sky, grinning wildly. "We have a legit sponsor, and it's not Arnold."

"It's not official until the paperwork has been signed," Yvette snipped, forever throwing a damp rag on any hint of joy she encountered.

"It's so weird that he came out of nowhere like that," Courtney said. "He seems really nice though. He's knowledgeable. And really tall. And not creepy…"

I grabbed hold of Vegas' reins and got ready to start walking him. "I told y'all it pays to be nice," I said, firmly taking the last word.

Erica

It all came down to this. Another ring, another class. One more winning check was all we needed to take us over the top. So routine by now. It might have almost felt like a formality, if not for the subtle shake of my hands as I fastened Soiree's girth. If not for the thudding bass of my heartbeat, as fast as a techno number. If not for the nervous energy flooding my bloodstream like an intravenous drug.

In lieu of a proper warm-up, I rode Soiree up and down the trails and footpaths of the Kentucky Horse Park, seeking the shade and comfort of the perfectly landscaped trees. Remaining just within earshot of the loudspeaker, we traipsed along, moving in and out of shadow. Soiree was relaxed and pure of mind. I tried to follow her lead.

Turning a corner, we came upon a mom and her young daughter, clearly out-of-state visitors to the park. The mom had a camera strapped around her neck, and the little girl was clutching a plastic bag from the gift shop.

I smiled at them. "Hi."

The little girl's mouth dropped open when she saw Soiree. "Your horse is so pretty!" She squeaked. "Can I pet her?"

"She's probably on her way somewhere, Faith," her mom said, although she too was looking at Soiree hopefully.

"You sure can." I halted the mare, letting the reins out to the buckle so Soiree could stretch her neck down to the little girl's level.

The little girl walked forward, placing a hand on Soiree's forehead. Gently and with the utmost care, Soiree nestled her head against the girl's body.

The little girl looked up at her in wonderment. "Do horses like to be *hugged?*"

I smiled. "Not a lot of them do. But this one does."

The little girl wrapped her arms around Soiree's head, though she had to stretch to fit them all the way around the circumference of Soiree's jaw. Beaming, the mom snapped a picture.

I heard the far-off loudspeaker announcement, and though I hated to break the moment, I knew it was time to go. "My number's on deck," I said regretfully. "I have to get to the ring."

The little girl stepped back. "Are you showing her? Can we watch?"

I saw no reason why not. "Sure. Just come with me, and when we get closer you'll see the stands. Just find a seat wherever."

Soiree walked briskly to the ring with her new admirers in tow. I watched to make sure they got to their seats safely, and then I waited for my turn.

My number was called, the in-gate swung open, and I rode into the ring to complete what would likely be my final hunter course on Soiree For Two.

I laid down my opening circle, noting that each time we stepped out on course, Soiree seemed to need less from me. I felt quite certain she could do it all without me, and the realization made me both glad and somewhat wistful.

But then, Soiree had always been who she was. Her talent came from somewhere within, and much like a recruiter I had merely paired her with a job at which she could excel.

No longer needed for things such as rating or other basic direction, I made it my mission to feel every second of this round. If I could, I wanted to absorb it into my skin where it would remain, accessible in a pinch, the sensation of riding a truly great horse.

The first outside line passed in a few leaps and bounds. Soiree turned the corner, skipping through a smooth lead change and heading for the diagonal line. She swept over the next fence, knees up to her chin, ears pricked toward the sky.

I found that instead of time slowing down for me to savor these final moments, it felt like someone had hit fast forward. The sand flowed from my hourglass, not in a trickle, but in a gush.

Soiree swapped leads again, her body bent flawlessly to meet the next set of fences. She was incandescent. I sat above her, mute and dumb, asking nothing of her while she laid down the performance of her career.

We crossed over the finish line, staring at the out gate. I asked her to walk, my hand skimming over the hair on her neck. "You did it, Soiree," I whispered.

Leaving the ring I caught the eye of the little girl and her mom in the stands. They hurried over to Soiree. I halted the mare, not caring if others were forced to cut a path around us.

"Thank you for letting us watch," the mom said. "She looked beautiful out there."

Soiree bent her head, pulling slightly on the bit, hoping for another hug. I fed her a length of rein, and she plopped her head happily into the little girl's outstretched arms.

"I'm glad you got to see it," I said. "This was my last time competing on her."

"How come?" The mom asked. "Is she retiring?"

I shook my head. "I actually ride jumpers. She was a laid-up ex-racehorse that my friend rescued from slaughter. I just found that she had a knack for the hunter ring. I qualified her for a big event, and now she'll go up for sale."

The little girl's eyes met mine. "You're *selling* her?"

"Yeah, unfortunately." I shifted in the saddle. "I love her, but I can't keep them all."

The little girl hugged Soiree even tighter. "If she were my horse, I would keep her *forever*."

I smiled through my tears, looking down at her youthful spirit and conviction. I thought of D.M. and how I just couldn't let him go, even when he had no future in my chosen sport. "I know exactly what you mean," I said.

Courtney

Hermione was on the hotwalker, her ears flopping slightly as she completed the endless circuits. I sat on the ground nearby, working saddle soap into her tack. Her bridle was gummy with sweat and accumulated dirt, and the saddle wasn't much better.

Lawrence ambled up out of nowhere. He must have come from the meeting with John and his lawyers because he was all buttoned-up in a suit and a nice white shirt. He'd already taken off the jacket and thrown it over one shoulder.

"Soon we won't have to do that anymore," he said, nodding at the filthy equipment I was scrubbing. "I don't understand a word of that lawyer-speak, but essentially what it boils down to is John is going to make sure our every need is met." He grinned steadily. "I really like that guy."

"I'm glad it went well." I reached for another rag, tossing the soiled one aside. "I don't really mind taking care of Hermione, though. Or cleaning tack. It's not like I have anything else going on."

Lawrence looked at me with a slight gleam in his eye. "You could."

"I could what?"

"Have something else going on."

I sighed. "I suppose you think I should go join a kickball league or something akin to that. Or get a membership at the Y?"

"Wrong and wrong." He studied me. "You really don't know what I'm getting at?"

I felt a welling ball of frustration in my esophagus. "Well clearly I don't. Clearly, I'm not *smart* enough to follow your subtle hints and weird posturing, so maybe you should just come out with whatever it is you're *getting at.*"

Lawrence turned his head slowly, leaning his whole body subtly in the same direction. Slowly, I followed his gaze. It landed on Dougie, half-hidden beside the stands, hunched over his iPhone.

I looked at Lawrence. "What does Dougie have to do with it?"

Lawrence rolled his eyes. "He likes you."

A little puff of air escaped my lungs. My heart knocked out a quick beat behind my breastbone.

Lawrence shrugged, seemingly unbothered by my sudden muteness. "Dougie likes you. I thought you should know."

He wandered off, leaving me sitting there with a mess of tack at my feet and an even bigger mess in my mind.

Elaine

I was leading one of the club ponies along a grassy lane, head turned back to carefully monitor his stride. Immersed in the soothing, slightly hypnotic rhythm of the cool-down process, I was reluctant to move my head when I heard my name called. My eyes broke away from the pony with a slight but noticeable effort, akin to the slap of your skull against the water as you break through the surface of the ocean.

My gaze landed on Lawrence. He stood leaning against the side of the barn, lazily waving me over. I sighed deeply, humoring him, extending the path I traveled with Lynx, the club pony I was cooling out.

The wind blew an errant strand of hair over his eye. "Have you met our money man yet?" Lawrence asked.

I shook my head. "No. I've been a little too busy doing my job, especially with all these new mouths to feed."

"Well you should introduce yourself. He'll be arriving shortly." Lawrence walked off, breeches and boots glinting in the sunlight.

I turned my attention back to Lynx, but with half my brain I listened and waited for the arrival of this sponsor Lawrence had spoken of. No name, to make him sound more mysterious. More impressive, like some superhero. *The money man.* I was pretty sure he was just a man, the same as all the others. With his own flaws, and the ability to send your body soaring or make you break down in quiet moments, tears sliding down your face and saturating the pillow, breathing inward in sporadic stifled sobs as he slept, oblivious, mere feet from all that suffering.

The quiet hum of an imported motor became audible. I turned and walked another circuit, touching my bare fingers to Lynx's chest to check his body temperature. When I faced the barn once again, I saw the man Lawrence had spoken of.

He cut a path through the grassy lane I walked on, hurrying along, eyes slightly downcast. He looked up as he neared me, nodding respectfully. He seemed to slow down, and I came to a complete standstill.

When his eyes met mine they sent a current of warmth and pressure surging through my body. My arms fell to my sides, and I was bound to him, unable to walk or utter a sound. The scenery whirled around me, everything fading to a blur while his strong, elegant frame stood out in Technicolor.

I realized with a jolt that this was almost the same spot where I first laid eyes on Lawrence six years before. All this past year, I'd been running from that moment and the period of insanity that followed it. I'd holed myself away in that storage room, throwing myself into my job, living with the ponies and isolating myself from people. All to smother the person I really was. *Lock her up and throw away the key.*

I understood now that I hadn't gained any ground. Not a single yard. I'd traveled in a circle, and now I was right back where I started. Only now, the roles were reversed. This time I was the one leading a pony.

The man stepped closer, reaching out to me. "Hello, I'm John Spencer."

I tucked my arms against my sides. I would not touch him. "Elaine Windzor."

He took his hand away, looking a bit shame-faced, as if he'd gone in for a grope instead of just trying to initiate a handshake.

I cleared my throat, trying to pull myself together. "Lawrence told me about you," I said. "You're a real godsend for Team Dark Horse."

John smiled in a way that could only be described as bittersweet. "It gives me something to do. Something to give my life meaning again. Get me out of the house."

I knew something had happened in his life, but I didn't want to delve into it. That would involve too much intimacy. "It's good to meet you," I said. "If you'll excuse me, I need to get back to work."

"Of course." John stepped aside, his eyes swiftly assessing Lynx's condition like a true horseman. "It was a pleasure to meet you." His gaze returned to me and remained there with a steadiness that was at once comforting and terrifying.

I clucked to Lynx, asking him to walk briskly forward. I shoved my eyes on him and didn't take them off. But there was a heavy rumble in my head that hadn't been there before. I tried to shut it out, but it was as difficult to ignore as a splitting migraine.

All at once, I felt the weight of every emotion I'd walled myself off from over this last year. Every basic human need I'd outlawed and gone without. My stomach made not a single shudder, but I couldn't even hear over the rumble of hunger in my head.

"No," I whispered, fingernails digging into the skin on my arm. "I can't go back to that."

I halted Lynx, who gazed out at the rows of paddocks, eyes bright and free of sorrow. I crouched down before him and leaned my head against his chest, allowing the salty drying sweat on his skin to soak into me. And I wondered, not for the first time, who was really the intelligent life form and who could be considered the beast of burden.

Courtney

The trailer doors banged open; the ramp was lowered. The first eight ponies were led out, snorting and dancing around after their long haul. Lawrence and Delaware clustered around the new arrivals, peeling off their shipping boots and exclaiming over them like kids at Christmas. Yvette stood back, not laying a hand on even one of the creatures, but her eyes scanned their bodies, noting their quality, and she nodded approvingly, a smile on her lips.

Argentinean ponies were generally considered the gold standard, but importing horses was a laborious process that required substantial paperwork and a lengthy quarantine period. Knowing time was of the essence, John had opted for the best U.S.-bred stock money could buy. They looked like they would do.

I was the only one on the team who wasn't invested in these new horses. My string was now my string alone, not shared with anyone else. I could divide the labor as I saw fit, and I knew each of my horses inside and out. So I left the welcoming to Lawrence and Delaware, and I went off in search of the person I needed to see.

Team Dark Horse

I found him in the first place I looked. He was easy to find once you knew to look in the corners.

"Hey," I said awkwardly, sitting myself down beside him in the stands.

"Courtney. Hi." He shoved his phone in his pocket, looking at me jumpily. "I thought you'd be checking out the new ponies."

"They're not mine," I said, drawing my knees up to my chest. "It's good for the team, though."

"Yeah, I guess you already have what you need," Dougie said. His hand lingered over the place where his phone was, like he didn't quite know what to do without it.

"My daddy always made sure of that. I never had to worry about money." I knew I wasn't making eye contact with Dougie, and I knew that was bad. But it was okay for me, being here with him side by side. And I got the sense that he was okay with it too.

I bit down on a nail. This was the hard part. I didn't know how this was done. *How do some people just know? It seems so effortless for them. Is there a code, some crucial social blueprint I somehow never learned? Or is there something wrong in my brain? Does it need an update? If I was a computer, would I be saddled with an archaic operating system and crippled by viruses?*

Dougie looked at me. His eyes were a muddy grey color. I tried to look at him, but it dialed up the intensity too much, so I had to just sort of stare through him. My eyes kept twitching around. I was sure I looked crazy.

"Lawrence said you like me," I blurted out.

Oh, terrific start, Courtney. "Lawrence said you like me." Ridiculous. Are we in third grade?

Dougie hung his head. "I knew he wouldn't keep his mouth shut." He looked at the trash-speckled ground far below us. "I'm not going to deny it or anything, because I think it's pretty obvious by now. But I wouldn't expect you to return the feeling. In fact, I pretty much expect you not to."

I twisted a lock of hair, letting it pull against my scalp a little. "I'm not upset that you like me. I think I'm okay with it."

He let out a slow exhale. "Good. That's a relief."

"And if you wanted to ask me out or something, I think I would be okay

332

with that too." My voice trembled.

Dougie's mouth parted. He'd gone slightly paler than usual.

I picked myself up and walked down to ground level into the warmth of sunshine. *I've done my part. I did a thing.*

I heard a commotion behind me and I turned back. Dougie scrambled to his feet, tripping down from the stands. He caught up with me, limping slightly.

"Did you change your mind in the last 10 seconds?" He asked, breathless.

I shook my head. "No."

"Then come over to my place tomorrow night. I'll make dinner." He looked slightly panicked. "If you want."

"That sounds fine."

Another trailer rumbled in, cutting a path right through the place we were standing, and we hurried to get out of the way.

Dougie

I'd been calling Amber all day, but she never answered. So when 4:30 came, I positioned myself right in the entryway, preparing to intercept Amber and Kelly as soon as they walked through the door.

Sure enough, the door flew open, nearly slamming into me. Amber rocked back on her heels, startled, looking perplexed. "The fuck are you doing here?"

"This is my house," I answered stiffly.

"No duh, I fucking know that. I meant what are you doing *here* in the goddamn entryway? Why aren't you in your chair?"

"That doesn't matter," I said. "I need you to clear out. You can't be here tonight."

Amber gawked at me. "Why? You have a hot date or something?"

"*Yes*," I answered, my teeth chattering together as a fresh wave of anxiety hit me. "I need peace and quiet. I need to not be disturbed. So I need you and your girlfriend to clear out."

"What girlfriend?" Amber spat with venom. "Do you see anyone else here with me?"

Stupidly, I peered behind her. For the first time, I realized Kelly wasn't there. "What happened?"

"Doesn't matter," Amber barked, her face set. "Seeing as how I've got to *clear out* anyway. I'll just be going."

"Wait, Amber." My face felt hot. I was actually perspiring a little. "I feel bad kicking you out. I just don't want any interruptions. So if you could just stay in your room and avoid doing loud things, I think it'll be fine."

"Stay in my room and be *quiet*? Who are you, my mom?" Amber groused.

"At least I'm not kicking you out," I snapped. "Do what you want. Make a scene. Get in the way. I clearly can't stop you." I stalked away. "Now if you'll excuse me, I need to go stir this sauce."

"Ooh, whatcha making?" Amber asked eagerly, tagging along behind me. It was always really jarring when girls' moods did a complete 180 like that.

"Nothing you'd like," I said, returning to the kitchen. "It's got meat in it."

"Oh." Amber slouched away, officially uninterested. "I hope you enjoy eating lots of leftovers. Because I'm not touching that shit."

"I'll send some home with Courtney." I leaned over the pot, watching it simmer.

Amber's eyes jumped open. "Courtney? As in *Courtney Silva*?"

"The very one."

Amber looked at me with deep confusion and grudging awe. "How'd you manage *that*?"

Courtney

I rapped tentatively on the door, stealing one more furtive glance at Dougie's van sitting in the driveway. The houses on this block all looked exactly the same, so I was glad the van was there. It gave me visual confirmation that I wasn't about to go into the wrong house, which was something I would probably do, given the opportunity.

There was a slight commotion inside the house, and the door was pulled open. Dougie stepped back, allowing me through. The entryway was so narrow, we were practically on top of each other. I struggled out of my coat, tensing up whenever my body accidentally touched his, which was all the time.

He seemed to realize I needed a little room, and he broke away to the kitchen. I was aware of several pots and pans sizzling and steaming away on the stove. He had like six burners going at once.

The walls were all bare. It was a depressing bachelor's apartment, lacking furniture or décor, but it wasn't at all dirty. It was really clean and sterile, kind of like a hospital. Except it was cleaner, whiter, alarmingly clean, and empty.

"Something smells good," I said, my voice at a high pitch. I couldn't really breathe right then, so I couldn't really smell, but I was willing to hazard a guess that he knew what he was doing. Terrible-to-average cooks typically kept it to one or two burners max.

"If you want to sit down, I'll have dinner ready in like 10 minutes," Dougie said, his back to me.

I looked around in confusion. "Where...do I, uh, sit?"

Dougie glanced up, looking slightly embarrassed. "Right. You can, uh, go sit on the couch. In the living room. That room with all the electronics in it," he added, seeing my confused face. "We'll eat there. I, uh, don't have that much furniture."

I think I noticed that. "Okay, thanks!" I said shrilly, slinking away to the room with all the electronics in it.

I sat down on the couch, jittery as all get-out. I bounced my feet together like a little kid in the waiting room of a dentist's office, rocking back and forth slightly. All the electronics stared back at me, their wide, faceless monitors unblinking.

Dougie came hurrying into the room. From my seated position, he looked like he was walking on stilts, his legs were so long and ungainly. "Can I get you anything to drink?"

I wavered nervously. "What do you have?"

"Um, there's Mountain Dew, and I think my roommate has a six-pack of beer in the fridge," Dougie said.

"I don't really drink beer." I considered the options and couldn't bring myself to opt for the standard water fallback. "I guess I'll take a Mountain Dew."

"Okay." Dougie disappeared from view. I leaned my head back against the couch, realizing a caffeinated beverage was probably not the smartest choice I could have made for myself right now.

He came back into the room, setting down the soda bottle and following it up with a large plate of food, spaghetti and meatballs with garlic bread and green beans on the side. I looked down at the angel-hair pasta drenched in blood-red sauce, and when I breathed in I could discern a multitude of spices.

He watched intently as I twirled my fork around some strands of pasta and took a bite. I looked up at him, slightly stunned. "Wow. You could get a job at any kitchen in my hometown. This is superlative."

"I'm glad you like it." Dougie sat down beside me, eating from his own substantially smaller plate. "I don't cook nearly as much as I should. It's hard to get motivated when you're cooking just for yourself."

"What about your roommate?"

"Amber doesn't eat meat." Dougie shook his head slightly. "I don't even know what to say about that."

"Yeah, that's a tough one to work around." I chewed another bite, salivating the entire time. "You can only do so much with kale."

"True that." Dougie smiled wryly.

He finished eating well before I did and left to clean up the kitchen. I chewed the remains of my dinner, occasionally taking a sip of Mountain Dew. My earlier nerves, somewhat soothed by the comfort food, came rushing back, no doubt boosted by the array of harsh chemicals in the soda I'd been ingesting. I started to wonder about the part that came next. I really didn't know a lot about this next part, considering I hadn't ever really dated anyone before.

What happens next? What are people supposed to do on a date? The questions chafed at me so badly, I almost ran to one of Dougie's computers to fire off a frantic Google search. Only the thought of him walking in and seeing me typing "what do people do on a date" into the search engine was enough to keep me seated.

Dougie walked back into the room. My eyes skimmed over him frantically, trying to avoid landing on his large knobby knees, or the strange, abnormal length and shape of his thighs. Brain spinning in my head, I stood up wildly. He looked at me, appearing somewhat concerned.

Do I leave now? Can I just walk out the door and leave? No, that doesn't seem like a thing you can do. That can't be right. I stared at Dougie helplessly. *But what happens next?*

He shuffled his feet, placing one of top of the other. Then he leaned against the wall in that way people lean against the wall when they're trying to appear confident and relaxed but they're not really fooling anyone. He didn't seem to know any better than I did.

Something has to happen now. That much I knew for sure. I didn't know what was supposed to happen, but if nothing happened for much longer, and I had to stand here facing him with nothing happening, my heart was probably going to explode.

"Do you want to, um, go upstairs?" I asked meekly. My mouth was saying the words, and my brain was just barely on board with the whole consent thing. I realized how desperate this looked, but I really didn't know any other options.

Dougie's head shot up so fast I heard his neck crack. "Go upstairs, meaning like…"

"Uh-huh." I snatched the last of the Mountain Dew and chugged it.

"Oh man. Yeah. Of course." Dougie shook himself, taking my hand. It felt cold and clammy against my skin. "Just, uh, follow me."

We walked up the creaking stairs to his bedroom. It was depressingly empty, much like the rest of the house. There was a laptop on the bed, and Dougie shoved it off to the side. Then he turned to me, leaning down to kiss me. But he did it way too fast and overshot, scraping his front teeth against mine.

He pulled back, embarrassed. "Sorry."

"That's okay," I said, even though it wasn't really, and I was getting chills down my back now for all the wrong reasons. "Maybe go a little slower next time."

"Yeah." He bent down again, meeting my mouth correctly this time. Emboldened, he stuck his tongue fully in my mouth for a second and then broke away, which, again, is not how you kiss someone.

"Okay. That's enough of that." I stepped back, pulling my shirt over my head. My jeans came off next, and I was standing there in a bra and panties. The timing of this was awkward. In my somewhat limited experience, things usually moved quicker than they were moving right now.

I looked at Dougie, who was looking at me with his eyes glazed over. Now that was actually a look that felt familiar.

"Holy shit," Dougie breathed.

Dougie

Courtney stood before me, completely naked except for a hot pink bra and a matching thong, semi sheer. Her breasts rose in soft peaks above the lace edging.

"Holy shit," I choked out.

She didn't move away, so I stepped closer, my hands finding her body, clutching her sides below her bra and the swoop of her waist. Her hips moved when I touched them, and the first faint jiggle of flesh about did me in.

I had never had outlandish expectations of how women were supposed to look. It was kind of understood that real women were different from the ones you saw in porn. They didn't look quite the same, but they were no less exciting because they were real.

But here I was with a girl who looked like she'd walked straight out of my computer. It was exciting as hell, and awesome in theory, but I was having a bit of trouble keeping the excitement at a tolerable level.

I turned Courtney around, reaching for her ass, feeling faint. *How is it so round? And high? And how does it look even better and more perfect now than it did before?*

In a sudden kick of adrenaline I threw Courtney on the bed, moving in behind her, still fully clothed and without a clue what I was doing. My mind swam with possibilities, and my body slowly tightened up, fighting to maintain control.

I stared at Courtney on all fours on my bed, and I looked one more time at the perfectly round, full shape of her ass, and the thong that had almost entirely disappeared within it. My hold slipped, and after putting up a moment's fight, I surrendered to the inevitable and relinquished it entirely.

Courtney's head turned back. Her eyes met mine, slightly panicked. "Do we have protection?" She asked suddenly.

I shook my head as my body let go with a shudder. "I don't think we need to worry about that."

Courtney

I stared at Dougie blankly. My confusion was so deep you could have dug to China before you hit the bottom of it.

Dougie leaned back against the bed frame, his chest rising and falling rhythmically. His face behind the acne was somewhat flushed, his eyes half lidded.

It was a familiar look in a new context. And with the jarring sensation of being hit by a bus, I understood. Tucking my feet up, I sat there a second, thinking about what had just happened. *You can go down the only road you know, and still end up completely lost.*

Well, that could happen if you were me. I doubted it happened to anyone else.

I got up, carefully putting my clothes back on. Dougie didn't say a word to me, and I didn't offer anything up either.

Standing in the door frame, I paused. *I'm pretty sure I can just leave now. Since that happened. I know I want to.*

So I did.

Dougie

I stared at the wall, listening to Courtney's car leave my driveway. She didn't exactly burn rubber as she left, but I still didn't feel too great about my chances of ever seeing her again.

Not two seconds later, Amber appeared in my doorway. "That was quick."

"I don't need you to tell me that, Amber," I said bitterly. "I have no delusions about what just happened."

Her eyes lit on me and jumped open. "Are you still in your *clothes*?"

"What does it look like to you!" I shouted.

"Oh, man." Amber clapped a hand over her mouth. "Was she understanding about it?"

I rolled my eyes. "Why would she be understanding about it?"

"Yeah, I suppose girls do tend to get cut up about it when a dick doesn't function optimally." Amber folded her arms. "Maybe you should have taken it slow."

"I was *going* to. She offered to come upstairs. Was I supposed to say *no*?"

"Yeah, I guess that wouldn't have gone over too well either." Amber made a move to leave.

I rested my head against the metal bed frame, feeling the urge to just straight up beat it against a wall. I knew I was never going to get another chance with Courtney, and my endeavor with Team Dark Horse was also in jeopardy, especially since they had money behind them now. *And I also have to do laundry. Fuck.*

Amber's head popped into my room. "Should I be offended that you lasted longer with me?"

"We had an arrangement!" I yelled. "And you like girls anyway. What the hell do you care?"

Amber guffawed. "*It was a joke*, dude. Chillax."

I stared hatefully through the open door as she left. *Lawrence was right about you*, I thought bitterly. *You do make a sucky roommate.*

I threw myself facedown on the bed, where I lay in self-loathing and despair, until the stickiness got to be too much and I had to shower and change.

Erica

Soiree was sold. I'd screened potential buyers and found her a great home with a renowned hunter stable. She would compete in the Finals and would be campaigned for a few more years, after which she would be bred. She would live out her remaining years in peace and comfort on a sprawling piece of land with misting fans in the barn and irrigated grass in the fields. She would want for nothing.

Team Dark Horse had a sponsor and a real shot at making their dream happen. In many ways, all the pieces were falling together. Everything up to this point led neatly to where we were now.

My eyes drifted to Assault, his regal, defiant presence standing out amongst all the other horses. Walled off from the others, with more fresh, newly replaced fence boards on his section of fence than on all the other paddocks combined, he was quickly wearing an angry trench in the soil. He'd taken to pacing the fence line and snapping at the other horses, a habit that was quickly escalating to a full-blown vice.

I knew his surly nature and explosive tendencies were exacerbated by the lonely, caged-in life he lived. But with more freedom, I feared he would merely self-destruct, galloping until he pulled a tendon or his heart burst. A companion would give him an outlet to work off energy and frustration, but a horse as powerful as Assault could kick even the most stoutly built animal to pieces. It was a chance I couldn't take.

It was a conundrum that every trainer faced at some point. As a horse's value increased, the urge to bubble-wrap and isolate them became stronger, often to the detriment of the animal. Solitary confinement went against a horse's every basic need, but many of the most talented, brilliant performers were dealt that very sentence because they were too valuable to risk. It was an ugly side effect of success in the show ring, and the horses paid the price.

In some ways, I could understand Assault's sour attitude. He lived a life of structured exercise and restricted freedom. No matter where he went, he viewed the world from behind bars. He was confined to stalls, paddocks, and trailers. Even when he competed, the rails of the arena were all around. They were undeniably in his face. I could see how that would make him shut down.

With a heavy sigh, I walked past Assault. As I often did in moments like these, I went to D.M.

I didn't bother tacking him up, I just looped a lead rope through the rings on his halter, creating makeshift reins. Strapping on my helmet, I positioned him close to the arena fence, which I used as a mounting block. Even so, I had to throw myself awkwardly onto his bare back. I landed with a thump, but D.M. didn't protest. He remained stock still until I had hauled myself up and settled in for the ride. With a small squeeze of my legs, D.M. ambled out to the field. Ears up, he carried me steadily over the rolling hills and valleys, placing his big hooves carefully, mashing down the tall grass.

I urged him up to a canter, letting my legs dangle at his sides, following the rolling motion of his spine with my seat. With encouragement from me, he accelerated to a gallop, neck stretched out, topline flat. He screamed over the ground, and I leaned over his withers, holding loosely to the lead rope.

I could be vulnerable with D.M. I could trust him with my life, because he'd proven himself time and time again. We knew each other inside and out, and whenever I rode him, however infrequently, my body loosened and all the worries seeped out of me.

We were nearing the end of the field, and I sat up to rate him, giving the lead rope a tug. D.M. slowed down, obediently reducing his speed, conceding to the gentle pressure of the halter on his face.

I ruffled the hairs on his neck, and with a dull, achy kind of sadness, I thought how Assault would never get the chance to gallop through a field so large you couldn't see the end of it when you started.

Lawrence

The parking lot at Angelina's was packed, and I had to park my truck somewhat illegally. *Marla really must have revamped this place,* I thought. There was actually a line at the door.

I wandered around until I spotted the girls. Yvette stood in line, her arms folded. Courtney was darting around and bouncing in and out of line, apologizing whenever she inadvertently brushed against someone. Delaware appeared to be chatting up the bouncer.

I sidled up to Yvette and Courtney. "I invited John to come with us," I said. "He should be here pretty soon."

"That was kind of you," Yvette said snarkily. "Considering if he comes, he will most certainly pay the tab."

"Well, yeah, I did think about that," I admitted. "But I mostly just wanted to include him in something. The guy seems lonely."

"While we are on the subject of people who should be included, where exactly is your girlfriend?" Yvette asked, giving me considerable side-eye. "I would have thought she would be joining us."

"She just sold a horse, and she wants to see her off," I said. "Make sure she loads okay and that sort of thing."

"I see." Yvette returned her eyes to the unmoving line in front of her.

"Speaking of someone who should probably be here, where the hell is Dougie?" I searched for his gawky frame without success. "Shouldn't he be documenting our every move?"

"I have no idea." Yvette gave a dainty shrug. "I have not seen him for a few days. Perhaps he has quit on us."

"I don't believe that." I scanned the crowd some more, coming up empty. "Hey, Court!" I hollered. "Have you seen Dougie lately?"

Courtney jolted to a stop, flashing panicked eyes at me. "No! Why would you think that?"

"I dunno, just taking a stab in the dark." I raised my hands. "He follows you more closely than the rest of us. I figured if anyone knew what was up, it would be you."

"Plus I just texted him, 'Dougie, get your ass down to Angelina's right now', and he responded with 'Is Courtney there?'" Yvette cut in. "And when I said she was here, his response was 'I'm busy'."

I raised my eyebrows. "Oh, what happened there?"

"Yes, Courtney, what happened?" Yvette asked, pointing her industrial-laser-strength gaze at Courtney.

"It wasn't my fault, okay!" Courtney wailed. "We went out once, and it didn't end well. That's all there is to it, okay?"

Delaware backed up a step or two, drawn away from her conversation with the bouncer. "Ooh, what happened?"

I took a wild guess. "Was there premature ejaculation involved?"

"I don't want to talk about it!" Courtney yelped. "Can't you guys just leave well enough alone? Please?"

"I am sure Lawrence hit the nail on the head," Yvette stated confidently. She looked at Courtney almost maternally. "See, I told you to go careful there."

"Ugh." Courtney buried her face in her hands. "Why did I even come here with you people?"

"You should probably send Dougie a text or something," Delaware pointed out. "You don't have to ever go out with him again, but you should at least try to make him feel less embarrassed."

"Yeah, because we don't want to lose our PR guy over this," I said, preparing to backpedal as Courtney's shocked face stared at me. "And also, it's the right thing to do."

"What's the deal with this line?" Delaware asked, turning back to the bouncer. "I thought this place almost shut down last year."

"It's this new headlining performer," someone in line piped up. "She does, like, artistic pole dancing. Fully clothed, no nudity, sometimes not that much sexuality. But it's heavy shit. It'll rip your heart out."

"Yeah, she's phenomenal," the girl's companion added. "I heard she works at a horse stable. Who would have thought?"

"There she is!" Someone shouted. Heads whipped around and camera phones were pulled out as a dark-haired girl with short, jagged hair and empty eyes cut through the parking lot, darting in the back entrance of the club.

I glanced around at the girls, who were staring in the same direction as everyone else. "Was that *Elaine*?"

Erica

I took the whole afternoon off to prepare Soiree for her trailer ride. I bathed her and let her dry in the sun, massaging detangler through her mane and tail, fingering each individual strand until I could shake out her long, full tail and meet not a single snag. Then I brushed her coat until she sparkled, leaning into every brushstroke with the fervor of a person performing CPR.

Eventually, my nervous energy ran out and I collapsed, sitting down with her lead rope on my lap. Soiree grazed in a tight circle around me, and I let the sun parch my skin, breathing in the humid air.

Amber's Harley barreled in right on schedule. She jumped down from the cab, catching sight of the tableau Soiree and I made. Without hesitating, she walked over and sat down on the grass beside me.

"When is the trailer coming?" Amber asked, even though she knew.

"They should be here in half an hour." My shoulders sagged a little. "I need to put on her shipping boots and stuff."

"I'll go get it." Amber jumped up, jogging to the barn and returning with a massive armload of protective gear. With great care she fastened the puffy, snow pants-sounding shipping boots to Soiree's legs, followed by a body sheet to protect her from sustaining any possible abrasions.

"Head up, Soiree," Amber instructed. The mare raised her head, and Amber slipped the head bumper over her ears, fastening it to her halter to shield the mare's poll.

"She's ready." I smiled wanly. "I wish I was."

Amber nodded, eyes downcast. "I know I'll never be. I don't want to see this horse go."

We lapsed into silence, sitting side by side. We didn't talk, we just stared at Soiree like she was a crown jewel. All too soon, I heard the rumble of a large rig on the dirt road. One look confirmed it was Soiree's ride. The driver slowed way down, making an expert turn into the narrow driveway.

Amber's eye's fell on me. "They're early," she said.

I nodded. "The one time I don't want them to be," I said.

With a heaviness in my heart that extended to all my limbs, I stood up, clucking to Soiree. She followed us eagerly, and when she saw the trailer, her eyes brightened. Soiree had come to know what a trailer ride meant. She would go to a new place, and she would show off and be adored.

I was glad Soiree was happy and not apprehensive about getting on this huge, strange rig. But her eagerness felt like a stab to my heart.

"Stay here with her," I said to Amber. "I have to go get her papers."

I walked to the house, where I lifted a folder off the table. Everything was up to date, but I rifled through it one last time, buying myself another 30 seconds.

When I got back outside, the driver had joined Amber. He was letting Soiree sniff him, taking his time getting acquainted with her. I could see he was a proper horseman. Where she was going, I knew Soiree would never encounter anything less.

"All the paperwork is signed over, and here's the proof of her current Coggins and vaccinations," I said as I handed him the folder. He flipped through the contents, noting the dates.

"Everything looks good," he said, nodding. "Are we all set, then?"

"Yes," I said, not allowing myself to hesitate. It would hurt now or it would hurt later, even if I waited a million years.

"Come along, mare," he said pleasantly, taking her lead rope. She hopped onto the trailer and stood for him to tie her lead rope in a quick-release knot. No fuss. Soiree was as serene in this brand-new trailer with its brand-new smells as she had been when she was grazing on the lawn.

The driver closed the doors, and I could no longer see her.

"Have a good trip," I said throatily.

"Thank you." The driver looked at me with sympathy in his eyes. "I'll make sure you're notified when we reach our destination."

"Thanks," I said.

The guy made a move to leave. Beside me, Amber clutched her arms around herself. I looked one more time at the trailer, and back to the driver, who had paused on his way to the cab.

The tears let go, and I didn't fight them. "When you get there," I said thickly, "will you give them a message?"

The guy nodded. "Of course."

I swallowed. "You tell them that when she wins the Hunter Derby Finals, they need to tell anyone who'll listen how she was pulled off a double-decker trailer headed for a Mexican slaughterhouse. They need to know where she's been, what she's endured, and how far she's come. People need to hear her story."

The driver smiled. "I will certainly pass that along. And I'm sure they'll be happy to put the word out."

He climbed in the cab and started the truck. Over the smooth roar of its engine, I could just make out Soiree's nicker.

Lawrence

Marla appeared at the door, painted into a slinky gold minidress. "What are you doing out here?" She asked, bemused, waving us in. "You should have just cut ahead in line."

"I didn't know that was an option," I said, following her into the pulsating club with the three girls in tow.

"Of course it's an option," Marla said, smiling. "You'll always be a VIP here, Cavanaugh."

"I'll text John and tell him to cut in line when he gets here," Delaware said, whipping out her phone.

Marla glanced back, her interest piqued. "Who is John?"

"Our money man," I answered. "I invited him out with us. The guy doesn't have a lot going on right now."

"That's kind of you," Marla said. "Since this John fellow is undoubtedly picking up the tab, do you want something to drink?"

"Jameson, straight up," I said.

"I'll be back in a flash," Marla purred, hustling over to the bar.

Delaware looked up from her phone. "Why didn't she take any of our orders?"

"I will hazard a guess and say it is because none of us have penetrated her," Yvette deadpanned, fishing around in her clutch for a lip balm.

Courtney was fitful, hopping from one foot to the other. Yvette sent her a hard glance. "Try to relax, Courtney. Dougie is not going to show his face here. In fact, you will probably never have to see him again."

"That's *not* what I'm worried about," Courtney snapped, and she went right back into her little anxiety jig.

Out of the corner of my eye, I saw John make an entrance. He stood still for a second, looking around, and I waved him over. He cleared a path without saying a word, without raising a hand. He wore a fine suit exceptionally well, but his overall manner was so quiet, so unassuming, that he would have faded into the background if not for the sheer size of him.

"Good evening," I said, clapping him on the back. "Glad you could make it."

"It was my pleasure," John said warmly. "I appreciate you inviting me along."

"Are you kidding? You're always welcome to hang with us," Delaware interjected.

"Indeed, as much as you can endure it," Yvette added, throwing in a twisted smile.

"Does everyone have drinks?" John asked. "Order whatever you want. It's my treat."

"I think we're going to grab some seats by the stage," I said. "The show's about to start soon."

"I'll save your places if you'd like," John offered. "You can get drinks and meet me there in time for the show."

"*Awww*, that's so nice of you," Delaware exclaimed. "Can I order you anything?"

"Just a Coke would be perfect. Thank you, Delaware."

"No problem." She sidled off to the bar as Marla returned, bearing my drink.

"That looks more like a double shot," I said, nodding at the full glass.

"It's on the house," Marla said sweetly. "You shouldn't look a free shot in the mouth. Besides," she added, "you can hold your liquor."

I downed the shot and handed her the empty glass.

"So where's this John fellow?" She asked, looking around.

"Over by the stage." I pointed him out.

Her lips slackened, revealing a glistening mouth. "I think I need to make his acquaintance," she said.

I shrugged. "Follow me."

We walked over to where John stood. "John, this is Marla St. James," I said, stepping back. "Marla is a good friend of mine. She owns this club."

John smiled politely, grasping Marla's hand. "John Spencer. Pleased to meet you, Ms. St. James."

Marla's gaze rippled with heat. "Tell me, is there a Mrs. Spencer?" She asked, cutting right to the chase.

The lines around John's eyes seemed to deepen slightly. "No. I'm afraid not."

"I see." Marla failed to notice the strain in his voice, barreling on full speed ahead with her mission. "What do you like to do around here, John?"

"Admittedly, not a whole lot." He smiled humorlessly. "I clean my house, but I've had to ease up on that or I'll put my housemaids out of a job. I read a lot or prepare meals. Sometimes I'll go for a ride. And lately, of course, I've been coming out to watch the team practice. They've really been a godsend to me."

"Sounds like something's missing," Marla said. "Companionship. Someone to share your bed and tell you what to do."

"Oh, yes." John smiled gravely. "But such a person is hard to come by."

"It can't be, for you." Marla gazed up at John, angling her body in toward him, as close as she could be without directly touching him.

John's eyes stared through her, facing the stage. "When you've had someone you love - truly - it makes starting over incalculably difficult. Everything feels hollow after that, when you've already had your one great love. It seems like a fallacy that you could ever hope to experience that anew. It becomes almost easier to tough it out and wait for the other side." The corner of his mouth turned down. "It would surely take someone very special for me to ever consider coming out of hibernation."

In the next moment, Delaware came trotting over, handing John his soda as she sipped on some cheap whiskey. Yvette followed her, holding an elaborate cocktail at arm's length, as if it had somehow displeased her.

"Where's Courtney?" I asked, as a horde of people clustered around us, angling for a better view of the stage. "The show's about to start."

"She went outside with her phone," Yvette said, rolling her eyes. "She said it was important."

The lights dimmed, and a person who was most definitely Elaine walked out onstage. A resounding cheer rose from the crowd. She looked right through them, already completely in character or just in her own head, fighting it out with the usual demons.

She wore a close-fitting blouse with large buttons and a black A-line skirt that ended in a sheer panel, revealing several inches of trim, toned thigh. With a leap that looked effortless, she took to the pole.

The music started, and she twisted, pulling, grasping, and struggling in a way that was somewhat terrifying even though I knew it had to be choreographed. She interpreted the lyrics perfectly, and when she flung herself on the stage at the end, I saw from the tremor in her muscles that she'd given everything.

She rose to her feet, bowing slightly. Her face didn't change now, and I knew she wasn't playing a character. This was all her.

Delaware whistled approvingly. "Way to go, Elaine!" She hollered, then turned to John. "What did you think?" She asked eagerly.

John didn't answer. He was standing, shoulders squared, applauding without stopping. His eyes were on Elaine, and even in the seedy club lighting I could tell they were more alive than I'd ever seen them.

Dougie

New SMS message.
Sent from: Courtney

Team Dark Horse

I'm sorry the other night didn't go well. I probably moved too fast, but that's not really the point. What happened isn't really my fault, and it isn't your fault either. It's just a thing that happened, and now we have to go on from here. Whether or not we have a relationship isn't important. What's important is that you do the right thing for yourself, and if you want to continue with Team Dark Horse, don't let anything stop you. The team wants you here, and I even want you here, even though it's going to be really embarrassing for a while, and I'm probably not going to be able to look you in the eye. Not that I was ever really good at that. Just don't give up on your dreams. Don't hide in your depressingly clean house because something embarrassing might happen. Come with us, and try new things. We're moving to Wellington soon, and it won't be the same if you're not there. Please don't let me ruin everything for you. I'm sorry.
Reply
I appreciate the sentiment. I'm sorry too.
Send
New SMS Message
So will you come to Wellington with us?
Reply
Maybe. I'll have to think on it. It's a big commitment to up and move across the country. There's a lot that has to go into that decision.
Send
New SMS Message
But what do you WANT?
Reply
I want to go to Wellington with Team Dark Horse.
Send
New SMS Message
So do it. Don't make a big decision. Just decide.
Reply
Okay. I'm doing it. I decided.
Send

Team Dark Horse

Elaine

Team Dark Horse was done for the day. I led four ponies up and down a grassy lane, two lead ropes in each hand. They were too spent to really pick on each other, but I still kept a watchful eye out.

Wilson popped up from out of nowhere, eyeing my tenuous hold. "Don't worry," I said, my voice slightly parched. "I've got it under control."

"You haven't taken a break all afternoon," Wilson said as he intercepted me. "You need to rest. You'll run yourself ragged."

"Isn't that the nature of the job?" I asked dryly.

"Let me take over for a little while." Wilson stepped in front of me, forcing me to halt the ponies. "You rest. Have a sip of water. I can't have you fainting away from heatstroke out here."

"Women only faint in soap operas and Harlequin novels, Wilson." I rolled my eyes, but he wouldn't budge, so I threw the lead ropes at him. "Fine."

"You'll thank me when you realize how dehydrated you are," Wilson said to my back as I sped away.

I hung a left into the barn, running some tap water into a paper cup. Downing it in a single gulp, I looked around for my cereal. *I know I picked some up last night.*

It wasn't anywhere I looked, so I figured it was probably still in my truck, which meant it would be a sticky, melted mess by now. I jogged out to the parking lot, looking for the vehicle. It was an eyesore, but at least it was easy to find.

I saw its looming, battle-scarred frame come into view, but something was different. I couldn't see through the cab, couldn't see the outline of a maple tree in the space where the doors should have been.

I stopped dead, blood burning in my eardrums. *What has he done?*

Brand-new doors. My truck had brand-new doors that locked, and a brand-new key fitted on the key ring. A quick glance around the parking lot revealed a cobalt blue Lamborghini, which meant he was on the premises. And I took off at a run.

He was easy to pick out of a crowd, powerful, tall and perfect, so large he blocked out the sun. He was out on the field with Delaware, helping her stomp the divots back into the turf, a somewhat mundane task she really liked to do for some reason. They appeared to be having a contest to see who could reach the end of the field first. She laughed uproariously while he watched her with a smile on his handsome face.

I ran onto the field at full speed, shoving into him, forcing him to take a step backward. "*What* the *hell* have you done?"

He looked at me, his eyes shocked, the color leaving his face. "I'm sorry..." he began.

"*Who do you think you are?*" I shouted, my blood throbbing angrily in my veins. "You think you can just make improvements on my vehicle without my knowledge? Without even *asking* me? *You think that's okay?*"

He hung his head, subdued by my reaction. "I thought it would be a nice gesture. I didn't mean anything by it. I thought you would appreciate it, but of course, I was wrong to do it without your permission. I'm very sorry."

I should have backed down right then. I should have stopped, but I couldn't. I kept advancing on him, backing him into a corner.

"You think I need your *help*?" I said viciously. "That I'm some dumb girl who can't support herself? I work hard, and I make my own money. I don't need you or any man to support me. I've been down that road before, and it almost fucking killed me. I will *never* do that again."

"I didn't mean anything by it," John repeated, face ashen. "It was just...a token of appreciation. For all you do for the team."

I stared at him, feeling an undercurrent of pure rage, the kind that had propelled me to punch a hotel room wall in fury until I split my knuckles open.

"What the fuck is wrong with you people?" I demanded, my voice nearing a scream. "You think you can come around and woo me with presents and *tokens* and all this stuff...throwing your money around like it means something." I shook my head at him, grinning like a maniac as hot, angry tears threatened to spill out of my eyes. "I guess you just think you can fix everything with money."

John's expression turned as quickly as someone flicking a light switch.

Team Dark Horse

The hair on his head seemed to bristle. His hands didn't clench into fists, but his whole body went as tight as a live wire.

"My wife had cancer," he said, his voice low and ragged. "I was with her for 10 years, and she developed cancer. I flew her around the country and around the world. I took her to the best doctors and paid for every cutting-edge treatment there was. I funded clinical trials for new drugs if there was even the slightest hope that something would cure her. She held on for two years, and then she wasted away and died as I was holding her hand." He looked directly at me, his lower lip trembling. "Believe me, I know as well as anyone that you can't fix everything with money."

He walked off the field, shoulders hunched, hands shoved in his pockets. I sank to my knees, staring at the ravaged ground, my stomach heaving.

Delaware came over to me. I didn't move my head, so I couldn't see anything but her boots. "You didn't know," she said. "None of us knew."

I shook my head. "That doesn't make it better."

"You could apologize," Delaware said.

"I can never speak to John again."

She wandered off and I remained, head bent beneath the brilliant sun, wishing it would melt me down, feeding my body to the grass, where at least I could do some good.

Erica

Lawrence and I lay in bed, carelessly draped around each other. I felt the soft scratchiness of his hairy leg, while he undoubtedly felt the prickle of my calf, where I was overdue for a shave.

"Everyone's all set for the move," Lawrence said. "All the players are on board."

"And Amber's going to stay out here and take care of the horses that aren't coming to Wellington," I said. "She said she needed a break for the track since she and Kelly broke up."

"She'll do a good job," Lawrence said. "Maybe she'll even clean the house."

"She'll probably just complain about how messy it is," I said, smiling. "But she'll take good care of the horses. I told her to take D.M. out anytime."

"It's going to be weird for you not to have him around," Lawrence said.

I shrugged dismissively. "It is what it is. It was hard putting Soiree on that trailer too. That's the horse business for you."

Lawrence cupped the back of my head with his hand. "I'm really proud of you, Erica. For achieving your goals with Soiree, and for persevering with Assault. And now you're ready to make your dream happen."

"Well, we'll see," I allowed. "I haven't made it to the Grand Prix ring yet."

"You'll kill it," Lawrence said, winking. "You've been so solid through this whole year and all the craziness with building the team. You've kept this place going through it all. You've kept a roof over our heads. And now it's all going to pay off for you."

"And for you," I said warmly.

"This is it," Lawrence said, pulling me closer, enveloping me in his strength. "This is where we go from here."

I kissed him, finding the slickness of his mouth, gasping softly as his body sank into mine. "I'll follow you," I murmured around his tongue. "I'll follow you anywhere."

Team Dark Horse

Part Four

Lawrence

The white-hot sun radiated down from the sky, filling the air with heat so heavy you felt the impact as you moved through it. Head tipped back, I allowed the sun's rays to pierce my brain, my eyes shielded by plastic Wayfarers. Muscles loose and lazy, I opened the driver's side door and slid into the cab of my truck, sitting down carefully on the scorching upholstery. I turned the key in the ignition and the truck rattled to life, taking me down the road, which was all I could ask for.

The International Polo Club entrance opened up before me, a welcoming stretch of pavement unmarred by a single crack or pothole. Palm trees, strategically planted on either side in precise rows, gently shimmied in the scalding breeze, dwarfing the American flags that stood beside them. Gleaming, imported cars were scattered everywhere they could fit, loitering with the palm trees, some parallel, others perpendicular, tires resting on grass while their hoods nearly stuck out into the driveway.

I kept going, past the tennis courts, the spa entrance, and the Infinity pool, its calm, chlorinated water bluer than the sky. Everywhere I looked, people were gathered under awnings, clustered in the artificial shade, sipping drinks and studiously avoiding the burning sun. They were here for the atmosphere, and I was here for the game.

I parked my truck near the stables, my real destination. Tossing my keys on the seat, I walked into the barn. The ponies had been brought in for the afternoon, sparing them from the heat of the day. Huge industrial fans stood at both ends of the aisle, creating a steady current of cool air, while the misting system installed in the ceiling rained a gentle spray of water on the ponies every fifteen minutes, preventing them from wilting like iceberg lettuce in the produce section.

Team Dark Horse

The ponies on my string were stalled together, a neat row of workmanlike faces and lean muscles. Harry was on the far end, his boldly-marked head standing out in this lineup of plain chestnuts and bays. He was the only one I truly knew inside and out. I'd given Delaware the ride on Vegas. She was the least experienced on our team, and would be dealing with the most pressure and uncertainty. I wanted a familiar horse under her, and I knew Vegas could be trusted to carry her through.

I glanced into each stall, giving the ponies a quick once-over. I'd worked with the grooms here before, and I trusted they were competent. But it never hurt to keep a close eye on things. Maybe it was Wilson's influence creeping out in me.

When my string was unloaded, I'd given the staff many instructions, but one in particular. I would be responsible for Harry's care. No one else would touch him unless they found him cast in his stall or in the throes of colic. He was the only horse on my string who was really mine. We had a bond that was hard-won, cemented in terror and triumph. It was important for me to remain the person he relied on for food, shelter, and freedom. It was vital that nothing changed.

Harry's eyes watched me with a laser-like focus as I set out his saddle, bridle, and brushes. I clipped a lead to his halter and led him to the cross ties, standing back to eyeball his condition. He'd put on weight again since the move; his hindquarters and chest were rounded and filled out, not angular. It was a good thing. I needed to step up his workouts again. Harry had a few things yet to learn, and with every passing day we drew closer to stepping onto the field as a team, with the scoreboard live, the competition intense, and a game that was ours to win or lose.

Few players understood my need to take care of my horses. Most regarded it as a big waste of time, and there was maybe some truth to that. In the hours I spent feeding, watering, and grooming, I could have been practicing. Time spent in the barn was time lost on the stick and balling field. In the minds of my colleagues, I was pissing away a large portion of my time and energy on duties that should have been left to a groom.

The truth was, polo wasn't all about technique. A good bit of it was, and if you didn't keep your reflexes fast and your edge sharp, you'd soon be in trouble out there. But there had been times when I'd been in the last chukker of a close game, with bedlam all around and the ground soaking in sweat from the riders and ponies. Bone-weary and hemmed in on all sides, miles from the ball, I'd looked out at the crush of players surrounding me, and I'd been certain there was no way to win.

In times like that, it didn't matter how much you practiced or how well you could hit. You looked to your horse, and you gave them free rein to find a way out.

Eloise had always answered. With little more than a twitch of her shoulder, she'd bowl her way through, taking me where I needed to go. No matter how tired we were, no matter how bleak the situation appeared, she would always find a way.

She put in that extra effort because I did. What I gave to her in the barn she returned to me on the field. No amount of time devoted to horse care is wasted, because a good horse will always repay you.

That was one thing I knew that other players didn't. It was the only thing that set me apart.

Smoothing the last Velcro strap in place, I led Harry outside. The air closed in around us like an oven, but Harry's feet moved quickly, ringing out over the blacktop. His body swept through the hazy atmosphere, glinting black like a crow in mid-flight.

I mounted up at the stick and ball field, settling into Harry's excited stride, mallet swinging on my right side. To the west, the sky crackled with heat lightning. As usual, we tuned everything out, two minds on a single track, two heads bent, looking forward to the line of the ball.

Erica

I stopped at the Shell station to fill my tank and pick up an extra-large blue raspberry Icee. The Icee actually ranked higher than the gas in importance. Nothing, not even ice cream, could relieve the Florida heat as effectively as one of those slushy soda concoctions.

Sipping from the ridiculously tall Styrofoam cup, I continued down the road to the show grounds, wondering how Assault was settling in.

I parked in the far reaches of the lot and began the lengthy walk to my assigned stabling, still holding the condensation-covered cup. The schooling ring was swarming with activity, a never-ending parade of horses bouncing over the practice fences in turn. A line consisting of grooms hanging onto fresh horses had formed by the designated longeing area.

With around 4,000 horses stabled on the premises at any given time, personal space and the freedom to move weren't merely luxuries. They straight up didn't exist.

I took a shortcut through one of the permanent barns, earning myself a hairy eyeball from several riders. This stabling was rickety at best, with slanting stalls and uneven aisles, and I was slightly glad I hadn't sprung for a stall in one of the barns. Not that it had ever really been an option financially. But even if it had, Assault would've soon torn the place down.

Then I was out in the open air, stepping straight into the first row of tents. Pulling a hand-drawn map out of my pocket, I cut through the rows, searching for Assault's spot. It was like trying to find my truck at the airport, except even more daunting and confusing. I didn't even have the "hit the Lock button and see if the horn beeps" method to fall back on. But I kept looking until I spotted my tent, marked number 28, in the middle of the final row.

I walked in the front of the tent, open partway to allow the air through. It was shady and reasonably cool inside. Letting my eyes adjust to the semi-darkness, I walked up to Assault.

The grass was torn up underneath him, full of scrape marks where his shod hooves had dug into the ground. He marched up to me, flipping his head in a warning gesture, shoving his neck and chest against the round pen panels. Solid steel, they held, which seemed to anger him more. He clanged his hoof against the panels, throwing up his head with a start at the sharp sound of metal on metal.

A gust of wind whipped through, causing the walls of the tent to snap back. Assault jumped in place and trembled, the underside of his neck bulging out in tension. The walls shook, and he flung himself into the gate, bashing his face into the metal. Undeterred, he tried it again, and to my horror, the entire round pen shifted slightly, threatening to collapse.

"*Hey!*" I shouted, fighting for his attention. I snatched up a lead rope and shoved it in between the panels, making a grab for his halter. "Easy. You're fine...."

Assault's ears flicked toward me for a second, then they snapped bolt upright again. His eyes darted around, unable to focus. Another current of wind rippled through the tent, fueling his fear. I managed to clip the lead rope on his halter, and with all my strength, I hauled his head around, forcing him to face me. "Assault. *Listen.*"

The wind picked up, causing the entire tent to sway. Then, in a split second the rain started, heavy drops as loud as hail on the plastic roof. Assault jolted, eyes large as softballs. I clung to the lead rope, anchoring it against the panel, holding him still. Assault's eye rolled in his head, lighting on me, and it narrowed.

With a single calculated pull, he jerked the lead rope out of my hands, wrenching himself away with enough force to slam me against the round pen. It knocked the breath out of me, and as I crumpled to the floor, I could feel a bruise blooming from my shoulder all the way to my hip. With an arrogant twitch of his head, Assault sidled over to the far corner, far from where I lay curled up on the ground.

When I could, I stood up, carefully straightening my battered body. I looked at Assault, suddenly huge and intimidating in this enclosed space. I looked at the portable panels and plastic sheeting that was supposed to contain him, and it all seemed like such a joke.

I went to open the gate to collect him, and I realized my hand was shaking. I had my hand on the pin that held the gate in place, and it was rattling.

I'd never been afraid of a horse before. Not even Assault. But when I raised my shirt and looked at the expanse of purple and blue under my skin, I felt faint.

Any horse had the capacity to seriously injure or kill a person. Even D.M., if he stepped wrong, got scared, or lost his balance, could take me out. No problem. I knew this, and I accepted the inherent risk involved, because I loved horses that much.

Assault's actions had been premeditated. He was angry. He wanted me to come to harm because he didn't want to be in this tent. He saw an opportunity, and he took it.

I stood inside the tent, listening to the roar of the rain pelting the plastic, and looked at Assault, safely on the other side of the panels. He was trapped, and I was free to go. I knew he resented me for it.

But my whole future was tied up in this horse. So even though I could walk away at any time, I remained, holding my bruised ribs and wondering where to go from here.

Elaine

I started getting requests for performances on different weeknights. Since I didn't have a binding contract with Angelina's I couldn't exactly say no. Some of the venues were pretty seedy, but as long as I got my tips at the end of the night I didn't care. None of the characters in these places worried me. I had far more skeletons in my past than they probably ever would.

This bar was no different. Dull hardwood floors, a distinctly sticky bar that people put their elbows on nonetheless, dart boards on every wall. The pool table saw a lot of action. The old men at the bar seemed more titillated by their game of cribbage than by my presence. I almost considered joining in until I remembered how much I hate games.

The pole was in the corner, skinnier and shorter than the one at Angelina's. I wouldn't be climbing it and flinging myself around. There was no room to work in here.

I started my warm-up anyway, doing a few half-hearted stretches and thinking of how I was going to revamp my entire routine. Not that it mattered all that much. Nobody was watching me. I bent over, touching my toes, and twisted my upper body back up. The door swung open, and I was looking right at John.

My breath snagged in my throat and I turned around slowly, as if I could keep him there by not making any sudden movements. As if I hadn't driven him off already. I expected him to walk out the door. Anyone would have after what I said. What I did.

He didn't acknowledge me one way or the other. Didn't nod or smile. But what he did spoke volumes. He pulled up a chair, away from the others, directly across from the pole. Hands folded, he watched me, waiting for my show.

My heart jolted, slamming around in my body. I looked at him in that chair, meticulously ironed slacks and dress shirt fitting him so well. I hadn't put much effort into my appearance for this gig. I wore jeans, boots, and a hoodie that I hadn't even bothered to remove yet.

A raunchy Rihanna song came on the stereo, an odd choice for this establishment, given the clientele. My body followed the beat without really meaning to. My hands grasped the pole, sliding rhythmically up and down its circumference.

Come in rude boy, boy can you get it up?

I locked my eyes on John, feeling my lower body unhinge. I worked myself on the pole, skimming against it, then grinding hard enough to feel the friction through my jeans. I felt a spark, a slight tremor from my nerve endings, so long ignored.

No. Not like that. I moved away from the pole, sliding in behind it, my back to John. Flattening myself against it, I bent over, head near the floor. Arms spread, I raised my fingers, letting my nails scratch against the floor.

Returning to the front, I mounted the pole, as far off the ground as I could get in the close quarters. My legs wrapped tightly around it, I moved with the beat, smoothly up and down. Again I stopped before things could get out of hand. Stepping off the pole, my eyes turned to John. He'd moved over to the bar and bought a drink, but his eyes hadn't left me. His gaze was so consuming, it felt like he was right on top of me. I felt my pulse throbbing in every part of me.

The song built to a climax, and I continued to dance, my careful choreography gradually slipping into something far more primal. My brain stopped dictating altogether and just shut down. Keeping my eyes on John, my movements sped up, both more rhythmic and less controlled. We watched each other from across the room, his large hands clutching a drink he hadn't taken one sip of, and for the first time I let myself think of what it would be like to have him inside me.

The song ended, and I wrenched myself away from the pole, suddenly aware that was swimming in wetness. I was about a hair's breadth away from coming. I waited a moment until the sensation ebbed, and then I walked out the door.

John

I needed to get on a plane to Wellington to make sure Team Dark Horse was doing alright in their first week at the International Polo Club. I could have just picked up the phone, but a personal visit went so much further. I found myself putting it off, though, trying to find things to occupy my time so I could be in Lexington on Friday night.

I had no reason to be at the polo club now that my team was in Florida, and I couldn't go there for the express purpose of seeing Elaine. She'd made it clear how she felt about me. She'd told me, not in so many words, that she had boundaries, and I'd already sullied them. I couldn't undo it, couldn't take back that foolish gesture I'd made. And since I reacted to her venom with anger, I was doubly sure she wanted nothing to do with me.

I spent a lot of time thinking of ways I could make it up to her, words I could say that might ease the damage. Inevitably, though, I ended up sitting back, glassy-eyed, imagining the smooth articulation of her slim thighs underneath her skirt.

I didn't know what it was about her that drew me in. She had a raw quality to her, and I sensed she'd gone to great lengths to wall herself off from the rest of the world. She was wild, almost feral, when you got her upset. And she moved with such a vast eloquence, it was hard not to be struck by the combination. Everything, down to the line of her fingertips, told volumes. When she performed, she worked the emotions of the people watching, leaving them spent and chilled by what they'd seen. Then as soon as she was done, the light in her eyes would shut down like someone had pulled a cord.

Perhaps that was what had me so absorbed. That fleeting light in her eyes, the flicker of joy on her face that disappeared so quickly. I wanted to capture it somehow and keep it there.

I shook my head. I was out of practice with this sort of thing. Since Sally died I'd been in a deep hibernation. No one had managed to pull me out of it, though many had tried. I couldn't muster any sort of interest in their advances.

Through word of mouth I'd heard Elaine was giving a performance at a small venue tonight. I decided I'd go and just try to have a quick word with her. I couldn't leave things this way. It didn't sit well with me.

I dressed and made the drive over. I recognized her truck sitting in the lot. She hadn't had the doors taken off. With a pinging in my chest, I stepped inside the squat, ramshackle bar.

I saw her instantly. There were only a few other patrons there and none were watching her. I pulled up a chair anyway, setting my hands in my lap.

Elaine's eyes landed on me. Unabashedly holding eye contact, she began to dance to a random song that came through the speakers. Hands on the pole, her body melded to it, moving in a guttural rhythm.

This wasn't her usual routine. Her previous work had relied heavily on emotion, delving into themes of abuse and heartache. This was different. This was complete, unapologetic sex. She moved with a purpose, her hips operating independently from her body. Her lips parted slightly, opening to a slick mouth. Abruptly, she pulled away.

I sat, enraptured, leaning forward, eyes straining to see her next move.

She slipped in behind the pole, bending down, her legs close together. Her fingers swept across the floor, nails digging in. I thought of how they'd feel on my back, and my spine shuddered. I stood up in a daze, walking over to the bar.

"What can I get you?" The bartender inquired.

"Jack and Coke," I said distractedly. I had no intention of drinking it, so it didn't matter. I fumbled in my wallet for my card, slapping it down.

When I looked up again she'd moved to the front of the pole. Wrapping herself around it, she slid against it in deliberate strokes. Her body was so tight to the pole, she had to feel the sensation of it against her. I slipped my hands around the drink I'd ordered, my lower body obscured by the bar, my erection hidden from view.

She dropped down from the pole, her feet on the floor. Maintaining eye contact, she ground against it, hands smoothing down the fabric of her sweatshirt and lingering at her lower belly, stopping just short of touching herself. My eyes whirled in my head, taking in the frenzied motion of her hips. I glanced at her face, her eyes distant and unfocussed, her mouth slightly slack. She wasn't pretending. This was real.

My whole body was on alert, waiting to see her come. I stared so intently I thought my retinas might burst, but at the last second the song died out and she stopped, breathing hard. Before I could speak or even move, she marched out of the bar.

I knew there was no use trying to follow her. I stayed seated for a minute, then walked to my car with the certainty that she would already be gone. In the driver's seat I shifted, relieving some of the pressure of my erection pressing into my pants. I knew it wouldn't be going away anytime soon.

I reached for my phone and dialed, my head flopped back against the seat.

"Maria, could you ring up Andrew and have him run the pre-flight checklist on the plane? I need to go to Wellington."

"I'll get right on it, John."

"Thank you." I hung up the phone.

I drove home, my mind turning in circles the whole way. If I hadn't understood Elaine before, I *really* didn't now.

I undressed and stepped into the shower, where I closed my eyes and thought of Elaine, her body, and her face, alive with pleasure. And I slipped my hand around myself, finding some relief that I knew was strictly temporary.

Erica

After staring at Assault for a while, I gave up. I left enough hay and water in front of him to keep him alive, and I hauled my bruised body back through the maze of tents and into my truck, deep breathing and repeating a time-honored mantra. *If something just isn't working, best to leave it alone and come back to it tomorrow.*

It was a statement that normally applied to lead changes or leg yielding, not simply removing my horse from his pen, but it was all I had to cling to right now. I clung to it like I was hanging off the edge of a building 80 floors above the ground. The remnants of my Icee had turned to watery soda. I sipped it anyway, tossing the empty cup in the passenger side floor well where it could linger for a while.

I turned in the drive at the International Polo Club, my new home base. It was sort of an unspoken courtesy that John was putting me up with the team even though I contributed precious little to the enterprise of Team Dark Horse. It wasn't as if I was costing him all that much sharing a room with Lawrence (although with all the room service orders I placed on an average day, my presence didn't exactly come cheap). I still felt vaguely out of place whenever I set foot on these grounds. I had the sensation that I was a groupie, or some sort of hanger-on, rather than a contributor.

I parked and went off in search of Lawrence. He wasn't answering his phone, but that didn't tell me all that much. I wondered if he'd had a more successful day than I had, although I'd set the bar so low, the answer to that query was a distinct "probably".

I tried the stables first, but a quick inventory of his ponies told me he was done for the day. They were all in paddocks, cropping grass or basking underneath shade trees, unwinding after a day of practice. I lingered by Harry's paddock, and he came and stood with me. I scratched his blaze, but he sensed my distracted presence and shook me off, returning to the grass. I sighed and went back to my search.

Lawrence wasn't in our room or any of the restaurants he usually frequented. I walked back outside, the slightly nervous patter of my pulse fueling me to continue my search even as the heat and exhaustion of the day threatened to melt me down. I rounded a corner, stepping in front of the Infinity pool, and spotted him in the most unlikely of places.

He was on the other side of the artificial water. I saw him, but he didn't see me, and for the moment we stood in our separate little worlds, held apart by the width of the pool. He was in his polo finery, sipping from a tall shot glass of icy bourbon. It was remarkable that I could even pick him out of the crowd, because he was surrounded, hemmed in on all sides by women.

They ranged in ages from late teens to perhaps mid-forties and beyond, all of them in as few clothes as possible; short, tight sundresses and bikinis abounded. Uncannily, they all had the same body language: pelvises tilted inward, chests thrust out, mouths slightly parted. They seemed to hang on his every word, and those who were close enough to him went even further, attaching themselves to his extremities as if he were public domain.

He took to it effortlessly, perfectly at ease in this environment. I realized he'd seen it all before. This wasn't his first time in Wellington. But I found myself asking, *Shouldn't it be different now?*

I limped around the pool's edge, making my presence known. He spotted me and detached himself from his fans, coming over to my side. "Hey. How'd it go with Assault?"

"I don't wanna talk about it." I lowered my voice, wavering under the weight of 20 pairs of harsh, judgmental female eyes. "Let's just get out of here."

"Okay." He took my hand and we skirted the pool, slowly making our way back to the hotel. I wondered if he'd pick up on my limp, but he didn't.

I was accustomed to maintaining a low profile at the IPC. I made not even a blip on most people's radar here. I could come and go without exchanging a single pleasantry. Without lifting even one person's eyes off their shoes or their phone.

Walking with Lawrence was an entirely different sensation. There wasn't a single girl we passed by who didn't give him at least a once-over. Most often, it was the slow-burn gaze, a bold, sustained look carrying enough heat to fry an egg.

They all did this, even though I was right there, holding his hand and timidly laying my claim on him. And the most disturbing part of it all, worse even than their total lack of respect for our union, was that each time one of them went by, I couldn't tell if they were looking at him that way because they had been with him, or simply because they wanted to be.

It was an unnaturally long walk to the hotel, longer than the rim of the Grand Canyon, the Sahara desert. When we got to the oasis of our room I moved away from him, hunting for more comfortable clothes. Lawrence saw me as I took off my shirt, the angry blue bruise staining my skin where Assault had slammed me up against those panels.

He marched over, his eyes tight with concern. "Erica. What happened?"

I shrugged, avoiding his gaze. "Just Assault...being Assault."

Lawrence grabbed me gently around the waist, being mindful of my bruise. "Did he throw you?"

"No. I didn't even get on him. Tomorrow's another day...." My voice trailed off and I reached for a pajama top, resting the cool satiny material against my chest.

"You have to be careful, Erica. He could seriously injure you." Lawrence's eyes were nearly pinched shut.

"I won't get hurt," I said defiantly. I slipped away from his grasp, putting the pajama top on and trying not to cry.

Lawrence looked at me critically. "It looks like you're already getting hurt."

"It's just a little bruise." I recognized the total absurdity of the statement as soon as it left my mouth.

"How far does it go, anyway?" Lawrence wanted to know.

I sighed, laying the pajama top down again, peeling off my breeches, standing naked before him. Lawrence drew in a sharp breath, his face grey.

I flinched away from his stare. "It's *just* a bruise," I said, making a move to cover up again.

"Don't." Lawrence peeled back the covers on the bed, inviting me in. "You should rest for a while."

"I'm not tired," I said as I got in, even though my head felt like it was full of wet cement and my body was still smarting.

"Rest anyway." I heard a rustle, and Lawrence slid in behind me, his arms settling around my body. In a minute or two he was inside me, and I dutifully let it happen. He moved slowly, his touch gentle.

"Are you okay?" He murmured around a soft moan, his lips against my ear. "I don't want to if you're too sore."

"I'm okay," I assured him, and I went on pretending it didn't hurt, like I'd gotten so accustomed to doing.

Delaware

I'd had my introduction to polo in Lexington, a sort of crash course before I moved up to the big leagues. Nothing could've prepared me for Wellington. It was on another level.

The International Polo Club was a hotbed of activity. Since John had put us up in the hotel, we were right there, right in the middle of the action. The place truly centered around polo. The patron's social lives revolved around polo. If you looked at an overhead view of the place, the polo fields were front and center, huge, a focal point, and the rest of it was sort of squeezed in around the edges of the fields.

John had arrived earlier in the day by private jet, and he'd probably traveled around the club five times, watching practices and tending to various orders of business. Even now that our practice was done for the day, he still hung out by the field, watching our ponies intently for signs of lameness. Seeming satisfied that they were all in tip-top shape, he finally turned away.

Giving Vegas a final pat, I turned him over to a waiting groom. Yvette's sharp eyes noticed the transfer. "Turning high-society already, Podunk?" She asked, her voice full of barbs as usual. "I was under the impression you were in the 'take care of your own horse' camp."

"Usually, that's the case," I explained nicely. "But I have to meet John for a quick bite, and he's running on a tight schedule."

Yvette's thin eyebrows raised. "He is meeting with you alone, and not the team?"

"It appears that way," I said, mimicking her way of talking. "Like I said, he's on a tight schedule, so I've gotta run."

I walked away, somewhat satisfied by the knowledge that Yvette was probably chewing off the inside of her face.

I rinsed the sweat off my body and put on a summer frock, then hurried to meet John at the 7th Chukker Bar and Grill. He was there already, seated at the bar with a Coke bottle in his hand. He pushed back his chair and stood up to greet me.

"Thank you for agreeing to meet with me," he said.

"Oh, no problem!" I chirped, going in for a hug. "It's my pleasure."

His strong arms settled around me, then released me. "Would you prefer to eat here or in the dining room?"

"Here is good." I liked this bar, with its elegant stone inlay and leather chairs. A row of flat screens played on the wall, framed in wood trim.

John pulled out a chair for me, and I sat down. I ordered a drink, and the bartender fetched it for me, along with two menus. I passed one to John.

"This all sounds so good," I marveled as I skimmed the menu. "But I think anything called 'Seventh Deadliest Sin Mac and Cheese' is something I have to try."

The bartender looped back around. "Have you made your selection, or do you need a minute?"

"I'm good," I said, handing in my menu. "I'll have the mac and cheese."

"All-American girl." He smiled at me. "And for you, sir?"

"The Kobe sirloin, please."

The bartender disappeared, leaving us alone together. I turned to John. "So, what's on your mind?"

He looked embarrassed. "Have I been that transparent?"

"Well, I kinda figured you didn't ask me here just for my company. Although I do make great company." I smiled fully. "And you look like something's wearing you down."

John sighed. He looked troubled. "It's none of my business, of course. I should leave well enough alone. But something has been weighing on me, and I thought you might be able to help shed some light on it."

"I'll do my absolute best." I leaned forward, looking at him straight on.

John hesitated, then came out with it. "You were there when Elaine and I...when we came to verbal blows."

I nodded, but I didn't offer anything up.

John's temple creased. "I've been struggling ever since...I feel terribly about what happened. And I can't help but wonder...did she say anything to you after I left? Did she give any indication on how she was feeling?"

"She was upset," I said. "I came over to try and talk to her, and she was a mess. I tried to tell her it was okay, that she didn't know any better, but she wouldn't listen. I told her she could apologize, but she said she could never speak to you again."

His face shadowed. "Because of how I behaved?"

I shook my head. "No. Because of how *she* treated *you*."

His chin dropped as a tightly held breath whistled out of him. "I just don't know how it can be made right. So much about her doesn't make sense. But I want to make sense of it...."

I patted his arm in sympathy. "Here's what I know about Elaine," I said. "She's been through a lot. I don't even know the half of it. But there are some things that went on in her life that would curl your hair. Things she did, and things she allowed to happen. Her past life was scandalous, and she's just now coming back from that. But she's a prickly mess, and I don't know how invested you are. If you aren't in too deep, you might want to cut your losses and run."

John looked at me as if from underwater. "I don't care what she's done," he said in a low, soft tone, like the warble of a bird or a mother speaking to an infant.

I nodded. "Then you need to go see her. Find a way to move past this."

Our food arrived and I dug into my mac and cheese. John stared at his beautifully garnished plate without touching it. I could almost see his mind boarding the plane and heading back to Lexington, where he really wanted to be.

Elaine

It was the part of my job that was the most grueling and the most invigorating. Just me and a semi-trailer loaded with 400 bales of hay that needed to be put up in the barn. When I first started working for Wilson I was too weak to lift a hay bale. So, even though the task was laborious and altogether pretty boring, I enjoyed the sheer physicality of it, because it meant my body, if not my head, was in good working order.

It was too hot for long sleeves, so I wore a tank top, scratches be damned. The rhythm of the work and the smothering heat had a calming, stupefying effect. Throw a layer of bales off the trailer. Pick them up and carry them into the barn. Stack them tightly, one by one.

Sweat gathered on my chest, attracting every fine piece of chaff like a magnet, covering my skin in tiny leaves the color of camouflage. I was about halfway done, and the area between my shoulder blades was starting to knot up. As usual, I ignored it. Some people took a lot of breaks on the job. Once I started a task, I worked until I either finished it or dropped dead.

Or, until Wilson tracked me down and forced me to stop for a while. Some of his disgruntled workers liked to call Wilson a dick behind his back, but Wilson was nothing of the sort. He was an overbearing mom, forever obsessed with cleanliness and alert for signs of heat exhaustion. His somewhat snappish lectures came from a place of love and concern. Which didn't make them any less annoying. So, when I heard footsteps behind me, I immediately went on the muscle.

"I *already* took a break 10 minutes ago," I asserted, even though I'd done nothing of the sort. "I'm not going to faint away. Go back to your office."

I said all that without turning around. Belatedly, I did. My shocked eyes landed on the silhouette of John standing beside the rear tire of the flatbed trailer.

"Oh my God. I'm sorry. I thought you were Wilson," I explained in string of fragmented sentences.

"It's quite alright. You were focused on your work." John stepped to the side, eyeing the stacked bales. "Looks like you've been working hard."

"It's what I'm good for," I said. "That, and not much else."

John's eyes settled on me, carrying enough heat to strip off my clothes. "I can't believe that."

"Believe what you want to," I said, moving to the next bale. "This hay isn't going to stack itself."

John appeared flustered, fiddling with his cufflinks. "Would you like some help?"

I dropped the bale on the ground. I almost laughed out loud. "You can't be serious."

"I don't make offers I don't intend to fulfill," John said. His eyes conveyed a slight challenge.

Now I did laugh a little. "*You* want to stack hay? Don't you have better things to do?"

"Even if I did, I wouldn't want to be doing them right now."

I shook my head at him. I should have told him off right then and there, but I couldn't bring myself to. He meant well, and if he genuinely wanted to help, I saw no reason not to let him.

I would have been content just to work in his shadow, if he would keep looking at me that way. Like a little kid with a lighter, I kept inching closer and closer to the flame, wanting to feel the heat, the excitement, knowing all the time I would eventually get burned.

"Okay, if you really want to, you can help." I picked up the same bale of hay for the second time. "But I work at a fast pace, and I don't take breaks. So try and keep up."

As I hauled the bale into the barn, I saw John hastily unbutton his suit coat. Rolling up his sleeves and removing the Rolex from his wrist, he worked alongside me in his dress shirt and trousers, face furrowed in concentration. We didn't speak the entire time, but he never slacked off the pace and he didn't falter, his unnervingly steady presence telling me that nothing had changed for him.

Erica

For my own safety, I approached Assault differently now. He was not allowed to bully me or show aggression. Until he behaved differently he would be stuck in solitary confinement. I wasn't messing around.

I gave him food and water, but that was it. If I showed up with a body brush or longeline and he gnashed his teeth or raised his hoof, I turned around and marched out of there. I'd loiter by the ring, watching the pros at work, and I'd come back in an hour or so. I could only hope he'd catch on sooner or later.

This amounted to an inordinate amount of time spent trudging back and forth under the scorching Florida sun, or sometimes in the rain, peering at my sullen horse in his increasingly filthy pen and wondering how long we could sustain this. I hadn't exercised him since we'd arrived in Wellington. My gear sat in a heap in the corner, brushes and leg wraps and a saddle and bridle that were proving about as useful as the proverbial Trojan horse.

I tried to sneak around, hoping no one would see me duck into Assault's tent and make the connection that I was the neglectful owner of the surly bay gelding in tent #28. As an up-and-coming unknown rider, I pretty much ranked lower than dirt in the minds of the established competitors. They had better things to think about than what I was doing wandering around all day long in boots and breeches and never actually getting on a horse. But still, I was mortified. This was not the auspicious debut I had wanted. This was pretty much a living nightmare.

I tried to make the best of it by watching and learning during the hours I spent giving Assault a time-out. Leaning on the rail and attempting to look studious, I watched the workmanlike riders sail around on their fit, athletic horses, legs wrapped in open-front leather boots or bright polos, matching or contrasting with equally loud saddle pads and polo shirts. I kept tabs on the array of bits used, from elevators to gag snaffles to the occasional pelham or mechanical hackamore. I paid attention to the warm-up routines, and how they piloted their horses over a course, turning, rating, and jumping at angles. I let it all soak into my brain, hoping I could put it to good use if I ever got my horse out of his box.

I check the time on my phone, deciding it was time to give Assault another chance. Making the long walk back to tent #28, I avoided the sidelong glances of everyone I passed.

Standing in front of Assault once again, I offered him a choice, holding a longeline out where he could see it. He looked at me with a cranky expression, but not outright venom. I took a deep breath, steadying myself. *This might be my best chance.*

Not allowing myself a second of hesitation, I opened the gate and marched right into his pen. Soggy manure, ground into the grass by his incessant pacing, squished under my boots. I clipped the line onto his halter, removing the frayed, manure-stained lead rope he'd worn and trodden on this whole time, suppressing the memories of what had happened the last time I attempted to hold this horse's strength in my hands. "Come on," I said with authority. "We're going to have a nice longe."

Assault followed me outside, raising his head and blinking against the sun's harsh glare. He tottered around on tiptoe, hyper-aware of his surroundings, careening past me with a snort and a flagging tail whenever one of the tents rustled, snapped, or shimmied. I let him bounce around and then calmly reeled him back in, and he'd walk somewhat sedately at my side until something spooked him again.

As we approached the longeing area there was a line of grooms holding tightly to impatient horses. There was always a line. I prepared to join it, feeling several pairs of eyes on me. Cold and impassive, the waiting grooms quickly took stock of me and Assault.

I glanced at the gelding. Manure was packed in his hooves. Flecks of it clung to his legs and even his back. His mane was starting to thin in places where he'd taken to rubbing it out of frustration or simple itchiness.

What kind of rider can't be bothered to give her horse a pass with a brush? I could see the accusation in their stares, and it was entirely warranted. I couldn't tell them this wasn't who I really was. I couldn't pull out my phone and show them photos of D.M. back in his heyday, when I'd put the polish on the old-fashioned way, with elbow grease and a rub rag, going over every inch of his bright bay coat while he stood in a deep, appreciative slumber.

Standing in line with Assault under control, I thought about the notion of victory. How it was always portrayed as this giant, earth-shattering moment, a tremendous achievement that even the most casual bystander could perceive as being impressive.

Those who worked with horses knew differently. Sometimes a victory could be as subtle as a grain of sand, nearly indistinguishable to the naked eye. A victory could be quiet as a whisper. A small gain of trust, or one good transition. Things you worked months for that seemed negligible, but in the long run, added up into something extraordinary.

Today victory was when Assault waited patiently in line at the longeing area. When it was finally our turn, I sent him out on the circle and he stepped into a canter, bounding through the churned-up sand, expending all his pent-up energy and anxiety. I stood in the middle holding the line, watching the graceful crest of his neck and breathing out in time with his stride, knowing maybe, just maybe, we could go from here.

Dougie

I sat in a shady corner at the far edge of the pool, accessing the Twitter app on my phone. I was seated on a wicker chair, and I couldn't decide whether to put my feet up or keep them planted on the ground. As I tweeted on behalf of Team Dark Horse, I mentally debated the assorted pros and cons of the two positions. They were both awkward, but for different reasons. Feet up made it look like I was trying too hard to appear nonchalant, and feet on the ground made it seem like I was prepared to leap up and scurry away at any minute. Which meant it was more authentic, but also sadder.

Lawrence ambled over, flanked by a slim black girl in a neon bikini. "Tanysha, this is Dougie," he said.

I nodded at Tanysha. "Hey," I said, looking at her for a few moments and then letting my eyes slide back to my phone.

Tanysha smiled big before flouncing away and taking a dive into the pool, which her friends enthusiastically applauded. Lawrence shook his head at me. I could feel the judgment rolling off him like a blast of heat from an oven. "That would have been easy."

"It *was* easy. We said hello, and she went back to her friends. What part of that was difficult?"

"You *know* what I mean." Lawrence leaned against the edge of an awning, extending a leg out, displaying close-fitting leather boots and white breeches, the polo duds he was constantly wearing now. "You could have Tanysha or any one of those girls out there."

"That's a ridiculous statement." I was actually bothered enough to set my phone down. "Why would any of them want to be with a guy like me?"

Lawrence waved the question aside with a toss of his head, hair falling over his forehead in a thick lock. "Girls like that think fucking is a numbers game."

I was almost speechless. "Well, thanks for the boost to my self esteem."

"I didn't mean it that way." Lawrence rolled his eyes, standing upright once again. "I'm just saying, it's not as hard as you think it is. There's a lot of that going on here. And you could be in on it."

"I'm here to work," I said, hunching over my phone and typing furiously to drive the point home. "Not to plow the fields, or peel me off some of that, or whatever it is you'd call it."

"I thought you were here to expand your box," Lawrence said.

"I *am* expanding my box," I said heatedly. "I'm *outside*, aren't I?"

"You're hiding in a dark corner," Lawrence said, walking away, chin jutted out in victory.

I tried to get back to the tweet I'd been composing, but I couldn't concentrate. I got up and walked away from the pool, inclining my body away from Tanysha and her inquisitive eyes and barely-there bikini top.

I hurried into the hotel, grateful for the quiet and also for the wave of AC that hit me as soon as I stepped inside. The hotel lobby was dim compared to the ultra-watt Florida sun, with what could only be described as eclectic décor: couches in plain suede and zebra-print, gilt-framed posters on the walls, and mid-century modern lamps.

I got on the elevator and pressed my thumb to the number 5. Without really thinking, I bypassed my room and kept walking. I got to room #114 and knocked.

The door opened. Courtney and I stood face to face, alive and in the flesh. I hadn't looked at her since our ill-fated date, except through a camera lens. She hadn't spoken to me since then, except via text message.

"Can I watch *Celebrity Dog Swap* with you?" I asked, baring my soul.

Her eyes shifted uncertainly. "Does that...*mean* anything?"

I shook my head. "I just want to watch *Celebrity Dog Swap* and I'd like to not be alone."

Courtney nodded. "Okay. I'd like that too."

She let me into the room and found the appropriate channel. I sat on the chair in the corner, and she lay on the bed, both of us expanding our requisite boxes just enough to allow room for each other.

Erica

I came armed with a fully-stocked brush box containing every grooming tool known to man. I tied Assault up short and put a currycomb to him, leaning into every stroke until my arms got wobbly, scrubbing the accumulated filth off his coat. I followed it up with a body brush, and I followed that up with a rub rag. The whole time, Assault's pointed stare and pinched eyeball let me know he was seething.

"I don't care," I told him, crouching down to polish his hock, ever mindful of his stance. If he raised a hoof, I was out of there. "You're going to look presentable out there even if it kills me. Go ahead and have your tantrum."

Assault twisted his head, pulling the rope this way and that. Testing for a weak point, just like he did when I rode him.

"Break your own neck if you so desire," I said in a singsong voice. "But you're *going* to be clean and shiny when they haul your carcass out of here."

Assault relented, staring hatefully forward at the metal post he was tied to and standing motionless.

"That's a good boy." I wrapped up my polishing and brought out a freshly-washed, spotless saddle pad. For the first time since we'd arrived in Wellington, I went through the motions of tacking up my horse. I tightened the girth gradually in between strapping on his open-front boots, tucking the leather billets into their keepers. Last came the bridle, which I slipped on hurriedly, buckling the throatlatch and cavesson a little tighter than I normally would.

    I grabbed my helmet and shoved it on my head, picking up my jumping bat as we exited the tent. Assault plodded beside me in an ill temper, not even glancing at his surroundings. He looked like a world-weary campaigner who'd been pushed too hard, jumped too much, and gone sour. It was a welcome change from his earlier theatrics, when he'd jumped out of his skin at every little noise, but I knew Assault well enough to be wary of this sudden shutdown. His mood could change faster than the flick of a light switch.

    We passed by tents, threading a careful course through the close quarters. Open flaps revealed horses being saddled and unsaddled or standing for the farrier. I looked ahead to the practice ring, picking the shortest route and walking briskly, pulling Assault along with me.

    As we rounded a corner, I saw the path I'd intended to take was momentarily blocked. A groom was rolling up a water hose that lay in coils on the muddy, water-spattered ground. I made a move to turn around, but my eyes landed on another groom holding a freshly-bathed horse, and I lost all momentum.

    She was an average-looking horse on the ground, not especially tall or regal. Well-built, with a leg at each corner, but somewhat narrow, with a skinny, graceless neck, the muscles oriented in the wrong direction. Her sopping-wet coat gleamed, dark as mahogany, but she was actually a deep chestnut.

    She was the chestnut mare. The one I could've had for my very own, the one I foolishly passed up on trying out. The one who'd hauled a parade of increasingly incompetent riders around courses, slaying D.M. and me. The one I'd had the ride on once, a glorious sensation I'd never experience again, because in the very next instant she was sold, and we parted ways.

    She'd had a lot of miles since I'd last seen her, and she'd grown up a bit. But I still knew it was her. I'd know her anywhere.

Her eyes latched onto me, and she gave me an inquisitive stare. There was no way she remembered me from before. But her deeply-set eyes remained on me for so long, I got chills.

The second groom returned, slopping through the mud. With a path cleared, they led the chestnut mare away.

I shook myself and gave Assault's reins a tug, leading him onward. He clomped through the mud, splattering his legs and my breeches. I didn't care. We reached the practice ring and I led him in the gate. He stood reluctantly as I got on, his ears swiveling, catching the sounds of perhaps two dozen horses clattering by in every direction.

I moved Assault toward the quarterline, ceding the rail to the faster-moving horses, intending to let him walk for a while. But the flow of traffic was so quick, I found myself creating a roadblock at every turn. I had no choice but to urge Assault on, joining the fray of horses moving at a quick canter that verged on a hand gallop.

I held firmly to Assault, knowing what a loose cannon he could be in the warm-up ring. Every time a horse cut in front of him or passed by him closely I gave the outside rein a strong pull, until his head was practically in my lap. His eyes bugged out of his head and the veins were visible on his neck, along with a light sheen of sweat. He cantered along tightly beneath me, his back rigid beneath the saddle tree.

I looked for a space to circle or perform some sort of figure, but each time one opened up, it quickly vanished. The only relief from this endless circuit of the rail would be to take a practice fence. There were two of them, each on a diagonal line in the center of the arena. They were both set at the maximum height.

Feeling myself go pale, I took a bead on one of the fences. There was an opening, and I took it. I pointed Assault and let him go.

Assault sat back and looked at it. I felt him take interest as he assessed it. The height, the challenge. The freedom. He pounded forward, all his energy on a straight track. All his ire, for once, focused.

He barreled down to the jump, ears flattened in concentration, neck snaking forward. He gathered and pushed, leaving the ground at the optimal place, cracking his back over the jump as he snapped his knees up to his chest so tightly I heard the thud of his hooves on his belly. His hind feet snapped out as he stretched to clear the fence, creating a hiss of air that sounded like the crack of a whip. He landed in balance, his legs underneath him, neck and withers elevated, so feather light I could rate and turn him with a flick of my wrist.

I walked him down to the gate and halted him, allowing the other riders chart a course around me for a moment while I let my fingers sink into the soft muscle of Assault's neck.

"No more," I said, rubbing him. "Tomorrow's another day."

Yvette

"Stupid fucking bullshit," I muttered, adjusting the strap on my evening gown.

"That's the spirit," Lawrence sang out as he lounged in a chair, having already put on his suit and tie. He had not bothered to run a comb through his hair or to shave.

"I will never understand why we are required to attend these things," I said, taking a long look in the mirror. "We are serious athletes. We spend long hours practicing our craft. Why are we then forced to stay up late into the night and hobnob?"

"Because polo isn't just a sport, it's also a way of life for a lot of people. For the people who fund the sport. We wouldn't be here if it weren't for them." Lawrence settled back, watching me fume, with a smile on his face.

"Yeah, most sponsors aren't like John," Courtney said, swiftly taking Lawrence's side. "They aren't in it for the love of the sport. They want a party."

"Well, I think it's nice," Delaware chimed in from the bathroom. She hadn't bothered to shut the door, she'd just pulled it closed. "It's always fun to go out and meet new people."

I sighed, her chipper demeanor needling at me already. "They may be new to you, Podunk, but I can assure you they are not new to me. And I can assure you they are huge asswipes."

Lawrence smirked. "You have a point there."

Delaware bounced out of the bathroom wearing the same bronze sequined hoochie dress she'd worn to the gala in Lexington, causing me to take a sharp breath. "*No*. You are *not* wearing that. Get your redneck ass back in there and change into something appropriate."

Delaware stared at me. "But I don't have any other dresses."

"It does not matter. Wear a terry cloth robe if you have to. It will look classier than what you have on now."

Lawrence rolled his eyes. "Yvette, quit nitpicking and let's get out of here. She looks fine."

"It is not about looks," I snapped. "There is nothing to that dress. If she walks past Delgrange showing that much exposed skin, she will contract herpes."

Delaware turned her eyes on me, grinning slightly. "It's sweet that you're trying to defend my honor," she said cloyingly. "But I'll be just fine. I know how a lady deports herself."

Courtney made a move to correct Delaware, but I silenced her with my eyes. "Let's just get this over with," I said, snatching my clutch.

The four of us entered the elevator, riding it down several floors until it opened up. We walked down the hallway to the ballroom. Potted palm trees lined the room, and tiki torches provided outrageously cheesy mood lighting. The floor was dotted with wicker tables and chairs that looked as if they had been swiped from poolside.

"It's *beautiful*!" Delaware exclaimed right on cue.

"A word, please," I said, grabbing her arm firmly and dragging her into the hallway.

Lawrence looked at me sharply. "Do I need to join you two?"

"I will be nice," I told him, and for some reason he believed me. Disappearing into the throes of the party, he left me alone with Delaware.

"Now then," I said, taking hold of her wrist. "Allow me to take a moment to explain the ways of the world to you."

"Oh, I'm all ears," Delaware chirped.

"You may think that things will go a certain way," I said to her. "You may believe that you will waltz in there and that everyone will love you. I am here to tell you otherwise."

"All those people," I said, waving an arm, "could give a single fuck about you. The fact that you were named rodeo queen at the Podunk County Fair three years running does not mean shit here."

Delaware nodded patiently. She didn't seem the least bit worked up.

I raised my voice slightly. *"You are nothing here,"* I said, emphasizing each word.

Delaware looked at me, puzzled. "Am I supposed to be upset right now?" She asked, always slow to catch on.

"Some would say so," I allowed.

Delaware shrugged, maddeningly indifferent. "Well I guess that's the main difference between you and me. Because I really don't care how I rank in the minds of all those people. And I can tell that you do."

Before I could assure her that was most definitely not the case, she flounced away, hurtling into the ballroom to make a fool of herself. I could not bring myself to follow her, so instead I went for a walk. When I returned to the stuffy ballroom I had no trouble picking her out of the crowd. She was easily the most cheaply dressed, her sequined minidress picking up the light from the tiki torches and sparkling violently.

It took me a moment to realize that she was surrounded by a group of patrons. She appeared to be telling a story, and I watched closely, waiting for signs of ridicule and condescension from the group she addressed.

"She's doing well, I think," Courtney whispered, having materialized at my side. "They like her."

My head swung around to look at her. *"Why?"* I demanded in a higher tone of voice than I'd intended.

Courtney shrugged. "You know I don't understand how this stuff works. I dunno. Maybe they like that she's folksy."

"I don't understand," I muttered. "I thought she would be eaten alive here."

Courtney glanced at me. "I know you don't like Delaware that much, but she's actually pretty likeable. Objectively speaking," she added hastily, seeing my face.

I didn't follow up with a retort, distracted by a newcomer who'd stepped into Delaware's little audience. "Now what is *that* fucker doing?"

Courtney squinted at the tall and swarthy figure who was introducing himself to Delaware. "Facundo Alvarez? Why is he a fucker?"

"They are all fuckers," I said, referring to high-goal polo players of a certain gender. "Every last one of them."

"Okay, but why him in particular? Did he do something really bad?" Courtney leaned into me, her voice soft and shrill. "*Does he have herpes*?"

"Not that I know of," I shrugged. "I am sure he is not to be trusted, of course. But I have not heard anything particularly damning."

"Well he seems to like Delaware." Courtney watched as he slowly separated her from the crowd. "Look, I think he's going to invite her to dance."

"I have lost interest," I said, moving away. "I am going to drink now."

"There's no open bar," Courtney warned from behind me.

"Those cheap cocksuckers," I snapped, digging my nails into my palm. "I hope you brought Daddy's credit card."

"It's up in my room," Courtney said, clasping her hands as she fretted. "I'll have to go get it."

"Hurry," I said.

She left the ballroom at a nervous shuffle, while my eyes found Delaware and Alvarez on the dance floor. She moved teasingly to a seductive Timbaland beat, and his hands settled on her hips, eyes on her body as if held by a magnet.

I walked out to the hallway to find some air that was not in contention. Courtney was not reliable. I could send her around the corner to the ice machine, a two-minute walk both ways, and it would be hours before she returned with some half-melted ice and those big, apologetic eyes of hers.

I settled in for a long wait, arms crossed in front of me to ward off any possible exchanges with passersby. Lawrence soon found me, as he was apt to do. He stood at my side, a shot glass in his hand.

"How did *you* get a drink?" I asked.

"I just opened a tab in John's name," Lawrence said, tipping the shot back.

"Oh." I looked away, disinterested. "I thought perhaps your girlfriend bought it for you."

"She's not here," Cavanaugh said.

I glanced his way. "That is odd. Why did you not invite her?"

"This isn't really her scene," Lawrence explained. "I don't think she's all that comfortable here."

"It is hard to imagine anyone being less comfortable here than I presently am," I said. "Yet I manage to make an appearance."

"You know who *is* comfortable here?" Lawrence asked, grinning lopsidedly. "Delaware."

"Is Alvarez still rubbing his sweaty hands all over that tacky, sequined monstrosity of a dress?" I asked, mainly out of boredom.

"Come see for yourself," Lawrence said, beckoning me into the ballroom.

I followed him to the entrance, where I could just make out Delaware and Alvarez seated in a back corner, leaning close together, talking animatedly.

"He's been by her side most of the night," Lawrence said. "And the times he wasn't by her side, he was looking at her."

"She is doing better than I thought," I said with caution.

Lawrence looked at me fully. "Everyone loves her," he said.

I walked to the lobby, putting some distance between myself and Cavanaugh. Sending Courtney to get her credit card had been foolish. Had I gone myself, I would have been drunk by now. Instead, I sat on a tacky zebra-print couch, sober in more ways than one.

The sound of a throat being cleared reached my ears. Somehow melodic, it rang out in a soft warble, with not a hint of coarseness or gravel. I looked around for the maker of the sound, finding him some distance behind me. Tight-fitting polo shirt, pressed khakis, bulbous Rolex around one wrist, rings on four different fingers and a gold chain around his neck. Thick, defined arms without a single hair on them, and a meticulously-coiffed head of light brown hair and a matching beard.

"Javier," I said.

"You are being antisocial again," he said, moving around to the front of the couch.

"There is no open bar," I explained, though I did not owe him anything, much less an explanation. "I have sent Courtney on a mission to collect her gold card, but she appears to have fallen down the rabbit hole once again."

"I would buy you a drink," Javier said, his eyes pouring over me like liquid.

I shook my head. "I would never allow myself to be in your debt."

"What if it were a gift? A nice gesture?" He hounded, undeterred.

A sliver of a smile crossed my mouth. "I've got a nice gesture for you." Slowly, I raised my middle finger, twisting my wrist so it faced him.

A sigh rippled through Javier's body. His shirt was so tight I could see the outlines of his muscles shifting when he breathed. "You are always so mean, Yvette. Everyone wonders why I continue to associate with you. They ask me."

"What do you tell them?" I queried.

"I let them think what they want to," he said, contemplative. "I let them draw their own conclusions, as wild and dangerous as they desire. For some people, that is all the pleasure they have."

"We should go to the party." I stood up, walking briskly. He kept up with me easily. At the door to the ballroom, I paused. Courtney was nowhere to be seen.

Javier bent down, the scruff of his beard brushing my ear. "Your new teammate is very well liked," he intoned.

I followed his gaze. Delaware was out on the dance floor with Alvarez. She spotted me, waving and smiling a beauty-queen smile. Big and fake.

I pulled Javier out of the room, summoning the elevator. He smiled at me, his eyes and mouth lazy. "Your place or mine?" He quipped.

"Yours," I said, crossing my arms before me. "So that I can leave."

Slightly disgruntled, he pressed the appropriate button, his face settling into a frown.

We entered his suite, large enough to house a family of six. I walked around turning on lights, unafraid of the stark lighting. Javier watched me, his hands at his hips, trying to appear distrustful.

"I thought you said you were done with me," he called out, his voice a little rougher now that we were alone.

"I am done with you." I walked up to him, sinking to my knees. "That is why I am doing this, instead of fucking you. It is less intimate."

"It's *more* intimate," he argued.

I eyed him critically, my hands at his fly. "Do you want this or not?"

He nodded almost imperceptibly, stripping off his shirt, revealing a thick, hairless body. I reached inside his pants, bringing him out into the open, warming him with my breath, lips open just enough to take him inside, but I didn't yet.

"You've been waxing again," I murmured against his shaft.

"The girls like it," Javier said, his voice a heavy rumble in his throat.

"It does make this easier," I said, sliding my tongue along the underside of him, just enough to awaken all the nerve endings. I lingered at his head before taking my mouth away again, blowing cool air on the slick wetness I'd left behind.

Javier's body shivered. "I will never understand you."

"What is there to understand?" I put my mouth on him, shoving him all the way back to break the catch in my throat, wrapping my lips around the base. Holding my breath, I moved my head back and forth in the rhythm I knew would undo him the most. Feeling his eyes on me, I stared up at him, holding eye contact as his control steadily slipped.

"Make it last," he pleaded, his voice at a guttural pitch.

I shook my head, corkscrewing my mouth around him. In the final moments, I pulled my head back, moaning softly against the top half of his shaft as I felt him come.

I detached myself from him. With no theatrics, I swallowed and dabbed the corners of my mouth with a napkin.

"What now?" Javier asked, breathing heavily.

"Now? Now, I leave."

"You shouldn't leave right after," Javier argued. "It's bad etiquette."

"I told you," I said, preparing to make my exit. "Less intimate."

"More intimate," he insisted.

"You are wrong." I turned back, fully engaged in the debate. "Is it intimate when I suck on a straw, or swallow a bite of filet mignon? I think not."

"That's sustenance," Javier asserted. "You need it to live. This is different. You're giving pleasure to someone else, and you don't get anything out of it except for the satisfaction of making them feel good. It's selfless. Therefore, it's more intimate."

"Who said I get nothing out of it?" I said, and I left him standing there with his dick hanging out.

Erica

Every day, I rode. There were no days off, no aborted workouts. My first Grand Prix class was in less than a week. Whether Assault felt like it or not, I dragged him to the ring each day and put him through his paces. He was sour and edgy on the rail, a tight bundle of nerves. When I pointed him at a fence he attacked it, powering through with a jumping effort that left me breathless. He was clearly uncomfortable in this environment, and he gave every horse that passed us a hateful stare. Over fences, though, he had never felt better.

There were still unanswered questions. Space constraints meant I couldn't ride him over a full course, and when we finally stepped in the ring we would have seconds to join together as a team and take on the challenge. There were so many factors I couldn't prepare for. But strangely, I felt a new sense of calmness settle over me. Perhaps I had little reason to feel confident, but somehow I did. I'd never had so much faith in Assault. Through all the pain he'd put me through, all the battles we'd faced, one truth remained, staring me in the face. His ability, his insane, inborn gift over fences. It was the one thing that had kept me from tossing him aside like his old owner had. And now that we were in Wellington, he was coming into his own. All his fear and frustration was channeled into boundless energy, supercharging his every muscle. He put it all into every jump, stretching and pushing, no longer slacking off. And it was beautiful.

It was something I could cling to after every ride, when I stripped off

Assault's tack and attempted to cool him out. Some days he was fine. Other days, I saw a certain look in his eye that chilled my heart and made me very, very cautious. My right side, now yellow-green, was still tender to the touch, a constant reminder of his destructive propensity.

I bent on one knee, unfastening his jumping boots while keeping a close eye on his body. If the line of his muscles shifted, I knew to get out of the way. He remained still, but there was a certain tightness to his body that told me to exercise caution.

I started leading him, legs slogging through the humid air. Assault lagged behind me, and when I asked him to step up, I met resistance. Hauling him to a stop in the middle of the tents, I cracked his chest with the end of the lead rope. "*Back,*" I growled.

Assault rocked back on his haunches, stamping his front hooves threateningly as he minced backward. I held myself up tall, ignoring the warning bells in my head. *This is all intimidation. If I show strength, he'll back down.*

I backed him up nearly to the lip of my tent, asking him to walk on again. Assault shook his head, planting his hooves in the dirt.

I breathed deeply, taking stock of the situation. Assault's chest and back were soaked with sweat, creating a neat outline of the saddle and breast collar. I wanted to walk him down to one of the barns and hose him off. Assault, for whatever reason, wanted to stay in his hated tent. I looked at the path to the barn, an intolerably long, dangerous walk I'd taken with him far too many times. I looked at the mouth of the tent, so near, so accessible. And I caved. Tossing my strict horse-care regimen in the gutter for the umpteenth time, I turned Assault around and marched him into the tent, chucking him into his narrow, dim little pen. "Have fun rotting in there," I said caustically to the gelding. "And don't you dare tie up."

He turned his butt to me, ears laid back. *Bitch.*

I stepped out into the sunlight, grateful to be leaving him. *I hope that sweat doesn't dry in a crust and leave him covered in salt,* I thought with slight regret. *But I guess even if it does, no one will see it once he's saddled,* I decided once and for all as I prepared to slink away.

"Riding him hard and putting him away wet?" A voice asked, jolting me.

Team Dark Horse

I turned around slowly, looking into the eyes of one of the riders. The twinkle in his eye said he was joking, but it didn't ease the horror in my heart. I wasn't as invisible as I thought.

"It's my dirty little secret," I said without a hint of humor.

The rider, a guy about my age in a polo shirt, jeans and a tweed ball cap, looked chagrined. "I'm only joking," he said. "Everyone I've talked to says the same thing. That horse is trouble."

"Really?" I couldn't fathom how Assault could be a topic of conversation around here.

"I've seen him in the schooling ring. Let's just say I'm glad I'm not you." He laughed, cutting it short when he saw I still wasn't amused. "You handle him well, though. And his jump is scary good."

"He's usually better in the show ring. That's where he shines." I glanced back at the tent that had obscured Assault from view. "It's hard to exercise him with all these other horses milling around. He doesn't do crowds. Today when I tried to lead him around, he flat-out said 'fuck you' and parked himself by his tent."

"Is this your first time here?" The guy asked me.

I nodded.

"Mine too." He smiled ruefully. "It's not like it is at home. It's a stressful environment, and it's hard on the horses. It sucks. But when you get in the ring, it's all worth it." He smiled at me. "When's your first class?"

"Saturday."

"Good luck. I'll be rooting for you, as long as you don't beat me." He smiled fully. "No, in all seriousness, I do wish you the best of luck."

"You're riding on Saturday?" I asked. "In the Budweiser Challenge?"

"That very one," he said, nodding. "On her."

I followed his head as it turned. I looked where he looked, and I saw the chestnut mare standing in between the rows of tents, cropping grass while a groom followed her around, holding the lead rope loosely.

I could've said something. I could have told him, "I know that horse," or asked about her. He was a nice guy, and I could've kept speaking with him. I might have even learned something. Instead, I stood staring at the chestnut mare standing under the spotlight-bright orb of the sun, collecting the light in every shaft of her coat, completely mute and rotting with envy.

Lawrence

Since the gala, Delaware had spent every second on her phone, texting Facundo Alvarez. She walked with her phone and ate with her phone right by her water glass, snatching it up every time it buzzed. Even now, at 5:30 in the morning, she sat on Vegas' back with her reins draped over his neck, using both hands to text Alvarez while Vegas stood there with his ears drooping and one hind leg cocked like a cow pony.

"Delaware!" I hollered as Harry's feet shuffled around, performing a series of intricate pirouettes, expending as much energy as he could within the confines of my hold on the reins. "Wrap it up already. Let's get this show on the road!"

"One sec," she promised, typing furiously. Vegas' head dropped even lower. His nose was about a foot off the ground.

"Why did we have to be out here so early, anyway?" Courtney asked, stifling a yawn. "I'm not even awake yet."

"I already told you," Yvette snipped. "We must prepare for our upcoming exhibition, and it is crucial that our routine remains a secret. Otherwise, what would be the point?"

"Exactly," I said, laying a hand on Harry's neck to soothe him. "Exhibition prep takes priority this week. We're going to show everyone what we're made of."

"*If* we can ever get Podunk off her phone," Yvette pointed out sourly. "This is precisely what I feared would happen. I have seen it so many times. You have these young women, these promising players with everything it takes to succeed. Then you expose them to Argentinean polo gods like Alvarez, and the next thing you know, they lose all drive."

"It is quite a startling change," Courtney said, shaking her head at Delaware's hunched posture and flying fingers.

Yvette gave Courtney a sidelong glance. "He appears to have fucked the brains right out of her. What little she had to begin with."

"That's enough," I ordered. Nudging Harry into a trot, I rode up behind Delaware. Easing my mallet back, I whacked Vegas on the rear, just hard enough to make that popping sound and wake him up. The gelding scooted forward, causing Delaware's upper body to fall back. Fighting for balance, she snatched up the reins and shoved her phone in her pocket.

"*Okay!*" She shouted.

"What is Alvarez doing up this early, anyway?" Courtney wanted to know. "Shouldn't he be asleep still?"

"We stayed up *all night* just talking," Delaware said, smiling big. "We can't get enough of each other. It's *so* romantic."

"Wait until you fuck him, and he loses interest completely, until he becomes bored enough to call you again," Yvette declared. "You will feel like you are a cheap fling, and for once you will be right."

Courtney stared listlessly at the ongoing battle. "I could still be in bed," she murmured.

"Wrap it up, you two." I stared daggers at Yvette. "We need to get on with this practice."

"First, we need to decide what we are riding to," Yvette turned her pony on a dime and rode up to me. "Then we will build the choreography from there, and we will practice it until it is perfect."

"I suppose you think you're going to pick the song," I said, rolling my eyes.

"We cannot leave the choice to Courtney." Yvette sneered. "Not unless we want to ride to 'Oh my soda pop, watch it fizz and pop'."

"That's not fair," Courtney protested. "*Of course* you're going to bring up the lamest possible Britney song as an example, when she has a whole body of work that speaks to generations..."

"Right. Because 'Born To Make You Happy' is a work of genius." Yvette snorted quietly into her gloved hand.

"Excuse me." Delaware rode up, thrusting Vegas into our midst. "How about the dog days song?"

Yvette turned her head, eyeing Delaware sharply. "'Dog Days Are Over', by Florence & The Machine?"

Delaware shrugged. "Yeah. The one you play in your car a lot. That one."

Yvette looked at Delaware, keenly assessing her. "That is actually an excellent idea, Podunk."

"I don't know which song you're talking about," I said.

Yvette turned her eyes on me. "I will play it for you," she said.

Courtney

I got back to my room at 8 and slumped on my bed. It took me a second to realize Dougie was still in it.

"Holy shit!" I said aloud.

Dougie stirred, slipping his fully-clothed body out from under the covers. "I didn't realize you left."

"I didn't realize you slept over." I watched him walk to the bathroom, marveling at how startlingly tall he was when he wasn't crunching his spine over an electronic device.

"We stayed up really late watching *Celebrity Dog Swap*, and then we watched that Britney documentary. I think eventually we just fell asleep where we were lying."

"Were we in the same bed?" I asked.

"I mean..." Dougie was watching me. He looked nervous. "I mean...yeah."

"Oh." I picked up my room phone, preparing to order room service. "I guess that's okay."

I placed my order, getting the next size up, in case Dougie wanted some. When I got off the phone, he was still looking at me.

"I got eggs Benedict," I said, placing it back on the nightstand. "Do you like eggs Benedict?"

"It's fine." Dougie seemed distracted. "So...that can happen again? Or just the one time?"

I looked at him in confusion. "Eggs Benedict?"

He shook his head, his face coloring in patches. "No. Sleeping together.

Platonically, I mean," he added frantically.

"Oh. That." I considered it for a moment. "I guess so. I mean, it didn't hurt anything." *I didn't even know it was happening at the time.*

"Good." The corners of Dougie's mouth turned up slightly. "I'd like it if it happened again."

"Exactly the same as last time though, right?" I asked, my wobbly tone announcing my unease. "No...extra stuff thrown in?"

"Of course. No extra stuff. I know my limits." Dougie smiled at me in a way that might've been flirtatious if it hadn't been so sad.

"You're not still feeling bad about what happened, are you?" I asked, veering into slightly dangerous territory.

Dougie looked at me levelly. "I'm a guy, Courtney. Of course I'm still upset about what happened."

My eyes popped open. "But that was my fault! I went too fast."

"You just have a really nice body," Dougie mumbled, his face turning red again. "There's nothing you can do about it."

I sat on the bed, chagrined, until room service knocked on the door and I had to go collect the eggs Benedict.

"Are you going to eat?" I asked.

"Yeah, I'll have some." Dougie scooted over, grabbing a fork.

I chewed a mouthful, contemplative and sleep-deprived. "I'm sorry you didn't get to lose your virginity," I said, appalled by the words as soon as they left my mouth.

"I'm not a virgin," Dougie said.

"Oh." *Oh.* I scrambled for a response. "I'm sorry..."

"Don't be. It's a common misconception." Dougie chewed another bite. "I have had sex. And I've kissed someone. Well, you." He looked away. "But I haven't done the stuff in between."

"Oh," I said again. With part of my brain, I realized that was probably the reason he sucked at kissing.

"What about you?" Dougie asked, seeming to fully commit to the awkwardness of the conversational track I'd unwittingly steered us onto. "How many guys have you been with?"

"Just two. Lawrence, and a guy from high school." I dropped the topic like a lead balloon.

We ate the rest of our breakfast in silence, and I set the dishes on the tray. "I think I'm gonna go to the fitness center," I said. "Hit the treadmill for an hour."

Dougie looked pained. Exercise wasn't really his thing. "Have fun with that. I'm going back to bed. That Britney show took a lot out of me."

"It was pretty insane, wasn't it?" I bent down, lacing up my running shoes. "Back in her heyday, everyone went nuts over her. Everyone was how I am. Now, no one is."

"You are how you are." Dougie peeled the covers back, crawling into bed. "And I like it."

His phone was on the nightstand. He reached for it as I left, but not a second before.

I walked through the muggy air to the fitness center. I stepped through the doors and was immediately intercepted by Yvette. "There you are, finally. Where were you when I needed someone to spot me? I had to ask Cavanaugh." She glared in his direction. He was by the elliptical, being chatted up by a female trainer with back dimples as large as quarters and a high blonde ponytail.

Lawrence saw me and abandoned the conversation with a friendly wave. "Where in the hell is Dougie?" He said as he came up to me. "I haven't seen him all morning. And he's not updating our pages."

"He is not in his room, either," Yvette added.

"He's in my room," I said without thinking.

Both sets of eyes landed on me. "You slept with Dougie?" Lawrence blurted.

"*Platonically*," I said, stressing the importance of the word. "We stayed up late watching TV, and we fell asleep in the same bed. *Platonically*."

Lawrence grinned widely. "I bet he still got off, though."

Yvette glanced at him sideways. "That is a cheap shot."

Lawrence smirked. "Yeah, but it was funny."

"Yes, it was." Yvette turned to me. "What did he say afterward?"

"He asked if it could happen again." I glared at Lawrence, whose grin was a mile wide.

"I am sure he did," Yvette said in that annoyingly superior way of hers.

"We're *only* sleeping together platonically!" I wailed. "No touching or extra stuff! We discussed it!"

"That is what they all say." I could never understand how Yvette managed to look down on me when she was 8 inches shorter. "Sooner or later he will roll over, and you will wake up with a dick poking you in the back."

"You guys suck!" I yelled, storming out of the fitness center. "I'm leaving!" I bellowed as I went, for emphasis that was strictly unnecessary.

Instead of exercising on a treadmill in a climate-controlled room, I went for a run in the boiling heat, perspiring from every pore, from the roots of my hair to the soles of my feet. Nearing heat exhaustion, I continued my run in the hotel, going up 5 flights of stairs and falling on my door. I left a slick of sweat on it.

Dougie looked up as I staggered into the room, alarm registering on his face. "Wow. When you work out, you clearly don't mess around."

"I have to drink some fluids," I mumbled, my brain in an electrolyte-starved haze. "But before I do that, I have to shower."

Dougie sat up in bed. "Mind if I join you? Platonically, of course."

My eyes popped open, and I stared at him, almost trembling. My heartbeat had resumed its mid-sprint pace.

Dougie chuckled, seeing my face. "I'm just kidding. You go shower. I'll call room service and have them bring some Gatorade."

Elaine

John attended my show religiously every Friday night at Angelina's. I could pick him out of the crowd the moment he walked in, no matter how many souls milled around the club, filling it to capacity. Whether he was seated right next to the stage or fifty rows back, I found him with my eyes, and they would remain on him for the length of my performance. Then I would leave. He never sought me out, never forced his way backstage like some of my other fans. He was waiting for me.

He would be waiting forever. I would never accept what he was offering, what he had so generously laid out before me. I wasn't a fool. I knew what he possessed. He could woo me better than Arnold ever had, and he could maybe even satisfy my most primal needs. Each time I looked at him, I could feel the promise of his body, his hands, his very nature. I could feel my head liquefying with warmth and desire.

That was how I knew to keep my distance. I'd felt this overwhelming, forceful passion before. When I finally got my life together, I told myself that if I ever felt it again, I would run. Ever since I met John, I had been running. Even when I stood right next to him, I was still running, keeping the wheels in my head spinning, not allowing them to land on any particular thought. If they tried catching, I forced them to perform another revolution. I was relentless. But so was he.

As I wrapped up my performance, I saw Marla edge her way through the crowd. She leaned into John, whispering something into his ear. At the same time, she pressed her breasts into him very strategically.

I stared at them with so much hope, I almost slipped out of my routine. *Give in to her,* I thought. *She'll satisfy you. Give in to her, and forget about me.*

He remained impassive as she writhed up against him, murmuring undoubtedly dirty things in his ear. All the while, his eyes remained on me, steady and faithful as the slow rotation of the earth.

Disgusted, I leapt off the pole, landing with all the grace of a trucker stepping down from the cab of his big rig. I stomped off the stage before my routine had even ended.

Applause ensued anyway. I was an established artist, and my fans accepted everything I did as art, even when it bordered on the insane. Grabbing my coat, I hurried out the back entrance, running through the parking lot in heels, seeking the sanctuary of my truck.

"*Elaine.*" John intercepted me, smoothly impeding my path. "Please slow down. I need to talk to you."

"I have nothing to say." I tried to cut past him, but he was large and suddenly ruthless. "I just want to get out of here."

John looked at me, his face regretful. I could make out the tiny flecks of gold in his eyes even in the semi-darkness. "I know you saw Marla talking to me. I'm sorry if it upset you. But you should know there is nothing between us. Her attraction is one-sided. I hope you understand that."

My shoulders slumped forward. Angry, frustrated tears spilled out of my eyes. "You *should* start something with Marla. You should be with her. Work whatever this is out of your system."

"I don't want Marla," John murmured, his voice soft. "I want *you*." He reached out a hand, wanting to pull me closer.

I shoved it away. "Why can't you understand?" I shouted. "I *want* you to want her. I want you to fuck Marla, or someone else! Anyone else! Why is that so hard to understand?"

John held steady this time. He didn't shrink back.

"I cheated on my husband," I said, a jagged edge in my voice. "I married him for his money, and I cheated on him with a guy who had zero interest in fucking me. But I hounded him and made him an offer he couldn't refuse. I gave him eight hundred grand of my husband's money." I looked at John, my eyes hard. "Now do you understand what I'm telling you? *You don't want me.*"

I was shaking a little, teetering on the edge of rage that threatened to give way to tears. Just like before, I pleaded with John in my head. *Walk away. Leave. You don't want me.*

John laid a hand on my trembling shoulder, steadying my whole body with one touch. "What do *you* want, Elaine?"

My eyes filled, heavy drops clinging to my lashes. "I don't get to decide what I want. I lost that privilege a long time ago."

John nodded, patiently going along with my twisted logic, seeming to know he couldn't change it. "But if you could, would you choose me?"

My body gave a small shudder. "I couldn't not choose you," I said.

"Then as long as you're here, I won't see anyone else." John smiled tenderly.

I shook my head, horrified. "Don't do that," I said urgently. "Don't sideline yourself for me. It's just a waste."

"You don't get to decide what I want," John said, and he got in his car, flipping on the headlights and pulling out of the parking lot.

I watched his tail lights fade into the distance, feeling a wave of sickness hit me as I wondered what would happen if he could stand still longer than I could run.

Erica

I sat upright in bed with a jolt, wrestling Lawrence's arm off me, convinced I had somehow slept through my class. When I looked at my phone, it was three hours before my alarm was even set to go off.

I lay back down, moving over to the edge of the bed, leaving some space between Lawrence's sleeping form and me. He rolled over the other way, spooning one of the hotel pillows. I lay on my back, facing the ceiling. Closing my eyes would be futile, and I knew it. I wasn't getting back to sleep.

I glanced over at Lawrence, sleeping and snoring lightly, seemingly without a care in the world. The noise in my head was building, the force of a million thoughts grappling for my attention creating a pressure point right behind my eyes.

I wondered, as I often did, how two people sharing each other's lives could be so different. How one person could think and feel and worry every second, while the other person simply assumed everything would work out.

Maybe there was no right or wrong way. Maybe it didn't mean they were any more or less invested.

I held my phone up before me, and I deleted old text messages and did other mindless tasks for a while. After I ran out of things to do I just watched the hours go by, and I shut my alarm off before it had even begun to sound.

Team Dark Horse

Erica again

Normally, the morning of a big event like this, I would spend hours primping and polishing the horse I was competing on. Because Assault was Assault, I'd had to break the massive grooming effort up into small chunks over the course of the past week. I'd pulled his mane one day, banged his tail the next. He'd been re-shod on Thursday. Now I pored over his feet, tapping the metal hardware with a small hammer, making sure the clinches were still tight.

With Assault standing tied, I went over every piece of equipment, every inch of supple leather. I tested everything, inspecting buckles for rust and keepers for wear. Wherever leather was stitched to leather, I gave it a good yank, testing the stitching. I was diligent. I could not afford a tack malfunction now, on the most important day of my career.

Everything passed inspection, and with a mighty sigh, I began tacking up Assault. He didn't put up a fight, he merely stood there, drawn up to his full height and appearing even more imposing than usual. He was a great wall of a horse, and he cut a large, statuesque shadow. When I tacked him up and dabbed the final polish on his hooves and the glinting hardware on his tack, I had to admit he looked impressive, if not happy.

We made our way down to the show ring. It was an indoor stadium, walled in on all sides, with seats full of spectators all around. Assault had never competed under the lights before. Yet another thing we couldn't prepare for.

We stepped over the threshold, right into a scene of chaos. It resembled an anthill, but with horses, riders, and grooms milling around everywhere. I waited my turn for the warm-up ring, holding tightly to an edgy horse. I looked around for the chestnut mare, but I didn't see her. Perhaps she'd already come and gone. I wanted to see her in action, but not today. I needed a clear head when I started on course, and she had a way of clouding it.

As the horses cycled through, we drew nearer to the warm-up ring. It had seemed perfectly adequate when I'd glimpsed it earlier in the day during the course walk. As I swung onto Assault, I realized it had the capacity of a teacup. *We might as well have warmed up in the tent*, I thought as we entered through the narrow gate.

There was enough room for a 10-meter circle, and that was about it. I turned Assault both ways, suppling him on each side and throwing in transitions to try and distract him from the fact that he kept almost running up against the fence.

With our allotted warm-up time drawing to a close, the rider before us started on course. Thus far, I'd been maintaining perfect tunnel vision, focusing on Assault and watching none of the rides. But something about the frenzied cheers echoing from the stands, and the hushed reverence that followed, caused me to glance into the ring, my concentration shattered.

I saw the chestnut mare bolt over the starting line. Body hugging the ground like a race car, she paused before the first fence, exploding into the air. On the landing side, she continued, moving like a demon was after her. Her rider was competent, but she was tremendous. She hadn't lost an ounce of her drive. If anything, she seemed more compelled to win now than ever before.

She was self-sufficient, cunning, and bold. Watching her, I realized you could say many of those same things about Assault. But while Assault had his own conflicting agenda, the chestnut mare only wanted to jump fast and true. She brought to mind the infamous Belmont Stakes call - "Secretariat is running like a tremendous machine!" The chestnut mare was a tremendous machine in the jumper ring, and I could only watch helplessly.

She blew over the finish line, the clock displaying a blistering time, stark numbers on a digital board. Staring me in the face. It was my job to beat that time. No one else had even come close. Established professionals, all of them. They ceded the win to her.

Assault could win. If he jumped like he had been jumping, if his energy and deep resentment all got in line on a straight track, he could crush her time. I'd never felt what this horse was truly capable of. He'd quickly gotten bored and burned out in every division along the path to Grand Prix. I'd never felt the bottom of him. I hadn't reached it.

I rode Assault down the narrow lane that led to the stadium. He crept

Team Dark Horse

along, his head nearly in my face, ears pricked hard, listening to the raucous cheers. The gate swung open, and his hooves touched down on sparkling, cream-colored footing and crushed rubber. Spectators were seated all around us, in stands so close it felt like they squeezed against the ring in a crush, hemming us in on all sides. Long strips of fluorescent lights blazed overhead, casting a sickly grayish tinge on everything, from the brightly-painted jumps to Assault's formerly radiant coat. The ring opened up before us, huge and welcoming in contrast to the jam-packed schooling ring and the tiny warm-up. No longer having to battle for space, I almost felt at home here. Confident. Collected. Only the sheer heft of the fences I was staring at could bring me back down to size.

They were painted in every color of the rainbow, with standards in the shape of beer cans or killer whales. Much of the course was maxed out in terms of height. The designer hadn't given anyone an easy trip. Each line posed a question, and when I walked the course, I'd only been able to answer some of them.

I patted Assault's shoulder soothingly. "Now or never," I said to the bay gelding.

He twitched his skin, shrugging me off. I gathered my reins and let him fly.

I chose an aggressive ride to the first fence, knowing the first line would be the easiest. I waited, poised above Assault, waiting to feel the pause and the takeoff. He jumped it cleanly, with the gusto he'd been applying since we got to Florida. I smiled.

The next two fences were on a slight diagonal. I rode it as a simple bending line, and we got through clean. Then there was a slice to the fourth fence, the first real test of the course. The beer can standards.

I put my heels into Assault, giving him a strong, forward ride to the base of the jump, knowing the strange shape and glaring metallic nature of the fence could cause him to back off. He barely gave it a sidelong glance as he powered over it, tossing me forward a little. If anything, he seemed to be building momentum.

We hurtled along to the next fence, a tricky double combination set at an awkward angle. This had been one of my sticking points during the course walk, but Assault took over and got us through. I allowed myself a glance at the clock. We were doing well. *This could be within our grasp*, I thought.

A maxed-out spread came next, and Assault stretched out over it, snapping his feet behind him to clear the rails. He landed and immediately rocketed forward, clipping himself with a hind foot and bobbling slightly. I checked him with the outside rein. "Slow down," I hissed.

He shook his head, and I felt the slow roll of his back humping underneath the saddle. A distinct threat, and a sign his mind wasn't entirely with me.

There wasn't much I could do in the middle of the course. I turned him to the next fence, looking ahead to the line I wanted to ride. The Shamu standards stared back at me.

Assault locked onto the jump and bolted forward, scooting his butt underneath him, his tail flagging. Too late, I realized he was going much too fast. He was sure to run out, or tangle with the fence. I abandoned my calm, professional presentation and went to the good old-fashioned pulley rein, one hand planted at the withers, holding mane, the other hand raised above his neck, bringing his head around.

With all my strength, I managed to drag his head back to face my stirrup. Assault's red-rimmed eyes stared at me, nearly clenched shut and pulsing with fury. Neck bent back like a deformed creature, he gnashed his teeth against my hold and continued on a straight track to disaster. And I realized something about Assault, perhaps the fatal flaw in our union, even more so than his aggression or general hatred of me.

He always complied when I asked for more. More speed, more daring. Higher fences. But that was all he complied with. When I needed to rate him, when I asked him to slow down, I had nothing. He was arrogant, sure of himself. He did not listen. And all I could do was hold on and pray.

The fence was right in front of us, and in a last-ditch effort to save him from himself, I flung the reins forward. If I kept holding onto him, if he fell, he could break his neck. *Now it's up to you*, I thought grimly. *You wanted control. Now you have to get us out of this.*

I knew he wouldn't run out, or stop, or do any of the sensible things. I knew all along that he would jump. And he did. Nearly sitting down, he gathered all the power he could muster, throwing his body up over the 5-foot fence from an impossible spot.

He twisted his body in midair, fighting to clear the fence. He knocked down the top two rails, and one Shamu standard teetered on its base, but it stayed up somehow. When he landed, he hyper-extended a leg. I saw the fetlock joint sink all the way into the sand, and I knew, by instinct, by feel, and with absolute, dreadful certainty, that the next step he took would be a lame step.

Assault lurched forward, holding one foreleg off the ground. He careened around on three legs, spinning in circles, giving a sickening hop each time his injured leg touched down. And still he wouldn't listen. He ceded nothing to me, even as I sobbed on his neck, pulling on him with all my adrenaline-fueled strength.

Lawrence leapt down from the stands, planting his body in front of Assault's face. With a single hand, he pulled Assault's nose around. "You're done," he said to the gelding.

Assault gave up, sighing like a deflated balloon, pointing his injured foreleg. I threw my weight off him, and we made the slow, halting walk out of the ring and into the stabling area, where we were descended upon by vets. Probing his leg, feeling it for heat and noting the location of the swelling, they worked silently, lining the foreleg with ice packs and securing it with copious amounts of vetwrap.

"Is it a break?" I asked tremulously, my hand on Assault's neck. His head hung by his knees, even though they hadn't given him any drugs. His adrenaline gone, the pain had taken over, and instinct had finally kicked in. He stood quietly, unnervingly docile, his body clinging to whatever energy reserves he had left.

The lead vet shook his head. "It's a tendon. We won't know for sure which structures are damaged, or how badly, until we ultrasound it. For now, we need to ice it and load him with NSAIDs. We have to keep the swelling under control, or the damage will worsen."

I nodded, feeling a dreadful iciness in my stomach, mixed with nausea.

"Is he stabled near here?" Another vet asked.

I shook my head, my eyes watering. "No. We're way out in the tents."

Her face fell. "We really shouldn't move him right now. But I guess we don't have a choice."

"Excuse me," a male voice cut in. The vets and I looked up from Assault's ravaged leg. The chestnut mare's rider was standing there.

"I have a spare stall in this barn," he said. "I've been using it for equipment storage, but I can make other arrangements for the time being."

I nodded, letting out a shaky breath. "Thank you."

"You shouldn't have to move an injured horse," he said. "I'll take you to it."

Lawrence left Assault's head, stripping the stall of all equipment and adding a thick bed of shavings. Once Assault had limped his way inside, I stripped off his tack, while the lead veterinarian inserted an IV line into his neck.

Assault's head hung below his knees. He looked miserable. The big, robust gelding had shrunk down to the size of a large pony, his mood was so low.

"This is good," the vet said, nodding at the stricken gelding. "At least he's not fighting."

"We'll change the ice packs in a couple hours, and we'll examine the leg further at that time," the lead vet told me. "From there, we'll be able to give you a clearer picture of the injury, as well as prognosis and recovery time."

I nodded. "Sounds good."

I moved around the stall, checking to ensure no nails were sticking out. It was an old habit, and it gave me something to do. Assault still hadn't moved. I sat by his head, massaging his poll. I couldn't tell if he liked it or not.

"You've really made a mess of it this time," I said to him. "Now we have to find out how big of a mess it is."

Assault shifted, twitching his lip back, exposing his incisors. I scrambled up and left the stall. He didn't have to tell me twice.

I sat on the concrete and awaited the verdict, thinking of everything that had led me here. All the years of hard work, a careful culmination of hopes and dreams I'd aligned to bring me to Grand Prix.

"You've really made a mess of it, too," I told myself, and I started to cry. Horses and riders walked past me, eyes averted. No longer invisible, I was now a casualty of the sport, and no one wanted to see that.

Delaware

Facundo and I sat at a small, intimate table set up by the polo field. Most of it was covered in a sprawling flower arrangement in the center. The sun had gone down, and the light was flattering, smoothing out his features until he looked like some kind of marble sculpture. He gazed at me, taking a long sip from his wineglass.

"This pinot is quite good," he remarked, nodding at the thin golden liquid as he swirled in in the glass.

I nodded, though I'd always been more of a whiskey girl. "It's kinda light. Summery."

He flashed a smile. "See, you're already becoming a connoisseur."

"I can appreciate the finer things and still enjoy the simple pleasures," I said, taking a swig of the wine.

Facundo blinked slowly, his dark lashes fanning out over his face. His eyes returned to me. "I think you represent the best of both."

"Why, thank you," I said, placing my hand on my chest like a good old-fashioned debutante.

A server arrived, setting out plates of ornate china, robin's egg blue in color, contrasting with the burnt orange of the tablecloth.

"Roasted leg of lamb with fennel and asparagus," he said, nodding at the plate.

"Looks delicious." It was a large piece of meat, and I wasn't sure where to start with it. In my family, a fancy meal was a rotisserie chicken from Wal-Mart, and we usually ate it with plastic utensils. Undaunted, I turned it this way and that, trying to find the grain of the meat.

"Here, I'll get that." Facundo took a knife and fork, gently sinking it into the meat and cutting it as finely as a deli slicer. I stacked three pieces on my fork and swirled them around, letting them soak up the juices. He watched as I took a bite. "Is it satisfactory?"

"Very." I nodded with enthusiasm.

"Good." He cut me enough pieces to last a while before going back to his own plate.

"How are things going with your team?" He asked. "Is everyone getting along?"

"More or less. A few dustups here and there, but nothing along the lines of the Cold War." I chuckled. "We're getting ready for our exhibition, so that's the big priority right now."

"I will be there." Facundo smiled, the corners of his eyelids crinkling. "I look forward to seeing it."

"It'll blow your socks off," I promised, before filling my mouth with some more lamb.

Facundo hesitated. "I know you have a very arduous training schedule, but I wondered if you might take some time off next weekend. The week after your exhibition, of course."

"What for?" I asked around the lamb.

Facundo pushed his chair back so he could look at me fully over the huge flower arrangement. "I wondered if you would like to join me for dinner with my family. My parents."

I swallowed quickly, nearly choking myself.

He continued. "It would involve getting on a plane, however, as they live at home in Argentina. They do not care to travel, as I do."

"Gee." I folded my hands on the table, fiddling with my wineglass. "I've never been out of the country. Doesn't that require all sorts of paperwork?"

"I will give you the money for an expedited passport," Facundo said. He studied me. "That is, if you want to go."

"I do! I do want to go," I assured him, reaching across the table to grasp his hand. "It's so nice that you asked."

"Then what is your hesitation?" Facundo asked, his voice steady and gentle.

"I just…" I looked across the table, over the white picket fence, to the field, empty and open. Everything here was so clean and shiny. Everything was the best of its kind. I'd never considered myself or my upbringing low-class. We hadn't had it fancy, but we had it good. But being in this crazy place with this world-famous polo player, I couldn't not get sucked into doubting myself.

I turned to Facundo, my eyes getting a little dewy. "I'm not what they're expecting," I said softly. "I'm not sure they'll approve of me. I don't know all the rules and intricacies of living at this level. I might say or do the wrong thing, and I don't want them to look down on me." I bit my lip, looking down at the thin strips of lamb my hands couldn't cut.

Facundo sighed, taking my chin in his hand, forcing me to look at him. Tenderly, he wiped the teardrops off my eyelashes.

"They will love you," he said, looking at me from the depths of his dark eyes. "Because I do."

I sniffed hard, pulling myself together. "Okay," I said, nodding. "I guess I'll get that passport."

Erica

The vet held the ultrasound probe to Assault's tendon, peering intently at the readout on the screen. I had never been adept at reading ultrasounds - the blurry, wavy grey images all looked the same to me. I waited for the vet's assessment.

"What you have here is a moderate injury due to some tearing of the fibers from the superficial digital flexor tendon," the vet said, continuing to run the probe up and down the leg. "When he hyper-extended that leg, he caused some damage, or perhaps exacerbated a pre-existing weak point due to everyday wear and tear. It's hard to know for sure. What we can say is that the prognosis for these types of injuries is fairly good. I had feared the worst, given his initial reaction."

"He's always had a low pain threshold," I said, glancing at the sullen gelding. He was back to his dark moods and intimidation now that the steady drip of anti-inflammatory into his bloodstream had reduced his discomfort.

"At any rate, the tendon is intact, so no surgical intervention will be necessary. Instead, we're looking at good old-fashioned rest. Keep the leg wrapped and check it daily. If swelling or heat increases, ice it and Bute him. Strict stall rest for two months, absolutely no exercise or turnout of any kind. Hopefully he tolerates it." He picked up the ultrasound machine and backed out of the stall, keeping a wary eye on Assault.

"Feed him as much hay as he'll eat to keep him occupied. I recommend trying to find a lower-quality 'filler' hay, so he doesn't put on too much weight. That leg doesn't need any additional strain on it. You could also consider using a slow feeder. Lots of horses enjoy them, and it will make his hay last longer. It'll also help preserve his digestive health during this confinement."

I nodded. "I'll get him a Nibble Net." *And hope he doesn't rip it apart in a fit of rage.* "When can I start controlled exercise?"

"If all goes well and the ultrasound checks out, you can begin 10-minute handwalks starting month three, gradually increasing the time to 30 minute walks. Around the fourth month, you could start to add in a little trotting. Again, if all goes as planned. If you have any doubts along the way, I'd advise going back to strict stall rest until you can schedule an ultrasound." He packed up his equipment and straightened up. "Any further questions?"

"No. I think I have a good idea of how to proceed."

He sighed, dropping his professional demeanor for a moment as he leaned against the stall door. "You prepare so much, and then this happens right in the middle of your season. It's heartbreaking every time I see it." He smiled ruefully. "Hopefully your year-end standings won't be too dismal."

I looked at him, the skin around my mouth sagging. "This was my first Grand Prix."

He shook his head. "Rough."

I left the stall, going out in search of a slow feeder. I was pretty sure I'd seen some at the local feed store. Lawrence intercepted me as I walked through the parking area, hell-bent on finding my truck.

"Hey." I let him keep walking with me, intent on my mission. "I got my marching orders on Assault's rehab."

"How bad is the injury?"

"Moderate tearing of the superficial digital flexor tendon. No surgery needed. Just lots of rest." I grimaced a little.

"Well, that's good," Lawrence said. "It could've been a lot worse."

"It could've been better," I said. "I just keep thinking what I could've done differently. All those times I should have ridden him, and I put it off…tendons fail because muscles fail to protect them. I didn't condition him properly, and he was out of his depth."

Lawrence let out a short sigh. "Erica. You exercised him plenty, as much as you could. He was always tricky. What worked for the average horse didn't work with him. I saw him in the ring, okay? He was fit and in great shape. He looked like dynamite out there. Then he got cocky, and he pushed too hard. He messed *himself* up, okay? You had nothing to do with it. Don't beat yourself up."

The explanation didn't sit well with me, but I was too tired to fight with Lawrence. I let it go. "I have to go shop for a slow feeder," I said wearily.

Lawrence nodded. "I was actually trying to flag you down for a reason. I have to take off to Lexington in an hour or two."

My jaw dropped. "You have to take off right *now*? Why?"

"John wants to meet with me and Dougie to discuss the future of the team. I think he wants to know where all this PR is heading. Be more involved." He shrugged. "So I have to go meet with him."

"Why can't he come here?" I asked, my voice coming out in a strangled squeak.

Lawrence's eyes ticked upward. "Because he's the money man, and he sent a plane for me already. I just have to do it, Erica. I'm sorry." He touched my arm, softening a little. "I know this is a really wretched time for you, and I don't want to leave you here by yourself. But I don't have a choice. John's bankrolling the team, and if he wants a private meeting with me, I get on a plane."

"I understand," I said, wrapping my arms around myself. *The team. The fucking team.*

"I'll tell him what happened with Assault, and we'll keep it brief," Lawrence promised, laying a kiss on my forehead. "I love you, okay?"

I gave an imperceptible nod, and he was gone.

Dougie

My feet fell into their typical path, a direct line to the hotel elevator. My thumb found the number 5. Once the doors opened, it was a blessedly short walk to the sanctuary of her room, the sounds of Britney trickling out into the hallway. I knocked on the door as my pulse knocked away in my throat, feeling that familiar, intoxicating mix of joy and terror.

She didn't come to the door right away, so I knocked again, thinking she hadn't heard. In the silence that remained when I took my knuckles away from the door, I realized she'd shut off the music.

I slumped against the door, the air entering my lungs like a razor blade. I pictured her sitting on her bed, feet tucked up, her huge eyes darting around like a trapped animal as she pretended she wasn't there.

I pulled out my phone and typed a message.

What did I do?

I hit *Send*, and the agonizing wait began. Anyone who said technology made life easier had obviously never endured the wait for a response to a critical text.

My phone buzzed, and I looked at it.

Nothing. I just shouldn't be leading you on.

You're not leading me on, I typed. *I like how it is. I don't need anything more.*

Yvette doesn't believe that. She's on my ass about every little thing again.

Yvette shouldn't matter. This is between you and me.

I just can't right now. Until I figure out who I'm leading on. You, or myself.

I don't understand.

Of course you don't understand. That was a string of sentence fragments that added up to nothing but hodgepodge. That's why I have to figure things out.

Can't I be there while you figure things out? I pressed my thumbs into the screen so hard, I expected it to shatter.

If I could figure things out with you there, we wouldn't be having this conversation.

The air left my lungs in a puff, and I struggled for breath for a second, realizing this was almost the exact sensation of being slammed against a locker.

Okay, I wrote. *I'm going.*

I got on the elevator and rode up two more floors, swiping my room key for the first time in a week. The space revealed itself to me, open and empty, my trademark non-home.

I found a Britney station on Pandora and let the ache intensify. Feeling the buzz of my phone at my hip, I snatched it up, hoping, for a rash second, that it was Courtney, telling me to come back.

Incoming Call

Lawrence

I pressed the button to receive the call. "What?" I asked, too upset for good manners.

"You need to get on a plane," he said.

Lawrence

Dougie followed me mutely into the waiting cab, his hunched figure and oversized sweatshirt creating the image of a person who'd given up on life. He'd sat in silence the entire flight, and I was beginning to regret bringing him along. Sitting next to him in a confined space had turned this unexpected errand into an unbearable drag.

"What is the deal with you right now?" I asked as the driver sped off to who-knows-where, having already been given his marching orders by John.

"I have depression." Dougie stared out the window, thankfully not turning the full force of his dreary, hangdog expression on me. "Most of the time it's just normal, sometimes it's crippling. Right now it's crippling."

"Ah," I said. "Well you need to snap out of it, because we need to meet with John, and you being a big, silent mope isn't exactly going to sell him on the whole thing."

"My work speaks for itself," Dougie said, finding the energy to fight back even as his head dropped lower and lower. "I do a good job, and John doesn't pay anything to keep me around besides my room and board."

"Why are you in such a funk anyway?" I asked him. "Did Courtney flake out on you?"

Dougie's shoulders sagged while his sweatshirt remained in place like a flimsy exoskeleton. "She's trying to figure things out."

"Oh," I said, nodding gravely. "That never ends well."

"I'm so tired," Dougie murmured, resting his acne-ravaged face on the taxi window. "I just want to sleep forever."

"You can sleep on the flight home," I said as the taxi driver made a familiar turn. "We have business to attend to."

The driver ground to a stop, and I opened my door, stepping onto a loose chunk of asphalt. Reluctantly, Dougie followed my lead, his eyes squinting in the low light of dusk. "Are you sure this is the right place?"

I nodded, taking in the flickering neon sign and the paint-peeling exterior of Angelina's. "I'm sure."

We started off across the parking lot, Dougie's long legs getting tripped up by potholes. He spied the line by the door and threw on the brakes. "This is a club."

"Yeah? So?" I doubled back, annoyed by the interruption.

Dougie stared balefully at me. "There will be people in there. Lots of people. I can't do lots of people right now."

"Too bad. You're going." I gripped his elbow and strong-armed him into Angelina's, cutting in line like I always did. I sat him down at the bar and looked around for John.

"I cannot believe you dragged me here today," Dougie said, his face ashy as he curled his body up around the bar like a turtle in a shell.

"Believe it." I walked away from him, scanning the floor. Already it was packed with patrons.

"What is going on here?" I asked a random girl. "I thought Elaine performed on Friday night."

"Special weekend performance," Marla said, her body slithering out from the crowd. "She's in demand."

"I guess." I glanced at the people milling around. "Have you seen John?"

"If I had, I wouldn't be standing here talking to you," Marla said, her voice oozing with flirtatiousness even as she insulted me.

"Maybe he's not here yet." I shrugged my shoulders. "I'm supposed to meet with him. He wanted to talk to me and our PR guy."

Marla cocked her head to the side. "I don't think I know your PR guy."

"He doesn't do crowds," I said. "He's over at the bar looking like he wants to curl up and die."

Marla peered over at Dougie's near-comatose form. "I'll perk him up," she said with an evil smile.

She walked over to Dougie, her hip-swing calculated and forceful. "Hello there, PR guy. I'm Marla."

He looked like he swallowed his tongue. "Dougie," he said after a lengthy pause.

"Lawrence tells me you don't like crowds," Marla said, leaning over Dougie, her breasts in his face.

"No," he admitted, keeping his eyes in line with hers, although they wavered heavily. "I prefer dark corners."

"A lot can happen in a dark, quiet corner," Marla said, leaning over his shoulder, brushing her lips against his neck, right below his ear. "You can get into all sorts of mischief."

I saw Dougie's body quiver, and I knew she'd hit him with the full force of her breath on his neck. With a canary-eating smile, Marla sashayed away from Dougie. Her eyes lit on a tall figure entering the club, and with the way her head snapped up at attention, I knew it had to be John.

"He's here," I said to Dougie, sitting down beside him. "Can you pull yourself together?"

"I don't know," Dougie admitted, his eyes a thick glaze.

The club lights dimmed, and the audience grew silent. "What's happening?" Dougie hissed.

"The show must be starting," I whispered back. "I guess we're staying for the show and meeting with John after."

"Weird," Dougie said. "Why would he pick this venue? And this time?"

I shrugged my shoulders. "He's the money man. I don't question the logic of someone who's bankrolling my team."

"I guess that's a fair point," Dougie said, his eyes on the stage. "Who's performing."

"My *former* money man," I said with a smile.

Elaine walked out onstage, head down. She wore a gingham dress that would have been very youthful and innocent, if not for the 6 or 7 inches of thigh it showed.

Dougie glanced at me. "Isn't that Elaine? The girl from the stable?"

I nodded.

Dougie's eyes returned to the stage. "I'm confused."

I saw John take a seat by the stage, sitting up with ramrod-straight posture. Suddenly, several things became clear to me.

"I'm not," I said to Dougie.

The music started up, a repetitive, dreamy, mood-setting number. As Elaine's body entwined with the pole, I saw Marla slip into the seat beside John. She leaned in close, her long hair flopping over his shoulder.

My eyes ticked back to Elaine. I couldn't help but notice her body was moving differently than it had in her past routines. Before, she'd steered away from anything remotely sexual. Now, her limbs were moving with a heavy, distinct sensuality. Her face was as closed-off as ever, but her body was blooming. Her hips moved in a rhythm that was clear and purposeful, a signal as strong as a flower releasing pollen.

Below the stage, Marla leaned into John, giving him a signal that was equally hard to miss. I saw her whisper something into his ear, breathing purposefully down that pleasure pathway from earlobe to neck.

I watched to see how he'd react, but John was as solid and impassive as a concrete wall. If anything, he leaned away from her, his body inclined forward toward the stage.

"How is he doing that?" Dougie asked, transfixed, not by Elaine, but by Marla.

"Doing what?" I asked. "He's not doing anything."

"Exactly." Dougie hunched forward, staring intently at the unfolding scene. "She put her body on him. *She breathed on his neck*...in that spot where, you know...things happen."

"Yes, I know about the spot," I said patiently.

"How is he not going after her?" Dougie asked, incredulous. "She wants him. She's all over him. And he's not paying any attention to her."

"It is curious," I agreed. "Very curious."

Elaine finished her act, winding her way down the pole and coming to rest at its base, her fair, muscular legs wrapped around it.

In the seconds that followed, I saw John take Marla's hands, which had wandered to his thigh. Politely, he gathered them up, folded them, and set them back in her lap. Then he stood up and applauded, leaving Marla sitting, disgruntled, in the line of his shadow.

Elaine stood up, giving her fans a sharp little bow. Then she went offstage, walking as fast as she could without actually breaking into a run.

"What was that?" Dougie mouthed at me.

I shook my head. "Marla's out of luck," I told Dougie, a slight frown on my face. "And from the looks of it, so is John."

Erica

I loitered in the barn aisle, stealing glances at Assault. He'd finally convinced himself that the Nibble Net I'd hung up in his stall wasn't a black, hay-stuffed demon, and now he was ripping pieces of hay out with enough force to pull the Nibble Net down from the wall, and maybe take the wall with it.

The chestnut mare's owner, Bruce, was exercising her in the schooling ring, and her stall was vacant. I looked at the fresh manure piles sitting in the sawdust, so easily accessible. There was a wheelbarrow nearby, and a manure fork propped up against the wall. Without really thinking about it, I snatched up the fork and parked the wheelbarrow in the open doorway. I picked up the piles, then sifted through the sawdust, picking up the little shards of manure the morning stall-cleaner had failed to remove. Then I raked the sawdust, pulling it out from the corners so it made a nice, even bed.

Bruce had two other jumpers stabled here, and their stalls were worse than the chestnut mare's. After a moment's hesitation, I picked up a halter, moving a grey gelding to the chestnut mare's stall. I cleaned his stall and threw down some fresh shavings, then moved the third horse, a striking bay tobiano. His stall was the worst by far, and I had to go for more shavings.

When I returned, Bruce was standing there, having handed the chestnut mare off to his grooms. He watched me with an amused smile and a slight tilt of his head.

My hand flew to my mouth, even though it was covered in faint traces of manure. "Oh God. I'm so sorry." I stared at him, mortified. "I should not have touched your equipment, and I definitely should not have moved your horses. I am so sorry. I just wanted to help."

He stepped toward me, his face soft with concern. "It's okay, Erica. I'm not mad. Why would I be mad about that?"

"I don't know." I lapsed into silence, staring at my hands. "I've just had a really bad week."

"Well, that much is clear." He came up alongside me. "Here, let's go sit somewhere. I feel like you could use a supportive ear."

I nodded, following him over to a bale of hay. He sat down without worrying about getting chaff stuck to his expensive breeches. That meant he was actually a horseman, not just a competitive rider.

"How is your horse?" He asked me.

I shrugged. "He's fine. He's not being too much of an ass, and the tendon hasn't flared up. It's just...this isn't what I wanted."

"Of course not," Bruce agreed. "It's a terrible thing to have your season taken away from you."

"But if I was at home, I'd have other horses, I'd have clients. Something to take my mind off things. But I don't have that anymore. I sold my hunter mare, and I don't have any other jumper prospects. I left my home base. I put everything into this, and now all I can do is sit on my hands. All I can do is stare at a horse that hates me, and shove flakes of hay into a Nibble Net." I looked over at Bruce. "That's why I did what I did. I had to do something. I have to feel like I'm achieving *something*, even if it's as basic as stripping a stall. I can't be in this limbo."

He nodded. "I have my own help, though, Erica. I can hardly see putting you to work when they have their marching orders. It wouldn't be fair to you."

I stared at him. "Please. Just let me pitch in. I can come in first thing in the morning and clean stalls. At least let me do that. The morning help does a lousy job."

Bruce smiled. "I will let you pitch in. But I'm not going to make you my stall-cleaning flunky. This isn't *The Saddle Club*. I'm not Veronica DiAngelo looking down my nose at you and letting you do the dirty work."

"You read those books?" I asked, grinning a little.

He laughed. "I sure did, and my guy friends never let me live it down at the time."

"I'm good at cleaning stalls, though," I reasoned with him. "I don't mind doing grunt work. It would at least give me a sense of purpose."

Bruce shook his head. "It's still a firm *no*. You're better than that, and I need your help with something else."

"What is it?" I asked, my interest piqued.

Bruce crossed one leg over the other. "Look, I'm a busy guy. I'm keeping three horses tuned up, all while juggling clients and keeping my barn staff in line. Sometimes I'm just running from horse to horse, and it feels like I'm going through the motions, not really giving them the ride they deserve. I don't like it. It drives me nuts. But that's the reality of the sport. I have more things demanding my time than I have time to give."

"I could oversee your barn staff," I said, nodding my head. "I know how to run a stable. And I'm here all the time anyway."

"That's not what I was thinking," Bruce said.

"What were you thinking?" I asked, my curiosity rising along with my pulse.

"Those days when I'm slammed, I want you to take the ride on one of my horses. Do flatwork, put in a jump school, whatever you feel needs to be done. You understand what goes into tuning up a jumper. You've done the whole process. I know I can trust you to do a good job. And it would be a huge weight off my shoulders."

I stared at him, my heart fluttering unnaturally high in my body cavity. "You would really trust me with your horses? After I *broke* my horse?"

He rolled his eyes. "You didn't *break* him. He hyper-extended. Shit happens." His face turned serious again. "Bottom line. I've seen enough of you in the schooling ring to realize you know what you're doing. And if you can take the ride on one of my horses, it'll benefit both of us. You'll stay in practice, and I won't be as rushed with my other two."

My voice was hushed as I said, "Which one?"

His head turned as the chestnut mare was led in, dripping wet from her bath. "Doesn't matter to me. You can ride her if you want. She's a lot of fun." He smiled, hopping up from the hay bale.

"I know," I whispered, but he was already out of earshot. The chestnut mare's eye fell on me, and I sat there trembling under her gaze.

Yvette

We gathered for a rehearsal in the early morning light. Of course, it was held up by Delaware's incessant chattering.

"He's just so generous, you know what I mean?" She asked, beaming from the saddle of her pony, Vegas. "He really knows how to treat a girl right."

"I am sure he does," I said, fiddling with my reins as my blood boiled. "Most men are capable of treating a woman right, until they become complacent and their slobbish true colors appear."

Delaware picked up a trot, her ponytail bouncing in time with Vegas' stride. "He makes me feel so *expensive!*" She called out, her face set in a grin.

"Now what could *that* possibly mean?" I snapped, vexed by the interruption and her silly behavior.

Delaware turned in the saddle as she passed me. "You said he'd make me feel cheap, but that didn't happen. He makes me feel *expensive!*"

"The opposite of feeling cheap," Lawrence cut in, a shit-eating grin on his face. "Get it, Yvette?"

I turned on him, wielding my mallet in a threatening gesture. "Can we *just* get moving?" I said icily.

Courtney pressed play on the boom box, and the rest of us quickly moved into formation. She joined us, and we completed a few run-throughs of the exhibition number.

"I think that will suffice," I said, halting my pony, a rich bay mare named Accolade. "We do not want to over-rehearse."

Cavanaugh nodded. "We should keep it fresh. The unbridled energy is a huge part of this performance. Plus, if we keep drilling it, these ponies will start to anticipate. He already is," he said, pointing at Harry.

"We will be in good shape for Saturday," I said, riding away.

I was still close enough to hear Delaware speak up. "Hey, Lawrence? Would it be possible for me to get some time off next weekend?"

He shrugged. "I don't see why not. You've been working hard. Keep up the good work, and you should be fine. I'll keep your ponies legged up for you."

Now, I was curious, which meant I was also resentful. "What could you possibly require time off for, Podunk?" I said less than kindly.

She tightened right up upon hearing my tone. "If you must know, Yvette, Facundo invited me to visit his parents with him. They live in Argentina, so I had to get a passport and everything. It's a *big* deal," she added.

"Wow," Courtney said from her perch on Hermione. "Meeting the parents. That's big."

"I know!" Delaware leaned over, her face excited. "*He said he loved me*," she mouthed.

"Wow," Courtney said again, like a parakeet with only a scant few phrases to choose from. "That's big too."

I dismounted, looking around for a groom. There was one waiting by the sidelines, but he walked right past me, taking Delaware's pony instead just for the chance to ogle her ass.

Her feet on the ground, Delaware suddenly looked small and unsure of herself. She flagged down Lawrence as he rode by. "Do you know the proper way to use silverware at a fancy dinner?" She asked him.

Lawrence snorted. "I used to, but I didn't even follow the rules back then. I can't remember any of that shit now."

Delaware chewed a nail, looking uncharacteristically nervous. "Okay. Thanks anyway."

"You could look it up on your phone," Lawrence offered. "Or have Dougie look it up."

"I kind of need someone to walk me through it and show me," Delaware said. "I learn better by doing stuff than reading."

Lawrence shrugged. "Sorry I can't be more helpful."

Once our ponies had been collected, the three of us walked to the Mallet Grille for breakfast. Lawrence remained behind, hosing off Harry.

We sat down at a table, Delaware across from me. She picked at her pancakes somewhat listlessly while I wielded my knife and fork with precision, looking her in the eye the entire time.

Courtney

Come over.

I wrote the text, and then I did everything in my power not to send it. I ran for hours, then grazed Hermione until my shoulders tingled with sunburn. I listened to Delaware gush about Facundo, and I listened to Yvette harp about Delaware. But when the night fell I was powerless to ignore the waiting message.

I hit *Send*, and in a startlingly short amount of time, Dougie was at my door.

"Did you figure your shit out?" He asked, heaving for breath as he leaned on the door frame.

"I'll never figure my shit out," I told him honestly. "But I missed having you here. So that must mean something."

"It's good enough for me," Dougie said, and he came in and sat down.

We watched VH1 for a while, and then I curled up under the covers. Dougie did the same, and we lay there on our separate sides, similarly wide awake.

I was the first to speak up, and my voice surprised me even as it came out of me. "We could...maybe we could cuddle," I said in a low squeak.

Dougie rolled over cautiously. "Yeah, that could happen..."

I flipped on my side, assuming the spooning position.

He moved in close, lingering behind me, not quite touching. "You know, if we cuddle, even though it's *purely* in the platonic sense of the word... certain things may still happen, Courtney. In fact, I'm almost positive they will."

I shrugged off his hesitation. "Are you talking about the whole dick-in-the-back thing? Yvette already gave me a full lecture about it."

"So you're okay with it then?" Dougie asked.

"I'll just deal with it," I said stiffly.

"Okay then." Dougie settled in, pulling me close and wrapping his arms around my mid-section.

I had thought I would tense up in some way or feel uncomfortable. All my previous instincts had told me I wasn't attracted to Dougie, and although I acknowledged that he was a nice guy, I didn't necessarily *like* like him. I'd made a concession to him by offering this. I'd gone out on a limb, and I'd expected to regret that, as I regretted most of my decisions concerning the opposite sex.

But as he surrounded me with his warmth and I felt his hands on my belly, my skin didn't crawl. Instead, curiously, my brain was enveloped with a sense of calm, a powerful wash of relaxation. And a short time later, when I felt the inevitable dick in my back, I didn't shy away from it.

I actually liked it.

Erica

The chestnut mare kept eluding me. Now, with the scintillating promise of riding her dangled in front of me, I remained on constant alert. I kept my phone close to my side at all times. I didn't let the battery life drop below two bars. I dialed my voicemail number in case my phone had somehow failed to inform me of an incoming message. And still my phone didn't ring.

I walked around the lavish grounds of the International Polo Club, taking in none of the sights. I didn't watch any of the polo or meet any of the minor and major celebrities who passed through these grounds. I ate alone at restaurants, my phone keeping me company, silent as a tomb.

Without a horse to put my all into, I was rudderless, utterly at loose ends. Skulking through the blistering sun, passing by pool parties and spa parties and heavily attended polo matches, I had to face reality. I had become the girl waiting by the phone.

While traipsing past the pool, an empty Styrofoam cup in my hand, I spotted Dougie. He'd tucked himself into a little corner and was typing away, his fingers bouncing all over the keypad with admirable dexterity.

He looked up when he saw me and gave me a smile and a nod. At the same time, he kept typing without losing any momentum.

"Erica. Hi."

"Hey, Dougie." I moved into the shade, standing beside him.

"What are you doing out here?" He asked, his eyes on the keypad.

"Just looking for a garbage receptacle," I explained, waving my empty cup in the air. "I can't seem to find a single one on these grounds, and it's starting to drive me crazy."

"There's one in the Mallet Grille," Dougie said. "And in the 7th Chukker."

"I know, but I feel tacky going in there just to deposit trash." I sighed. "I'll just go back to the hotel."

Dougie glanced at me. "You seem kind of frustrated."

I smiled wryly. "Yeah, I am. I didn't plan on spending so much time here. But since all I can do with my horse is stare at his leg and put food and water in front of him, I haven't wanted to spend too much time at the barn either."

Dougie nodded. "Yeah, Lawrence mentioned that. It's a tough break."

"I've just been chugging Icees and wandering around." I laughed humorlessly. "I'm really making good use of my time in the horse capitol of the nation."

"Can't you teach lessons or something?" Dougie asked.

I shook my head. "I was planning to once I established myself as a competitor. But then this happened."

Dougie's fingers slowed down on his phone, then picked back up. His eyes were on my gigantic cup. "Where do you go for Icees?" He asked, completely rerouting the conversation.

"I usually go to the Shell station," I said.

Dougie shook his head. "See, that's a mistake. I used to go there, but then I randomly went to the 7-Eleven one day and found out they're way cheaper. 75 cents instead of a dollar."

My eyes widened. "Seriously?"

"Yup. And you wouldn't think it, but that quarter you save adds up. For every three you buy at 75 cents versus a dollar, you pay for your next one in savings."

"That's serious money," I said.

"You bet it is."

I realized I hadn't checked my phone in the past 10 minutes, so of course I checked it. Nothing. I gathered myself up and prepared to leave. "Well, thanks for the tip, Dougie. I appreciate it."

"No problem, Erica." He smiled, his eyes meeting mine in a rare moment. "Sometimes a good Icee can be the only thing that gets you through the day."

I smiled, walking out to the main entrance, where my truck was parked among palm trees and Porsches. I'd throw out my empty cup at the 7-Eleven. It was turning out to be a two-Icee kind of day.

I wound my way to the gas station, fighting the midday traffic. When I rolled up to the green and white façade, I parked my truck out front, tossing the empty Shell cup into an easily-accessible garbage can before stepping inside. I walked to the soda fountain with a purpose, grinning brightly when I spotted the sign. *75 Cent Icees: Any Size.*

Grabbing an XL cup, I turned the lever, squeezing out the blue raspberry-flavored slushy goodness. Walking up to the counter, I slapped down a dollar.

The gas station clerk was a 20-something guy with a short stature and stocky build. He rang me up, handing back my change, which I accepted giddily. "I can't believe I didn't know about this place," I said. "This whole time I've been overpaying for Icees."

He looked at me, a grin stretching over his face. "Well, we can't have that."

"It's such a small thing, but it's making me so happy," I explained, taking a long sip from my beverage. "And I needed some happiness this week."

The guy regarded me fully, not in that half-paying-attention, mind-elsewhere way of the typical store clerk. "So I take it you'll be back for more?"

I nodded, gulping down the cold drink. "Most definitely."

He nodded, keeping his eyes on me. "Good."

Lawrence

The day of our exhibition dawned with a fierce storm, winds blowing sideways and raindrops that stung like hail. Yvette paced the barn aisle, fuming and swearing. "We will be rained out for sure," she said, her face slightly green in the gloomy light.

"No, we won't," I said. "They're moving us to a nearby venue, an indoor arena with ample seating. We'll be fine."

"How can you say that when we are now forced to perform in a venue we have never practiced in? On footing that may be substandard!" Yvette's eyes whirled in her head.

"The footing is fine," I said. "I already inspected it. And the venue may actually work to our advantage. The lighting will be much more dramatic, and our horse-handling skills will be shown off more effectively in a confined space."

"No one will show up," Yvette sniffed, grinding the soles of her boots into the floor, as if she could stomp out all her frustration that way. "They will not make the drive to see us. We will perform to an empty stadium. Empty seats. Empty walls."

"They will come," I promised patiently. "Trust me. We haven't gone entirely unnoticed in our stint here. The powers that be are curious. The spectacle of three girls and one guy on a team is hard to pass up."

"We are not a *spectacle*," Yvette hissed murderously.

"And we will show them that today," I said, turning away to prepare Harry for the short van ride.

Getting ready was a relatively simple task. We had only four ponies, one for each of us. After ensuring they were spotless, I loaded them onto the trailer. We wore our uniforms: white breeches, black shirts and helmets with white lettering. Dougie had our music; he would be in charge of the sound and lighting.

Once there, we unloaded the ponies and put them up in stalls. Yvette stalked around the arena, turning this way and that, eyeballing the footing suspiciously, like she expected the Loch Ness monster to come scrabbling out from a hidden sinkhole.

"*Yvette*! It's fine!" I yelled. "Come help us get these ponies tacked up."

With a withering glance, she abandoned her mission and came back to the stabling area, slapping a saddle onto Accolade. "Why do we not have a groom doing this?" She asked acidly.

"They can't leave IPC property. I guess it's a weird insurance thing." I shrugged. "It's not a big deal though."

"Not all of us enjoy this process," Yvette countered, applying polos with a scowl on her face.

"I think it's nice," Delaware piped up from the stall next to Yvette. "It gives us a little bonding moment before we ask them to perform."

"They do this because it is their job, not because of some sense of gratitude," Yvette grunted as she crouched under Accolade's belly.

"Yeah, but sometimes the extra effort does pay off." I clucked to Harry, leading him out.

As we began our warm-up, acclimating the ponies to the new space, the stands were already filling up. Strange and familiar faces stared down at us, some of them almost on our level. The ponies walked along, necks telescoping out in front of them, eyes rotating, taking in the gathering audience. They fed on the growing energy surrounding us, and it made them walk taller, move bolder.

At last, we left the arena, gathering in the narrow lane that fed into it. Yvette touched her heels to Accolade's sides, walking out and taking her place in the center of the arena, standing beneath a single spotlight. Eyes up, arm at her side, she nodded to Dougie up in the sound booth.

Happiness hit her like a train on a track...

At the opening chords, we cued the ponies to move out into the arena. Some distance apart, we gained on Yvette, Harry, Vegas, and Hermione traveling in a slow, lilting passage. Just as I'd hoped, the charged atmosphere ignited the ponies, and they moved better than they ever had in practice, with halting, bouncy steps, arched necks, and controlled energy. We reached Yvette, falling into line with her.

Run fast for your mother, run fast for your father...

As the chorus took off, so did our ponies. In one consecutive leap, their polished dressage paces transitioned into pure horsepower. At a speed that would be considered daring even in our galloping sport, the four animals pelted around the ring, cornering with precision, separated by inches. We stood in the stirrups, letting them run. Trusting them. The faces in the stands blurred and swirled into one big, abstract mess.

The horses are coming, so you better run.

The song faded to a halt, and we hit the centerline, the ponies coming to a stop from a dead gallop in unison. They stood in line, legs square, then fanned out as we cued them to step over. They turned on their haunches, moving together again.

Happiness hit her like a bullet in the back...

The song revved up, and the ponies burst forth like shrapnel, propelled off the ground by sheer energy and adrenaline. Bolting across the short side of the arena, nearly running up against the sideboards, they turned at the last second, executing a neat 180. In one effortless unit, they completed the sharp change of direction several more times, each time coming closer to the wall, nearer to the crowd, dusting them with dirt kicked up by their churning feet. Those in the stands felt the spray of sand and the wild, reckless energy of the ponies.

As we rode up against the stands, I saw Gerard Montague sitting a few rows above my level. Time slowed down, and I stared at him, my eyes communicating our history. His eyes lingered on Harry with so much regret, he looked ill.

More faces stood out to me, too. Jean-Phillipe, Yvette's former sponsor.

She had to see him, and I knew from the set of her face that his presence had spurred her on to ride faster and better. I saw former teammates and acquaintances. I saw old flames.

They all saw Team Dark Horse. They were seeing us at our best.

The song slowed again before the big climax, and we gathered our ponies back, reeling them in softly. They listened, tilting back on their hindquarters, their energy contained. They trotted in place, legs snapping up like pistons, bodies rounded up in the shape of a crescent, snorting and arch-necked, holding it all in.

Harry's energy rolled beneath my seat, his body growing and changing shape. In the center of the tight group of four, he rose up, leaping into a gallopade, hooves raining down in a perfect canter rhythm without breaking from the formation. I held him back with a single hand, reins light as strings.

As always, he went the extra mile.

I looked up into the stands, finding Erica's face effortlessly. She watched Harry, her eyes misty, hands clasped in front of her.

At the key change, the ponies surged forward on cue, taking a last victory lap around. Delaware rode in front on Vegas, who managed to stay elevated even at a full gallop. She looked around at the rest of us, her face in a grin, and for a moment we forgot about the performance and simply beamed at each other, riding out the thrill of the moment. Even Yvette had gotten caught up in it, and her loose, relaxed face looked as radiant as I'd ever seen her.

We halted, and the lights cut out. Whether it was Dougie's idea of a dramatic end, or simply the power going out from the electrical storm, I didn't know or care. The applause rained down, heavy as the downpour outside. I looked around at my teammates, their eyes bright in the sudden darkness.

"We came to play," I said. "They know that now."

"We will do more than play," said Yvette. "We will do much harm to their season."

"If we ride like we did today, we will," I agreed.

"We don't know any other way," Delaware spoke up, and for once, Yvette didn't correct her.

Team Dark Horse

Erica

I had my feet up, and I lay half underneath the covers, clothed in mismatched socks, a T-shirt, and a pair of Lawrence's boxers that were so old, faded, and stretched out that they actually fit me. I had conceded to my status as a loser, and I welcomed it with open arms, much as I embraced the mild stench I emitted after sitting for too long.

I no longer answered my phone when people from home called me, which wasn't very often. No one needed to know what I was up to now, because what I was up to consisted of brief check-ins with Assault and long stretches of guzzling Icees and watching back-to-back Animal Planet shows.

My phone buzzed, hidden somewhere in the chaos of sheets and comforter. I managed to grab it, and I opened it just in time to receive the call. "Hello?"

"Erica, hi. It's Bruce Ligfield."

I clutched the phone to my face so hard it made my ear tingle. "Hi. What's up?"

"I'm slammed today. I have to meet the farrier and look into possibly adding wedge pads for my gelding, and then I have to jet off to give some lessons." I heard him shift the phone around to his other ear. "Is there any way you can give my mare a jump school?"

"Yes. Absolutely," I said, my heart slamming up against my breast bone.

"Great. You'll see her equipment in the corner. It's the figure-eight noseband with the mullen mouth D-ring. Her saddle is the faded Stubben."

"Okay." I scrambled up, banging my knee on the bedside table and not feeling a thing.

"I really appreciate you doing this," Bruce said before hanging up.

I hastily searched for my riding clothes, finding them after excavating one of the growing piles of clothing on the floor. Pulling them on, I snatched up my keys and power-walked down to the elevator. As I pressed the button for the ground floor, Courtney appeared, jogging up the stairs. Of course she would take the freaking stairs.

"Hi, Erica!" She called, waving. I could have said something in return, but the doors opened and I jumped on the elevator without even acknowledging that I'd heard her.

Assault glowered at me when I hurried past his stall, but I ignored his withering glance. The chestnut mare stood in the very next stall, face pressed up against the bars, ears at attention. She watched me set out her equipment and stepped back as I opened the stall door, allowing me in.

I slipped the halter over her nose, carefully moving her satiny ears out of the way. Poring over her with a brush, I examined the fine bone structure in her head, gently probing her muscle groups for signs of soreness. She stood without moving a hair, her eyes giving me a slightly impatient, resigned look that reminded me of Eloise. This mare was just as I remembered her. All business. She wasn't in it for cuddles, kisses, or even food. She was a worker with the simple, determined mind and tenacity of the hardworking draft horses who toiled in the trenches, pulling logs and plowing fields. Only her job was highly skilled and hotly in demand. She had the drive and principles of a laborer, but she soared above all that.

With the chestnut mare tacked up, I led her out to the schooling ring. Miraculously, it was the emptiest I'd ever seen it. Wide stretches of sand were visible, dotted with hundreds of hoof prints. I swung onto her back. At just barely over 16 hands, she was an easy reach.

I took my time with her, taking her around at an easy walk, allowing ample time for her muscles to stretch and loosen. Then I moved her up to a long trot, leaving loops in my reins, allowing her to stretch downward. Rising into a half-seat, I asked her to canter.

The one time I'd been on her, she'd struck me as an average mover, even slightly deficient in certain basics like straightness and rhythm. She was no different now, even with another season and increased maturity under her girth. She moved slightly canted to the side, and her neck was as lank and skinny as ever. She was nothing like Assault, who carried enough power to bust through the side of a building packaged into every stride. She didn't feel like she could leap and spin and soar her way around a maxed-out course. But I knew she could.

Satisfied with my warm-up, I turned her onto the diagonal. It was then that I felt the afterburners come chugging on. She saw the fence and grew two hands taller. Her neck even looked fuller, shapelier. She saw her line and drove onward, and I had nothing to do but sit up and stay out of her way. She needed no fiddling or tinkering. She just wanted to jump.

Did I really think it would make a difference to her? The chestnut mare didn't care who was on her back, whether it was me, Bruce, or even a total stranger. She took charge in any situation.

She locked onto the jump and rose upward. I had the sensation that I was on an elevator, or strapped into a man lift. She cleared the jump with such utter ease and smoothness that the feeling was almost alien. She wasn't so much a horse, a breathing animal, as she was a machine, properly lubricated and well-maintained. She was that reliable.

I moved her back onto the rail, instinctively cautious, shying away from over-jumping her. After fighting to prevent burnout with Assault, I'd fallen into the habit of doing too little, never pushing, always quitting early. I'd get in a couple good jumps and then flee.

The chestnut mare raised her head, a mild show of passive resistance. Her eyes twitched, drawing my eye to where she looked. Her earlier crookedness returning, her whole body slanted toward the jump.

I turned her off the rail, leaving my legs off her sides, allowing the reins to float forward. She took off for the fence in a strong, measured pace, moving in a straight track. With no encouragement, she bounced over it.

I let her jump until I lost count, and each time I realized it felt more and more like that easy, weightless sensation of pumping a swing to the highest it could go, then letting the chains buck and snap.

Delaware

I was sitting in the lobby on one of those zebra couches when Yvette tracked me down. She pulled me into an empty conference room and sat me down at a big, wide table.

"I will only do this once," she said haughtily. "So pay attention the first time, Podunk."

Spreading her arms wide, she set out an array of silverware around a china plate. Two different forks, two different knives, two spoons and another fork that was randomly over with the spoons.

"You will start out here," she said, waving a hand at the silverware furthest away from the plate, "and work your way inward. The fork and knife closest to the plate are for the main course. Do not begin by using those, or you will look like an unpolished redneck idiot."

I nodded. "That seems pretty straightforward."

Yvette turned her sharp eye on me. "Now, we need to practice proper use of cutlery. You need to learn to use a knife and fork without fumbling or shaking the entire table while you ineffectively saw at a fine cut of meat."

"Facundo cuts my meat for me," I said brightly.

"Because having to watch you cut meat must make his eyes bleed." Yvette sighed, setting out a salami and placing a knife and fork in my hands. With careful strokes, she guided my hands, giving me the feel for the proper technique.

"You must let the knife do the work," she told me, sitting back and letting me take over.

I sliced it up in little even chunks, propping up the knife and fork on the edge of my plate. She nodded approvingly. "That is much better, Podunk. As much of an improvement as can be expected." She stood up, gathering the silverware. "I hope you will be better prepared now, though this gathering is admittedly out of your depth. You seem hell-bent on going anyway, so I could not leave you out in the cold, much as I wanted to."

I watched her for a minute, thinking how much she was like a porcupine. All sharp, spiny quills on the outside, and a voice full of barbs, but occasionally her soft underbelly would show.

I sat there, pleased. "You love me," I said.

"I most fervently do not," Yvette said.

"Yes, you do." I pushed back my chair, looking her in the eye. "You act like you don't, but when I needed you, you came through for me. You don't do that for someone you hate."

"It is not in the best interest of the team to have you running around like a bumpkin and making a fool of yourself," Yvette said stiffly.

"It doesn't matter if I'm a bumpkin, it matters how I play," I countered. "You're helping me out on a personal level. You don't do that for just anyone." I eyed her with a smile on my face. "You see, I've got you figured out. You act like you hate everyone, but you really don't. It's all just an act, a big false show of intimidation. You're like a little dog with a loud bark, trying to act all dangerous. When in reality, you're doing all this posturing just to comfort yourself."

"I would advise that you skip *Dr. Phil* and go back to *Springer* and *Maury*, Podunk." She made a move for the door.

I kept going, ignoring her completely. "And the people you're the meanest to, those are the people you love the most."

"You are speaking utter nonsense."

She tried to leave again, and I darted in front of her, stopping her cold. "You *love* me!" I said in a singsong voice, throwing my arms around her resistant, bony little frame.

"Okay. That is enough." She patted me awkwardly with one hand.

"You love me," I said again, driving the point home.

She relaxed in my arms for one second, then her body boarded up again. "If you do not stop, I will bite your left ear off, and you will practice cutting *that* instead of a salami."

"Okay," I said, releasing her. "But you still love me."

She stalked away, her shoulders hiked up by her ears. I watched her go, smiling fondly. I'd seen the man behind the curtain, and Yvette didn't scare me anymore.

Erica

Bruce walked into the barn, finding me sitting on a tack trunk and applying more duct tape to Assault's ravaged Nibble Net.

"Aren't those things under warranty?" He asked me wryly.

"Only under normal wear and tear," I said, looking up at him. "My horse is a natural disaster."

He shook his head ruefully, looking in at Assault. Now that his hay was gone, the gelding had turned tail and was refusing to look at anyone. "How's Vinnie treating you?"

"Vinnie?" I looked at him in confusion.

"The chestnut mare," he clarified. "Her show name's Invincible, we call her Vinnie. It's dumb."

"It is kind of...undignified." I thought of her plain face, her workmanlike attitude. "But it sort of almost fits her." I tore off the final strip of duct tape and smoothed it down. "She's been great. She's a phenomenal horse."

"I'm glad you're enjoying her," Bruce said. "She's got such a work ethic and she likes a nice long school. I hate to shortchange her when I'm busy."

"I know the feeling," I said. "Juggling clients, bills, and trying to keep competition horses legged up can feel like a lose-lose situation."

Bruce sat down on another tack trunk across the aisle from me, stretching his long legs out. "I mean, it's great to have multiple horses in competition, in case one gets injured. But I don't want to increase the odds of that happening because I half-assed my conditioning, you know?"

I nodded, uncomfortably aware of Assault's grumpy presence behind me.

"Bottom line is I have no right to complain. I'm living the dream right now." Bruce took in his small string with a sweeping glance. "But sometimes I wonder why I had to get so ambitious. The days of riding just to ride are over. I don't feel like I have a real bond with my horses, because it's not my passion, it's my business. I'm never truly present when I'm with them. You're always thinking ahead to the next show. And I think they sense that."

"If it was easy, everyone would be doing it." I smiled at Bruce. "I think you're doing just fine, though. Your horses are happy and healthy, and they seem to like their jobs. You may be hard on yourself, but you're doing a lot right."

He nodded. "It's nice to talk to someone who understands. I feel like your words carry more weight than my girlfriend's. She's an accountant, so she does what she does and she doesn't really get the whole horse thing."

"That would be hard," I said, stretching out a kink in my back muscles. "I can't imagine dating someone who wasn't into horses. I feel like there would be a giant gap of understanding, and it might be too hard to bridge.

To find common ground."

Bruce nodded. "I thought the same thing. To be honest, it's actually kind of a relief sometimes. This world - particularly the fishbowl that is Wellington - can be so consuming. It's nice to come home at night to someone who isn't as invested in it. Someone who can bring some perspective to the situation." He leaned back, placing his hands on his knee. "And when you have separate interests, you can know for sure that you're in it for the right reasons. You're in it for each other, not a common interest."

"I never thought about it that way," I said, biting down on a nail.

My phone vibrated, and I picked it up, seeing Lawrence's name on the screen. I opened it warily, poised for disappointment. If he was calling me, it meant he probably had news I wasn't too keen on hearing.

"Hey," I said shortly.

"Hey. I have to go to Lexington," Lawrence said abruptly, without even trying to soften me up first.

"Why?" I demanded. "You just went there."

"I know. John wants me there again, and I have to get it out of the way so I can be back by this weekend. Delaware's going out of town, and I told her I'd keep her ponies legged up."

"I see." I stared at the floor for a second. "Well I guess you'd better go."

"Thanks for understanding," Lawrence said. "I'll be back as soon as I can." I heard the little beep that told me he'd hung up on his end.

Lawrence

Instead of meeting me at Angelina's, or some mutually impersonal venue like a coffee shop, John had me driven straight from the airport to his house. I knew it had to be his house from the sheer scope and elegance of the thing, all wood paneling and floor-to-ceiling windows. John opened the door for me with a smile. "Cavanaugh. I appreciate you coming here."

"Not a problem," I said, stepping into the huge foyer. The house was filled with natural light, making the hardwood floors and walls glow. Most people seemed afraid of light, shutting it out with blinds and shutters, closing themselves in. John seemed to welcome and embrace it.

"Can I get you anything?" John asked, moving into the kitchen. "You must be hungry after your flight."

I shook my head. "I'm actually more interested in what you need from me. I don't want to take too much time away from Florida, so I'd rather get down to business."

John appeared in the doorway, looking somewhat chagrined. "I must admit I didn't bring you here on business. I needed to ask you something…personal."

"Okay," I shrugged. "I'll give it my best shot."

John made a move to sit down on a leather couch, but changed his mind. "Come with me."

He took me outside, making a right turn. I could see some outbuildings standing among the trees in the distance, and they looked distinctly like stables.

"I thought you'd be more comfortable here," he explained as we walked inside the barn, built in wood and painted dark chocolate with white trim. "Would you care to go for a ride?"

A pair of black Friesians peered out of their stalls, big, bold heads with long, wavy manes and forelocks that reached halfway down their faces. Eyes large and dark as coal, they blinked at me, every shaft of hair glistening even in the low light.

I nodded, grinning at John. "Definitely."

We saddled the horses and headed out on a trail cut through John's property. My mount had to be at least 16 hands, but John's gelding was bigger, so he still towered over me. We rode in silence for the first few minutes, and I didn't offer to break it, concentrating instead on the sweep of my horse's stride. I was more used to compact, fast-stepping polo ponies, and this gelding was as broad and smooth as an ocean liner.

Eventually, I fell into the rhythm, turning to look at John with one hand on the reins. "So. What did you need to ask?"

John turned his eyes on me, gathering up the reins. His gelding mouthed the bit, his neck curling into a crescent. His stride grew more animated, heavy, feathered legs moving in double time.

"You and Elaine were...involved, previously," he said.

I looked at him, a slight unease crawling into my esophagus. "How much do you know?"

"I know that you shared a bed with her, for a time, in exchange for a string of polo ponies," John said.

I looked straight ahead. "Well, we did more than share a bed, but if you're going with the more polite way to phrase it, then yes, that's how it went."

John's eyes were on me. "And I take it this was not your idea?"

I shook my head vehemently. "It was very much her idea. But I went along with it," I added, claiming my fair share of the blame.

John nodded. "I knew all this, but I wanted to hear it from you. I needed to understand the history between you. Particularly, I need to understand what happened at the end of your arrangement. How you parted."

"We parted badly," I said, chewing the inside of my lip. "Very badly."

"How so?"

"I ended it early, before I left for Florida. I told her I couldn't stand it anymore. I said some very nasty things. I was immature, and I didn't handle the situation well. She got very upset. I don't know what happened after I left, except that she spiraled down from there. We had one brief conversation on the phone, after which her husband threw her out on the street. I didn't speak to her again until I found her one day on the corner of Hewitt and Aachen. I picked her up and brought her to the LPC. I got her where she is, and she's been there ever since."

John studied me, his face intent. "Something is holding her back. Something has her running scared. She is simply terrified. And I can't figure it out."

I looked down at my horse's head, the thick black mane swinging with his stride, heavy hair covering half his neck.

"I think it is something in her past. Perhaps the way you ended things. She may still be hung up on you, and until that is resolved, there is no way for her to move forward." John's voice was as strong and inevitable as his words.

"There's a possibility," I agreed cautiously, unsure of what I was getting myself into.

John looked down at me from his lofty perch on his mount. The gelding seemed even more massive now, with as much menace and regal bearing as a medieval charger in times of war.

"I wonder if you might talk to her," John said, his careful phrasing communicating an option, his strong tone suggesting it was mandatory. "I understand it can be painful to dredge up old wounds. But it can be vital to the healing process."

I swallowed, though my mouth was pretty much dry. "I can give it a go," I said, knowing I was steering onto a road that was a fucking quagmire. What was I supposed to do? I couldn't turn down John, and I couldn't turn my back on Elaine either.

John smiled, the lines on his face assembling in a way that assured me it was genuine. "We should have a canter," he said, and he moved down the trail on his big black horse as if nothing had changed.

Erica

I lay awake, watching embarrassing reality shows and straying further and further away from sleep. After a while, I surrendered to the inevitable and flipped on the lights again, conceding to my wakefulness. An all-nighter wouldn't hurt me. After all, it wasn't as if I had to be at my best the next morning. I had to stagger blearily to the barn and feed Assault, and that was about it.

I thought about calling room service, but I wasn't really hungry or thirsty. I was something in between, and I knew exactly where to go for the in-between.

I put on some pants and rode the elevator down to the lobby. It was occupied by people getting in from somewhere or on their way somewhere. Regardless of the direction they traveled, they were undeviatingly glammed up. The sleepy desk clerk eyeballed my sweatpants and oversized T-shirt, giving a little disapproving shake of her head.

It was really remarkable how much nightlife there was on these grounds. Had I wanted to, I could've moved from party to party, never burning up any gas or putting miles on my vehicle. I looked around at the happy, drunken scene, and I couldn't muster an ounce of interest in any of it.

I was a homebody. I just had to accept it. I was a confirmed homebody, and this place felt nothing like home.

I turned my back on it, driving to the blazing fluorescent lights of the 7-Eleven. Through the window, I saw the same guy who was normally there during the day. I wondered if he actually worked round-the-clock, or if he was just stuck in swing-shift hell.

He blinked at me as I walked in the door. "I didn't expect to see you here at this hour."

I smiled wryly. "Well, I'm giving up on being a responsible adult. It hasn't been working out so great for me anyway."

He nodded. "We all have those days."

My cheeks stiffened, and I moved off to the soda fountain. "Well I'm having one of those years."

He watched me fill my cup, resting his elbows on the counter, leaning his body over it. "That sounds like it might take more than an Icee to fix."

"You may be right." I brought it up to the counter, setting the cup down. "But it's all I have to go on right now."

The guy remained in position, not hurrying to ring me up. "You're not from around here, are you?" He said.

I shook my head. "I'm from Kentucky. That's where my family is. I had a life there, and I thought I could just move it and set up shop here. But it didn't happen that way."

"What happened?" He asked. He was surprisingly alert and attentive, given the late hour and the soul-sapping quality of the compact fluorescents above his head.

"I ride horses," I explained. "I compete in show jumping at the Olympic level. Well, I tried. My horse got injured in my first competition here. He's laid up for two months, and then we start the rehab. It'll be the better part of a year before he can jump again."

"Wow." He shook his head. "That's really tough."

"I worked really hard for this." I leaned on the counter, mirroring the guy's position. "I worked 14-hour days training and teaching lessons. I sold my hunter mare who I adored. I left my other horse at home - my favorite horse - all to focus on campaigning this gelding. Now I can't focus on him. It's too harsh, too painful. So I give him the care he needs, and then I get out of there. It's sad."

The guy eyed me, standing up decisively. "I think this situation calls for more than an Icee," he said, moving to the case of shooters on the counter.

I watched as he pulled out an array of little bottles. "There's a reason why I got excited about 75 cent Icees," I said ruefully. "Pretty much all my money goes to my horse. And I'm not exactly earning any right now."

He looked at me head-on. "Did you really think I would charge you?"

I wavered in confusion. "Isn't that your job?"

He laughed slightly. "They can subtract it from my paycheck. I've worked 14 hours of overtime this week, and on this last night before my day off, I want to sit here with you and I want us to drink this whole case of shooters. It may not be the responsible thing, but it's the fun thing, and sometime's that's important too."

I moved behind the counter, and he brought out a chair for me. I selected my first shooter, picking utterly at random. "What's your name?" I asked, after scanning his shirt for a name tag and finding none.

He smiled. "My name's Kurt. I hate wearing a name tag. It's sitting over there," he said, pointing.

I smiled back. "I'm Erica."

He unscrewed the top of a shooter of Jack, drinking it in one gulp.

I took a daintier sip of mine, which was some kind of vodka. "What's the story if some customer asks why I'm here? What do we tell them?"

"You're security," Kurt said without hesitation. "You'll give them a beatdown if they cause trouble. And they'll like it."

I grinned, my Icee melting in its cup as we drank the night away, lining up tiny plastic bottles on the countertop and listening to classic rock on the radio.

Lawrence

Dusk settled over the polo field, a vast band of faded purple skyline visible beyond the greenery. My right arm hanging at my side, I galloped Delaware's pony in short bursts, asking her to push the pace, then rating her back to a forward canter. Spots of sweat dotted her chest and neck, and I felt a hesitation in her stride, a certain heaviness in her limbs that told me she was tired. She didn't protest or struggle. She was too well-bred for that. But every footfall lingered on the ground a second longer.

Drawing my spur along the line of her belly, just hard enough to ruffle the hair on her side, I asked her to give a little more. "Two more gallop sets," I murmured. "We've got to break through this plateau."

The pony scooted forward, picking up a rough gallop. I let her find her footing, and she eased into a smoother pace, making one circuit and returning to a canter when I lifted my rein hand. The patchy sweat on her neck had run together to form one large slick of damp, flattened hair. Monitoring her breathing, I asked her to move forward one more time. True to her breeding, she burst into a gallop, pushing herself admirably. But when I eased her back down to a canter, then a trot, I heard the raggedness of her breathing. I asked her to walk, slipping the reins out, and her head flopped low. Utterly spent, she poked along, her breathing gradually stabilizing, but not quickly enough for my liking.

"I need to talk to Delaware about conditioning," I said to the air. I couldn't really blame Delaware for her lack of knowledge. She'd never maintained a string of ponies before. But this level of fitness was unacceptable. You couldn't bring this mare on the field and throw her into a game. She would never have what it takes to win, and it would be borderline inhumane.

I stepped off the mare, walking beside her to monitor her condition as she cooled out. When Delaware got back from Argentina, I'd go over all the particulars of conditioning with her. Her ponies would be fit for our first game. We had time.

The lights around the practice field came on, and I looked at my watch.

It was getting late, and I had four more ponies to ride. I scanned my surroundings for a groom, but the lone figure coming out of the shadows did not resemble one of them. Invariably, they had the same shape, the same short, stocky build and unassuming manner. The silhouette I could make out was taller, more shapely, and she generated a vast presence in the night air.

"What brings you here?" I asked, halting the pony.

"I needed a change of scenery," Marla said, walking up to the edge of the field, her bare toes on the turf. "You know how I am."

"I thought you'd settled in Lexington," I said, happy to see her. "You seemed content there."

Marla shrugged. "I go where the best-looking men are," she said, looking me up and down.

"I've been splitting my time between here and there," I said. "And I've got to go back again soon."

Marla studied me. I couldn't see a single line on her face in this dusky light. "You don't seem happy about that."

"I'm not." I looked off into the distance. "I'm not exactly looking forward to what I have to do there. But I have my orders."

"Who's ordering you around?" Marla inquired.

"John," I said simply.

"Ah," Marla said, nodding deeply. "I suppose he does have a right to." She pulled her sarong around herself. It was made of a sparkly, thinly-woven thread. "What exactly are your marching orders?"

"I have to talk to Elaine. About us. About the past." I looked off into the distance. "I have to try to get her to move on."

Marla's face soured. "Best of luck with that," she growled.

"John asked me personally," I said, getting the pony moving again so she didn't stiffen up. "I have to try."

"I am sure you will try," Marla said, watching me. "Whether you will succeed is another matter."

"I just don't understand." I reined the mare in, looking at Marla. "If it's really about me…if it's some unresolved need for my love that's holding her back…*why*?" I shook my head, allowing my frustration to creep to the surface. "I wasn't even that good to her, Marla. I mean, I fucked her good, like she wanted, but that was about it. I never said one word to her. I didn't even make an effort to treat her like a human being. I acted like an immature baby all the time. Why would she want someone like that, Marla? Why would she want me still? I don't get it."

"You just have that effect on women," Marla said, her voice a whisper. She turned away, head bent, removing her shimmering body and hair from my line of vision, leaving me wondering whether I understood everything now, or nothing at all.

Courtney

Dougie and I lay in bed, his arms wrapped tightly around me, like we'd done for the past few weeks. I felt the usual dick-in-the-back sensations, and neither of us acknowledged it, or them, our eyes trained on the TV as we kind of half-watched *Celebrity Dog Swap* while not really watching it at all.

That was the good thing about Dougie. He was utterly safe, never making any sudden movements, because he didn't want me to kick him out of my room again. By default, any move-making fell to me. He wasn't about to chance it again. So we were in a stalemate of not making any moves, because I wasn't exactly good at move-making either. I was better at getting caught up in the moment and just being pulled along with someone else's move-making. That was more my thing.

So, we stayed like this for quite a while, neither one of us making a move in the literal or figurative sense of the word. I was good with this. This could pretty much just keep going on forever, as far as I was concerned. Dougie made no protestations either, if you didn't count the whole dick-in-the-back thing.

At some point we fell asleep, and the TV must have timed out and done its auto-shutdown thing, because I woke up to a dark room. In a sort of haze of half-wakefulness, I rolled over, facing Dougie, his bony frame melding to my body. I took in a whiff of pheromones, and I pressed my lips up against his.

    Instantly awake, Dougie's arms settled around me. A low moan echoed in his throat, and we kissed for a good minute, sort of working out a rhythm, but mostly not. It was awkward, for sure, but I didn't mind it. I had a certain level of comfort nailed down now, and any fumbling, loss of rhythm, or even an excess of saliva didn't phase me, because I was more tuned in to the particular taste of Dougie's mouth. That was the focal point, and everything else was just background.

    I took off my shirt, wondering in the back of my mind if things would end as abruptly as they had last time, but somehow knowing they wouldn't. Dougie's hands wandered to the band of my bra, and I obligingly unhooked it.

    His head dipped down, and in the faint, bluish light of late night I could just make out the shape of his head as he sucked on my nipple. "Do the other one," I murmured, and he obliged, taking his time as I lay back, quieted. I'd never taken it this slow before, never lingered in the early stages of foreplay. Usually it was a big rush, a frantic struggle to get me out of my clothes and on my back or whatever. It was heart-pounding, an adrenaline-soaked experience that left me confused and jittery afterward. This was relaxing, a slow burn of sensations. Nothing hurried or forced.

    Dougie moved lower, sliding off my sweatpants and my thong, turning me this way and that, admiring my shape in the dim light. I reached for him, pulling his hips into mine, reaching between us and feeling the hard outline of him through his jeans. A groan rumbled in his throat, and I heard the rustling and jangling of a belt being undone. I shifted underneath him, legs open, calm and welcoming.

    Dougie hesitated, pushing against my slickness, his whole body trembling. Then he pulled away. "I can't do this, Courtney. I can't go through with it. I'm sorry."

    "*Why?*" I demanded, persistent with need, tantalized by that one moment of contact.

    "You've been with Lawrence," Dougie said, his eyes skipping wildly from the pale blue glow of the window to my naked chest. "You can't possibly realize how intimidating that is. The stories I hear about him…the reputation that precedes him…" he looked into my eyes, his face pale. "I can't compare to that. I'll only fuck it up."

"I *want* you to fuck it up," I said loudly, in a moment of pure, hormone-fueled brazenness.

Dougie shook his head. "I can't do that to you. I want to so bad. But I can't."

I wriggled beneath him, a powerful ache developing. Dougie continued to stare at me longingly, but he showed no sign of relenting.

"Lawrence never went down on me," I said, not even recognizing my own voice as it spoke those words. "You could do that instead."

"Yeah, I could give that a go." Easily convinced, Dougie moved low, hooking an arm around one of my thighs and rearranging my limbs to accommodate his head and torso. At first, he seemed kind of lost down there, and I considered calling it off. Then he hit a nerve that sent up a little spark, and I moaned softly in encouragement. He remained in precisely the right spot, keeping a dead-perfect rhythm, and eventually I lost all sense of time and place and just lay there with my back arching and my limbs limp, in a puddle of endorphins as thick and binding as quicksand.

Erica

My cell phone vibrated to life, waking me abruptly from a firm slumber. It was stationed right up against my temple, which would've been a vexing sensation on a good day, but due to the fact that I happened to be slightly hungover, the vibrations rattled my head with what felt like the force of a jackhammer.

"Hello?" I said thickly, holding onto my head with my free hand as I brought my phone up to my ear.

"Hey, it's Bruce. Can you give Vinnie a school today?" His voice sounded clipped and polished, the hallmark of those semi-frequent days when he was "slammed".

"Sure." I rolled myself out of bed, kicking at the sheets that had wound themselves around my fully-clothed legs. Once I'd extricated myself from the bedding, I looked around for some ibuprofen.

"Super. Thanks a bunch," Bruce said before hanging up.

I located a bottle of Advil in the bathroom. One of the perks of a fancy hotel was the fully-stocked medicine cabinet in every room. I chugged the maximum recommended dose and threw on my breeches before heading down to the lobby to scope out the continental breakfast. I couldn't take that much Advil on an empty stomach, but anything heavy or greasy was a definite no-go right now.

I made a pass through the breakfast buffet, selecting a piece of white toast. It lasted me the whole walk to the parking lot as I ate it in polite nibbles, gingerly ingesting the bland material. My truck was in its usual spot. I'd waited to sober up, spending time talking with Kurt as I lingered behind the counter. When it was safe for me to drive, I'd pulled out of the parking lot, feeling a sense of loss as I left the green and white exterior behind.

I drove to the barn, my head full of excitement, anticipating the unique, weightless sensation of taking the chestnut mare over fences. Before setting out her tack, I dutifully repaired Assault's Nibble Net and stuffed more hay in, making sure his water was clean and his leg wasn't puffy. He cooperated tenuously, holding four to the floor and keeping his teeth to himself, even when it was clear he would've preferred not to.

My daily obligation complete, I turned my attention to the chestnut mare. I liked to take my time with her, using all the grooming tools in the proper order: curry, body brush, finishing brush. I thoroughly inspected her legs and feet, melding my fingers into every groove, every junction of tendon and bone. I had all the time in the world, and I used it on her. She didn't have much patience for these long, drawn-out proceedings, but she was too polite to act up. Instead, she kept her frustration to herself, occasionally releasing it through her nostrils in a loud, fluttering sigh.

It was good to have a horse again, a creature with particular needs, likes, and dislikes. The process of setting out equipment and putting it on piece by piece grounded me, showing me, once again, that horses were a way of life I couldn't divorce myself from. As my fingers moved with dexterity, fastening all the buckles, manipulating the sliders and keepers, I felt a little less displaced, a little less homesick. Home was wherever the barn was, as long as I could make myself useful.

I walked the chestnut mare to the schooling ring. She moved in quick, reaching strides, her shoulder in line with my body, her eyes focused on the enclosed ring, sandy footing interspersed with standards and poles.

The morning was cool and pleasant by Florida standards, with only a hint of mugginess in the air. The chestnut mare moved with an additional thrust in her step, keen and impatient. With each revolution of the arena, her feet danced higher, and her skinny neck bobbed faster. With every avenue of communication she had, the chestnut mare was telling me to let her go.

I conceded to her longing, slipping the reins and putting my trust in her. She sailed into a canter, remaining on the rail at first, as if she was running her own pre-flight checklist. *Hocks, stifles, ready and engaged. All systems go.*

She rolled on her hindquarters, making a neat turn off the rail. Doubling her speed in a smooth leap, she poured herself at the jump, body flat to the ground, aerodynamic. Just as quickly, she gathered herself up, redistributing her weight to her hindquarters as she met the fence.

There it was, that addicting, gravity-defying sensation, that adrenaline-spiking thrill. She was a theme park ride, a car on a metal track zooming up and away, engineered for speed and daring. She was a unique animal. I'd known it from the first time I sat on her, and she reiterated it for me every time she left the ground.

Completing the first leap and subsequent landing, the chestnut mare swung back, eschewing the rail, making a quick turn and lining herself up with the other practice fence. She continued as she'd started, laying down a series of intricate loops interspersed with grand jumping efforts. I hadn't touched her with hand or leg. It was all her doing.

If I stepped off and simply let her go, without a rider on her back, would she keep jumping? I wondered. I had to think that she would.

As the morning heated up and she showed so signs of slowing down, I sat up, engaging my core muscles, asking her to come back to me. She ceded to my aids and returned to the rail, making several circuits at a long trot before dropping to a walk. I gave her the reins, and she stretched her neck forward and down, her body swinging. She was mellow. Happy.

When she'd had ample time to cool down, I halted her in the middle of the arena. Shoulders bent forward, I rubbed her neck, my gloved fingers skimming over her spiny withers and slightly straight shoulder. She bent her head, content to stand there, knowing the ride was over. Her job done well.

The ring had cleared out, and by some miracle it was just the two of us, accompanied by the heavy, yellow sun off in the distance. I lingered in the saddle, not wanting to break the moment. It was beautiful and sad at the same time, the hallmark of real life.

I wanted to sit here forever. I wanted to spend all day brushing her, bathing her, and then grazing her on the lawn. I wanted to stay up late at night reading into various supplements and therapeutic saddle pads, all for her benefit. And when she had a problem, when she got hurt or sick or simply had an off day, I wanted to feel the throb of anxiety in the pit of my stomach.

I couldn't do things halfway. It had always been an integral part of my nature, and there were times when I wished I could rip off that particular part of me and throw it away. But it was always going to be there, which is why I had to tell Bruce I couldn't help him with Vinnie anymore.

She was beautiful, talented, and vital. She was the epitome of what a competition horse could be. But she would never be mine.

Lawrence

Dougie appeared in my doorway, holding tightly to his iPhone. The door was propped open, and I was packing a suitcase.

"Where are you running off to?" Dougie asked, leaning up against the door frame.

"I have to go to Lexington," I said, the force of my words conveying just how much I didn't want to be doing that. "John needs me to do a thing."

Dougie cracked a smile. "*Again*? Who does that guy think he is, asking for favors all the time?" He grinned at me, his eyebrows crinkling with mirth.

You're in an awfully good mood, I thought, eyeing him suspiciously. It was weird to see Dougie like that. Normally I would've pressed him about it, but I was too wrapped up in my own shit to start delving into other people's.

"What is he having you do?" Dougie wanted to know, his eyes trained on his phone.

"I have to talk to Elaine," I said, throwing one more pair of socks into my luggage. "I have to convince her that she's not still in love with me, or whatever." I zipped up the bag, feeling myself descend into a black mood.

"Is that what he thinks is going on with her?" Dougie asked, suddenly alert.

"He thinks she has unresolved shit from her past that's holding her back. And it just so happens I'm it." I rolled my eyes, moving for the door.

"Just tread carefully there," Dougie said, his eyes following me. "I'm not sure you really know what you're dealing with."

I shot him a livid glance. "Oh, I'm *pretty* sure I do."

"She's suicidal," Dougie said, catching me off-guard. I jolted to a stop and looked at him.

"She's suicidal," Dougie repeated, his murky grey eyes serious. "And if you don't know that, you haven't been paying attention. I know what it looks like. It's in her eyes, it's all over her. And even if you can't see it in her face, you should certainly see it in her choices."

"What are you talking about?" I demanded.

Dougie looked at me, his face set. "You know how you found her on the street, all skin and bones, within days of death?"

I nodded, my throat drying up at the memory.

"She didn't have to get like that," Dougie said, his eyes blazing slightly. "She's an intelligent, able-bodied woman. She ran her husband's estate, managed millions of dollars in assets. You're telling me she couldn't have gotten a job somewhere? And besides that, there are shelters, there are programs for women to help them get back on their feet. She didn't have to be on the street. She *chose* that." Dougie sighed, turning away. "She chose an agonizing existence and a slow, inevitable death. For some reason, she sought that out. And you need to figure out why. Because until you do, she won't truly get better."

He looked at me again, and I knew he was speaking from experience. "She looks good now, and she's gotten her life together. But she's suicidal. She's still that way. You don't just stop."

Elaine

Marla appeared backstage as I shrugged into my coat, her jet-setting surprisingly short-lived. I gave her a smile as I tied off the waist of my trench coat. "Back so soon?" I inquired.

"I realized the things I needed to say couldn't be said in Florida," Marla said, folding her arms around her midsection. "Or rather, the person I need to say them to is not in Florida."

"Interesting," I said, a strange foreboding creeping into my mind. I made a move to slip out the back, and her hand snaked out, holding fast to my wrist.

"You and I need to have words," Marla said firmly.

"I finished my set. I'm leaving. I owe you nothing." *Now let me go before I start thrashing in your grasp like a marlin.*

"I have something to say to you, and you'll hear it," Marla said icily.

"Fine." I ripped my arm out of her grip and stood with my hands on my hips, like a child awaiting a time-out. "Say it and let's be done."

"Just fuck him already," Marla said, her face resigned, her voice strong.

"*Who?*" I asked, though I knew I was only drawing out this conversation by playing dumb.

Marla rolled her eyes. "*John.* Just fuck him already. I can see you want to."

"I told you. You can have him." I moved away, my eyes downcast.

"That's the thing," Marla said. "I *can't* have him, because he only wants you. He's made it abundantly clear to me on numerous occasions. I can't take any more humiliation."

"So maybe you should find another man, and stop worrying about John. And maybe you should *stop worrying about me*," I said, lowering my voice several octaves.

Marla shook her head, golden-red hair swaying like a palm tree. "See, I can't do that. Because I look at him, and I look at you, holding onto this stupid notion of abstinence, and all I can think is *what a waste*. I can't abide it."

"I'm done here," I snapped, picking up my bag. "Good luck keeping this place going without your headliner."

I sped out the back, fumbling with my key and wrenching my door open. Teeth rattling in my head, rage and tears spilling down my cheeks, I burned rubber on my way out of the parking lot, taking a hard right onto a back road.

The engine strained, reaching my ears in a loud whine, but I didn't ease my foot off the accelerator. I kept building speed, and eventually I was flying down the two-lane road at 80 miles per hour. My truck skipped and lurched over potholes and joins in the pavement. I kept my eyes trained forward through the windshield. Nothing would stop me.

I rounded a hairpin turn, my truck fishtailing on some gravel scattered over the road. I moved my foot to the brake, and then I saw what lay ahead.

A mother doe and her adolescent fawn were standing in the middle of the road, necks snapped upright, their large, round eyes shining bright white, reflecting my headlights. I had no room to stop in time. And they didn't move.

I made no conscious choice. It was pure reflex. I cranked the wheel to the left as hard as I could, my tires spinning and catapulting off the road.

There was a tiny guardrail, but my truck made short work of it, crushing it down and ricocheting off it. I could make out trees and a river, their colors eerie and stark in the dark of night and the harsh glow of my high beams. Then I was rolling down the ravine, every part of me slamming up against the interior of the cab, jolts of pain firing in my limbs and body. All the while, I could hear the outside of my truck splintering, windows cracking, roof and walls being crunched in. The only things that held were the doors, new, rust-free, and reinforced. They made not a shiver, while everything else gave way.

After a minute that stretched on to an hour, a scene replayed over and over as my truck rotated, a helpless victim of gravity, the battered shell around me finally stopped moving. I was upside down, the seatbelt strangling me. I fought my way out of it, scrambling through the massive gap in the windshield, cutting myself on broken glass and only noticing the warmth and wetness of the blood.

I crawled on my hands and knees, standing up slowly, patting myself down lightly at first, then frantically. *I should be injured*, I thought, the stubborn and determined words repeating in my head. Giving up at last, I looked around.

I was in a valley, a quiet stretch of forestland near the banks of the river. My truck lay in pieces, a ghastly collection of scrap metal. Car parts and snapped-off trees marked its descent.

I fell to my knees, and I began crying hysterically, my body heaving with sobs that had no cutoff, no end. I should have been crying in gratitude, and the good Samaritans who found me likely thought I was. I let them believe what they wanted to believe.

But the only singular thought in my head, the only thing I could feel, was a curt, shameful question.

Why can't I be dead?

Erica

Lawrence had gone off to Lexington again. It was pretty much expected that he would be gone more than he was here, and I didn't get shook up about it anymore. Mostly, I just didn't know how I was going to occupy my time. Assault was still on strict stall rest, and since I'd informed Bruce that I couldn't ride Vinnie anymore, my hours at the barn were reduced to an occasional drive-by. I could only spend so much time at the 7-Eleven without looking like a full-on stalker, although Kurt seemed to appreciate my company, no matter how repetitive or drawn-out it was.

I spent my afternoons tooling around the International Polo Club, trying to muster the desire to try new things. The fitness center would've been a good place to start, but it seemed like Courtney was always there, running the treadmill at full blast without breaking a sweat, her boobs and blonde ponytail jouncing rhythmically. My next stop was always the spa, but I could never make myself set foot inside the door. It would've been nice in theory, but my mother's particular persuasions had left me with an irreversible bad taste in my mouth when it came to any sort of pampering.

    I really only had one option. Without the clout and competition record to recruit clients and train horses, I'd decided to start applying for grooming positions. I was more than qualified for a show groom's job, and it would give me something to do outside of lounging in bed, eating myself fat, and waiting for Lawrence. At least I would be a part of that world again. At least I would be on the inside, not skirting around the edges, guiltily slipping in to care for my laid-up horse, and retreating like a thief in the night.

    I left the spa behind, turning back to head for the parking area. Maybe I'd start my job search this afternoon. I was tired of inertia.

    I saw Dougie on my way there, and I gave him a short wave. He responded by steering himself directly into my path, forcing me to stop short. "What's up?" I asked him, trying to conceal the fact that I really wanted to get moving.

    "I'm supposed to find you," Dougie said. "And I'm supposed to tell you to go to the stables. The ones here, not your barn." He glanced at his phone, perhaps checking his notes. "Yeah. That's it."

    "Why?" I asked, reminding myself not to snap at the messenger. "What's going on?"

    Dougie dropped his head to my level. "Okay. I'm not supposed to tell you anything specific, so when certain people ask you about it, be sure to say it was a big surprise." His voice lowered. "Lawrence is sending you something. It's a gift of some sort, and it's a big deal. I'm supposed to make sure you're there when it arrives, and I'd better not screw this up. That's all he told me."

    "Wow." I stepped back, my brain whirling, trying to deduce what it might be. "Thanks a lot, Dougie. I appreciate you tracking me down and everything."

    "No problem," Dougie said, shuffling back by a few paces. "Hey, have you seen Courtney?"

    "I think she's in the fitness center," I told him.

"Great." He loped away, a jaunty spring in his long-legged step.

I walked to the stables, wondering what kind of a present awaited me. Maybe he'd arranged for me to get a polo lesson from some Argentinean hunk. *Nah, probably not. He's in Lexington right now, maybe he had Indulgence ship a cake for me! But why would he have it sent to the stable?* I wasn't getting anywhere with my guessing game, so I sat down on the pommel horse and waited for my mystery gift to show up.

A short while later, a commercial shipper rolled up the drive, large dually truck and slant-haul trailer. *One of the players must've bought some new ponies.* I paid it no mind.

But when no army of grooms appeared to collect the animals inside, I began to get a slight suspicion. The shipper stepped down from the cab, lowering the ramp and ducking inside the van. I heard no scuffle, not even a sound, then I heard the booming sound of heavy hooves on a metal floor.

The shipper came back down the ramp, followed by a blaze-faced behemoth of a horse. His coat was scruffy and sun-bleached, and the feathers on his legs had grown in. He had a slack, pot-bellied physique, far from his heyday, when I'd conditioned him every day and groomed him to a spit-shine. But he was my horse.

"D.M.," I whispered, coming over to hold his head in my hands. His breath warmed me, and I wrapped my arms around his jaw, breathing in his dusty, salty smell.

I stepped back and looked at him, strong, solid limbs and feet, and a good head on his shoulders. We had a lot of ground to make up when it came to conditioning, a lot of time lost that we'd never get back. But he was sound, healthy, and willing, and I knew what we had to do.

I knew what Lawrence was telling me. This gift wasn't free; it was contingent on whether I dared to try again.

"What do you think?" I said to D.M., tears shimmering in my eyes. "Can we give it one more go?"

He looked down his long nose at me, lowering his head and giving my arm a gentle bump with his soft nose.

I laughed through my tears, emotions soaring. "I have to agree," I said, hugging him again.

Team Dark Horse

Part Five

John

Leaning over the table, I took a long sip from a cup of coffee. The morning paper spread out before me, I read through the sports section, the TV playing quietly in the background. Seated in my usual spot, I awaited my eggs over easy and hash browns.

This diner wasn't exceptional, but it was comforting, and I appreciated the routine of coming here and listening to the banter and the clink of coffee cups. I had the capability of preparing a breakfast spread that exceeded the quality of anything served here, but it was difficult to justify going to such lengths when I was serving a party of one.

The morning news played on, curt, abridged stories without much detail. I didn't normally listen to it, but occasionally some snippet would find its way into my synapses.

"The victim of a one-car accident was treated and released yesterday. According to officers on scene, the vehicle left the road and rolled down an embankment, sustaining significant damage. The victim was treated for minor injuries. Excessive speed is thought to have been a factor, but the cause is still under investigation."

I turned around in my seat, craning my neck to see the screen. I saw just a flash of the footage before they cut to the next story.

A huge, white, rusted-out truck lay upside-down in a sickening heap, twisted and broken, the weight of the cab supported mainly by two brand-new doors, standing out in the chaos of the wreckage.

With a cold blast of fear in my heart, I leapt up from the table and strode out the door, blindly sliding into my car and driving away. The words *treated and released* meant nothing to me as I clutched the wheel, swerving through traffic. I just kept seeing that tangle of metal that had been her truck, the image growing and expanding behind my eyes and intensifying the stab of fear.

Yvette

Bicep quivering, I leaned back on the pommel horse, scattering the neat line of balls on the ground, going through the repertoire of shots while I waited for my pony to be warmed up. I could see her on the stick and balling field, an exercise rider on her back, completing the requisite tedious circuits of slow-paced work. I always imagined that would be the worst job, to sit astride a fine horse and guide it through the walk, trot, and canter, working out the kinks and stretching the muscles, only to hand it off once the animal was engaged and ready to fly.

Delaware sidled up the path, her slim, shapely figure drawing more than a few stares as she walked in uniform, chestnut ponytail flopping at her back.

I nodded dismissively in acknowledgment. To my chagrin, she took it as an open invitation, swinging onto the horse beside me. Failing to pick up a mallet, her intent was clear as she faced me, seated upon the horse as if it were a couch. She was here to gab, not to practice her shots.

There was little else in the world that could annoy me more.

"What do you want from me, Podunk?" I asked curtly, flicking my wrist and sending a ball flying sideways. It hit a passerby sharply on the shin, and he sent me a dirty stare. I nearly cracked a smile.

"Oh, nothing in particular. I just thought I'd join you while they get my pony ready." She gave me a big grin.

"Did I appear lonely to you?" I inquired acidly, firing another shot into the walkway and seeing if I could get two in a row. "Because the only commodity in my life that remains at a premium is solitude."

Delaware shook her head. "You might find it surprising, Yvette, but my main motivation in life isn't to piss you off."

"Then you must be a natural," I said.

We lapsed into silence, punctuated by the thwack of my mallet as it dispersed the balls. Having hit every last one, I waited for them to be replaced, propping my mallet up on the side of the horse. My hands idle, I decided to throw Delaware a bone.

"How was your time in Argentina?" I asked convivially. "Did his family accept you with open arms?"

Delaware beamed at me. "They sure did," she enthused. "They thought I was charming, and they wanted to hear all about my rodeo days. I guess foreigners are really into the Western culture," she added as an aside.

"Good for you," I said.

"And they were impressed by my table manners," Delaware threw in with a Cheshire-cat grin.

"Good for me, then," I said, returning her smirk.

One of the workers stepped in, setting down a line of balls next to my horse. *It has taken you long enough,* I thought in irritation. As he moved out of the way, I hit the first ball. My arm scissored relentlessly as I displaced them in a matter of seconds. In the moment of calmness that followed, I looked around, my eyes locating Javier as he walked up the path. Hips undulating in a swagger that plowed right over the borderline of overkill, he cut a fine form nonetheless, muscle groups bursting through a uniform that was skintight. He wore his clothes like a preteen girl would - everything tight and revealing, appearance carefully cultivated to attract attention, regardless of how positive or negative it was.

He saw me and gave me a slow-burn smile, thrusting out his hips as he walked, accentuating the bulge created by his tight breeches and contoured briefs.

I would have knocked a ball right into his ankles, but I was out of ammunition. I settled for chopping a divot out of the ground, marring a perfectly fine patch of grass and watching the groundskeeper sigh in agitation.

"You are getting sloppy," Javier said as he walked by. "Divots are the mark of an amateur."

"My amateur is better than you on your best day," I retorted. "You will see when we finally share a field."

He strode off, intensifying his swagger, treating the narrow lane as his runway. Delaware watched him leave, sighing a little.

"They sure make them different out here," she said.

"Than in Indiana?" I asked, my nose curling. "I should hope so."

"So, you and him, are you like a thing?" Delaware asked, eyes brightening as she gave me an inquisitive stare.

"We are not a *thing*," I refuted, keeping my eyes trained straight ahead. "He is, occasionally, a means to an end for me. And nothing more."

"I see," Delaware nodded. "But isn't that kind of empty?"

"That is the thing with these men, Podunk," I said, dismounting from the horse as my pony was pulled to a halt in the distance. "They appear slick and polished on the outside, and they will offer you all sorts of promises, but their heads are as empty and vacant as a cupboard laid bare. They know just enough to hurt you, and to deny it later."

Erica

D.M. stood in the cross ties, feet planted as he dozed off. Cocking a hind leg, he let one hip slump, a sigh whistling through his body. After hours of scrubbing and rinsing, I'd managed to get all the dirt out of his coat. Now I wielded a pair of Oster clippers, starting at his head and working my way down. Tufts of hair collected on the floor and on my eyeballs, but I was relentless, stopping only to apply more lubricant to the blades. Moving in smooth, slow strokes, I left behind a velvety surface, with no lines or uneven spots.

My hand cramped up after I finished clipping his neck and shoulders, and when I moved to his broad body, my whole arm followed suit. I worked through the pain, incapable of stopping and leaving D.M. a half-clipped disaster. The OCD groomer in me wouldn't allow it.

Three hours later, every inch of D.M. was sleek and spotless. His hairy legs were clean-shaven again, and I'd evened off the scraggly ends of his tail so it appeared fuller. Body aching, I leaned against a tie post, leaning this way and that to work the knots out. I was in need of a full chiropractic workup, but at least my horse looked presentable.

Team Dark Horse

Lawrence had somehow managed to secure a stall for D.M. in the IPC barn, so D.M. lived with the polo ponies, standing out like a lovable sore thumb. He clearly didn't belong, but his gentle nature and good manners had given him an easy "in" with the barn staff. They always found paddock space for him if I requested it, and oftentimes I'd find him on the end of a lead, with one of the grooms hand-grazing him.

I even had my own locker for D.M.'s equipment, although his extra-large saddle barely fit in there. Closing the door was always interesting. Inevitably, I ended up shoving it closed with my ample hip, leaning the bulk of my body against the door and forcing it to comply.

With my grooming duties drawn to a close, I decided it was time to ride. I needed to feel a horse under me, and D.M. needed the exercise. If we were going to get back in the game, we needed to get moving.

I saddled D.M., noting that his saddle no longer sat flush with his back but dipped too low in front, the custom-made tree now too wide for his bony withers. I slipped some shim pads underneath, improving the fit to some degree, but not enough for my liking. D.M. had been fitted for this saddle when he was in his prime, a robust athlete with plenty of muscle tone. Now, he was anything but.

I wrapped his legs and bridled him, letting him lap up the bit from my hand like he always did. Placing my helmet on my head, I led him outside.

Unlike the equestrian center where I kept Assault, the IPC had ample land to ride on, from the outskirts of the grounds to the meandering fields nearby. I let D.M. pick a gentle pace and just watched the scenery go by, allowing him a long warm-up while I sat there in relaxation.

As we rounded a corner to a small incline, I asked D.M. to trot. Pushing me out of the saddle with short, jarring strides, he scrambled up the hill.

"Easy," I murmured, sitting up and taking back on the outside rein, attempting to connect his body. He huffed along, loading his front hooves with every step as his hindquarters floated along, drifting far behind him.

This was a feeling I'd become all too familiar with in the early days of D.M.'s training. I'd struggled for months to teach him to carry himself properly. Naturally weak in the hind end, D.M. wasn't blessed like some horses were. I'd worked every day to help him develop strength and work more efficiently, and my work had paid off in the end. But after having sat all summer, his physique had taken a turn for the worse. The hard-earned muscle had melted off, replaced by flab, and even though the bulk of our training remained in his head, D.M. simply couldn't comply with my request. The will to please was still there, but his body wasn't able to follow through.

I kept him trotting through a long straightaway, rising off his back in two-point to ease the jarring. D.M.'s head dropped down, exerting a heavy pull on my hands as he leaned on the bit, his body pummeling along in a pile-driver stride, not the airy, lofty movement of a horse that was fully engaged. This was the desperate plodding of a distance runner in the final stretch of a race, just waiting to break the tape and collapse across the finish line.

I let him walk, and his head flopped low, nostrils wide, sucking in air. Light patches of sweat were blooming on his freshly clipped coat after one short-lived trot set. The hard-to-condition draft horse in D.M. had come out in full force after his time off, and as I touched his skin, I felt the heat rising off it. The extra weight he carried sucked up the Florida heat, making D.M. feel hot as an oven.

We had a lot of work to do.

Elaine

I held Penny Dreadful's lead shank, spraying her down with the hose after a morning workout. Wilson had tried to get me to take some time off after my accident, but after a while, he saw the foolishness in arguing with me and left me alone in my room. My life wasn't altered by the wreck. My life was small enough that very few things could alter it anymore. The only things I'd lost in the accident were my truck and maybe a pint of blood.

Some people would say losing my vehicle was a setback, but I didn't look at it that way. Since I'd quit my side gig at Angelina's, the barn was my focal point once again. It was better that way. Lawrence had tried to expand my life, but I had found that it was better to keep myself hemmed in. I was like a high-strung horse recovering after a serious injury. You couldn't trust me with too much freedom.

I heard someone fishtail into the driveway at what sounded like 90 miles per hour. "Who would be out here this early?" I said to Penny as I rinsed off her neck. She turned her head delicately away from the mist of water, blinking her eye furiously and laying her ears to the side. I took pity on her and soaked a rag in water, using that to wash her poll instead.

Angry footsteps descended on me. John stood in the mire of grass and mud that surrounded Penny, his leather shoes soaking up the water. "What has gotten into you?" He said, his voice low.

I pointedly ignored the question concentrating on the water droplets rolling off Penny's rump, where she was driest. I thought of ducks, how the water rolls off their backs, and how they always look happy, even in the rain.

"I saw it on the news. Your accident." John turned away from me, pacing a narrow strip, his footsteps squishy on the waterlogged ground. "What the hell happened?"

"My truck left the road," I said with a hint of irony.

He looked at me, his eyes irate. "It's not funny."

"I was treated and released, which I'm sure you heard on the news. What are you getting so worked up about?" I asked, turning off the hose and reaching for the sweat scraper.

"I'm concerned that you're acting dangerously. You're self-destructing," John said.

"Well, since I totaled my truck, I doubt I'll be getting into any more car accidents." Starting at Penny's back, I whisked the water off her. "So I'll have to get creative."

John shook his head, a deep crease forming between his eyebrows. "This isn't a joke, Elaine." He resumed his squelchy pacing. "Marla said you quit your engagement at Angelina's."

I eyed him warily. "What else did Marla tell you?"

"Nothing I haven't heard many times over from her." John slipped his hands into his pockets. "Can I ask why you quit?"

"I just figured I needed to reevaluate my life," I said, running the metal scraper gently over Penny's bony shoulders. "I decided I can't be on a pole anymore."

John's eyes lingered on me. "But you have such a talent," he said, as if I didn't know that already. There wasn't a lot that slipped by me, except for those few things I chose to overlook when it suited me.

"Talent has nothing to do with it," I said, gathering up Penny's lead shank and leaving John standing in the mud. He had to feel it in his shoes, but he still watched me walk away before he moved to dry ground.

Courtney

Dougie and I met up in the lobby, in the tranquil corner over by the vending machine. A forlorn vessel containing trail mix and beef jerky, it didn't get much business, while the Gatorade machine on the other side of the room remained a hotbed of activity.

"Hey, Courtney," Dougie said, leaning down and kissing me. Our bodies were close enough to touch, and I didn't separate us.

"Hey," I whispered back, resting my hands on either side of his slim midsection.

"So I was thinking we could go to the 7th Chukker for dinner if you want," Dougie offered, gazing down at me.

"Maybe." I considered whether I wanted food, and it lagged behind a few other things on my priority list. "Or we could just go upstairs."

"You want to?" Dougie asked, looking utterly hopeful.

"Yeah." I nodded, and he took my arm and brought me to the elevator.

Inside my room, his arms settled around me, his hands roaming, gently gathering and squeezing my flesh. We made out for a good 20 minutes before he took off my clothes and laid me on my back, slipping a finger inside me, his head between my legs.

When he resurfaced, wiping his face off on his sleeve, I looked up at him blearily. "Thanks," I said, from somewhere deep within my orgasm-induced stupor.

He grinned slowly. "You're very welcome, Courtney. I enjoyed it." He nuzzled up to me, lying down and turning me on my side.

I stirred, feeling the dick-in-the-back and the inevitable guilt that came along with it now that he was working so hard at pleasing me. "What about you?" I said, deciding to act on my feelings instead of just stewing about it forever.

"What about me?" Dougie asked, breathing in my ear.

"You know." I scrunched my face up, trying to employ a phrase that wasn't awkward as all get-out. "Your needs. And all that."

"Oh, Courtney." Dougie sighed, taking my chin in his hand and bringing my face around to kiss me. "You don't have to worry about my needs. My needs are just fine."

"But I want to be worried about it," I said, looking at him. "That's what a good girlfriend would do."

I shut up, staring at Dougie in slight terror. My words had done that thing where they jump off a cliff and leave me wondering how that just happened.

"Is that what you want?" Dougie asked me. "To be my girlfriend?"

"I mean, if you even want us to be boyfriend and girlfriend," I said, muddling through the conversation and hoping it didn't take a bad turn, which would mean a very unpleasant throwing on of clothes and storming out the door for me. "But if you don't want that, that's fine."

Still cupping my face in his hand, Dougie looked in my eyes. "Of course I want us to be boyfriend and girlfriend," he said tenderly.

I smiled at him. "Well, then we can be that," I said, inevitably finding the least romantic way of putting things.

Lawrence

The plane touched down in Lexington at half past eight, the sun burning a dull cast of bronze in the sky. Stepping onto the tarmac, I made my way to the cab, weary all the way to my shoes. This wasn't a good way to begin, feeling like I'd already waged a small war. I just outright dreaded this meeting. I couldn't begin to rally myself for the effort. I knew it would involve dredging up old wounds, and I wanted nothing to do with that. I wanted to believe that Elaine would be just fine without my intervention. All the while,

Dougie's words rattled away in my head.

Was she suicidal? I couldn't say for sure. All I knew was that Elaine's behavior and her choices leading up to me finding her on the street never really made sense. I'd never stopped to consider it before, but Dougie had shone an ultra-watt light on the situation, and now I couldn't look away.

I got in the cab and the driver sped off, knowing exactly where he was going. I lay back with my head on the seat like a child, wishing I could execute John's request with that much certainty.

The LPC drive opened up before me, its grounds small and quaint compared to the International Polo Club's scale and extravagance. I said a clipped "thank you" to the driver and stepped out into an empty parking lot.

We'd have our privacy; that was for sure. I walked on the grass, searching for Elaine. The sunset had intensified, throwing streaks of hot pink and blood orange over the treetops. I had the strange sense that there were flames at my back, urging me on, though there was little heat in the air, only the cool, slightly damp sensation of dusk.

Elaine

It was that waiting time in between evening chores and night check. My day not yet done but no pressing tasks to occupy my time. It was time I could have spent on myself, and I usually spent it grazing Free Bird, the elderly retired polo maven of the barn. Hip bones showing through her coat, she needed all the green grass she could stomach. I normally took her out on a daily basis, and even when I didn't feel like it, the haughty looks she gave me from her stall convinced me to change my plans.

My strange proclivities did make me a better horse servant. Everyone is good at something.

Zoning out, I followed Free Bird as she wandered, snatching up the grass and spitting out the occasional weed. Allowing her to pull me along, I took no notice of anything until Free Bird suddenly raised her head, ears pricked and eyes staring forward. She gathered herself up like a doe preparing to leap into the woods.

I turned, seeing Lawrence approaching me, hands shoved in his pockets, a dark, slim figure against the slow burn of the sunset. He walked up to me, a flicker of light held in his eyes, his face solemn.

"What are you doing here?" I asked, gathering up Free Bird's lead shank.

"We need to talk," Lawrence said, his jaw in a firm line.

"John put you up to this," I said angrily, turning away to take Free Bird in.

"So what if he did?" Lawrence said to my back, his voice a sharp edge. "We still need to talk."

"Let me put this pony away, and then I'll talk all you want," I said, stomping away with Free Bird at my shoulder.

I locked her in her stall, resting my hands on the wood paneling. Heaving a fractured sigh, I walked outside.

"What does John want you to tell me?" I said, rising up on tiptoe like a prizefighter entering the ring, ready to do some damage. "And since when are you his little messenger boy?"

"John didn't hand me a script, if that's what you think this is," Lawrence sent a returning shot over my bow. "We need to talk about what happened with us. How fucked-up it was, and how it's still fucking you."

"You really think you have that kind of power over me?" I said, my voice shaking with impotent rage as I recalled all those months he practically spoon-fed me like a baby bird.

"Unfortunately, I do." Lawrence stepped forward, a shock of hair falling over his forehead. "And I don't understand why."

"What does it matter?" I asked. "You have Erica. You shouldn't concern yourself with me. You did your part."

"See, I thought that, but I think I was wrong." Lawrence bent down on one knee and retied his bootlace. "You need to move on, Elaine."

"And by 'move on', you mean that I should fuck John?" I asked, my voice rising.

"If that's what you both want, then yes," Lawrence said, looking at me straight on.

"I'm not doing that again," I said stiffly, breaking away from him.

"Why not?" Lawrence followed me, now actively chasing me down. "You're not married. He's not married. You're both consenting adults. What the hell is your holdup here?"

I shook my head, walking away from him as my blood pressure rose. The grassy lane I walked on wasn't big enough, and the sky was darkening as his words hemmed me in, making me feel claustrophobic, like I'd descended into a manhole.

"I know I messed you up," Lawrence said. His words clawed at my back like some rabid animal. "Those things I said…the way I left…I know it was bad. I shouldn't have done that. But you can't let it end your life."

I jolted, turning back. "You think you have all the power here?" I said. "All the responsibility?" I shook my head, suddenly manic. "You know *nothing*, Lawrence."

"Well maybe you should tell me all these things I don't know." Lawrence stood still, his face cast in shadow.

"I don't think so," I said coolly, and continued walking.

He was right beside me in a flash. "Why would you let yourself get that way?" He demanded.

His words threw me off balance, and I struggled to right myself. "What are you talking about?"

"Why did you let yourself starve?" He looked at me, eyes on fire, chunks of smoldering coal in the near darkness. "Why did you almost die out there? You knew there were options. Resources. Why didn't you use them?" He was gaining on me, relentless. "Did you *want* to die?"

I wrapped my arms around myself, putting up a wall against the onslaught of his questioning. "So what if I did?" I said, huddling. "You made it better. You pulled me out of it and set me up here. You can absolve yourself of any guilt."

"It's not that simple," he said, lingering. "This is still affecting you. You're not well."

I looked at him, seeing the hard line of his face, the stubborn set of his eyes. I felt the first flicker of fear, the first inkling that he might never give up until I told him the truth.

"You should leave," putting up a fight even as the energy seeped out of me.

"No." He held firm. "Tell me what's going on. Tell me what you've been trying to keep from me this whole time."

I found myself at the hay barn, so I unbolted the door and slid it open. Sitting down on a partially stacked row of bales, I folded my hands in my lap, looking down at the floor, layers of fallen chaff and strands of dried grass.

Lawrence sat beside me, his body inclined toward me. "Why did you want to die?" He asked.

"It's not your fault," I said, taking a quivering breath. "That's what you should know."

I laid my hands flat on my thighs, looking at my scarred knuckles.

"When we parted ways, I was extremely upset," I said. "I spiraled down. I drank too much. I had a meltdown. That much is true. But I wasn't as bad as when you found me. Something else happened..." I looked away.

"What happened?" Lawrence said gently, urging me on, his voice applying steady pressure like a human calf against a horse's side.

"I started getting really sick, and I thought it was just from the liquor. But something wasn't right." My thumbnail dug into the fleshy palm of my hand, a steady prick of physical pain to offset the dull roar of anguish in my head. "So, I went to the doctor, and it turned out I was pregnant."

I saw the flare of white in Lawrence's eyes, and I knew that was the last thing he had expected.

"I didn't know what to do. I panicked." My voice floated somewhere far above me, my brain distancing itself from the words. "I didn't think it through, and I thought it was my only option. So I scheduled a procedure." My voice broke, and I stopped to put it back together.

Lawrence took a shuddering breath. "And you are absolutely sure it was mine and not Arnold's." He didn't phrase it as a question, but it clearly was.

I looked at him levelly. "It could not have been Arnold's," I said. "There is no possible chance."

"Okay." He breathed out, his face whiter than usual. "You had a procedure, then. So it never happened. There is no baby."

"Right," I said, remaining stock still. "It never happened."

"Is that what you wanted?" Lawrence asked, his voice soft.

I shook my head, feeling the tears starting. "No. I wanted to keep it. But I went through with it anyway. It's the worst thing I've ever done."

Lawrence leaned over me, draping an arm around my shoulders. "Why didn't you tell me?"

Tears ran down my cheeks in a steady current. "Because I would rather dismember myself limb by limb than hurt you."

He stared at me, deep lines of concern forming on his face. "You should have told me. Why did you feel you had to be alone in this? It wasn't your fault. I was responsible too."

"I knew how much you hated me," I said thickly, clutching tightly to my upper arms. "I couldn't drag you into that mess. How were we supposed to raise a child together? I couldn't tell you; I couldn't tell Arnold. I was alone, and I couldn't see a way out of it. Until I'd already gone through with it. Then I realized I could've found another way." I smiled bitterly.

Lawrence hiked his knees up to his chest, his eyes world-weary and bloodshot. I fell silent, realizing what I'd done. I'd placed a weight on him that would never come off.

"You've got to stop denying yourself the things you want," he said, his voice light as air. "You made some bad mistakes in the past, and you weren't a good person for a long time. But you've done nothing but good work for Wilson, and for Marla at the club. You're not doing anything wrong, and you're still treating yourself like a felon." He looked over at me. "I know you're scared you'll screw up again, and yeah, you might. But John can handle it. He's solid and powerful and just inherently *good*, and you deserve that. You need it."

"I don't get to have needs anymore," I said, clinging fitfully to my notions of right and wrong.

"You can't divorce yourself from basic human nature," Lawrence said, standing up. "You can't ignore away the hunger. You think it's gone, but it's there, just buried. You should let yourself give in to it."

He faded into the darkness, and I sat there shivering, my body's instinct taking over to prevent me from getting a chill.

I wondered what would happen if I followed my other instincts. If my brain was truly fit to rule, or if it had been what was holding me back this entire time.

Lawrence

I landed in Wellington, feeling jet-lagged and utterly scrambled, like I'd sustained a concussion. My balance was even affected. I couldn't walk straight, couldn't see straight. Basic human functions were lost to me after Elaine's confession.

It changed nothing. It wasn't like she'd come at me with a kid. I wasn't on the hook for child support or dad duty. But everything was different now. It colored this whole past year in a different shade.

It was utterly my fault. I placed the blame solely on myself for putting her in that situation. I had always been careful. You couldn't live the lifestyle I used to live and *not* be careful, unless you wanted to go through a paternity test every other week. I wasn't careful one time, and that single moment of carelessness changed Elaine's life forever.

There was nothing I could do. I had to just move on and hope she could do the same. I drove underneath the palm trees, remembering the first time I'd entered these prestigious grounds in my rusty truck with Eloise in tow, gleeful and grinning at the wheel. All the while, Elaine had been carrying my child.

I shook off the thought and went looking for Erica. Fortunately, her horse was easy to spot. Big as a barn, he stood at least two full hands taller than the polo ponies milling around. I walked toward them, and she dismounted, throwing her arms around me. I held onto her tightly, breathing in the scent of her neck and letting it restore some of my sanity.

"Do you like your present?" I asked, stepping back to look at her.

"It's the best thing you could've done," Erica said, beaming at D.M. "I can't believe you would go to that much trouble."

"Well I couldn't leave you without a horse," I said, grinning. "Not in Wellington, Florida, for fuck's sake." I walked around, taking in D.M.'s condition and steady demeanor. "He looks like he's settled in quite well."

"D.M.'s right at home anywhere he goes," Erica said. "What's difficult is putting the muscle back on him."

I followed her gaze, putting my hands on D.M. and feeling the soft layer of flab with my hands. His hindquarters had shrunk visibly, and his chest jiggled when I touched it. He had developed the horsey equivalent of a beer gut in his downtime.

Erica's mouth formed a thin line. "It's not pretty," she said, reading my mind.

"No, it's not," I agreed. "But it can be fixed."

I swung onto D.M.'s broad back, adjusting to the feel of a large horse under me. I walked him out to the fields with Erica trailing behind.

"This is why I arranged to have him stabled here and not at the show barn," I said, urging D.M. into a ground-covering walk that hustled. "You can't effectively condition a horse in those places. You need room to move."

With Erica's eyes absorbing everything I did, I rode D.M. through the simple, measured drills of speed and rest, long trots interspersed with walk breaks. When he was warmed up, I moved him up to a canter, asking for speed in short bursts and dropping back to a walk in between. D.M. huffed beneath me, sweat staining his coat, but I pushed him on, knowing he had to stretch himself. There was a certain heartlessness required in the early stages of conditioning, which was why I'd chosen to get in the saddle.

If there was one thing about D.M., it was that he had endless drive. He struggled, but he never said "no".

I patted him, pulling him up and dismounting, walking him on foot for what would undoubtedly be a lengthy cooldown. He looked like a wilted flower, wet and bedraggled all the way to his drooping ears. I caught Erica's worried eye as I walked past her.

"He can do this," I said. "It's tough, but you've got to believe in him a little more. You've got to push him. He can't stay like this. If he's going to be an athlete, you have to treat him like one."

I turned back to D.M., feeling his chest for heat, listening to his breathing with a well-tuned ear, his large presence grounding me and leaving me wondering what might've become of me if I hadn't wandered into that stable so many years ago.

Erica

D.M. labored beneath me, his large ears hooked backward in concentration and slight discomfort. His life had become a continuous stretch of interval training, and I knew he probably longed for the days when he had sat idle. Every day without fail I tacked him up and took him out to the fields. We started out slow and easy, with two-minute trot sets followed by two minutes of walking, and we built up to short breezes at a hand gallop.

There was nothing fun about this. We weren't skipping around jump courses or trotting poles. It didn't have the grace or the mental stimulation of dressage. This was pure, aerobic exercise, the equivalent of a person on a treadmill. A means to an end, a necessary evil performed with a stiff upper lip and not a hint of a smile.

Fresh from my stint with Assault, I rode in a defensive posture, holding my breath whenever I asked D.M. to pick up the pace. Subconsciously, I expected him to rebel. But D.M. knew only the value of honest work, and he plugged away, never looking for an easy way out even though his muscles undoubtedly ached.

It was the draft horse in D.M. that kept him going through the hard spots, when the sensitive Thoroughbred in him would have liked to shut down. He toiled away like a draft horse working in the fields or on the logging trails, and I marveled at the irony in play. It was the lesser half of his lineage, responsible for so many of his problems, but in the end, the cold-blooded, steady, determined draft horse in D.M. might be what would get him through.

Over D.M.'s rapid breathing, I could hear a quick patter of hoof beats. Lawrence appeared at my side on Harry. Short, lean, and quick as a whip, Harry kept up easily with D.M.'s generous stride.

"D.M. hates these drills," I said, raising my voice over the thud of both horses on the grass.

"He'll learn to love them," Lawrence said, eyes trained ahead. "It's what

I do with my polo ponies to get them fit and dangerous. He's got to be fitter than he ever has been if he's going to perform at the maximum capacity."

"I just wonder if it's fair to him," I said, looking down at his shoulders, pumping away in time with his stride. "All this misery. What if I'm just fitting a square peg in a round hole like I always do?"

"Look, I've seen you work him over fences," Lawrence said, checking Harry before he could overtake D.M. and make conversation difficult. "He can jump great. He's got the ability, and the will to please. But his reaction time has got to be quicker. That's what this is about. To truly get him fit, it's not just about making sure he can get around the ring without breaking out in a flop sweat. It's about shaving every ounce of spare fat off him and replacing it with hard muscle. You want him leaner, faster, stronger. Carve him down to his essence. *Then* you'll see what kind of horse you're dealing with."

I checked my watch, allowing D.M. a walk break. Lawrence pulled Harry up too and looked at me.

"And yeah, you might get to the end and realize that he just doesn't have it, and he never will. It's a possibility. But with Assault laid up, why not take the chance? Why not exhaust every option and see if you can make the Grand Prix with D.M.?"

I nodded. "I always did wonder. I believed in him so much, and it took us so far. Farther than I ever expected."

"Believe in him a little more, and see where it takes you," Lawrence said, easing Harry forward and letting him cruise, until they disappeared around a bend and left me alone with my thoughts.

I touched D.M. with my heels, letting myself relax, knowing he would be there for me. A little sigh moved through him, and he stepped forward, his body looser. I realized I'd been holding him back, and I gave him the reins and urged him on, looking between his newly-pricked ears.

Elaine

A few days after Lawrence left, John arrived in precisely the same spot, walking through the dusk. I had expected it, and I had prepared myself mentally, cauterizing every inch of me so nothing would break open.

The only thing I couldn't know was if Lawrence had reported back to John, and how much detail his report had contained. I didn't imagine he would tell John about the baby, but I wasn't in the habit of trusting people, so I took nothing for granted.

John halted some distance away from me, measurably beyond the usual two or three feet of space that was standard in a conversation between acquaintances. I took notice of this but assigned no meaning to it.

"Didn't Cavanaugh give you the answers you wanted?" I asked him, my voice haughty. "Have you come here yourself to shake them out of me?"

John shook his head, shame spreading on his face. "I came only to tell you that I am done interfering. After tonight, I will never question you again, or argue my case to you."

Just like that, he disassembled my carefully prepared façade. "I don't understand," I said, drawing a breath.

John looked at me, his eyes and face old. "I should never have sent Cavanaugh here, questioned Delaware about you, or any of the things I've done. I was foolish, and I got carried away. I let my need for you take over and render me senseless. But it is not right for me to carry on this way when you have told me many times over that you do not wish to be with me. It is time for me to respect that."

I stood there gulping air like a fish, feeling a surge of emotions slam into me, powerful as an oncoming train.

"It was wrong for me to push for this when you were clearly not ready. I was arrogant, blinded by desire, and I thought I could make you come around. That is not what a man does. That is not respectable behavior. I'm truly sorry for it, and it ends today."

"What?" My voice whispered, a ghostly sliver of sound that barely reached his ears.

"You won't see me again," John said, and he turned away, long strides carrying him away from me. His absence brought no relief, only a cold harshness I hadn't felt since those long days lying on the pavement, my brittle bones throbbing as I forgot how to execute every basic human function.

I'd really only remembered enough to just barely survive. I wasn't actually living.

Erica

I descended upon the 7-Eleven, eschewing the soda fountain and letting my elbows rest on the counter. Kurt saw me and abandoned his project, organizing the scratch-off tickets. He walked over, an amiable grin on his face.

"I haven't seen you around these parts in a while," he said, his voice perhaps the slightest bit suggestive. I dismissed the notion immediately. I'd been living with Lawrence for too long, and I was obviously projecting his inborn traits onto every guy I talked to.

"I know," I lamented. "I got a new horse. Well, not a new horse. A different horse. My old horse, actually. My boyfriend had him shipped here," I added after a slight pause, realizing this was the first time I'd used the *boyfriend* bomb around Kurt.

He didn't bat an eye. "That was considerate of him," Kurt said. "He must know it's important to you."

What had I expected? Jealousy? For him to tell me it *wasn't* a nice gesture? I rolled my eyes at myself inwardly and returned to the conversation. "We have so much ground to make up. I took him to one show this spring, and then I barely rode him all summer. Now I have to get him in shape and see if we can even make the Grand Prix."

"Why did you choose the other horse over this one?" Kurt asked.

"He was more suited to the sport," I said. "Well, physically, he was more suited. He had talent. Mentally, he was an accident waiting to happen."

"Which is more important?" Kurt asked. "Physical or mental aptitude?"

I considered the answer carefully before responding. It was a question I'd asked myself many times over.

"Both can make or break you," I said, flexing my knuckles as I looked down at my hands. "I don't think you can have one without the other. I think you need a balance."

"The horse you're working with now," Kurt began. "Does he have a balance?"

"I don't know," I said. "But I'll give him every chance to prove it to me."

Lawrence

The three girls rode in front of me on the field, crisscrossing and circling each other. At times, they appeared as if they would crash head-on, but the ponies seamlessly parted ways, coming around to meet each other once again. There was such an established rhythm between these ponies and riders, an effortless flow and pacing to their workouts. They moved amongst each other like old friends, secure in their own space and also willing to share it.

I'd been wanting to discuss strategy with them, but there were always a few railbirds lurking around who couldn't be privy to that information. Mostly, their eyes were trained on Delaware, our secret weapon. Between her brilliant performance at our exhibition and her budding romance with Facundo Alvarez, she'd jetted her way into becoming the talk of the IPC.

Today, the sidelines were empty, except for Dougie, playing with his zoom lens as he waited for us to finish warming up.

"We need to talk about our strategy going into our first game," I said, pulling Harry up. "Specifically, the strategy I believe we should employ."

"We have been working on our strategy this entire time," Yvette pointed out. "Honing our team until it is an unbeatable force."

"Well, yeah, our ultimate strategy is to make Team Dark Horse as strong as it can be," I relented. "But there's another piece of the puzzle we haven't worked in yet."

"And what is that?" Yvette asked trimly.

"One word. Fouls." I shifted Harry over with my leg, keeping his feet moving so he would stay happy. "If there's one thing that really chaps my ass, it's fouls. When you foul the other team, they get a clear shot at goal. And when they have a clear shot at goal, they don't often miss."

"They miss more than you might think," Yvette said. "I have witnessed players the likes of Alvarez miss a penalty shot. It is always comical."

"Well, be that as it may, I'd rather not leave it up to chance." I took Harry up to a slow canter. "If you don't foul people, they don't get penalty shots. If they don't get penalty shots, they don't get free points."

"Yeah, but isn't it, like, *really* hard not to foul people in a sport like this?" Delaware cut in.

"It's a consequence of the game," Courtney agreed. "It's fast and it's brutal. Fouls happen. It's almost impossible to avoid them."

"*Almost* impossible," I said. "Look back at my game footage. Any game will do. Do you see me fouling anyone?"

"You say that like it is easy," Yvette countered. "I suppose you also think it is easy to keep a ball off the ground for half the length of the field."

I looked at her in surprise. "Was that almost a compliment I just heard?"

"You are scum," Yvette said daintily, "and you will always be scum in my eyes. Just as you will always be a top-notch player."

"Well, thanks, Yvette. That was touching." I looked back at the three women. "Anyway, avoiding fouls. Simple, not easy. You've got to raise your awareness. Open your field of vision. Don't get too focused on one thing. You've got to disassociate your mind from the pursuit of the ball, and look everywhere at once. You've got to be *everywhere*."

"Wow," Delaware said, tugging the elastic on her ponytail. "Talk about easier said than done."

"We've got to practice with a full field of ponies," I said. "Fortunately, the fields get more crowded the closer we get to the season opener."

"The top players will keep their distance," Yvette said. "They will not want to show their cards, so to speak. Getting them on a field with us will not be easy."

I glanced at Delaware, sitting up tall on her pony, long chestnut hair falling down her spine, her eyes warm and hospitable. "I can think of one way we might draw them in," I said.

Dougie

The heavy camera banged against my chest as I walked, the thick strap gradually cutting into the back of my neck. The practice was winding down, and I was eager to get out of the hot sun and into Courtney's bed. Inevitably, we spent our afternoons there, snuggled up under the blankets with the AC cranked, turning the room into an icebox.

The ponies were walking with their reins draped carelessly over their shoulders, a sure sign that the practice was over. I made an attempt to slip away, eyes on my phone to make it look like I was working, when I was actually getting in a quick round of *Night Of The Gummies*.

I saw Lawrence's head swivel in my direction. Quick as night, he kicked Harry up into a canter. Aided by his horse's speed, he overtook me in seconds.

"Where are you running off to?" Lawrence asked, stopping Harry just short of running into me.

"I need to go input these files," I said confidently. Usually, if I hit him with a bunch of jargon, that did the trick.

"Mmm hmm," Lawrence said, eyeing me. "Yvette tells me your page updates haven't been as frequent in recent weeks."

"That's because Team Dark Horse is becoming more established. People watch and wait for our content."

"They shouldn't have to wait for it," Lawrence said, pivoting Harry on his hindquarters. "That's why you're here. To provide them with a steady stream of content. Remember that," he added semi-threateningly, and galloped Harry back into the group.

I sighed, trudging up to my room and setting up my Macbook. I imported the files and started fucking with them, wishing I was doing anything but.

I'd made good progress and was starting to get back in the rhythm when there was a hurried knock on the door. I popped out of my chair and opened it, glad for the interruption.

Courtney stood before me, still wearing her uniform, her hair taken out of its ponytail, shimmering around her face. It made me want to grab my camera and take a candid, but mostly it made me want to throw her on the bed and lose myself in the taste of her.

"What did Lawrence say to you?" Courtney asked worriedly. "I saw him ride over to you when we were done."

I shrugged. "Oh, he made a lot of threatening noises about how if I don't step it up with my updates, he'll get rid of me, or something."

Courtney stared at me. "Do you think he *knows*?"

"He has no idea," I said. "He probably just thinks I'm playing *Night Of The Gummies* all the time instead of working."

"Is that a real game?" Courtney asked, scrunching up her nose.

"Unfortunately, yes," I said.

"Okay, well, I guess I should leave," Courtney said.

I looked at her. "Why?"

"So I won't distract you and you won't get fired," Courtney said, her voice in that higher pitch it climbed to when she got nervous.

"Oh, fuck that," I said, holding her face in my hands and kissing her.

"What about Lawrence?" Courtney asked, her voice slightly muffled, as I gently steered her to the bed.

"Let him fire me," I said, fiddling with her belt and peeling off her breeches. "He doesn't pay me anything anyway."

Courtney lay back, sighing in contentment. "I suppose if he did fire you, I could just use Daddy's credit card to pay for your room."

"Do me a favor, Court, and don't talk about your Daddy right now," I said, the last word muffled as my tongue settled into her flesh.

Erica

D.M. flattened out over the gently sloping terrain of the fields, steamrolling over the parched grass, his shoulders and neck foaming up with every stride. He'd figured out the game of interval training, and he pushed himself to the maximum each time, knowing there was a break in store for him. If nothing else, this system was melting the fat off him. D.M.

was actually a relatively hard keeper. His metabolism took a leaf out of the Thoroughbred book, and I'd already had to increase his grain to account for these pounding workouts under the Florida sun.

As the training went on, the intervals would increase and the breaks would decrease, contributing to an increase of both speed and stamina. It seemed like overkill, but there was no sense in turning back now. If D.M. needed to be fit enough for a 7-minute polo chukker to succeed in Grand Prix jumping, I would faithfully follow this system to the bitter end.

D.M. motored up a small hill, abandoning his efficient gallop for a lurching scramble, clawing his way up with his front end. The tail end of our sessions were always the hardest for me to sit through. D.M. started out with so much energy, and the training slowly sapped the life out of him until he felt like he had the first time I'd ridden him in Florida. An ungainly, trembling mess.

I stopped him and slid off, landing with my knees bent. I walked him the long way back to the stable, knowing he'd be cool by the time we got there.

I parked him in the cross ties and stripped off his tack, picking up his feet and stretching his legs, feeling his muscles for tender spots. D.M. was stoic, and he never gave much of a reaction. He wasn't the type to pin his ears or swing his head around with bared teeth. About all he gave was a twitch of his shoulder muscles, and when that happened, I made careful note of it.

The aftercare almost exceeded the time spent under saddle. I was logging many hours spent with D.M. in the barn aisle, massaging tight spots and grooming him with care, applying a concoction of liniments containing herbs and cooling menthol to his legs and large muscle groups. Finally, when I put him away, I had to tend to Assault.

It was inconvenient having two horses stabled in two different places, but it made things easier in one way. During the hours I spent pampering and polishing D.M., I didn't have Assault's hateful glare on me while he sat in a stall, increasingly scruffy and unloved.

I felt the inevitable shame and guilt whenever I went to see the gelding, giving him a quick once-over and refilling his hay net. But I still turned away from his face and walked out as soon as my cursory check was done.

Delaware

I knew what time Facundo's team normally practiced because that was the time of day when his steady flow of text messages would stop coming in. So, I had Vegas saddled up at the right time, and I rode to the stick and balling field.

Facundo and his teammates were all out there, just getting started. I rode nonchalantly onto the field, seeing them scatter and come to a halt as soon as they spotted me. Facundo rode over to me, his face both pleased and wary.

"What are you doing here, my one and only?" He asked sweetly, leaning over from his saddle to plant a kiss on me.

"I'm extending an offer," I said, giving him a little peck on the lips. "We'd like to share a practice with you guys. We feel it would be a good experience to work with a full field in preparation for our first competition." I smiled at him.

Facundo's teammates seemed to noticeably bristle at the suggestion that they share the field. Facundo reacted more reasonably, but even he boarded up a bit, glancing back at his compatriots and noting their lack of goodwill.

"You know I would do anything for you," Facundo said, rallying to try and save face with both me and his teammates in one fell swoop. "But I'm afraid this sort of field-sharing just isn't done around here."

"Oh, I know," I interrupted, waving a hand. "You guys have to keep your secrets close at hand; you can't give up your strategy, blah blah blah."

"So you do understand," Javier said, pleasantly surprised.

"Oh, absolutely," I said, picking up the reins. Vegas prepared to move off, and I held him back for a moment. "We have our secrets, too. And our secrets are a lot more secretive than yours, considering we've never had a televised game or anything. But if you guys would rather not get an inside peek at what we're made of, I guess you can just wait until we meet in competition. You'll find out for sure then."

I fed Vegas a length of rein and gave him a touch of leg. He cantered away, leaving Facundo and his team to watch my back as it drifted further away, and to consider their next move.

Yvette

I lingered at the 7th Chukker bar, waiting to order some sherry. It was crowded, crawling with people, a good number of whom were larger and louder than I was. Staring at the bobbing, shoving mass of people standing between the alcohol, and me, I hungered for a drink even more than when I had first set foot in this place.

I edged my way through to the front of the line, elbows out protectively. Should anyone threaten my hard-fought space, they would soon experience a sharp and unpleasant jab to the ribs.

"Your finest sherry," I said to the bartender, a guy with a scruffy beard and sandy hair falling in soft curls.

"Sweet or dry?" He asked, reaching for a bottle.

"Very dry," I said.

He poured me a glass, flexing his wrist. I was about to tell him to put it on John's tab when someone slapped a Gold card down in front of me.

"I've got it," said a polished voice with a Spanish accent.

I turned my head to see Javier, wearing pressed jeans and a tan cashmere sweater with a deep V-neck. A gold chain caressed his hairless chest. He stood directly behind me, so close he nearly pushed me into the bar.

"I do not need you to buy me a drink," I said, turning my back on him and taking my glass.

"I do not see Silva anywhere in this bar," Javier said, following me through the crowd, his breath on my neck.

"I have many ways of attaining alcohol," I said, cutting away from the throng of bar goers and sipping my sherry in the corner.

"Do they involve sexual favors?" Javier asked me, his voice low and his pelvis tilted inward, facing me.

I peered up at him coolly, taking more of the liquid into my mouth. "So you liked what you got, then."

"That much was obvious," Javier said primly, folding his arms over his bulky chest.

"I do enjoy how I can demolish your stamina," I said, licking the rim of the glass where a few droplets clung to it. "You revert to an inexperienced teenager when you are in my mouth."

"I wish you would let me fuck you," Javier murmured, moving behind me, pressing himself against my ass and holding my hips in his broad hands. I considered shrugging him off, but I wanted to get his hopes up before I did so.

"Have Facundo and the rest of your team given any thought to our proposition?" I asked him, remaining still.

"Your proposition?" He rumbled, still deep within the throes of lust.

"Sharing a field," I said, putting a stop to this nonsense.

"It is an intriguing offer," Javier said. "Admittedly, I would enjoy it myself. I believe Alvarez wishes to make it a reality as well."

"What about the other two?" I asked.

Javier frowned. "They are not on board."

"Get them on board," I said. "And perhaps I will warm up to the possibility of sharing your bed again."

"I am sure you are already warm for me," Javier said, leaning over, his breath tickling my ear. "If I touched you, I would find out."

"Touch me once, and I'll snap your wrist," I said, downing the rest of my drink. "*Get them on board.*"

Erica

I traveled the aisles of the supermarket, quietly resenting the fact that I was pushing a shopping cart. It always made me feel prematurely old and matronly, much like the first time someone called me "Ma'am", an entirely unpleasant milestone, which, incidentally, also occurred in a grocery store.

I had to pick up a few essentials, but I skirted the produce section in favor of the inner aisles. I only needed a couple things: Cookies 'n Cream Crunch, and feminine products. The hotel supplied me with almost everything I needed, but it fell flat in both cereal selection and availability of tampons.

I moved down the cereal aisle, picking up a black-and-white themed box of Cookies 'n Cream Crunch and setting it in my cart. I cut through the spices aisle, rather than taking the long way around, and I spotted a familiar face that made me grin. I was also very glad that my cart did not yet contain a Tampax box.

"Kurt!" I said, giving him a wave. He smiled at me, abandoning his perusing of the Italian seasonings.

"Erica. Hey." He spontaneously went in for a hug, and I let him, noting how my head fit in over his shoulder and how warm his body was.

"They finally let you out of work," I said, stepping back to look at him. "Or do you work here too?"

He hung his head, slightly embarrassed. "No, it's my day off. I have no food in my house, so I came here to pick up a few things for dinner."

I glanced in his cart, even though it was rude of me to do so. It was piled high with fresh produce, herbs, and mozzarella, not the shredded kind in the bag, but the fancy kind that you have to shred yourself.

I looked up at him in surprise. "Looks like more than a few things."

"Well, when I do it, I do it big," he said, reaching for a pepper grinder.

"It looks like you've got enough here to feed a family of four," I commented.

Kurt shrugged. "Yeah, it's a lot of effort to go through just to feed myself. Then again, I do end up with enough leftovers to last me a week straight." Now he looked in my cart. "What have you got there? *Cereal*?"

"*Hey*," I said, laughing, "I live in a four-star hotel. I order room service every meal of the day. They just happen to have a poor selection of cereal."

"The perks of having a polo star for a boyfriend," Kurt said, smiling. "I would feed you just as well, though," he added, with just a hint of a challenge in his eyes.

I grinned at him. "I'd say 'prove it', but then you'd have to make me dinner."

Team Dark Horse

"I wouldn't mind that," Kurt said, steering his cart away. I hurried down the aisle.

"Really?" I asked, my interest unmistakably piqued.

Kurt shrugged. "Sure. I'm going straight home after I check out to get started on dinner. You can follow me if you want. I drive a vintage Ford Ranger," he said, turning into a checkout line. "It's very blue."

I stumbled into a line, making my singular purchase and keeping an eye on Kurt's progress. He was still a ways off from making it out the door, so I went back and bought tampons on the stealth, hiding them in a paper bag.

When I came out, the old Ranger was idling near the exit door. It was, indeed, very blue. I jumped in my F-150 and followed the turquoise-and-chrome Ranger out of the parking lot.

We drove to a nearby cul-de-sac, side-by-side duplexes in neutral colors with small, well-maintained yards. Some were better decorated than others, with flowers growing in elaborate planters. Kurt turned into the driveway of a pale grey house, parking off to one side and shutting off his motor. I pulled in beside him.

He unlocked the door, carrying in the groceries and setting them on the counter. His kitchen was immaculate, with a gleaming range and countertops and a center island that looked like it had been built by hand.

"Have a seat," Kurt said, nodding to the living room that adjoined the kitchen. "Put some music on if you want."

I went in and sat down on a cushy leather couch, noting the strange progression of our relationship. When we began, we had only interacted with a counter between us, and now I was inside his house.

I selected a classic rock station on Pandora and leaned my head back. It was nice to be in someone's home again. I'd grown weary of hotel rooms, particularly when my only company consisted of 500 channels on cable TV.

I heard the quiet sizzle of oil warming up in a pan. Kurt appeared in the doorway, holding a chef's knife and still managing to look endearing. "Can I get you anything to drink? I have bourbon, whiskey…"

"I'll rummage through your cupboards," I said, standing up and moving into the kitchen.

"Right on." He grinned at me, returning to the cutting board where he was dicing up some onions.

I looked through the liquor cabinet, selecting a bottle and pouring myself a glass. With admirable precision, Kurt had set up an assembly line of ingredients. With all four burners firing, he stirred, flipped, and tasted things, setting out plates and ladling carefully proportioned servings into them.

"Wow," I said, watching him in slight awe. "You're like a professional at this."

Kurt glanced at me. "Well, I certainly don't intend on working at the 7-Eleven forever," he said, applying a final garnish of mint leaves. "Actually, I'm saving to open a restaurant. That's the goal. My five-year plan."

"You sure have the talent for it," I said, nodding approvingly.

"Taste it," Kurt said, nodding at my plate.

I took a bite, and it confirmed my suspicions. It was complex, light, and decadent. It put room service to shame, that was for sure.

"It's good," I said, nodding and putting some more into my mouth.

We lingered in the kitchen, eating over the countertop and listening to Kurt's laptop play. With the warm burn of the liquor in my throat, I found myself looking at Kurt in a different way. He wasn't showy, but there was something about him that commanded attention.

As the night wore on, and I ate a good bit of the food that would've otherwise kept Kurt fed throughout his work week, I wondered what exactly he had in mind for the evening. I never really forgot about Lawrence when I was hanging out with Kurt; I just didn't think about him. I wondered if Kurt thought I was willing to forget about him entirely.

He cleared the plates and did the dishes while I sat there, the alcohol wearing off and my anxiety kicking in. When the water stopped running and he appeared in the doorway, I braced myself.

"So, I should probably get going," I said, standing up, my hands twitchy and my face slightly flushed.

Kurt nodded. He didn't appear disappointed. "I figured you needed to get home. Thanks for having dinner with me, though," he said, coming over to where I stood, my flustered legs rooted to the ground. "I like when you keep me company."

He put his arms around me again, and though he didn't kiss me, this hug was both slower and more deliberate. Just as I felt confident that I knew the feel of him, he stepped back, allowing me some distance and a clear path to the door.

I found I didn't want to leave.

Lawrence

All around the pool, the tiki torches were lit, their glow reminding me of bar lighting. A great number of the people gathered around held cocktails, contributing to the drunken atmosphere. Delaware was bobbing around in the turquoise water, wearing a red sequined bikini, her arms and legs wrapped around Alvarez. He whispered in her ear, undoubtedly trying to convince her that they should get out here. I was sure she was making him sweat.

Yvette was in a lawn chair with her usual scowl and a tall glass of sherry. Her thorny demeanor earned her an ample dose of personal space. The partygoers fanned out around her like a wave, and she sat in contentment, exchanging small talk with no one.

Courtney, I suspected, was in her room, lost in the throes of Britney, the soundtrack to her life. What interested me more was where Dougie had run off to. Normally, he would be in the shadows, at least snapping a few candids before hightailing it out of the party. But he was nowhere to be found. Perhaps it was time to step up my threats and get to the bottom of what was causing these long absences.

The complimentary drinks at this party were the same as always, frothy, beachy cocktails popular with the wealthy polo set around here. I could never stomach them, so inevitably, I was the most sober person at these get-togethers. Alvarez's teammate, Javier, sipped the girlie drinks at will, but he also waxed the hair off his chest, so we didn't really see eye to eye on much of anything.

A chic redhead in a sarong and a midnight blue one-piece with a cutout that exposed her cleavage came sauntering out of the crowd. Her red hair and dark blue eyes made her look like a doll, or a mercilessly retouched fashion model in an ad. She was one of my notable conquests from my first season in Wellington. The wife of an oil baron who sponsored many of the top players, she did her share of playing the field, and they seemed to have an agreement that he would look the other way.

Like many of the women here, she specialized in 9- to 10-goal players. There was a certain status symbol associated with bedding a top player. It was just another game people played around here.

"Rebecca," I said, giving her a one-armed hug. "Glad to see you're still in fine form."

She smiled, her cobalt eyes on me. "I could say the same to you."

The light from the nearest tiki torch collected in her cleavage, and she popped her chest out to emphasize the smooth, round fullness of her breasts. Like any good trophy wife, she knew exactly how to work the lighting.

"Giving it another try with a brand-new team," she said, her eyes taking in Yvette and Delaware. "I bet no one is asking you if you're comfortable working with women."

"I make it work," I shrugged, grinning comically.

"I do need you to address a particularly disturbing rumor I've heard," she said, keeping her eyes on me.

I rolled my eyes. "Are they *still* saying that I fuck horses?"

"Specifically, they were talking about Eloise. But no, I haven't heard that one in a while." She reached out, her fingers clasping the stem of a martini glass from a tray as it headed past her. "I heard you're shacked up. Settled down with some girl."

"That one's true," I said. "It's been over a year now."

"Get out of here." Rebecca gave me a sharp stare, her delicate eyebrows arching. "Since when do you do monogamy?"

"Since I found the right woman," I said confidently, causing her to take a step back.

"That just doesn't seem like you," Rebecca said, crossing her arms in front of her. "You really think this is right for you?"

"I have no complaints so far," I said, pulling up a chair and putting my feet up. "I think I wanted that for a long time and just didn't realize it. Once I did, though...there was no going back."

"Relationships aren't as easy as you think," Rebecca said, resting her butt on the arm of my chair, letting me feel the firmness of her cheek as it slid against my hand. "You might think that you'll never want anyone else, but time changes that. Things can get pretty grim after a few years of staring at the same person. Things you didn't notice in the beginning can jump out at you, as loud as a foghorn. You start to hate them for simple things, even the way they chew their food or breathe."

"Sounds like *your* relationship is pretty rocky," I said, resting my hands behind my head. "My relationship is fine."

"You don't know what you're getting into," Rebecca said, shaking her head. Her cobalt eyes drifted up and down my body as her hand slipped to my thigh. I was reminded of what Marla had said. *You just have that effect on women.*

"Regardless," I said, standing up and leaving her teetering on the arm of an empty chair, "I'm not getting into you."

I walked back to the hotel in the nightfall, eager to find Erica. When I got to our room, her shape wasn't in the bed. I settled in under the covers anyway, but I didn't fall asleep. I heard the swipe of a key card a few minutes later.

"Where were you?" I asked, sitting up in bed, the sheet sliding down my torso.

"I was having dinner," Erica said, setting her keys on the night table as she undressed with her back to me.

"I thought you usually get room service," I said, watching her as more and more flesh was uncovered.

"Sometimes, I don't feel like sitting alone in here," Erica said. She slipped beneath the covers, facing away. "Sometimes, I want more than that."

I rolled over to her, gently taking hold of her thigh, while my other hand gripped her waist.

I heard her sigh. "Can we skip it tonight? I'm pretty tired."

"Sure," I said, even though I couldn't remember a time when she'd turned me down, and it came as more than a slight shock to my system.

"We'll just do this," I said, and I snuggled up to her back, drifting off into sleep with ease even though I hadn't achieved release, owing it all to the smell of her and the comforting weight of her body in my arms.

Some time later, my phone buzzed, and I held it up, my eyes squinting blearily to read the incoming text message.

We will join you tomorrow morning at 6, it read. *No cameras. No spectators. Just my team and yours.*

Sender: Alvarez

Courtney

In the early morning mist, we rode onto the field, our ponies moving shoulder to shoulder in a neat formation, their hooves moisturized by the dew clinging to the short stems of grass. Any railbirds that would have normally gathered here were absent, sleeping off last night's overabundance of mango cocktails.

Alvarez and Javier sat on their ponies, shoulders erect, eyes forward. They were joined by Romero and Ruiz, and the four of them eyed us suspiciously, carrying visible tension in their necks and upper bodies as they rode forward to say hello.

"Are we alone here?" Ruiz asked haughtily, pulling up his pony harshly, so the animal raised its head, opening its mouth to relieve the pressure. Hermione's eyes widened in alarm.

"I'm capable of reading and comprehending simple instructions," Lawrence said, the hint of a bristle in his voice. "I followed them to the letter."

"All the same," Ruiz said, turning his pony away. "One cannot be too careful."

Javier stared at Yvette, trying to get her to acknowledge him. As usual, she looked the other way, and he sat in disgruntled silence, a frown punctuating his smooth, chiseled face.

"Morning, Facundo," Delaware said sweetly, giving him a lingering, doe-eyed stare.

"It is a good morning," Facundo affirmed. "It was even better half an hour ago."

The two of them grinned sickeningly at each other, while the rest of us shifted uncomfortably in our saddles, trying to act like we hadn't just heard things that undoubtedly alluded to morning sex.

"Can we get started?" Lawrence asked in a voice that was surprisingly snappish.

"We will be happy to," Facundo said, and his team fanned out. Team Dark Horse followed suit as a waiting groom threw in the ball, rolling it precisely down the center of the field.

Snapping to attention, we raised our sticks, and our ponies picked up the pace, shooting furtive glances at each-other, loathe to be the last one standing once the charge ensued.

Delaware sat lightly on Vegas, her eyes front and center, deadly serious. She was the one who would benefit most from this joint practice. I knew that was why Lawrence had lobbied so hard for it. She needed the chance to work with a full field of ponies, to learn what she was up against. I knew once she started playing against Alvarez and his team, our practices would seem like child's play in comparison. These men played rough, and they weren't about to spare her. Even Alvarez's face was set, and he passed her like she wasn't there.

Welcome to high-stakes polo, I thought. Yvette glanced at Delaware, watching for her reaction.

Delaware picked up the reins, and I sensed what she was about to do. Without pausing for Alvarez to build up speed, she kicked Vegas into a gallop, capturing the ball and taking charge of the game. Grinning maniacally, Yvette hurried to back her up, fending off Javier with a handy block. Lawrence accelerated up the field on offense, while I moved into defense, feeling Hermione board her body up as she crouched low to the ground, turning herself into an impenetrable wall. Pushing Ruiz off his line, she maintained her defensive position, knocking him further off course.

I heard a solid whack, and I saw Delaware had hit the ball into the goal. Lawrence neatly took possession of it as Facundo came tearing up the field, ready to reclaim it. Evenly matched in skill and determination, they steamrolled down the field, their ponies leaning on each other, shoving and grunting like linemen.

Delaware positioned herself alongside Lawrence, giving him a wide opening to pass the ball to her. Javier took notice, and took chase, barreling down on her, ready to intervene. He pushed himself into her space, and she rode him off expertly, slamming Vegas into his pony's shoulder. Floating the reins, delegating the task of throwing off Javier to Vegas, she scanned the field, her stick at the ready. Lawrence shot the ball to the side, and she collected it, turning the ball and booting Vegas in the side, coaxing a burst of speed out of him. She hit a forehand shot straight into the goal as Javier and Alvarez both stared dumbly at her.

"Brilliant, Delaware!" Lawrence shouted in encouragement, his face animated. She smiled like a beauty queen, but her eyes were sharply focused. Taking aim, she passed the ball, inexplicably, to Alvarez.

"What are you *doing*, Podunk?" Yvette roared as Alvarez hit the ball powerfully forward. "You had the advantage. You gave it up!"

Delaware ignored her, launching Vegas into a gallop, chasing down Alvarez as the rest of us milled around, sort of providing defense while mostly watching to see what would happen.

"She's lost her fucking mind," Yvette muttered, toying with Javier and preventing him from making a move.

"I'm sure she has her reasons," Lawrence said, forever steadfast in his faith in Delaware. "This is a practice, not a live game. She wants to practice all the scenarios."

"But you do not just *pass* the ball to your opponent," Ruiz said in thinly veiled contempt.

Lawrence glanced at him. "You do if they can't get it from you," he said with a smirk.

"Facundo is playing nice because it is his lady on the field," Romero assayed.

"Really?" Lawrence watched the ensuing chase between Delaware and Facundo. "It looks like he's working as hard as he can to keep her from scoring."

Vegas had made up an impressive amount of ground, gaining on

Facundo's sleek black pony with every stride. I watched as Delaware began cutting in on him at an angle, slowly throwing him off his line. They blew past the goal without scoring. The next few crucial seconds would decide who came out on top.

"Any bets?" Lawrence asked, his voice laced with a challenge.

"Delaware will get it," I said.

Yvette's eyes turned on me, and I could tell she didn't agree. She kept her mouth shut for the sake of team unity, but the look on her face was not generous.

"She is out of her depth," Romero stated confidently.

"We'll see about that," I said.

Facundo collected his pony, pausing to take stock of the situation. He had options. Forehand or backhand shot, feint and try to bamboozle Delaware, or simply choose momentum and hope it would be enough to get around her. Delaware watched his every move, poised in the saddle. Vegas' hocks were fully engaged, and his muscles twitched. Both ponies and riders remained on a hair trigger.

Alvarez went for the deception route, feinting to the side and acting like he was about to take a backhand shot. But the strategist in Delaware knew a forehand shot was the most efficient way. She shot out in front just as Facundo changed course and swung his mallet. He saw her, and his eyes widened helplessly. It was too late for him to stop. Pure momentum carried his swing through, and the ball landed next to Vegas' flying hooves. The gelding swung his haunches out, lining her up with the ball, and she picked it up, lightly flicking her wrist to keep it above the turf.

Lawrence sat there grinning like a Cheshire cat as Facundo's teammates abandoned what they were doing and just stared at Delaware, performing the most difficult maneuver in the polo playbook with a smile on her face. Vegas skipped along, maintaining a steady pace, making her job easier, like a good team player.

When she got near enough, she passed the ball to Yvette, who fired it into the goal as an afterthought. No one was really keeping score anymore.

Delaware eased Vegas down to a walk, giving him a well-deserved break. He strutted, almost breaking into a jig, his excitement running over.

"Well done, Podunk," Yvette began, looking almost shame-faced.

Delaware nodded coolly at her, turning in the saddle and seeking out Facundo as he traipsed up the field.

"No hard feelings, I hope?" She asked him, treading carefully where his male ego was concerned like a true Southern belle.

He shook his head, looking at her fondly. "I am unaccustomed to being in this position. It isn't often that I am shown up on the field like I was just now." He shrugged his shoulders. "But you are a true force to be reckoned with on this field. You belong here."

He leaned over in the saddle, kissing her boldly in front of his teammates. Javier's eyes shifted to Yvette, and she shot him down with a flick of her lashes.

"We have some work to do," Facundo said, addressing Ruiz, Romero, and Javier. "Please give us some privacy."

We moved off the field, allowing them their space. We could not rest until our first game. There was work to be done, and we could never be too fast, too versatile. But we left with the sense that we were no longer scrambling from the bottom. We were easing our way up on an increasingly level playing field.

Erica

I walked into the 7-Eleven, my heart palpitating a little. When I saw Kurt in his usual position behind the counter, it palpitated a little more. Kurt had a line of customers to deal with, so I charted a direct course to the Icee machine, keeping my head down.

When the line cleared, I went up to the counter, knees slightly shaky. I wasn't sure how to handle the recent shift in our casual friendship. What had been a safe zone for me, an easy outlet, had become something much more confusing. I cared more now, and I wasn't sure what to make of that.

I set my Icee down on the counter, waiting for him to take the conversational lead.

"Hi, Erica." He scanned my cup like nothing out of the ordinary had taken place. A tightly held breath seeped out of me. Nothing was going on. It was the same as always.

"Last night was fun," I said, because it was true, and I couldn't think of anything else to say.

"It was," Kurt said, his elbows on the counter. "I enjoyed having you over."

"It was really nice of you to cook for me," I said, just full-on blabbering now. "I'm sorry I ate so much of your food, though. I kind of have an issue with portion control. You could have stopped me. I didn't mean to leave you without leftovers."

Kurt's dark eyes remained on me, and a smile graced his mouth. "I would cook for you every day of the week," he said.

"But don't you work a lot?" I asked, continuing with the babbling. There was always more where that came from.

Kurt looked me up and down in a way that managed not to be sleazy, while still being very pointed and deliberate. "I'd make the time," he said.

Delaware

I went up to Facundo's room dressed in my best summer frock, a pink plaid number that cinched in at the waist. It had a low scooped neckline, and I wore a gold locket around my neck. Clutching my handbag, I made my way to the door and knocked lightly.

I hoped he wouldn't be too cross with me after the morning's events. He had seemed okay on the field, but who knew what his teammates had said to him after I left. If they had taunted him all day long about it, his mood might well have taken a turn for the worse by now.

There was a slight rustling around on the other side of the door, and Facundo opened it. He smiled coolly at me, but that was the only acknowledgment he gave.

"Can I come in?" I asked, fanning out my skirt with my hands.

"Of course," he said, stepping aside to let me enter. I realized this was probably his way - polite, reserved, not showing all his cards when he was pissed off. It was a far cry from the screaming, hooting and carrying on that some of my exes were prone to, but it was unsettling all the same.

"Did your friends give you a hard time about being beat by a girl?" I teased, trying to lighten the mood.

"They know better than to question me," Facundo said, his back to the wall. "As the team captain, I am to be respected, not ridiculed."

"Ah," I said, thinking of how Yvette would lay into Lawrence all the time and call him everything from scum to motherfucker, depending on her mood. "Well, that's good they aren't giving you grief about it."

He nodded, pouring himself a drink of tequila. He held the crystalline tumbler in his hand and stared out the window.

"Are you sure you're okay?" I asked, coming up alongside him.

Facundo's dark eyes looked at me for the first time since I'd stepped into the room. "I suppose I was unprepared for the reality of sharing a field with the girl I love. The simplicity of the game is gone for me. I am accustomed to seeing everyone simply as opponents, obstacles in my way. It is different now, with you there. I am not sure I like it."

"You don't have to treat me any differently out there," I said, twisting a lock of hair. "I wasn't exactly easy on you."

"No, you certainly were not," he admitted, the slightest hint of pride in his eyes. "I was impressed, and mortified at the same time."

"We can be brutal competitors on the field," I said. "And once we step off, we can be lovers again."

"I am not sure it is as easy as you make it sound," Facundo said. "But we will have to try."

"Are you upset that I dominated you out there?" I asked. "Are you going to resent me for that?"

Facundo took a step back, considering me, his eyes sweeping from my windblown hair to my form-fitting dress, and finally, to the delicate straps of my wedge sandals.

"Not really," he said, moving up closer. "As long as I can still dominate you in here."

He lifted me up, setting me against the wall as my hands interlaced behind his neck. My legs wrapped around his waist, he supported me with one arm as he reached down, undoing his fly.

"Are you wearing panties?" He whispered in my ear.

"As luck would have it, no." I grinned at him.

He made a low sound in his throat and lifted my skirt up, opening my legs wider to accommodate him. He pushed into me, and I felt myself get wet, the initial friction replaced by the easy glide of our bodies joining. He shoved me gently into the wall, moving in and out of me, listening for the quickening of my breath. When it began, he pulled my hips into his, staying deep inside me and grinding in a slow circular rhythm, until my quick breaths became whimpers and he resumed his earlier urgency, moving quicker and harder, rattling my body against the wall until his face dropped into my neck and he leaned on me, body stilled and quivering.

After giving himself a moment, he lifted me up again, carrying me and laying me on the bed. Moving in beside me, he tucked me into his arms, and we lay like that for a while.

"Do you still wish it were different?" I said. "That we didn't have to share a field?"

"No," Facundo said, holding me to him. "It may be complicated for me, and there will be times when I may find it untenable. But you are worth the inconvenience. You are something different, and I am willing to leave my depth for you."

"I'll still try my best to win," I said.

"As will I," Facundo promised, his face hidden from view, his words both daunting and reassuring.

Courtney

The soles of my Nikes pounding the treadmill, I ran faster to complete my mileage and get back to my room. I could feel the sweat exuding from my pores, and I knew the shower would be my next stop. The machine began my automated cooldown, and I jogged, then walked, until it shut off. I jumped down, picking up my gym bag and getting ready to rinse off.

"Silva! Where are you running to?" Yvette barked, her voice loud and jarring among the quiet hum of machines and running feet.

"I need to hit the shower," I said, fiddling with my bag. It contained a fresh thong, as well as a bra that showed cleavage and didn't mash my boobs into one large, graceless mass.

"Normally, you do not sweat when you run," Yvette said, noting the sheen on my skin. "It appears you are losing condition at a most inopportune time."

"My condition's fine," I said, trying to shake her off. "I was just pushing the pace a little."

"Why?" Yvette demanded, as small and tenacious as a mosquito. "So you can sustain an overexertion injury and leave us fucked right before our season opener?"

"I won't get injured," I whined. "Will you just let me take my shower?"

"That would be a good idea," Yvette said, her mood changing markedly. "And then you will come with us to the 7th Chukker."

"Who is us?" I asked.

"You, myself, and Podunk," Yvette announced. "We are going to eat lunch as a team. Minus Cavanaugh, because he is otherwise involved."

"What is he doing?"

"Giving his pony a fresh clip," Yvette said, rolling her eyes delicately. "Because of course the grooms here are too unskilled and oblivious to wield a set of clippers without slicing the carotid artery."

"Oh, right, his 'no one touches Eloise but me' rule," I said, nodding. "Except now it's Harry."

"Get in the shower," Yvette said, her patience tenuous, as always.

"I was really just planning on going back to my room," I began.

"Of course you were," Yvette said. "But unless you have some pressing engagement going on there that I am not aware of, I see no reason why you cannot attend lunch with your team." Her beady eyes challenged me to contradict her.

It was a challenge I would never take on. "Okay," I conceded, slumping off to the showers. I texted Dougie on the way to let him know I was being held up. He responded with a sad face emoticon. My face was a lot sadder when I emerged from the showers with wet hair and followed Yvette to the 7th Chukker.

Delaware was waiting in a corner booth, and she jumped up like a Labrador, waving enthusiastically at us. I sat down with a thump and buried my face in a menu, even though I wasn't interested in any of the options.

"How did Alvarez take to being bested by you?" Yvette asked Delaware, obviously hoping for an unfavorable outcome. "Did it test your love?"

"Our love is just fine," Delaware said sweetly, taking a sip from her water glass. "Courtney, have you tried the mac and cheese here? It's *so* good."

I shook my head, hiding deeper behind my menu.

"Has anybody seen Dougie today?" Delaware asked, looking around. "I haven't seen him all day."

"I have not," Yvette said, laying her menu open. "But I would not expect to."

"Why?" I said loudly, flying into a complete panic with total disregard for the potential consequences of that action. "Did Lawrence get rid of him? Did you hear something? Is he leaving for good?"

Yvette and Delaware both gave me a slow stare of confusion. "I have heard nothing of the sort," Yvette said, her voice low. "And why would you be so concerned? I was under the impression you did not like Dougie."

"Yeah, is something going on there?" Delaware asked, eyes alight. "Are you hooking up?"

"No!" I denied shakily, feeling more shortness of breath than I'd experienced on the treadmill. "Why would you ask that?"

"Well, you did go out with him once," Delaware explained reasonably. "It wouldn't be all that crazy if you went out with him again."

"But it went terribly the last time you tried it," Yvette said, skimming through the emotions projected on my face. "You probably wouldn't want to go through that again. Unless something changed..."

"Okay, fine," I said, perspiring all over my newly-showered skin. "We are...involved. Me and him."

"Oh my gosh!" Delaware squealed, hugging me from across the table. "That's so great! You guys are so awkward and cute together!"

"Are you fucking?" Yvette wanted to know, blunt as ever.

"Um." I looked down at my lap as Delaware released me, unsure of the phrasing. "Kind of. In a way."

"In *what* way?" Yvette asked pointedly.

"Yeah, how many ways are there even?" Delaware asked.

"More than you know," Yvette shot back at her.

"Well, he doesn't want to have sex with me, because of Lawrence's reputation or whatever." I scrunched down in my seat, wishing this conversation were happening in a more private place. Like my room, or a back corner of the barn, basically anywhere but a busy restaurant during the lunch rush. "He doesn't think he'll measure up."

"He will not," Yvette agreed, arms folded neatly.

"Anyway. So we don't really have sex." I applied pressure to my ribs with one hand in a sort of calming mechanism. "He'll only go down on me."

"Are you serious?" Delaware asked, nearly sliding off the edge of her seat. "That's the best part! How did you get so lucky?"

"Does he make you reciprocate?" Yvette asked with a sort of scientific curiosity, nothing more.

I shook my head. "No. He said he doesn't care."

"Oh, man," Delaware said, shaking her head. "Hang onto this one, Court. In fact, you should probably have a quickie wedding and take his last name. What even is his last name?"

"What's going on here?" Lawrence's voiced asked, and then Lawrence's body slid into the booth next to me. I made wild throat-slashing gestures at Yvette, which she strategically ignored.

"Silva and your PR boy are going at it," she told Lawrence, smiling and showing all her teeth while I buried my face in my hands.

"No shit." Lawrence considered this development. "So that's why he's been slacking. He's putting it to Silva."

"Well, actually…" Yvette's eyebrows curled up deviously.

"What does that mean?" Lawrence asked, suspicious. "Don't tell me they're into some weird shit."

"It's not especially *weird*," Yvette amended. "But it is a little one-sided." She glanced at me as I huddled in my little corner of mortification.

Team Dark Horse

"Courtney?"

"He'll only go down on me," I said, vaguely directing my words at Lawrence, but I was way beyond being able to look him in the eye. "Because of you and your reputation."

"That's bullshit," Lawrence said, standing up with aplomb. "I'm putting a stop to this nonsense."

"No!" Delaware shouted, lunging for him. "You'll ruin it!"

He swept out of the café, and I fumbled for my phone, thinking to give Dougie a heads-up. The screen was black when I picked it up, and no amount of button pressing would reactivate the battery.

"Stupid iPhone 4," I muttered. "Does anyone have a compatible charger?"

Yvette and Delaware held up their outdated flip phones apologetically.

Dougie

A knock sounded on the door. Thinking it was Courtney, fresh from her lunch ordeal and in need of some de-stressing, I flung it open without glancing through the peephole.

"I thought I'd find you here," Lawrence said, handily obliterating my excitement.

"Who told you?" I asked, sitting down on Courtney's bed in defeat.

"Yvette let it slip at lunch just now," Lawrence said, taking a turn about the room. "She's an instigator, but I'm glad she told me, because I'm ending this right now."

"I will walk," I said, standing up. "I'll pay for my own hotel room, and I'll make my own money. If you want to end my arrangement with Team Dark Horse, that's fine. But I'm not leaving Courtney."

"I'm not asking you to do either of those things," Lawrence said, catching me off guard. "I mean, yeah, you could take a break from eating her out now and again and actually slap some content on our pages, but I know firsthand how addicting it is when you start. It's hard to focus on anything else."

"I'll do better with the pages," I promised, hoping against hope to be rid of him. But he kept sauntering around the room in a way that told me he was in no hurry to let me off the hook.

"Oh, I'm not done," Lawrence said, confirming my fears. "So what's this about you not fucking Silva?"

"I'm being safe," I muttered, knowing the avenue of deception wasn't likely to work, but determined to try it anyway.

"Bullshit," said Lawrence. "There are ways to be safe that don't involve abstinence."

"Look," I said, facing him, "we're both happy with how it is. Why do you think you need to meddle in other people's shit all the time? You may be the boss on the field, but it ends there. You don't get to rule our lives."

"The only reason I came over here is because Courtney said you're too intimidated by my reputation to seal the deal with her," Lawrence started in on me again. "And that's bullshit. If Courtney wants you, you should get on that."

I shook my head. "I'm happy with things as they are. And even if I wasn't, I would never let you tell me what to do."

Lawrence cocked an eyebrow. "Except on things involving files."

"Except for that," I said, and I made myself look busy at my computer until he walked out.

Elaine

I made my way through the barn, sweeping cobwebs that weren't there. My eyes searched for any dust grains, but I couldn't find any. I went outside and fired up the riding mower, turning it in slow circles on the lawn out in front. The grass never grew past an inch anymore. The rotating blades were merciless, and sitting atop the loud hub of plastic, turning the wheel hand over hand, so was I.

The months I'd toiled away at this job, giving it my singular focus, had made me so efficient that I was done with chores in half the time. Wilson knew now to look out for the familiar shape of me barging into his office and

Team Dark Horse

demanding tasks to fill my hours. It had begun with scrubbing the walls, and it had progressed to mowing, painting, even landscaping, applying river rock to the borders of the walkways because one of the patrons said it would look nicer that way.

These "extras" filled up my day, keeping me occupied in that limbo between morning and evening chores. Some of the jobs were tedious, requiring painstaking detail, while others consisted of simple grunt work. But when I was finished, I could step back and appreciate the difference it made. My efforts were tangible. They made the place look more beautiful, and as I stood and took it all in, I could take pride in that.

I never stood still for very long. I'd look for a few seconds, and I'd move on to the next thing. By the time I fell into bed after night check, I was so exhausted that I fell into a blank haze of sleep almost immediately.

That was why I did it. I didn't really care about pleasing the patrons, or making a difference. I was still running, even though no one was chasing me.

The mowing done, I put the riding mower back in the shed and locked it up. Without glancing at the newly shaved grass, I headed into Wilson's office to get more marching orders.

He looked at me blearily from behind his usual mountain of paperwork. He looked none too pleased to see me, but I didn't let it concern me, intent on my mission.

"Any extras today?" I asked brightly.

Wilson thumped the desk with his fist. "No. Your orders are to take the afternoon off."

My head whipped back, stung. "But...why?"

"You're working too hard," Wilson snapped, shuffling his papers around and managing to make an even bigger mess. "I was appreciative at first, but now it has to end. You need a life outside of work. You need rest and relaxation. And if I have to force you to do it, I will. Because I've had enough of watching you run yourself ragged."

"But I like working," I said, feeling my pulse creep up like an addict facing an intervention.

"Do you really?" Wilson asked, fine lines drawn at his eyes and mouth.

"Or are you just using it to avoid your problems?"

"Why can't you just be grateful?" I asked, throwing my hands up incredulously. "You have to chase most of your employees to get them to work at half the speed I do. The ponies are sound and comfortable. Your buildings are clean. Your club looks beautiful. Why can't you just say 'thank you'?"

"You're running away from your problems," Wilson said, rolling his chair back from the desk. "I won't have that in my stable. You'll be a danger to yourself and everyone around you if you keep going this way."

"So you're *firing* me?" I demanded, my voice flat with rage.

"I'm telling you to take an afternoon off," Wilson said, his hands tightening into fists. "Or you *will* be fired."

"This is absurd," I said, twisting in a circle. "This is bullshit."

Wilson glared at me, hunkering down in his chair like he was bracing for a hurricane. "Get out of my office," he said.

Lawrence

I turned out of Courtney's room, walking to the elevator. My phone shrilled at my hip, and I was about to press *Ignore* when I saw the California area code.

I accepted the call and answered warily. "Hello?" I said into the phone. Purely professional, an impersonal greeting.

"Lawrence, it's your mother," my mom's voice told me.

"Mom. Hey." I came to a stop in the hallway, my progress stalled. "What's going on?"

"Your father and I are in the process of finalizing our divorce," she said, adopting the pinched, slightly nasally, pissed-off way of speaking she used whenever he entered the conversation. "While dividing our possessions, we've come upon a few things we agree you should have. We'd like to give them to you in person."

"So you're asking me to come out there?" I asked. "Our season opener is a few weeks away."

Team Dark Horse

"That's why I called when I did," she said. "I know it will be harder to get away once your season starts. I had hoped you could come out sometime soon, even just for a day or two."

"I'd have to talk to our sponsor," I said. "About arranging a flight."

"I'll happily pay the airfare for you to come out here," she said.

"I don't want you to have to do that." I looked down at the grey carpeting. "I'll ask John."

"And Harry?" She hesitated but didn't correct herself. "You don't have to see your father if you don't want to. You'll only have to deal with me."

"Okay," I said. "Let me call John."

She let me go. I leaned against the wall next to the elevator, listening to the binging and watching the people come and go. I dialed John's number, letting it ring. At the last moment, he picked up.

"Cavanaugh. What can I do for you?" He said, business as usual.

"I hate to ask you this." I stalled for a moment, then got on with it. "Is there any way I could use your plane? I need to go to California for a couple days."

"Certainly," John said, catching me off guard.

"Don't you want to know the reason?" I asked.

"If you're asking, I'm sure there's a good reason," John said. "And it's not my place to poke around in your personal matters."

"How do you know it's personal?"

I heard John chuckle. "You don't look at newsstands much, do you?"

"I make it a point not to," I said.

He lapsed into silence, a drawn-out pause. "The Wilder divorce is all over the papers. Not just the gossip rags, but the *New York Times* as well. Anyway, they've been running photos of the Wilders and their teenage son, Harrison. Circa 2006. The resemblance is uncanny, and the timing adds up. Right about the time Harrison stopped getting photographed, Lawrence Cavanaugh turned up in Lexington."

He gave me a minute to process it all, and I didn't argue a single point he had made.

"I don't think anyone else has picked up on it," John said in my ear. "But I noticed it. And I'm happy to send my plane to pick you up. It's time you

504

sorted it all out."

I hung up the phone and pressed the elevator button, wondering if it even could be, after all this time.

Elaine

Wilson didn't say how I was supposed to take an afternoon off when I had no vehicle and it was a hundred degrees, too hot to be walking on the side of the road, baking on the asphalt. But he'd left the keys to his old Chevy hanging in plain sight, so I took them and fired it up, listening to the ominous wheeze of the engine. I drove it with care, easing up slowly to highway speed and pissing off the people behind me, a growing parade of angry drivers in a hurry to get nowhere.

I drove around town, but I didn't see anything that made me want to stop. I couldn't see myself going into the beauty parlor or the bakery. Taking myself out to lunch was out of the question. I preferred to eat in private, so no one could question my lack of vigor, the halting crunch as I chewed my food just enough so I could swallow it.

I drove myself out to the ghetto, the paint-peeling, broken-window part of town. It was a small, out of the way subsection of an otherwise thriving community. It was where I'd crawled away to die.

I left Wilson's Chevy by the curb and walked to the corner of Hewitt and Aachen. I stood above the pavement I'd lain on, trying to understand myself.

I'd thought the problem was Lawrence, or John. That was the idea I latched onto. I had to get away from them, and everything would be fine. I had what I wanted now. I had Lawrence off my back. I had John off my back. They were both gone, and I was left alone to do my job and live my semblance of a life.

Something was crying out in me now, some insatiable need I couldn't stomp out. It hadn't vanished when John did. It lived on, that ghastly part of me that just couldn't be killed.

I settled into the pavement, considering the cold, gritty feel of it against my skin. Being alone was the only real option for me. I truly believed that. But the hunger got worse every day, and now that I was still and quiet, I could feel it needling away at me. I'd tried everything but giving in.

Erica

I'd taken to getting up early, a full two hours before my usual 6 a.m. ritual, tacking up in the near darkness, riding when it was cool and the dew shimmered underfoot. The polo ponies knew me by now, and with the exception of a few hungry, hopeful nickers, they barely stirred when I moved past their stalls. D.M. waited at the end of the row, reaching over the top of his door with his long neck, waiting to press his muzzle into my palms and warm my chilled hands with his breath.

I set him up in the middle of the aisle, not bothering to attach the cross ties to his halter, letting his lead rope drop to the floor. He stood there with his legs spread, as if he was still a little sleepy and in danger of toppling over. He picked his feet up in turn, holding still as I tapped the clinches and hooked my hoof pick into the grooves of his shoes, ensuring they still held firmly to his feet. I wrapped his legs in cotton polos, moving up to place the saddle on his back. It seemed a little snug, so I removed the shim pads, nodding in approval as it settled into his back, hugging the gentle slope from his withers to his spine. Slipping the bit into his mouth, I fastened the throatlatch and cavesson, donning my helmet before we headed down the aisle, D.M.'s shod feet patting the cement floor, his sharp, metallic hoof beats echoing in the quiet barn.

I led him over to a fence rail, adjusting the girth one final time and then clambering up the boards, reducing the distance between the ground and his back. Even so, I had to stretch to throw my leg over his back. D.M. waited patiently for me to settle in and adjust my stirrups, starting out for the fields at my cue. He walked along, hooves touching down on lush, irrigated grasses, moving smoothly over the undulating terrain. A far cry from our first conditioning ride, when he'd staggered and stutter-stepped at every small hill and dip.

I checked my watch, keeping tabs on the length of our warm-up. When sufficient time had passed, I moved him into a trot, reins forward so he could stretch down. He opened his throatlatch, neck telescoping out, taking the contact. His stride propelled me out of the saddle, my posting steady and rhythmic. I could leave him to his own devices now, and he would get the job done.

I looked around the fields, yellow-green, the first peek of morning sun setting them aglow. Lawrence had done right by bringing D.M. here. There was no hubbub, no distractions. We simply disappeared into the fields, silent as a puff of vapor. Away from the world, I looked inward, focusing on every footfall, every muscle flexing and stretching. I was fully present, invested, and in return, so was he. I approached our training with a vigor I hadn't been able to access in a while. D.M. restored what Assault had taken away from me, and horses were my joy and comfort once again.

I lifted D.M. with my seat, bringing him into a canter. The straightness of my posture and the set of my hands told D.M. that the real work for the day was about to commence. He didn't argue, steaming ahead with pricked ears, almost prompting me to check him.

I kept the first few intervals relatively easy, equal parts canter and walk. The fourth time, I pressed my calves into him, increasing the swing of my seat over the saddle. D.M. burned forward, his body lengthening and lowering just a hair. I crouched above his withers, bringing my weight off his back, and he picked up the pace even more, causing the wind to whip in my ears.

Ever so sneakily, D.M. was changing. He was a different animal now, evolving into something more athletic and powerful. His gallop was quicker, yet his feet danced lightly over the ground. His shoulders had lightened and lifted. He was still enormous, but he was more streamlined, able to corner and change direction more effectively. His Thoroughbred side had come to the party, edging out his draft lineage once and for all.

I glanced at my watch, realizing we'd exceeded our mark. Excitedly, I let him go on just a little longer, feeling the kind of power I had in my hands. D.M. felt limitless, charging onward in the daybreak, shoulder muscles cut and angular.

I sat back and half-halted, slowing him to a walk. Body undulating, he strode out freely, almost breaking into a jig. Ears flicking, he looked around at the scenery, eyes bright and clear. It was as if he'd come alive.

If he could take on a jump course with this much fire in his eyes and life in his feet, I might have a Grand Prix horse after all.

Lawrence

My head leaning against the window, I watched the clouds change shape, occasionally resting my eyes. Sleep wasn't going to happen. Neither was reading, although there was a magazine spread out across my lap. It just sat there for me to occasionally flip through, so I was doing something with my hands.

An announcement came on over the intercom. *"We're about 10 minutes out from landing,"* the pilot's distorted voice told me. I couldn't decide if this flight had dragged on or gone by like a bullet. The last 10 minutes did seem long, maybe because I was counting them.

The plane landed, and I undid my seatbelt, collecting the small satchel I'd brought with me. I'd packed light, knowing I wouldn't be staying long. I would just get in, get whatever it was they wanted to give me, and get out of there.

I turned my phone on as I exited the plane, moving down the stairs. I was about to dial my mom and ask her for a ride, when I saw a black Mustang sitting conspicuously alongside the landing strip.

A girl wearing a tight pantsuit walked up to me, handing me the keys. "Enjoy your visit," she said, with a practiced smile that creased none of the lines on her face.

"Thank you," I said equally stiffly. I walked to the car and set my bag on the passenger seat, sliding into the immaculate interior, all black leather and chrome. I turned the key in the ignition, hearing the smooth turnover of the engine, the strong hum promising considerable horsepower.

I fiddled with the sound system, turning up the bass until the music threatened to split the plastic on the dash, rattling the rearview mirrors. I shifted it into Drive and pressed the accelerator down to the floor, causing the tires to squeal and shudder until they found purchase and rotated smoothly, taking me down the road.

I got on the freeway, accessing the skills I'd once had when I was an unlicensed kid driving my girlfriend's car around. The traffic was thick and congested, but with a V-8 engine on your side, you found your way through the tight spots and got where you needed to go.

The roads here were frequented by countless convertibles and the occasional Hummer. Leaving the interstate, I turned into my old neighborhood. It was much the same as I remembered, mansions standing shoulder to shoulder, with so many stories they blocked out the skyline, protected by wrought-iron or electric fences. Palm trees grew near the sidewalks, and vans of tourists drove up and down the streets, maps in hand, hoping for a glimpse of some A-lister. The paparazzi were staked out, lying in wait, their hungry eyes following every passing car.

A line of photographers, 10 deep, led the way to my old house. I pulled up to the gate, barely decelerating, sending them scattering. I reached out and typed in the old code, wondering if it was null and void now. The gates snapped open with a clank, so I guessed it still worked.

I parked my rental car, walked up to the back door and rang the doorbell. I could just barely hear it as it chimed through the house. Moments later, the door opened.

"Welcome home," my mother said, embracing me. Her eyes looked tired and battle-weary, a bit like the old days.

I nodded, stepping through the door into the great, mostly empty depths of the house. It took me a second to realize it really was empty. All my parents' possessions were gone.

"Everything had to be sold and the money divided," she told me, resting her arm on the granite countertop. "There were a few things we agreed you should have. We set them aside for you."

"Is he out of town?" I asked, moving around the empty shell of a house.

"No, he is staying nearby for the time being," my mother said. "I figured if you wanted to see him, you should have the choice, not have it forced on you."

"I don't want to see him," I said. "But I feel like I should."

She nodded. "If you tell me, I'll make the call."

I thought about what John had said, and all the unanswered questions I had that pressed on me when I stayed motionless long enough for them to catch up. "You should make the call," I said.

Erica

It was officially hot by the time D.M. and I returned to the stable. The usual flurry of activity was starting, clusters of ponies being tacked up and taken out to the fields. I dumped D.M.'s tack in my locker and hurried out of there, seeking the relative peace of the wash rack.

I aimed the hose at D.M., spraying him with a fine mist of water that saturated his coat, turning him the darkest of chocolate. Once he was rinsed off, I hurried to scrape the water off him before it could heat up on his skin and raise his body temperature all over again.

Leading him over to a patch of grass, I set him up, squaring his feet underneath him and stepping back to the end of the lead shank to get a good look at him. He blinked back at me, seemingly unsure why he couldn't just start mowing down the grass, but he held his pose.

The intense workouts in the hot sun had melted the flab off D.M. faster than I could believe. His formerly sagging belly was tucked up, while his shoulders and croup stood out, the bone structure visible, covered in a thin layer of smooth muscle. He was leaner than I'd ever seen him, undeniably fit. He looked like a racing Thoroughbred with larger, stronger legs and feet. Even his plain head seemed more cut, the noble, slightly Roman profile of a war horse.

I remembered what Lawrence had said. *You'll see what kind of animal you have underneath you.*

D.M. was a different animal now. He could run, and he could turn. All that remained was to see if he could soar.

Lawrence

My mother came out of the living room, tucking her cell phone back into her pocket. "He's on his way," she said, sitting down at the counter.

I wanted to rummage through the cabinets for a drink, but I figured there were certain times that called for a clear head, and this was probably one of them.

"How's Erica?" My mom asked, hands folded, face eager.

"She's good," I said. "The horse she brought to Wellington got injured, so I sent for her old horse, and he's coming along well. She kind of wrote him off earlier this year, but I think he might have what it takes."

"And your ponies are doing well?" She inquired.

"They're fit and ready," I said. "We just had a test practice with one of the teams we'll face, and we smoked them. It's not a guarantee, but it bodes well for our first season."

"I've already pre-ordered the tickets," my mother said, her eyes alight. "Fiske and I will be in the stands to watch your first game."

"You didn't have to do that," I said, casting my eyes downward, trying not to let on how pleased I was. "I know it's a long way to travel."

My mother reached over, taking my hand. "I wanted to."

The back door opened with a sharp click, and we both froze, the happy moment shattered. My mother and I stood at attention, artificially posed in the empty room.

My father walked in, a heavy overcoat covering his body, Wayfarers over his eyes. Slowly, he shed the conspicuous camouflage and laid it over the back of a chair.

My mother eased out of the room, leaving me alone with him.

I eyed the bulk of his body, his heavy arms and hands, the close-cropped light brown hair on his head. He looked down at me from his height of six foot three, and I was slender beside him, taking after my mother in complexion and body mass.

"Harrison," my father said, unclasping his watch and sliding it around on his wrist. "Back from the dead."

"I suppose I was dead to you," I agreed, moving away from him. If I kept my feet moving, perhaps I could keep my fists still.

"I see you've made a name for yourself," he said. "Lawrence Cavanaugh. Polo legend. Tell me, does it say that on your ID?"

Wordlessly, I handed him my license. He looked at it in surprise. "How did you manage that?"

"You can manage a lot when you're young and charming," I said. "I got a license, a new Social Security number, everything."

"I see you've done very well for yourself," my father said, nodding. "You took to the runaway life effortlessly."

"It's not as if it was easy," I said, my hackles raising. My father shut up fast, taking a circuitous route around conflict. That was always his early strategy, until his temper took over the steering wheel, bowling over everything in its path.

"Your mother set aside a few things for you," he said, picking up his overcoat. "I'll let her do the honors."

I watched him gather his things and prepare to clear out. The veins in my arms and neck throbbed, and I wondered why he'd even come at all. He was dancing the quickstep, swerving every possible intersection that might lead to unpleasant questions, to necessary answers.

"We're not done here," I said.

Javier

Reclining on my bed, feet on the duvet, I poured a glass of sherry, watching the sunset-orange liquor swirl and bubble. Taking a sip, I felt the light sweetness on my tongue, the slow burn of it against my throat.

This room was my home for so many months out of the year that I had my own art brought in, sensuous sculptures of couples embracing, and oil paintings of Spanish vistas. The lighting was substandard too, so I had augmented it with bedside lamps that featured various settings, from very dim to fairly bright, but always flattering.

My phone lit up beside me with a steady stream of text messages, some of them containing graphic photos. Had I wanted, I could have walked down this hallway, making a stop at almost every room. I had spent many a night doing just that, and it was satisfactory. But I was hungry for the company of one girl in particular.

I would have called her, but I knew from experience she would not answer. So, I accessed my camera roll and selected a photo, enclosing it in a message to her. I waited.

Minutes later, I heard what were surely her knuckles raining heavily on my door. I sat up, putting my feet on the floor, and let her in.

Her arms folded tightly around her small chest, she stared up at me in contempt. "You have sent me a dick pic," she growled.

I grinned slowly at her. "You must have liked what you saw. You are here."

"I am here to slap some sense into you," she said, slipping past me into the room.

"So you want it rough," I said, nodding.

She took a sip of sherry from the bottle, spitting it out into a plastic hotel cup. "This is disgusting. How can you stomach this foul fruity shit?"

"I prefer drinking to be a pleasant experience," I said as I poured myself another glass. "I do not feel the urge to assert my masculinity by pounding back hard, bitter liquors. I have other ways of flexing my muscles."

"What you mean is, you cannot take the burn," Yvette said, walking away. "The burn of your laser zit zapper, perhaps, but not the burn of a nice hard scotch or whiskey."

"Men are evolving," I said, setting my drink down. "We can now uphold a higher standard than before. We can wear better clothes, cultivate our appearance more. What used to be regarded as 'manly' is now seen as slovenly."

"Yet you insist on taking photos of your penis," Yvette said, her voice ending in a sigh. "You still think women will like it."

"Are you denying that you do?" I asked.

Yvette rolled her eyes. "Women are not visual like men. A little show of skin is not enough to make us titillated. Women need to be wooed."

"I have tried wooing you," I said heatedly. "You would not take it."

Yvette gave me a slow stare. "Then perhaps you should take a hint."

"The other night," I said. "Why did you do it?"

Yvette's small body heaved a sigh. "Be pleased that it happened, Javier. Do not analyze it."

"I can't help it," I said, following her. "I need to know why you would do such a thing if you do not want me."

"I never said I did not want you," Yvette said, her back to me. "I do not want any man. Occasionally, I have needs, and they must be fulfilled. That is the extent of it."

"I could meet your needs," I said, bending down to suck on her earlobe. "You know I can."

"You want something more," Yvette said, ducking away from me. "You get too attached."

"I can be cold," I promised. "You will see how cold I can be."

"You are a classless individual," Yvette said, picking up one of my statues. "This is how you choose to surround yourself? With crass naked-people art and stereotypical landscape paintings?"

"I surround myself with things I find beautiful," I said, moving in behind her. "Regardless of whether others agree."

"Such a clear low blow," Yvette said, laughing. "An attempt to chip at my self esteem so I will reconsider going to bed with you?"

"You are determined to see evil in everyone," I said. "The world is not such a dark place as you make it out to be."

"You are a sheltered polo prince with all the riches in the world," Yvette said. "Your corner of the world is brighter than the rest."

"You could occupy it with me," I said. "Just for tonight."

"I could occupy it with you as much as I wanted," Yvette said. "Do not attempt to be coy."

"Will you spend the night with me?" I asked, dimming the bedside lights, taking her face in my hands.

A sigh rippled through her. "I am still here, aren't I?" She said.

I unzipped her sweatshirt, finding a bare torso underneath. She shed her jeans while I hurried out of my clothes, and we faced each other. Wasting no time, she gripped my erection, steering me onto the bed and laying me on my back. Her thighs settled on either side of my face, and she drove herself on, augmenting the motions of my tongue with the steady roll of her hips. She leaned forward, changing the angle and taking me in her mouth. Her tongue wrapped around my head, I had to fight to maintain focus and hold my rhythm. I moaned with my mouth against her, and she pressed her hips down, her body stilled.

After achieving release, she resumed her activities, her mouth corkscrewing slowly up and down my shaft. Only taking me so far in, never quickening the pace or the intensity, she kept me in a holding pattern, intensely aroused but unable to reach the peak.

"Please," I murmured, pulling away from her. "Can't I be inside you?"

"Of course you *can*," she said, drawing her knees up delicately, effectively slamming an iron door in my face. "It's whether I will allow you to be."

"Can't you let me?" I quavered, moving up on her. "I'll make it worth your while."

"You had better," she threatened, spreading her knees.

I picked her up, feeling her slickness on my belly as her legs settled around me, her hands exploring my contours. I set her on her back on the dresser, reaching for her legs, lifting her hips up and sliding into her. Easing my way in at first, I went deeper each time, until I was filling every crevice of her, stroking the innermost point, brushing the sensitive nerve endings at first, then with her throaty encouragement, pushing more forcefully, driving into her, until her head flopped back and her eyes glazed over, her body shuddering. A few more quick thrusts, and I was over the brink too, leaning over her, both of us panting.

When I could trust myself to be steady on my feet, I picked her up and carried her to the bed, a softer place for her to lie in the afterglow. She didn't protest when I tucked her in and crawled in behind her, wrapping her small, sharp body in my arms. I lay in peace and comfort, savoring the moment, knowing when I woke up in the morning she would already be gone.

Lawrence

My father turned. "I thought you only came here for the things we wanted to give you," he said sharply.

"That's what I told myself," I said. "But more than that, I came here for answers."

"Answers," my father said. "What could you possibly want to know?"

"Maybe I'd like to know how you could focus so much on your career, how you could fight and strive for every detail to be perfect in the eyes of the outside world, when on the inside, your family was falling apart," I said, my blood steaming. "Maybe I'd like to know how you could abandon your son and leave him to fend for himself out on the streets."

"You ran away from home," he said, his thick neck tightening. "You made the choice to leave. It's not as if I kicked you out. I'm not some monster."

"Is that how you justify it," I said flatly. I turned away.

"It's the truth," he insisted. "You ran away! Are you saying you didn't?"

"I did run away," I said, breathing in and out. "That much is true. But you haven't seen me in over seven years, and you shoulder the blame for that."

He took a turn around the room, hands on his hips, like he was striking a pose. There was nothing in the empty house for him to fiddle with, nothing for him to do with his hands. "I didn't think you wanted to see me. I figured you ran away for a reason."

"Yeah, that's true," I said bitterly. "But you know what? That doesn't absolve you."

"What was I supposed to do?" He asked me. "You were a rebellious child, a troubled teenager. You never wanted to be around me. I figured you were better off wherever you were."

"That's the thing," I said, making the turn for home, getting right to the bare bones of it. "You had no idea where I was. What had happened to me. You didn't even know if I was alive."

"I assumed you were fine," my father said neatly.

I gripped the edge of the countertop, my hand straining against the smooth, cold marble. "What kind of father lets his kid run away and doesn't even go *looking* for him?"

His eyes tipped up toward the high ceiling, and he sighed, as if this was so tedious. "So that's what this is all about. You're hurt because I didn't check up on you."

"It would've been nice," I said. "Because you know what? It wasn't easy. It wasn't romper room out there. I could've easily gone a bad way, down a bad path. It was all luck that I ended up in that stable, do you understand? It was all dumb luck, and if that hadn't happened, I probably wouldn't be here today. And the fact that I am here today has everything to do with Wilson, and the saving grace of those horses. It has absolutely nothing to do with you, because as far as I'm concerned, you left me to die."

My father wavered, swaying in my watery vision like a palm tree. "I thought I was doing what you wanted," he said. "You wanted me to leave you alone. You didn't want to be controlled. I decided I would respect your wishes."

"I was *fourteen*," I said, advancing on him. "How the hell was I supposed to know what I wanted? I didn't know shit. You were the adult, and I was the punk kid. You were supposed to be there for me!"

"So you're saying I failed you," my father said slowly. "Add it to my list of failures. I've failed everyone."

"Well, you didn't let down your fans," I said. "I'm sure your ugly divorce is providing a lot of drama and entertainment for them. And that's really all you ever cared about. Being adored and followed by the public."

"That's not true," he argued weakly, with about as much heft as a limp-wristed slap.

"Isn't it?" I stepped up to him, squaring my shoulders. "I was your teenage son, always in the papers, always in compromising positions. Driving without a license, underage drinking, sometimes both at the same time. Partying, doing drugs, having sex in public places. I had a juvie record as long as my arm by the summer I turned fourteen. Then I made a break for it and hit the road. It was a relief, wasn't it?" I asked, studying his face.

"It wasn't," he said, a polished line, an easy deception.

"Yes, it was," I said, blinking away the last of my tears, hardening once again. "I was a liability, and you were glad to be rid of me. You weren't respecting my wishes. You were celebrating your windfall."

Lawrence again

In the ensuing calm and quiet after my father left, my mother and I sat in the kitchen, seeking out the one small corner of the house I'd grown up in that felt at all like home. She baked biscuits, and we spread butter and jam on them, watching it melt and drip onto the countertop, creating a sticky mess we didn't bother to clean up.

After a while, my mother went upstairs and gathered the few items I'd come for. The first two were childhood relics that would probably end up stuffed in a drawer, but I knew why she hadn't thrown them out, and I knew why I wouldn't either.

As I set aside the toys, she pressed a small white box into my hand. I opened it up, staring at a blindingly bright diamond ring. The large, square stone looked like it had been cut from glass. You could almost see through it, the clarity was so high.

"What…ranking is that?" I said stupidly.

"Oh, it's about five full carats," my mother said. She placed her hand over mine. "When I dropped in on you this spring and met Erica, the idea began to form in my mind. She impressed me immediately. She's the kind of girl you want in your life, the kind you ought not to let slip through your fingers. So I spoke with your father, and he agreed that you should have this ring, so that when you're ready, you can give it to her."

The blood whooshed in my head, moving in and out like waves, gently slapping my subconscious. I hadn't really thought about marrying Erica, but now that my mom had suggested it, the idea stood out in my head, a focal point as big as a billboard.

"Thank you," I said, still a little stunned. "This is really generous."

"It's the best we could do for fucking up your childhood," my mother said offhandedly. She smiled, looking off into the distance. "As bad as things got with your father, the night he gave me that ring was always a fond memory.

It's beautiful, and as silly as the custom may be, offering trinkets to supposedly cement your love, it was still breathlessly exciting."

She stood up, gathering her purse, checking her phone. "I just thought something good should come of it. That you should take it and make your own memories. Ones that will last."

Erica

Ashley's number played across my phone's screen as it vibrated gently on the seat. I picked it up eagerly, steering myself onto a quiet side street and parking by the curb. I was on my way back from the equestrian center where Assault was stabled, and I had no pressing duties awaiting me. This conversation was long overdue, and I pressed the green button, waiting to hear her voice.

"Erica! You live," Ashley said as I answered the phone.

"I could say the same to you," I said happily. "Your communication hasn't exactly been forthcoming."

"Yeah, yeah," Ashley said, impatient. "I'm not the one who up and moved to Florida." She took a pause. "So how are things going?"

"Pretty mixed, but definitely looking up," I said. "Assault hurt himself his first time out on course, so he's laid up for a good half year. But I've got another up-and-coming prospect that's looking quite promising."

"Who's your new prospect?" Ashley inquired.

"None other than the tried and true D.M.," I said, smiling.

"You really think he's got what it takes?" Ashley said.

"I haven't tried him on a course yet," I admitted. "But the Florida heat and Lawrence's polo pony-approved workouts have transformed him into a fierce athlete."

"Whoa," Ashley said. "Who knew D.M. could get ripped."

"He's ripped, alright," I said. "Wait 'til you see him. I'll text you a pic later."

"Speaking of ripped," Ashley began, "how's your boyfriend?"

"He's...good," I said, a little absentmindedly. "He's been running around a lot. He just jet-setted off to California for no apparent reason. I don't always see him a lot."

"He must be really busy getting ready for the start of the season," Ashley said. "Considering he's working with a brand new team and everything. It's a lot of pressure."

"It is a different world down here," I said. "My dad was absolutely right when he said it's like a wormhole. The circuit at home doesn't even compare to this. It's like peewee football, and this is the NFL."

"Using football comparisons?" Ashley teased. "Really?"

"It's just way different out here," I shrugged.

"So is it true what they say about the International Polo Club?" Ashley asked. "That it's just party central?"

"Oh, yeah," I said, disinterested. "It's always hopping over here."

"Are you making up for some lost opportunities in your high school years?" Ashley pressed on.

"Not really," I admitted.

"Aw, man," Ashley whined. "I thought you'd at least have some good stories for me."

"I've mostly been hanging out with a guy who works at the 7-Eleven," I said, verging into semi-dangerous territory.

I could almost hear Ashley roll her eyes. "That's sad."

"Not really," I said again. "He's actually a great guy. He's saving to open a restaurant, and I think he's made for the restaurant life. He's an awesome cook..."

"Okay, blah blah blah," Ashley interrupted. "I can't believe you're telling me you haven't been to any sweet parties!"

"I just don't care for that scene," I defended myself. "Particularly since most of that scene is comprised of women who want to bang my boyfriend."

"Of course they do!" Ashley said. "He's a high-ranked player. You do know that's a thing, right?"

"I know it's a thing," I said. "I'm just a little weary of it."

"Well, it goes along with the lifestyle," Ashley said. "It can't all be glamorous. You take the good with the bad."

"That's what I try to tell myself," I said, sighing into the phone. "But some days, Ash...some days I just really think about what it would be like to be with a normal guy."

"Wait, what do you mean 'normal guy'?" Ashley demanded. "Define 'normal guy'."

"You know," I said, broadly waving an arm, even though she was hundreds of miles away and couldn't possibly read my body language. "Just a guy. Without the big career, without the rabid fans, hoopla, and billions of exes swarming everywhere. Just a nice, normal guy."

"You have one picked out already, don't you," Ashley said, her tone as sharp as a razor.

"No, I don't," I retorted, starting up my truck. "I'm just saying, sometimes it seems like a nice alternative."

"Say what you will," Ashley said, with that lofty tone she adopted when she was convinced she was right. "No girl in a decent relationship thinks about leaving, unless she has someone else in mind. You're sparking with someone else, I know it."

I remained silent on my end of the phone as I drove past the 7-Eleven, smiling inwardly as I took in its green-and-white façade and Kurt's very blue vintage Ranger parked in a far-off corner of the lot.

Lawrence

The weight of my mother's engagement ring pressed at my hip, a constant, insistent reminder. I'd carried it with me ever since I'd returned from California. I started toting it around because I was afraid to leave it sitting just anywhere, but mostly, I kept it close at hand so when I felt the time was right, I could go down on one knee and present it to Erica, saying whatever dippy thing came to my brain at the time.

With two weeks left until our first game, the preseason press tour had picked up from zero to sixty. Reporters were swirling around the grounds, questioning every player they could flag down. As usual, they hit up the 10-goalers, polo royalty such as Alvarez and Javier. But the most enterprising among them were increasingly determined to get a sit-down interview with the members of Team Dark Horse. Regardless of whether they respected us, controversy was king, and nothing brought controversy like a budding team consisting of mostly female players.

Yvette and Courtney were familiar with the media circus, well versed in the preseason press tour from their days in the Women's Polo Federation. Courtney never interviewed well, but Yvette, with her cutting tongue and salacious remarks, made up for the pizzazz that her teammate lacked.

There was one name that left the reporters' lips more often than any other. One figure who filled up their eager lenses more than her fair share. Delaware was a nobody, a charming girl with a face and body that photographed exceedingly well and a growing reputation. Alvarez and his teammates had kept their dismal showing against us tight-lipped, but I suspected someone had vented to the wrong person, and Delaware's triumph had spread like wildfire. No longer regarded simply as a curiosity, she commanded respect wherever she went. She had become an overnight celebrity, and everyone was clamoring for a sit-down interview with her.

Previously ignored, our practice sessions were frequented by the press, hanging on the sidelines in rows three deep. Our tranquil field had become a fishbowl, and it could be a struggle to ignore everyone tapping on the glass. Everyone coped, but an air of tension circulated through our practices. It wasn't the same as before.

Success always came at a price, and I had to be sure that we didn't lose sight of why we were here.

I headed into the barn, giving Harry's stall a quick mucking out. He stepped to the side, moving his feet delicately out of the way as I wielded the manure fork.

I walked the wheelbarrow back to the muck heap, seeing a pair of long, shapely legs out of the corner of my eye. Setting the wheelbarrow down sharply, I turned to see Delaware standing there.

"Surprised to see me here?" She asked with a smile.

"Very," I admitted, walking over to her.

"The photographers don't come back here," she explained. "If I need a little break, the best place to find peace and quiet is by the shit pile."

"Makes sense," I said. "They like to find the dirt, but they don't like to get dirty." I leaned against the barn, the metal almost uncomfortably hot against my T-shirt. "How are you holding up?"

"I never imagined I would be such a big deal," Delaware said, staring at the clouds. "I'm just a girl."

"You have a very compelling story," I said. "You intrigue people. They want to root for you."

"It's a nice feeling," she said. "But it's scary at the same time. How do you handle it?"

"You just have to play for you," I said. "Don't try to play for anyone else. Just play for you."

"What should I do for my big interview?" She asked me, her chestnut hair fanning out in the breeze. "I don't want to let the team down. What should I say?"

I reached over, hugging her gently. "Just be Delaware," I said. "Be genuinely who you are. You don't need to be anything else."

Erica

D.M.'s hind hoof slipped a little on the edge of the ramp. "Slow, easy," I said to him, steadying him with the lead rope. He repositioned his feet and backed down carefully, deliberately. Eyes wide, he took in the bustling sights and sounds of the equestrian center, confirming that it was, indeed, just another barn. Head low, he followed me into the stable, treading softly, his big body taking up the entire aisle.

Bruce was there with Vinnie, overseeing the farrier as he fit her for new shoes. He did a double take as he spotted me leading D.M. "You got a new horse!"

I smiled. "No, I got an old horse. I made him like new again."

"You certainly did," Bruce said, eyeing him up and down. "He's massive. What's his breeding?"

"Nondescript Thoroughbred and Shire," I said proudly, setting D.M. up in the cross ties. I returned to the trailer, bringing his gear with me. With quick fingers, I tacked him up, readying myself for the moment of truth.

"Are you just hauling in for the day?" Bruce asked.

"Yeah," I said. "I have him stabled nearby, but the facility really isn't set up for jumping. I just want to take him over a fence or two, to see if our conditioning paid off."

"Well, it's your lucky day," Bruce said. "The practice ring's set up with a full course. There's a hell of a line to ride in it, but once you wait your turn, you get 10 minutes to ride a full course set at your chosen height."

My mouth went dry as a trickle of sweat dripped from my temple. I hadn't ridden a full course since Assault tore his tendon. D.M. hadn't jumped in a year. Were we setting ourselves up for disaster?

Bruce grinned at me, seemingly reading my mind. "Ride to the jump, and let the horse do the rest," he said. "It's like riding a bike. It comes right back to you."

I nodded, taking D.M.'s reins and joining the line, standing among pawing, snorting horses and riders on their cell phones, waiting to learn if our work had paid off, or if our bid for Grand Prix would take us no further than this arena.

Interview with Yvette Sauvage and Courtney Silva Transcript

Dan Mickelson, Polo Weekly: It's a pleasure to have both of you ladies in the same room again. Many saw it as an unfortunate decision when you left the Women's Polo Federation, but would you say you've moved on to bigger and better things?

Yvette Sauvage: I can assure you I would not have left for lesser and worse things. I am not some foolhardy bitch.

Courtney Silva: Yvette doesn't do anything if it's not worth doing. That's why I joined her. Because I knew she was onto something.

DM: So it was Yvette's decision to leave, and not yours?

CS: Yes. I wouldn't have done it on my own.

DM: Yvette, there was a lot of talk when you left the Women, rumors of bad blood and such. Any truth to those?

Team Dark Horse

YS: I left because I wanted to play on equal footing with the men. The Women's Federation had no challenge left for me. It was not personal.

DM: But your former teammates were surely hurt by your decision.

YS: If they were, that is between them and their therapists. I am here to play polo, not to validate anyone.

DM: Courtney, do you agree?

CS: What? Yes, of course.

DM: You two had quite a long hiatus after leaving the Women. Then you joined forces with Lawrence Cavanaugh, and things progressed quickly. Was he in your plans all along?

YS: No. We put out a few feelers, and that one happened to work out.

DM: Delaware Freeman, your number 2 offensive player, is dating Facundo Alvarez, one of your fiercest rivals. Doesn't that create a lot of strife in the relationship?

YS: I do not share a bed with them. You would have to talk to Alvarez or Delaware.

DM: Such potential for fraternization is a big part of why the Federation has fought to keep women and men on separate fields. They feel it will make an already difficult game even more complicated.

YS: I can assure you Alvarez will still fight like a mad dog to beat Delaware. And I can assure you the reverse is equally true.

DM: But doesn't that create a lot of unnecessary strain on the relationship?

YS: If it does, so be it. That is their choice, and they have made it. If it is important enough to them to be together, they will overcome the strain. Or they will fall apart like so many do. But this discussion has no relevance. We are here to play polo, not to play house.

DM: Does your previous romantic involvement with Lawrence Cavanaugh make your working relationship more difficult?

CS: Whoa!

YS: As I said before, this is irrelevant. If you would like to discuss strategy, I would be happy to oblige, but if you insist on continuing with these intrusive, meaningless questions, we will need to step out.

DM: Do you care to comment on your rumored relationship with top-ranked player Javier -

YS: That is it. We are leaving. Come, Courtney.

CS: Thanks for your time, Mr. Mickelson.

YS: Do not thank the man, Courtney. He does not deserve your pleasantries.

CS: It's polite.

YS: Is it so polite that he has wasted our time on drivel? Come along, Courtney.

Erica

The rider on course before me approached the big combination. His horse rated, attacked the fence, and pelted on flawlessly, moving in the punctuated rhythm so often seen in the big jumper classes. They made up time whenever they could, slowing down only when necessary to avoid overtaking a fence. I sat up watching, awaiting our turn. D.M. was a mountainous presence beneath me, standing still as the breeze ruffled his mane.

The previous rider had set the course at a generous height. It wasn't a monster course, but it was a solid, Grand Prix-worthy test. I thought of our combined time off, and I wondered, once again, what I was getting us into.

The rider exited the gate, clearing the arena. Ready or not, it was mine for the next 10 minutes.

"Would you like to reset the jumps?" The steward asked me as I approached the gate.

I looked into the ring, taking in the brightly striped, spindly poles. They could be jumped in any order, and I could skip however many I wanted to. I could pull up at any time.

D.M. took a step through the gate, ears up, standing tall on familiar footing. I knew I hadn't lost a single day of training as far as D.M.'s mind was concerned. Once he learned something, he took it to heart, and even after a long hiatus, he would rally himself for the effort.

"No," I said, deciding. "I'll take them as they are."

Team Dark Horse

The time started running on the clock, seconds falling like dominoes.

I took D.M. to the rail and moved him out, stretching his muscles. The other riders in line watched me incredulously as I frittered away my precious course time. But I only needed one run-through, perhaps a minute and a half of jumping. I needed D.M. to be loose and supple. I wanted no chance of injury, no regrets. I wanted to know I had given him every chance.

D.M.'s soft eyeball blinked in confusion as we traveled an avoidance course away from the jumps. I patted him softly. "In due time," I said. He cantered along like a rocking horse, laying down an easy, lofty pace. I rose off his back, adopting a half seat, and he switched into galloping mode.

I looked at the array of fences, creating a plan in my head. And I rode D.M. to the jump. I didn't pick or pull. I rode forward, and I waited to see D.M.'s essence.

He picked his big, oafish head up, surveying the obstacle. Turning on a burst of speed, he ate up the distance. I wondered if he'd keep running flat out, or if he'd take the smart approach.

Nearing the base of the fence, D.M. dropped back off the pace, slowing himself without losing an ounce of momentum. With a powerful push, he left the ground, clodhopper hooves tucked gracefully up toward his belly. Kicking his hind feet clear, he landed with the fence intact, looking around, waiting for my direction.

In a sort of dreamlike state, I steered him vaguely toward the second fence I'd planned to take on. He sped up, belly low to the ground, legs churning. Again, he set back on the approach and jumped clean.

Abandoning my simple route, I challenged him, asking him to bend himself in two and jump a narrow in-and-out. He pivoted sharply, anchoring himself with one hind hoof like a reining horse performing a spin. Tail flagging in the air, he launched himself at the combination, bouncing through it with quick feet.

I made him take all the fences that posed a question. The triple combination, the spread. The three verticals on a bending line. Anything tricky or trappy, I rode him over. I didn't make it easy for him.

His sluggish feet that used to land us outside the ribbons every time had gotten a boost from muscle and adrenaline. His strapping height had always been his saving grace. He truly had a big jump in him. But he'd never been this sharp. He'd never skipped through a course before, pushing the pace and finding it easy. His body had failed him, not for lack of talent, but simply because he hadn't been fit enough for the task.

I took him over every jump at least once, until the time ran out on my clock and the cries of dissent from the waiting riders started. I pulled D.M. up and walked him through the gate, ignoring their icy stares and generously thumping his neck, feeling light chills run from my neck all the way down my spine.

Bruce spotted us and rode over, mounted on his gelding. "How was it?" He inquired.

I smiled, a bloom of color creeping out on my cheeks. "Grand Prix, here we come."

Delaware

The time on the little digital nightstand clock alerted me that it was time to get ready. "I'm gonna be late for my interview," I said, giving Facundo a little shove so he would slide off me.

He rolled over, smoothing a sheet over his naked body, watching me as I hunted for my clothes. "Are you nervous?"

"Gee, I don't know," I said, placing my breasts in the cups of my bra and fastening the band. "Maybe. It's my first interview with a major publication. It's kind of a big deal."

"You will be sensational," Facundo assured me, reaching for the little bottle of liquor on the nightstand.

"The guy who's interviewing me sounds like kind of a dick," I said. "Yvette warned me about him. She said he would ask stupid questions."

"They always ask stupid questions," Facundo said, tossing his chin-length hair back. "It's all in how you answer them."

"I suppose," I relented, brushing a trace of lint off my skirt. "You just gotta make the most of it."

"You have the power here," Facundo said, his eyes on me. "Never forget that."

"I appreciate your words of wisdom," I said, moving over to lay a kiss on him. "But now I really have to go."

I turned down the hallway, getting on the elevator and pressing the button for the main floor. I made a left turn and knocked on one of the conference room doors.

The door whipped open, and a guy around five six stood there beaming at me. His build was slim but soft, and his sandy hair was generously speckled with grey.

"Ms. Freeman," he said, taking my hand in his. "It's wonderful to finally make your acquaintance. Dan Mickelson," he added, as if I didn't already know what his name was.

"It's a pleasure to meet you," I said. He gave me a handshake that was so limp my father would've beat the stuffing out of him for it.

"Are we ready to get started?" He asked, stepping back.

"I'm ready," I said brightly. "I can't speak on your behalf."

He threw his head back and laughed like it was the funniest thing ever. "Alright then. Would you care to sit down?"

I glanced in the direction he pointed, glimpsing a long, impersonal rectangular table with a chair on either side. I didn't feel like sitting in a stuffy room. I couldn't be me in a stuffy room.

"Let's take a walk instead," I said decisively, remembering what Facundo had said about the power.

"Sounds about right to me," he said, picking up his tape recorder. "Lead the way."

"I'll be happy to," I said, leaving the conference room behind.

We headed down the lane, past the Mallet Grille and up toward the stable. The sun was heavy on the back of my neck, causing my skin to prickle as it deepened my tan.

"Ask me a question," I said to Dan Mickelson.

He clicked the Record button on his little device, getting right to it. "Everyone knows the rags-to-riches story of Lawrence Cavanaugh finding you in a cornfield of all places and recruiting you for his team. But I want to hear *your* version of it."

"Okay," I said, thinking back. "Well, it was just a nice spring day in Indiana."

"Did you have any inkling of what might be in store?" Dan interrupted. "Did you sense that everything was about to change?"

"Of course not," I said, laughing. "No, it was just a normal day. I ate breakfast, and then I went to shoot a ball around on my dad's old roping horse, Toby."

"Just for fun? Did it serve a purpose?"

I shrugged. "Nope, it was just plain enjoyable. The fair season hadn't started up yet, so I didn't have to buckle down and run my barrel patterns. I was too old to try out for rodeo queen, so I'd let up on my formal practices. Stick and balling was just something fun to do. I didn't know it was stick and balling. I didn't know it was a sport."

Dan nodded, his short legs working double time to keep up with me. "Fascinating. So, Lawrence Cavanaugh pulls off the road and comes to talk to you. Did you know who he was? What did you think in that moment?"

"Oh, I had no idea who he was," I said, thinking back. "He was sure good-looking, though. I sure didn't mind having him come to my cornfield."

Dan chuckled. "What did he say to you?"

"He asked if I knew I was practicing polo," I said. "I didn't really know what it was, to be honest. Like most people, I just knew the brand. I'd seen it on the commercials, but I'd never seen a full game. I didn't know what I was missing."

"Then he asks you to drop everything, leave your family, and come try out for his team. What was your reaction?"

"I was excited," I said. "It was an adventure. What is life if you don't have adventures? Drudgery?"

"You weren't nervous?"

"No," I said, laughing. "Though I really didn't know what I was getting myself into."

"Once you did know, did you regret making the journey?"

"Hell no," I said. "I had doubts, for sure, but no regrets."

"Where did your doubts originate?" Dan prompted.

"I wondered if I could play on a level with Courtney and Yvette," I said.

"These ladies are intense."

"They certainly are," Dan replied. "But you hadn't had any formal experience. Certainly, they understood that."

"There wasn't much of a grace period for me," I said. "We didn't have time to muck around. Our season was coming up fast, and it was either get with the program or be left in the dust."

"Sounds pretty cutthroat," Dan said.

"They didn't baby me," I said. "They soon found out they didn't have to."

"You rose to the occasion," Dan inferred.

"I did what I needed to do," I said.

"What can we expect from you this season, Ms. Freeman?" Dan pressed. "What can we expect from Team Dark Horse?"

"You can expect us to function as a single unit," I said. "You can expect fast, fair play from all of us. You can expect us to hold our own with any of the all-male teams out there. You can expect all that, and you should."

"Does that allude to the commonly held belief that women players are at a disadvantage on the men's field?"

"Nailed it," I said, grinning at him.

"What are your thoughts on this?" Dan asked. "Does it bother you to hear the naysayers bring your team down?"

"No one ever wants to change their beliefs," I said. "The earth is flat. Women shouldn't vote. People are stubborn this way, until enough momentum builds for a certain cause, and the tide turns. Then it becomes cool to root for change. You can say *I was there when this happened. I was in support of it.* You just have to wait out the bad parts and get ready for when the shift happens. Because when it does, suddenly you're on top of the world, and everyone wants to boost you up."

"That's what's coming for Team Dark Horse?" Dan inquired.

"Yes," I said, without a doubt in my mind.

Yvette

"I cannot believe Podunk's feature turned out so well," I groused to

Team Dark Horse

Courtney as I flipped through the spread. "This is everything I wanted for our article. Instead, Mickelson did his best to turn it into a sad piece of work fit only for a gossip rag."

"He asked her way better questions," Courtney agreed, thumbing through her copy. "I can't believe he never even asked her about her relationship with Alvarez. I thought he would've jumped all over that."

"You would think, the way he grilled me incessantly about every two-bit one-night stand I have ever indulged in," I said bitterly, tossing the magazine aside. Delaware's face on the cover irked me, and I flipped it over. The back cover consisted of one of Javier's endorsement deals, a glossy full-page ad for tingling lubricant.

"Javier was more than a two-bit one-night stand," Courtney commented, studiously averting her eyes from the advertisement that featured him shirtless on a Friesian horse.

"Barely," I said, lying back with my head on a pillow.

"Well, at least we got one good article out of this ordeal," Courtney said. "Leave it to Delaware to salvage Team Dark Horse's good name."

"Of course it would be her," I said. "Tell me, Courtney. Why does everyone bow and scrape to kiss her corn-fed ass, while they treat us like shit?"

"Delaware's lovable," Courtney said. "I guess we're not."

"That is bullshit," I said. "If one has to act like a pageant princess to be considered lovable, then I will never qualify."

Courtney's phone buzzed, and she picked it up. "Looks like Dougie's done with his work for the day," she said, snatching up her bag.

"Are the two of you still abstaining?" I asked.

"Yes," Courtney said, head down, cheeks red.

"Hmm," I said. "Well, I suppose he has had a lot of practice."

"That was mean," Courtney huffed, and she walked out.

I settled back into the covers, but my mind was too restless for sleep. My body felt as though it was hovering above the mattress, muscles tight, with currents of energy zipping through.

I gave up, exiting my room and taking a walk down to the hotel bar, eschewing the crowded elevator for the solitude and endurance-boosting capacity of the stairs. Beginning slowly, I built my pace until my feet and legs were a blur, and I felt the dampness of sweat breaking out on my back and temple. At last, my feet found the ground floor, and I proceeded to the bar, lingering in the doorway. My eyes found Javier easily. He wore a letterman jacket, an egregious fashion choice that was once again all the rage among men with poor taste and large egos. Tipping a glass of liquor into his mouth, he did not notice me. I remained out of his line of sight, waiting to make my move.

A lone flame-haired figure separated herself from the throng of women swaying drunkenly to the music. Her hourglass form accentuated by a tight, backless dress, she danced her way over to Javier.

Marla, I thought, recognizing her. She'd had a job as a polo journalist before, and she slept with polo players like it was her job. She had been a favorite of Lawrence's in the past, before he became a born-again good guy.

A break formed in the tipsy crowd, and I prepared to step into it. Marla leaned in close to Javier, brushing her exposed cleavage against his chest. She whispered in his ear, stepping back to let him have a good look at her.

Without waiting even a second or two, he closed the distance between them, gathering up her ass in his hands. They moved to the music together for a beat or two, and without fanfare, he took her by the arm and began guiding her out of the bar.

I tucked myself up close to the wall, and they passed by, never laying eyes on me. I watched as they left, his stupid letterman jacketed arm tucking her into him as they increased their pace, fighting to get to the elevator.

In the quiet calm of their absence, I marched myself up to the bar, thankful I'd thought to tuck Courtney's Gold card into my pocket.

I ordered a line of top-shelf shots, and I drained them one by one to the resounding cheers of the other patrons, feeling my coordination steadily slip away and caring increasingly less after each one.

Erica

With D.M. safely back in the land of polo enjoying some free time in a paddock, I unloaded his gear, carefully stowing it in my locker. I leaned my elbows on the fence, watching D.M. as he ambled about, his vibrant coat flooded with light from the evening sun. I remembered how I'd observe him in the early years of our relationship. I was always watching him. Whenever I led him anywhere, whenever he took a step, I kept one eye on him, until I could discern his mood and his soundness in a single glance. I learned him so completely, he was as familiar as a family member or my childhood home. In fact, had someone blindfolded me and left me to fend for myself inside the towering walls of my parents' home, I might have struggled to find my way around, but I could close my eyes, listening to the beat of D.M.'s stride, and hear any wobble, any slight hesitation.

I could have stayed at the fence rail, but the knowledge that I still needed to unhitch my trailer and take care of my other duties at the equestrian center chafed at me until I relented and walked to my truck. Heading down the familiar route, I held the wheel with one hand, pushing the speed limit and decelerating sharply around turns now that my trailer no longer held precious cargo.

At the equestrian center, I backed my trailer up into its assigned spot, threading the needle through the narrow gap between its neighboring rigs. I freed my truck and left it standing there, noting with pride that it was one of the straightest and best parking jobs I could see in the row.

With that chore taken care of, I walked into the barn, humming softly to myself. The barn was empty except for the resident horses, and I allowed myself a little celebratory skip in my step, still high from D.M.'s comeback.

I came to Bruce's section, Vinnie and the two geldings poking their heads out hopefully. As usual, Assault remained huddled in the back of his stall. His malevolent look erased my chipper mood.

It was hard, but I forced myself to look at him. I'd fallen into the habit of merely glancing in, confirming he was still on his feet. I didn't let myself do that this time. I turned my horseman's eye on him, and I looked over every inch of him without stopping, without turning back.

A vision of neglect hit me in the face. Assault's coat was dull, faded at the tips, matted to his skin with manure in places. His hooves, bare now that I'd pulled his shoes, were at least a week overdue for a trim. His thick black tail fell in a tangled mess, twisting itself into mismatched strands of dreadlocks.

I let myself into the stall, leaving the door partially open, enough for an escape route if I should need it. Assault remained in place, and though his eye twitched toward me in hatred, it was a reserved, tempered fury. The slackness of his shoulder muscles and the low set of his head told me he'd given up. He'd accepted his lot in life, and he wasn't trying anymore.

I sat down in the corner underneath his water bucket, hugging my knees. He looked out through the bars, watching Vinnie as she rustled around in her pile of hay. I looked at Assault, thinking what potential he had possessed as a young horse. What dreams his breeder must have had for him. With the conformation, gaits, and power he'd been blessed with, he could have succeeded anywhere. He could have done anything.

Now, in the prime of his life, he was a spoiled horse with a poor temperament, a reckless distaste for authority, and a serious injury. He'd had everything, and now he had nothing.

I shifted forward, balancing on my knees, stretching out a hand to Assault. He ignored me pointedly, ears sagging to the side in disinterest. I leaned against the wall again, hands folded in my lap.

I'd spent a lot of time thinking about all the ways Assault had gone wrong. I'd spent a lot of time blaming Assault's old owner and his old trainers, but I'd never really stopped to think about how I was responsible, too.

Maybe it had taken the stark contrast of my careful management of D.M. to shine a floodlight on how much I'd slacked off with Assault. Maybe I didn't realize it at the time because it hadn't happened overnight. It had been a slow shift over time as I made concessions and endless justifications.

I thought of all the times I'd skipped training rides because I was exhausted, and more insidiously, all the times I'd quit for the day because things were going *well enough*. I let Assault take over, and I stopped cracking down on him for the little things like rooting at the bit or barging against my leg aid. Battle weary or just plain complacent, I let him get away with things I never would've stood for in the past. I stopped getting into the nitty-gritty of training, and started merely skimming the surface.

Assault was a horse who needed constant, firm corrections. He needed to be kept on a short leash, and if I wasn't physically and mentally capable of doing that, I should have passed him on to someone who was. I'd been blinded by the sheer magnitude of his talent, and I'd convinced myself we were ready for Grand Prix when I had no right to even be jumping a horse I couldn't control on the flat.

My dad had been right all along. Assault wasn't safe for me. It wasn't that I couldn't ride out his shenanigans, it was that we were too disconnected from each other. We didn't have a partnership, and after what had happened now, we probably never would.

"I'm sorry," I told Assault, a tear trickling down my cheek. Hugging myself, I sniffled quietly in the corner, taking a moment to grieve. My dream of attaining Grand Prix might still be alive, but my dream of reforming Assault lay dead in the water.

With a heavy sigh, Assault lowered his knees, sinking to the floor with a thud that rattled the walls. Whether his lying down in my presence was just another sign of his having given up on life, or a small gesture of trust, I couldn't say. But I remained in my corner for quite some time, if only to show him that I was there now, and I would no longer look the other way.

Elaine

In the middle of the day, in that strange lag time between morning and evening chores, I came to a decision. I didn't take it lightly. I'd done everything in my power to avoid it, after all.

Wilson was in his office, typing away, when I went to see him. His head turned to me, drawn in by my shape in his doorway. His eyes, vexed by my sudden appearance, creased at the edges. He seemed to age visibly whenever I came around, and I knew that despite the high standard of work I maintained, I was indisputably a thorn in Wilson's side.

"Elaine, I have no jobs for you," he began, his voice rising precipitously. "You'll have to find something to do, because I can't keep coming up with nonsense to keep you occupied. This is a working stable, not a city park. If I see you laying in any more river rock, I'll throw one at your head."

"I know," I told Wilson patiently. "I was coming to see if I could borrow your keys."

"Just my keys, or do you also want my vehicle?" Wilson snapped, not quite able to quash his foul mood now that it had gained such momentum.

"Well, both."

"I see." Wilson leaned back, hands behind his head. "Will you be doing something constructive?"

I took a breath. "I'll be doing what everyone thinks...what I think I need."

"Very well," Wilson said, handing them over. "Come back with a better attitude."

"I'll try," I said, leaving his office with the light jingle of keys at my side. I gathered myself and stepped into Wilson's Chevy, coaxing it to life with a turn of the key and a push of the accelerator, easing down the road.

I made the requisite turns, wondering if it was all for nothing. I peered through the windshield like a coal mine canary brought back up to the light. The sun was too bright, the world too loud, and though I yearned for the stimulation, some shy, frail part of me still fought to scurry back underground.

A certain comfort came with being on the bottom. When you had good things in your life, they were accompanied by the imminent threat of loss. When you had nothing, you could at least be secure in that. I was shaking it up now, and it could all come crashing down on me.

I parked Wilson's Chevy out on the road, leaving the keys in it. John didn't have any close neighbors. His acreage spread far and wide, bordered by a short iron fence. The gate wasn't locked, so I tried it, and it came open in my hands. I shut it behind me and walked forward on trembling legs. You couldn't see his house from here, only trees, massive and beautiful specimens, weeping willows and oaks. Stationed on either side of the driveway, they formed a canopy, hemming me in and driving me onward. My legs buckled, as if I were fighting through sludge instead of walking on firm ground. I hadn't felt this kind of a tremble since my walk to the clinic, but this tremble came for a different reason, and I fought through it with the knowledge that this time, I was doing the right thing.

As I went on, the trees thinned out, situated as you would find them in a park, with large openings to allow the light through. John's house appeared through gaps in their formation. It was huge and simple, with varnished wood walls and floor-to-ceiling windows. Astoundingly beautiful, it collected every shaft of light, glowing like a diamond in the middle of the old-growth forest.

My hand reaching out clumsily for the railing, I pulled myself up the front steps, standing on the wraparound porch. I hesitated, taking a moment to breathe and collect myself like a young horse faced with a trailer ramp. I took the doorknob in both hands and turned it, finding my way in.

The interior was spectacular. It was sparsely furnished, allowing the astonishingly simple design of the house to remain the focal point. Waxed hardwood floors stretched on before me, the sunlight all around, dancing off every surface. I pivoted in place, taking stock of the unfamiliar surroundings, searching for him. My first instinct was to call out, but my feet took over, ushering me to the staircase. I took the stairs two at a time, blood hurtling through my veins, my heart thudding and my head swaying, knowing I was close to him, and soon I would be closer than ever before.

I reached the top of the stairs. What had started as a brisk walk had become a dead run. I hit the hallway, whirling like a crazed animal, unsure of which direction I should take.

John must have heard me, because he came out of one of the rooms, slowly placing the bulk of his body in my field of vision. I froze, clutching my hands in front of me, seeking him out with eyes that demanded to know if I was still everything he wanted.

He started toward me, and I ran for him, slamming into him with force that would've knocked a lesser man down. He gathered me up, lifting me like I weighed nothing, like I was still a skeleton. He made a small noise of contentment and took the back of my head in one hand, bringing my face up to his. Our wet mouths slid together, tongues thrashing in a messy, broken rhythm. I could feel him fighting to neaten it up, and I redoubled my intensity, dragging him along with me.

He steered us into the bedroom, laying me down on a lavish bedspread. Settling over me, he pulled off his T-shirt, revealing a thick, rippled torso. I licked my way down the hard outline of his abs, tracing every groove with my tongue. He pulled me up, undressing me slowly, his eyes faithfully remaining on every part of me. Wrapping my legs around his waist, I felt his strong arms holding me close as he kissed me and rubbed my back. I could feel the rigid length of his shaft pressing against me through his slacks, tantalizingly close. I shifted so I could feel it more directly, moving against it, quickening my pace. John reached around, stroking me from behind, and I moved against his hand instead, shaking with need.

"Please," I hissed, clutching the back of his neck with my hands, a guttural whisper conveying all the instincts I'd squelched over the past year. Everything I'd been holding back.

John nodded, laying me down on the bed, stripping off his slacks and boxers, taking my legs in his hands and tucking my knees up toward my chest. He settled in between them, pressing his erection into my thigh, then sinking just the first few inches inside me. He held still for a moment, letting me adjust to his width, setting a lingering kiss on my lips. Then he slid all the way in, gasping, his shuddering body colliding with mine.

Voices rising, we moved together, him slamming into me at my prompting, the bed creaking as he drove into me faster, always stilling himself and pausing when he began to lose control. I lay back on a nest of pillows, watching him pull out and thrust into me over and over, feeling the velvety softness of his skin against me as he pulled at my hips, repositioning my limbs so it would feel different, and better than before.

"You can come, you know," I murmured, stroking his face as he pulled out once again, with only the tip inside me. "I have, many times."

"I know," John said, looking down at me, his eyes perfectly focused on mine. "I'm just not ready for this to be over."

"It won't be," I said. "There will be other times."

"With you, I can't be sure," John said, watching me knowingly, his eyes both trusting and guarded.

I moved away from him, rising up on my knees. Realizing what I wanted, John settled on his back, surrendering to me. I eased a leg on either side of him and took him in my hand, bringing him into me. Moving steadily up and down his length, I leaned back, letting him watch. His muscles tightened and released, and he came silently, pulling me into him as his body lurched.

I lay on his shoulder as he drifted into sleep and I remained wide awake, wondering if I could make good on my word.

Erica

I walked across the IPC grounds, dodging numerous parties already in full swing. I was quickly becoming the social pariah of the International Polo Club, but all I cared about was getting to the stables to tuck D.M. in for the night. Several drunk girls waved bottles of booze at me invitingly. I gave them the thumbs-up as I passed and kept walking.

The pool parties were always the most raucous, and I glanced up as the shrieking and splashing assaulted my ears. One tall, shapely figure drew my eye more than the others. Her very presence reviled me, and I hurried to get away She saw me anyway and separated herself from the crowd, hunting me down like I was a sitting duck.

Since our first meeting when she'd made it clear she was out to take Lawrence back, my opinion of Marla would forever be sullied with blackness. Her habit of turning up without warning did her no favors in my eyes either. This jet-setting lifestyle might've been fun for her, but it irked me to see her bouncing back and forth whenever she saw fit, spending precious money and resources just to fuck with people.

"In a hurry to see your beau?" She said, voice oozing with irony. "The hotel's that way."

"I'm going to see my horse," I said flatly.

"Oh," Marla said, smiling for a faint second. "I thought when I saw you on the run like that, it would be in the direction of the one you desire."

"If I was truly on the run, you'd see me running out the gate," I said without humor. "And out of this place."

"Why don't you?" Marla said, her playfulness gone.

"Why don't *you* just settle somewhere," I snapped, unable to hold back my loathing for one second longer. "And while you're at it, quit stalking my boyfriend. We all know that's what all your traveling is about. Don't pretend otherwise."

Marla cracked a smile, shaking her head, her coppery hair twinkling in the faint blue glow of the pool. "You're no better than any of us, Erica," she said, catching me off guard.

"What?" I demanded, still teetering on the brink of outright rage, but now more confused than anything.

"All these women," she answered, waving an arm around. "Me. Rebecca." She pointed to a stunningly beautiful redhead with sapphire eyes and a conspicuous wedding band. "Silva. Sauvage. And countless others. You look down on us all, don't you see? You practically sneer as you walk by. You treat us like cheap sluts, when you're no better. You're not."

"I don't see how..." I began.

"You think you're special, don't you?" Marla asked, a tired smile on her face. "You think you're a cut above. You're a *good girl*. You waited. He's your *first and your only*, isn't he?" Marla inquired, studying my face. "In your mind, you're the cat's ass, because he picked you out of the litter. He's *going steady* with you. You know what, Erica? Nobody gives a damn."

"Well, that much I know," I said, thinking of all the times I'd seen Marla or some other girl pressing her body up against his like he was some piece of state land they all had free access to.

"You don't get points for waiting," Marla said cruelly, "and you don't get points for being exclusive. Not when you walk around with your nose in the air, looking down on all of us from your bullshit palace like we're second-class citizens. No one respects you, and no one likes you."

"Lawrence likes me," I said, my voice thin and reedy.

"Well, thank heaven for that," Marla said sardonically. "Because you don't have a single friend here."

"I'm well aware of that," I said thickly.

"Good," Marla said, walking away. "Maybe you should think about why that is."

Lawrence

Harry's white-emblazoned face greeted me as I walked into the stable. He bobbed his head eagerly, bumping his chest against the stall door. "Quit that," I ordered, without much malice in my words. He settled back down, and I reached over to rub his face, mixing the white hairs with the surrounding black.

His bare neck and sculpted muscles created the picture of a fit, healthy pony. I'd given the ponies an easy day of work, and now on the last night before our first game, I wanted to take a quiet moment for us to savor the calm before the storm. Tomorrow, everything would be different. We would be in the middle of it.

I unbolted the stall door, and Harry swept back, respectfully giving me space. I clipped a lead onto his halter. His coat was black as an oil slick. No fine sand grains clung to it. Fastening the ends of the lead to his halter's D-rings to form a makeshift bridle, I led him out into the dusk, vaulting onto his back. We stood above it all, watching the swirling masses of people gathered around the twinkle lights and tiki torches.

I touched him with my leg, and he turned, heading for the fields, my hips following the swing of his back, my seat bones oriented on either side of his spine. There was something comforting about taking a meandering bareback ride. It was down to just you and your horse, flesh and bone animals at their essence. Without all the bullshit, I was reminded of what was most important. The basics. Rhythm. Trust. Connection.

Harry picked his way through the hills and gullies, leaving my mind free to wander, my hand idle on the makeshift reins. I felt the ring box at my hip, a small item and a big step.

It didn't really worry me, though. I didn't have doubts. I couldn't remember being this sure about any one thing in my lifetime. My main concern was how I was going to pop the question. What I would say, how it would go down. I couldn't decide how I wanted it to go. My head was blank when I tried to picture it.

Maybe I would just do it tomorrow, right after our first game. Maybe I'd invite her out on the field and do it in front of everyone. That seemed like a good time and place. It would mean something. It might even be romantic.

I decided it felt right, and I walked Harry back to the stable. He walked slowly, not hurrying, seeming to know nothing awaited him except another boring night in a stall.

Tonight was just a night. Tomorrow was everything.

Erica

I shoved through the elevator doors as soon as they started to open, still seething from my altercation with Marla. I stomped down the hall, my feet making more noise than they had a right to, digging in my pocket for my key card.

I saw the leg of a pink Nike tracksuit coming around the corner, and Courtney jogged her way up to me. Her tied-back hair was doing that full-rotation swish thing, and her feet bounced soundlessly off the floor.

"Hi, Erica!" Courtney said brightly, giving me a friendly wave. Ignoring her fully, I continued on my way, not noticing she had turned back until she was suddenly right in front of me.

"What is your problem?" I snapped, inadvertently lashing her with the full brunt of my bad mood. *Courtney isn't the problem here*, I reminded myself. *She's just really annoying.*

"What is *your* problem?" Courtney wailed, her face screwing up. "What did I ever do to you?"

Oh, hell. I watched the tears wobble in her huge eyes, hoping a full-on meltdown wasn't in store. "I had a bad day, I'm sorry. I didn't mean to take it out on you."

"Yes, you did!" Courtney howled. "You're *always* this way to me. Every time I try to be friendly, you act like I'm not there. Why don't you like me?"

"Not everyone likes everyone," I said, attempting to sidestep her. "Welcome to life."

"It's because I slept with Lawrence," Courtney said, wiping her eyes. "You hate everyone who slept with him before you. I can't do anything to get you to like me because of what happened before we even met."

"That's not how I am," I said angrily.

"You're nice to Delaware," Courtney said, staring me in the face. "She's the only one you'll talk to."

"What do you care, anyway?" I challenged. "You have your life, and I have mine. Who cares if we like each other? Who gives a fuck?"

Courtney looked down, crestfallen. "I just thought we could be friends."

Now I was really thrown. "You thought we could be *friends*?" I asked, my voice shrill.

"Yeah," Courtney said, standing up to me although her voice quavered. "We're a lot alike, you know. I met you, and you seemed like you would understand where I'm coming from. So I tried to be friendly. I tried so many times to be your friend, and you shot me down every single time."

"You say we're a lot alike," I said heavily. "Are you saying we're both *athletic girls*, so we both know the curse that comes with being painted with that brush? Are you saying we share the same struggles, the same fight to be respected as an athlete, while, at the same time, still being seen as feminine and worthy?"

"Yes!" Courtney said, her face bright. "Exactly!"

"*Get out of my sight*," I said, my voice low.

Courtney fell back, aghast. "What? Why?"

"You have *no idea* what it's like to be me," I said. "Look at you. You never had a problem getting attention. You have it all, Courtney, and seeing you pretend to have *athletic girl problems* so you can bond with me is *really* pissing me off."

Fat tears welled in Courtney's eyes. "I'm sorry," she began.

"You know nothing," I said. "Get the fuck out of my face."

Courtney fled, and I changed course, suddenly wanting nothing to do with this hotel, these rooms, this life. I made a critical decision, and I followed it faithfully, never once looking back.

Dougie

Courtney burst into her room, tears streaming down her face. Sniffling and hiccupping, she launched herself into my arms, curling up to me in abject misery.

"Baby, what happened?" I said, listening to her struggle to breathe through her sobs. "Did someone attack you? What's going on?"

"Erica is mean," Courtney whimpered, wiping her face on her Nike-emblazoned sleeve. "I just tried to be her friend, and she jumped all over me. Why are girls so mean?" She wailed, starting to cry again.

"Oh, Courtney," I said, snuggling her and patting her hair. "I don't think she means to be mean. I think she's just not happy here."

"Then why blame me for it?" Courtney asked. "Why not just leave?"

"It's hard for people to make those choices sometimes," I said. "You were just in the wrong place at the wrong time, and you took the fall for whatever's bothering her. You should try to feel better. It isn't anything you did."

She still looked crestfallen, so I took her hand and pulled her up to a sitting position. "Hey," I said, looking in her eyes. "You know what we should do?"

"What?" Courtney asked, inching closer.

"We should go out for a drink," I said. "Tomorrow's your big game. Let's have some fun. Let's celebrate how far we've come, and what's in store for us."

"Yvette will murder me if I show up hungover," Courtney said, her eyes widening.

"We won't get hungover," I said confidently. "We'll just get tipsy."

Courtney

Sometime shortly after closing, we staggered to the elevator, pressing buttons wildly until the right one lit up. I leaned against the wall, letting it anchor me, and when the elevator opened on our floor, I stumbled out just far enough to find another wall to lean on. Dougie's coordination had held up much better than mine, but he was laughing a lot at things you wouldn't normally find funny, like the ice machine sign, for instance.

"What's so funny?" I said loudly, looking around.

"Everything," Dougie said, and he laughed some more.

"Why did those guys keep buying us drinks?" I asked, feeling my way along the wall like a blind person. *Oh, so that must be where the phrase "blind drunk" came from. Neat.*

"Because you're sexy," Dougie slurred, pressing his body up against me.

"How are you still hard?" I asked unnecessarily loudly. "I thought alcohol was supposed to interfere with that."

Dougie shrugged. "I'm 23," he said.

"Ah," I said, fishing around for my room key. "Is this my room?" I asked, squinting up at the number on the door. I looked at my card. "I think it matches."

"If the numbers match, that's a good sign," Dougie said, giggling again.

"I'll give her a go," I said, swiping the card. The light strip blinked green, and I twisted the handle in triumph.

I turned to Dougie, throwing my purse, phone and key card down on the nightstand. Most of it bounced off and hit the floor. "Now what?"

Dougie pushed me lightly, landing on top of me on the bed. He unzipped my dress and peeled it off, unhooking my bra and sliding my thong down to my ankles in a matter of seconds. I kicked it off the rest of the way as he pulled off his shirt. It landed on my head, blinding me for a moment, and I heard the frantic jangling of a belt being unfastened. As I removed the article of clothing from my eyes, Dougie reached for the nightstand drawer, returning with the unmistakable shape of a condom packet in his hand.

"You had one of those all along?" I demanded, rising up on my elbows, my head clearing miraculously, allowing me to be in the moment.

"Well, I couldn't keep up this nonsense forever," Dougie said, staring down at me tenderly. "Look at you, Courtney."

Team Dark Horse

He rolled it on, and I drew my legs up, settling back with my head on the pillow. He fell forward on his knees, pushing against me and going all the way this time, groaning as my tightness enveloped him.

"Fuck, Court," he gasped, his breath coming in short bursts. I dug my nails into his back in encouragement, and his hips bucked against me until he toppled over, shouting obscenities and almost sliding off me, his head on my shoulder.

"Sorry," he hastened to say as he struggled for breath. "I know that wasn't awesome…"

"It was better than the first time we tried it," I said. "And it'll keep getting better."

Dougie's arm snaked around me. "So that can happen again?"

"It had better," I said threateningly.

He kissed my hair and promptly fell asleep. I held him tightly in my arms and thought about how I should really hydrate, and then I fell asleep too.

Erica

Of all the places I could've gone in Wellington, all the natural wonders and hopping nightclubs, the 7-Eleven just happened to be my go-to. Providing more comfort and better companionship than even the barn, it was a true example of the company you keep being more important than the setting for your adventures.

Kurt looked sleepily at me from the counter, standing up straight when I walked in the door. "It's the season opener tomorrow," he said. "Shouldn't you be at some swingin' party?"

"The mood I'm in, the only thing swinging at one of those parties would be my fists," I said truthfully, pulling up a chair.

Kurt whistled. "Who's got you all worked up?"

"Everyone," I said.

"Well, I guess I should steer clear of you, then," Kurt said, though he didn't move a muscle.

I shook my head. "You're not everyone."

"Who am I, then?" Kurt asked, his eyes on me.

"My lifeline," I said.

A customer walked in, and our eyes broke apart. I fiddled with my hands, cracking my knuckles, until they had come and gone.

"Are you at the end of your six-day stretch?" I asked Kurt.

He nodded. "You'll be at the game tomorrow, I'm sure."

"I don't know," I said, twisting my hands. "I feel disconnected. I can't get excited about it."

He leaned over the counter. "Why do you think that is?"

"Because I hate it here," I said truthfully. "I thought I would like it, but I don't. Nothing here is mine. I don't work for a living, I'm with the team. But I'm not really a part of it. I'm just there because Lawrence wants me there. But he wants other things more."

"Why do you say that?"

"Because we don't spend time together." I sighed, letting a neon sign take over my field of vision. "Our lives used to be together. They used to go together. Now, we pass like ships in the night."

"Maybe you should think about what you want," Kurt said. "That's what matters most."

My eyes watered. "I think I want something different too."

"Like what?"

"Like you." I put it all out there, a gutsy move or a suicide, depending on how this next part went.

Kurt remained in front of me, close enough to embrace, but he didn't lay a hand on me. "I'm not going to tell you what to do. If you're going to leave your boyfriend, it should be for the right reasons. Only you can figure out what those are." He looked at me directly. "But I'm sure you know how I feel about you. And I'm not about to blow smoke up your ass and tell you I wouldn't be thrilled to be your boyfriend."

I reached across the counter, feeling his chest, his ribcage, the firm expanse of his stomach. Before I could go further, he took my hands in his, holding them gently, keeping me honest.

"Figure your shit out first," he said. "Then you'll see how much I want you."

Team Dark Horse

Delaware

The morning of our first game dawned dimly, the sun barely making an appearance before creeping back into the clouds. The atmosphere was chilly and misty as we changed into our uniforms, stripping and dressing silently in separate rooms. My hands shook as I tied my ponytail, and I shook my head harder, beating back the nerves. "Nope, not right now," I said, my trusty phrase from back in my rodeo queen years. All this stuff was mind over matter. You had to keep a strong head on your shoulders.

I stepped onto the sidelines, flanked by Courtney, Yvette, and Lawrence. We walked in stride together, gathering on our side of the field. Our ponies were being warmed up, their heads and tails high, energized by the cold weather.

I saw immediately that it was different out here during a live game. Officials with clipboards stalked around; reporters and film crews filled the sidelines instead of just the usual railbirds. Fans sat down in the stands, bundled up like it was 30 degrees out. I suppose by Florida standards, it was.

When the time came, the exercise riders dismounted, holding our ponies for us. I stroked Vegas' muzzle, glad Lawrence had selected him for the first chukker. I knew him the best, and I knew he would make up for any beginner mistakes I made as I found my footing.

Courtney huddled in the saddle, looking visibly ill.

"You appear hungover," Yvette remarked, riding around Courtney in a circle like a vulture. "I sincerely hope you are not."

"Hope all you want," Courtney hissed back at her. "It won't change anything."

Yvette turned to Lawrence. She appeared to be chewing the inside of her cheek. "Your number 4 is hungover," she declared.

"As long as she does her job out there, I don't care what she did last night," Lawrence snapped. "At least she's going out and being a real person for once."

"Ugh," Courtney said, shuddering. "Never again."

549

Lawrence steered his pony away, standing tall in the stirrups, looking up into the stands. "Have you guys seen Erica?"

"No," I said, surprised. "Haven't you?"

"This is your five-minute warning," the ref cut in. "You should begin to make your way to the field."

Tapping Vegas' sides, I led the way onto the field, flat and green with tiny sideboards. Cameras hummed and snapped all around me. Every pair of eyes in the stands and the surrounding area were looking at me.

This is the real deal, I thought. *If we do our job like we practiced, we will have arrived.*

On the opposite end of the field, Team Pony Express made their entrance. The tall, strapping men gathered up their reins, prompting their ponies to jig and prance in anticipation. Flexing their muscles, the men appeared smug and confident.

I looked at my teammates, especially the two women. Their mouths formed hard lines, their shoulders looked so tight they might crack. It felt like a dome had settled over the field, the stands, and the sidelines, filled with enough pressurized air that a single pinprick would cause it to explode.

The referee threw in the ball, and the overwhelming silence became a rumble.